Fantasy Masterworks

'Some of the finest heroic fantasy ever written' *SF Chronicle*

'A writer who is . . . still the greatest of us all' Michael Moorcock

'The most literate and important sword and sorcery series'
Mike Ashley

'Most fantasy writers, if asked, admit that Fritz Leiber is our
spiritual father, and for the most part we're sweating to keep up,
let alone overtake him' Raymond E. Feist

'[A] writer of major importance' *The Encyclopedia of Fantasy*

D0861021

ALSO BY FRITZ LEIBER

Novels

Conjure Wife (1943)

Gather, Darkness! (1950)

The Green Millennium
   (1953)

Destiny Times Three (1957)

The Big Time (1961)

The Silver Eggheads (1962)

The Wanderer (1964)

Tarzan and the Valley of Gold
   (1966)

A Specter is Haunting Texas
   (1969)

Our Lady of Darkness (1977)

Short Story Collections

Night's Black Agents (1947)

Shadows with Eyes (1962)

Ships to the Stars (1964)

A Pail of Air (1964)

The Night of the Wolf (1966)

The Secret Songs (1968)

Night Monsters (1969)

You're All Alone (1972)

The Book of Fritz Leiber (1974)

The Best of Fritz Leiber (1974)

The Worlds of Fritz Leiber (1976)

Bazaar of the Bizarre (1978)

The Change War (1978)

Heroes and Horrors (1978)

Ship of Shadows (1979)

The Leiber Chronicles: Fifty
   Years of Fritz Leiber (1990)

The First Book of Lankhmar
   (2001)

Poetry

The Demons of the Upper Air
   (1969)

Sonnets to Jonquil and All (1978)

FANTASY MASTERWORKS

THE SECOND BOOK
OF LANKHMAR

FRITZ LEIBER

This edition published in Great Britain in 2001 by
Gollancz
An imprint of the Orion Publishing Group
Orion House, 5 Upper St Martin's Lane,
London WC2H 9EA

10 9 8 7 6 5 4 3 2

A CIP catalogue record for this book is available
from the British Library

ISBN 978 0 575 07358 6

Typeset at The Spartan Press Ltd,
Lymington, Hants

Printed in Great Britain by
Clays Ltd, St Ives plc

The Orion Publishing Group's policy is to use papers that
are natural, renewable and recyclable products and
made from wood grown in sustainable forests. The logging
and manufacturing processes are expected to conform to
the environmental regulations of the country of origin.

www.orionbooks.co.uk

CONTENTS

THE SWORDS
OF LANKHMAR

AUTHOR'S NOTE

Fafhrd and the Mouser are rogues through and through, though each has in him a lot of humanity and at least a diamond chip of the spirit of true adventure. They drink, they feast, they wench, they brawl, they steal, they gamble, and surely they hire out their swords to powers that are only a shade better, if that, than the villains. It strikes me (and something might be made of this) that Fafhrd and the Gray Mouser are almost at the opposite extreme from the heroes of Tolkien. My stuff is at least equally as fantastic as his, but it's an earthier sort of fantasy with a strong seasoning of 'black fantasy' – or of black humor, to use the current phrase for something that was once called gallows' humor and goes back a long, long way. Though with their vitality, appetites, warm sympathies, and imagination, Fafhrd and the Mouser are anything but 'sick' heroes.

One of the original motives for conceiving Fafhrd and the Mouser was to have a couple of fantasy heroes closer to true human stature than supermen like Conan and Tarzan and many another. In a way they're a mixture of Cabell and Eddison, if we must look for literary ancestors. Fafhrd and the Mouser have a touch of Jurgen's cynicism and anti-romanticism, but they go on boldly having adventures – one more roll of the dice with destiny and death. While the characters they most parallel in *The Worm Ouroboros* are Corund and Gro, yet I don't think they're touched with evil as those two, rather they're rogues in a decadent world where you have to be a rogue to survive; perhaps, in legendry, Robin Hood comes closest to them, though they're certainly a pair of lone-wolf Robin Hoods . . .

Fritz Leiber

I

'I see we're expected,' the small man said, continuing to stroll toward the large open gate in the long, high, ancient wall. As if by chance, his hand brushed the hilt of his long, slim rapier.

'At over a bowshot distance how can you—' the big man began. 'I get it. Bashabeck's orange headcloth. Stands out like a whore in church. And where Bashabeck is, his bullies are. You should have kept your dues to the Thieves Guild paid up.'

'It's not so much the dues,' the small man said. 'It slipped my mind to split with them after the last job, when I lifted those eight diamonds from the Spider God's temple.'

The big man sucked his tongue in disapproval. 'I sometimes wonder why I associate with a faithless rogue like you.'

The small man shrugged. 'I was in a hurry. The Spider God was after me.'

'Yes, I seem to recall he sucked the blood of your lookout man. You've got the diamonds to make the payoff now, of course?'

'My purse is as bulging as yours,' the small man asserted. 'Which is exactly as much as a drunk's wineskin the morning after. Unless you're holding out on me, which I've long suspected. Incidentally, isn't that grossly fat man – the one between two big-shouldered bravos – the keeper of the Silver Eel tavern?'

The big man squinted, nodded, then rocked his head disgustedly. 'To make such a to-do over a brandy tab.'

'Especially when it couldn't have been much more than a yard long,' the small man agreed. 'Of course there were those two full casks of brandy you smashed and set afire the last night you were brawling at the Eel.'

'When the odds are ten to one against you in a tavern fight, you have to win by whatever methods come easiest to hand,' the big man protested. 'Which I'll grant you are apt at times to be a bit bizarre.'

He squinted ahead again at the small crowd ranged around the square inside the open gate. After awhile he said, 'I also make out Rivis Rightby the swordsmith . . . and just about all the other creditors any two men could have in Lankhmar. And each with his hired thug or three.' He casually loosened in its scabbard his somewhat huge weapon, shaped like a rapier, but heavy almost as a broadsword. 'Didn't you settle *any* of our bills before we left Lankhmar the last time? I was dead broke, of course, but you must have had money from all those earlier jobs for the Thieves Guild.'

'I paid Nattick Nimblefingers in full for mending my cloak and for a new gray silk jerkin,' the small man answered at once. He frowned. 'There must have been others I paid – oh, I'm sure there were, but I can't recall them at the moment. By the by, isn't that tall rangy wench – half behind the dainty man in black – one you were in trouble with? Her red hair stands out like a . . . like a bit of Hell. And those three other girls – each peering over her besworded pimp's shoulder like the first – weren't you in trouble with them also when we last left Lankhmar?'

'I don't know what you mean by trouble,' the big man complained. 'I rescued them from their protectors, who were abusing them dreadfully. Believe me, I trounced those protectors and the girls laughed. Thereafter I treated them like princesses.'

'You did indeed – and spent all your cash and jewels on them, which is why you were broke. But one thing you didn't do for them: you didn't become their protector in turn. So they had to go back to their former protectors, which has made them justifiably angry at you.'

'I should have become a pimp?' the big man objected. 'Women!' Then, 'I see a few of *your* girls in the crowd. Neglect to pay them off?'

'No, borrowed from them and forgot to return the money,' the small man explained. 'Hi-ho, it certainly appears that the welcoming committee is out in force.'

'I told you we should have entered the city by the Grand

Gate, where we'd have been lost in the numbers,' the big man grumbled. 'But no, I listened to you and came to this god-forsaken End Gate.'

'Wrong,' the other said. 'At the Grand Gate we wouldn't have been able to tell our foes from the bystanders. Here at least we know that everyone is against us, except for the Overlord's gate watch, and I'm not too sure of them – at the least they'll have been bribed to take no notice of our slaying.'

'Why should they all be so hot to slay us?' the big man argued. 'For all they know we may be coming home laden with rich treasures garnered from many a high adventure at the ends of the earth. Oh, I'll admit that three or four of them may also have a private grudge, but—'

'They can see we haven't a train of porters or heavily-laden mules,' the small man interrupted reasonably. 'In any case they know that after slaying us, they can pay themselves off from any treasure we may have and split the remainder. It's the rational procedure, which all civilized men follow.'

'Civilization!' the big man snorted. 'I sometimes wonder—'

'—why you ever climbed south over the Trollstep Mountains and got your beard trimmed and discovered that there were girls without hair on their chests,' the small man finished for him. 'Hey, I think our creditors and other haters have hired a third S besides swords and staves against us.'

'Sorcery?'

The small man drew a coil of thin yellow wire from his pouch. He said, 'Well, if those two graybeards in the second-story windows aren't wizards, they shouldn't scowl so ferociously. Besides, I can make out astrological symbols on the one's robe and see the glint of the other's wand.'

They were close enough now to the End Gate that a sharp eye could guess at such details. The guardsmen in browned-iron mail leaned on their pikes impassively. The faces of those lining the small square beyond the gateway were impassive too, but grimly so, except for the girls, who smiled with venom and glee.

The big man said grumpily, 'So they'll slay us by spells and incantations. Failing which, they'll resort to cudgels and gizzard-cutters.' He shook his head. 'So much hate over a little cash. Lankhmarts are ingrates. They don't realize the tone we give their city, the excitement we provide.'

The small man shrugged. 'This time they're providing the excitement for us. Playing host, after a fashion.' His fingers were deftly making a slipknot in one end of the pliant wire. His steps slowed a trifle. 'Of course,' he mused, 'we don't have to return to Lankhmar.'

The big man bristled. 'Nonsense, we must! To turn back now would be cowardly. Besides, we've done everything else.'

'There must be a few adventures left outside Lankhmar,' the small man objected mildly, 'if only little ones, suitable for cowards.'

'Perhaps,' the big man agreed, 'but big or little, they all have a way of beginning in Lankhmar. Whatever are you up to with that wire?'

The small man had tightened the slipknot around the pommel of his rapier and let the wire trail behind him, flexible as a whip. 'I've grounded my sword,' he said. 'Now any death-spell launched against me, striking my drawn sword first, will be discharged into the ground.'

'Giving Mother Earth a tickle, eh? Watch out you don't trip over it.' The warning seemed well-advised – the wire was fully a half score yards long.

'And don't you step on it. 'Tis a device Sheelba taught me.'

'You and your swamp-rat wizard!' the big man mocked. 'Why isn't he at your side now, making some spells for us?'

'Why isn't Ningauble at your side, doing the same?' the small man counter-asked.

'He's too fat to travel.' They were passing the blank-faced guardsmen. The atmosphere of menace in the square beyond thickened like a storm. Suddenly the big man grinned broadly at his comrade. 'Let's not hurt any of them too seriously,' he said in a somewhat loud voice. 'We don't want our return to Lankhmar beclouded.'

As they stepped into the open space walled by hostile faces, the storm broke without delay. The wizard in the star-symboled robe howled like a wolf and lifting his arms high above his head, threw them toward the small man with such a force that one expected his hands to come off and fly through the air. They didn't, but a bolt of bluish fire, wraithlike in the sunlight streamed from his out-flung fingers. The small man had drawn his rapier and pointed it at the wizard. The blue bolt crackled along the slim blade and then evidently did discharge itself into the ground, for he only felt a stinging thrill in his hand.

Rather unimaginatively the wizard repeated his tactics, with the same result, and then lifted his hands for a third bolt-hurling. By this time the small man had got the rhythm of the wizard's actions and just as the hands came down, he flipped the long wire so that it curled against the chests and faces of the bullies around the orange-turbaned Bashabeck. The blue stuff, whatever it was, went crackling into them from the wire and with a single screech each they fell down writhing.

Meanwhile the other sorcerer threw his wand at the big man, quickly following it with two more which he plucked from the air. The big man, his own outsize rapier drawn with surprising speed, awaited the first wand's arrival. Somewhat to his surprise, it had in flight the appearance of a silver-feathered hawk stooping with silver talons forward-pointing to strike. As he continued to watch it closely, its appearance changed to that of a silvery, long knife with this addition: that it had a silvery wing to either side.

Undaunted by this prodigy and playing the point of his great rapier as lightly as a fencing foil, the big man deftly deflected the first flying dagger so that it transfixed the shoulder of one of the bullies flanking the keeper of the Silver Eel. He treated the second and third flying dagger in the same fashion, so that two other of his foes were skewered painfully though unfatally.

They screeched too and collapsed, more from terror of such supernatural weapons than the actual severity of their wounds. Before they hit the cobbles, the big man had snatched a knife from his belt and hurled it left-handed at his sorcerous foe. Whether the graybeard was struck or barely managed to dodge, he at any rate dropped out of sight.

Meanwhile the other wizard, with continuing lack of imagination or perhaps mere stubbornness, directed a fourth bolt at the small man, who this time whipped upwards the wire grounding his sword so that it snapped at the very window from which the blue bolt came. Whether it actually struck the wizard or only the window frame, there was a great crackling there and a bleating cry and that wizard dropped out of sight also.

It is to the credit of the assembled bullies and bravoes that they hesitated hardly a heartbeat at this display of reflected death-spells but urged on by their employers – and the pimps by their whores – they rushed in, lustily trampling the wounded and thrusting and slashing and clubbing with their various weapons. Of course, they had something of a fifty-to-two advantage; still, it took a certain courage.

The small man and the big man instantly placed themselves back-to-back and with lightning-like strokes stood off the first onset, seeking to jab as many faces and arms as they could rather than make the blows deep and mortal. The big man now had in his left hand a short-handled ax, with whose flat he rapped some skulls for variety, while the small man was supplementing his fiendishly pricking rapier with a long knife whose dartings were as swift as those of a cat's paw.

At first the greater number of the assaulters was a positive hindrance to them – they got into each other's way – while the greatest danger to the two fighting back-to-back was that they might be overwhelmed by the mere mass of their wounded foes, pushed forward enthusiastically by comrades behind. Then the battling got straightened out somewhat, and for awhile it looked as if the small and big man would have to use more deadly strokes – and perhaps nevertheless be cut down. The clash of tempered iron, the stamp of boots, the fighting-snarls from twisted lips, and the excited screeches of the girls added up to a great din, which made the gate guard look about nervously.

But then the lordly Bashabeck, who had at last deigned to take a hand, had an ear taken off and his collarbone on that side severed by a gentle swipe of the big man's ax, while the girls – their sense of romance touched – began to cheer on the outnumbered two, at which their pimps and bullies lost heart.

The attackers wavered on the verge of panic. There was a sudden blast of six trumpets from the widest street leading into the square. The great skirling sound was enough to shatter nerves already frayed. The attackers and their employers scattered in all other directions, the pimps dragging their fickle whores, while those who had been stricken by the blue lightning and the winged daggers went crawling after them.

In a short time the square was empty, save for the two victors, the line of trumpeters in the street mouth, the line of guards outside the gateway now facing away from the square as if nothing at all had happened – and a hundred and more pairs of eyes as tiny and red-glinting black as wild cherries, which peered intently from between the grills of street drains and from various small holes in the walls and even from the rooftops. But who counts or even notices rats? – especially in a city as old and vermin-infested as Lankhmar.

The big man and the small man gazed about fiercely a bit longer. Then, regaining their breaths, they laughed uproariously, sheathed their weapons, and faced the trumpeters with a guarded yet relaxed curiosity.

The trumpeters wheeled to either side. A line of pikemen behind them executed the same movement, and there strode forward a venerable, clean-shaven, stern-visaged man in a black toga narrowly bordered with silver.

He raised his hand in a dignified salute. He said gravely, 'I am chamberlain of Glipkerio Kistomerces, Overlord of Lankhmar, and here is my wand of authority.' He produced a small silver wand tipped with a five-pointed bronze emblem in the form of a starfish.

The two men nodded slightly, as though to say, 'We accept your statement for what it's worth.'

The chamberlain faced the big man. He drew a scroll from his toga, unrolled it, scanned it briefly, then looked up. 'Are you Fafhrd the northern barbarian and brawler?'

The big man considered that for a bit, then said, 'And if I am—?'

The chamberlain turned toward the small man. He once more consulted his parchment. 'And are you – your pardon, but it's written here – that mongrel and long-suspected burglar, cutpurse, swindler, and assassin, the Gray Mouser?'

The small man fluffed his gray cape and said, 'If it's any business of yours – well, he and I might be connected in some way.'

As if those vaguest answers settled everything, the chamberlain rolled up his parchment with a snap and tucked it inside his toga. 'Then my master wishes to see you. There is a service which you can render him, to your own considerable profit.'

The Gray Mouser inquired, 'If the all-powerful Glipkerio Kistomerces has need of us, why did he allow us to be assaulted and for all he might know slain by that company of hooligans who but now fled this place?'

The chamberlain answered, 'If you were the sort of men who would allow yourselves to be murdered by such a mob, then you would not be the right men to handle the assignment, or fulfill the commission, which my master has in mind. But time presses. Follow me.'

Fafhrd and the Gray Mouser looked at each other and after a moment they simultaneously shrugged, then nodded. Swaggering just a little, they fell in beside the chamberlain, the pikemen and the trumpeters fell in behind them, and the cortège moved off the way it had come, leaving the square quite empty.

Except, of course, for the rats.

2

With the motherly-generous west wind filling their brown triangular sails, the slim war galley and the five broad-beamed grain ships, two nights out of Lankhmar, coursed north in line ahead across the Inner Sea of the ancient world of Nehwon.

It was late afternoon of one of those mild blue days when sea and sky are the same hue, providing irrefutable evidence for the hypothesis currently favored by Lankhmar philosophers: that Nehwon is a giant bubble rising through the waters of eternity with continents, islands, and the great jewels that at night are the stars all orderly afloat on the bubble's inner surface.

On the afterdeck of the last grain ship, which was also the largest, the Gray Mouser spat a plum skin to leeward and boasted luxuriously, 'Fat times in Lankhmar! Not one day returned to the City of the Black Toga after months away adventuring and we get this cushy job from the Overlord himself – and with an advance on pay too.'

'I have an old distrust of cushy jobs,' Fafhrd replied, yawning and pulling his fur-trimmed jerkin open wider so that the mild wind might trickle more fully through the tangle hair-field of his chest. 'And we were rushed out of Lankhmar so quickly that we had not even time to pay our respects to the ladies. Nevertheless I must confess that we might have done worse. A full purse is the best ballast for any man-ship, especially one bearing letters of marque against ladies.'

Ship's master Slinoor looked back with hooded appraising eyes at the small lithe gray-clad man and his tall, more gaudily accoutred barbarian comrade. The master of *Squid* was a sleek black-robed man of middle years. He stood beside the two stocky black-tunicked bare-legged sailors who held steady the great high-arching tiller that guided *Squid*.

'How much do you two rogues really know of your cushy job?' Slinoor asked softly. 'Or rather, how much did the arch-noble Glipkerio choose to tell you of the purpose and dark antecedents of this voyaging?' Two days of fortunate sailing seemed at last to have put the closed-mouthed ship's master in a mood to exchange confidences, or at least trade queries and lies.

From a bag of netted cord that hung by the taffrail, the Mouser speared a night-purple plum with the dirk he called Cat's Claw. Then he answered lightly, 'This fleet bears a gift of grain from Overlord Glipkerio to Movarl of the Eight Cities in gratitude for Movarl's sweeping the Mingol pirates from the Inner Sea and mayhap diverting the steppe-dwelling Mingols from assaulting Lankhmar across the Sinking Land. Movarl needs grain for his hunter-farmers turned cityman-soldiers and especially to supply his army relieving his border city of Klelg Nar, which the Mingols besiege. Fafhrd and I are, you might say, a small but mighty rearguard for the grain and for certain more delicate items of Glipkerio's gift.'

'You mean those?' Slinoor bent a thumb toward the larboard rail.

Those were twelve large white rats distributed among four silver-barred cages. With their silky coats, pale-rimmed blue eyes, and especially their short, arched upper lips and two huge upper incisors, they looked like a clique of haughty, bored, inbred aristocrats, and it was in a bored aristocratic fashion that they were staring at a scrawny black kitten which was perched

13

with dug-in claws on the starboard rail, as if to get as far away from the rats as possible, and staring back at them most worriedly.

Fafhrd reached out and ran a finger down the black kitten's back. The kitten arched its spine, losing itself for a moment in sensuous delight, but then edged away and resumed its worried rat-peering – an activity shared by the two black-tunicked helmsmen, who seemed both resentful and fearful of the silver-caged afterdeck passengers.

The Mouser sucked plum juice from his fingers and flicked out his tongue-tip to neatly capture a drop that threatened to run down his chin. Then, 'No, I mean not chiefly those high-bred gift-rats,' he replied to Slinoor and kneeling lightly and unexpectedly and touching two fingers significantly to the scrubbed oak deck, he said, 'I mean chiefly *she* who is below, who ousts you from your master's cabin, and who now insists that the gift-rats require sunlight and fresh air – which strikes me as a strange way of cosseting burrow- and shadow-dwelling vermin.'

Slinoor's cropped eyebrows rose. He came close and whispered, 'You think the Demoiselle Hisvet may not be merely the conductress of the rat-gift, but also herself part of Glipkerio's gift to Movarl? Why, she's the daughter of the greatest grain-merchant in Lankhmar, who's grown rich selling tawny corn to Glipkerio.'

The Mouser smiled cryptically but said nothing.

Slinoor frowned, then whispered ever lower, 'True, I've heard the story that Hisvet has already been her father Hisvin's gift to Glipkerio to buy his patronage.'

Fafhrd, who'd been trying to stroke the kitten again with no more success than to chase it up the aftermast, turned around at that. 'Why, Hisvet's but a child,' he said almost reprovingly. 'A most prim and proper miss. I know not of Glipkerio, he seems decadent' – the word was not an insult in Lankhmar – 'but surely Movarl, a Northerner albeit a forest man, likes only strong-beamed, ripe, complete women.'

'Your own tastes, no doubt?' the Mouser remarked, gazing at Fafhrd with half-closed eyes. 'No traffic with child-like women?'

Fafhrd blinked as if the Mouser had dug fingers in his side. Then he shrugged and said loudly, 'What's so special about these rats? Do they do tricks?'

'Aye,' Slinoor said distastefully. 'They play at being men. They've been trained by Hisvet to dance to music, to drink from cups, hold tiny spears and swords, even fence. I've not seen it – nor would care to.'

The picture struck the Mouser's fancy. He visioned himself small as a rat, dueling with rats who wore lace at their throats and wrists, slipping through the mazy tunnels of their underground cities, becoming a great connoisseur of cheese and smoked meats, perchance wooing a slim rat-queen and being surprised by her rat-king husband and having to dagger-fight him in the dark. Then he noted one of the white rats looking at him intently through the silver bars with a cold inhuman blue eye and suddenly his idea didn't seem amusing at all. He shivered in the sunlight.

Slinoor was saying, 'It is not good for animals to try to be men.' *Squid*'s skipper gazed somberly at the silent white aristos.

'Have you ever heard tell of the legend of—' he began, hesitated, then broke off, shaking his head as if deciding he had been about to say too much.

'A sail!' The call winged down thinly from the crow's nest. 'A black sail to windward!'

'What manner of ship?' Slinoor shouted up.

'I know not, master. I see only sail top.'

'Keep her under view, boy,' Slinoor commanded.

'Under view it is, master.'

Slinoor paced to the starboard rail and back.

'Movarl's sails are green,' Fafhrd said thoughtfully.

Slinoor nodded. 'Ilthmar's are white. The pirates' were red, mostly. Lankhmar's sails once were black, but now that color's only for funeral barges and they never venture out of sight of land. At least I've never known . . .'

The Mouser broke in with, 'You spoke of dark antecedents of this voyaging. Why dark?'

Slinoor drew them back against the taffrail, away from the stocky helmsman. Fafhrd ducked a little, passing under the

15

arching tiller. They looked all three into the twisting wake, their heads bent together.

Slinoor said, 'You've been out of Lankhmar. Did you know this is not the first gift-fleet of grain to Movarl?'

The Mouser nodded. 'We'd been told there was another. Somehow lost. In a storm, I think. Glipkerio glossed over it.'

'There were two,' Slinoor said tersely. 'Both lost. Without a living trace. There was no storm.'

'What then?' Fafhrd asked, looking around as the rats chittered a little. 'Pirates?'

'Movarl had already whipped the pirates east. Each of the two fleets was galley-guarded like ours. And each sailed off into fair weather with a good west wind.' Slinoor smiled thinly. 'Doubtless Glipkerio did not tell you of these matters for fear you might beg off. We sailors and the Lankhmarines obey for duty and the honor of the City, but of late Glipkerio's had trouble hiring the sort of special agents he likes to use for second bowstrings. He has brains of a sort, our overlord has, though he employs them mostly to dream of visiting other world bubbles in a great diving-bell or sealed metallic diving-ship, while he sits with trained girls watching trained rats and buys off Lankhmar's enemies with gold and repays Lankhmar's ever-more-greedy friends with grain, not soldiers.' Slinoor grunted. 'Movarl grows most impatient, you know. He threatens, if the grain comes not, to recall his pirate patrol, league with the land-Mingols and set them at Lankhmar.'

'Northerners, even though not snow-dwelling, league with Mingols?' Fafhrd objected. 'Impossible!'

Slinoor looked at him. 'I'll say just this, ice-eating Northerner. If I did not believe such a league both possible and likely – and Lankhmar thereby in dire danger – I would never have sailed with this fleet, honor and duty or no. Same's true of Lukeen, who commands the galley. Nor do I think Glipkerio would otherwise be sending to Movarl at Kvarch Nar his noblest performing rats and dainty Hisvet.'

Fafhrd growled a little. 'You say both fleets were lost without a trace?' he asked incredulously.

Slinoor shook his head. 'The first was. Of the second, some wreckage was sighted by an Ilthmar trader Lankhmar-bound.

The deck of only one grain ship. It had been ripped off its hull, splinteringly – how or by what, the Ilthmart dared not guess. Tied to a fractured stretch of railing was the ship's master, only hours dead. His face had been nibbled, his body gnawed.'

'Fish?' the Mouser asked.

'Seabirds?' Fafhrd inquired.

'Dragons?' a third voice suggested, high, breathless, and as merry as a schoolgirl's. The three men turned around, Slinoor with guilty swiftness.

The Demoiselle Hisvet stood as tall as the Mouser, but judging by her face, wrists, and ankles was considerably slenderer. Her face was delicate and taper-chinned with small mouth and pouty upper lip that lifted just enough to show a double dash of pearly tooth. Her complexion was creamy pale except for two spots of color high on her cheeks. Her straight fine hair, which grew low on her forehead, was pure white touched with silver and all drawn back through a silver ring behind her neck, whence it hung unbraided like a unicorn's tail. Her eyes had china whites but darkly pink irises around the large black pupils. Her body was enveloped and hidden by a loose robe of violet silk except when the wind briefly molded a flat curve of her girlish anatomy. There was a violet hood, half thrown back. The sleeves were puffed but snug at the wrists. She was barefoot, her skin showing as creamy there as on her face, except for a tinge of pink about the toes.

She looked at them all three one after another quickly in the eye. 'You were whispering of the fleets that failed,' she said accusingly. 'Fie, Master Slinoor. We must all have courage.'

'Aye,' Fafhrd agreed, finding that a cue to his liking. 'Even dragons need not daunt a brave man. I've often watched the sea monsters, crested, horned, and some two-headed, playing in the waves of outer ocean as they broke around the rocks sailors call the Claws. They were not to be feared, if a man remembered always to fix them with a commanding eye. They sported lustily together, the man dragons pursuing the woman dragons and going—' Here Fafhrd took a tremendous breath and then roared out so loudly and wailingly that the two helmsmen jumped – '*Hoongk! Hoongk!*'

'Fie, Swordsman Fafhrd,' Hisvet said primly, a blush

mantling her cheeks and forehead. 'You are most indelicate. The sex of dragons—'

But Slinoor had whirled on Fafhrd, gripping his wrist and now crying, 'Quiet, you monster-fool! Know you not we sail tonight by moonlight past the Dragon Rocks? You'll call them down on us!'

'There are no dragons in the Inner Sea,' Fafhrd laughingly assured him.

'There's something that tears ships,' Slinoor asserted stubbornly.

The Mouser took advantage of this brief interchange to move in on Hisvet, rapidly bowing thrice as he approached.

'We have missed the great pleasure of your company on deck, Demoiselle,' he said suavely.

'Alas, sir, the sun mislikes me,' she answered prettily. 'Now his rays are mellowed as he prepared to submerge. Then too,' she added with an equally pretty shudder, 'these rough sailors—' She broke off as she saw that Fafhrd and the master of *Squid* had stopped their argument and returned to her. 'Oh, I meant not you, dear Master Slinoor,' she assured him, reaching out and almost touching his black robe.

'Would the Demoiselle fancy a sun-warmed, wind-cooled black plum of Sarheenmar?' the Mouser suggested, delicately sketching in the air with Cat's Claw.

'I know not.' Hisvet said, eyeing the dirk's needlelike point. 'I must be thinking of getting the White Shadows below before the evening's chill is upon us.'

'True,' Fafhrd agreed with a flattering laugh, realizing she must mean the white rats. 'But 'twas most wise of you, Little Mistress, to let them spend the day on deck, where they surely cannot hanker so much to sport with the Black Shadows – I mean, of course, their black free commoner brothers, and slim delightful sisters, to be sure, hiding here and there in the hold.'

'There are no rats on my ship, sportive or otherwise,' Slinoor asserted instantly, his voice loud and angry. 'Think you I run a rat-brothel? Your pardon, Demoiselle,' he added quickly to Hisvet. 'I mean, there are no common rats aboard *Squid*.'

'Then yours is surely the first grain ship so blessed,' Fafhrd told him with indulgent reasonableness.

The sun's vermilion disk touched the sea to the west and flattened like a tangerine. Hisvet leaned back against the taffrail under the arching tiller. Fafhrd was to her right, the Mouser to her left with the plums hanging just beyond him, near the silver cages. Slinoor had moved haughtily forward to speak to the helmsmen, or pretend to.

'I'll take that plum now, Dirksman Mouser,' Hisvet said softly.

As the Mouser turned away in happy obedience and with many a graceful gesture, delicately palpating the net bag to find the most tender fruit, Hisvet stretched her right arm out sideways and without looking once at Fafhrd slowly ran her spread-fingered hand through the hair on his chest, paused when she reached the other side to grasp a fistful and tweak it sharply, then trailed her fingers lightly back across the hair she had ruffled.

Her hand came back to her just as the Mouser turned around. She kissed the palm lingeringly, then reached it across her body to take the black fruit from the point of the Mouser's dirk. She sucked delicately at the prick Cat's Claw had made and shivered.

'Fie, sir,' she pouted. 'You told me 'twould be sun-warmed and 'tis not. Already all things grow chilly with evening.' She looked around her thoughtfully. 'Why, Swordsman Fafhrd is all gooseflesh,' she announced, then blushed and tapped her lips reprovingly. 'Close your jerkin, sir. 'Twill save you from catarrh and perchance from further embarrassment a girl who is unused to any sight of man-flesh save in slaves.'

'Here is a toastier plum,' the Mouser called from beside the bag. Hisvet smiled at him and lightly tossed him back-handed the plum she'd sampled. He dropped that overboard and tossed her the second plum. She caught it deftly, lightly squeezed it, touched it to her lips, shook her head sadly though still smiling, and tossed back the plum. The Mouser, smiling gently too, caught it, dropped it overboard and tossed her a third. They played that way for some time. A shark following in the wake of the *Squid* got a stomach-ache.

The black kitten came single-footing back along the starboard rail with a sharp eye to larboard. Fafhrd seized it instantly as any good general does opportunity in the heat of battle.

'Have you seen the ship's catling, Little Mistress?' he called, crossing to Hisvet, the kitten almost hidden in his big hands. 'Or perhaps we should call the *Squid* the catling's ship, for she adopted it, skipping by herself aboard just as we sailed. Here, Little Mistress. It feels sun-toasted now, warmer than any plum,' and he reached the kitten out sitting on the palm of his right hand.

But Fafhrd had been forgetting the kitten's point of view. Its fur stood on end as it saw itself being carried toward the rats and now, as Hisvet stretched out her hand toward it, showing her upper teeth in a tiny smile and saying, 'Poor little waif,' the kitten hissed fiercely and raked out stiff-armed with spread claws.

Hisvet drew back her hand with a gasp. Before Fafhrd could drop the kitten or bat it aside, it sprang to the top of his head and from there onto the highest point of the tiller.

The Mouser darted to Hisvet, crying meanwhile at Fafhrd, 'Dolt! Lout! You knew the beast was half wild!' Then, to Hisvet, 'Demoiselle! Are you hurt?'

Fafhrd struck angrily at the kitten and one of the helmsmen came back to bat at it too, perhaps because he thought it improper for kittens to walk on the tiller. The kitten made a long leap to the starboard rail, slipped over it, and dangled by two claws above the curving water.

Hisvet was holding her hand away from the Mouser and he was saying, 'Better let me examine it, Demoiselle. Even the slightest scratch from a filthy ship's cat can be dangerous,' and she was saying, almost playfully, 'No, Dirksman, I tell you it's nothing.'

Fafhrd strode to the starboard rail, fully intending to flick the kitten overboard, but somehow when he came to do it he found he had instead cupped the kitten's rear in his hand and lifted it back on the rail. The kitten instantly sank its teeth deeply in the root of his thumb and fled up the aftermast. Fafhrd with difficulty suppressed a great yowl. Slinoor laughed.

'Nevertheless, I will examine it,' the Mouser said masterfully and took Hisvet's hand by force. She let him hold it for a moment, then snatched it back and drawing herself up said frostily, 'Dirksman, you forget yourself. Not even her own physician touches a Demoiselle of Lankhmar, he touches only the body of her maid, on which the Demoiselle points out her pains and symptoms. Leave me, Dirksman.'

The Mouser stood huffily back against the taffrail. Fafhrd sucked the root of his thumb. Hisvet went and stood beside the Mouser. Without looking at him, she said softly, 'You should have asked me to call my maid. She's quite pretty.'

Only a fingernail clipping of red sun was left on the horizon. Slinoor addressed the crow's nest: 'What of the black sail, boy?'

'She holds her distance, master,' the cry came back. 'She courses on abreast of us.'

The sun went under with a faint green flash. Hisvet bent her head sideways and kissed the Mouser on the neck, just under the ear. Her tongue tickled.

'Now I lose her, master,' the crow's nest called. 'There's mist to the northwest. And to the northeast . . . a small black cloud . . . like a black ship specked with light . . . that moves through the sir. And now that fades too. All gone, master.'

Hisvet straightened her head. Slinoor came toward them muttering, 'The crow's nest sees too much.' Hisvet shivered and said, 'The White Shadows will take a chill. They're delicate, Dirksman.' The Mouser breathed, 'You are Ecstasy's White Shadow, Demoiselle,' then strolled toward the silver cages, saying loudly for Slinoor's benefit, 'Might we not be privileged to have a show of them, Demoiselle, tomorrow here on the afterdeck? 'Twould be wondrous instructive to watch you control them.' He caressed the air over the cages and said, lying mightily, 'My, they're fine handsome fellows.' Actually he was peering apprehensively for any of the little spears and swords Slinoor had mentioned. The twelve rats looked up at him incuriously. One even seemed to yawn.

Slinoor said curtly, 'I would advise against it, Demoiselle. The sailors have a mad fear and hatred of all rats. 'Twere best not to arouse it.'

'But these are aristos,' the Mouser objected, while Hisvet only repeated, 'They'll take a chill.'

Fafhrd, hearing this, took his hand out of his mouth and came hurrying to Hisvet, saying, 'Little Mistress, may I carry them below? I'll be gentle as a Kleshite nurse.' He lifted between thumb and third finger a cage with two rats in it. Hisvet rewarded him with a smile, saying, 'I wish you would, gallant Swordsman. The common sailors handle them too roughly. But two cages are all you may safely carry. You'll need proper help.' She gazed at the Mouser and Slinoor.

So Slinoor and the Mouser, the latter much to his distaste and apprehension, must each gingerly take up a silver cage, and Fafhrd two, and follow Hisvet to her cabin below the after-deck. The Mouser could not forbear whispering privily to Fafhrd, 'Oaf! To make rat-grooms of us! May you get rat-bites to match your cat-bite!' At the cabin door Hisvet's dark maid Frix received the cages, Hisvet thanked her three gallants most briefly and distantly and Frix closed the door against them. There was the muffled thud of a bar dropping across it and the jangle of a chain locking down the bar.

Darkness grew on the waters. A yellow lantern was lit and hoisted to the crow's nest. The black war galley *Shark*, its brown sail temporarily furled, came rowing back to fuss at *Clam*, next ahead of *Squid* in line, for being slow in getting up its masthead light, then dropped back by *Squid* while Lukeen and Slinoor exchanged shouts about a black sail and mist and ship-shaped small black clouds and the Dragon Rocks. Finally the galley went bustling ahead again with its Lankhmarines in browned-iron chain mail to take up its sailing station at the head of the column. The first stars twinkled, proof that the sun had not deserted through the waters of eternity to some other world bubble, but was swimming as he should back to the east under the ocean of the sky, errant rays from his lighting the floating star-jewels in his passage.

After moonrise that night Fafhrd and the Mouser each found private occasion to go rapping at Hisvet's door, but neither profited greatly thereby. At Fafhrd's knock Hisvet herself opened the small grille set in the larger door, said swiftly, 'Fie, for shame, Swordsman! Can't you see I'm undressing?' and closed it instantly. While when the Mouser asked softly for a moment with 'Ecstasy's White Shadow', the merry face of the dark maid Frix appeared at the grille, saying, 'My mistress bid me kiss my hand good night to you.' Which she did and closed the grille.

Fafhrd, who had been spying, greeted the crestfallen Mouser with a sardonic, 'Ecstasy's White Shadow!'

'Little Mistress!' the Mouser retorted scathingly.

'Black Plum of Sarheenmar!'

'Kleshite Nurse!'

Neither hero slept restfully that night and two-thirds through it the *Squid*'s gong began to sound at intervals, with the other ships' gongs replying or calling faintly. When at dawn's first blink the two came on deck, *Squid* was creeping through fog that hid the sail top. The two helmsmen were peering about jumpily, as if they expected to see ghosts. The sails were barely filled. Slinoor, his eyes dark-circled by fatigue and big with anxiety, explained tersely that the fog had not only slowed but disordered the grain fleet.

'That's *Tunny* next ahead of us, I can tell by her gong note. And beyond *Tunny*, *Carp*. Where's *Clam*? What's *Shark* about? And still not certainly past the Dragon Rocks! Not that I want to see 'em!'

'Do not some captains call them the Rat Rocks?' Fafhrd interposed. 'From a rat-colony started there from a wreck?'

'Aye,' Slinoor allowed and then grinning sourly at the Mouser, observed. 'Not the best day for a rat-show on the afterdeck, is it? Which is some good from this fog. I can't abide the lolling white brutes. Though but a dozen in number they remind me too much of the Thirteen. Have you ever heard tell of the legend of the Thirteen?'

'I have,' Fafhrd said somberly. 'A wise woman of the Cold Waste once told me that for each animal kind – wolves, bats, whales, it holds for all and each – there are always thirteen individuals having almost manlike (or demonlike!) wisdom and skill. Can you but find and master this inner circle, the Wise Woman said, then through them you can control all animals of that kind.'

Slinoor looked narrowly at Fafhrd and said, 'She was not an altogether stupid woman.'

The Mouser wondered if for men also there was an inner circle of Thirteen.

The black kitten came ghosting along the deck out of the fog forward. It made toward Fafhrd with an eager mew, then hesitated, studying him dubiously.

'Take for example, cats,' Fafhrd said with a grin. 'Somewhere in Nehwon today, mayhap scattered but more likely banded together, are thirteen cats of superfeline sagacity, somehow sensing and controlling the destiny of all catkind.'

'What's this one sensing now?' Slinoor demanded softly.

The black kitten was staring to larboard, sniffing. Suddenly its scrawny body stiffened, the hair rising along its back and its skimpy tail a-bush.

'*Hoongk!*'

Slinoor turned to Fafhrd with a curse, only to see the Northerner staring about shut-mouthed and startled. Clearly *he* had not bellowed.

3

Out of the fog to larboard came a green serpent's head big as a horse's, with white dagger teeth fencing red mouth horrendously agape. With dreadful swiftness it lunged low past Fafhrd on its endless yellow neck, its lower jaw loudly scraping the deck, and the white daggers clashed on the black kitten.

Or rather, on where the kitten had just been. For the latter seemed not so much to leap as to lift itself, by its tail perhaps, onto the starboard rail and thence vanished into the fog at the top of the aftermast in at most three more bounds.

The helmsmen raced each other forward. Slinoor and the Mouser threw themselves against the starboard taffrail, the unmanned tiller swinging slowly above them affording some sense of protection against the monster, which now lifted its nightmare head and swayed it this way and that, each time avoiding Fafhrd by inches. Apparently it was searching for the black kitten or more like it.

Fafhrd stood frozen, at first by sheer shock, then by the thought that whatever part of him moved first would get snapped off.

Nevertheless he was about to jump for it – besides all else the monster's mere stench was horrible – when a second green dragon's head, four times as big as the first with teeth like scimitars, came looming out of the fog. Sitting commandingly atop this second head was a man dressed in orange and purple, like a herald of the Eastern Lands, with red boots, cape, and helmet, the last with a blue window in it, seemingly of opaque glass.

There is a point of grotesquerie beyond which horror cannot go, but slips into delirium. Fafhrd had reached that point. He began to feel as if he were in an opium dream. Everything was unquestionably real, yet it had lost its power to horrify him acutely.

He noticed as the merest of quaint details that the two greenish yellow necks forked from a common trunk.

Besides, the gaudily garbed man or demon riding the larger head seemed very sure of himself, which might or might not be a good thing. Just now he was belaboring the smaller head, seemingly in rebuke, with a blunt-pointed, blunt-hooked pike he carried, and roaring out, either under or through his blue red helmet, a gibberish that might be rendered as:

'*Gottverdammter Ungeheuer!*'*

The smaller head cringed away, whimpering like seventeen puppies. The man-demon whipped out a small book of pages and after consulting it twice (apparently he could see *out* through his blue window) called down in broken, outlandishly accented Lankhmarese, 'What world is this, friend?'

Fafhrd had never before in his life heard that question asked, even by an awakening brandy guzzler. Nevertheless in his opium-dream mood he answered easily enough, 'The world of Nehwon, oh sorcerer!'

'*Got sei dank!*'† the man-demon gibbered.

Fafhrd asked, 'What world do *you* hail from?'

The question seemed to confound the man-demon. Hurriedly consulting his book, he replied, 'Do you know about other worlds? Don't you believe the stars are only huge jewels?'

Fafhrd responded, 'Any fool can see that the lights in the sky are jewels, but we are not simpletons, we know of other worlds. The Lankhmarts think they're bubbles in infinite waters. *I* believe we live in the jewel-ceilinged skull of a dead god. But doubtless there are other such skulls, the universe of universes being a great frosty battlefield.'

* 'Goddam monster!' German is a language completely unknown in Nehwon.
† 'Thank God!'

The tiller, swinging as *Squid* wallowed with sail a-flap, bumped the lesser head, which twisted around and snapped at it, then shook splinters from its teeth.

'Tell the sorcerer to keep it off!' Slinoor shouted, cringing.

After more hurried page-flipping the man-demon called, 'Don't worry, the monster seems to eat only rats. I captured it by a small rocky island where many rats live. It mistook your small black ship's cat for a rat.'

Still in his mood of opium-lucidity, Fafhrd called up, 'Oh sorcerer, do you plan to conjure the monster to your own skull-world, or world-bubble?'

This question seemed doubly to confound and excite the man-demon. He appeared to think Fafhrd must be a mind reader. With much frantic book-consulting, he explained that he came from a world called simply Tomorrow and that he was visiting many worlds to collect monsters for some sort of museum or zoo, which he called in his gibberish *Hagenbeck's Zeitgarten*.* On this particular expedition he had been seeking a monster that would be a reasonable facsimile of a wholly mythical six-headed sea-monster that devoured men off the decks of ships and was called Scylla by an ancient fantasy writer named Homer.

'There never was a Lankhmar poet named Homer,' muttered Slinoor.

'Doubtless he was a minor scribe of Quarmall or the Eastern Lands,' the Mouser told Slinoor reassuringly. Then, grown less fearful of the two heads and somewhat jealous of Fafhrd holding the center of the stage, the Mouser leapt atop the taffrail and cried, 'Oh, sorcerer, with what spells will you conjure your Little Scylla back to, or perhaps I should say ahead to, your Tomorrow bubble? I myself know somewhat of witchcraft. Desist, vermin!' This last remark was directed with a gesture of lordly contempt toward the lesser head, which came questing curiously toward the Mouser. Slinoor gripped the Mouser's ankle.

The man-demon reacted to the Mouser's question by slap-

* Literally, in German, 'Hagenbeck's Time garden,' apparently derived from *Tiergarten*, which means animal-garden, or zoo.

ping himself on the side of his red helmet, as though he'd forgotten something most important. He hurriedly began to explain that he traveled between worlds in a ship (or space-time engine, whatever that might mean) that tended to float just above the water – 'a black ship with little lights and masts' – and that the ship had floated away from him in another fog a day ago while he'd been absorbed in taming the newly captured sea-monster. Since then the man-demon, mounted on his now-docile monster, had been fruitlessly searching for his lost vehicle.

The description awakened a memory in Slinoor, who managed to nerve himself to explain audibly that last sunset *Squid's* crow's nest had sighted just such a ship floating or flying to the northeast.

The man-demon was voluble in his thanks and after questioning Slinoor closely announced (rather to everyone's relief) that he was now ready to turn his search eastward with new hope.

'Probably I will never have the opportunity to repay your courtesies,' he said in parting. 'But as you drift through the waters of eternity at least carry with you my name: Karl Treuherz of Hagenbeck's.'

Hisvet, who had been listening from the middeck, chose that moment to climb the short ladder that led up to the afterdeck. She was wearing an ermine smock and hood against the chilly fog.

As her silvery hair and pale lovely features rose above the level of the afterdeck the smaller dragon's head, which had been withdrawing decorously, darted at her with the speed of a serpent striking. Hisvet dropped. Woodwork rended loudly.

Backing off into the fog atop the larger and rather benign-eyed head, Karl Treuherz gibbered as never before and belabored the lesser head mercilessly as it withdrew.

Then the two-headed monster with its orange-and-purple mahout could be dimly seen moving around *Squid's* stern eastward into thicker fog, the man-demon gibbering gentlier what might have been an excuse and farewell: '*Es tut mir sehr leid! Aber dankeschoen, dankeschoen!*'*

* It was: 'I am so very sorry! But thank you, thank you so nicely!'

With a last gentle '*Hoongk!*' the man-demon dragon-dragon assemblage faded into the fog.

Fafhrd and the Mouser raced a tie to Hisvet's side, vaulting down over the splintered rail, only to have her scornfully reject their solicitude as she lifted herself from the oaken middeck, delicately rubbing her hip and limping for a step or two.

'Come not near me, Spoonmen,' she said bitterly. 'Shame it is when a Demoiselle must save herself from toothy perdition only by falling helter-skelter on that part of her which I would almost shame to show you on Frix. You are no gentle knights, else dragons' heads had littered the afterdeck. Fie, fie!'

Meanwhile patches of clear sky and water began to show to the west and the wind to freshen from the same quarter. Slinoor dashed forward, bawling for his bosun to chase the monster-scared sailors up from the forecastle before *Squid* did herself an injury.

Although there was yet little real danger of that, the Mouser stood by the tiller, Fafhrd looked to the mainsheet. Then Slinoor, hurrying back aft followed by a few pale sailors, sprang to the taffrail with a cry.

The fogbank was slowly rolling eastward. Clear water stretched to the western horizon. Two bowshots north of *Squid*, four other ships were emerging in a disordered cluster from the white wall: the war galley *Shark* and the grain ships *Tunny*, *Carp*, and *Grouper*. The galley, moving rapidly under oars, was headed toward *Squid*.

But Slinoor was staring south. There, a scant bowshot away, were two ships, the one standing clear of the fogbank, the other half hid in it.

The one in the clear was *Clam*, about to sink by the head, its gunwales awash. Its mainsail, somehow carried away, trailed brownly in the water. The empty deck was weirdly arched upward.

The fog-shrouded ship appeared to be a black cutter with a black sail.

Between the two ships, from *Clam* toward the cutter, moved a multitude of tiny, dark-headed ripples.

Fafhrd joined Slinoor. Without looking away, the latter said simply, 'Rats.' Fafhrd's eyebrows rose.

The Mouser joined them, saying, '*Clam*'s holed. The water swells the grain, which mightily forces up the deck.'

Slinoor nodded and pointed toward the cutter. It was possible dimly to see tiny dark forms – rats surely! – climbing over its side from out of the water. 'There's what gnawed holes in *Clam*,' Slinoor said.

Then Slinoor pointed between the ships, near the cutter. Among the last of the ripple-army was a white-headed one. A second later a small white form could be seen swiftly mounting the cutter's side. Slinoor said, 'There's what commanded the hole-gnawers.'

With a dull splintering rumble the arched deck of *Clam* burst upward, spewing brown.

'The grain!' Slinoor cried hollowly.

'Now you know what tears ships,' the Mouser said.

The black cutter grew ghostlier, moving west now into the retreating fog.

The galley *Shark* went boiling past *Squid*'s stern, its oars moving like the legs of a leaping centipede. Lukeen shouted up, 'Here's foul trickery! *Clam* was lured off in the night!'

The black cutter, winning its race with the eastward-rolling fog, vanished in whiteness.

The split-decked *Clam* nosed under with hardly a ripple and angled down into the black and salty depths, dragged by its leaden keel.

With war trumpet skirling, *Shark* drove into the white wall after the cutter.

Clam's masthead, cutting a little furrow in the swell, went under. All that was to be seen now on the waters south of *Squid* was a great spreading stain of tawny grain.

Slinoor turned grim-faced to his mate. 'Enter the Demoiselle Hisvet's cabin, by force if need be,' he commanded. 'Count her white rats!'

Fafhrd and the Mouser looked at each other.

Three hours later the same four persons were assembled in Hisvet's cabin with the Demoiselle, Frix and Lukeen.

The cabin, low-ceilinged enough so that Fafhrd, Lukeen, and the mate must move bent and tended to sit hunch-shouldered, was spacious for a grain ship, yet crowded by this company together with the caged rats and Hisvet's perfumed, silver-bound baggage piled on Slinoor's dark furniture and locked sea chests. Three horn windows to the stern and louver slits to starboard and larboard let in a muted light.

Slinoor and Lukeen sat against the horn windows, behind a narrow table. Fafhrd occupied a cleared sea chest, the Mouser an upended cask. Between them were racked the four rat-cages, whose white-furred occupants seemed as quietly intent on the proceedings as any of the men. The Mouser amused himself by imagining what it would be like if the white rats were trying the men instead of the other way round. A row of blue-eyed white rats would make most formidable judges, already robed in ermine. He pictured them staring down mercilessly from very high seats at a tiny cringing Lukeen and Slinoor, round whom scuttled mouse pages and mouse clerks and behind whom stood rat pikemen in half armor holding fantastically barbed and curvy-bladed weapons.

The mate stood stooping by the open grille of the closed door, in part to see that no other sailors eavesdropped.

The Demoiselle Hisvet sat cross-legged on the swung-down sea-bed, her ermine smock decorously tucked under her knees, managing to look most distant and courtly even in this attitude. Now and again her right hand played with the dark wavy hair of Frix, who crouched on the deck at her knees.

Timbers creaked as *Squid* bowled north. Now and then the bare feet of the helmsmen could be heard faintly slithering on the afterdeck overhead. Around the small trapdoor-like hatches leading below and through the very crevices of the planking came the astringent, toastlike, all-pervasive odor of the grain.

Lukeen spoke. He was a lean, slant-shouldered, cordily muscled man almost as big as Fafhrd. His short coat of browned-iron mail over his simple black tunic was of the finest links. A golden band confined his dark hair and bound to his forehead the browned-iron five-pointed curvy-edged starfish emblem of Lankhmar.

'How do I know *Clam* was lured away? Two hours before dawn I twice thought I heard *Shark*'s own gong-note in the distance, although I stood then beside *Shark*'s muffled gong. Three of my crew heard it too. 'Twas most eerie. Gentlemen, I know the gong-notes of Lankhmar war galleys and merchantmen better than I know my children's voices. This that we heard was so like *Shark*'s I never dreamed it might be that of another ship – I deemed it some ominous ghost-echo or trick of our minds and I thought no more about it as a matter for action. If I had only had the faintest suspicion . . .'

Lukeen scowled bitterly, shaking his head, and continued, 'Now I know the black cutter must carry a gong shaped to duplicate *Shark*'s note precisely. They used it, likely with someone mimicking my voice, to draw *Clam* out of line in the fog and get her far enough off so that the rat-horde, officered by the white one, could work its will on her without the crew's screams being heard. They must have gnawed twenty holes in her bottom for *Clam* to take on water so fast and the grain to swell so. Oh, they're far shrewder and more persevering than men, the little spade-toothed fiends!'

'Midsea madness!' Fafhrd snorted in interruption. 'Rats make men scream? And do away with them? Rats seize a ship and sink it? Rats officered and accepting discipline? Why, this is the rankest superstition!'

'You're a fine one to talk of superstition and the impossible, Fafhrd,' Slinoor shot at him, 'when only this morning you talked with a masked and gibbering demon who rode a two-headed dragon.'

Lukeen lifted his eyebrows at Slinoor. This was the first he'd heard of the Hagenbeck episode.

Fafhrd said, 'That was travel between worlds. Another matter altogether. No superstition in it.'

Slinoor responded skeptically. 'I suppose there was no superstition in it either when you told me what you'd heard from the Wise Woman about the Thirteen?'

Fafhrd laughed. 'Why, I never believed one word the Wise Woman ever told me. She was a witchy old fool. I recounted her nonsense merely as a curiosity.'

Slinoor eyed Fafhrd with slit-eyed incredulity, then said to Lukeen, 'Continue.'

'There's little more to tell,' the latter said. 'I saw the rat-battalions swimming from *Clam* to the black cutter. I saw, as you did, their white officer.' This with a glare at Fafhrd. 'Thereafter I fruitlessly hunted the black cutter for two hours in the fog until cramp took my rowers. If I'd found her, I'd not boarded her but thrown fire into her! Aye, and stood off the rats with burning oil on the waters if they tried again to change ships! Aye, and laughed as the furred murderers fried!'

'Just so,' Slinoor said with finality. 'And what, in your judgment, Commander Lukeen, should we do now?'

'Sink the white archfiends in their cages,' Lukeen answered instantly, 'before they officer the rape of more ships, or our sailors go mad with fear.'

This brought an instant icy retort from Hisvet. 'You'll have to sink me first, silver-weighted, oh Commander!'

Lukeen's gaze moved past her to a scatter of big-eared silver unguent jars and several looped heavy silver chains on a shelf by the bed. 'That too is not impossible, Demoiselle,' he said, smiling hardly.

'There's not one shred of proof against her!' Fafhrd exploded. 'Little Mistress, the man is mad.'

'No proof?' Lukeen roared. 'There were twelve white rats yesterday. Now there are eleven.' He waved a hand at the stacked cages and their blue-eyed haughty occupants. 'You've all counted them. Who else but this devilish Demoiselle sent the white officer to direct the sharp-toothed gnawers and killers that destroyed *Clam*? What more proof do you want?'

'Yes, indeed!' the Mouser interjected in a high vibrant voice that commanded attention. 'There is proof aplenty . . . *if* there were twelve rats in the four cages yesterday.' Then he added casually but very clearly, 'It is my recollection that there were eleven.'

Slinoor stared at the Mouser as though he couldn't believe his ears. 'You lie!' he said. 'What's more, you lie senselessly. Why, you and Fafhrd and I all spoke of there being twelve white rats!'

The Mouser shook his head. 'Fafhrd and I said no word about the exact number of rats. *You* said there were a dozen,' he informed Slinoor. 'Not twelve, but . . . a dozen. I assumed you were using the expression as a round number, an approximation.' The Mouser snapped his fingers. 'Now I remember that when you said a dozen I became idly curious and counted the rats. And got eleven. But it seemed to me too trifling a matter to dispute.'

'No, there were twelve rats yesterday,' Slinoor asserted solemnly and with great conviction. 'You're mistaken, Gray Mouser.'

'I'll believe my friend Slinoor before a dozen of you,' Lukeen put in.

'True, friends should stick together,' the Mouser said with an approving smile. 'Yesterday I counted Glipkerio's gift-rats and got eleven. Ship's Master Slinoor, any man may be mistaken in his recollections from time to time. Let's analyze this. Twelve white rats divided by four silver cages equals three to a cage. Now let me see . . . I have it! There was a time yesterday when between us, we surely counted the rats – when we carried them down to this cabin. How many were in the cage you carried, Slinoor?'

'Three,' the latter said instantly.

'And three in mine,' the Mouser said.

'And three in each of the other two,' Lukeen put in impatiently. 'We waste time!'

'We certainly do,' Slinoor agreed strongly, nodding.

'Wait!' said the Mouser, lifting a point-fingered hand. 'There was a moment when all of us must have noticed how many rats there were in one of the cages Fafhrd carried – when he first lifted it up, speaking the while to Hisvet. Visualize it. He lifted it like this.' The Mouser touched his thumb to his third finger. 'How many rats were there in that cage, Slinoor?'

Slinoor frowned deeply. 'Two,' he said, adding instantly, 'and four in the other.'

'You said three in each just now,' the Mouser reminded him.

'I did not!' Slinoor denied. 'Lukeen said that, not I.'

'Yes, but you nodded, agreeing with him,' the Mouser said, his raised eyebrows the very emblem of innocent truth-seeking.

'I agreed with him only that we wasted time,' Slinoor said. 'And we do.' Just the same a little of the frown lingered between his eyes and his voice had lost its edge of utter certainty.

33

'I see,' the Mouser said doubtfully. By stages he had begun to play the part of an attorney elucidating a case in court, striding about and frowning most professionally. Now he shot a sudden question, 'Fafhrd, how many rats did you carry?'

'Five,' boldly answered the Northerner, whose mathematics were not of the sharpest, but who'd had plenty of time to count surreptitiously on his fingers and to think about what the Mouser was up to. 'Two in one cage, three in the other.'

'A feeble falsehood!' Lukeen scoffed. 'The base barbarian would swear to anything to win a smile from the Demoiselle, who has him fawning.'

'That's a foul lie!' Fafhrd roared, springing up and fetching his head such a great hollow thump on a deck beam that he clapped both hands to it and crouched in dizzy agony.

'Sit down, Fafhrd, before I ask you to apologize to the deck!' the Mouser commanded with heartless harshness. 'This is solemn civilized court, no barbarous brawling session! Let's see – three and three and five make . . . eleven. Demoiselle Hisvet!' He pointed an accusing finger straight between her red-irised eyes and demanded most sternly, 'How many white rats did you bring aboard *Squid*? The truth now and nothing but the truth!'

'Eleven,' she answered demurely. 'La, but I'm joyed someone at last had the wit to ask me.'

'That I know's not true!' Slinoor said abruptly, his brow once more clear. 'Why didn't I think of it before? – 'twould have saved us all this bother of questions and counting. I have in this very cabin Glipkerio's letter of commission to me. In it he speaks verbatim of entrusting to me the Demoiselle Hisvet, daughter of Hisvin, and twelve witty white rats. Wait, I'll get it out and prove it to your faces!'

'No need, Ship's Master,' Hisvet interposed. 'I saw the letter writ and can testify to the perfect truth of your quotations. But most sadly, between the sending of the letter and my boarding of *Squid*, poor Tchy was gobbled up by Glippy's giant boarhound Bimbat.' She touched a slim finger to the corner of her eye and sniffed. 'Poor Tchy, he was the most winsome of the twelve. 'Twas why I kept to my cabin the first two days.' Each time she spoke the name Tchy, the eleven caged rats chittered mournfully.

'Is it Glippy you call our overlord?' Slinoor ejaculated, genuinely shocked. 'Oh shameless one!'

'Aye, watch your language, Demoiselle,' the Mouser warned severely, maintaining to the hilt his new role of austere inquisitor. 'Any familiar relationship between you and our overlord the arch-noble Glipkerio Kistomerces does not come within the province of this court.'

'She lies like a shrewd subtle witch!' Lukeen asserted angrily. 'Thumbscrew or rack, or perchance just a pale arm twisted high behind her back would get the truth from her fast enough!'

Hisvet turned and looked at him proudly. 'I accept your challenge, Commander,' she said evenly, laying her right hand on her maid's dark head. 'Frix, reach out your naked hand, or whatever other part of you the brave gentleman wishes to torture.' The dark maid straightened her back. Her face was impassive, lips firmly pressed together, though her eyes searched around wildly. Hisvet continued to Slinoor and Lukeen, 'If you know any Lankhmar law at all, you know that a virgin of the rank of Demoiselle is tortured only in the person of her maid, who proves by her steadfastness under extreme pain the innocence of her mistress.'

'What did I tell you about her?' Lukeen demanded of them all. 'Subtle is too gross a term for her spiderwebby sleights!' He glared at Hisvet and said scornfully, his mouth a-twist, 'Virgin!'

Hisvet smiled with cold long-suffering. Fafhrd flushed and although still holding his battered head, barely refrained from leaping up again. Lukeen looked at him with amusement, secure in his knowledge that he could bait Fafhrd at will and that the barbarian lacked the civilized wit to insult him deeply in return.

Fafhrd stared thoughtfully at Lukeen from under his capping hands. Then he said, 'Yes, you're brave enough in armor, with your threats against girls and your hot imaginings of torture, but if you were without armor and had to prove your manhood with just one brave girl alone, you'd fall like a worm!'

Lukeen shot up enraged and got himself such a clout from a deck beam that he squeaked shudderingly and swayed. Nevertheless he gripped blindly for his sword at his side. Slinoor grasped that wrist and pulled him down into his seat.

'Govern yourself, Commander,' Slinoor implored sternly,

seeming to grow in resolution as the rest quarreled and quibbled. 'Fafhrd, no more dagger words. Gray Mouser, this is not your court but mine and we are not met to split the hairs of high law but to meet a present peril. Here and now this grain fleet is in grave danger. Our very lives are risked. Much more than that, Lankhmar's in danger if Morvarl gets not his gift-grain at this third sending. Last night *Clam* was foully murdered. Tonight it may be *Grouper* or *Squid*, *Shark* even, or no less than all our ships. The first two fleets went warned and well guarded, yet suffered only total perdition.'

He paused to let that sink in. Then, 'Mouser, you've roused some small doubts in my mind by your eleven-twelving. But small doubts are nothing where home lives and home cities are in peril. For the safety of the fleet and of Lankhmar we'll sink the white rats forthwith and keep close watch on the Demoiselle Hisvet to the very docks of Kvarch Nar.'

'Right!' The Mouser cried approvingly, getting in ahead of Hisvet. But then he instantly added, with the air of sudden brilliant inspiration, '*Or* . . . better yet . . . appoint Fafhrd and myself to keep unending watch not only on Hisvet but also on the eleven white rats. That way we don't spoil Glipkerio's gift and risk offending Movarl.'

'I'd trust no one's mere watching of the rats. They're too tricksy,' Slinoor informed him. 'The Demoiselle I intend to put on *Shark*, where she'll be more closely guarded. The grain is what Movarl wants, not the rats. He doesn't know about them, so can't be angered at not getting them.'

'But he does know about them,' Hisvet interjected. 'Glipkerio and Movarl exchange weekly letters by albatross-post. La, but Nehwon grows smaller each year, Ship's Master – ships are snails compared to the great winging mail-birds. Glipkerio wrote of the rats to Movarl, who expressed great delight at the prospective gift and intense anticipation of watching the White Shadows perform. Along with myself,' she added, demurely bending her head.

'Also,' the Mouser put in rapidly, 'I must firmly oppose – most regretfully, Slinoor – the transfer of Hisvet to another ship. Fafhrd's and my commission from Glipkerio, which I can produce at any time, states in clearest words that we are to attend the Demoiselle at all times outside her private quarters. He makes us wholly responsible for her safety – and also for that of the White Shadows, which creatures our overlord states, again in clearest writing, that he prizes beyond their weight in jewels.'

'You can attend her in *Shark*,' Slinoor told the Mouser curtly.

'I'll not have the barbarian on my ship!' Lukeen rasped, still squinting from the pain of his clout.

'I'd scorn to board such a tricked-out rowboat or oar-worm,' Fafhrd shot back at him, voicing the common barbarian contempt for galleys.

'*Also*,' the Mouser cut in again, loudly, with an admonitory gesture at Fafhrd, 'it is my duty as a friend to warn you, Slinoor, that in your reckless threats against the White Shadows and the Demoiselle herself, you risk incurring the heaviest displeasure not only of our overlord but also of the most powerful grain merchant in Lankhmar.'

Slinoor answered mostly simply, 'I think only of the City and the grain fleet. You know that,' but Lukeen, fuming, spat out a 'Hah!' and said scornfully, 'The Gray Fool has not grasped that it is Hisvet's very father Hisvin who is behind the rat-sinkings, since he thereby grows rich with the extra nation's-ransoms of grain he sells Glipkerio!'

'Quiet, Lukeen!' Slinoor commanded apprehensively. 'This dubious guesswork of yours has no place here.'

'Guesswork? Mine,' Lukeen exploded. 'It was *your* suggestion, Slinoor – Yes, and that Hisvin plots Glipkerio's overthrow – Aye, and even that he's in league with the Mingols! Let's speak truth for once!'

'Then speak it for yourself alone, Commander,' Slinoor said most sober-sharply. 'I fear the blow's disordered your brain. Gray Mouser, you're a man of sense,' he appealed. 'Can you not understand my one overriding concern? We're alone with mass murder on the high seas. We must take measures against it. Oh, will none of you show some simple wit?'

'La, and I will, Ship's Master, since you ask it,' Hisvet said brightly, rising to her knees on the sea-bed as she turned toward Slinoor. Sunlight striking through a louver shimmered on her silver hair and gleamed from the silver ring confining it. 'I'm but

37

a girl, unused to problems of war and rapine, yet I have an all-explaining simple thought that I have waited in vain to hear voiced by one of you gentlemen, wise in the ways of violence.

'Last night a ship was slain. You hang the crime on rats – small beasties which would leave a sinking ship in any case, which often have a few whites among them, and which only by the wildest stretch of imagination are picturable as killing an entire crew and vanishing their bodies. To fill the great gaps in this weird theory you make me a sinister rat-queen, who can work black miracles, and now even, it seems, create my poor doting daddy an all-powerful rat-emperor.

'Yet this morning you met a ship's murderer if there ever was one and let him go honking off unchallenged, La, but the man-demon even confessed he'd been seeking a multi-headed monster that would snatch living men from a ship's deck and devour them. Surely he lied when he said his this-world foundling ate small fry only, for it struck at me to devour me – and might earlier have snapped up any of you, except it was sated!

'For what is more likely than that the two-headed long-neck dragon ate all *Clam*'s sailors off her deck, snaking them out of the forecastle and hold, if they fled there, like sweetmeats from a compartmented comfit-box, and then scratched holes in *Clam*'s planking? Or perhaps more likely still, that *Clam* tore out her bottom on the Dragon Rocks in the fog and at the same time met the sea-dragon? These are sober possibilities, gentlemen, apparent even to a soft girl and asking no mind-stretch at all.'

This startling speech brought forth an excited medley of reactions. Simultaneously the Mouser applauded. 'A gem of princess-wit, Demoiselle; oh, you'd make a rare strategist.' Fafhrd said stoutly, 'Most lucid, Little Mistress, yet Karl Treu-herz seemed to me an honest demon.' Frix told them proudly, 'My mistress outthinks you all.' The mate at the door goggled at Hisvet and made the sign of the starfish. Lukeen snarled, 'She conveniently forgets the black cutter,' while Slinoor cried them all down with, 'Rat-queen you say jestingly? Rat-queen you are!'

As the others grew silent at that dire accusation, Slinoor gazing grimly fearful at Hisvet, continued rapidly, 'The Demoi-selle has recalled to me by her speech the worst point against her. Karl Treuherz said his dragon, living by the Rat Rocks, ate only rats. It made no move to gobble us several men, though it had every chance, yet when Hisvet appeared it struck at her at once. It knew her true race.'

Slinoor's voice went shudderingly now. 'Thirteen rats with the minds of men rule the whole rat race. That's ancient wisdom from Lankhmar's wisest seers. Eleven are these silver-furred silent sharpies, hearing our every word. The twelfth celebrates in the black cutter his conquest of *Clam*. The thirteenth' – and he pointed a finger – 'is the silver-haired, red-eyed Demoiselle herself!'

Lukeen slithered to his feet at that, crying, 'Oh, most shrewdly reasoned, Slinoor! And why does she wear such modest shrouding garb except to hide further evidence of the dread kinship? Let me but strip off that cloaking ermine smock and I'll show you a white-furred body and ten small black dugs instead of proper maiden breasts!'

As he came snaking around the table toward Hisvet, Fafhrd sprang up, also cautiously, and pinned Lukeen's arms to his sides in a bear-hug, calling, 'Nay, and you touch her, you die!'

Meantime Frix cried, 'The dragon was sated with *Clam*'s crew, as my mistress told you. It wanted no more coarse-fibered men, but eagerly seized at my dainty-fleshed darling for a dessert mouthful!'

Lukeen wrenched around until his black eyes glared into Fafhrd's green ones inches away. 'Oh most foul barbarian!' he grated. 'I forego rank and dignity and challenge you this instant to a bout of quarterstaves on middeck. I'll prove Hisvet's taint on you by trial of battle. That is, if you dare face civilized combat, you great stinking ape!' And he spat full in Fafhrd's taunting face.

Fafhrd's only reaction was to smile a great smile through the spittle running gummily down his cheek, while maintaining his grip of Lukeen and wary lookout for a bite at his own nose.

Thereafter, challenge having been given and accepted, there was naught for even the head-shaking, heaven-glancing Slinoor to do but hurry preparation for the combat or duel, so that it might be fought before sunset and leave some daylight for taking sober measures for the fleet's safety in the approaching dark of night.

As Slinoor, the Mouser and mate came around them, Fafhrd released Lukeen, who scornfully averting his gaze instantly went on deck to summon a squad of his marines from *Shark* to second him and see fair play. Slinoor conferred with his mate and other officers. The Mouser, after a word with Fafhrd, slipped forward and could be seen gossiping industriously with *Squid*'s bosun and the common members of her crew down to cook and cabin boy. Occasionally something might have passed rapidly from the Mouser's hand to that of the sailor with whom he spoke.

4

Despite Slinoor's urging, the sun was dropping down the western sky before *Squid*'s gongsman beat the rapid brassy tattoo that signalized the imminence of combat. The sky was clear to the west and overhead, but the sinister fogbank still rested a Lankhmar league (twenty bowshots) to the east, paralleling the northward course of the fleet and looking almost as solid and dazzling as a glacier wall in the sun's crosswise rays. Most mysteriously neither hot sun nor west wind dissipated it.

Black-suited, brown-mailed, and brown-helmeted marines facing aft made a wall across *Squid* to either side of the mainmast. They held their spears horizontal and crosswise at arm's length down, making an additional low fence. Black-tunicked sailors peered between their shoulders and boots, or sat with their own brown legs a-dangle on the larboard side of the foredeck, where the great sail did not cut off their view. A few perched in the rigging.

The damaged rail had been stripped away from the break in the afterdeck and there around the bare aftermast sat the three judges: Slinoor, the Mouser, and Lukeen's sergeant. Around them, mostly to larboard of the two helmsmen, were grouped *Squid*'s officers and certain officers of the other ship on whose presence the Mouser had stubbornly insisted, though it had meant time-consuming ferrying by ship's boat.

Hisvet and Frix were in the cabin with the door shut. The

Demoiselle had wanted to watch the duel through the open door or even from the afterdeck, but Lukeen had protested that this would make it easier for her to work an evil spell on him, and the judges had ruled for Lukeen. However the grille was open and now and again the sun's rays twinkled on a peering eye or silvered fingernail.

Between the dark spear-wall of marines and the afterdeck stretched a great square of white oaken deck, empty save for the crane-fittings and like fixed gear and level except for the main hatch, which made a central square of deck a hand's span above the rest. Each corner of the larger square was marked off by a black-chalked quarter circle. Either contestant stepping inside a quarter circle after the duel began (or springing on the rail or grasping the rigging or falling over the side) would at once forfeit the match.

In the forward larboard quarter circle stood Lukeen in black shirt and hose, still wearing his gold-banded starfish emblem. By him was his second, his own hawkfaced lieutenant. With his right hand Lukeen gripped his quarterstaff, a heavy wand of close-grained oak as tall as himself and thick as Hisvet's wrist. Raising it above his head he twirled it till it hummed. He smiled fiendishly.

In the after starboard quarter circle, next to the cabin door, were Fafhrd and his second, the mate of *Carp*, a grossly fat man with a touch of the Mingol in his sallow features. The Mouser could not be judge and second both, and he and Fafhrd had diced more than once with *Carp*'s mate in the old days at Lankhmar – losing money to him, too, which at least indicated that he might be resourceful.

Fafhrd took from him now his own quarterstaff, gripping it cross-handed near one end. He made a few slow practice passes with it through the air, then handed it back to *Carp*'s mate and stripped off his jerkin.

Lukeen's marines sniggered to each other at the Northerner handling a quarterstaff as if it were a two-headed broadsword, but when Fafhrd bared his hairy chest *Squid*'s sailors set up a rousing cheer and when Lukeen commented loudly to his second, 'What did I tell you? A great hairy-pelted ape, beyond question,' and spun his staff again, the sailors booed him lustily.

'Strange,' Slinoor commented in a low voice. 'I had thought Lukeen to be popular among the sailors.'

Lukeen's sergeant looked around incredulously at that remark. The Mouser only shrugged. Slinoor continued to him, 'If the sailors knew your comrade fought on the side of rats, they'd not cheer him.' The Mouser only smiled.

The gong sounded again.

Slinoor rose and spoke loudly: 'A bout at quarterstaves with no breathing spells! Commander Lukeen seeks to prove on the overlord's mercenary Fafhrd certain allegations against a Demoiselle of Lankhmar. First man struck senseless or at mercy of his foe loses. Prepare!'

Two ship's boys went skipping across the middeck, scattering handfuls of white sand.

Sitting, Slinoor remarked to the Mouser, 'A pox on this footling duel! It delays our action against Hisvet and the rats. Lukeen was a fool to bridle at the barbarian. Still, when he's drubbed him, there'll be time enough.'

The Mouser lifted an eyebrow. Slinoor said lightly, 'Oh, didn't you know? Lukeen will win; that's certain,' while the sergeant, nodding soberly, confirmed, 'The Commander's a master of staves. 'Tis no game for barbarians.'

The gong sounded a third time.

Lukeen sprang nimbly across the chalk and onto the hatch, crying, 'Ho, hairy ape! Art ready to double-kiss the oak? – first my staff, then the deck?'

Fafhrd came shambling out, gripping his wand most awkwardly and responding, 'Your spit has poisoned my left eye, Lukeen, but I see some civilized target with my right.'

Lukeen dashed at him joyously then, feinting at elbow and head, then rapidly striking with the other end of his staff at Fafhrd's knee to tumble or lame him.

Fafhrd, abruptly switching to conventional stance and grip, parried the blow and swung a lightning riposte at Lukeen's jaw.

Lukeen got his staff up in time so that the blow hit only his cheek glancingly, but he was unsettled by it and thereafter Fafhrd was upon him, driving him back in a hail of barely-parried blows while the sailors cheered.

Slinoor and the sergeant gaped wide-eyed, but the Mouser only knotted his fingers, muttering, 'Not so fast, Fafhrd.'

Then, as Fafhrd prepared to end it all, he stumbled stepping off the hatch, which changed his swift blow to the head into a slow blow at the ankles. Lukeen leaped up so that Fafhrd's staff passed under his feet, and while he was still in the air rapped Fafhrd on the head.

The sailors groaned. The marines cheered once, growlingly.

The unfooted blow was not of the heaviest, nonetheless it three-quarters stunned Fafhrd and now it was his turn to be driven back under a pelting shower of swipes. For several moments there was no sound but the rutch of soft-soled boots on sanded oak and the rapid dry musical *bong* of staff meeting staff.

When Fafhrd came suddenly to his full senses he was falling away from a wicked swing. A glimpse of black by his heel told him that his next inevitable backward step would carry him inside his own quarter circle.

Swift as thought he thrust far behind him with his staff. Its end struck deck, then stopped against the cabin wall, and Fafhrd heaved himself forward with it, away from the chalk line, ducking and lunging to the side to escape Lukeen's blows while his staff could not protect him.

The sailors screamed with excitement. The judges and officers on the afterdeck kneeled like dice-players, peering over the edge.

Fafhrd had to lift his left arm to guard his head. He took a blow on the elbow and his left arm dropped limp to his side. Thereafter he had to handle his staff like a broadsword indeed, swinging it one-handed in whistling parries and strokes.

Lukeen hung back, playing more cautiously now, knowing Fafhrd's one wrist must tire sooner than his two. He'd aim a few rapid blows at Fafhrd, then prance back.

Barely parrying the third of these attacks, Fafhrd riposted recklessly, not with a proper swinging blow, but simply gripping the end of his staff and lunging. The combined length of Fafhrd and his staff overtook Lukeen's retreat and the tip of Fafhrd's staff poked him low in the chest, just on the nerve spot.

Lukeen's jaw dropped, his mouth stayed open wide, and he wavered. Fafhrd smartly rapped his staff out of his fingers and as it clattered down, toppled Lukeen to the deck with a second almost casual prod.

The sailors cheered themselves hoarse. The marines growled surlily and one cried, 'Foul!' Lukeen's second knelt by him, glaring at Fafhrd. *Carp*'s mate danced a ponderous jig up to Fafhrd and wafted the wand out of his hands. On the afterdeck *Squid*'s officers were glum, though those of the other grain ships seemed strangely jubilant. The Mouser gripped Slinoor's elbow, urging, 'Cry Fafhrd victor,' while the sergeant frowned prodigiously, hand to temple, saying, 'Well, there's nothing I know of in the *rules* . . .'

At that moment the cabin door opened and Hisvet stepped out, wearing a long scarlet, scarlet-hooded silk robe.

The Mouser, sensing climax, sprang to starboard, where *Squid*'s gong hung, snatched the striker from the gongsman and clanged it wildly.

Squid grew silent. Then there were pointings and questioning cries as Hisvet was seen. She put a silver recorder to her lips and began to dance dreamily toward Fafhrd, softly whistling with her recorder a high haunting tune of seven notes in a minor key. From somewhere tiny tuned bells accompanied it tinklingly. Then Hisvet swung to one side, facing Fafhrd as she moved around him, and the questioning cries changed to ones of wonder and astonishment and the sailors came crowding as far aft as they could and swinging through the rigging, as the procession became visible that Hisvet headed.

It consisted of eleven white rats walking in single file on their hind legs and wearing little scarlet robes and caps. The first four carried in each forepaw clusters of tiny silver bells which they shook rhythmically. The next five bore on their shoulders, hanging down between them a little, a double length of looped gleaming silver chain – they were very like five sailors lugging an anchor chain. The last two each bore slantwise a slim silver wand as tall as himself as he walked erect, tail curving high.

The first four halted side by side in rank facing Fafhrd and tinkling their bells to Hisvet's piping.

The next five marched on steadily to Fafhrd's right foot. There their leader paused, looked up at Fafhrd's face with upraised paw, and squeaked three times. Then, gripping his

44

end of the chain in one paw, he used his other three to climb Fafhrd's boot. Imitated by his four fellows, he then carefully climbed Fafhrd's trousers and hairy chest.

Fafhrd stared down at the mounting chain and scarlet-robed rats without moving a muscle, except to frown faintly as tiny paws unavoidably tweaked clumps of his chest-hair.

The first rat mounted to Fafhrd's right shoulder and moved behind his back to his left shoulder, the four other rats following behind in order and never letting slip the chain.

When all five rats were standing on Fafhrd's shoulders, they lifted one strand of the silver chain and brought it forward over his head, most dexterously. Meanwhile he was looking straight ahead at Hisvet, who had completely circled him and now stood piping behind the bell-tinklers.

The five rats dropped the strand, so that the chain hung in a gleaming oval down Fafhrd's chest. At the same instant each rat lifted his scarlet cap as high above his head as his foreleg would reach.

Someone cried, 'Victor!'

The five rats swung down their caps and again lifted them high, and as if from one throat all the sailors and most of the marines and officers cried in a great shout: '*Victor!*'

The five rats led two more cheers for Fafhrd, the men aboard *Squid* obeying as if hypnotized – though whether by some magic power or simply by the wonder and appropriateness of the rats' behavior, it was hard to tell.

Hisvet finished her piping with a merry flourish and the two rats with silver wands scurried up onto the afterdeck and standing at the foot of the aftermast where all might see, began to drub away at each other in most authentic quarterstaff style, their wands flashing in the sunlight and chiming sweetly when they clashed. The silence broke in rounds of exclamation and laughter. The five rats scampered down Fafhrd and returned with the bell-tinklers to cluster around the hem of Hisvet's skirt. Mouser and several officers were leaping down from the after-deck to wring Fafhrd's good hand or clap his back. The marines had much ado to hold back the sailors, who were offering each other bets on which rat would be the winner in this new bout.

Fafhrd, fingering his chain, remarked to the Mouser, 'Strange

45

that the sailors were with me from the start,' and under cover of the hubbub the Mouser smilingly explained, 'I gave them money to bet on you against the marines. Likewise I dropped some hints and made some loans for the same purpose to the officers of the other ships – a fighter can't have too big a claque. Also I started the story going round that the whiteys are anti-rat rats, trained exterminators of their own kind, sample of Glipkerio's latest device for the safety of the train fleets – sailors eat up such tosh.'

'Did you first cry victor?' Fafhrd asked.

The Mouser grinned. 'A judge take sides? In *civilized* combat? Oh, I was prepared to, but 'twasn't needful.'

At that moment Fafhrd felt a small tug at his trousers and looking down saw that the black kitten had bravely approached through the forest of legs and was now climbing him purposefully. Touched at this further display of animal homage, Fafhrd rumbled gently as the kitten reached his belt, 'Decided to heal our quarrel, eh, small black one?' At that the kitten sprang up his chest, sunk his little claws in Fafhrd's bare shoulder and, glaring like a black hangman, raked Fafhrd bloodily across the jaw, then sprang by way of a couple of startled heads to the mainsail and rapidly climbed its concave taut brown curve. Someone threw a belaying pin at the small black blot, but it was negligently aimed and the kitten safely reached the mast-top.

'I forswear all cats!' Fafhrd cried angrily, dabbling at his chin. 'Henceforth rats are my favored beasties.'

'Most properly spoken, Swordsman!' Hisvet called gaily from her own circle of admirers, continuing, 'I will be pleased by your company and the Dirksman's at dinner in my cabin an hour past sunset. We'll conform to the very letter of Slinoor's stricture that I be closely watched and the White Shadows too.' She whistled a little call on her silver recorder and swept back into her cabin with the nine rats close at her heels. The quarterstaving scarlet-robed pair on the afterdeck broke off their drubbing with neither victorious and scampered after her, the crowd parting to make way for them admiringly.

Slinoor, hurrying forward, paused to watch. *Squid*'s skipper was a man deeply bemused. Somewhere in the last half hour the white rats had been transformed from eerie poison-toothed monsters threatening the fleet into popular, clever, harmless animal-mountebanks, whom *Squid*'s sailors appeared to regard as a band of white mascots. Slinoor seemed to be seeking unsuccessfully but unceasingly to decipher how and why.

Lukeen, still looking very pale, followed the last of his disgruntled marines (their purses lighter by many a silver smerduk, for they had been coaxed into offering odds) over the side into *Shark*'s long dinghy, brushing off Slinoor when *Squid*'s skipper would have conferred with him.

Slinoor vented his chagrin by harshly commanding his sailors to leave off their disorderly milling and frisking, but they obeyed him right cheerily, skipping to their proper stations with the happiest of sailor smirks. Those passing the Mouser winked at him and surreptitiously touched their forelocks. *Squid* bowled smartly northward a half bowshot astern of *Tunny*, as she'd been doing throughout the duel, only now she began to cleave the blue water a little more swiftly yet as the west wind freshened and her after sail was broken out. In fact, the fleet began to sail so swiftly now that *Shark*'s dinghy couldn't make the head of the line, although Lukeen could be noted bullying his marine-oarsmen into back-cracking efforts, and the dinghy had finally come to signal *Shark* herself to come back and pick her up – which the war galley achieved only with difficulty, rolling dangerously in the mounting seas and taking until sunset, oars helping sails, to return to the head of the line.

'*He*'ll not be eager to come to *Squid*'s help tonight, or much able to either.' Fafhrd commented to the Mouser where they stood by the larboard middeck rail. There had been no open break between them and Slinoor, but they were inclined to leave him the afterdeck, where he stood beyond the helmsmen in benthead converse with his three officers, who had all lost money on Lukeen and had been sticking close to their skipper ever since.

'Not still expecting *that* sort of peril tonight, are you, Fafhrd?' the Mouser asked with a soft laugh. 'We're far past the Rat Rocks.'

Fafhrd shrugged and said frowningly, 'Perhaps we've gone just a shade too far in endorsing the rats.'

'Perhaps,' the Mouser agreed. 'But then their charming

mistress is worth a fib and false stamp or two, aye and more than that, eh, Fafhrd?'

'She's a brave sweet lass,' Fafhrd said carefully.

'Aye and her maid too,' the Mouser said brightly. 'I noted Frix peering at you adoringly from the cabin entryway after your victory. A most voluptuous wench. Some men might well prefer the maid to the mistress in this instance. Fafhrd?'

Without looking around at the Mouser, the Northerner shook his head.

The Mouser studied Fafhrd, wondering if it were politic to make a certain proposal he had in mind. He was not quite certain of the full nature of Fafhrd's feelings toward Hisvet. He knew the Northerner was a goatish man enough and had yesterday seemed quite obsessed with the love-making they'd missed in Lankhmar, yet he also knew that his comrade had a variable romantic streak that was sometimes thin as a thread yet sometimes grew into a silken ribbon leagues wide in which armies might stumble and be lost.

On the afterdeck Slinoor was now conferring most earnestly with the cook, presumably (the Mouser decided) about Hisvet's (and his own and Fafhrd's) dinner. The thought of Slinoor having to go to so much trouble about the pleasures of three persons who today had thoroughly thwarted him made the Mouser grin and somehow also nerved him to take the uncertain step he'd been contemplating.

'Fafhrd,' he whispered, 'I'll dice you for Hisvet's favors.'

'Why, Hisvet's but a girl—' Fafhrd began in accents of rebuke, then cut off abruptly and closed his eyes in thought. When he opened them, they were regarding the Mouser with a large smile.

'No,' Fafhrd said softly, 'for truly I think this Hisvet is so balky and fantastic a miss it will take both our most heartfelt and cunning efforts to persuade her to aught. And, after that, who knows? Dicing for such a girl's favors were like betting when a Lankhmar night-lily will open and whether to north or south.'

The Mouser chuckled and lovingly dug Fafhrd in the ribs, saying, 'There's my shrewd true comrade!'

Fafhrd looked at the Mouser with sudden dark suspicions.

'Now don't go trying to get me drunk tonight,' he warned, 'or sifting opium in my drink.'

'Hah, you know me better than that, Fafhrd,' the Mouser said with laughing reproach.

'I certainly do,' Fafhrd agreed sardonically.

Again the sun went under with a green flash, indicating crystal clear air to the west, though the strange fogbank, now an ominous dark wall, still paralleled their course a league or so to the east.

The cook, crying, 'My mutton!' went racing forward past them toward the galley, whence a deliciously spicy aroma was wafting.

'We've an hour to kill,' the Mouser said. 'Come on, Fafhrd. On our way to board *Squid* I bought a little jar of wine of Quarmall at the Silver Eel. It's still sealed.'

From just overhead in the rat-lines, the black kitten hissed down at them in angry menace or perhaps warning.

5

Two hours later the Demoiselle Hisvet offered to the Mouser, 'A golden rilk for your thoughts, Dirksman.'

She was on the swung-down sea-bed once more, half reclining. The long table, now laden with tempting viands and tall silver wine cups, had been placed against the bed. Fafhrd sat across from Hisvet, the empty silver cages behind him, while the Mouser was at the stern end of the table. Frix served them all from the door forward, where she took the trays from the cook's boys without giving them so much as a peep inside. She had a small brazier there for keeping hot such items as required it and she tasted each dish and set it aside for a while before serving it. Thick dark pink candles in silver sconces shed a pale light.

The white rats crouched in rather disorderly fashion around a little table of their own set on the floor near the wall between the sea-bed and the door, just aft of one of the trapdoors opening down into the grain-redolent hold. They wore little black jackets open at the front and little black belts around their middles. They seemed more to play with than eat the bits of food Frix set before them on their three or four little silver plates and they did not lift their small bowls to drink their wine-tinted water but rather lapped at them and that not very industriously. One or two would always be scampering up onto the bed to be with Hisvet, which made them most difficult to count, even for Fafhrd, who had the best view. Sometimes he got eleven, sometimes ten. At intervals one of them would stand up on the pink coverlet by Hisvet's knees and chitter at her in cadences so like those of human speech that Fafhrd and the Mouser would have to chuckle.

'Dreamy Dirksman, two rilks for your thoughts!' Hisvet repeated, upping her offer. 'And most immodestly I'll wager a third rilk they are of me.'

The Mouser smiled and lifted his eyebrows. He was feeling very light-headed and a bit uneasy, chiefly because contrary to his intentions he had been drinking much more than Fafhrd. Frix had just served them the main dish, a masterly yellow curry heavy with dark-tasting spices and originally appearing with 'Victor' pricked on it with black capers. Fafhrd was devouring it manfully, though not voraciously, the Mouser was going at it more slowly, while Hisvet all evening had merely toyed with her food.

'I'll take your two rilks, White Princess,' the Mouser replied airily, 'for I'll need one to pay the wager you've just won and the other to fee you for telling me *what* I was thinking of you.'

'You'll not keep my second rilk long, Dirksman,' Hisvet said merrily, 'for as you thought of me you were looking not at my face, but most impudently somewhat lower. You were thinking of those somewhat nasty suspicions Lukeen voiced this day about my secretest person. Confess it now, you were!'

The Mouser could only hang his head a little and shrug helplessly, for she had most truly divined his thoughts. Hisvet laughed and frowned at him in mock anger, saying, 'Oh, you are most indelicate minded, Dirksman. Yet at least you can see that Frix, though indubitably mammalian, is not fronted like a she-rat.'

This statement was undeniably true, for Hisvet's maid was all dark smooth skin except where black silk scarves narrowly circled her slim body at breasts and hips. Silver net tightly confined her black hair and there were many plain silver bracelets on each wrist. Yet although garbed like a slave, Frix did not seem one tonight, but rather a lady-companion who expertly played at being a slave, serving them all with perfect yet laughing, wholly unservile obedience.

Hisvet, by contrast, was wearing another of her long smocks, this of black silk edged with black lace with a lace-edged hood half thrown back. Her silvery white hair was dressed high on her head in great smooth swelling sweeps. Regarding her across the table, Fafhrd said, 'I am certain that the Demoiselle would be no less than completely beautiful to us in whatever shape she chose to present herself to the world – wholly human or somewhat otherwise.'

'Now that was most gallantly spoken, Swordsman,' Hisvet said with a somewhat breathless laugh. 'I must reward you for it. Come to me, Frix.' As the slim maid bent close to her, Hisvet yet twined her white hands round the dark waist and imprinted a sweet slow kiss on Frix's lips. Then she looked up and gave a little tap on the shoulder to Frix, who moved smiling around the table and, half kneeling by Fafhrd, kissed him as she had been kissed. He received the token graciously, without unmannerly excitement, yet when Frix would have drawn back, prolonged the kiss, explaining a bit thickly when he released her: 'Somewhat extra to return to the sender, perchance.' She grinned at him saucily and went to her serving table by the door, saying, 'I must first chop the rats their meat, naughty barbarian.' While Hisvet discoursed, 'Don't seek too much, Bold Swordsman. That was in any case but a small proxy reward for a small gallant speech. A reward with the mouth for words spoken with the mouth. To reward you for drubbing Lukeen and vindicating my honour were a more serious matter altogether, not to be entered on lightly. I'll think of it.'

At this point the Mouser, who just had to be saying something but whose fuddled brain was momentarily empty of suitably venturesome yet courteous wit, called out to Frix, 'Why chop you the rats their mutton, dusky minx? 'Twould be rare sport to see them slice it for themselves.' Frix only wrinkled her nose at him, but Hisvet expounded gravely, 'Only Skwee carves with any great skill. The others might hurt themselves, particularly with the meat shifting about in the slippery curry. Frix, reserve a single chunk for Skwee to display us his ability. Chop the rest fine. Skwee!' she called, setting her voice high. 'Skwee-skwee-skwee!'

A tall rat sprang onto the bed and stood dutifully before her with forelegs folded across his chest. Hisvet instructed him, then took from a silver box behind her a most tiny carving set of knife, steel, and fork in joined treble scabbard and tied it carefully to his belt. Then Skwee bowed low to her and sprang nimbly down to the rats' table.

The Mouser watched the little scene with clouded and heavy-lidded wonder, feeling that he was falling under some sort of spell. At times thick shadows crossed the cabin; at times Skwee grew tall as Hisvet or perhaps it was Hisvet tiny as Skwee. And then the Mouser grew small as Skwee, too, and ran under the bed and fell into a chute that darkly swiftly slid him, not into a dark hold of sacked or loose delicious grain, but into the dark spacious low-ceilinged pleasance of a subterranean rat-metropolis, lit by phosphorus, where robed and long-skirted rats whose hoods hid their long faces moved about mysteri-ously, where rat-swords clashed behind the next pillar and rat-money clinked, where lewd female rats danced in their fur for a fee, where masked rat-spies and rat-informers lurked, where everyone – every-furry-one – was cringingly conscious of the omniscient overlordship of a supernally powerful Council of Thirteen, and where a rat-Mouser sought everywhere a slim rat-princess named Hisvet-sur-Hisvin.

The Mouser woke from his dinnerdream with a jerk. Some-how he'd surely drunk even more cups than he'd counted, he told himself haltingly. Skwee, he saw, had returned to the rats' table and was standing before the yellow chunk Frix had set on the silver platter at Skwee's end. With the other rats watching him, Skwee drew forth knife and steel with a flourish. The Mouser roused himself more fully with another jerk and shake and was inspired to say, 'Ah, were I but a rat, White Princess, so that I might come as close to you, serving you!'

The Demoiselle Hisvet cried, 'A tribute indeed!' and laughed with delight, showing – it appeared to the Mouser – a slim pink tongue half splotched with blue and an inner mouth similarly pied. Then she said rather soberly, 'Have a care what you wish, for some wishes have been granted,' but at once continued gaily, 'nevertheless, 'twas most gallantly said, Dirksman. I must reward you. Frix, sit at my right side here.'

The Mouser could not see what passed between them, for Hisvet's loosely smocked form hid Frix from him, but the merry eyes of the maid peered steadily at him over Hisvet's shoulder, twinkling like the black silk. Hisvet seemed to be whispering into Frix's ear while nuzzling it playfully.

Meanwhile there commenced the faintest of high *skirrings* as Skwee rapidly clashed steel and knife together, sharpening the latter. The Mouser could barely see the rat's head and shoulders and the tiny glimmer of flashing metal over the larger table intervening. He felt the urge to stand and move closer to observe the prodigy – and perchance glimpse something of the interesting activities of Hisvet and Frix – but he was held fast by a great lethargy, whether of wine or sensuous anticipation or pure magic he could not tell.

He had one great worry – that Fafhrd would out with a cleverer compliment than his own, one so much cleverer that it might even divert Frix's mission to him. But then he noted that Fafhrd's chin had fallen to his chest, and there came to his ears along with the silvery *klirring* the barbarian's gently rumbling snores.

The Mouser's first reaction was pure wicked relief. He re-membered gloatingly past times he'd gamboled with generous, gay girls while his comrade snored sodden. Fafhrd must after all have been sneaking many extra swigs or whole drinks!

Frix jerked and giggled immoderately. Hisvet continued to whisper in her ear while Frix giggled and cooed again from time to time, continuing to watch the Mouser impishly.

Skwee scabbarded the steel with a tiny *clash*, drew the fork with a flourish, plunged it into the yellow-coated meat-chunk, big as a roast for him, and began to carve most dexterously.

Frix rose at last, received her tap from Hisvet, and headed around the table, smiling the while at the Mouser.

Skwee stood up with a paper-thin slice of mutton on his fork and flapped it this way and that for all to see, then brought it close to his muzzle for a sniff and a taste.

The Mouser in his dreamy slump felt a sudden twinge of apprehension. It had occurred to him that Fafhrd simply couldn't have sneaked *that* much extra wine. Why, the Northerner hadn't been out of his sight the past two hours. Of course blows on the head sometimes had a delayed effect.

All the same his first reaction was pure angry jealousy when Frix paused beside Fafhrd and leaned over his shoulder and looked in his forward-tipped face.

Just then there came a great squeak of outrage and alarm from Skwee and the white rat sprang up onto the bed, still holding carving knife and fork with the mutton slice dangling from it.

From under eyelids that persisted in drooping lower and lower, the Mouser watched Skwee gesticulate with his tiny implements, as he chittered dramatically to Hisvet in most man-like cadences, and finally lift the petal of mutton to her lips with an accusing squeak.

Then, coming faintly through the chittering, the Mouser heard a host of stealthy footsteps crossing the middeck, converging on the cabin. He tried to call Hisvet's attention to it, but found his lips and tongue numb and unobedient to his will.

Frix suddenly grasped the hair of Fafhrd's forehead and jerked his head up and back. The Northerner's jaw hung slackly, his eyes fell open, showing only whites.

There was a gentle rapping at the door, exactly the same as the cook's boys had made delivering the earlier courses.

A look passed between Hisvet and Frix. The latter dropped Fafhrd's head, darted to the door, slammed the bar across it and locked the bar with the chain (the grille already being shut) just as something (a man's shoulder, it sounded) thudded heavily against the thick panels.

That thudding continued and a few heartbeats later became much more sharply ponderous, as if a spare mast-section were being swung like a battering ram against the door, which yielded visibly at each blow.

The Mouser realized at last, much against his will, that something was happening that he ought to do something about. He made a great effort to shake off his lethargy and spring up.

He found he could not even twitch a finger. In fact it was all he could do to keep his eyes from closing altogether and watch through lash-blurred slits as Hisvet, Frix, and the rats spun into a whirlwind of silent activity.

Frix jammed her serving table against the jolting door and began to pile other furniture against it.

Hisvet dragged out from behind the sea-bed various dark long boxes and began to unlock them. As fast as she threw them open the white rats helped themselves to the small blue-iron weapons they contained: swords, spears, even most wicked-looking blued-iron crossbows with belted cannisters of darts. They took more weapons than they could effectively use themselves. Skwee hurriedly put on a black-plumed helmet that fitted down over his furry cheeks. The number of rats busy around the boxes was ten – that much the Mouser noted clearly.

A split appeared in the middle of the piled door. Nevertheless Frix sprang away from there to the starboard trapdoor leading to the hold and heaved it up. Hisvet threw herself on the floor toward it and thrust her head down in the dark square hole.

There was something terribly animal-like about the movements of the two women. It may have been only the cramped quarters and the low ceiling, but it seemed to the Mouser that they moved by preference on all fours.

All the while Fafhrd's chest-sunk head kept lifting very slowly and then falling with a jerk as he went on snoring.

Hisvet sprang up and waved on the ten white rats. Led by Skwee, they trooped down through the hatch, their blued-iron weapons flashing and once or twice clashing, and were gone in a twinkling. Frix grabbed dark garments out of a curtained niche. Hisvet caught her by the wrist and thrust the maid ahead of her down the trap and then descended herself. Before pulling the hatch down above her, she took a last look around the cabin. As her red eyes gazed briefly at the Mouser, it seemed to him that her forehead and cheeks were grown over with silky white hair, but that may well have been a combination of eyelash-blur and her own disordered hair streaming and streaking down across her face.

The cabin door split and a man's length of thick mast boomed through, overturning the bolstering table and scattering the furniture set on and against it. After the mast-end came piling in three apprehensive sailors followed by Slinoor, holding a cutlass low, and Slinoor's starsman (navigation officer) with a crossbow at the cock.

Slinoor pressed ahead a little and surveyed the scene swiftly yet intently, then said, 'Our poppy-dust curry has taken Glipkerio's two lust-besotted rogues, but Hisvet's hid with her nymphy slave-girl. The rats are out of their cages. Search, sailors! Starsman, cover us!'

Gingerly at first, but soon in a rush, the sailors searched the cabin, tumbling the empty boxes and jerking the quilts and mattresses off the sea-bed and swinging it up to see beneath, heaving chests away from walls and flinging open the unlocked ones, sweeping Hisvet's wardrobe in great silken armfuls out of the curtained niches in which it had been hanging.

The Mouser again made a mighty effort to speak or move, with no more success than to widen his blurred eye-slits a little. A sailor louted into him and he helplessly collapsed sideways against an arm of his chair without quite falling out of it. Fafhrd got a shove behind and slumped face-down on the table in a dish of stewed plums, his great arms outsweeping unconsciously, upsetting cups and scattering plates.

The starsman kept crossbow trained on each new space uncovered. Slinoor watched with eagle eye, flipping aside silken fripperies with his cutlass point and using it to overset the rats' table, peering the while narrowly.

'There's where the vermin feasted like men,' he observed disgustedly. 'The curry was set before them. Would they had gorged themselves senseless on it.'

'Likely they were the ones to note the drug even through the masking spices of the curry, and warn the women,' the starsman put in. 'Rats are prodigiously wise to poisons.'

As it became apparent neither girls nor rats were in the cabin, Slinoor cried with angry anxiety, 'They can't have escaped to the deck – there's the sky-trap locked below besides our guard above. The mate's party bars the after hold. Perchance the sternlights—'

But just then the Mouser heard one of the horn windows behind him being opened and *Squid*'s arms-master call from there, 'Naught came this way. Where are they, captain?'

'Ask someone wittier than I,' Slinoor tossed him sourly. 'Certain they're not here.'

'Would that these two could speak,' the starsman wished, indicating the Mouser and Fafhrd.

'No,' Slinoor said dourly. 'They'd just lie. Cover the larboard trap to the hold. I'll have it up and speak to the mate.'

Just then footsteps came hurrying across the middeck and *Squid*'s mate with blood-streaked face entered by the broken door, half dragging and half supporting a sailor who seemed to be holding a thin stick to his own bloody cheek.

'Why have you left the hold?' Slinoor demanded of the first. 'You should be with your party below.'

'Rats ambushed us on our way to the after hold,' the mate gasped. 'There were dozens of blacks led by a white, some armed like men. The sword of a beam-hanger almost cut my eye across. Two foamy-mouthed springers dashed out our lamp. 'Twere pure folly to have gone on in the dark. There's scarce a man of my party not bitten, slashed or jabbed. I left them guarding the foreway to the hold. They say their wounds are poisoned and talk of nailing down the hatch.'

'Oh monstrous cowardice!' Slinoor cried. 'You've spoiled my trap that would have scotched them at the start. Now all's to do and difficult. Oh scarelings! Daunted by rats!'

'I tell you they were armed!' the mate protested and then, swinging the sailor forward, 'Here's my proof with a spearlet in his cheek.'

'Don't drag her out, captain, sir,' the sailor begged as Slinoor moved to examine his face. ' 'Tis poisoned too, I wot.'

'Hold still, boy,' Slinoor commanded. 'And take your hands away, I've got it firm. The point's near the skin. I'll drive it out forward so the barbs don't catch. Pinion his arms, mate. Don't move your face, boy, or you'll be hurt worse. If it's poisoned, it must come out the faster. There!'

The sailor squeaked. Fresh blood rilled down his cheek.

' 'Tis a nasty needle indeed,' Slinoor commended, inspecting the bloody point. 'Doesn't look poisoned. Mate, gently cut off the shaft aft of the wound, draw out the rest forward.'

'Here's further proof, most wicked,' said the starsman, who'd been picking about in the litter. He handed Slinoor a tiny crossbow.

Slinoor held it up before him. In the pale candlelight it gleamed bluely, while the skipper's dark-circled eyes were like agates.

'Here's evil's soul,' he cried. 'Perchance 'twas well you were ambushed in the hold. 'Twill teach each mariner to hate and fear all rats again, like a good grain-sailor should. And now by a swift certain killing of all rats on *Squid* wipe out today's traitorous foolery, when you clapped for rats and let rats lead your cheers, seduced by a scarlet girl and bribed by that most misnamed Mouser.'

The Mouser, still paralysed and perforce watching Slinoor aslant as Slinoor pointed at him, had to admit it was a well-turned reference to himself.

'First off,' Slinoor said, 'drag those two rogues on deck. Truss them to mast or rail. I'll not have them waking to botch my victory.'

'Shall I up with a trap and loose a dart in the after hold?' the starsman asked eagerly.

'You should know better,' was all Slinoor answered.

'Shall I gong for the galley and run up a red lamp?' the mate suggested.

Slinoor was silent two heartbeats, then said, 'No. This is *Squid*'s fight to wipe out today's shame. Besides, Lukeen's a hothead botcher. Forget I said that, gentlemen, but it is so.'

'Yet we'd be safer with the galley standing by,' the mate ventured to continue. 'Even now the rats may be gnawing holes in us.'

'That's unlikely with the Rat-Queen below,' Slinoor retorted. 'Speed's what will save us and not standby ships. Now hearken close. Guard well all ways to the hold. Keep traps and hatches shut. Rouse the off watch. Arm every man. Gather on middeck all we can spare from sailing. Move!'

The Mouser wished Slinoor hadn't said 'Move!' quite so vehemently, for the two sailors instantly grabbed his ankles and dragged him most enthusiastically out of the littered cabin and across the middeck, his head bumping a bit. True, he couldn't feel the bumps, only hear them.

To the west the sky was a quarter globe of stars, to the east a mass of fog below and thinner mist above, with the gibbous moon shining through the latter like a pale misshapen silver ghost-lamp. The wind had slackened. *Squid* sailed smoothly.

One sailor held the Mouser against the mainmast, facing aft, while the other looped rope around him. As the sailors bound him with his arms flat to his sides, the Mouser felt a tickle in his throat and life returning to his tongue, but he decided not to try to speak just yet. Slinoor in his present mood might order him gagged.

The Mouser's next divertissement was watching Fafhrd dragged out by four sailors and bound lengthwise, facing inboard with head aft and higher than feet, to the larboard rail. It was quite a comic performance, but the Northerner snored through it.

Sailors began to gather then on middeck, some palely silent but most quipping in low voices. Pikes and cutlasses gave them courage. Some carried nets and long sharp-tined forks. Even the cook came with a great cleaver, which he hefted playfully at the Mouser.

'Struck dumb with admiration of my sleepy curry, eh?'

Meanwhile the Mouser found he could move his fingers. No one had bothered to disarm him, but Cat's Claw was unfortunately fixed far too high on his left side for either hand to touch, let alone get out of its scabbard. He felt the hem of his tunic until he touched, through the cloth, a rather small flat round object thinner along one edge than the other. Gripping it by the thick edge through the cloth, he began to scrape with the thin edge at the fabric confining it.

The sailors crowded aft as Slinoor emerged from the cabin with his officers and began to issue low-voiced orders. The Mouser caught, 'Slay Hisvet or her maid on sight. They're not women but were-rats or worse,' and then the last of Slinoor's orders: 'Poise your parties below the hatch or trap by which you enter. When you hear the bosun's whistle, move!'

The effect of this 'Move!' was rather spoiled by a tiny *twing* and the arms-master clapping his hand to his eye and screaming. There was a flurry of movement among the sailors. Cutlasses struck at a pale form that scurried along the deck. For an instant a rat with a crossbow in his forepaws was silhouetted on the starboard rail against the moonpale mist. Then the starsman's crossbow twanged and the dart winging with exceptional accuracy or luck knocked the rat off the rail into the sea.

'That was a whitey, lads!' Slinoor cried. 'A good omen!'

Thereafter there was some confusion, but it was quickly settled, especially when it was discovered that the arms-master had not been struck in the eye but only near it, and the beweaponed parties moved off, one into the cabin, two forward past the mainmast, leaving on deck a skeleton crew of four.

The fabric the Mouser had been scraping parted and he most carefully eased out of the shredded hem an iron tik (the Lankhmar coin of least value) with half its edge honed to razor sharpness and began to slice with it in tiny strokes at the nearest loop of the line binding him. He looked hopefully toward Fafhrd, but the latter's head still hung at a senseless angle.

A whistle sounded faintly, followed some ten breaths later by a louder one from another part of the hold, it seemed. Then muffled shouts began to come in flurries, there were two screams, something thumped the deck from below, and a sailor swinging a rat squeaking in a net dashed past the Mouser.

The Mouser's fingers told him he was almost through the first loop. Leaving it joined by a few threads, he began to slice at the next loop, bending his wrist acutely to do it.

An explosion shook the deck, stinging the Mouser's feet. He could not conjecture its nature and sawed furiously with his sharpened coin. The skeleton crew cried out and one of the helmsmen fled forward but the other stuck by the tiller. Somehow the gong clanged once, though no one was by it.

Then *Squid*'s sailors began to pour up out of the hold, half of them without weapons and frantic with fear. They milled about. The Mouser could hear sailors dragging *Squid*'s boats, which were forward of the mainmast, to the ship's side. The Mouser gathered that the sailors had fared most evilly below, assaulted by battalions of black rats, confused by false whistles, slashed and jabbed from dark corners, stung by darts, two struck in the eye and blinded. What had completed their rout was that, coming to a hold of unsacked grain, they'd found the air above it choked with grain dust from the recent churnings and scatterings of a horde of rats, and Frix had thrown in fire from beyond, exploding the stuff and knocking them off their feet though not setting fire to the ship.

At the same time as the panic-stricken sailors, there also came on deck another group, noted only by the Mouser – a most quiet and orderly file of black rats that went climbing around him up the mainmast. The Mouser weighed crying an alarm, although he wouldn't have wagered a tik on his chances of survival with hysterical be-cutlassed sailors rat-slashing all around him.

In any case his decision was made for him in the negative by Skwee, who climbed on his left shoulder just then. Holding on by a lock of the Mouser's hair, Skwee leaned out in front of him, staring into the Mouser's left eye with his own two wally blue ones under his black-plumed silver helmet. Skwee touched pale paw to his buck-toothed lips, enjoining silence, then patted the little sword at his side and jerked his rat-thumb across his rat-throat to indicate the penalty for silence broken. Thereafter he retired into the shadows by the Mouser's ear, presumably to watch the routed sailors and wave on and command his own company – and keep close to the Mouser's jugular vein. The Mouser kept sawing with his coin.

The starsman came aft followed by three sailors with two white lanterns apiece. Skwee crowded back closer between the Mouser and the mast, but touched the cold flat of his sword to the Mouser's neck, just under the ear, as a reminder. The Mouser remembered Hisvet's kiss. With a frown at the Mouser the starsman avoided the mainmast and had the sailors hang their lanterns to the aftermast and the crane fittings and the forward range of the afterdeck, fussing about the exact positions. He asserted in a high babble that light was the perfect military defense and counter-weapon, and talked wildly of light-entrenchments and light palisades, and was just about to set the sailors hunting more lamps, when Slinoor limped out of the cabin bloody-foreheaded and looked around.

'Courage, lads,' Slinoor shouted hoarsely. 'On deck we're still masters. Let down the boats orderly, lads, we'll need 'em to fetch the marines. Run up the red lamp! You there, gong the alarm!'

Someone responded, 'The gong's gone overboard. The ropes that hung it – gnawed!'

At the same time thickening waves of fog came out of the east, shrouding *Squid* in deadly moonlit silver. A sailor moaned. It was a strange fog that seemed to increase rather than diminish the amount of light cast by the moon and the starsman's lantern. Colors stood out, yet soon there were only white walls beyond the *Squid*'s rails.

Slinoor ordered, 'Get up the spare gong! Cook, let's have your biggest kettles, lids, and pots – anything to beat an alarm!'

There were two splashing thumps as *Squid*'s boats hit the water.

Someone screamed agonizingly in the cabin.

Then two things happened together. The mainsail parted from the mast, falling to starboard like a cathedral ceiling in a gale, its lines and ties to the mast gnawed loose or sawed by tiny swords. It floated darkly on the water, dragging the boom wide. *Squid* lurched to starboard.

At the same time a horde of black rats spewed out of the cabin door and came pouring over the taffrail, the latter presumably by way of the stern lights. They rushed at the humans in waves, springing with equal force and resolution whether they landed on pike points or tooth-clinging to noses and throats.

The sailors broke and made for the boats, rats landing on their backs and nipping at their heels. The officers fled too. Slinoor was carried along, crying for a last stand. Skwee out with his sword on the Mouser's shoulder and bravely waved on his suicidal soldiery, chittering high, then leaped down to follow in their rear. Four white rats armed with crossbows knelt on the crane fittings and began to crank, load, and fire with great efficiency.

Splashings began, first two and then three, then what sounded like a half dozen together, mixed with screams. The Mouser twisted his head around and from the corner of his eye saw the last two of *Squid*'s sailors leap over the side. Straining a little further around yet, he saw Slinoor clutch to his chest two rats that worried him and follow the sailors. The four white-furred arbalesters leaped down from the crane fittings and raced toward a new firing position on the prow. Hoarse human cries

62

came up from the water and faded off. Silence fell on *Squid* like the fog, broken only by the inevitable chitterings – and those few now.

When the Mouser turned his head aft again, Hisvet was standing before him. She was dressed in close-fitting black leather from neck to elbows and knees, looking most like a slim boy, and she wore a black leather helmet fitting down over her temples and cheeks like Skwee's silver one, her white hair streaming down in a tail behind making her plume. A slim dagger was scabbarded on her left hip.

'Dear, dear Dirksman,' she said softly, smiling with her little mouth, 'you at least do not desert me,' and she reached out and almost brushed his cheek with her fingers. Then, 'Bound!' she said, seeming to see the rope for the first time and drawing back her hand. 'We must remedy that, Dirksman.'

'I would be most grateful, White Princess,' the Mouser said humbly. Nevertheless, he did not let go his sharpened coin, which although somewhat dulled had now sliced almost halfway through a third loop.

'We must remedy that,' Hisvet repeated a little absently, her gaze straying beyond the Mouser. 'But my fingers are too soft and unskilled to deal with such mighty knots as I see. Frix will release you. Now I must hear Skwee's report on the after-deck. Skwee-skwee-skwee!'

As she turned and walked aft the Mouser saw that her hair all went through a silver-ringed hole in the back top of her black helmet. Skwee came running past the Mouser and when he had almost caught up with Hisvet he took position to her right and three rat-paces behind her, strutting with forepaw on sword-hilt and head held high, like a captain-general behind his empress.

As the Mouser resumed his weary sawing of the third loop, he looked at Fafhrd bound to the rail and saw that the black kitten was crouched fur-on-end on Fafhrd's neck and was slowly raking his cheek with the spread claws of a forepaw while the Northerner still snored garglingly. Then the kitten dipped its head and bit Fafhrd's ear. Fafhrd groaned piteously, but then came another of the gargling snores. The kitten resumed its cheek-raking. Two rats, one white, one black, walked by and the kitten wailed at them softly yet direly. The rats stopped and stared, then scurried straight toward the afterdeck, presumably to report the unwholesome condition to Skwee or Hisvet.

The Mouser decided to burst loose without more ado, but just then the four white arbalesters came back dragging a brass cage of frightened cheeping wrens the Mouser remembered seeing hanging by a sailor's bunk in the forecastle. They stopped by the crane fittings again and started a wren-shoot. They'd release one of the tiny terrified flutterers, then as it winged off bring it down with a well-aimed dart – at distances up to five and six yards, never missing. Once or twice one of them would glance at the Mouser narrowly and touch the dart's point.

Frix stepped down the ladder from the afterdeck. She was now dressed like her mistress, except she had no helmet, only the tight silver hairnet, though the silver rings were gone from her wrists.

'Lady Frix!' the Mouser called in a light voice, almost gaily. It was hard to say how one should speak on a ship manned by rats, but a high voice seemed indicated.

She came toward him smiling, but, 'Frix will do better,' she said. 'Lady is such a corset title.'

'Frix then,' the Mouser called, 'on your way would you scare that black witch cat from our poppy-sodden friend? He'll rake out my comrade's eye.'

Frix looked sideways to see what the Mouser meant, but still kept stepping toward him.

'I never interfere with another person's pleasure or pains, since it's hard to be certain which are which,' she informed him, coming close. 'I only carry out my mistress's directives. Now she bids me tell you be patient and of good cheer. Your trials will soon be over. And this withal she sends you as a remembrancer.' Lifting her mouth, she kissed the Mouser softly on each upper eyelid.

The Mouser said, 'That's the kiss with which the green priestess of Djil seals the eyes of those departing this world.'

'Is it?' Frix asked softly.

'Aye, 'tis,' the Mouser said with a little shudder, continuing briskly, 'So now undo me these knots, Frix, which is something your mistress has directed. And then perchance give me a livelier smack – after I've looked to Fafhrd.'

'I only carry out the directives of my mistress's own mouth,' Frix said, shaking her head a little sadly. 'She said nothing to me about untying knots. But doubtless she will direct me to loose you shortly.'

'Doubtless,' the Mouser agreed, a little glumly, forbearing to saw with his coin at the third loop while Frix watched him. If he could but sever at once three loops, he told himself, he might be able to shake off the remaining ones in a not impossibly large number of heartbeats.

As if on cue, Hisvet stepped lightly down from the afterdeck and hastened to them.

'Dear mistress, do you bid me undo the Dirksman his knots?' Frix asked at once, almost as if she wanted to be told to.

'I will attend to matters here,' Hisvet replied hurriedly. 'Go you to the afterdeck, Frix, and harken and watch for my father. He delays overlong this night.' She also ordered the white cross-bow-rats, who'd winged their last wren, to retire to the afterdeck.

6

After Frix and the rats had gone, Hisvet gazed at the Mouser for the space of a score of heartbeats, frowning just a little, studying him deeply with her red-irised eyes.

Finally she said with a sigh, 'I wish I could be certain.'

'Certain of what, White Princessship?' the Mouser asked.

'Certain that you love me truly,' she answered softly yet downrightly, as if he surely knew. 'Many men – aye and women too and demons and beasts – have told me they loved me truly, but truly I think none of them loved me for myself (save Frix, whose happiness is being a shadow) but only because I was young or beautiful or a Demoiselle of Lankhmar or dreadfully clever or had a rich father or was dowered with power, being blood-related to the rats, which is a certain sign of power in more worlds than Nehwon. Do you truly love me for myself, Gray Mouser?'

'I love you most truly indeed, Shadow Princess,' the Mouser said with hardly an instant's hesitation. 'Truly I love you for yourself alone, Hisvet. I love you more dearly than aught else in Nehwon – aye, and in all other worlds too and heaven and hell besides.'

Just then Fafhrd, cruelly clawed or bit by the kitten, let off a most piteous groan indeed with a dreadful high note in it, and the Mouser said impulsively, 'Dear Princess, first chase me that were-cat from my large friend, for I fear it will be his blinding and death's bane, and then we shall discourse of our great loves to the end of eternity.'

'*That* is what I mean,' Hisvet said softly and reproachfully. 'If you loved me truly for myself, Gray Mouser, you would not care a feather if your closest friend or your wife or mother or child were tortured and done to death before your eyes, so long as my eyes were upon you and I touched you with my fingertips. With my kisses on your lips and my slim hands playing about you, my whole person accepting and welcoming you, you could watch your large friend there scratched to blindness and death by a cat – or mayhap eaten alive by rats – and be utterly content. I have touched few things in this world, Gray Mouser. I have touched no man, or male demon or larger male beast, save by the proxy of Frix. Remember that, Gray Mouser.'

'To be sure, Dear Light of my Life!' the Mouser replied most spiritedly, certain now of the sort of self-adoring madness with which he had to deal, since he had a touch of the same mania and so was well acquainted with it. 'Let the barbarian bleed to death by pinpricks! Let the cat have his eyes! Let the rats banquet on him to his bones! What skills it while we trade sweet words and caresses, discoursing to each other with our entire bodies and our whole souls!'

Meanwhile, however, he had started to saw again most fiercely with his now-dulled coin, unmindful of Hisvet's eyes upon him. It joyed him to feel Cat's Claw lying against his ribs.

'That's spoken like my own true Mouser,' Hisvet said with most melting tenderness, brushing her fingers so close to his cheek that he could feel the tiny chill zephyr of their passage. Then, turning, she called. 'Holla, Frix! Send to me Skwee and the White Company. Each may bring with him two black comrades of his own choice. I have somewhat of a reward for them, somewhat of a special treat. Skwee! Skwee-skwee-skwee!'

What would have happened then, both instantly and ulti-
mately, is impossible to say, for at that moment Frix hailed,
'Ahoy!' into the fog and called happily down, 'A black sail! Oh
Blessed Demoiselle, it is your father!'

Out of the pearly fog to starboard came the shark's-fin
triangle of the upper portion of a black sail, running alongside
Squid aft of the dragging brown mainsail. Two boathooks, a
small ship's length apart, came up and clamped down on the
starboard middeck rail while the black sail flapped. Frix came
running lightly forward and secured to the rail midway between
the boathooks the top of a rope ladder next heaved up from the
black cutter (for surely this must be that dire craft, the Mouser
thought).

Then up the ladder and over the rail came nimbly an old man
of Lankhmar dressed all in black leather and on his left shoulder
a white rat clinging with right forepaw to a checkflap of his black
leather cap. He was followed swiftly by two lean bald Mingols
with faces yellow-brown as old lemons, each shoulder-bearing a
large black rat that steadied itself by a yellow ear.

At that moment most coincidentally, Fafhrd groaned again,
more loudly, and opened his eyes and cried out in the faraway
moan of an opium-dreamer, 'Millions of black monkeys! Take
him off, I say! 'Tis a black fiend of hell torments me! Take him
off!'

At that the black kitten raised up, stretched out its small evil
face, and bit Fafhrd on the nose. Disregarding this interruption,
Hisvet threw up her hand at the newcomers and cried clearly,
'Greetings, oh Co-commander my Father! Greetings, peerless
rat-captain Grig! *Clam* is conquered by you, now *Squid* by me,
and this very night, after small business of my own attended to,
shall see the perdition of all this final fleet. Then it's Movarl
estranged, the Mingols across the Sinking Land, Glipkerio
hurled down, and the rats ruling Lankhmar under my overlordship and yours!'

The Mouser, sawing ceaselessly at the third loop, chanced to
note Skwee's muzzle at that moment. The small white captain
had come down from the afterdeck at Hisvet's summoning
along with eight white comrades, two bandaged, and now he
shot Hisvet a silent look that seemed to say there might be

doubts about the last item of her boast, once the rats ruled Lankhmar.

Hisvet's father Hisvin had a long-nosed, much wrinkled face patched by a week of white, old-man's beard, and he seemed permanently stooped far over, yet he moved most briskly for all that, taking very rapid little shuffling steps.

Now he answered his daughter's bragging speech with a petulant sideways flirt of his black glove close to his chest and a little impatient 'Tsk-tsk!' of disapproval, then went circling the deck at his odd scuttling gait while the Mingols waited by the ladder-top. Hisvin circled by Fafhrd and his black tormentor ('Tsk-tsk!') and by the Mouser (another 'Tsk!') and stopping in front of Hisvet said rapid and fumingly, still crouched over, jogging a bit from foot to foot, 'Here's confusion indeed tonight! You catsing and romancing with bound men! – I know, I know! The moon coming through too much! (I'll have my astrologer's liver!) *Shark* oaring like a mad cuttlefish through the foggy white! A black balloon with little lights scudding above the waves! And but now ere we found you, a vast sea monster swimming about in circles with a gibbering demon on his head – it came sniffing at us as if we were dinner, but we evaded it!

'Daughter, you and your maid and your little people must into the cutter at once with us, pausing only to slay these two and leave a suicide squad of gnawers to sink *Squid*!'

'Yeth, think *Thquid*!' the Mouser could have sworn he heard the rat on Hisvin's shoulder lisp shrilly in Lankhmarese.

'Sink *Squid*?' Hisvet questioned. 'The plan was to slip her to Ilthmar with a Mingol skeleton crew and there sell her cargo.'

'Plans change!' Hisvin snapped. 'Daughter, if we're not off this ship in forty breaths, *Shark* will ram us by pure excess of blundering energy or the monster with the clown-clad mad mahout will eat us up as we drift here helpless. Give orders to Skwee! Then out with your knife and cut me those two fools' throats! Quick, quick!'

'But, Daddy,' Hisvet objected. 'I had something quite different in mind for them. Not death, at least not altogether. Something far more artistic, even loving—'

'I give you thirty breaths each to torture ere you slay them!'

Hisvin conceded. 'Thirty breaths and not one more, mind you! I know your somethings!'

'Dad, don't be crude! Among new friends. *Why* must you always give people a wrong impression of me? I won't endure it longer!'

'Chat-chat-chat! You pother and pose more than your rat-mother.'

'But I tell you I won't endure it. This time we're going to do things *my* way for a change!'

'Hist-hist!' her father commanded, stooping still lower and cupping hand to left ear, while his white rat Grig imitated his gesture on the other side.

Faintly through the fog came a gibbering. '*Gottverdammter Nebel! Freunde, wo sind Sie?*'*

' 'Tis the gibberer!' Hisvin cried under his breath. 'The monster will be upon us! Quick, daughter, out with your knife and slay, or I'll have my Mingols dispatch them!'

Hisvet lifted her hand against that villainous possibility. Her proudly plumed head literally bent to the inevitable.

'I'll do it,' she said. 'Skwee, give me your crossbow. Load with silver.'

The white-rat captain folded his forelegs across his chest and chattered at her with a note of demand.

'No, you can't have him,' she said sharply. 'You can't have either of them. They're mine now.'

Another curt chitter from Skwee.

'Very well, your people may have the small black one. Now quick with your crossbow or I'll curse you! Remember, only a smooth silver dart.'

Hisvin had scuttled to his Mingols and now he went around in a little circle, almost spitting. Frix, smiling, glided to him and touched his arm but he shook away from her with an angry flirt.

Skwee was fumbling into his cannister rat-frantically. His eight comrades were fanning out across the deck toward Fafhrd, snarling defiance.

Fafhrd himself was looking about bloody-faced but at last

* 'Goddman fog! Friends, where are you?' Evidently Karl Treuherz's Lankhmar-ese dictionary was unavailable to him at the moment.

lucid-eyed, drinking in the desperate situation, poppy-languor banished by nose-bite.

Just then there came another gibber through the fog, '*Gottverdammter Nirgendswelt!*'*

Fafhrd's bloodshot eyes widened and brightened with a great inspiration. Bracing himself against his bonds, he inflated his mighty chest.

'*Hoongk!*' he bellowed. '*Hoongk!*'

Out of the fog came eager answer, growing each time louder: 'Hoongk! *Hoongk! Hoongk!*'

Seven of the eight white rats that had crossed the deck now returned carrying stretched between them the still-snarling black kitten, spread-eagled on its back, one to each paw and ear while the seventh tried to master but was shaken from side to side by the whipping tail. The eighth came hobbling behind on three legs, shoulder paralysed by a deep-stabbing cat-bite.

From cabin and forecastle and all corners of the deck, the black rats scurried in to watch gloatingly their traditional enemy mastered and delivered to torment, until the middeck was thick with their bloaty dark forms.

Hisvin cracked a command at his Mingols. Each drew a wavy-edged knife. One headed for Fafhrd, the other for the Mouser. Black rats hid their feet.

Skwee dumped his tiny darts on the deck. His paw closed on a palely gleaming one and he slapped it in his crossbow, which he hurriedly handed up toward his mistress. She lifted it in her right hand toward Fafhrd, but just then the Mingol moving toward the Mouser crossed in front of her, his kreese point-first before him. She shifted crossbow to left hand, whipped out her dagger, and darted ahead of the Mingol.

Meanwhile the Mouser had snapped the three cut loops with one surge. The others still confined him loosely at ankles and throat, but he reached across his body, drew Cat's Claw, and slashed out at the Mingol as Hisvet shouldered the yellow man aside.

The dirk sliced her pale cheek from jaw to nose.

The other Mingol, advancing his kreese toward Fafhrd's

* 'Goddam Nowhere-World!'

throat, abruptly dropped to the deck and began to roll back across it, the black rats squeaking and snapping at him in surprise.

'*Hoongk!*'

A great green dragon's head had loomed from the moon-mist over the larboard rail just at the spot where Fafhrd was tied. Strings of slaver trailed on the Northerner from the dagger-toothed jaws.

Like a ponderous jack-in-the-box, the red-mawed head dipped and drove forward, lower jaw rasping the oaken deck and sweeping up from it a swath of black rats three rats wide. The jaws crunched together on their great squealing mouthful inches from the rolling Mingol's head. Then the green head swayed aloft and a horrid swelling traveled down the greenish yellow neck.

But even as it poised there for a second strike, it shrank in size by comparison with what now appeared out of the mist after it – a second green dragon's head fourfold larger and fantastically crested in red, orange, and purple (for at first sight the rider seemed to be part of the monster). This head now drove forward as if it were that of the father of all dragons, sweeping up a black-rat swath twice as wide as had the first and topping off its monster gobble with the two white rats behind the rat-carried black kitten.

It ended its first strike so suddenly (perhaps to avoid eating the kitten) that its parti-colored rider, who'd been waving his pike futilely, was hurled forward off its green head. The rider sailed low past the mainmast, knocking aside the Mingol strik-ing at the Mouser, and skidded across the deck into the starboard rail.

The white rats let go of the kitten, which raced for the mainmast.

Then the two green heads, famished by their two days of small fishy pickings since their last real meal at the Rat Rocks, began methodically to sweep *Squid*'s deck clean of rats, avoiding humans for the most part, though not very carefully. And the rats, huddled in their mobs, did little to evade this dreadful mowing. Perhaps in their straining toward world-dominion they had grown just human and civilized enough to experience imaginative, unhelpful, freezing panic and to have acquired something of humanity's talent for inviting and enduring destruction. Perhaps they looked on the dragons' heads as the twin red maws of war and hell, into which they must throw themselves willy-nilly. At all events they were swept up by dozens and scores. All but three of the white rats were among those engulfed.

Meanwhile the larger people aboard *Squid* faced up variously to the drastically altered situation.

Old Hisvin shook his fist and spat in the larger dragon's face when after its first gargantuan swallow it came questing toward him, as if trying to decide whether this bent black thing were (ugh!) a very queer man or (yum!) a very large rat. But when the stinking apparition kept coming on, Hisvin rolled deftly over the rail as if into bed and swiftly climbed down the rope ladder, fairly chittering in consternation, while Grig clung for dear life to the back of the black leather collar.

Hisvin's two Mingols picked themselves up and followed him, vowing to get back to their cozy cold steppes as soon as Mingolly possible.

Fafhrd and Karl Treuherz watched the melee from opposite sides of the middeck, the one bound by ropes, the other by out-wearied astonishment.

Skwee and a white rat named Siss ran over the heads of their packed apathetic black fellows and hopped on the starboard rail. There they looked back. Siss blinked in horror. But Skwee, his black-plumed helmet pushed down over his left eye, menaced with his little sword and chittered defiance.

Frix ran to Hisvet and urged her to the starboard rail. As they neared the head of the rope ladder, Skwee went down it to make way for his empress, dragging Siss with him. Just then Hisvet turned like someone in a dream. The smaller dragon's head drove toward her viciously. Frix sprang in the way, arms wide, smiling, a little like a ballet dancer taking a curtain call. Perhaps it was the suddenness or seeming aggressiveness of her move that made the dragon sheer off, fangs clashing. The two girls climbed the rail.

Hisvet turned again, Cat's Claw cut a bold red line across her face, and sighted her crossbow at the Mouser. There was the faintest silvery flash. Hisvet tossed the crossbow in the black sea and followed Frix down the ladder. The boathooks let go, the flapping black sail filled, and the black cutter faded into the mist.

The Mouser felt a little sting in his left temple, but he forgot it while whirling the last loops from his shoulders and ankles. Then he ran across the deck, disregarding the green heads lazily searching for last rat morsels, and cut Fafhrd's bonds.

All the rest of that night the two adventurers conversed with Karl Treuherz, telling each other fabulous things about each other's worlds, while Scylla's sated daughter slowly circled *Squid*, first one head sleeping and then the other. Talking was slow and uncertain work, even with the aid of the little *Lankhmarese-German German-Lankhmarese Dictionary for Space-Time and Inter-Cosmic Travelers*, and neither party really believed a great deal of the other's tales, yet pretended to for friendship's sake.

'Do all men dress as grandly as you do in Tomorrow?' Fafhrd once asked, admiring the German's purple and orange garb.

'No, Hagenbeck just has his employees do it, to spread his time zoo's fame,' Karl Treuherz explained.

The last of the mist vanished just before dawn and they saw, silhouetted against the sea silvered by the sinking gibbous moon, the black ship of Karl Treuherz hovering not a bowshot west of *Squid*, its little lights twinkling softly.

The German shouted for joy, summoned his sleepy monster by thwacking his pike against the rail, swung astride the larger head, and swam off calling after him, '*Auf Wiedersehen!*'

Fafhrd had learned just enough Gibberish during the night to know this meant, 'Until we meet again.'

When the monster and the German had swum below it, the space-time engine descended, somehow engulfing them. Then a little later the black ship vanished.

'It drove into the infinite waters toward Karl's Tomorrow bubble,' the Gray Mouser affirmed confidently. 'By Ning and by Sheel, the German's a master magician!'

Fafhrd blinked, frowned, and then simply shrugged.

The black kitten rubbed his ankle. Fafhrd lifted it gently to eye level, saying, 'I wonder, kitten, if you're one of the Cats'

Thirteen or else their small agent, sent to wake me when waking was needful?' The kitten smiled solemnly into Fafhrd's cruelly scratched and bitten face and purred.

Clear gray dawn spread across the waters of the Inner Sea, showing them first *Squid*'s two boats crowded with men and Slinoor sitting dejected in the stern of the nearer but standing with uplifted hand as he recognized the figures of the Mouser and Fafhrd; next Lukeen's war galley *Shark* and the three other grain ships *Tunny*, *Carp*, and *Grouper*; lastly, small on the northern horizon, the green sails of two dragon-ships of Movarl.

The Mouser, running his left hand back through his hair, felt a short, straight, rounded ridge in his temple under the skin. He knew it was Hisvet's smooth silver dart, there to stay.

7

Fafhrd awoke consumed by thirst and amorous yearning, and with a certainty that it was late afternoon. He knew where he was and, in a general way, what had been happening, but his memory for the past half day or so was at the moment foggy. His situation was that of a man who stands on a patch of ground with mountains sharp-etched all around, but the middle distance hidden by a white sea of ground-mist.

He was in leafy Kvarch Nar, chief of the Eight, so-called Cities – truly, none of them could compare with Lankhmar, the only city worth the name on the Inner Sea. And he was in his room in the straggling, low, unwalled, yet shapely wooden palace of Movarl. Four days ago the Mouser had sailed for Lankhmar aboard *Squid* with a cargo of lumber which the thrifty Slinoor had shipped, to report to Glipkerio the safe delivery of four-fifths of the grain, the eerie treacheries of Hisvin and Hisvet, and the whole mad adventure. Fafhrd, however, had chosen to remain awhile in Kvarch Nar, for to him it was a fun-place, not least because he had found a fun-loving, handsome girl there, one Hrenlet.

More particularly, Fafhrd was snug abed but feeling somewhat constricted – clearly he had not taken off his boots or any other of his clothing or even unbelted his short-ax, the blade of which, fortunately covered by its thick leather sheath, stuck into his side. Yet he was also filled with a sense of glorious achievement – why, he wasn't yet sure, but it was a grand feeling.

Without opening his eyes or moving any part of him the thickness of a Lankhmar penny a century old, he oriented himself. To his left, within easy arm-reach on a stout night table would be a large pewter flagon of light wine. Even now he could sense, he thought, its coolth. Good.

To his right, within even easier reach, Hrenlet. He could feel her radiant warmth and hear her snoring – very loudly, in fact.

Or was it Hrenlet for certain? – or at any rate *only* Hrenlet? She had been very merry last night before he went to the gaming table, playfully threatening to introduce him intimately to a red-haired, and hot-blooded female cousin of hers from Ool Hrusp, where they had great wealth in cattle. Could it be that . . . ? At any rate, good too, or even better.

While under his downy thick pillows— Ah, there was the explanation for his ever-mounting sense of glory! Late last night he had cleaned them all out of every golden Lankhmarian rilk, every golden Kvarch Nar gront, every golden coin from the Eastern Lands, Quarmall, or elsewhere! Yes, he remembered it well now: he had taken them all – and at the simple game of sixes and seven, where the banker wins if he matches the number of coins the player holds in his fist; those Eight-City fools didn't realize they tried to make their fists big when they held six golden coins and tightened them when they held seven. Yes, he had turned all their pockets and pouches inside out – and at the end he had crazily matched a quarter of his winnings against an oddly engraved slim tin whistle supposed to have magical properties . . . and won that too! And then saluted them all and reeled off happily, well-ballasted by gold like a treasure galleon, to bed and Hrenlet. Had he had Hrenlet? He wasn't sure.

Fafhrd permitted himself a dry-throated, raspy yawn. Was ever man so fortunate? At his left hand, wine. At his right a beauteous girl, or more likely two, since there was a sweet strong farm-smell coming to him under the sheets; and what is juicier than a farmer's (or cattleman's) redhead daughter? While under his pillows— He twisted his head and neck luxuriously; he couldn't quite feel the tight-bulging bag of golden coins – the pillows were many and thick – but he could imagine it.

He tried to recall why he had made that last hare-brained successful wager. The curly-bearded braggart had claimed he had the slim tin whistle of a wise woman and that it summoned thirteen helpful beasts of some sort – and this had recalled to Fafhrd the wise woman who had told him in his youth that each sort of animal has its governing thirteen – and so his sentimentality had been awakened – and he had wanted to get the whistle as a present for the Gray Mouser, who doted on the little props of magic – yes, that was it!

Eyes still shut, Fafhrd plotted his course of action. He suddenly stretched out his left arm blind and without any groping fastened it on the pewter flagon – it was even bedewed! – and drained half of it – nectar! – and set it back.

Then with his right hand he stroked the girl – Hrenlet, or her cousin? – from shoulder to haunch.

She was covered with short bristly fur and, at his amorous touch, she mooed.

Fafhrd wide-popping his eyes and jackknifed up in the bed, so that sunlight, striking low through the small unglazed window, drenched him yellowly and made a myriad wonder of the hand-polished woods paneling the room, their grains an infinitely varied arabesque. Beside him, pillowed as thickly as he was – and possibly drugged – was a large, long-eared, pink-nostriled auburn calf. Suddenly he could feel her hooves through his boots, and drew the latter abruptly back. Beyond her was no girl – or even other calf – at all.

He dove his right hand under his pillows. His fingers touched the familiar double-stitched leather of his pouch, but instead of being ridgy and taut with gold pieces, it was, except for one thin cylinder – that tin whistle – flat as an unleavened Sarheenmar pancake.

He flung back the bedclothes so that they bellied high and wild in the air, like a sail torn loose in a squall. Thrusting the burgled purse under his belt, he vaulted out of bed, snatched up his long-sword by its furry scabbard – he intended it for spanking purposes – and dashed through the heavy double drapes out the door, pausing only to dump down his throat the last of the wine.

Despite his fury at Hrenlet, he had to admit, as he hurriedly quaffed, that she had dealt honestly with him up to a point: his bed-comrade was female, red-haired, indubitably from the farm and – for a calf – beauteous, while her now-alarmed mooing had nevertheless a throaty amorous quality.

The common-room was another wonder of polished wood – Movarl's kingdom was so young that its forests were still its chief wealth. Most of the windows showed green leaves close beyond. From walls and ceiling jutted fantastic demons and winged warrior-maidens all wood-carved. Here and there against the wall leaned beautifully polished bows and spears. A wide doorway led out to a narrow courtyard where a bay stallion moved restlessly under an irregular green roof. The city of Kvarch Nar had twenty times as many mighty trees as homes.

About the common-room lounged a dozen men clad in green and brown, drinking wine, playing at board-games, and conversing. They were dark-bearded brawny fellows, a little shorter – though not much – than Fafhrd.

Fafhrd instantly noted that they were the identical fellows whom he had stripped of their gold-pieces at last night's play. And this tempted him – hot with rage and fired by gulped wine – into a near-fatal indiscretion.

'Where is that thieving, misbegotten Hrenlet?' he roared, shaking his scabbarded sword above his head. 'She's stolen from under my pillows all my winnings!'

Instantly the twelve sprang to their feet, hands gripping sword hilts. The burliest took a step toward Fafhrd, saying icily, 'You dare suggest that a noble maiden of Kvarch Nar shared your bed, barbarian?'

Fafhrd realized his mistake. His liaison with Hrenlet, though obvious to all, had never before been remarked on, because the women of the Eight Cities are revered by their men and may do what they wish, no matter how licentious. But woe betide the outlander who put this into words.

Yet Fafhrd's rage still drove him beyond reason. 'Noble?' he cried. 'She's a liar and a whore! Her arms are two white snakes, a-crawl 'neath the blankets – for gold, not man-flesh! Despite which, she's also a shepherd of lusts and pastures her flock between my sheets!'

A dozen swords came screeching out of their scabbards at that and there was a rush. Fafhrd grew logical, almost too late. There seemed only one chance of survival left. He sprinted straight for the big door, parrying with his still-scabbarded sword the hasty blows of Movarl's henchmen, raced across the courtyard, vaulted into the saddle of the bay, and kicked him into a gallop.

He risked one backward look as the bay's iron-shod hooves began to strike sparks from the flinty narrow forest road. He was rewarded by a vivid glimpse of his yellow-haired Hrenlet leaning bare-armed in her shift from an upper window and laughing heartily.

A half-dozen arrows whirred viciously around him and he devoted himself to getting more speed from the bay. He was three leagues along the winding road to Klelg Nar, which runs east through the thick forest close to the coast of the Inner Sea, when he decided that the whole business had been a trick, worked by last night's losers in league with Hrenlet, to regain their gold – and perhaps one of them his girl – and that the arrows had been deliberately winged to miss.

He drew up the bay and listened. He could hear no pursuit. That pretty well confirmed it.

Yet there was no turning back now. Even Movarl could hardly protect him after he had spoken the words he had of a Lankhmar lady.

There were no ports between Kvarch Nar and Glelg Nar. He would have to ride at least that far around the Inner Sea, somehow evading the Mingols besieging Klelg Nar, if he were to get back to Lankhmar and his share of Glipkerio's reward for bringing all the grain ships save *Clam* safe to port. It was most irksome.

Yet he still could not really hate Hrenlet. This horse was a stout one and there was a big saddlebag of food balancing a large canteen of wine. Besides, its reddish hue delightfully echoed that of the calf. A rough joke, but a good one.

Also, he couldn't deny that Hrenlet had been magnificent between the sheets – a superior sort of slim unfurred cow, and witty too.

He dipped in his pancake-flat pouch and examined the tin whistle, which aside from memories was now his sole spoil from Kvarch Nar. It had down one side of it a string of undecipherable characters and down the other the figure of a slim feline beast couchant. He grinned widely, shaking his head. What a fool was a drunken gambler! He made to toss it away, then remembered the Mouser and returned it to his pouch.

He touched the bay with his heels and cantered on toward Klelg Nar, whistling an eerie but quickening Mingol march.

Nehwon – a vast bubble leaping up for ever through the waters of eternity. Like airy champagne . . . or, to certain moralists, like a globe of stinking gas from the slimiest, most worm-infested marsh.

Lankhmar – a continent firm-seated on the solid watery inside of the bubble called Nehwon. With mountains, hills, towns, plains, a crooked coastline, deserts, lakes, marshes too, and grainfields – especially grainfields, source of the continent's wealth, to either side of the Hlal, greatest of rivers.

And on the continent's northern tip, on the east bank of the Hlal, mistress of the grainfields and their wealth, the City of Lankhmar, oldest in the world. Lankhmar, thick-walled against barbarians and beasts, thick-floored against creepers and crawlers and gnawers.

At the south of the City of Lankhmar, the Grain Gate, its twenty-foot thickness and thirty-foot width often echoing with the creak of ox-drawn wagons bringing in Lankhmar's tawny, dry, edible treasure. Also the Grand Gate, larger still and more glorious, and the smaller End Gate. Then the South Barracks with its black-clad soldiery, the Rich Men's Quarter, the Park of Pleasure and the Plaza of Dark Delights. Next Whore Street and the streets of other crafts. Beyond those, crossing the city from the Marsh Gate to the docks, the Street of the Gods, with its many flamboyantly soaring fanes of the Gods *in* Lankhmar and its single squat black temple of the Gods *of* Lankhmar – more like an ancient tomb except for its tall, square, eternally silent bell-tower. Then the slums and the windowless homes of the thick-tree-trunks chopped off evenly. Finally, facing the Inner Sea to the north and the Hlal to the west, the North

Barracks, and on a hill of solid, sea-sculptured rock, the Citadel and the Rainbow Palace of the Overlord Glipkerio Kistomerces.

An adolescent serving maid balancing on her close-shaven head with aid of a silver coronet-ring a large tray of sweetmeats and brimming silver goblets, strode like a tightrope walker into a green-tiled antechamber of the Blue Audience Chamber of that palace. She wore black leather collars around her neck, wrists, and slender waist. Light silver chains a little shorter than her forearms tied her wrist-collars to her waist-collar – it was Glipkerio's whim that no maid's finger should touch his food or even its tray and that every maid's balance be perfect. Aside from her collars she was unclothed, while aside from her short-clipped eyelashes, she was entirely shaven – another of the fantastic monarch's dainty whims, that no hair should drop in his soup. She looked like a doll before it is dressed, its wig affixed, and its eyebrows painted on.

The sea-hued tiles lining the chamber were hexagonal and big as the palm of a large hand. Most were plain, but here and there were ones figured with sea creatures, a mollusk, a cod, an octopus, a sea-horse.

The maid was almost halfway to the narrow, curtained archway leading to the Blue Audience Chamber when her gaze became fixed on a tile in the floor a long stride from the archway ahead but somewhat to the left. It was figured with a sea lion. It lifted the breadth of a thumb, like a little trapdoor, and eyes with a jetty gleam a finger-joint apart peered out at her.

She shook from toes to head, but her tight-bitten lips uttered no sound. The goblets chinked faintly, the tray began to slide, but she got her head under its center again with a swift sidewise ducking movement, and then began to go with long fearful steps around the horrid tile as far as she could to the right, so that the edge of the tray was hardly a finger's breadth from the wall.

Just under the edge of the tray, as if that were a porch-roof, a plain green tile in the wall opened like a door and a rat's black face thrust out with spade-teeth bared.

The maid leaped convulsively away, still in utter silence. The tray left her head. She tried to get under it. The floor-tile clattered open wide and a long-bodied black rat came undulating out. The tray struck the dodging maid's shoulder, she strained toward it futilely with her short-chained hands, then it struck the floor with a nerve-shattering clangor and all the spilled goblets rang.

As the silver reverberations died, there was else only the rapid soft *thump* of her bare feet running back the way she had come. One goblet rolled a last turn. Then there was desert stillness in the green antechamber.

Two hundred heartbeats later, it was broken by another muted thudding of bare feet, this time those of a party returning the way the maid had run. There entered first, watchful-eyed, two shaven-headed, white-smocked, browny cooks, each armed with a cleaver in one hand and a long toasting-fork in the other. Second, two naked and shaven kitchen boys, bearing many wet and dry rags and a broom of black feathers. After them, the maid, her silver chains gathered in her hands, so that they would not chink from her trembling. Behind her, a monstrously fat woman in a dress of thick black wool that went to her redoubled chins and plump knuckles and hid her surely monstrous feet and ankles. Her black hair was dressed in a great round beehive stuck through and through with long black-headed pins, so that it was as if she bore a prickly planet on her head. This appeared to be the case, for her puffed face was weighted with a world of sullenness and hate. Her black eyes peered stern and all-distrustful from between folds of fat, while a sparse black moustache, like the ghost of a black centipede, crossed her upper lip. Around her vast belly she wore a broad leather belt from which hung at intervals keys, thongs, chains, and whips. The kitchen boys believed she had deliberately grown mountain-fat to keep them from clinking together and so warn them when she came a-spying.

Now the fat kitchen-queen and palace mistress stared shrewdly around the ante-chamber, then spread her humpy palms, glaring at the maid. Not one green tile was displaced.

In like dumb-show, the maid nodded vehemently, pointing from her waist at the tile figured with a sea-lion, then threaded tremblingly forward between the spilled stuff and touched it with her toe.

One of the cooks quickly knelt and gently thumped it and the surrounding tiles with a knuckle. Each time the faint sound was equally solid. He tried to get the tines of his fork under the sea lion tile from every side and failed.

The maid ran to the wall where the other glazed door had opened and searched the bare tiles frantically, her slim hands tugging uselessly. The other cook thumped the tiles she indicated without getting a hollow sound.

The glare of the palace mistress changed from suspicion to certainty. She advanced on the maid like a storm cloud, her eyes its lightning, and suddenly thrusting out her two ham-like arms, snapped a thong to a silver ring in the maid's collar. That snap was the loudest sound yet.

The maid shook her head wildly three times. Her trembling increased, then suddenly stopped altogether. As the palace mistress led her back the way they had come, she drooped her head and shoulders, and at the first vindictive downward jerk dropped to her hands and knees and padded rapidly, dog-fashion.

Under the watchful eyes of one of the cooks, the kitchen boys began swiftly to clean up the mess, wrapping each goblet in a rag ere they laid it on the platter, lest it chink. Their gazes kept darting fearfully about at the myriad tiles.

The Gray Mouser, standing on *Squid*'s gently-dripping prow, sighted the soaring Citadel of Lankhmar through the dispersing fog. Beyond it to the east there soon came into view the square-topped minarets of the Overlord's palace, each finished in stone of different hue, and to the south the dun granaries like vast smokestacks. He hailed the first sea-wherry he saw to *Squid*'s side. With the black kitten spitting at him reproachfully, and against Slinoor's command – but before Slinoor could decide to have him forcibly restrained – he slid down the long boathook with which the prow wherryman had caught hold of *Squid*'s rail. Landing lightly in the wherry, he gave an approving shoulder-pat to the astonished hook-holder, then commanded, promising a fat fee, that he be rowed with all speed to the palace dock. The hook was shipped, the Mouser wove his way to the slender craft's stern, the three wherrymen out-oared and the craft raced east over the silty water, brown with mud from the Hlal.

The Mouser called consolingly back to Slinoor, 'Never fear, I will make a marvelous report to Glipkerio, praising you to the skies – and even Lukeen to the height of a low raincloud!'

Then he faced forward, faintly smiling and frowning at once in thought. He was somewhat sorry he had had to desert Fafhrd, who had been immersed in an apparently endless drinking and dicing bout with Movarl's toughest henchmen when *Squid* had sailed from Kvarch Nar – the great oafs died of wine and their losses each dawn, but were reborn in the late afternoon with thirst restored and money-pouches miraculously refilled.

But he was even more pleased that now he alone would bear Glipkerio Movarl's thanks for the four shiploads of grain and be able all by himself to tell the wondrous tale of the dragon, the rats, and their human masters – or colleagues. By the time Fafhrd got back from Kvarch Nar, broken-pursed and likely broken-pated too, the Mouser would be occupying a fine apartment in Glipkerio's palace and be able subtly to irk his large comrade by offering him hospitalities and favors.

He wondered idly where Hisvin and Hisvet and their small entourage were now. Perhaps in Sarheenmar, or more likely Ilthmar, or already lurching by camel-train from that city to some retreat in the Eastern Lands, to be well away from Glipkerio's and Movarl's vengeance. Unwilled, his left hand rose to his temple, gently fingering the tiny straight ridge here. Truly, at this already dreamy distance, he could not hate Hisvet or the brave proxy-creature Frix. Surely Hisvet's vicious threats had been in part a kind of love-play. He did not doubt that some part of her yearned for him. Besides, he had marked her far worse than she had marked him. Well, perhaps he would meet her again some year in some far corner of the world.

These foolishly forgiving and forgetting thoughts of the Mouser were in part due, he knew himself, to his present taut yearning for any acceptable girl. Kvarch Nar under Movarl had proved a strait-laced city, by the Mouser's standards, and during his brief stay the one erring girl encountered – one Hrenlet – had chosen to err with Fafhrd. Well, Hrenlet had been something of a giantess, albeit slender, and now he was in Lankhmar, where he knew a dozen score spots to ease his tautness.

The silty-brown water gave way abruptly to deep green. The sea-wherry passed beyond the outflow of the Hlal and was darting along atop the Lankhmar Deep, which dove down sheer-walled and bottomless at the very foot of the wave-pitted great rock on which stood the citadel and the palace. And now the wherrymen had to row out around a strange obstruction: a copper chute wide as a man is tall that, braced by great brazen beams, angled down from a porch of the palace almost to the surface of the sea. The Mouser wondered if the whimmy Glipkerio had taken up aquatic sports during his absence. Or perhaps this was a new way of disposing of unsatisfactory servants and slaves – sliding them suitably weighted into the sea. Then he noted a spindle-shaped vehicle (if it was that) thrice as long as a man and made of some dull gray metal poised at the top of the chute. A puzzle.

The Mouser dearly loved puzzles, if only to elaborate on them rather than solve them, but he had no time for this one. The wherry had drawn up at the royal wharf, and he was haughtily exhibiting to the clamoring eunuchs and guards his starfish-emblemed courier's ring from Glipkerio and his parchment sealed with the cross-sworded seal of Movarl.

The latter seemed to impress the palace-fry most. He was swiftly bowed across the dock, mounted a dizzily tall, gaily-painted wooden stair, and found himself in Glipkerio's audience chamber – a glorious sea-fronting blue-tiled room, each large triangular tile bearing a fishy emblem in bas-relief.

The room was huge despite the blue curtains dividing it now into two halves. A pair of naked and shaven pages bowed to the Mouser and parted the curtains for him. Their sinuous silent movements against that blue background made him think of mermen. He stepped through the narrow triangular opening – to be greeted by a rather distant but imperious 'Hush!'

Since the hissing command came from the puckered lips of Glipkerio himself and since one of the beanpole monarch's hand-long skinny fingers now rose and crossed those lips, the Mouser stopped dead. With a fainter hiss the blue curtains fell together behind him.

It was a strange and most startling scene that presented itself. The Mouser's heart missed a beat – mostly in self-outrage that his imagination had completely missed the weird possibility that was now staged before him.

Three broad archways led out onto a porch on which rested the pointy-ended gray vehicle he had noted balanced at the top of the chute. Now he could see a hinged manhole toward its outjutting bow.

At the near end of the room was a large, thick-bottomed, close-barred cage containing at least a score of black rats, which chittered and wove around each other ceaselessly and sometimes clattered the bars menacingly.

At the far end of the sea-blue room, near the circular stair leading up into the palace's tallest minaret, Glipkerio had risen in excitement from his golden audience couch shaped like a sea-shell. The fantastic overlord stood a head higher than Fafhrd, but was thin as a starved Mingol. His black toga made him look like a funeral cypress. Perhaps to offset this dismal effect, he wore a wreath of small violet flowers around his blond head, the hair of which clustered in golden ringlets.

Close beside him, scarce half his height, hanging weightlessly on his arm like an elf and dressed in a loose robe of pale blonde silk, was Hisvet. The Mouser's dagger-cut, stretching from her left nostril to her jaw, was still a pink line and would have given her a sardonic expression, except that now as her gaze swung to the Mouser she smiled most prettily.

Standing almost midway between the audience couch and the caged rats was Hisvet's father Hisvin. His skinny frame was wrapped in a black toga, but he still wore his tight black leather cap with its long cheek-flaps. His gaze was fixed fiercely on the caged rats and he was weaving his bony fingers at them hypnotically.

'Gnawers dark from deep below . . .' he began to incant in a voice that whistled with age yet was authoritatively strident.

At that instant a naked young serving maid appeared through a narrow archway near the audience couch, bearing on her shaven head a great silver tray laden with goblets and temptingly-mounded silver plates. Her wrists were chained to her waist, while a fine silver chain between her narrow black anklets prevented her from taking steps more than twice as long as her narrow pink-toed feet.

Without a 'Hush!' this time, Glipkerio raised a narrow long

palm to her and once again put a long skinny finger to his lips. The slim maid's movements ceased imperceptibly and she stood silent as a birch tree on a windless day.

The Mouser was about to say, 'Puissant Overlord, this is evilest enchantment. You are consorting with your dearest enemies!' – but at that instant Hisvet smiled at him again and he felt a frightening delicious tingling run down his cheek and gums from the silver dart in his left temple to his tongue, inhibiting speech.

Hisvin recommended in his commanding Lankhmarese that bore the faintest trace of an Ilthmar lisp and reminded the Mouser of the lisping rat Grig:

> *'Gnawers dark from deep below*
> *To ratty grave you now must go!*
> *Blear each eye and drag each tail!*
> *Fur fall off and heartbeat fail!'*

All the black rats crowded to the farthest side of their cage from Hisvin, chittering and squeaking as if in maddest terror. Most of them were on their hind feet, clawing toward the bars like a panicky human crowd.

The old man, now swiftly weaving his fingers in a most complex, mysterious pattern, continued relentlessly:

> *'Blur your eyesight, stop your breath!—*
> *By corrupting spell of Death!*
> *Your brains are cheese, your life is fled!*
> *Spin once around and drop down dead!'*

And the black rats did just that – spinning like amateur actors both to ease and dramatize their falls, yet falling most convincingly all the same with varying *plops* onto the cage floor or each other and lying stiff and still with furry eyelids a-droop and hairless tails slack and sharp-nailed feet thrust stiffly up.

There was a curious slow-paced slappy clapping as Glipkerio applauded with his narrow hands which were long as human feet. Then the beanpole monarch hurried to the cage with strides so lengthy that the lower two-thirds of his toga looked like the silhouette of a tent. Hisvet skipped merrily at his side, while Hisvin came circling swiftly.

'Didst see that wonder, Gray Mouser?' Glipkerio demanded in piping voice, waving his courier closer. 'There is a plague of rats in Lankhmar. You, who might from your name be expected to protect us, have returned somewhat tardily. But – bless the Black-Boned Gods! – my redoubtable servant Hisvin and his incomparable sorcerer-apprentice daughter Hisvet, having conquered the rats which menaced the grain fleet, hastened back in good time to take measures against our local rat-plague – magical measures which will surely be successful, as has now been fully demonstrated.'

At this point the fantastical overlord reached a long thin naked arm from under his toga and chucked the Mouser under the chin, much to the latter's distaste, though he concealed it. 'Hisvin and Hisvet even tell me,' Glipkerio remarked with a fluty chuckle, 'that they suspected *you* for awhile of being in league with the rats – as who would not from your gray garb and small crouchy figure? – and kept you tied. But all's well that ends well and I forgive you.'

The Mouser began a most polemical refutation and accusation – but only in his mind, for he heard himself saying, 'Here, Milord, is an urgent missive from the King of the Eight Cities. By the by, there was a dragon—'

'Oh, that two-headed dragon!' Glipkerio interrupted with another piping chuckle and a roguish finger-wave. He thrust the parchment into the breast of his toga without even glancing at the seal. 'Movarl has informed me by albatross post of the strange mass delusion in my fleet. Hisvin and Hisvet, master psychologists both, confirm this. Sailors are a woefully superstitious lot, Gray Mouser, and 'tis evident their fancies are more furiously contagious than I suspected – for even you were infected! I would have expected it of your barbarian mate – Favner? Fafrah? – or even of Slinoor and Lukeen – for what are captains but jumped-up sailors? – but you, who are at least sleazily civilized . . . However, I forgive you that too! Oh, what a mercy that wise Hisvin here thought to keep watch on the fleet in his cutter!'

The Mouser realized he was nodding – and that Hisvet and,

in his wrinkle-lipped fashion, Hisvin were smiling archly. He looked down at the piled stiff rats in their theatrical death-throes. Issek take 'em, but their droopy-lidded eyes even looked whitely glazed!

'Their fur hasn't fallen off,' he criticized mildly.

'You are too literal,' Glipkerio told him with a laugh. 'You don't comprehend poetic license.'

'Or the devices of humano-animal suggestion,' Hisvin added solemnly.

The Mouser trod hard – and, he thought, surreptitiously – on a long tail that drooped from the cage bottom to the tiled floor. There was no atom of response.

But Hisvin noted and lightly clicked a fingernail. The Mouser fancied there was a slight stirring deep in the rat-pile. Suddenly a nauseous stink sprang from the cage. Glipkerio gulped. Hisvet delicately pinched her pale nostrils between thumb and ring-finger.

'You had some question about the efficacy of my spell?' Hisvin asked the Mouser most civilly.

'Aren't the rats corrupting rather fast?' the Mouser asked. It occurred to him that there might have been a tight-sealed sliding door in the floor of the cage and a dozen long-dead rats or merely a well-rotted steak in the thick bottom beneath.

'Hisvin kills 'em doubly dead,' Glipkerio asserted somewhat feebly, pressing his long hand to his narrow stomach. 'All processes of decay are accelerated!'

Hisvin waved hurriedly and pointed toward an open window beyond the archways to the porch. A brawny yellow Mingol in black loincloth sprang from where he squatted in a corner, heaved up the cage, and ran with it to dump it in the sea. The Mouser followed him. Elbowing the Mingol aside with a shrewd dig at the short ribs and leaning far out, supporting himself with his other hand reaching up and gripping the tiled window-side, the Mouser saw the cage tumbling about and fall with a white splash into the blue waters.

At the same instant he felt Hisvet, who had rapidly followed him, press closely with her silken side against his from armpit to ankle bone.

The Mouser thought he made out small dark shapes leaving

the cage and swimming strongly underwater toward the rock as the iron rat-prison sank down and down, out of sight.

Hisvet breathed in his ear. 'Tonight when the evening star goes to bed. The Plaza of Dark Delight. The grove of closet trees.'

Turning swiftly back, Hisvin's delicate daughter commanded the black-collared, silver-chained maid, 'Light wine of Ilthmar for his Majesty! Then serve us others.'

Glipkerio gulped down a goblet of sparkling colorless ferment and turned a shade less green. The Mouser selected a goblet of darker, more potent stuff and also a black-edged tender beef cutlet from the great silver tray as the maid dropped gracefully to both knees while keeping her slender upper body perfectly erect.

As she rose with an effortless-seeming undulation and moved mincingly toward Hisvin, the short steps enforced by her silver ankle-chains, the Mouser noted that although her front had been innocent of both raiment and ornamentation, her naked back was crisscrossed diamond-wise by a design of evenly-spaced pink lines from nape to heels.

Then he realized that these were not narrow strokes painted on, but the weals of a whiplashing. So stout Samanda was maintaining her artistic disciplines! The unspoken torment-conspiracy between the lath-thin effeminate Glipkerio and the bladder-fat palace mistress was both psychologically instructive and disgusting. The Mouser wondered what the maid's offense had been. He also pictured Samanda sputtering through her singeing black woolen garb in a huge white-hot oven – or sliding with a leaden weight on her knee-thick ankles down the copper chute outside the porch.

Glipkerio was saying to Hisvin, 'So it is only needful to lure out all the rats into the streets and speak your spell at them?'

'Most true, O sapient Majesty,' Hisvin assured him, 'though we must delay a little, until the stars have sailed to their most potent stations in the ocean of the sky. Only then will my magic slay rats at a distance. I'll speak my spell from the blue minaret and slay them all.'

'I hope those stars will set all canvas and make best speed,' Glipkerio said, worry momentarily clouding the childish delight in his long, low-browed face. 'My people have begun to fret at me to do something to disperse the rats or fight 'em back into their holes. Which will interfere with luring them forth, don't you think?'

'Don't trouble your mighty brain with that worry,' Hisvin reassured him. 'The rats are not easily scared. Take measures against them in so far as you're urged to. Meanwhile, tell your council you have an all-powerful weapon in reserve.'

The Mouser suggested, 'Why not have a thousand pages memorize Hisvin's deadly incantation and shout it down the rat-holes? The rats, being underground, won't be able to tell that the stars are in the wrong place.'

Glipkerio objected, 'Ah, but it is necessary that the tiny beasts also see Hisvin's finger-weaving. You do not understand these refinements, Mouser. You have delivered Movarl's missive. Leave us.

'But mark this,' he added, fluttering his black toga, his yellow-irised eyes like angry gold coins in his narrow head. 'I have forgiven you once your delays, Small Grey Man, and your dragon-delusions and your doubts of Hisvin's magical might. But I shall not forgive a second time. Never mention such matters again.'

The Mouser bowed and made his way out. As he passed the statuesque maid with crisscrossed back, he whispered, 'Your name?'

'Reetha,' she breathed.

Hisvet came rustling past to dip up a silver forkful of caviar, Reetha automatically dropping to her knees.

'Dark delights,' Hisvin's daughter murmured and rolled the tiny black fish eggs between her bee-stung upper lip and pink and blue tongue.

When the Mouser was gone, Glipkerio bent down to Hisvin, until his fingers somewhat resembled a black gibbet. 'A word in your ear,' he whispered. 'The rats sometimes make even me . . . well, nervous.'

'They are most fearsome beasties,' Hisvin agreed somberly, 'who might daunt even the gods.'

Fafhrd spurred south along the stony sea-road that led from

Klelg Nar to Sarheenmar and which was squeezed between steep, rocky mountains and the Inner Sea. The sea's dark swells peaked up blackly as they neared shore and burst with unending crashes a few yards below the road, which was dank and slippery with their spray. Overhead pressed low dark clouds which seemed less water vapor than the smoke of volcanoes or burning cities.

The Northerner was leaner – he had sweated and burned away weight – and his face was grim, his eyes red-shot and red-rimmed from dust, his hair dulled with it. He rode a tall, powerful, gaunt-ribbed gray mare with dangerous eyes, also red-shot – a beast looking as cursed as the landscape they traversed.

He had traded the bay with the Mingols for this mount, and despite its ill temper got the best of the bargain, for the bay had been redly gasping out its life from a lance thrust at the time of the trade. Approaching Klelg Nar along the forest road, he had spied three spider-thin Mingols preparing to rape slender twin sisters. He had managed to thwart this cruel and unaesthetic enterprise because he had given the Mingols no time to use their bows, only the lance, while their short narrow scimitars had been no match for Graywand. When the last of the three had gone down, sputtering curses and blood, Fafhrd had turned to the identically-clad girls, only to discover that he had rescued but one – a Mingol had mean-heartedly cut the other's throat before turning his scimitar on Fafhrd. Thereafter Fafhrd had mastered one of the tethered Mingol horses despite its fiendish biting and kicking. The surviving girl had revealed among her other shriekings that her family might still be alive among the defenders of Klelg Nar, so Fafhrd had swung her up on his saddlebow despite her frantic struggles and efforts to bite. When she quieted somewhat, he had been stirred by her slim sprawly limbs so close and her lemur-large eyes and her repeated assertion, reinforced by horrendous maidenly curses and quaint childhood slang, that all men without exception were hairy beasts, this with a sneer at Fafhrd's luxuriously furred chest. But although tempted to amorousness he had restrained himself out of consideration for her coltish youth – she seemed scarce twelve, though tall for her age – and recent bereavement.

Yet when he had returned her to her not very grateful and strangely suspicious family, she had replied to his courteous promise to return in a year or two with a wrinkling of her snub nose and a sardonic flirt of her blue eyes and slim shoulders, leaving Fafhrd somewhat doubtful of his wisdom in sparing her his wooing and also saving her in the first place. Yet he had gained a fresh mount and a tough Mingol bow with its quiver of darts.

Klelg Nar was the scene of bitter house-to-house and tree-to-tree street fighting, while Mingol campfires glowed in a semi-circle to the east every night. To his dismay Fafhrd had learned that for weeks there had not been a ship in Klelg Nar's harbor, of which the Mingols held half the perimeter. They had not fired the city because wood was wealth to the lean dwellers of the treeless steppes – in fact, their slaves dismantled and plucked apart houses as soon as won and the precious planks and lovely carvings were instantly carted off east, or more often dragged on travoises.

So despite the rumor that a branch of the Mingol horde had bent south, Fafhrd had set off in that direction on his vicious-tempered mount, somewhat tamed by the whip and morsels of honeycomb. And now it seemed from the smoke adrift above the sea-road that the Mingols might not have spared Sarheenmar from the torch as they had Klelg Nar. It also began to seem certain that the Mingols had taken Sarheenmar, from the evidence of the wild-eyed, desperate, ragged, dust-caked refugees who began to crowd the road in their flight north, forcing Fafhrd to tour now and again up the hillside, to save them from his new mount's savage hooves. He questioned a few of the refugees, but they were incoherent with terror, babbling as wildly as if he sought to waken them from nightmare. Fafhrd nodded to himself – he knew the Mingol penchant for torture.

But then a disordered troop of Mingol cavalry had come galloping along in the same direction as the escaping Sarheen-marts. Their horses were lathered with sweat and their skinny faces contorted by terror. They appeared not to see Fafhrd, let alone consider attacking him, while it seemed not from malice but panic that they rode down such refugees as got in their way.

Fafhrd's face grew grim and frowning as he cantered on, still against the gibbering stream, wondering what horror would daunt Mingol and Sarheenmart alike.

Black rats kept showing themselves in Lankhmar by day – not stealing or biting, squealing or scurrying, but only showing themselves. They peered from drains and new-gnawed holes, they sat in window slits, they crouched indoors as calmly and confident-eyed as cats – and as often, proportionately, in milady's boudoir as in the tenement-cells of the poor.

Whenever they were noted, there was a gasping and thin shrieking, a rush of footsteps, and a hurling of black pots, be-gemmed bracelets, knives, rocks, chessmen, or whatever else might be handy. But often it was a time before the rats were noted, so serene and at home they seemed.

Some trotted sedately amidst the ankles and swaying black togas of the crowds on the tiled or cobbled streets, like pet dwarf dogs, causing sharp human eddies when they were recognized. Five sat like black, bright-eyed bottles on a top shelf in the store of the wealthiest grocer in Lankhmar, until they were spied for what they were and hysterically pelted with clumpy spice-roots, weighty Hrusp nuts, and even jars of caviar, whereupon they made their leisurely exit through a splinter-edged rat doorway which had not been in the back of the shelf the day before. Among the black marble sculptures lining the walls of the Temple of the Beasts, another dozen posed two-legged like carvings until the climax of the ritual, when they took up a fife-like squeaking and began a slow, sure-foot weaving through the niches. Beside the blind beggar Naph, three curled on the curb, mistaken for his soot-dirty rucksack, until a thief tried to steal it. Another reposed on the jeweled cushion of the pet black mar-moset of Elakeria, niece of the overlord and a most lush devourer of lovers, until she absently reached out a plump hand to stroke the beastie and her nail-gilded fingers encoun-tered not velvet fur, but short and bristly.

During floods and outbreaks of the dread Black Sickness, rats had in remembered times invaded the streets and dwellings of Lankhmar, but then they had raced and dodged or staggered in curves, never moved with their present impudent deliberation.

Their behavior made old folks and storytellers and thin-bearded squinting scholars fearfully recall the fables that there had once been a humped city of rats large as men where imperial Lankhmar had now stood for three-score centuries; that rats had once had a language and government of their own and a single empire stretching to the borders of the unknown world, coexistent with man's cities but more united; and that beneath the stoutly mortared stones of Lankhmar, far below their customary burrowings and any delvings of man, there was a low-ceilinged rodent metropolis with streets and homes and glow-lights all its own and granaries stuffed with stolen grain.

Now it seemed as if the rats owned not only that legendary sub-metropolitan rodent Lankhmar, but Lankhmar above ground as well, they stood and sat and moved so arrogantly.

The sailors from *Squid*, prepared to awe their sea-tavern cronies and get many free drinks with their tales of the horrid rat-attack on their ship, found Lankhmar interested only in its own rat plague. They were filled with chagrin and fear. Some of them returned for refuge to *Squid*, where the starsman's light-defenses had been renewed and both Slinoor and the black kitten worriedly paced the poop.

8

Glipkerio Kistomerces ordered tapers lit while the sunset glow still flared in his lofty sea-footed banquet hall. Yet the beanpole monarch seemed very merry as with many a giggle and whinnying laugh he assured his grave, nervous councillors that he had a secret weapon to scotch the rats at the peak of their insolent invasion and that Lankhmar would be rid of them well before the next full moon. He scoffed at his wrinkle-faced Captain General, Olegnya Mingolsbane, who would have him summon troops from the outlying cities and towns to deal with the furry attackers. He seemed unmindful of the faint patterings that came from behind the gorgeously figured draperies whenever a lull in the conversation and clink of eating tools let it be heard, or of the occasional small, hunchbacked, four-footed shadow cast by the tapers' light. As the long banquet went its bibulous course, he seemed to grow more merry and carefree yet – *fey*, some whispered in their partners' ears. But twice his right hand shook as he lifted his tall-stemmed wine glass, while beneath the table his ropy left fingers quivered continuously, and he had doubled his long skinny legs and hooked the heels of his gilded boots over a silver rung of his chair to keep his feet off the floor.

Outdoors the rising moon, gibbous and waning, showed small, low, humped shapes moving along each roof-ridge of the city, except those on the Street of the Gods, both the many temples of the Gods *in* Lankhmar and the grimy cornices of the temple of the Gods *of* Lankhmar and its tall, square bell-tower which never issued chimes.

The Gray Mouser scuffed moodily up and down the pale sandy path that curved around the grove of perfumy closet trees. Each tree was like a huge, upended, hemispherical basket, its bottom and sides formed by the thin, resilient, closely-spaced branches which, weighted with dark green leaves and pure white blooms, curved widely out and down, so that the interior was a single bell-shaped, leaf-and-flower-walled room, most private. Fire-beetles and glow-wasps, and night-bees supping at the closet flowers dimly outlined each natural tent with their pale, wink-ing, golden and violet, and pinkish lights.

From within two or three of the softly iridescent bowers already came the faint murmurings of lovers, or perhaps, the Mouser thought with a vicious stab of the mind, of thieves who had chosen one of these innocent and traditionally hallowed privacies to plot the night's maraudings. Younger or on another night, the Mouser would have eavesdropped on the second class of privacy-seekers, in order to loot their chosen victims ahead of them. But now he had other rats to roast.

High tenements to the east hid the moon, so that beyond the twinkling twilight of the closet trees, the rest of the Plaza of Dark Delights was almost gropingly black, except where some small dim sheen marked store or stand, or ghostly flames and charcoal glow showed hot food and drink available, or where some courtesan rhythmically swung her tiny scarlet lan-tern as she sauntered.

Those last lights mightily irked the Mouser at the moment,

though there had been times when they had drawn him as the closet bloom does the night-bee and twice they had jogged redly through his dreams as he had sailed home in *Squid*. But several most embarrassing visits this afternoon – first to fashionable female friendlets, then to the city's most titillating brothels – had demonstrated to him that his manhood, which he had felt so ravenously a-leap in Kvarch Nar and aboard *Squid*, was limply dead except – he first surmised, now rather desperately hoped – where Hisvet was concerned. Every time he had embraced a girl this disastrous half-day, the slim triangular face of Hisvin's daughter had got ghostily in the way, making the visage of his companion of the moment dull and gross by comparison, while from the tiny silver dart in his temple a feeling of sick boredom and unjoyful satiety had radiated through all his flesh.

Reflected from his flesh, this feeling filled his mind. He was dully aware that the rats, despite the great losses they had suffered aboard *Squid*, threatened Lankhmar. Rats were deterred even less than men by numerical losses and made them up more readily. And Lankhmar was a city for which he felt some small affection, as of a man for a very large pet. Yet the rats menacing it had, whether from Hisvet's training or some deeper source, an intelligence and organization that was eerily frightening. Even now he could imagine troops of black rats footing it unseen across the lawns and along the path of the Plaza beyond the closet trees' glow, encircling him in a great ambush, rank on black rank.

He was aware too that he had lost whatever small trust the fickle Glipkerio had ever had in him and that Hisvin and Hisvet, after their seemingly total defeat, had turned the tables on him and must be opposed and defeated once again, just as Glipkerio's favor must be re-won.

But Hisvet, far from being an enemy to be beaten, was the girl to whom he was in thrall, the only being who could restore him to his rightful, calculating, selfish self. He touched with his fingertips the little ridge the silver dart made in his temple. It would be the work of a moment to squeeze it out point-first through its thin covering of skin. But he had a dread of what would happen then: he might not lose only his bored satiety, but the juice of all feeling, or even life itself. Besides, he didn't want to give up his silver link with Hisvet.

A tiny treading on the gravel of the path, a very faint rutching that was nevertheless more than that of one pair of footsteps, made him look up. Two slim nuns in the black robes of the Gods *of* Lankhmar and in the customary narrow, jutting hoods which left faces totally shadowed were approaching him, long-sleeved arm in arm.

He had known courtesans in the Plaza of Dark Delights to adopt almost any garb to inflame the senses of their customers, new or old, and capture or recapture their interest: the torn smock of a beggar girl, the hose and short jerkin and close-cropped hair of a page, the beads and bangles of a slave-girl of the Eastern Lands, the fine chain mail and visored helmet and slim sword of a fighting prince from those same areas of Nehwon, the rustling greenery of a wood nymph, the green or purplish weeds of a sea nymph, the prim dress of a schoolgirl, the embroidered garb of a priestess of any of the Gods *in* Lankhmar – the folk of the City of the Black Toga are rarely or never disturbed by blasphemies committed against such gods, since there are thousands of them, and easily replaced.

But there was one dress that no courtesan would dare counterfeit: the simple, straight-falling black robes and hood of a nun of the Gods *of* Lankhmar.

And yet . . .

A dozen yards short of him, the two slim black figures turned off the path toward the nearest closet tree. One parted its rustling, pendant branches, black sleeve hanging from her arm like a bat's wing. The other slipped inside. The first swiftly followed her, but not before her hood had slipped back a little, showing for an instant by a wasp's violet pulse the smiling face of Frix.

The Mouser's heart leaped. So did he.

As the Mouser arrived inside the bower amid an explosion of dislodged white blooms, as if the tree herself were throwing flowers to welcome him, the two slim black figures faced around toward him and dropped back their hoods. The same as he had last seen it aboard *Squid*, Frix's dark hair was confined by a silver net. The smile still curved her lips, though her gaze was distant and grave. But Hisvet's hair was itself a silver-blonde wonder, her lips pouted enticingly, as if blowing him a kiss, while her gaze danced all over his person with naughty merriment.

She moved toward him a step.

With a happy roaring shout only he could hear, blood rushed through the Mouser's arteries toward his center, reviving his limp manhood in a mere moment, as a magically summoned genie offhandedly builds a tower.

The Mouser imitated his blood, rushing blindly to Hisvet and clapping his arms around her.

But with a concerted movement like a half circling in a swift dance, the two girls had changed places, so that it was Frix he found himself embracing, and with cheek pressed to cheek, for at the last moment she had swayed her head aside.

The Mouser would have disengaged himself then, murmuring courteous and indeed almost sincere excuses, for through her robe Frix's body felt slimly enticing and most interestingly embossed, except that at that instant Hisvet leaned her head over Frix's shoulder and tipping her elfin face sideways, planted her half-parted lips on the Mouser's mouth, which instantly began to imitate that of the industrious bee sipping nectar.

It seemed to him that he was in the Seventh Heaven, which is reserved for only the most youthful and beauteous of the gods.

When at last Hisvet removed her lips from his, keeping her face so close that the fresh scar Cat's Claw had made was a blue-edged pink ribbon from magnificent nostril to velvet-rounded slender jaw, it was instantly to murmur to him, 'Rejoice, delicious Dirksman, for you have kissed with your own the actual lips of a Demoiselle of Lankhmar, which is a familiarity almost beyond imagining, and you have kissed *my* lips, an intimacy which passeth all understanding. And now, Dirksman, embrace Frix closely while I preoccupy your eyes and solace your face, which is truly the noblest area of the skin, the very soul's vizard. It is demeaning work for me, to be sure, as if a goddess should scrub and anoint with oil a common soldier's dirty boot, yet know that I do it right gladly.'

Meanwhile Frix's slim fingers were unbuckling his ratskin belt. With the faintest slither and tiniest double *thunk*, it slipped with Scalpel and Cat's Claw to the springy close-cropped turf bleached almost white by the closet tree's perpetual shade.

'Remember, your eyes on *me* only,' Hisvet whispered with the faintest yet firmest note of reproach. 'I remain unjealous of Frix only so long as you disregard her utterly.'

Though the light was still velvet soft, it seemed brighter inside the closet tree's bower than without. Perhaps the gibbous moon had risen. Perhaps the glimmer of the nectar-supping fire-beetles and glow-wasps and night-bees was concentrated here. A few of them circled lazily inside the bower, winking on and off like flirtatious gem moons.

The Mouser clapped his arms more tightly around Frix's slim waist, meanwhile murmuring to Hisvet, 'Oh, White Princess . . . Oh, icy directress of desire . . . Oh, frosty goddess of the erotic . . . Oh, satanic virgin . . .' as she all the while planted tiny kisses on his eyelids and cheeks and free ear, and raked them with the long silvery lashes of her blinking eyes, so that the plant of love was tenderly cultivated and grew and grew. The Mouser sought to return these favors, but she stopped his mouth with hers. As his tongue caressed her teeth, he noted that her two center front incisors were somewhat overlarge, but in his infatuated state this difference seemed only one more point of beauty. Why, even if Hisvet turned out to have some of the appurtenances of a dragon or a giant white spider – or a rat, for that matter – he would love and cosset them each and all. Even if there lifted over her head from behind the joint-masted white moist sting of a scorpion, he would honor it with a loving kiss – well, he mightn't go quite so far as that, he decided abruptly . . . still and on the other hand, he almost might, for at that instant Hisvet's eyelashes tickled the ridge of skin over the silver dart in his temple.

This was ecstasy indeed, he assured himself. It seemed to him that he was now in the Ninth and topmost Heaven, where a few select heroes luxuriate and dream and submit themselves to almost unendurable pleasures, at whiles glancing down with lazy amusement at all the gods toiling at their sparrow-watching and incense-sniffing and destiny-directing on the many tiers below.

The Mouser might never have known what happened next –

and it might have been a direly different happening too – if it had not been that, never satisfied even with the most supreme ecstasy, he decided once more to disobey Hisvet's explicit injunction and steal a glance at Frix. Up to this moment he had been obediently disregarding her with eye and ear, but now it occurred to him that it would twist the launching cords of the catapult of pleasure a notch tighter if he observed both faces of his – after a fashion – two-headed light-of-love.

So when Hisvet once again nuzzled his outside ear with her slender pink and blue tongue and while he encouraged her to keep at it with small twistings of his head and moanings of delight, he rolled his eyes in the other direction, gazing surreptitiously at the face of Frix.

His first thought was that she had her neck bent at an angle that could hardly be anything but uncomfortable, to keep her head quite out of the way of the Mouser's and her mistress's. His second thought was that although her cheeks were passionately inflamed and her perfumy breath was panting through her yawn-slack lips, her gaze was coolly sad, distantly melancholy, and fixed on something worlds away, perhaps a chess game in which she and the Mouser and even Hisvet were less than pawns, perhaps a scene from an unimaginably remote child-hood, perhaps—

Or perhaps she was watching something a little closer than that, something behind him and not quite worlds away—

Although it discourteously took his ear away from Hisvet's maddening tongue, he rolled his whole head in the direction he had his eyeballs and glancing over shoulder saw, blackly out-lined against the pale pulsating wall of closet-blooms, the edge of a crouching silhouette with half-outstretched arm and some-thing gleaming blue-grey at the end of that.

Instantly the Mouser crouched himself, rudely drawing back from Frix, and then half spun around, flailing out backhanded with his left hand, which had an instant earlier embraced Hisvet's maid.

It was a blow barely in time and of necessity imperfectly aimed. As the back of his left fist crashed against the lean wrist of the other hand holding the knife, he felt the sting of its point in his forearm. But then his right fist smashed into the Mingol's face, stirring it at least for a moment from its taut-skinned impassiveness.

As the snugly black-clad figure staggered backward under the impact, it seemed to divide in two, like some creature of slime reproducing itself, as a second dagger-armed Mingol circled from behind the first and moved toward the Mouser who was snatching up his belt and its pendant scabbards with a curse, drawing his dirk Cat's Claw, because the pommel of that weapon came first to hand.

Frix, who still stood dreamily in her black draperies, was saying in a husky, faraway voice, 'Alarums and excursions. Enter two Mingols,' while behind her Hisvet was exclaiming petulantly, 'Oh, my accursed, spoilsport father! He always ruins my most aesthetic creations in the realms of delight, whether from some vile and most unfatherly jealousy, or from—'

By now the first Mingol had recovered and the two rushed warily toward the Mouser, flickering their knives ahead of their slit-eyed yellow faces as they came in. The Mouser, Cat's Claw poised a little ahead of his chest, drove them back with a sudden swishing swing of his belt held in his other hand. The weighted scabbard of his sword Scalpel took one of them in the ear, so that he winced in pain. Now would be the time to leap forward and finish them – with a single dagger-thrust apiece if he were lucky.

But the Mouser didn't. He had no way of knowing that these Mingols were the only two, or whether Hisvet and Frix might not leave off their playacting – if it had been altogether that – and leap upon him with knives of their own as he attacked his lean black assassins. Moreover, his left arm was dripping blood and he could not yet tell how bad that wound was. Finally, it was being borne in reluctantly on his proud mind that he was faced with dangers which might be a mite too much for even his great cunning, that he was blundering about in a situation he did not wholly understand, that he had even now, drunken-sensed, risked his very life against an admittedly unusual ecstasy, that he dared not depend longer on fickle luck, and that – especially in the absence of brawny Fafhrd – he badly needed wise counsel.

In two heartbeats he had turned his back on his assailants, darted past a somewhat startled-looking Frix and Hisvet, and burst out through the branchy wall of the closet-bower amidst a second and even larger explosion of white blooms.

Five heartbeats more and as he scurried north across the Plaza of Dark Delights in the light of the new-risen moon, he had buckled on his belt and withdrawn from a small pouch pendant on it a bandage which he began deftly to wrap tightly about his wound.

Five more heartbeats and he was hastening through a narrow cobbled alleyway that led in the direction of the Marsh Gate.

For he had decided that, much as he hated to admit it to himself, the time had come when he must venture across the treacherous, malodorous Great Salt Marsh and seek the advice of his sorcerous mentor, Sheelba of the Eyeless Face.

Fafhrd spurred his tall gray mare south through the burning streets of Sarheenmar, since no road led around that city fronted by the Inner Sea and backed by desert mountains. Through those latter dry, craggy hills the only trail led east to the land-locked desert-girt Sea of Monsters, by which stood the lonely City of Ghouls, avoided by all other men.

It was smoke-clouded night and the sole light was that of the flames gushing in streamers and roaring sheets from the roofs, doors, and windows of buildings once noted for their coolness, firing their thick walls of dried-clay bricks to red heat and a beauteous, rippling porcelain-like gloss where they did not melt and topple entirely.

Though the wide street was empty, Fafhrd's bloodshot eyes were watchful in his haggard, smoke-stained, sweat-riveted face. He had loosened his sword in its scabbard and his short-ax in its wide sheath, strung his Mingol bow and held it ready in his left hand, and slung the quiver of its arrows high behind his right shoulder. His lightened saddlebag and half-full canteen thumped against his mount's ribs, while his flat pouch, still empty except for the ridiculous tin whistle, flapped about.

For a wonder the mare was not panicked by the fire all around. Fafhrd had heard that the Mingols, by stark-real tests, inured their horses to all manner of horrors almost as sternly as they did themselves, slaying without mercy those who still quailed on the seventh attempt of a beast or the second of a man.

Yet now Fafhrd's mount suddenly stopped dead, just short of a narrow side street, snorting her lathered nostrils and glaring her great eyes more wild and bloodshot than Fafhrd's. Heel-thuds on her ribs would not put her in motion again, so Fafhrd dismounted and began to drag her forward by brute force down the center of the smoke-swirled, flame-walled street.

Then there came rushing from around the burning corner ahead what looked at first glance to be a gang of exceptionally tall and skinny red-litten skeletons, each wearing a skimpy harness and brandishing in either bony hand a short tapering double-edged needle-pointed sword.

After an instant's shock, Fafhrd realized these must be Ghouls, whose flesh and inner organs, he had heard – with much skepticism, but now no longer – were transparent except where the skin became sallowly or rosily translucent on the genital organs and on the lips and small breasts of their women.

It was said also that they ate only flesh, human by preference, and that it was strange indeed to watch the raw gobbets they gulped course down and churn within the bars of their ribs, gradually turning to mush and fading from sight as their sight-less blood assimilated and transformed the food – granting that a mere normal man might ever have opportunity to watch Ghouls feast without becoming a supply of gobbets himself.

Fafhrd was filled with dread, but also indignation, that he, clearly a neutral in a Ghoul-Sarheenmart-Mingol war, should be thus ambushed – for now the leading skeleton hurled his right-hand sword and Fafhrd had to weave swiftly aside as it came cartwheeling through the smoky air.

Whipping his hand over shoulder, he set arrow to bow and dropped the foremost Ghoul with a shot that transfixed his ribs just to the left of his breastbone. Somewhat to his surprise, he discovered that having a skeleton for foe and target made it easier to aim for a vital part. Now as the Ghouls approached closer, uttering horrendous war-shrieks, he noted the flame-light glinting here and there from their glassy hides and realized that even counting their flesh as solid, they were an exception-ally skinny, though rangy, folk.

He brought down two more of his charging foes, the last with a dart into a black eye socket, then dropped his bow, whirled out short-ax and sword, and made a long lunge with the latter as the four remaining Ghouls, their speed unchecked, were upon him.

Graywand took a Ghoul under the chin, jolting him to a dying stop. It was weird to see the skeleton collapse without rattle of bone. The short-ax next licked out, decapitating another enemy, whose glassy-fleshed skull went spinning off, but whose torso, louting forward, drenched the Northerner's ax-hand with invisible, warm, silky fluid.

These grisly events gave the third Ghoul time to run around his stricken comrades and get in on Fafhrd a thrust which, fortunately coming from above, glanced off his left ribs without wounding him deeply.

The long smarting sword-slice, however, turned Fafhrd's indignation wholly to fury and he smote that Ghoul so deeply in the skull that the short-ax stuck and was jerked from Fafhrd's hand. His fury became an almost blinding red rage, not lacking sexual undertones, so that when he noted that the fourth and last Ghoul carried pale breasts on her white ribs like two roses pinned there, he knocked the weapons from her hands with short disarming sword-swipes as she came darting toward him; then as she faltered stretched her full-length on the road with a left-handed punch to her jaw.

He stood panting, closely eyeing the scattered skeletons for sign of movement – there was none – and glaring all about for evidence of other parties of Ghouls. None also.

The horror-inured gray mare had hardly shifted an iron-shod hoof during the melee. Now she tossed her gaunt head, writhed back her black lips from her huge teeth and whinnied snicker-ingly.

Sheathing Graywand, Fafhrd knelt warily by the female skeleton and pressed two fingers into the invisible flesh under the hinges of her jaw. He felt a slow pulse. Without ceremony he hoisted her by the waist. She weighed a little more than he anticipated so that her slenderness surprised him as did also the resilience and smooth texture of her invisible skin. Cold-head-edly leashing his hot vengeful impulses, he dumped her over his saddlebow so that her legs dangled on one side and her trunk on the other. The mare glared back over shoulder and again lip-writhingly bared her yellowish teeth, but did no more than that.

Fafhrd bandaged his wound, rocked his hand-ax from its bony trap and sheathed it, gathered up his bow, mounted the mare and cantered on down the fire-fence street through the wreaths of smoke and swirls of stinging sparks. He was constantly peering for more ambushes, yet glancing down once he found himself disconcerted that there should appear to be a bare white pelvic girdle on his saddlebow, just a fantastically-finned large loose bony knot to the eyes, even though hitched on either side by misty sinews and other cloudy gristle to the balance of a skeleton. After a bit he slung his strung bow over her left shoulder and rested his left hand on the slim warm invisible buttocks, to reassure himself there was a woman there.

The rats were looting by night in Lankhmar. Everywhere in the age-old city they were pilfering, and not only food. They filched the greenish bent brass coins off a dead carter's eyes and the platinum-set nose, ear, and lip jewels from the triply locked gem chest of Glipkerio's wraith-thin aunt, gnawing in the thick oak a postern door neat as a fairy tale. The wealthiest grocer lost all his husked Hrusp nuts, gray caviar from sea-sundered Ool Plerns, dried larks' hearts, strength-imparting tiger meal, sugar-dusted ghostfingers, and ambrosia wafers, while less costly dainties were untouched. Rare parchments were taken from the Great Library, including original deeds to the sewerage and tunneling rights under the most ancient parts of the city. Sweetmeats vanished from bedside tables, toys from princes' nurseries, tidbits from gold-inlaid silver appetizer trays, and flinty grain from horses' feedbags. Bracelets were unhooked from the wrists of embracing lovers, the pouches and snugly-flapped pockets of crossbow-armed rat watchers were picked, and from under the noses of cats and ferrets their food was stolen.

Ominous touch, the rats gnawed nothing except where it was needful to make entries, they left no dirty, clawed tracks or fluted toothmarks, and they befouled nothing, but left their dark droppings in neat pyramids, as if taking an absent owner's care for a house they might decide to occupy permanently.

The most cunning traps were set, subtle poisons laid out invitingly, ratholes stoppered with leaden plugs and brazen plates, candles lit in dark corners, unwinking watch kept in every likely spot. All to no avail.

Shiversomely, the rats showed a human sagacity in many of their actions. Of their few doorways discovered, some looked sawed rather than gnawed, the sawed-out part being replaced like a little door. They swung by cords of their own to dainties hung from ceilings for safety, and a few terrified witnesses claimed to have seen them hurling such cords over their hanging places like bolas, or even shooting them there attached to the darts of tiny crossbows. They seemed to practice a division of labor, some acting as lookouts, others as leaders and guards, others as skilled breakers and mechanics, still others as mere burden-bearers docile to the squeak of command.

Worst of all, the humans who heard their rare squeaking and chitterings claimed they were not mere animal noises, but the language of Lankhmar, though spoken so swiftly and pitched so high that it was generally impossible to follow.

Lankhmar's fears grew. Prophecies were recalled that a dark conquerer commanding a countless horde of cruel followers who aped the manners of civilization but were brutes *and wore dirty furs*, would some day seize the city. This had been thought to refer to the Mingols, but it could be construed as designating the rats.

Even fat Samanda was inwardly terrorized by the depredation of the overlord's pantries and food lockers, and by a ceaseless invisible pattering. She had all the maids and pages routed from their cots two hours before dawn and in the cavernous kitchen and before the roaring fireplace, big enough to roast two beefs and heat two dozen ovens, she conducted a mass interrogation and whipping to quiet her nerves and divert her thoughts from the real culprits. Looking like slim copper statues in the orange light each shaven victim stood, bent, knelt or lay flat before Samanda, as directed, and endured her or his artistically laid-on welting, afterwards kissing the black hem of Samanda's skirt or gently patting her face and neck with a lily-white towel, chilled with ice water and wrung out, for the ogress plied her whip until the sweat trickled down from the black sphere of her hair and dripped in beads from her moustache. Slender Reetha was lashed once more, but she had a revenge by slipping a fistful of finely ground white pepper into the icy basin when she returned the towel to it; true, this resulted in a quadrupling of the next victim's punishment, but when one achieves revenge, the innocent perforce suffer.

The spectacle was watched by a select audience of white-smocked cooks and grinning barbers, of whom not a few were needed to shave the palace's army of servants. They guffawed and giggled appreciatively. It was also observed by Glipkerio from behind curtains in a gallery. The beanpole overlord was entranced and his aristocratically long nerves as much soothed as Samanda's – until he noted in the kitchen's topmost gloomy shelves the hundred of paired pinpoints of the eyes of uninvited onlookers. He raced back to his well-guarded private chambers with his black toga flapping like a sail torn loose in a squall from a tall-masted yacht. Oh, he thought, if only Hisvin would work his master spell! But the old grain-merchant and sorcerer had told him that one planet was not quite yet in the proper configuration to reinforce his magic. Events in Lankhmar had begun to look like a race between some star and the rats. Well, if worse came to worst, Glipkerio told himself, at once giggling and panting in his swirly flight, he had an infallible way of escaping from Lankhmar and Nehwon too, and winning his way to some other world, where he would doubtless quickly be proclaimed monarch of all or at any rate an ample principality to begin with – he was a very reasonable overlord, Glipkerio felt – and thereby have some small solace for the loss of Lankhmar.

9

Sheelba of the Eyeless Face reached into the hut without turning his hooded head and swiftly found a small object and held it forth.

'Here is your answer to Lankhmar's Rat Plague,' he said in a voice deep, hollow, rapid and grating as round stones thudding together in a moderate surf. 'Solve that problem, you solve all.'

Gazing from more than a yard below, the Gray Mouser saw silhouetted against the paling sky a small squat bottle pinched between the black fabric of the overlong sleeve of Sheelba, who chose never to show his fingers, if they were that. Silvery dawn-light shivered through the bottle's crystal stopper.

The Mouser was not impressed. He was bone-weary and be-mired from armpit to boots, which were now sunk ankle-deep in sucking muck and sinking deeper all the time. His coarse gray silks were be-slimed and ripped, he feared, beyond the most cunning tailor's repair. His scratched skin, where it was dry, was scaled with the Marsh's itching muddy salt. The bandaged wound in his left arm ached and burned. And now his neck had begun to ache too, from having to peer craningly upward.

All around him stretched the dismal reaches of the Great Salt Marsh, acres of knife-edged sea grass hiding treacherous creeks and deadly sink-holes and pimpled with low hummocks crowded with twisted, dwarfed thorn trees and bloated prickly cactuses. While its animal population ran a noxious gamut from sea leeches, giant worms, poison eels and water cobras to saw-beaked, low-flapping cadaver birds and far-leaping, claw-footed salt-spiders.

Sheelba's hut was a black dome about as big as the closet-tree bower in which the Mouser had last evening endured ecstasy and attempted assassination. It stood above the Marsh on five crooked poles or legs, four spaced evenly around its rim, the fifth central. Each leg was footed with a round plate big as a cutlassman's shield, concave upward, and apparently enve-nomed, for ringing each was a small collection of corpses of the Marsh's deadly fauna.

The hut had a single doorway, low and top-rounded as a burrow entrance. In it now Sheelba lay, chin on bent left elbow, if either of those were those, stretching out the squat bottle and seeming to peer down at the Mouser, unmindful of the illogicality of one called the Eyeless peering. Yet despite the sky-rim now pinkening to the east, the Mouser could see no hint of face of any sort in the deep hood, only midnight dark. Wearily and for perhaps the thousandth time, the Mouser wondered if Sheelba were called the Eyeless because he was blind in the ordinary way, or had only leathery skin between nostrils and pate, or was skull-headed, or perhaps had quivering antennae where eyes should be. The speculation gave him no shiver of fear, he was too angry and fatigued – and the squat bottle still didn't impress him.

Batting aside a springing salt-spider with the back of his gauntleted hand, the Mouser called upward, 'That's a mighty small jug to hold poison for all the rats of Lankhmar. Hola, you in the black bag there, aren't you going to invite me up for a drink, a bite, and a dry-out? I'll curse you otherwise with spells I've unbeknownst stolen from you!'

'I'm not your mother, mistress, or nurse, but your wizard!' Sheelba retorted in his harsh hollow sea-voice. 'Cease your childish threats and stiffen your back, small gray one!'

That last seemed the ultimate and crushing indignity to the Mouser with his stiff neck and straining spine. He thought bitterly of the sinew-punishing, skin-smarting night he'd just spent. He'd left Lankhmar by the Marsh Gate, to the frightened amazement of the guards, who had strongly advised against solo Marsh sorties even by day. Then he'd followed the twisty cause-way by moonlight to the lightning-blasted but still towering grey Seahawk Tree. There after long peering he'd spotted Sheelba's hut by a pulsing blue glow coming from its low door-way, and plunged boldly toward it through the swordish sea grass. Then had come nightmare. Deep creeks and thorny hum-mocks had appeared where he didn't expect them and he had speedily lost his usually infallible sense of direction. The small blue glow had winked out and finally reappeared far to his right, then seemed to draw near and recede bafflingly time after time. He had realized he must be walking in circles around it and guessed that Sheelba had cast a dizzying enchantment on the area, perhaps to ensure against interruption while working some particularly toilsome and heinous magic. Only after twice almost perishing in quicksands and being stalked by a long-legged marsh leopard with blue-glinting eyes which the Mouser once mistook for the hut, because the beast seemed to have a habit of winking, had he at last reached his destination as the stars were dimming.

Thereafter he had poured out, or rather up, to Sheelba all his recent vexations, suggesting suitable solutions for each problem:

a love potion for Hisvet, friendship potions for Frix and Hisvin, a patron potion for Glipkerio, a Mingol-repellent ointment, a black albatross to seek out Fafhrd and tell him to hurry home, and perhaps something to use against the rats, too. Now he was being offered only the last.

He rotated his head writhingly to unkink his neck, flicked a sea cobra away with Scalpel's scabbard-tip, then gazed up sourly at the little bottle.

'How am I supposed to administer it?' he demanded. 'A drop down each rathole? Or do I spoon it into selected rats and release them? I warn you that if it contains seeds of the Black Sickness, I will send all Lankhmar to extirpate you from the Marsh.'

'None of those,' Sheelba grated contemptuously. 'You find a spot where rats are foregathered. Then you drink it yourself.'

The Mouser's eyebrows lifted. After a bit he asked, 'What will that do? Give me an evil eye for rats, so my glance strikes them dead? Make me clairvoyant, so I can spy out their chief nests through solid earth and rock? Or wondrously increase my cunning and mental powers?' he added, though truth to tell, he somewhat doubted if the last were possible to any great degree.

'Something like all those,' Sheelba retorted carelessly, nodding his hood. 'It will put you on the right footing to cope with the situation. It will give you a power to deal with rats and deal death to them too, which no complete man has ever possessed on earth before. Here.' He let go the bottle. The Mouser caught it. Sheelba added instantly, 'The effects of the potion last but nine hours, to the exact pulsebeat, which I reckon at a tenth of a million to the day, so see that all your work be finished in three-eighths that time. Do not fail to report to me at once thereafter all the circumstances of your adventure. And now farewell. Do not follow me.'

Sheelba withdrew inside his hut, which instantly bent its legs and by ones and twos lifted its shield-like feet with sucking *plops* and walked away – somewhat ponderously at first, but then more swiftly, footing it like a great black beetle or water bug, its platters fairly skidding on the mashed-down sea grass.

The Mouser gazed after it with fury and amazement. Now he understood why the hut had been so elusive, and what had *not* gone wrong with his sense of direction, and why the tall Seahawk Tree was no longer anywhere in sight. The wizard had led him a long chase last night, and doubtless a merry one from Sheelba's viewpoint.

And when it occurred to the bone-tired, be-mired Mouser that Sheelba could readily now have transported him to the vicinity of the Marsh Gate in his traveling hut, he was minded to peg at the departing vehicular dwelling the lousy little bottle he'd got.

Instead he knotted a length of bandage tightly around the small black container, top to bottom, to make sure the stopper didn't come out, put the bottle in the midst of his pouch, and carefully tightened and tied the pouch's thong. He promised himself that if the potion did not solve his problems, he would make Sheelba feel that the whole city of Lankhmar had lifted up on myriad stout legs and come trampling across the Great Salt Marsh to pash the wizard in his hut. Then with a great effort he pulled his feet one after the other out of the muck into which he'd sunk almost knee-deep, pried a couple of pulsing sea slugs off his left boot with Cat's Claw, used the same dagger to slay by slashing a giant worm tightening around his right ankle, drank the last stinging sup of wine in his wine-flask, tossed that away, and set out toward the tiny towers of Lankhmar, now dimly visible in the smoky west, directly under the sinking, fading gibbous moon.

The rats were harming in Lankhmar, inflicting pain and wounds. Dogs came howling to their masters to have needle-like darts taken out of their faces. Cats crawled into hiding to wait it out while rat-bites festered and healed. Ferrets were found squealing in rat-traps that bruised flesh and broke bones. Elakeria's black marmoset almost drowned in the oiled and perfumed water of his mistress' deep, slippery-sided silver bath-tub, into which the spidery-armed pet had somehow been driven, befouling the water in his fear.

Rat-nips on the face brought sleepers screamingly awake, sometimes to see a small black form scuttling across the blanket and leaping from the bed. Beautiful or merely terrified women took to wearing while they slept full masks of silver filigree or tough leather. Most households, highest to humblest, slept by candlelight and in shifts, so that there were always watchers. A shortage of candles developed, while lamps and lanterns were priced almost out of sight. Strollers had their ankles bitten; most streets showed only a few hurrying figures, while alleys were deserted. Only the Street of the Gods, which stretched from the Marsh Gate to the granaries on the Hlal, was free of rats, in consequence of which it and its temples were crammed with worshipers rich and poor, credulous and hitherto atheist, praying for relief from the Rat Plague to the ten hundred and one Gods *in* Lankhmar and even to the dire and aloof Gods *of* Lankhmar, whose bell-towered, ever-locked temple stood at the granaries-end of the street, opposite the narrow house of Hisvin the grain-merchant.

In frantic reprisal, ratholes were flooded, sometimes with poisoned water. Fumes of burning phosphorus and sulfur were pumped down them with bellows. By order of the Supreme Council and with the oddly ambivalent approval of Glipkerio, who kept chattering about his secret weapons, professional rat-catchers were summoned en masse from the grainfields to the south and from those to the west, across the river Hlal. By command of Olegnya Mingolsbane, acting without consultation with his overlord, regiments of black-clad soldiers were rushed at the double from Tovilyis, Kartishla, even Land's End, and issued on the way weapons and items of uniform which puzzled them mightily and made them sneer more than ever at their quartermasters and at the effete and fantasy-minded Lankhmar military bureaucracy: long-handled three-tined forks, throwing balls pierced with many double-ended slim spikes, lead-weighted throwing nets, sickles, heavy leather gauntlets and bag-masks of the same material.

Where *Squid* was docked at the towering granaries near the end of the Street of the Gods, waiting fresh cargo, Slinoor paced the deck nervously and ordered smooth copper disks more than a yard across set midway up each mooring cable, to baffle any rat creeping up them. The black kitten stayed mostly at the mast-top, worriedly a-peer at the city and descending only to scavenge meals. No wharf-cats came sniffing aboard *Squid* or were to be seen prowling the docks.

In a green-tiled room in the Rainbow Palace of Glipkerio Kistomerces, and in the midst of a circle of fork-armed pages and guardsmen officers with bared dirks and small one-hand crossbows at the cock, Hisvin sought to cope with the hysteria of Lankhmar's beanpole monarch, whom a half-dozen slim naked serving maids were simultaneously brow-stroking, finger-fondling, toe-kissing, plying with wine and black opium pills tiny as poppy seeds, and otherwise hopefully soothing.

Twisting away from his delightful ministrants, who moderated but did not cease their attentions, Glipkerio bleated petulantly, 'Hisvin, Hisvin, you must hurry things. My people mutter at me. My Council and Captain General take measures over my head. There are even slavering mad-dog whispers of supplanting me on my seashell throne, as by my idiot cousin Radomix Kistomerces-Null. Hisvin, you've got your rats in the streets by day and night now, all set to be blasted by your incantations. When, oh when, is that planet of yours going to reach its proper spot on the starry stage so you can recite and finger-weave your rat-deadly magic? What's delaying it, Hisvin? I command that planet to move faster! Else I will send a naval expedition across the unknown Outer Sea to sink it!'

The skinny, round-shouldered grain-merchant sorrowfully sucked in his cheeks beneath the flaps of his black leather cap, raised his beady eyes ceilingward, and in general made a most pious face.

'Alas, my brave overlord,' he said, 'that star's course may not yet be predicted with absolute certainty. It will soon arrive at its spot, never fear, but exactly how soon the most learned astrologer cannot foretell. Benign waves urge it forward, then a malign sky-swell drives it back. It is in the eye of a celestial storm. As an iceberg-huge jewel floating in the blue waters of the heavens, it is subject to their currents and ragings. Recall also what I've told you of your traitorous courier, the Gray Mouser, who it now appears is in league with powerful witch doctors and fetishmen working against us.'

Nervously plucking at his black toga and slapping away with his long flappy fingers the pink hand of a maid who sought to rearrange the garment, Glipkerio spat out peevishly, 'Now the Mouser. Now the stars. What sort of impotent sorcerer are you? Methinks the rats rule the stars as well as the streets and corridors of Lankhmar.'

Reetha, who was the rebuffed maid, uttered a soundless philosophic sigh and softly as a mouse inserted her slapped hand under her overlord's toga and began most gently to scratch his stomach, meanwhile occupying her mind with a vision of herself girdled in three leather loops with Samanda's keys, thongs, chains, and whips, while the blubbery palace mistress knelt naked and quaking before her.

Hisvin intoned, 'Against that pernicious thought, I present you with a most powerful palindrome: Rats live on no evil star. Recite it with lips and mind when your warlike eagerness to come to final grips with your furry foes makes you melancholy, oh most courageous commander in chief.'

'You give me words; I ask for action,' Glipkerio complained.

'I will send my daughter Hisvet to attend you. She has now disciplined into instructive erotic capers a new dozen of silver-caged white rats.'

'Rats, rats, rats! Do you seek to drive me mad?' Glipkerio squeaked angrily.

'I will at once order her to destroy her harmless pets, good scholars though they be,' Hisvin answered smoothly, bowing very low so that he could make a nasty face unseen. 'Then, your overlordship wishing, she shall come to soothe your battle-strung brazen nerves with mystic rhythms learned in the Eastern Lands. While her maid Frix is skilled in subtle massages known only to her and to certain practitioners in Quarmall, Kokgnab, and Klesh.'

Glipkerio lifted his shoulders, pouted his lips, and uttered a little grunt midway between indifference and unwilling satisfaction.

At that instant, a half-dozen of the officers and pages crouched together and directed their gazes and weapons at a doorway in which had appeared a little low shadow.

At the same moment, her mind overly absorbed and excited by imagined squeals and groans of Samanda forced to crawl about the kitchen floor by jerks of her globe-dressed black hair and by the jabs of the long pins taken from it, Reetha inadvertently tweaked a tuft of body hair which her gently scratching fingers had encountered.

Her monarch writhed as if stabbed and uttered a thin, piercing shriek.

A dwarf white cat had trotted nervously into the doorway, looking back over shoulder with nervous pink eyes, and now when Glipkerio screamed, disappeared as if batted by an unseen broom.

Glipkerio gasped, then shook a pointing finger under Reetha's nose. It was all she could do not to snap with her teeth at the soft, perfumed object, which looked as long and loathsome to her as the white caterpillar of a giant moon moth.

'Report yourself to Samanda!' he commanded. 'Describe to her in full detail your offense. Tell her to inform me beforehand of your hour of punishment.'

Against his own rule, Hisvin permitted himself a small, veiled expression of his contempt for his overlord's wits. In his solemn professional voice he said, 'For best effect, recite my palindrome backwards, letter by letter.'

The Mouser snored peacefully on a thick mattress in a small bedroom above the shop of Nattick Nimblefingers the tailor, who was furiously at work below cleaning and mending the Mouser's clothing and accouterments. One full and one half-empty wine-jug rested on the floor by the mattress, while under the Mouser's pillow, clenched in his left fist for greater security, was the small black bottle he'd got from Sheelba.

It had been high noon when he had finally climbed out of the Great Salt Marsh and trudged through the Marsh Gate, utterly spent. Nattick had provided him with bath, wine, and a bed – and what sense of security the Mouser could get from harboring with an old slum friend.

Now he slept the sleep of exhaustion, his mind just beginning to be tickled by dreams of the glory that would be his when, under the eyes of Glipkerio, he would prove himself Hisvin's superior at blasting rats. His dreams did not take account of the fact that Hisvin could hardly be counted a blaster of rats, but rather their ally – unless the wily grain-merchant had decided it was time to change sides.

*

Fafhrd, stretched out in a grassy hilltop hollow lit by moonlight and campfire, was conversing with a long-limbed recumbent skeleton named Kreeshkra, but whom he now mostly addressed by the pet name Bonny Bones. It was a moderately strange sight, yet one to touch the hearts of imaginative lovers and enemies of racial discrimination in all the many universes.

The somewhat oddly-matched pair regarded each other tenderly. Fafhrd's curly, rather abundant body hair against his pale skin, where his loosened jerkin revealed it, was charmingly counterpointed by the curving glints of camp-fire reflected here and there from Kreeshkra's skin against the background of her ivory bones. Like two scarlet minnows joined head and tail, her mobile lips played or lay quivering side by side, alternately revealing and hiding her pearly front teeth. Her breasts mounted on her rib cage were like the stem-halves of pears, shading from palest pink to scarlet.

Fafhrd thoughtfully gazed back and forth between these colorful adornments.

'Why?' he asked finally.

Her laughter rippled like glass chimes. 'Dear stupid Mud Man!' she said in her outlandishly-accented Lankhmarese. 'Girls who are not Ghouls – all your previous women, I suppose, may they be chopped to still-sentient raw bits in Hell! – draw attention to their points of attraction by concealing them with rich fabric or precious metals. We, who are transparent-fleshed and scorn all raiment, must go about it another way, employing cosmetics.'

Fafhrd chuckled lazily in answer. He was now looking back and forth between his dear white-ribbed companion and the moon seen through the smooth, pale gray branches of the dead thorn tree on the rim of the hollow, and finding a wondrous content in *that* counterpoint. He thought how strange it was, though really not so much, that his feelings toward Kreeshkra had changed so swiftly. Last night, when she had revived from her knockout a mile or so beyond burning Sarheenmar, he had been ready to ravage and slay her, but she had comported herself with such courage and later proven herself such a spirited and sympathetic companion, and possessed of a ready wit, though somewhat dry, as befitted a skeleton, that when the pink rim of dawn had added itself to and then drunk the city's flames, it had seemed the natural thing that she should ride pillion behind him as he resumed his journey south. Indeed, he'd thought, such a comrade might daunt without fight the brigands who swarmed around Ilthmar and thought Ghouls a myth. He had offered her bread, which she refused, and wine, which she drank sparingly. Toward evening his arrow had brought down a desert antelope and they had feasted well, she devouring her portion raw. It was true what they said about Ghoulish digestion. Fafhrd had at first been bothered because she seemed to hold no grudge on behalf of her slain fellows and he suspected that she might be employing her extreme amiability to put him off guard and then slay him, but he had later decided that life or its loss was likely accounted no great matter by Ghouls, who looked so much like skeletons to begin with.

The gray Mingol mare, tethered to the thorn tree on the hollow's rim, threw up her head and nickered.

A mile or more overhead in the windy dark, a bat slipped from the back of a strongly winging black albatross and fluttered earthward like an animate large black leaf.

Fafhrd reached out an arm and ran his fingers through Kreeshkra's invisible, shoulder-length hair. 'Bonny Bones,' he asked, 'why do you call me Mud Man?'

She answered tranquilly, 'All your kind seem mud to us, whose flesh is as sparkling clear as running water in a brook untroubled by man or rains. Bones are beautiful. They are made to be seen.' She reached out a skeleton-seeming soft touching hand and played with the hair on his chest, then went on seriously, staring toward the stars. 'We Ghouls have such an aesthetic distaste for mud-flesh that we consider it a sacred duty to transform it to crystal-flesh by devouring it. Not yours, at least not tonight, Mud Man,' she added, sharply tweaking a copper ringlet.

He lightly captured her wrist. 'So your love for me is most unnatural, at least by Ghoulish standards,' he said with a touch of argumentativeness.

'If you say so, master,' she answered with a sardonic, mock-submissive note.

'I stand, or rather lie, corrected,' Fafhrd murmured. 'I'm the lucky one, whatever your motives and whatever name we give them.' His voice became clearer again. 'Tell me, Bonny Bones, how in the world did you ever come to learn Lankhmarese?'

'Stupid, *stupid* Mud Man,' she replied indulgently. 'Why, 'tis our native tongue' – and here her voice grew dreamy – 'deriving from those ages a millennium and more ago when Lankhmar's empire stretched from Quarmall to the Trollstep Mountains and from Earth's End to the Sea of Monsters, when Kvarch Nar was Hwarshmar and we lonely Ghouls alley-and-graveyard thieves only. We had another language, but Lankhmarese was easier.'

He returned her hand to her side, to plant his own beyond her and stare down into her black eye sockets. She whimpered faintly and ran her fingers lightly down his sides. Fighting impulse for the moment, he said, 'Tell me, Bonny Bones, how do you manage to *see* anything when light goes right through you? Do you see with the inside of the back of your skull?'

'Questions, questions, questions,' she complained moaningly.

'I only want to become less stupid,' he explained humbly.

'But I *like* you to be stupid,' she answered with a sigh. Then raising up on her elbow so that she faced the still blazing camp-fire – the thorn tree's dense wood burnt slowly and fiercely – she said, 'Look closely into my eyes. No, without getting between them and the fire. Can you see a small rainbow in each? That's where light is refracted to the seeing part of my brains, and a very tiny real image formed there.'

Fafhrd agreed he could see twin rainbows, then went on eagerly, 'Don't stop looking at the fire yet; I want to show you something.' He made a cylinder of one hand and held an end of the cylinder to her nearest eye, then clapped his fingers, held tightly together, against the other end. 'There!' he said. 'You can see the fire glow through the edges of my fingers, can't you? So I'm part transparent. I'm part crystal, at least.'

'I can, I can,' she assured him with singsong weariness. She looked away from his hands and the fire at his face and hairy chest. 'But I *like* you to be mud,' she said. She put her hands on his shoulders. 'Come, darling, be dirtiest mud.'

He gazed down at the moonlit pearl-toothed skull and

blackest eye sockets in each of which a faint opalescent moon-bow showed, and he remembered how a wisewoman of the North had once told him and the Mouser that they were both in love with Death. Well, she'd been right, at least about himself, Fafhrd had to confess now, as Kreeshkra's arms began to tug at him.

At that instant there sounded a thin whistle, so high as to be almost inaudible, yet piercing the ear like a needle finer than a hair. Fafhrd jerked around, Kreeshkra swiftly lifted her head, and they noted that they were being watched not only by the Mingol mare, but also with upside-down eyes by a black bat which hung from a high gray twig of the thorn tree.

Filled with premonition, Fafhrd pointed a forefinger at the dangling black flier, which instantly fluttered down to the fleshly perch presented. Fafhrd drew off its leg a tiny black roll of parchment springy as thinnest tempered iron, waved the flutterer back to its first perch, and unrolling the black parchment and holding it close to the firelight and his eyes close to it, read the following missive writ in a white script:

> *Mouser in the direst danger. Also Lankhmar. Consult Ningauble of the Seven Eyes. Speed of the essence. Don't lose the tin whistle.*

The signature was a tiny unfeatured oval, which Fafhrd knew to be one of the sigils of Sheelba of the Eyeless Face.

White jaw resting on folded white knuckles, Kreeshkra watched the Northerner from her inscrutable black eye pits as he buckled on his sword.

'You're leaving me,' she asserted in a flat voice.

'Yes, Bonny Bones, I must ride south like the wind,' Fafhrd admitted hurriedly. 'A lifelong comrade's in immense peril.'

'A man, of course,' she divined with the same tonelessness. 'Even Ghoulish men save their great love for their male sword-mates.'

'It's a different sort of love,' Fafhrd started to argue as he untied the mare from the thorn tree, feeling at the flat pouch hanging from the saddlebow, to make sure it still held the thin tin cylinder. Then, more practically, 'There's still half the antelope to give you strength for your trudge home – and it's uncooked too.'

'So you assume my people are eaters of carrion, and that half a dead antelope is a proper measure of what I mean to you?'

'Well, I'd always heard that Ghouls . . . and no, of course, I'm not trying to *pay* you . . . Look here, Bonny Bones – I won't argue with you, you're much too good at it. Suffice it that I must course like the lonely thunderbolt to Lankhmar, pausing only to consult my master sorcerer. I couldn't take you – or anyone! – on that journey.'

Kreeshkra looked around curiously. 'Who asked to go? The bat?'

Fafhrd bit his lip, then said, 'Here, take my hunting knife,' and when she made no reply, laid it by her hand. 'Can you shoot an arrow?'

The skeleton girl observed to some invisible listener, 'Next the Mud Man will be asking if I can slice a liver. Oh well, I should doubtless have tired of him in another night and, on pretext of kissing his neck, bit through the great artery under his ear, and drunk his blood and devoured his carrion mud-flesh, leaving only his stupid brain, for fear of contaminating and making imbecilic my own.'

Abstaining from speech, Fafhrd laid the Mingol bow and its quiver of arrows beside the hunting knife. Then he knelt for a farewell kiss, but at the last instant the Ghoul turned her head so that his lips found only her cold cheek.

As he stood up, he said, 'Believe it or not, I'll come back and find you.'

'You won't do either,' she assured him, 'and I shan't be anywhere.'

'Nevertheless I will hunt you down,' he said. He had un-tethered the mare and stood beside it. 'For you have given me the weirdest and most wondrous ecstasy of any woman in the world.'

Looking out into the night, the Ghoulish girl said, 'Congratulations, Kreeshkra. Your gift to humanity: freakish thrills. Make like a thunderbolt, Mud Man. I dote on thrills too.'

Fafhrd shut his lips, gazed at her a moment longer. Then as

he whirled about him his cloak, the bat fluttered to it and hung there.

Kreeshkra nodded her head. 'I said the bat.' Fafhrd mounted the mare and cantered down the hillside.

Kreeshkra sprang up, snatched the bow and arrow, ran to the rim of the grassy saucer and drew a bead on Fafhrd's back, held it for three heartbeats, then turned abruptly and winged the arrow at the thorn tree. It lodged quivering in the center of the gray trunk.

Fafhrd glanced quickly around at the *snap, whir, tchunk!* A skeleton arm was waving him goodbye and continued to do so until he reached the road at the foot of the slope, where he urged the mare into a long-striding lope.

On the hilltop Kreeshkra stood in thought for two breaths. Then from her belt she detached something invisible, which she dropped in the center of the dying campfire.

There was a sputtering and a shower of sparks, when a bright blue flame shot straight up a dozen yards and burnt for as many heartbeats before it died. Kreeshkra's bones looked like blued iron, her glinting glassy flesh like scraps of tropic night-sky, but there was none to see this beauty.

Fafhrd watched the needlelike flare over shoulder as he sped rockingly along and he frowned into the wind.

The rats were murdering in Lankhmar that night. Cats died by swiftly sped crossbow darts that punctured slit-pupiled eye to lodge in brain. Poison set out for rats was cunningly secreted in gobbets of dogs' dinners. Elakeria's marmoset died, crucified to the head of the sandalwood bed of that plump wanton, just opposite her ceiling-tall mirror of daily-polished silver. Babies were bitten to death in their cradles. A few big folk were stung by deep-burrowing darts smeared with a black stuff and died in convulsions after hours of agony. Many drank to still their fears, but the unwatched dead-drunk bled to death from neat cuts that tapped arteries, Glipkerio's aunt, who was also Elakeria's mother, strangled in a noose hung over a dark deep stairs made slippery by spilled oil. A venturesome harlot was overrun in the Plaza of Dark Delights and eaten alive while no one heeded her screams.

So tricky were some of the traps the rats set and by circumstantial evidence so deft their wielding of their weapons, that many folk began to insist that some of them, especially the rare and elusive albinos, had on their forelegs tiny clawed hands rather than paws, while there were many reports of rats running on their hind legs.

Ferrets were driven in droves down ratholes. None returned. Eerily bag-headed, brown-uniformed soldiers rushed about in squads, searching in vain for targets for their new and much-touted weapons. The deepest wells in the city were deliberately poisoned, on the assumption that the city of rats went as deep and tapped those wells for its water supply. Burning brimstone was recklessly poured into ratholes and soldiers had to be detached from their primary duty to fight the resultant fires.

An exodus begun by day continued by night from the city, by yacht, barge, rowboat, and raft, also south by cart, carriage, or afoot through the Grain Gate and even east through the Marsh Gate, until bloodily checked by command of Glipkerio, advised by Hisvin and by the city's stiff-necked and ancient Captain General, Olegnya Mingolsbane. Lukeen's war galley was one of the several which rounded up the fleeing civilian vessels and returned them to their docks – that is, all but the most gold-heavy, bribe-capable yachts. Shortly afterwards, rumor spread as fast as news of a new sin, that there was a conspiracy to assassinate Glipkerio and set on his throne his widely-admired and studious pauper cousin, Radomix Kistomerces-Null, who was known to keep seventeen pet cats. A striking force of plain-clothes constables and Lankhmarines was sent from the Rainbow Palace through the torchlit dark to seize Radomix, but he was warned in time and lost himself and his cats in the slums, where he and they had many friends, both human and feline.

As the night of terror grew older at snail's pace, the streets emptied of civilian human traffic and grew peculiarly silent and dark, since all cellars and many ground floors had been abandoned and locked, barred, and barricaded from above. Only the Street of the Gods was still crowded, where the rats still had made no assault and where comfort of a sort was to be had against fears. Elsewhere the only sounds were the quick, nervous tramp of squads of constables and soldiers on night guard and patterings and chitterings that grew ever more bold and numerous.

Reetha lay stretched before the great kitchen fire, trying to ignore Samanda sitting in her huge palace mistress's chair and inspecting her whips, rods, paddles and other instruments of correction, sometimes suddenly whishing one through the air. A very long thin chain confined Reetha by her neck collar to a large, recessed, iron ring-bolt in the kitchen's tiled floor near the center of the room. Occasionally Samanda would eye her thoughtfully, and whenever the bell tolled the half hour, she'd order the girl to stand to attention and perhaps perform some trifling chore, such as filing Samanda's wine-tankard. Yet still she never struck the girl, nor so far as Reetha knew, had sent message to Glipkerio apprising him of the time of his maid's correction.

Reetha realized that she was being deliberately subjected to the torment of punishment deferred and tried to lose her mind in sleep and fantasies. But sleep, the few times she achieved it, brought nightmares and made more shockful the half-hourly wakenings, while fantasies of lording it cruelly over Samanda rang too hollow in her present situation. She tried to romance, but the material she had to work with was thin. Among other scraps, there was the smallish, gray-clad swordsman who had asked her her name the day she had been whipped for being scared by rats into dropping her tray. He at least had been courteous and had seemed to regard her as more than an animated serving tray, but surely he had long since forgotten her.

Without warning, the thought flashed across her mind that if she could lure Samanda close, she might if she were swift enough be able to strangle her with the slack of her chain – but this thought only set her trembling. In the end she was driven to a count of her blessings, such as that at least she had no hair to be pulled or set afire.

The Gray Mouser woke an hour past midnight feeling fit and ready for action. His bandaged wound didn't bother him, though his left forearm was still somewhat stiff. But since he could not favorably contact Glipkerio before daylight, and having no mind to work Sheelba'a anti-rat magic except in the overlord's admiring presence, he decided to put himself to sleep again with the remaining wine.

Operating silently, so as not to disturb Nattick Nimblefingers, whom he heard snoring tiredly on a pallet near him, he rather rapidly finished off the half jug and then began more meditatively to suck on the full one. Yet drowsiness, let alone sleep, perversely refused to come. Instead the more that he drank, the more tinglingly alive he became, until at last with a shrug and a smile he took up Scalpel and Cat's Claw with never a clink and stole downstairs.

There a horn-shielded lamp burning low showed his clothes and accouterments all orderly lying on Nattick's clean work-table. His boots and other leather had been brushed and scrubbed and then re-suppled with neat's-foot oil, and his gray silk tunic and cloak washed, dried, and neatly mended, each new seam and patch interlocked and double-stitched. With a little wave of thanks at the ceiling, he rapidly dressed himself, lifted one of the two large oil-filmed identical keys from their secret hook, unlocked the door, drew it open on its well-greased hinges, slipped into the night, and locked the door behind him.

He stood in deep shadow. Moonlight impartially silvered the age-worn walls opposite and their stains and the tight-shuttered little windows and the low, shut doors above the footstep-hollowed stone thresholds and the worn-down cobbles and the bronze-edged drain-slits and the scattered garbage and trash. The street was silent and empty either way to where it curved out of sight. So, he thought, must look the City of Ghouls by night, except that there, there were supposed to be skeletons slipping about on narrow ridgy ivory feet with somehow never a *clack* or *click*.

Moving like a great cat, he stepped out of the shadows. The swollen but deformed moon peered down at him almost blindingly over Nattick's scolloped roof-ridge. Then he was himself part of the silvered world, padding at a swift, long-striding walk on his spongy-soled boots along Cheap Street's center toward its curve-hidden intersections with the Street of the Thinkers and the Street of the Gods. Whore Street paralleled Cheap Street to the left and Carter Street and Wall Street to the right, all four following the curving Marsh Wall beyond Wall Street.

At first the silence was unbroken. When the Mouser moved like a cat, he made no more noise. Then he began to hear it – a tiny pattering, almost like a first flurry of small raindrops, or the first breath of a storm through a small-leafed tree. He paused and looked around. The pattering stopped. His eyes searched the shadows and discerned nothing except two close-set glints in the trash that might have been water-drops or rubies – or something.

He set out again. At once the pattering was resumed, only now there was more of it, as if the storm were about to break. He quickened his stride a little, and then all of a sudden they were upon him: two ragged lines of small low silvered shapes rushing out of the shadows to his right and from behind the trash-heaps and out of the drain-slits to his left and a few even squeezing under the scoop-thresholded doors.

He began to run skippingly and much faster than his foes, Scalpel striking out like a silver toad's tongue to pink one after another of them in a vital part, as if he were some fantastic trash collector and the rats animate small rubbish. They continued to close on him from ahead, but most he outran and the rest he skewered. The wine he'd bibbed giving him complete confidence, it became almost a dance – a dance of death with the rats figuring as humanity and he their grisly gray overlord, armed with rapier instead of scythe.

Shadows and silvered wall switched sides as the street curved. A larger rat got past Scalpel and sprang for his waist, but he deftly flicked it past him on Cat's Claw's point while his sword thrust through two more. Never in his life, he told himself gleefully, had he been so truly and literally the Gray Mouser, decimating a mouser's natural prey.

Then something whirred past his nose like an angry wasp, and everything changed. He recalled in a vivid flash the supremely strange night of decision aboard *Squid*, which had become almost a fantasy-memory to him, and the crossbow rats and Skwee with sword at his jugular, and he realized fully for the first time in Lankhmar that he was not dealing with ordinary or even extraordinary rats, but with an alien and hostile culture of intelligent beings, small to be sure, but perhaps more clever and surely more prolific and murder-bent than even men.

Leaving off skipping, he ran as fast as he could, slashing out repeatedly with Scalpel, but thrusting his dirk in his belt and grabbing in his pouch for Sheelba's black bottle.

It wasn't there. With sinking heart and a self-curse, he remembered that, wine-bemused, he'd left it under his pillow at Nattick's.

He shot past the black Street of the Thinkers with its taller buildings shutting out the moon. More rats poured out. His boot squished down on one and he almost slipped. Two more steel wasps buzzed past his face and – he'd never have believed it from another's lips – a small blue-flaming arrow. He raced past the lightless long wall of the building housing the Thieves' Guild, thinking chiefly of making more speed and hardly at all of rat-slashing.

Then almost at once, Cheap Street curving more sharply, there were bright lights ahead of him and many people, and a few strides later he was among them and the rats all gone.

He bought from a street vendor a small tankard of charcoal-heated ale to occupy the time while his dread and gasping faded. When his dry throat had been warmly and bitterly wetted, he gazed east two squares down the Street of the Gods to the Marsh Gate and then west more glittering blocks than he could clearly see.

It seemed to him that all Lankhmar was gathered here tonight by light of flaring torch and lamp and horn-shielded candle – and pole-lofted flare – praying and strolling, moaning and drinking, munching, and whispering fearful gossip. He wondered why the rats had spared this street only. Were they even more afraid of men's gods than men were?

At the Marsh Gate end of the Street of the Gods were only the hutments of the newest, poorest, and most slum-suited Gods *in* Lankhmar. Indeed most of the congregations here were mere curb-side gatherings about some scrawny hermit or leather-skinned death-skinny priest come from the deserts of the Eastern Lands.

The Mouser turned the other way and began a slow and

twisty stroll through the hush-voiced mob, here greeting an old acquaintance, there purchasing a cup of wine or a noggin of spirits from a street-seller, for the Lankhmarts believe that religion and minds half-fuddled, or at least drink-soothed, go nicely together.

Despite momentary temptation, he successfully got by the intersection with Whore Street, tapping the dart in his temple to remind himself that erotic experience would end in futility. Although Whore Street itself was dark, the girls young and old were out in force tonight, doing their business in the shadowed porticos, workmanlike providing man's third most potent banishment of fears after prayers and wine.

The farther he got from Marsh Gate, the wealthier and more richly served became the gods *in* Lankhmar whose establishments he passed – churches and temples now, some even with silver-chased pillars and priests with golden chains and gold-worked vestments. From the open doors came rich yellow light and heady incense and the drone of chanted curses and prayers – all against the rats, so far as the Mouser could make them out.

Yet the rats were not altogether absent from the Street of the Gods, he began to note. Tiny black heads peered down from the roofs now and again, while more than once he saw close-set amber-red eyes behind the grill of a drain in the curb.

But by now he had taken aboard enough wine and spirits not to be troubled by such trifles, despite his recent fright, and his memory wandered off to the strange season, years ago, when Fafhrd had been the penniless, shaven acolyte of Bwadres, sole priest of Issek of the Jug, and he himself had been lieutenant to the racketeer Pulg, who preyed on all priests and prayerful folk.

He returned to his complete senses near the Hlal end of the Street of the Gods, where the temples are all golden-doored and their spires shoot sky-high and the priests' robes are rainbow expanses of jewels. Around him was a throng of folk almost as richly clad, and now through a break in it he suddenly perceived, under green velvet hood and highpiled, silver-woven black hair, the merry-melancholy face of Frix with dark eyes upon him. Something pale brown and small and irregularly shaped dropped noiselessly from her hand to the pavement, here of ceramic bricks morticed with brass. Then she turned and was gone. He rushed after her, snatching up the small square of ball-crumpled parchment she'd dropped, but two aristos and their courtesans and a merchant in cloth of gold got shoulderingly in his way, and when he had broken free of them, resolutely curbing his wine-fired temper to avoid a duel, and got out of the press, no hooded green velvet robe was to be seen – or any woman in any guise looking remotely like Frix.

He smoothed the crumpled parchment and read it by the light of low-swinging, horn-paned oil street lamp.

> *Be of hero-like patience and courage.*
> *Your dearest desire will be fulfilled*
> *beyond your daringest expectations,*
> *and all enchantments lifted.*
>
> *Hisvet.*

He looked up and discovered he was past the last luxuriously gleaming, soaring temple of the Gods *in* Lankhmar and facing the lightless low square fane with its silent square bell-tower of the Gods *of* Lankhmar, those brown-boned, black-togaed ancestor-dieties, whom the Lankhmarts never gather to worship, yet fear and revere in their inmost sleeping minds beyond the sum of all the other gods and devils in Nehwon.

The excitement engendered in him by Hisvet's note momentarily extinguished by that sight, the Mouser moved forward from the last street lamp until he stood in the lightless street facing the lightless low temple. There crowded into his liquored compassless mind all he had ever heard of the dread Gods *of* Lankhmar: They cared not for priests, or wealth, or even worshipers. They were content with their dingy temple *so long as they were not disturbed.* And in a world where practically all other gods, including all the Gods *in* Lankhmar, seemed to desire naught but more worshipers, more wealth, more news of themselves to be dissipated to the ends of the world, this was most unusual and even sinister. They emerged only when Lankhmar was in direct peril – and even then not always – they rescued and then they chastised – not Lankhmar's foes but her folk – and after that they retired as swiftly as possible to their dismal fane and rotting beds.

There were no rat-shapes on the roof of *that* temple, or in the shadows crowding thick around it.

With a shudder the Mouser turned his back on it, and there across the street, shouldered by the great dim cylinders of the granaries and backgrounded by Glipkerio's palace with its rainbow minarets pastel in the moonlight, was the narrow, dark-stoned house of Hisvin the grain-merchant. Only one window in the top floor showed light.

The wild desires roused in the Mouser by Hisvet's note flared up again and he was mightily tempted to climb that window, however smooth and holdless looked the unadorned sooty stone wall, but common sense got the better of wild desire in him despite the fire of wine. After all, Hisvet had writ 'patience' before 'courage'.

With a sigh and a shrug he turned back toward the brightly lit section of the Street of the Gods, gave most of the coins in his pouch to a mincing, bejeweled slave-girl for a small crystal flask of rare white brandy from the walled tray hung from her shoulders just below her naked breasts, took one swig of the icily fiery stuff, and was by that swig emboldened to cut down pitch-black Nun Street, intending to go a square beyond the Street of the Thinkers and by way of Crafts Street, weave home to Cheap Street and Nattick's.

Aboard *Squid*, curled up in the crow's nest, the black kitten writhed and whimpered in his sleep as though racked by the nightmares of a full-grown cat, or even a tiger.

10

Fafhrd stole a lamb at dawn and broke into a cornfield north of Ilthmar to provide breakfast for himself and his mount. The thick chops, broiled or at least well-scorched on a thick green twig over a small fire, were delicious, but the mare as she chomped grimly eyed her new master with what seemed to him qualified approval, as if to say, 'I'll eat this corn, though it is soft, milky, and effeminate truck compared to the flinty Mingol grain on which they raised me and grew my stern courage, which comes of grinding the teeth.'

They finished their repast, but made off hurriedly when outraged shepherds and farmers came hooting at them through the tall green field. A stone slung by a shepherd who'd probably brained a few dozen wolves in his day, whizzed close above Fafhrd's ducked head. He attempted no reprisal, but galloped out of range, then reined in to an amble to give himself time to think before passing through Ilthmar, around which no roads led, and the quatty towers of which were already visible ahead, glinting deceptively golden in the new minted rays of the fresh sun.

Ilthmar, fronting the Inner Sea somewhat north of the Sinking Land which led west to Lankhmar, was an ill, treacherous, money-minded city. Though nearest Lankhmar, it stood at the crossroads of the known world, roughly equidistant from the desert-guarded Eastern Lands, and forested Land of the Eight Cities, and the steppes, where traveled about the great tent-city of the merciless Mingols. And being so situated, it forever sought by guile or secret force to levy toll on all travelers. Its land-pirates and sea-brigands, who split their take with its unruly governing barons, were widely feared, yet the great powers could never permit one of themselves to dominate such a strategic point, so Ilthmar maintained the independence of a middle-man, albeit a most thievish and untrustworthy one.

Central location, where the gossip of all Nehwon crossed tracks along with the world's travelers, was surely also the reason why Ningauble of the Seven Eyes had located himself in a mazy, enchantment-guarded cave at the foot of the little mountains south of Ilthmar.

Fafhrd saw no signs of Mingol raiding, which did not entirely please him. An alarmed Ilthmar would be easier to slip through than an Ilthmar pretending to laze in the sun, but with pig-eyes ever a-watch for booty. He wished now he'd brought Kreeshkra with him, as he'd earlier planned. Her terrifying bones would have been a surer guarantee of safe transit than a passport from the King of the East stamped in gold-sifted wax with his famed Behemoth Seal. What a fool, either to dote or to flee, a man was about a woman new-bedded! He wished also that he had not given her his bow, or rather that he'd had two bows.

However, he was three-quarters of the way through the trash-paved city with its bedbug inns and smiling little taverns of resinous wine, more often than not laced with opium for the unwary, before trouble pounced. A great gaudy caravan rousing itself for its homeward journey to the Eastern Lands doubtless attracted attention from him. The only decor of the mean buildings around him was the emblem of Ilthmar's rat-god, endlessly repeated.

The trouble came two blocks beyond the caravan and consisted of seven scarred and pockmarked rogues, all clad in black boots, tight black trousers and jerkins and black cloaks with hoods thrown back to show close-fitting black skullcaps. One moment the street seemed clear, the next all seven were around him, menacing with their wickedly saw-toothed swords and other weapons, and demanding he dismount.

One made to seize the mare's bridle near the bit. That was definitely a mistake. She reared and put an iron-shod hoof past his guard and into his skull as neatly as a duelist. Fafhrd drew Graywand and at the end of the drawing stroke slashed through the throat of the nearest black brigand. Coming down on her forehooves the mare lashed out a hind one and ruined the guts of an unchivalrous fellow preparing to launch a short javelin at Fafhrd's back. Then horse and rider were galloping away at a pace that at the southern outskirts of the city took them past Ilthmar's baronial guard before those slightly more respectable, iron-clad brigands could get set to stop them.

A half-league beyond, Fafhrd looked back. There was no sign as yet of pursuit, but he was hardly reassured. He knew his Ilthmar brigands. They were stickers. Fired now by revenge-lust as well as loot-hunger, the four remaining black rogues would doubtless soon be on his trail. And this time they'd have arrows or at least more javelins, and use them at a respectful distance. He began to scan the slopes ahead for the tricky, almost unmarked path leading to Ningauble's underground dwelling.

Glipkerio Kistomerces found the meeting of the Council of Emergency almost more than he could bear. It was nothing more than the Inner Council plus the War Council, which overlapped in membership, these two being augmented by a few additional notables, including Hisvin, who had said nothing so far, though his small black-irised eyes were watchful. But all the others, waving their toga-winged arms for emphasis, did nothing but talk, talk, talk about the rats, rats, rats!

The beanpole overlord, who did not look tall when seated, since all his height was in his legs, had long since dropped his hands below the tabletop to hide the jittery way they were weaving like a nest of nervous white snakes, but perhaps because of this he had now developed a violent facial tic which jolted his wreath of daffodils down over his eyes every thirteenth breath he drew – he had been counting and found the number decidedly ominous.

Besides this, he had lunched only hurriedly and meagerly and worse – not watched a page or maid being whipped or even slapped since before breakfast, so that his long nerves, finer drawn than those of other men by reason of his superior aristocracy and great length of limb, were in a most wretched state. It was all of yesterday, he recalled, that he had sent that one mincing maid to Samanda for punishment and still had got no word from his overbearing palace mistress. Glipkerio knew well enough the torment of punishment deferred but in this case it seemed to have turned into a torment of pleasure deferred – for himself. The beastly fat woman should have more imagination! Why, oh, why, he asked himself, was it only that watching a whipping could soothe him? He was a man greatly abused by destiny.

Now some black-togaed idiot was listing out nine arguments for feeing the entire priesthood of Ilthmar's rat-god to come to Lankhmar and make propitiating prayers. Glipkerio had grown so nervously impatient that he was exasperated even by the fulsome compliments to himself with which each speaker lengthily prefaced his speech, and whenever a speaker paused more than a moment for breath or effect, he had taken to quickly saying 'Yes,' or 'No,' at random, hoping this would speed things up, but it appeared to be working out the other way. Olegnya Mingolsbane had still to speak and he was the most boring, lengthiest, and self-infatuated talker of them all.

A page approached him and kneeled, holding respectfully out a scrap of dirty parchment twice folded and sealed with candle grease. He snatched it, glancing at Samanda's unmistakably large and thick-whorled thumbprint in the sooty grease, and tore it open and read the black scrawl.

She shall be lashed with white-hot wires
on the stroke of three. Do not be tardy, little
overlord, for I shall not wait for you.

Glipkerio sprang up, his thoughts for the moment concerned only with whether it was the half-hour or three-quarter hour after two o'clock he had last heard strike.

Waving the refolded note at his council – or perhaps it was only that his hand was wildly a-twitch – he said in one breath, glaring defiantly as he did so, 'Important news of my secret weapon! I must closet me at once with its sender,' and without waiting for reactions, but with a final tic so violent it jolted his daffodil wreath forward to rest on his nose, Lankhmar's overlord dashed through a silver-chased purple-wood arch out of the Council Chamber.

Hisvin slid out of his chair with a curt thin-lipped bow to the council and went scuttling after him as fast as if he had wheels under his toga, rather than feet. He caught up with Glipkerio in the corridor, laid firm hand on the skinny elbow high as his black-capped skull and after a quick glance ahead and back for eavesdroppers, called up softly yet stirringly, 'Rejoice, oh mighty mind that is Lankhmar's very brain, for the lagging planet has at last arrived at his proper station, made rendezvous with his starry fleet, and tonight I speak my spell that shall save your city from the rats!'

'What's that? Oh, yes. Good, oh, good,' the other responded, seeking chiefly to break loose from Hisvin's grasp, though meanwhile pushing back his yellow wreath so it was once more atop his blond-ringleted narrow skull. 'But now I must rush me to—'

'She will stand and wait for her thrashing,' Hisvin hissed with naked contempt. 'I said that tonight at the stroke of twelve I speak my spell that shall save Lankhmar from the rats, and save your overlord's throne too, which you must certainly lose before dawn if we beat not the rats tonight.'

'But that's just the point, she *won't* wait,' Glipkerio responded with agonizing agitation. 'It's *twelve*, you say? But that can't be. It's not yet three! – surely?'

'Oh wisest and most patient one, master of time and the waters of space,' Hisvin growled obsequiously, a-tiptoe. Then he dug his nails into Glipkerio's arm and said slowly, marking each word, 'I said that tonight's the night. My demonic intelligencers assure me the rats plan to hold off this evening, to lull the city's wariness, then make a grand assault at midnight. To make sure they're all in the streets and stay there while I recite my noxious spell from this palace's tallest minaret, you must an hour beforehand order all soldiers to the South Barracks and your constables too. Tell Captain General Olegnya you wish him to deliver them a morale-building address – the old fool won't be able to resist that bait. Do . . . you understand . . . me . . . my . . . overlord?'

'Yes, yes, oh, yes!' Glipkerio babbled eagerly, grimacing at the pain of Hisvin's grip, yet not angered but thinking only of getting loose. 'Eleven o'clock tonight . . . all soldiers and constables off streets . . . oration by Olegnya. And now, please, Hisvin, I must rush me to—'

'—to see a maid thrashed,' Hisvin finished for him flatly. Again the fingernails dug. 'Expect me infallibly at a quarter to midnight in your Blue Audience Chamber, whence I shall climb the Blue Minaret to speak my spell. You yourself *must* be there – and with a corps of your pages to carry a message of reassurance to your people. See that they are provided with wands of authority. I will bring my daughter and her maid to mollify you – and also a company of my Mingol slaves to supplement your pages if need be. There'd best be wands for them too. Also—'

'Yes, yes, dear Hisvin,' Glipkerio cut in, his babbling growing desperate. 'I'm very grateful . . . Frix and Hisvet, they're good ones . . . I'll remember all . . . quarter to midnight . . . Blue Chamber . . . pages . . . wands . . . wands for Mingols. And now I must rush me—'

'*Also*,' Hisvin continued implacably, his fingernails like a spiked trap. '*Beware of the Gray Mouser!* Set your guards on the watch for him! And now . . . be off to your flagellatory pastimes,' he added lightly, loosing his horny nails from Glipkerio's arm.

Massaging the dents they'd made, hardly yet realizing he was free, Glipkerio babbled on, 'Ah, yes, the Mouser – bad, bad! But the rest . . . good, good! Enormous thanks, Hisvin! And now I *must* rush me—' And he turned away with a lunging, improbably long step.

'—to see a maid—' Hisvin couldn't resist repeating.

As if the words stung him between the shoulders, Glipkerio turned back at this and interrupted with some spirit. 'To attend to business of highest importance! I have other secret weapons than yours, old man – and other sorcerers too!' And then he was swift-striding off again, black toga at extremest stretch.

Cupping bony hand to wrinkled lips, Hisvin cried after him sweetly, 'I hope your business writhes prettily and screams most soothingly, brave overlord!'

The Gray Mouser showed his courier's ring to the guards at the opal-tiled land entry of the palace. He half expected it not to work. Hisvin had had two days to poison silly Glip's mind against him. And indeed there were sidewise glances and a wait long enough for the Mouser to feel the full strength of his hangover and to swear he'd never drink so much, so mixed again. And to marvel too at his stupidity and good luck in venturing last night into the dark rat-infested streets and getting back silly-drunk to Nattick's through some of the darkest of them without staggering into a second rat-ambush. Ah, well, at least he'd found Sheelba's black vial safe at Nattick's, resisted the impulse to drink it while tipsy, and he'd got that heartening, titillating note from Hisvet. As soon as his business was finished here, he must hie himself straight to Hisvin's house and—

A guard returned from somewhere and nodded sourly. He was passed inside.

From the sneer-lipped third butler, who was an old gossip friend of the Mouser, he learned that Lankhmar's overlord was with his Emergency Council, which now included Hisvin. He resisted the grandiose impulse to show off his Sheelban rat-magic before the notables of Lankhmar and in the presence of his chief sorcerous rival, though he did confidently pat the black vial in his pouch. After all, he needed a spot where rats were fore-gathered for the thing to work and he needed Glipkerio alone best to work on *him*. So he strolled into the dim mazy lower corridors of the palace to waste an hour and eavesdrop or chat as opportunity afforded.

As generally happened when he killed time, the Mouser soon found himself headed for the kitchen. Though he dearly detested Samanda, he made a point of slyly courting her, because he knew her power in the palace and liked her stuffed mushrooms and mulled wine.

The plain-tiled yet spotless corridors he now traversed were empty. It was the slack half hour when dinner has been washed up and supper mostly not begun, and every weary servitor who can flops on a cot or the floor. Also, the menace of the rats doubtless discouraged wanderings of servant and master alike. Once he thought he heard a faint boot-tramp behind him, but it faded when he looked back, and no one appeared. By the time he had begun to smell foods and fire and pots and soap and dishwater and floorwater, the silence had become almost eerie. Then somewhere a bell harshly knelled three times and from ahead, 'Get out!' was suddenly roared in Samanda's harsh voice. The Mouser shrank back despite himself. A leather curtain bellied a score of paces ahead of him and three kitchen boys and a maid came hurrying silently into the corridor, their bare feet making no sound on the tiles. In the light filtering down from the tiny, high windows they looked like waxen nannikins as they filed swiftly past him. Though they avoided him, they seemed not to see him. Or perhaps that was only some whip-ingrained 'Eyes front!' discipline.

As silently as they – who couldn't even make the noise of a hair dropping, since this morning's barbering had left them none – the Mouser hurried forward and put his eye to the slit in the leather curtains.

The four other doorways to the kitchen, even the one in the gallery, also had their curtains drawn. The great hot room had only two occupants. Fat Samanda, perspiring in her black wool dress and under the prickly plum pudding of her piled black hair, was heating in the whitely blazing fireplace the seven wire lashes of a long-handled whip. She drew it forth a little. The strands glowed dull red. She thrust it back. her sparse, sweat-beaded black moustache lengthened and shed its salt rain in a smile as her tiny, fat pillowed eyes fed on Reetha, who stood with arms straight down her sides and chin high, almost in the room's center, half faced away from the blaze. The serving maid wore only her black leather collar. The diamond stripe patterns of her last whippings still showed faintly down her back.

'Stand straighter, my pet,' Samanda cooed like a cow. 'Or would it be easier if your wrists were roped to a beam and your ankles to the ring-bolt in the cellar door?'

Now the dry stink of dirty floorwater was strongest in the Mouser's nostrils. Glancing down and to one side through his slit, he noted a large wooden pail filled almost to the brim with a mop's huge soggy head, lapped around by gray, soap-foamy water.

Samanda inspected the seven wires again. They glowed bright red. 'Now,' she said, 'Brace yourself, my poppet.'

Slipping through the curtain and snatching up the mop by its thick, splintery handle, the Mouser raced at Samanda, holding the mop's huge, dripping Medusa-head between their faces in hopes that she would not be able to identify her assailant. As the fiery wires hissed faintly through the air, he took her square in the face with a big smack and a gray splash, so that she was driven back a yard before she tripped on a long grilling-fork and fell backwards on her hinder fat-cushions.

Leaving the mop lying on her face with its handle neatly down her front, the Mouser whirled around, noting as he did a watery yellow eye in the nearest curtain slit and also the last red winking out of the wires lying midway between the fireplace and Reetha, still stiffly erect and with eyes squeezed shut and muscles taut against the red-hot blow.

He grabbed her arm at its pit, she screamed with amazement and pent tension, but he ignored this and hurried her toward the doorway by which he had entered, then stopped short at the tramp of many boots just beyond it. He rushed the girl in turn toward the other leather-curtained doorways that hadn't an eye in their slits. More boots tramping. He sped back to the room's center, still firmly gripping Reetha.

Samanda, still on her back, had pushed the mop away and was frantically wiping her eyes with her pudgy fingers and squealing from soap-smart and rage.

The watery yellow eye was joined by its partner as Glipkerio strode in, daffodil wreath awry, black toga a-flap, and to either side of him a guardsman presenting toward the Mouser the gleaming brown-steel blade of a pike, while close behind came more guardsmen. Still others, pikes ready, filled the other three doorways and even appeared in the gallery.

Waving long white fingers at the Mouser, Glipkerio hissed, 'Oh most false Gray Mouser! Hisvin has hinted you work against me and now I catch you at it!'

The Mouser squatted suddenly on his hams and heaved muscle-crackingly with both hands on a big recessed iron ring-bolt. A thick square trapdoor made of heavy wood topped with tile, came up on its hinges. 'Down!' he commanded Reetha, who obeyed with commendably cool-headed alacrity. The Mouser followed hunched at her heels, and let drop the trap-door. It slammed down just in time to catch the blades of two pikes thrust at him, and presumably lever them with a jerk from their wielders' hands. Admirable wedges those tapering browned-iron blades would make to keep the trapdoor shut, the Mouser told himself.

Now he was in absolute darkness, but an earlier glance had shown him the shape and length of the stone stairs and an empty flagstoned area below abutting a niter-stained wall. Once again grasping Reetha's upper arm, he guided her down the stairs and across the gritty floor to within a couple of yards of the unseen wall. Then he let go the girl and felt in his pouch for flint, steel, his tinderbox, and a short thick-wicked candle.

From above came a muffled crack. Doubtless a pike-pole breaking as someone sought to rock out the trapped blade. Then someone commanded a muffled, 'Heave!' The Mouser grinned in the dark, thinking how that would wedge the browned-iron wedges tighter.

Tiny sparks showered, a ghostly flame rose from a corner of the tinderbox, a tiny round flame like a golden pillbug with a sapphire center appeared at the tip of the candle's wick and began to swell. The Mouser snapped shut the tinderbox and held up the candle beside his head. Its flame suddenly flared big and bright. The next instant Reetha's arms were clamped around his neck and she was gasping in dry-mouthed terror against his ear.

Surrounding them on three sides and backing them against the ancient stone wall with its pale crystalline splotches, were a dozen ranks of silent rats formed in a semicircle about a spear-length away – hundreds, nay thousands of blackest long-tails, and more pouring out to join them from a score of ratholes in the base of the walls in the long cellar, which was piled here and there with barrels, casks, and grain-sacks.

The Mouser suddenly grinned, thrust tinderbox, steel, and flint back in his pouch and felt there for something else.

Meanwhile he noted a tall, narrow rathole just by them, newly gnawed – or perhaps chiseled and pickaxed, to judge from the fragments of mortar and tiny shards of stone scattered in front of it. No rats came from it, but he kept a wary eye on it.

The Mouser found Sheelba's squat black bottle, pried the bandage off it and withdrew its crystal stopper.

The dull-brained louts in the kitchen overhead were pounding on the trapdoor now – another useless assault!

The rats still poured from the holes and in such numbers that they threatened to become a humpy black carpet covering the whole floor of the cellar except for the tiny area where Reetha clung to the Mouser.

His grin widened. He set the bottle to his lips, took an experimental sip, thoughtfully rolled it on his tongue, then upended the vial and let its faintly bitter contents gurgle into his mouth and down his throat.

Reetha, unlinking her arms, said a little reproachfully, 'I could use some wine too.'

The Mouser raised his eyebrows happily at her and explained, 'Not wine. Magic!' Had not her own eyebrows been shaven, they would have risen in puzzlement. He gave her a wink, tossed the bottle aside, and confidently awaited the emergence of his anti-rat powers, whatever they might be.

From above came the groan of metal and the slow cracking of tough wood. Now they were going about it the right way, with pry-bars. Likely the trap would open just in time for Glipkerio to witness the Mouser vanquishing the rat army. Everything was timing itself perfectly.

The black sea of hitherto silent rats began to toss and wave and from it came an angry chittering and a clashing of tiny teeth.

Better and better! – this warlike show would put some life into their defeat.

He idly noted that he was standing in the center of a large gray-bordered splotch of pinkish slime he must have overlooked before in his haste and excitement. He had never seen a cellar-mold quite like it.

His eyeballs seemed to him to swell and burn a little and suddenly he felt in himself the powers of a god. He looked up at Reetha to warn her not to be frightened at anything that might happen – say his flesh glowing with a golden light or two bright scarlet beams flashing from his eyes to shrivel rats or heat them to popping.

Then he was asking himself '*Up* at Reetha?'

The pinkish splotch had become a large puddle lapping slimily over the soles of his boots.

There was a splintering. Light spilled down from the kitchen on the crowded rats.

The Mouser gawked at them horror-struck. They were as big as cats! No, black wolves! No, furry black men on all fours! He clutched at Reetha . . . and found himself vainly seeking to encircle with his arms a smooth white calf thick as a temple pillar. He gazed up at Reetha's amazed and fear-struck giant face two stories above. There echoed evilly in his ears Sheelba's carelessly spoken, fiendishly ambiguous: '. . . put you on the right footing to cope with the situation . . .' Oh, yes, indeed!

The slime-puddle and its gray border had grown wider still and he was in it up to his ankles.

He clung to Reetha's leg a moment longer with the faint and ungracious hope that since his weapons and his clothing, which touched him, had shrunk with him, she might shrink too at his touch. He would at least have a companion. Perhaps to his credit, it did not occur to him to yell, 'Pick me up!'

The only thing that happened was that an almost inaudibly deep voice thundered down at him from Reetha's mouth, big as a red-edged shield, 'What are you doing? I'm scared. Start the magic!'

The Mouser jumped away from the fleshy pillar, splashing the nasty pink stuff and almost slipping in it, and whipped out his sword Scalpel. It was just a shade bigger than a needle for mending sails. While the candle, which he still held in his left hand, was the proper size to light a small room in a doll's house.

There was loud, confused, multiple padding and claw-clicking, chittering war-cries blasted ears, and he saw the huge black rats stampeding him from three sides, kicking up the gray border in puffs as if it wcre a powder and then splashing the pink slime and sending ripples across it.

Reetha, terror-struck, watched her inexplicably diminished rescuer spin around, leap over a shard of rock, land in a pink splash, and brandishing his tiny sword before him, shielding his doll's candle with his cloak, and ducking his head, rush into the rathole behind her and so vanish. Racing rats brushed her ankles and snapped at each other, to be first down the hole after the Mouser. Elsewhere the rat horde was swiftly disappearing down the other holes. But one rat stayed long enough to nip her foot.

Her nerve snapped. Her first footsteps splattering pink slime and gray dust, she shrieked and ran, rats dodging from under her feet, and dashed up the steps, clawed her way past several wide-eyed guardsmen into the kitchen, and sank sobbing and panting on the tiles. Samanda snapped a chain on her collar.

Fafhrd, his arms joined in a circle above and before his head to avoid skull-bump from rocky outcrops and also the unexpected brushings on face of cobwebs and wraithlike fingers and filmy wings, at last saw a jaggedly circular green glow ahead. Soon he emerged from the black tunnel into a large and many entranced cavern somewhat lit at the center of its rocky floor by a green fire which was being replenished with thin blood-red logs by two skinny, raggedly-tunicked, sharp-eyed boys, who looked like typical street urchins of Lankhmar or Ilthmar, or any other decadent city. One had a puckered scar under his left eye. On the other side of the fire from them sat on a low wide stone an obscenely fat figure so well cloaked and hooded that not a speck of his face or hands was visible. He was sorting out a large pile of parchment scraps and potsherds, pinching hold of them through the dark fabric of his overlong, dangling sleeves, and scanning them close-sightedly, almost putting them inside his hood.

'Welcome, my Gentle Son,' he called to Fafhrd in a voice like a quavering sweet flute. 'What happy chance brings you here?'

'*You* know!' Fafhrd said harshly, striding forward until he was glaring across the leaping green flames at the black oval defined by the forward edge of the hood. 'How am I to save the Mouser? What's with Lankhmar? And why, in the name of all the gods of death and destruction, is the tin whistle so important?'

'You speak in riddles, Gentle Son,' the fluty voice responded soothingly, as its owner went on sorting his scraps. 'What tin whistle? What peril's the Mouser in now? – reckless youth! And what *is* with Lankhmar?'

Fafhrd let loose a flood of curses, which rattled impotently among the stalactites overhead. Then he jerked free from his pouch the tiny black oblong of Sheelba's message and held it forward between finger and thumb that shook with rage. 'Look, Know-nothing One: I dumped a lovely girl to answer this and now—'

But the hooded figure had whistled warblingly and at that signal the black bat, which Fafhrd had forgot, launched itself from his shoulder, snatched with sharp teeth the black note from his finger-grip, and fluttered past the green flames to land on the paunchy one's sleeve-hidden hand, or tentacle, or whatever it was. The whatever-it-was conveyed to hoodmouth the bat, who obligingly fluttered inside and vanished in the coally dark there.

There followed a squeaky, unintelligible, hood-muffled dialogue while Fafhrd sat his fists on his hips and fumed. The two skinny boys gave him sly grins and whispered together impudently, their bright eyes never leaving him. At last the fluty voice called, 'Now it's crystal clear to me, Oh Patient Son. Sheelba of the Eyeless Face and I have been on the outs – a bit of a wizardly bicker – and now he seeks to mend fences with this. Well, well, well, first advances by Sheelba. Ho-ho-ho!'

'Very funny,' Fafhrd growled. 'Haste's the marrow of our confab. The Sinking Land came up, shedding its waters, as I entered your caves. My swift but jaded mount crops your stingy grass outside. I must leave within the half hour if I am to cross the Sinking Land before it resubmerges. *What do I do about the Mouser, Lankhmar, and the tin whistle?*'

'But, Gentle Son, I know nothing about those things,' the other replied artlessly.' 'Tis only Sheelba's motives are air-clear to me. Oh, ho, to think that he— Wait, wait now, Fafhrd! Don't rattle the stalactites again. I've ensorcled them against falling, but there are no spells in the universe which a big fellow can't sometimes break through. I'll advise you, never fear. But I must first clairvoy. Scatter on the golden dust, boys – thriftily now, don't waste it, 'tis worth ten times its weight in diamond unpowdered.'

The two urchins each dipped into a bag beside them and threw into the feet of the green flames a glittering golden swirl. Instantly the flames darkened, though leaping high as ever and sending off no soot. Watching them in the now almost night-dark cavern, Fafhrd thought he could make out the transitory, ever-distorting shadows of twisty towers, ugly trees, tall hunch-backed men, low-shouldered beasts, beautiful wax women melting, and the like, but nothing was clear or even hinted at a story.

Then from the obese warlock's hood came toward the darkened fire two greenish ovals, each with a vertical black streak like the jewel cat's eye. A half yard out of the hood they paused and held steady. They were speedily joined by two more which both diverged and went farther. Then came a single one arching up over the fire until one would have thought it was in great danger of sizzling. Lastly, two which floated in opposite directions almost impossibly far around the fire and then hooked in to observe it from points near Fafhrd.

The voice fluted sagely: 'It is always best to look at a problem from all sides.'

Fafhrd drew his shoulders together and repressed a shudder. It never failed to be disconcerting to watch Ningauble send forth his Seven Eyes on their apparently indefinitely extensible eye-stalks. Especially on occasions when he'd been coy as a virgin in a bathrobe about keeping them hidden.

So much time passed that Fafhrd began to snap his fingers with impatience, softly at first, then more cracklingly. He'd given up looking at the flames. They never held anything but the tan-talizing, churning shadows.

At last the green eyes floated back into the hood, like a mystic fleet returning to port. The flames turned bright green again, and Ningauble said, 'Gentle Son, I now understand your problem and its answer. In part, I have seen much, yet cannot explain all. The Gray Mouser, now. He's exactly twenty-five feet below the deepest cellar in the palace of Glipkerio Kistomerces. But he's not buried there, or even dead – though about twenty-four parts in twenty-five of him *are* dead, in the cellar I mentioned. But *he* is alive.'

'But *how*?' Fafhrd almost gawked, spreading his spread-fingered hands.

'I haven't the faintest idea. He's surrounded by enemies but near him are two friends – of a sort. Now about Lankhmar, that's clearer. She's been invaded, her walls breached everywhere and desperate fighting going on in the streets, by a fierce host which outnumbers Lankhmar's inhabitants by . . . my goodness . . . fifty to one – and equipped with all modern weapons.

'Yet you can save the city, you can turn the tide of battle – this part came through very clearly – if you only hasten to the temple of the Gods *of* Lankhmar and climb its bell-tower and ring the chimes there, which have been silent for uncounted centuries. Presumably to rouse gods. But that's only my guess.'

'I don't like the idea of having anything to do with that dusty crew,' Fafhrd complained. 'From what I've heard of them, they're more like walking mummies than true gods – and even more dry-spirited and unloving being sifted through like sand with poisonous senile whims.'

Ningauble shrugged his cloaked, bulbous shoulders. 'I thought you were a brave man, addicted to deeds of derring-do.'

Fafhrd cursed sardonically, then demanded, 'But even if I should go clang those rusty bells, how can Lankhmar hold out until then with her walls breached and the odds fifty to one against her?'

'I'd like to know that myself,' Ningauble assured him.

'And how do I get to the temple when the streets are crammed with warfare?'

Ningauble shrugged once again. 'You're a hero. You should know.'

'Well, then, the tin whistle?' Fafhrd grated.

'You know, I didn't get a thing on the tin whistle. Sorry about that. Do you have it with you? Might I look at it?'

Grumbling, Fafhrd extracted it from his flat pouch, and brought it around the fire.

'Have you ever blown it?' Ningauble asked.

'No,' Fafhrd said with surprise, lifting it to his lips.

'Don't!' Ningauble squeaked. 'Not on any account! Never blow a strange whistle. It might summon things far worse even than savage mastiffs or the police. Here, give it to me.'

He pinched it away from Fafhrd with a double fold of animated sleeve and held it close to his hood, revolving it clockwise and counterclockwise, finally serpentinely gliding out four of his eyes and subjecting it to their massed scrutiny at thumbnail distance.

At last he withdrew his eyes, sighed, and said, 'Well . . . I'm not sure. But there are thirteen characters in the inscription – I couldn't decipher 'em, mind you, but there *are* thirteen. Now if you take that fact in conjunction with the slim couchant feline figure on the other side . . . Well, I think you blow this whistle to summon the War Cats. Mind you, that's only a deduction, and one of several steps, each uncertain.'

'Who are the War Cats?' Fafhrd asked.

Ningauble writhed his fat shoulders and neck under their garments. 'I've never been quite certain. But putting together various rumors and legends – oh, yes, and some cave drawings north of the Cold Waste and south of Quarmall – I have arrived at the tentative conclusion that they are a military aristocracy of all the feline tribes, a bloodthirsty Inner Circle of thirteen members – in short, a dozen and one ailuric berserkers. I would assume – provisionally only, mind you – that they would appear when summoned, as perhaps by this whistle, and instantly assault whatever creature or creatures, beast or man, that seemed to threaten the feline tribes. So I would advise you not to blow it except in the presence of enemies of cats more worthy of attack than yourself, for I suppose you have slain a few tigers and leopards in your day. Here, take it.'

Fafhrd snatched and pouched it, demanding, 'But by God's ice-rimmed skull, when *am* I to blow it? How can the Mouser be two parts in fifty alive when buried eight yards deep? What vast, fifty-to-one host can have assaulted Lankhmar without months of rumors and reports of their approach? What fleets could carry—'

'No more questions!' Ningauble interposed shrilly. 'Your half hour is up. If you are to beat the Sinking Land and be in time to save the city, you must gallop at once for Lankhmar. Now no more words.'

Fafhrd raved for a while longer, but Ningauble maintained a stubborn silence, so Fafhrd gave him a last thundering curse, which brought down a small stalactite that narrowly missed bashing his brains out, and departed, ignoring the urchins' maddening grins.

Outside the caves, he mounted the Mingol mare and cantered, followed by hoof-raised dust-cloud, down the sun-yellowed, dryly rustling slope toward the mile-wide westward-leading isthmus of dark brown rock, salt-filmed and here and there sea-puddled, that was the Sinking Land. South-ward gleamed the placid blue waters of the Sea of the East, northward the restless gray waters of the Inner Sea and the glinting squat towers of Ilthmar. Also northward he noted four small dust-clouds like his own coming down the Ilthmar road, which he had earlier traveled himself. Almost surely and just as he'd guessed, the four black brigands were after him at last, hot to revenge their three slain or at least woefully damaged fellow-rogues. He narrowed his eyes and nudged the gray mare to a lively lope.

II

The Mouser was hurrying against a marked moist cool draft through a vast, low-ceilinged concourse close-pillared like a mine with upended bricks and sections of pike-haft and broom-handle, and lit by caged firebeetles and glow-worms and an occasional sputtering torch held by a rat-page in jacket and short trews lighting the way for some masked person or persons of quality. A few jewel-decked or monstrously fat rat-folk, likewise masked, traveled in litters carried by two or four squat, muscular, nearly naked rats. A limping, aged rat carrying two sacks which twitched a little from the inside was removing dim, weary firebeetles from their cages and replacing them with fresh bright ones. The Mouser hastened along on tiptoe with knees permanently bent, body hunched forward, and chin out-thrust. It made his legs in particular ache abominably, but it gave him, he hoped, the general silhouette and gait of a rat walking two-legged. His entire head was covered by a cylin-drical mask cut from the bottom of his cloak, provided with eye-holes only, and which, stiffened by a wire which had pre-viously stiffened the scabbard of Scalpel, thrust down several inches below his chin to give the impression that it covered a rat's long snout.

He worried what would happen if someone came close enough and were sufficiently observant to note that his mask and cloak too of course were made of tiny ratskins closely stitched together. He hoped that rats were plagued by propor-tionately tinier rats, though he hadn't noted any tiny rat-holes so far; after all, there was that proverb about little bugs having littler bugs, and so on; at any rate he could claim in a pinch that he came from a distant rat-city where such was the case. To keep the curious and watchful at a distance he hovered his gaunt-leted hands a-twitch above the pommels of Scalpel and Cat's Claw, and chittered angrily or muttered such odd oaths as 'All rat-catchers fry!' or 'By candle-fat and bacon-rind!' in Lankh-marese, for now that he had ears small and quick enough to hear, he knew that the language was spoken underground, and especially well by the aristos of these lower levels. And what more natural than that rats, who were parasites on man's farms and ships and cities, should copy his language along with many other items of his habits and culture? He had already noted other solitary armed rats – bravos or berserkers, presumably – who behaved in the irritable and dangerous manner he now put on.

His escape from the cellar-rats had been achieved by his own cool-headedness and his pursuers' blundering eagerness, which had made them fight to be first, so that the tunnel had been briefly blocked behind him. His candle had been most helpful in his descent of the first sharply down-angling, rough-hewn, then rough-digged passages, where he had made his way by sliding and leaping, checking himself on a rocky outcropping or by digging heel into dirt only when his speed became so great as to threaten a disastrous fall. The first rough-pillared concourse had also been pitch-dark, almost. There he had quickly thrown his cloak over his face to the eyes, for his candle had shown him numerous rats, most of them going naked on all fours, but a few of them hunchedly erect and wearing rough dark clothing, if only a pair of trews or a jacket or slouch hat or smock, or a belt for a short-bladed hanger. Some of these had carried pickax or shovel or pry-bar over shoulder. And there had been one rat fully clothed in black, armed with sword and dagger and wearing a silver-edged full-face vizard – at least the Mouser had assumed it was a rat.

He had taken the first passage leading down – there had been regular steps now, hewn in rock or cut in gravel – and had paused at a turn in the stairs by a curious though stenchful alcove. It contained the first he had seen of the firebeetle lamps and also a half-dozen small compartments, each closed by a door that left space below and above. After a moment's hesitation he had darted into one which showed no black hand paws or boots below and securely hooking the door behind, had instantly and rapidly begun to fabricate his ratskin mask. His instinctive assumption about the function of the compartments was confirmed by a large two-handled basket half full of rat droppings and a bucket of stinking urine. After his long-chinned vizard had been made and donned, he had shaken out his candle, pouched it and then relieved himself, at last per-mitting himself to wonder in amazement that all his clothes and belongings had been reduced in size proportionately with his body. Ah, he told himself, that would account for the wide gray border of the pink puddle which had appeared around his boots in the cellar above. When he'd been sorcerously shrunken, the excess motes or atomies of his flesh, blood, and bones had been shed downward to make the pink pool, while those of his gray clothing and tempered iron weapons had sifted away to make up the pool's gray border, which had been powdery rather than slimy, of course, because metal or fabric contains little or no liquid compared to flesh. It had occurred to him that there must be twenty times as much of the Mouser by weight in that poor abused pink pool overhead as there was in his present rat-small form, and for a moment he had felt a sentimental sadness.

Finishing his business, he had prepared to continue his downward course when there had come the descending clatter of paw- and boot-steps, quickly followed by a banging on the door of his compartment.

Without hesitation he had unhooked the door and opened it with a jerk. Facing him close there had been the black-clad, black-and-silver-masked rat he had seen on the level above, and behind him three bare-faced rats with drawn hangers that looked and probably were sharper than gross human fingers could ever hone.

After the first glance, the Mouser had looked lower than his pursuers' faces, for fear the color and shape and especially the placing of his eyes might give him away.

The vizarded one had said swiftly and clearly in excellent Lankhmarese, 'Have you seen or heard anyone come down the stairs? – in particular an armed human magically reduced to decent and normal size?'

Again without hesitation the Mouser had chittered most angrily, and roughly shouldering his questioner and the others aside, had spat out, 'Idiots! Opium-chewers! Nibblers of hemp! Out of my way!'

On the stairs he had paused to look back briefly, snarl loudly and contemptuously, 'No, of course not!' and then gone down the stairs with dignity, though taking them two at a time.

The next level had shown no rats in sight and been redolent of grain. He had noted bins of wheat, barley, millet, kombo, and wild rice from the River Tilth. A good place to hide – perhaps. But what could he gain by hiding?

The next level – the third down – had been full of military clatter and rank with rat-stink. He had noted rat pikemen drilling in bronze cuirasses and helmets and another squad being instructed in the crossbow, while still others crowded around a table where routes on a great map were being pointed out. He had lingered even a shorter time there.

Midway down each stairs had been a compartmented nook like the first he'd used. He had docketed away in his mind this information.

Refreshingly clean, moist air had poured out of the fourth level, it had been more brightly lit, and most of the rats strolling in it had been richly dressed and masked. He had turned into it at once, walking against the moist breeze, since that might well come from the outer world and mark a route of escape, and he had continued with angry chitters and curses to play his impulsively assumed role of crotchety, half-mad rat-bravo or rogue-rat.

In fact, he found himself trying so hard to be a convincing rat that without volition his eyes now followed with leering interest a small mincing she-rat in pink silk and pearls – mask as well as dress – who led on a leash what he took at first to be a baby rat and then realized was a dwarfish, well-groomed, fear-eyed mouse; and also an imperiously tall ratess in dark green silk sewn over with ruby chips and holding in one hand a whip and in the other the short leashes of two fierce-eyed, quick-breathing shrews that looked as big as mastiffs and were doubtless even more bloodthirsty.

Still looking lustfully at this striking proud creature as she passed him with green, be-rubied mask tilted high, he ran into a slow-gaited, portly rat robed and masked in ermine, which looked extremely coarse-haired now, and wearing about his neck a long gold chain and about his aldermanic waist a gold-studded belt, from which hung a heavy bag that chinked dulcetly at the Mouser's jolting impact.

Snapping a 'Your pardon, merchant!' at the wheezingly chittering fellow, the Mouser strode on without backward glance. He grinned conceitedly under his mask. These rats were easy to befool! – and perhaps reduction in size had sharpened finer his own sharp wits.

He was tempted for an instant to turn back and lure off and rob the fat fellow, but realized at once that in the human world the chinking goldpieces would be smaller than sequins.

This thought set his mind on a problem which had been obscurely terrifying him ever since he had plunged into the rat-world. Sheelba had said the effects of the potion would last for nine hours. Then presumably the Mouser would resume his normal size as swiftly as he had lost it. To have that happen in a burrow or even in the foot-and-a-half high, pillar-studded concourse would be disastrous – it made him wince to think of it.

Now, the Mouser had no intention of staying anything like nine hours in the rat-world. On the other hand, he didn't exactly want to escape at once. Dodging around in Lankhmar like a nimbly animate gray doll for half a night didn't appeal to him – it would be shame-making even if, or perhaps especially if, while doll-size he had to report his important intelligences about the rat-world to Glipkerio and Olegnya Mingolsbane – with Hisvet watching perhaps. Besides, his mind was already afire with schemes to assassinate the rats' king, if they had one, or foil their obvious project of conquest in some even more spectacular fashion on their home ground. He felt a peculiarly great self-confidence and had not realized yet that it was because he was fully as tall as the taller rats around, as tall as Fafhrd, relatively, and no longer the smallish man he had been all his life.

However, there was always the possibility that by some unforeseeable ill fortune he might be unmasked, captured, and imprisoned in a tiny cell. A panicking thought.

But even more unnerving was the basic problem of time. Did it move faster for the rats or slower? He had the impression that life and all its processes moved at a quicker tempo down here. But was that true? Did he now clearly hear the rat-Lankhmar-ese, which had previously sounded like squeaks, because his ears were quicker, or merely smaller, or because most of a rat's voice was pitched too high for human ears to hear, or even because rats spoke Lankhmarese only in their burrows? He surrepti-tiously felt his pulse. It seemed the same as always. But mightn't it be greatly speeded up and his senses and mind speeded up equally, so that he noted no difference? Sheelba had said something about a day being a tenth of a million pulsebeats. Was that rat or human pulse? Were rat-hours so short that nine of them might pass in a hundred or so human minutes? Almost he was tempted to rush up the first stairs he saw. No, wait . . . if timing was by pulse and his pulse seemed normal, then wouldn't he have one normal Mouser-sleep to work in down here? It was truly most confusing. 'Out upon it all, by cat-gut sausages and roasted dog's eyes!' he heard himself curse with sincerity.

Several things at any rate were clear. Before he dared idle or nap, let alone sleep, he must discover some way of measuring down here the passage of time in the above-ground world. Also, to get at the truth about rat-night and day, he must swiftly learn about rodent sleeping habits. For some reason his mind jumped back to the tall ratess with the brace of straining shrews. But that was ridiculous, he told himself. There was sleeping and sleeping, and that one had very little if anything to do with the other.

He came out of his thought-trance to realize fully what his senses had for some time being telling him: that the strollers had become fewer, the breeze more damp and cool and fresh, and sea-odorous too, and the pillars ahead natural rock, while through the doorways chiseled between them shone a yellowish light, not bright yet twinkling and quite unlike that of the fire-beetles, glow-wasps, and tiny torches.

He passed a marble doorway and noted white marble steps going down from it. Then he stepped between two of the rocky pillars and halted on the rim of a wonder-place.

It was a roughly circular natural rock cave many rats high and many more long and wide, and filled with faintly rippling sea-water which transmitted a mild flood of yellowish light that came through a great wide hole, underwater by about the length of a rat's pike, in the other end of the glitter-ceilinged cavern. All around this sea lake, about two rat-pikes above the water, went the rather narrow rock road, looking in part natural, in part chiseled and pickaxed, on which he now stood. At its distant end, in the shadows above the great underwater hole, he could dimly make out the forms and gleaming weapons of a half-dozen or so motionless rats, evidently on guard duty.

As the Mouser watched, the yellow light became yellower still, and he realized it must be the light of later afternoon, surely the afternoon of the day in which he had entered the rat-world. Since sunset was at six o'clock and he had entered the rat-world after three, he had spent fewer than three of his nine hours. Most important, he had linked the passage of time in the rat-world with that in the big world – and was somewhat startled at the relief he felt.

He recalled too the 'dead' rats which had seemed to swim away from the cage dropped from the palace window into the

Inner Sea after Hisvin's demonstration of his death-spell. They might very well have swum underwater into this very cavern, or another like it.

It also came to him that he had discovered the secret of the damp breeze. He knew the tide was rising now, an hour or so short of full, and in rising it drove the cave-trapped air through the concourse. At low tide the great hole would be in part above water, allowing the cavern air to be refreshed from outside. A rather clever if intermittent ventilation system. Perhaps some of these rats were a bit more ingenious than he had given them credit for.

At that instant there came a light, inhuman touch on his right shoulder. Turning around, he saw stepping back from him with naked rapier held a little to one side the black-masked, black-clad rat who had disturbed him in the privy.

'What's the meaning of this?' he chitteringly blustered. 'By God's hairless tail, why am I catted and ferreted? – you black dog!'

In far less ratlike Lankhmarese than the Mouser's, the other asked quietly. 'What are you doing in a restricted area? I must ask you to unmask, sir.'

'Unmask? I'll see the color of your liver first, mousling!' the Mouser ranted wildly. It would never do, he knew, to change character now.

'Must I call in my underlings to unmask you by force?' the other inquired in the same soft, deadly voice. 'But it is not necessary. Your reluctance to unmask is final confirmation of my deduction that you are indeed the magically shrunken human come as a spy into Lankhmar Below.'

'That opium specter again?' the Mouser raved, dropping his hand to Scalpel's hilt. 'Begone, mad mouse dipped in ink, before I cut you to collops!'

'Your threats and brags are alike useless, sir,' the other answered with a low and humorous laugh. 'You wonder how I became certain of your identity? I suppose you think you were very clever. Actually you gave yourself away more than once. First, by relieving yourself in that jakes where I first encountered you. Your dung was of a different shape, color, consistency, and odor than that of my compatriots. You should have sought out a water-privy. Second, although you did try to shadow your eyes, the eye-holes in your mask are too squintingly close together, as are all human eyes. Third, your boots are clearly made to fit human rather than rodent feet, though you have the small sense to walk on your toes to ape our legs and gait.'

The Mouser noted that the other's black boots had far tinier soles than his own and were of soft leather both below and above the big ankle-bend.

The other continued, 'And from the very first I knew you must be an utter stranger, else you would never have dared shoulder aside and insult the many times proven greatest duellist and fastest sword in all Lankhmar Below.'

With black-gloved left paw the other whipped off his silver-trimmed mask, revealing upstanding oval ears and long furry black face and huge, protuberant, wide-spaced black eyes. Baring his great white incisors in a lordly smirk and bringing his mask across his chest in a curt, sardonic bow, he finished, 'Svivomilo, at your service.'

At least now the Mouser understood the vast vanity – great almost as his own! – which had led his pursuer to leave his underlings behind in the concourse while he came on alone to make the arrest. Whipping out simultaneously Scalpel and Cat's Claw, purposely not pausing to unmask, the Mouser made his most rapid advance, ending in a tremendous lunge at the neck. It seemed to him that he had never before in his life moved as swiftly – small size certainly had its points.

There was a flash and a clash and Scalpel was deflected – by Svivomilo's dagger drawn with lightning speed. And then Svivomilo's rapier was on the offensive and the Mouser barely avoiding it by rapid parries with both his weapons and by backing off perilously along the water's brink. Now his involuntary thought was that his opponent had had a much longer time than he of being small and practising the swiftness it allowed, while his mask interfered with his vision and if it slipped a little would blind him altogether. Yet Svivomilo's incessant attacks gave him no time to whip it off. With sudden desperation he lunged forward himself, managing to get a bind with Scalpel on the rapier that momentarily took both weapons out of the fight, and an instant later lashed out with Cat's Claw at Svivomilo's dagger-stabbing wrist, and by accurate eye and good fortune cut its inner tendons.

Then as Svivomilo hesitated and sprang back, the Mouser disengaged Scalpel and launched it in another sinew-straining, long lunge, thrice dipping his point just under Svivomilo's double and then circle parries, and finally drove its point on in a slicing thrust that went through the rat's neck and ended grating against the vertebra there.

Scarlet blood pouring over the black lace at Svivomilo's throat and down his chest, and with only one short, bubbling, suffocated gasp, for the Mouser's thrust had severed windpipe as well as arteries, the rightly boastful but foolishly reckless duellist pitched forward on his face and lay writhing.

The Mouser made the mistake of trying to sheathe his bloodied sword, forgetting that Scalpel's scabbard was no longer wire-stiffened, which made the action difficult. He cursed the scabbard, limp as Svivomilo's now nerveless tail.

Four cuirassed and helmeted rats with pikes at the ready appeared at two of the rocky doorways. Brandishing his red-dripping sword and gleaming dirk, the Mouser raced through an untenanted doorway and with a chittering scream to clear the way ahead of him, sprinted across the concourse to the marble doorway he'd noted earlier, and plunged down the white stairway.

The usual nook in the turn of the stairs held only three compartments, each with a silver-fitted door of ivory. Into the central one there was going a white-booted rat wearing a voluminous white cloak and hood and bearing in his white-gloved right hand an ivory staff with a large sapphire set in its top.

Without an instant's pause the Mouser ended his plunging descent with a dash into the nook. He hurled ahead of him the white-cloaked rat and slammed and hooked fast behind them the ivory door.

Recovering himself, the Mouser's victim turned and with outraged dignity and brandished staff demanded through his white mask set with diamonds, 'Who dareth dithturb with rude thcufflingth Counthillor Grig of the Inner Thircle of Thirteen? Mithcreant!'

While a part of the Mouser's brain was realizing that this was the lisping white rat he had seen aboard *Squid* sitting on Hisvin's shoulder, his eyes were informing him that this compartment held not a box for droppings, but a raised silver toilet seat, up through which came the sound and odor of rushing seawater. It must be one of the water-privies Svivomilo had mentioned.

Dropping Scalpel, the Mouser threw back Grig's hood, dragged off his mask over his head, tripped the sputtering councillor and forced his head down against the far side of the privy's silver rim, and then with Cat's Claw cut Grig's furry white throat almost from ratty ear to ear, so that his blood gushed down into the rushing water below. As soon as his victim's writhings stilled, the Mouser drew off Grig's white cloak and hood, taking great care that no blood got on them.

At that moment he heard the booted footsteps of several persons coming down the stairs. Operating with demonic speed, the Mouser placed Scalpel, the ivory staff, and the white mask and hood and cloak behind the seat of the privy, then hoisted the dead body so that it sat on the same, and himself stood crouching on the silver rim, facing the hooked door and holding the limp trunk erect. Then he silently prayed with great sincerity to Issek of the Jug, the first god he could think of, the one whom Fafhrd had once served.

Wavy and hooked browned-iron pike-blades gleamed above the doorways. The two to either side were slammed open. Then after a pause, during which he hoped someone had peered under the central door just enough to note the white boots, there came a light rapping, and then a respectful voice inquiring, 'Your pardon, Nobility, but have you recently seen anything of a person in gray with cloak and mask of finest gray fur, and armed with rapier and dagger?'

The Mouser answered in a voice which he tried to make calm and dignifiedly benign, 'I have theen nothing, thir. About thicty breathth ago I heard thomeone clattering at thpeed down the thtairth.'

'Our humblest thanks, Nobility,' the questioner responded, and the booted footsteps continued rapidly down toward the fifth level.

The Mouser let off a long soft sigh and chopped short his

prayer. Then he set swiftly to work, for he knew he had a considerable task ahead of him, some of it most grisly. He wiped off and scabbarded Scalpel and Cat's Claw. Then he examined his victim's cloak, hood, and mask, discovering almost no blood on them, and set them aside. He noted that the cloak could be fastened down the front with ivory buttons. Then he dragged off Grig's tall boots of whitest suede and tried them on his own legs. Though their softness helped, they fitted abominably, the sole covering little more than the area under his toes. Still, this would keep him reminded to maintain a rat's gait at all times. He also tried on Grig's long white gloves, which fitted worse, if that were possible. Still, he could wear them. His own boots and gauntlets he tucked securely over his gray belt.

Next he undressed Grig and dropped his garments one by one into the water, retaining only a razor-sharp ivory-and-gold-fitted dagger, a number of small parchment scrolls, Grig's undershirt, and a double-ended purse filled with gold coins struck with a rat's head on one side, circled by a wreath of wheat, and on the other a complex maze (tunnels?) and a numeral followed by the initials *S.F.L.B.* 'Since the Founding of Lankhmar Below?' he hazarded brilliantly. He hung the purse over his belt, fixed the dagger to it by a gold hook on its ivory sheath, and thrust the scrolls unscanned into his own pouch.

Then with a grunt of distaste he rolled up his sleeves and, using the ivory-handled dagger, proceeded to dismember the furry corpse into pieces small enough to force through the silver rim so that they splashed into the water and were carried away.

This horrid task at last accomplished, he made a careful search for blood spatters, wiped them up with Grig's undershirt, used it to polish the silver rim, then dropped it after the other stuff.

Still not giving himself a pause, he pulled on again the white suede boots, donned the white cloak, which was of finest wool, and buttoned it all the way down the front, thrusting his arms through the slits in the cloak to either side. Then he put on the mask, discovered that he had to use the dagger to extend narrowly the eye-slits at their inner ends to be able to see at all with his own close-set human eyes. After that he tied on the hood, throwing it as far forward as practicable to hide the mask's mutilations and his lack of be-furred rat ears. Finally he drew on the long, ill-fitting white gloves.

It was well that he had worked as speedily as he had, allowing himself no time for rest, for now there came booted footsteps up the stairs and the nastily hooked pike blades a-wave again, while below the door of his compartment there appeared typically crooked rat-boots of fine black leather embossed with golden scroll-work.

There was a sharper knocking and a grating voice, polite yet peremptory, said, 'Your pardon, Councillor. This is Hreest. As Lieutenant Warden of the Fifth Level, I must ask you to open the door. You have been closeted a long while in there, and I must assure myself that the spy we seek is not holding a knife at your throat.'

The Mouser coughed, took up the sapphire-headed ivory staff, drew wide the door and majestically strode forth with a slight hobble. Resuming with tired legs the aching, tiptoe rat-gait had given him a sudden torturing cramp in his left calf.

The pike-rats knelt. The fancy-booted rat, whose black clothes, mask, gauntlets and rapier-scabbard were also covered with fine-lined golden arabesques, dropped back two steps.

Directing only a brief gaze at him, the Mouser said coolly, 'You dare dithturb and hathten Counthillor Grig at hith eliminathionth? Well, perhapth your reathonth are good enough. Perhapth.'

Hreest swept off his wide-brimmed hat plumed with the breast-feathers of black canaries. 'I am certain they are, Nobility. There is loose in Lankhmar Below a human spy, magically changed to our size. He has already murdered that skillful if unruly and conceited swordsman Svivomilo.'

'Thorry newth indeed!' the Mouser lisped. 'Thearch out thith thpy at onthe! Thpare no ecthpenthe in men or effort. I will inform the Counthil, Hreetht, if you have not.'

And while Hreest's voice followed him with ratly apologies, thanks, and reassurances, the Mouser stepped regally down the white marble stairs, his limp hardly noticeable due to the grateful support afforded by his ivory staff. The sapphire in its top twinkled like the blue star Ashsha. He felt like a king.

*

Fafhrd rode west through the gathering twilight, the ironshod hooves of the Mingol mare striking sparks from the flinty substance of the Sinking Land. The sparks were becoming faintly visible, just as were a few of the largest stars. The road, mere hoof dints, was becoming hard to discern. To north and south, the Inner Sea and the Sea of the East were sullen gray expanses, the former wave-flecked. And now finally, against the last dirty pink ribbon of sunset fringing the west, he made out the wavery black line of squat trees and towering cactuses that marked the beginning of the Great Salt Marsh.

It was a welcome sight, yet Fafhrd was frowning deeply – two vertical furrows springing up from the inside end of either eyebrow.

The left furrow, you might say, was for what followed him. Taking an unhurried look over shoulder, he saw that the four riders whom he had first glimpsed coming down the Sarheen-mar road were now only a bowshot and a half behind him. Their horses were black and they wore great black cloaks and hoods. He knew now to a certainty they were his four black Ilthmar brigands. And Ilthmar land-pirates hungry only for loot, let alone vengeance, had been known to pursue their prey to the very Marsh Gate of Lankhmar.

The right furrow, which was deepest, was for an almost imperceptible tilt, south lifting above north, in the ragged black horizon ahead. That this was actually a slight tilting of the Sinking Land in the opposite direction was proven when the Mingol mare took a lurch to the left. Fafhrd harshly kicked his mount into a gallop. It would be a near thing whether he reached the Marsh causeway before he was engulfed.

Lankhmar philosophers believe that the Sinking Land is a vast long shield, concave underneath, of hard-topped rock so porous below that it is exactly the same weight as water. Volcanic gases from the roots of the Ilthmar Mountains and also mephitic vapors from the incredibly deep-rooted and yeasty Great Salt Marsh gradually fill the concavity and lift the huge shield above the surface of the sea. But then an instability develops, due to the great density of the shield's topping. The shield begins to rock. The supporting gases and vapors escape in great alternate belches through the waters to north and south.

Then the shield sinks somewhat below the waves and the whole slow, rhythmic process begins again.

So it was that the tilting told Fafhrd that the Sinking Land was once more about to submerge. And now the tilt had increased so much that he had to pull a little on the mare's right bridle to keep her to the road. Looking back over right shoulder, he saw that the four black horsemen were also coming on faster, in fact somewhat faster than he.

As his gaze returned to his goal of safety, the Marsh, he saw the near waters of the Inner Sea shoot upward in a line of gray, foamy geysers – the first escape of vapors – while the waters of the Sea of the East drew suddenly closer.

Then very slowly the rock beneath him began to tilt in the opposite direction, until at last he was pulling on the mare's left bridle to keep her to the road. He was very glad she was a Mingol beast, trained to ignore any and all unnaturalness, even earthquake.

And now it was the still waters of the Sea of the East that exploded upward in a long, dirty, bubbling fence of escaping gas, while the waters of the Inner Sea came foaming almost to the road.

Yet the Marsh was very close. He could make out individual thorn trees and cactuses and thickets of giant sea-grass outlined against the now utterly bled west. And then he saw straight ahead a gap that – pray Issek! – would be the causeway.

Sparks sped whitely from under the mare's iron shoes. The beast's breath rasped.

But now there was a new disquieting change in the landscape, though a very slight one. Almost imperceptibly, the whole Great Salt Marsh was beginning to rise.

The Sinking Land was beginning its periodic submergence.

From either side, from north and south, gray walls were converging on him – the foam-fronted raging waters of the Inner Sea and the Sea of the East rushing to sink the great stone shield now its gaseous support was gone.

A black barrier a yard high loomed just ahead. Fafhrd leaned low in the saddle, nudging the mare's flanks with his heels, and with a great long leap the mare lifted them the needed yard and found them firm footing again, and with never a pause galloped on unchangingly, except that now instead of clashing sharply against the rock, the iron shoes struck mutedly on the tight-packed gravel of the causeway.

From behind them came a mounting, rumbling, snarling roar that suddenly rose to a crashing climax. Fafhrd looked back and saw a great starburst of waters – not gray now, but ghostly white in the remaining light from the west – where the waves of the Inner Sea had met the rollers of the Sea of the East exactly at the road.

He was about to look forward again and slow his mount, when out of that pale, churny explosion there appeared a black horse and rider, then another, then a third. But no more – the fourth had evidently been engulfed. The hair lifted on his back at the thought of the leaps the three other beasts had made with their riders, and he cursed the Mingol mare to make more speed, knowing that kind words went unheard by her.

12

Lankhmar readied herself for another night of terror as shadows lengthened toward infinity and the sunlight turned deep orange. Her inhabitants were not reassured by the lessening number of murderous rats in the streets; they smelled the electric calm before the storm and they barricaded themselves in upper stories as they had the night gone by. Soldiers and constables, according to their individual characters, grinned with relief or griped at bureaucracy's inanities when they got the news that they were to repair to the Southern Barracks one hour before midnight to be harangued by Olegnya Mingolsbane, who was reputed to make the longest and most tedious spittle-spraying speeches of any Captain General in Nehwon's history, and to stink with the sourness of near-senility besides that.

Aboard *Squid*, Slinoor gave orders for lights to burn all night and an all hands watch to be kept. While the black kitten, forsaking the crow's nest, paced the rail nearest the docks, from time to time uttering an anxious mew and eyeing the dark streets as if with mingled temptation and dread.

For awhile Glipkerio soothed his nerves by observing the

subtle torturing of Reetha, designed chiefly to fray her nerves rather than her flesh, and by auditing her hours-long questioning by well-trained inquisitors, who sought to hammer from her the admission that the Gray Mouser was leader of the rats – as his shrinking to rat-size seemed surely to prove – and also force her to divulge a veritable handbook of information on the Mouser's magical methods and sorcerous stratagems. The girl truly entranced Glipkerio: she reacted to threats, evil teasings, and relatively minor pain in such a lively, unwearying way.

But after awhile he nonetheless grew bored and had a light supper served him in the sunset's red glow on his sea-porch outside the Blue Audience Chamber and beside the head of the great copper chute where balanced the great leaden spindle, which he reached out and touched from time to time for assurance. He hadn't lied to Hisvin, he told himself smugly; he *did* have at least one other secret weapon, albeit it wasn't a weapon of offense, but rather the ultimate opposite. Pray, though, he wouldn't have to use it! Hisvin had promised that at midnight he would work his spell against the assaulting rats, and thus far Hisvin had never failed – had he not conquered the rats of the grain fleet? – while his daughter and her maid had ways of soothing Glipkerio that amazingly did not involve whippings. He had seen with his own eyes Hisvin slay rats with his spell – while on his own part he had arranged for all soldiers and police to be in the South Barracks at midnight listening to that tiresome Olegnya Mingolsbane. He had done his part, he told himself; Hisvin would do his; and at midnight his troubles and vexations would be done.

But it was such a long time until midnight! Once more boredom engulfed the black-togaed, purple-pansy-coroneted, beanpole monarch, and he began to think wistfully of whips and Reetha. Beyond all other men, he mused, an overlord, burdened by administration and ceremonies, had no time for even the most homely hobbies and innocent diversions.

Reetha's questioners, meanwhile, gave up for the day and left her in Samanda's charge, who from time to time described gloatingly to the girl the various all-out thrashings and other torments the palace mistress would visit on her as soon as her namby-pamby inquisitors were through with her. The much-abused maid sought to comfort herself with the thought that her madcap gray rescuer might somehow regain his proper size and return to work again her escape. Surely, and despite all the nasty insinuations she had endured, the Gray Mouser was rat-size against his will. She recalled the many fairy tales she had heard of lizard- and frog-princes restored to handsomeness and proper height by a maiden's loving kiss, and despite her miseries, her eyebrowless eyes grew dreamy.

The Mouser squinted through Grig's notched mask at the glorious Council Chamber and the other members of the Supreme Thirteen. Already the scene had become oppressively familiar to him, and he was damnably tired of lisping. Nevertheless, he gathered himself for a supreme effort, which at least was one that tickled his wits.

His coming here had been simplicity itself, and inevitability too. Upon reaching the Fifth Level after parting with Hreest and his pike-rats, rat-pages had fallen in beside him at the foot of the white marble stairs, and a rat-chamberlain had gone solemnly before him, ringing an engraved silver bell which probably once had tinkled from the ankle of a temple dancer in the Street of the Gods in the world above. Thus, footing it grandly himself with the aid of his sapphire-topped ivory staff, though still hobbling a little, he had been wordlessly conducted into the Council Chamber and to the very chair which he now occupied.

The chamber was low but vast, pillared by golden and silver candlesticks doubtless pilfered from palaces and churches overhead. Among them were a few of what looked like jeweled scepters of office and maces of command. In the background, toward the distant walls and half hid by the pillars, were grouped rat-pikemen, waiters, and other servants, litter-bearers with their vehicles, and the like.

The chamber was lit by golden and silver cages of firebeetles and night-bees and glow wasps large as eagles, and so many of them that the pulsing of their light was barely apparent. The Mouser had decided that if it became necessary to create a diversion, he would loose some of the glow-wasps.

Within a central circle of particularly costly pillars was set a great round table, about which sat evenly spaced the Thirteen, all masked and clad in white hoods and robes, from which white-gloved rat-hands emerged.

Opposite the Mouser and on a slightly higher chair sat Skwee, well remembered from the time he had crouched on the Mouser's shoulder threatening to sever the artery under his ear. On Skwee's right sat Siss, while on his left was a taciturn rat whom the rest addressed as Lord Null. Alone of the Thirteen, this grumpy Lord Null was clad in a robe, hood, mask, and gloves of black. There was something hauntingly familiar about him, perhaps because the hue of his garb recalled to the Mouser Svivomilo and also Hreest.

The remaining nine rats were clearly apprentice members, promoted to fill the gaps in the Circle of Thirteen left by the white rats slain aboard *Squid*, for they never spoke and when questions were voted, only bobbingly agreed with the majority opinion among Skwee, Siss, Lord Null, and Grig – that is, the Mouser – or if that opinion were split two to two, abstained.

The entire tabletop was hidden by a circular map of what appeared to be well-tanned and buffed human skin, the most delicate and finely pored. The map itself was nothing but innumerable dots: golden, silver, red, and black, and thick as fly-specks in the stall of a slum fruit-merchant. At first the Mouser had been able to think of nothing but some eerie, dense starfield. Then it had been revealed to him, by the references the others made to it, that it was nothing more or less than a map of all the ratholes in Lankhmar!

At first this knowledge hadn't made the map come to life for the Mouser. But then gradually he had begun to see in the apparently randomly clustered and twisty-trailed dots the out-lines of at least the principal buildings and streets of Lankhmar. Of course, the whole plot of the city was reversed, because viewed from below instead of above.

The golden dots, it had turned out, stood for ratholes unknown to humans and used by rats; the red, for holes known to humans yet still used by rats; the silver for holes unknown to humans, but not currently employed by the dwellers under-neath; while the black dots designated the holes known to humans and avoided by the rodents of Lankhmar Below.

During the entire council session, three slim female rat-pages silently went about, changing the color of ratholes and even dotting in new ones, according to information whispered them by rat-pages, who ceaselessly came and went on equally silent paws. For this purpose, the three females used rat-tail brushes each made of a single, stiffened horsehair frayed at the tip, which they employed most dexterously, and each had slung in a rack at the waist four inkpots of the appropriate colors.

What the Mouser had learned during the council session had been, simply yet horribly, the all-over plan for the grand assault on Lankhmar Above, which was to take place a half-hour before this very midnight: detailed information about the disposition of pike companies, crossbow detachments, dagger groups, poison-weapon brigades, incendiaries, lone assassins, child-killers, panic-rats, stink-rats, genital-snappers and breast-biters and other berserkers, setters of man-traps such as trip-cords and needle-sharp caltrops and strangling nooses, artillery brigades which would carry up piecemeal larger weapons to be assembled above ground, until his brain could no longer hold all the data.

He had also learned that the principal attacks were to be made on the South Barracks and especially on the Street of the Gods, hitherto spared.

Finally he learned that the aim of the rats was not to exterminate humans or drive them from Lankhmar, but to force an unconditional surrender from Glipkerio and enslave the overlord's subjects by that agreement and a continuing terror so that Lankhmar would go on as always about its pleasures and business, buying and selling, birthing and dying, sending out of ships and caravans, gathering of grain – especially grain! – but ruled by the rats.

Fortunately all this briefing had been done by Skwee and Siss. Nothing had been asked of the Mouser – that is, Grig – or of Lord Null, except to supply opinions on knotty problems and lead in the voting. This had also provided the Mouser with time to devise ways and means of throwing a cat into the rats' plans.

Finally the briefing was done and Skwee asked around the table for ideas to improve the grand assault – not as if he expected to get any.

But at this point the Mouser rose up – somewhat crippled,

since Grig's damnably ill-fitting rat-boots were still giving him the cramp – and taking up his ivory staff laid its tip unerringly on a cluster of silver dots at the west end of the Street of Gods.

'Why ith no aththault made here?' he demanded. 'I thuggetht that at the heighth of the battle, a party of ratth clad in black togath iththue from the temple of the Godth *of* Lankhmar. Thith will convinthe the humanth ath nothing elthe that their very godth – the godth of their thity – have turned againtht them – been tranthformed, in fact, to ratth!'

He swallowed hard down his raw, wearied throat. Why the devil had Grig had to have a lisp?

His suggestion appeared for a moment to stupefy the other members of the Council. Then Siss said, wonderingly, admiringly, enviously, and as if against his will, 'I never thought of that.'

Skwee said, 'The temple of the Gods *of* Lankhmar has long been avoided by man and rat alike, as you well know, Grig. Nevertheless . . .'

Lord Null said peevishly, 'I am against it. Why meddle with the unknown? The humans of Lankhmar fear and avoid the temple of their city's gods. So should we.'

The Mouser glared at the black-robed rat through his mask slits. 'Are we mithe or ratth?' he demanded. 'Or are we even cowardly, thuperthtitiouth men? Where ith your ratly courage, Lord Null? Or thovereign, thkeptical, ratly reathon? My thratagem will cow the humanth and prove forever the thuperior bravery of ratth! Thkwee! Thith! Ith it not tho?'

The matter was put to a vote. Lord Null voted nay, Siss and the Mouser and – after a pause – Skwee voted aye, the other nine bobbed, and so Operation Black Toga, as Skwee christened it, was hastily added to the battle plans.

'We have over four hours in which to organize it,' Skwee reminded his nervous colleagues.

The Mouser grinned behind his mask. He had a feeling that the Gods *of* Lankhmar, if ever roused, would side with the city's human inhabitants. Or would they? – he wondered belatedly.

In any case, his business and desire now was to get out of the Council Chamber as soon as possible. A stratagem instantly suggested itself to him. He waved to a page.

'Thummon a litter,' he commanded. 'Thith deliberathion hath tired me. I feel faint and am troubled by leg cramp. I will go for a thort while to my home and wife to retht me.'

Skwee looked around at him. 'Wife?' the white rat asked incredulously.

Instantly the Mouser answered, 'Ith it any buthineth of youth if it ith my whim to call my mithtreth my wife?'

Skwee still eyed him for a bit, then shrugged.

The litter arrived almost immediately, borne by two very brawny, half-naked rats. The Mouser rolled into it gratefully, laying his ivory staff beside him, commanded 'To my home!' and waved a gentle goodbye to Skwee and Lord Null as he was carried joggingly off. He felt himself at the moment to be the most brilliant mind in the whole universe and thoroughly deserving of a rest, even in a rat burrow. He reminded himself he had at least four hours to go before Sheelba's spell wore off and he became once more human size. He'd done his best for Lankhmar, now he must think of himself. He lazily wondered what the comforts of a rat home would be like. He must sample them before escaping above ground. It really had been a damnably tiring council session after all that had gone before.

Skwee turned to Lord Null as the litter disappeared by stages beyond the pillars and said through his be-diamonded white mask, 'So Grig has a mistress, the old misogynist! Perhaps it's she who has quickened his mind to such new brilliancies as Operation Black Toga.'

'I still don't like that one, though you outvoted me and I must go along,' chittered the other irritably from behind his black vizard. 'There's too much uncertainty tonight. The final battle about to be joined. A magically transformed human spy reported in Lankhmar Below. The change in Grig's character. That rabid mouse running widdershins a-foam at the jaws, outside the Council Chamber, and which squeaked thrice when you slew him. The uncustomary buzzing of the night-bees in Siss' chambers. And now this new operation adopted on the spur of the moment—'

Skwee clapped Lord Null on the shoulder in friendly fashion. 'You're distraught tonight, comrade, and see omens in every night-bug,' he said. 'Grig at all events had one most sound notion. We all could do with a little rest and refreshment. Especially you before your all-important mission. Come.'

And turning the table over to Siss, he and Lord Null went to a curtained alcove just off the Council Chamber, Skwee ordering on the way that food and drink be brought them.

When the curtains were closed behind them, Skwee seated himself in one of the two chairs beside the small table there and took off his mask. In the pulsing violet light of the three silver-caged glow-wasps illuminating the alcove, his long, white-furred, blue-eyed snout looked remarkably sinister.

'To think,' he said, 'that tomorrow my people will be masters of Lankhmar Above. For millennia we rats have planned and built, tunneled and studied and striven, and now in less than six hours – it's worth a drink! Which reminds me, comrade, isn't it time for your medicinal draught?'

Lord Null hissed with consternation, prepared to lift his black mask distractedly, dipped his black-gloved right fore-member into his pouch, and came up with a tiny white vial.

'Stop!' Skwee commanded with some horror, capturing the black-gloved wrist with a sudden grab. 'If you should drink *that* one now—!'

'I *am* nervous tonight, nervous to flusteration,' the other admitted, returning the white vial to his pouch and coming up with a black one. Before draining its contents, he lifted his black mask entirely. The face behind was not a rat's, but the seamed and beady-eyed visage, rat-small, of Hisvin the grain-merchant.

The black draught swallowed, he appeared to experience relief and easement of tension. The worry lines in his face were replaced by those of thought.

'Who is Grig's mistress, Skwee?' he speculated suddenly. 'No common slut, I'll swear, or vanity-puffed courtesan.'

Skwee shrugged his hunchy shoulders and said cynically, 'The more brilliant the enchanted male, the stupider the enchanting female.'

'No!' Hisvin said impatiently. 'I sense a brilliant and rapacious mind here that is not Grig's. He was ambitious once, you know, sought your position, then his fires sank to coals glowing through wintery ash.'

'That's true,' Skwee agreed thoughtfully.

'Who has blown him alight again?' Hisvin demanded, now with anxious suspicion. '*Who* is his mistress, Skwee?'

Fafhrd pulled up the Mingol mare before that iron-hearted beast should topple from exhaustion – and had trouble doing it, so resolute unto death was the grim creature. Yet once stopped, he felt her legs giving under her and he dropped quickly from the saddle lest she collapse from his weight. She was lathered with sweat, her head hung between her trembling forelegs, and her slatted ribs worked like a bellows as she gasped, whistlingly.

He rested his hand lightly on her shaking shoulders. She never could have made Lankhmar, he knew. They were less than halfway across the Great Salt Marsh.

Low moonlight, striking from behind, washed with a faint gold the gravel of the causeway road and yellowly touched the tops of thorn tree and cactus, but could not yet slant down to the Marsh's sea-grassed floor and black bottoms.

Save for the hum and crackle of insects and the calls of night birds, the moonlight-brushed area was silent – yet would not be so for long, Fafhrd knew with a shudder.

Ever since the preternatural emergence of the three black riders from the crash of waves over the Sinking Land and their drumming unshakable pursuit of him through the deepening night, he had been less and less able to think of them as mere vengeful Ilthmar brigands, and more and more conceived them as a supernatural black trinity of death. For miles now, besides, something huge and long-legged and lurching, though never distinctly seen, had been pursuing him through the Marsh, keeping pace with him at the distance of a spear cast. Some giant familiar or obedient djinn of the black horsemen seemed most likely.

His fears had so worked on him that Fafhrd had finally put the mare to her extremest gallop, outdistancing the hoof-noise of the pursuit, though with no effect on the lurching shape and with the inevitable present result. He drew Graywand and faced back toward the new-risen gibbous moon.

Then very faintly he began to hear it: the muted rhythmic drumming of hooves on gravel. They were coming.

At the same moment, from the deep shadows where the giant familiar should be, he heard the Gray Mouser call hoarsely, 'This way, Fafhrd! Toward the blue light. Lead your mount. Make it swift!'

Grinning even as the hairs lifted on his neck, Fafhrd looked south and saw a shaped blue glow, like a round-topped, smallish, blue-lit window in the blackness of the Marsh. He plunged down the causeway's slanting south side toward it, pulling the mare after him, and found underfoot a low ridge of firm ground rather than mud. He moved ahead eagerly through the dark, digging in his heels and leaning forward as he dragged his spent mount. The blue window looked a little above his head now. The drumming coming up from the east was louder.

'Shake a leg, Lazybones!' he heard the Mouser call in the same rasping tones. The Gray One must have caught a cold from the Marsh's damp or – the Fates forfend! – a fever from its miasmas.

'Tether your mount to the thorn stump,' the Mouser continued gruffly. 'There's food for her there and a water pool. Then come up. Speed, speed!'

Fafhrd obeyed without word or waste motion, for the drumming had become very loud.

As he leaped and caught hold of the blue window's bottom and drew himself up to it, the blue glow went out. He scrambled inside onto the reed-carpeted floor of whatever it was and swiftly squirmed around so he was looking back the way he'd come.

The Mingol mare was invisible in the dark below. The causeway's top glowed faintly in the moonlight.

Then round a cluster of thorn trees came speeding the three black riders, the drumming of the twelve hooves thunderous now. Fafhrd thought he could make out a fiendish phosphorescent glow around the nostrils and eyes of the tall black horses and he could faintly discern the black cloaks and hoods of the riders streaming in the wind of their speed. With never a pause they passed the point where he'd left the causeway and vanished behind another thorn grove to the west. He let out a long-held breath.

'Now get away from the door and brace yourself,' a voice that wasn't the Mouser's at all grated over his shoulder. 'I've got to be there to pilot this rig.'

The hairs that had just lain down on Fafhrd's neck erected themselves again. He had more than once heard the rockharsh voice of Sheelba of the Eyeless Face, though never seen, let alone entered, his fabulous hut. He swiftly hitched himself to one side, back against wall. Something smooth and round and cool touched the back of his neck. A wall-hung skull, it almost had to be.

A black figure crawled into the space he'd just vacated. Dimly silhouetted in the doorway, it's edge touched by moonlight, he saw a black cowl.

'Where's the Mouser?' Fafhrd asked with a wheeze in his voice.

The hut gave a violent lurch. Fafhrd grabbed gropingly for and luckily found two wall posts.

'In trouble. *Deep*-down trouble,' Sheelba answered curtly. 'I did his voice to make you jump lively. As soon as you've fulfilled whatever geas Ningauble has laid upon you – bells, isn't it? – you must go instantly to his aid.'

The hut gave a second lurch and a third, then began to rock and pitch somewhat like a ship, but in a swift rhythm and more joltingly, as if one were in a howdah on the slant back of a drunken giant giraffe.

'Go instantly where?' Fafhrd demanded, somewhat humbly.

'How should I know and why should I tell you if I did? I'm not your wizard. I'm just taking you to Lankhmar by secret ways as a favor to that paunchy, seven-eyed, billion-worded dilettante in sorcery who thinks himself my colleague and has gulled you into taking him as mentor,' the harsh voice responded from the hood. Then, relenting somewhat, though growing gruffer, 'Overlord's palace, most likely. Now shut up.'

The rocking of the hut and also its speed increased. Wind pushed in, flapping the edge of Sheelba's hood. Flashes of moon-dappled marsh shot by.

'Who were those riders after me?' Fafhrd asked, clinging to his wall posts. 'Ilthmar brigands? Acolytes of the grisly, scythe-armed lord?'

No reply.

'What *is* it all about?' Fafhrd persisted. 'Grand assault by a near numberless yet nameless host on Lankhmar. Nameless black riders. The Mouser deep-buried and woefully shrunk, yet alive. A tin whistle maybe summoning War Cats who are dangerous to the blower. None of it makes sense.'

The hut gave a particularly vicious lurch. Sheelba still said not a word. Fafhrd grew seasick and devoted himself to hanging on.

Glipkerio, nerving himself, poked his pansy-wreathed, gold-ringleted head on its long neck through the kitchen door's leather curtains and blinking his weak yellow-irised eyes at the fire's glare, grinned an archly amiable, foolish grin.

Reetha, chained once more by the neck, sat cross-legged in front of the fire, head a-droop. Surrounded by four other maids squatting on their heels, Samanda nodded in her great chair. Yet now, though no noise had been made, her snores broke off, she opened her pig-eyes toward Glipkerio, and said familiarly, 'Come in, little overlord, don't stand there like a bashful giraffe. Have the rats got you scared too? Be off to your cots, girls.'

Three maids instantly rose. Samanda snatched a long pin from her sphere-dressed hair and lightly jabbed awake the fourth, who had been asleep on her heels.

Silently, except for a single swift-stifled squeal from the pricked one, the four maids bobbed a bow at Glipkerio, two at Samanda, and hurried out like so many wax mannequins. Reetha looked around wearily. Glipkerio wandered about, looking anywhere but at her, his chin a-twitch, his long fingers jittery, twining and untwining.

'The restless bug bite you, little overlord?' Samanda asked him. 'Shall I make you a hot poppy-posset? Or would you like to see her whipped?' she asked, jerking a thick thumb toward Reetha. 'The inquisitors ordered me not to, but of course if you should command me—'

'Oh, no, no, no, of course not,' Glipkerio protested. 'But speaking of whips I've some new ones in my private collection I'd like to show you, dear Samanda, including one reputedly from Far Kiraay coated with rough-ground glass, if only you'd come with me. Also a handsomely embossed six-tined silver bull prod from—'

'Oh, so it's company you want, like all the other scared ones,' Samanda told him. 'Well, I'd be willing to oblige you, little overlord, but the 'quisitors told me I must keep an eye all night on this wicked girl, who's in league with the rats' leader.'

Glipkerio hemmed and hawed, finally said, 'Well, you could bring her along, I suppose, if you really have to.'

'So I could,' Samanda agreed heartily, at last levering her black-dressed bulk from her chair. 'We can test your new whips on her.'

'Oh, no, no, *no*,' Glipkerio once more protested. Then frowning and also writhing his narrow shoulders, he added thoughtfully, 'Though there are times when to get the hang of a new instrument of pain one simply must . . .'

'. . . simply must,' Samanda agreed, unsnapping the silver chain from Reetha's collar and snapping on a short leash. 'Lead the way, little overlord.'

'Come first to my bedroom,' he told her. 'I'll go ahead to get my guardsmen out of the way.' And he made off at his longest, toga-stretching stride.

'No need to, little overlord, they know all about your habits,' Samanda called after him, then jerked Reetha to her feet. 'Come, girl! – you're being mightily honored. Be glad I'm not Glipkerio, or you'd be rubbed with cheese and shoved down-cellar for the rats to nibble.'

When they finally arrived through empty silk-hung corridors at Glipkerio's bed-chamber, he was standing in mingled agitation and irritation before its open, jewel-studded, thick oaken door, his black toga a-rustle from his nervous jerking.

'There weren't any guardsmen for me to warn off,' he complained. 'It seems my orders were stupidly misinterpreted, extended farther than I'd intended, and my guardsmen have all gone off with the soldiers and constables to the South Barracks.'

'What need you of guardsmen when you have *me* to protect you, little overlord?' Samanda answered boisterously, slapping a truncheon hanging from her belt.

'That's true,' he agreed, only a shade doubtfully, and twitched a large and complex golden key from a fold of his toga. 'Now let's lock the girl in here, Samanda, if you please, while we go to inspect my new acquisitions.'

'And decide which to use on her?' Samanda asked in her loud coarse voice.

Glipkerio shook his head as if in shocked disapproval, and looking at last at Reetha, said in grave fatherly tones, 'No, of course not, it is only that I imagine the poor child would be bored at our expertise.'

Yet he couldn't quite keep a sudden eagerness from his tones, nor a furtive gleam from his eyes.

Samanda unsnapped the leash and pushed Reetha inside.

Glipkerio warned her in last-minute apprehension, 'Don't touch my night-draught now,' pointing at a golden tray on a silver night table. Crystal flagons sat on the tray and also a long-stemmed goblet filled with pale apricot-hued wine.

'*Don't touch one thing*, or I'll make you beg for death,' Samanda amplified, suddenly all unhumorously brutal. 'Kneel at the foot of the bed on knees and heels with head bent – servile posture three – and don't move a muscle until we return.'

As soon as the thick door was closed and its lock softly thudded shut and the golden key chinkingly withdrawn on the other side, Reetha walked straight to the night table, worked her cheeks a bit, spat into the night-draught, and watched the bubbly scum slowly revolve. Oh, if she only had some hairs to drop in it, she yearned fiercely, but there seemed to be no fur or wool in the room and she had been shaved this very morning.

She unstoppered the most tempting of the crystal flagons and carried it about with her, swigging daintily, as she examined the room, paneled with rare woods from the Eight Cities, and its ever rarer treasures, pausing longest at a heavy golden casket full of cut but unset jewels – amethysts, aquamarines, sapphires, jades, topazes, fire opals, rubies, gimpels, and ice emeralds – which glittered and gleamed like the shards of a shattered rainbow.

She also noted a rack of women's clothes, cut for someone very tall and thin, and – surprising beside these evidences of effeminacy – a rack of browned-iron weapons.

She glanced over several shelves of blown-glass figurines long enough to decide that the most delicate and costly-looking was, almost needless to say, that of a slim girl in boots and scanty jacket wielding a long whip. She flicked it off its shelf, so that it shattered on the polished floor and the whip went to powder.

What could they do to her that they weren't planning to do already? – she asked herself with a tight smile.

She climbed into the bed, where she stretched and writhed luxuriously, enjoying to the full the feel of the fine linen sheets against her barbered limbs, body, and head, and now and again trickling from the crystal flagon a few nectarous drops between her playfully haughty-shaped lips. She'd be damned, she told herself, if she'd drink enough to get dead drunk before the last possible instant. Thereafter Samanda and Glipkerio might find themselves hard-put to torment a limp body and blacked-out mind with any great pleasure to themselves.

13

The Mouser, reclining on his side in his litter, the tail of one of the fore-rats swaying a respectful arm's length from his head, noted that, without leaving the Fifth Level, they had arrived at a wide corridor stationed with pike-rats stiffly on guard and having thirteen heavily curtained doorways. The first nine curtains were of white and silver, the next of black and gold, the last three of white and gold.

Despite his weariness and grandiose feeling of security, the Mouser had been fairly watchful along the trip, suspecting though not very seriously that Skwee or Lord Null might have him followed – and then there was Hreest to be reckoned with, who might have discovered some clue at the water-privy despite the highly artistic job the Mouser felt he had done. From time to time there had been rats who might have been following his litter, but all these had eventually taken other turns in the mazy corridors. The last to engage his lazy suspicions had been two slim rats clad in black silken cloaks, hoods, masks, and gloves, but these without a glance toward him now disappeared arm-in-arm through the black-and-gold curtains, whispering together in a gossipy way.

His litter stopped at the next doorway, the third from the end.

So Skwee and Siss outranked Grig, but he outranked Lord Null. This might be useful to know, though it merely confirmed the impression he had got at the council.

He sat, then stood up with the aid of his staff, rather exaggerating his leg cramp now, and tossed the fore-rat a corn-wreathed silver coin he had selected from Grig's purse. He assumed that tips would be the custom of any species of being whatever, in particular rats. Then without a backward look he hobbled through the heavy curtains, noting in passing that they were woven of fine soft gold wire and braided fine white silk threads. There was a short, dim passageway similarly curtained at the other end. He pushed through the second set of curtains and found himself alone in a cozy-feeling but rather shabby square room with curtained doorways in each of the other three walls and lit by a bronze-caged firebeetle over each doorway. There were two closed cupboards, a writing desk with stool, many scrolls in silver containers that looked suspiciously like thimbles from the human world, crossed swords and a battle-ax fixed to the dingy walls, and a fireplace in which a single giant coal glowed redly through its coat of white ash. Above the fireplace, or rather brazier-nook, emerged from the wall a bronze-ringed hemisphere about as big as the Mouser's own rat-size head. The hemisphere was yellowish, with a large greenish-brown circle on it, and centered in this circle a black one. With a qualm of horror, the Mouser recognized it as a mummified human eye.

In the center of the room was a pillowed couch with the high back support of one who does a lot of reading lying down, and beside the couch a sizable low table with nothing on it but three bells, one copper, one silver, and one gold.

Putting his horror out of mind, for it is a singularly useless emotion, the Mouser took up the silver bell and rang it vigorously, deciding to see what taking the middle course would bring.

He had little more time than to decide that the room was that of a crusty bachelor with studious inclinations when there came backing through the curtains in the rear wall a fat old rat in spotless long white smock with a white cap on his head. This one turned and showed his silver snout and bleared eyes, and also the silver tray he was carrying, on which were steaming plates and a large steaming silver jug.

The Mouser pointed curtly at the table. The cook, for so he seemed to be, set the tray there and then came hesitantly toward the Mouser, as if to help him off with his robe. The Mouser waved him away and pointed sternly at the rear doorway. He'd be damned if he'd go to the trouble of lisping in Grig's own home. Besides, servants might have a sharper ear than colleagues for a false voice. The cook bowed bumblingly and departed.

The Mouser settled himself gratefully on the couch, deciding against removing as yet his gloves or boots. Now that he was reclining, the latter bothered him hardly at all. However, he did remove his mask and place it close by – it was good to get more than a squinty view of things – and set to at Grig's dinner.

The steaming jug turned out to contain mulled wine. It was most soothing to his raw, dry throat and wearied nerves, though excessively aromatic – the single black clove bobbing in the jug was large as a lime and the cinnamon stick big as one of the parchment scrolls. Then, using Cat's Claw and the two-tined fork provided, he began cutting up and devouring the steaming cutlets of beef – for his nose told him it was that and not, for instance, baby. From another steaming plate he sampled one of the objects that looked like small sweet potatoes. It turned out to be a single grain of boiled wheat. Likewise, one of the yellowish cubes about as big as dice proved a grain of coarse sugar, while the black balls big as the end joint of his thumb were caviar. He speared them one at a time with his fork and munched, alternating this with mouthfuls of the beef. It was very strange to eat good tender beef, the fibers of which were thick as his fingers.

Having consumed the meaty portions of Grig's dinner and drunk all the mulled wine, the Mouser resumed his mask and settled back to plot his escape to Lankhmar Above. But the golden bell kept teasing his thoughts away from practical matters, so he reached out and rang it. Yield to curiosity without giving the mind time to get roiled, was one of his mottoes.

Hardly had the sweet *chinks* died away when the heavy curtains of one of the side doors parted and there appeared a slim straight rat – or ratess, rather, he judged – dressed in robe, hood, mask, slippers and gloves all of fine lemon yellow silk.

This one, holding the curtains parted, looked toward him and said softly, 'Lord Grig, your mistress awaits you.'

The Mouser's first reaction was one of gratified conceit. So Grig did have a mistress, and his spur-of-the-moment answer to Skwee's 'Wife?' question at the council had been a brilliant stroke of intuition. Whether human-large or rat-small, he could outsmart anyone. He possessed Mouser-mind, unequaled in the universe.

Then the Mouser stood up and approached the slender, yellow clad figure. There was something cursedly familiar about her. He wondered if she were the ratess in green he'd seen leading short-leashed the brace of shrews. She had a pride and poise about her.

Using the same stratagem he had with the cook, he silently pointed from her to the doorway that she should precede him. She acquiesced and he followed close behind her down a dim twisty corridor.

And cursedly attractive too, he decided, eyeing her slender silhouette and sniffing her musky perfume. Rather belatedly, he reminded himself that she was a rat and so should waken his extremest repugnance. But was she necessarily a rat? He had been transformed in size, why not others? And if this were merely the maid, what would the mistress be? Doubtless lard-fat or hag-hairy, he told himself cynically. Still his excitement grew.

Sparing a moment's thought to orient himself, he discovered that the side door they'd gone out by led toward the black-curtained apartments of Lord Null – presumably – rather than to those of Siss and Skwee.

At last the yellow-clad ratess parted gold-heavy black drapes, then light violet silken ones. The Mouser passed her and found himself staring about through the notched eye-holes of Grig's mask at a large bedroom, beautifully and delicately furnished in many ways, yet the weirdest and perhaps the most frightening he had ever seen.

It was draped and carpeted and ceilinged and upholstered all in silver and violet, the latter color the exact complement of the yellow of his conductress' gowning. It was lit indirectly from below by narrow deep tanks of slimy glow-worms big as eels, set against the walls. Against these tanks were several vanity tables, each backed by its large silver mirror, so that the Mouser saw more than one reflection of his white-robed self and his slim cicerone, who had just let the silken violet curtains waft together again. The tabletops were strewn with cosmetics and the tools of beauty, variously colored elixirs and tiny cups – all except one, near a second silver-draped door, which held nothing but two score or so black and white vials.

But between the vanity tables there hung on silver chains, close to the walls and brightly lit by the glow-worm's upjutting effulgence, large silver cages of scorpions, spiders, mantises, and suchlike glittering vermin, all large as puppy dogs or baby kangaroos. In one spacious cage coiled a Quarmall pocket-viper huge as a python. These clashed their fangs or hissed, according to their kind, while one scorpion angrily clattered its sting across the gleaming bars of its cage, and the viper darted its trebly forked tongue between those of its own.

One short wall, however, was bare except for two pictures tall and wide as doors, the one depicting against a dusky background a girl and crocodile amorously intertwined, the other a man and a leopardess similarly preoccupied.

Almost central in the room was a large bed covered only by a tight-drawn white linen sheet, the woven threads looking coarse as burlap, yet inviting nonetheless, and with one fat white pillow.

Lying supine and at ease on this bed, her head propped against the pillow to survey the Mouser through the eyeholes of her mask, was a figure somewhat slighter than that of his guide, yet otherwise identical and identically clad, except that the silk of her garb was finer still and violet instead of yellow.

'Well met below ground. Sweet greetings, Grey Mouser,' this one called softly in a familiarly silvery voice. Then, looking beyond him, 'Sweetest slave, make our guest comfortable.'

Softest footsteps approached. The Mouser turned a little and saw that his conductress had removed her yellow mask, revealing the merry yet melancholy-eyed dark face of Frix. Her black hair this time hung in two long plaits, braided with fine copper wire.

Without more ado than a smile, she began deftly to unbutton Grig's long white robe. The Mouser lifted his arms a little and let himself be undressed as effortlessly as in a dream, and with even less attention paid the process, for he was most eagerly scanning the violet-masked figure on the bed. He knew to a certainty who it must be, beyond all contributing evidence, for the silver dart was throbbing in his temple and the hunger which had haunted him for days returned redoubled.

The situation was strange and almost beyond comprehension. Although guessing that Frix and the other must have used an elixir like Sheelba's, the Mouser could have sworn they were all three human size, except for the presence of the familiar vermin, scuttlers and slitherers, so huge.

It was a great relief to have his cramping rat-boots deftly drawn off, as he lifted first one leg, then the other. Yet although he submitted so docilely to Frix's ministrations, he kept hold of his sword Scalpel and of the belt it hung from and also, on some cloudy impulse, of Grig's mask. He felt the smaller scabbard empty on the belt and realized with a pang of apprehension that he had left Cat's Claw behind in Grig's apartment along with the latter's ivory staff.

But these worries vanished like the last snowflake in spring when the one on the bed asked cajolingly, 'Will you partake of refreshment, dearest guest?' and when he said, 'I will most gladly,' lifted a violet-gloved hand and ordered, 'Dear Frix, fetch sweetmeats and wine.'

While Frix busied herself at a far table, the Mouser whispered, his heart-a-thump, 'Ah, most delectable Hisvet – For I deem you are she?'

'As to that, you must judge for yourself,' the tinkling voice responded coquettishly.

'Then I shall call you Hisvet,' the Mouser answered boldly, 'recognizing you as my queen of queens and princess of princesses. Know, delicious Demoiselle, that ever since our raptures 'neath the closet tree were so rudely broken off by an interruption of Mingols, my mind, nay, my mania has been fixed solely on you.'

'That were some small compliment—' the other allowed, lolling back luxuriously, 'if I could believe it.'

'Believe it you must,' the Mouser asserted masterfully, stepping forward. 'Know, moreover, that it is my intention that on this occasion our converse not be conducted over Frix's shoulder, dear companion that she is, but at the closest range. I am fixedly desirous of all refreshments, omitting none.'

'You cannot think I am Hisvet!' the other countered, starting up in what the Mouser hoped was mock indignation. 'Else you would never dare such blasphemy!'

'I dare for more!' the Mouser declared with a soft amorous growl, stepping forward more swiftly. The vermin hanging round about moved angrily, striking against their silver bars and setting their cages a little a-swing, and clashing, clattering, and hissing more. Nevertheless the Mouser, dropping his belt and sword by the edge of the bed and setting a knee thereon, would have thrust himself directly upon Hisvet, had not Frix come bustling up at that moment and set between them on the coarse linen a great silver tray with slim decanters of sweet wine and crystal cups for its drinking and plates of sugary tidbits.

Not entirely to be balked, the Mouser darted his hand across and snatched away the vizard of violet silk from the visage it hid. Violet-gloved hand instantly snatched the mask back from him, but did not replace it, and there confronting him was indeed the slim triangular face of Hisvet, cheeks flushed, red-irised eyes glaring, but pouty lips grinning enough to show the slightly over-large pearly upper incisors, the whole being framed by silver-blonde hair interwoven like that of Frix, but with even finer wire of silver, into two braids that reached to her waist.

'Nay,' she said laughingly, 'I see you are most wickedly presumptuous and that I must protect myself.' Reaching down on her side of the bed, she procured a long slender-bladed gold-hilted dagger. Waving it playfully at the Mouser, she said, 'Now refresh yourself from the cups and plates before you, but have a care of sampling other sweetmeats, dear guest.'

The Mouser complied, pouring for himself and Hisvet. He noted from a corner of his eye that Frix, moving silently in her silken robe, had rolled up Grig's white boots and gloves in his white hood and robe and set them on a stool near the floor-to-ceiling painting of the man and the leopardess and that she had made as neat a bundle of all the rest of the Mouser's garb – his own garb, mostly – and set them on a stool next to the first. A most efficient and foresighted maid, he thought and most devoted to her mistress – in fact altogether too devoted: he wished at this moment she would take herself off and leave him private with Hisvet.

But she showed no sign of so doing, nor Hisvet of ordering her away, so without more ado the Mouser began a mild love-play, catching at the violet-gloved fingers of Hisvet's left hand as they dipped toward the sweetmeats or plucking at the ribbons and edges of her violet robe, in the latter case reminding her of the discrepancy in their degree of undress and suggesting that it be corrected by the subtraction of an item or two from her outfit. Hisvet in turn would deftly jab with her dagger at his snatching hand, as if to pin it to tray or bed, and he would whip it back barely in time. It was an amusing game, this dance of hand and needle-sharp dagger – or at least it seemed amusing to the Mouser, especially after he had drained a cup or two of fiery colorless wine – and so when Hisvet asked him how he had come into the rat-world, he merrily told her the story of Sheelba's black potion and how he had first thought its effects a most damnably unfair wizardly joke, but now blessed them as the greatest good ever done him in his life – for he twisted the tale somewhat to make it appear that his sole objective all along had been to win to her side and bed.

He ended by asking, as he parted two fingers to let Hisvet's dagger strike between them, 'How ever did you and dear Frix guess that I was impersonating Grig?'

She replied, 'Most simply, gracious gamesman. We went to fetch my father from the council, for there is still an important journey he, Frix and I must make tonight. At a distance we heard you speak and I divined your true voice despite your clever lispings. Thereafter we followed you.'

'Ah, surely I may hope you love me as dearly, since you trouble to know me so well,' the Mouser warbled infatuatedly, slipping hand aside from a cunning slash. 'But tell me, divine one, how comes it that you and Frix and your father are able to live and hold great power in the rat-world?'

With her dagger she pointed somewhat languidly toward the vanity table holding the black and white vials, informing him,

'My family has used the same potion as Sheelba's for countless centuries, and also the white potion, which restores us at once to human-size. During those same centuries we have interbred with the rats, resulting in divinely beautiful monsters such as I am, but also in monsters most ugly, at least by human standards. Those latter of my family stay always below ground, but the rest of us enjoy the advantages and delights of living in two worlds. The inter-breeding has also resulted in many rats with human-like hands and minds. The spreading of civilization to the rats is largely our doing, and we shall rule as chiefs and chief tesses paramount, or even goddesses and gods, when the rats rule men.'

This talk of interbreeding and monsters startled the Mouser somewhat and gave him to think, despite his ever more firmly gyved ensorcelment by Hisvet. He recalled Lukeen's old suggestion, made aboard *Squid*, that Hisvet concealed a she-rat's body under maiden robes and he wondered – somewhat fearfully yet most curiously – just what form Hisvet's slim body did take. For instance, did she have a tail? But on the whole he was certain that whatever he discovered under her violet robe would please him mightily, since now his infatuation with the grain-merchant's daughter had grown almost beyond all bounds.

However, he outwardly showed none of this wondering, but merely asked, as if idly, 'So your father is also Lord Null, and you and he and Frix regularly travel back and forth between the big and little worlds?'

'Show him, dear Frix,' Hisvet commanded lazily, lifting slim fingers to mask a yawn, as though the hand-and-dagger game had begun to bore her.

Frix moved back against the wall until her head with its natural jet-black sheath and copper-gleaming plaits, for she had thrown back her hood, was between the cages of the pocket-viper and the most enraged scorpion. Her dark eyes were a sleep-walker's, fixed on things infinitely remote. The scorpion darted his moist white sting between the bars rat-inches from her ear, the viper's trifid tongue vibrated angrily against her cheek, while his fangs struck the silver rounds and dripped venom that wetted oilily her yellow silken shoulder, but she seemed to take no note whatever of these matters. The fingers of her right hand, however, moved along a row of medallions decorating the glow-worm tank behind her, and without looking down she pressed two at once.

The painting of the girl and crocodile moved swiftly upward, revealing the foot of a dark steep stairway.

'That leads without branchings to my father's and my house,' Hisvet explained.

The painting descended. Frix pressed two other medallions and the companion painting of man and leopardess rose, revealing a like stairway.

'While that one ascends directly by way of a golden rathole to the private apartments of whoever is Lankhmar's seeming overlord, now Glipkerio Kistomerces,' Hisvet told the Mouser as the second painting slid down into place. 'So you see, beloved, our power goes everywhere.' And she lifted her dagger and touched it lightly to his throat. The Mouser let it rest there a space before taking its tip between fingers and thumb and moving it aside. Then he as gently caught hold of the tip of one of Hisvet's braids, she offering no resistance, and began to unweave the fine silver wires from the finer silver-blonde hairs.

Frix still stood like a statue between fang and sting, seeming to see things beyond reality.

'Is Frix one of your breed? – combining in some fashion the finest of human and ratly qualities,' the Mouser asked quietly, keeping up with the task which, he told himself, would eventually and after an admittedly weary amount of unbraiding, allow him to arrive at his heart's desire.

Hisvet shook her head languorously, laying aside her dagger. 'Frix is my dearest slave and almost sister, but not by blood. Indeed she is the dearest slave in all Nehwon, for she is a princess and perchance by now a queen in her own world. While a-travel between worlds, she was shipwrecked here and beset by demons, from whom my father rescued her, at the price that she serve me for ever.'

At this, Frix spoke at last, though without moving else but her lips and tongue, not even her eyes to look at them. 'Or until, sweetest mistress, I three times save your life at entire peril of my own. That has happened once now, aboard *Squid*, when the dragon woud have gobbled you.'

'You would never leave me, dear Frix,' Hisvet said confidently.

'I love you dearly and serve you faithfully,' Frix replied. 'Yet all things come to an end, O blessed Demoiselle.'

'Then I shall have the Gray Mouser to protect me, and you unneeded,' Hisvet countered somewhat pettishly, lifting on an elbow. 'Leave us for the nonce, Frix, for I would speak privately with him.'

With merriest smile Frix came from between the deadly cages, made a curtsy toward the bed, resumed her yellow mask and swiftly went off through the second unsecret doorway, curtained with filmy silver.

Still lifted on her elbow, Hisvet turned towards the Mouser her slender form and her taper-face alight with beauty. He reached toward her eagerly, but she captured his questing hands in her cool fingers and fondling them asked, or rather stated, her eyes feeding on his, 'You will love me for ever, will you not, who dared the dark and fearsome tunnels of the rat-world to win me?'

'That will I surely, O Empress of Endless Delights,' the Mouser answered fervently, maddened by desire and believing his words to the ends of the universe of his feelings – almost.

'Then I think it proper to relieve you of *this*,' Hisvet said, putting the fingers of her two hands to his temple, 'for it would be an offense against myself and my supreme beauty to depend on a charm when I may now wholly depend on *you*.'

And with only the tiniest tweak of pain inflicted, she deftly squeezed with her fingernails the silver dart from under the Mouser's skin, as any woman might squeeze out a blackhead or whitehead from the visage of her lover. She showed him the dart gleaming on her palm. He for his part felt no change in his feelings whatever. He still adored her as divinity – and the fact that previously in his life he had never put any but momentary trust in any divinity whatever seemed of no importance at all, at least at this moment.

Hisvet laid a cool hand on the Mouser's side, but her red eyes were no longer languorously misty; they were sparklingly bright. And when he would have touched her similarly she prevented him, saying in most businesslike fashion, 'No, no, not quite yet! First we must plan, my sweet – for you can serve me in ways which even Frix will not. To begin, you must slay me my father, who thwarts me and confines my life unbearably, so that I may be imperatrix of all and you my most favored consort. There will be no end to our powers. Tonight, Lankhmar! Tomorrow, all Nehwon! Then . . . the conquest of other universes beyond the waters of space! The subjugation of the angels and demons, of heaven itself and hell! At first it may be well that you impersonate my father, as you have Grig – and done most cleverly, by my own witnessing, pet. You are of men the most like me in the world for deceptions, darling. Then—'

She broke off at something she saw in the Mouser's face. 'You will of course obey me in all things?' she asked sharply, or rather asserted.

'Well . . .' the Mouser began.

The silver drape billowed to the ceiling and Frix dashed in on silent silken slippers, her yellow robe and hood flying behind her.

'Your masks! Your masks!' she cried, ' 'Ware! 'Ware!' And she whirled over them to their necks an opaque violet coverlet, hiding Hisvet's violet-robed form, the Mouser's unclad body, and the tray between them. 'Your father comes with armed attendants, lady!' And she knelt by the head of the bed nearest Hisvet and bowed her yellow-masked head, assuming a servile posture.

Hardly were the white and violet masks in place and the silver curtains settled to the floor than the latter were jerked rudely aside. Hisvin and Skwee appeared, both unmasked, followed by three pike-rats. Despite the presence of the huge vermin in their cages, the Mouser found it hard to banish the illusion that all the rats were actually five feet and more tall.

Hisvin's face grew dusky red as he surveyed the scene. 'Oh, most monstrous!' he cried at Hisvet. 'Shameless filth! Loose with my own colleague!'

'Don't be dramatic, Daddy,' Hisvet countered, while to the Mouser she whispered tersely, 'Slay him now. I'll clear you with Skwee and the rest.'

The Mouser, fumbling under the coverlet over the side of the bed for Scalpel, while presenting a steady white be-diamonded mask at Hisvin, said blandly, 'Calm yourself, counthillor. If your divine daughter chootheth me above all other ratth and men, ith it my fault, Hithvin? Or herth either? Love knowth no ruleth.'

'I'll have your head for this, Grig,' Hisvin screeched at him, advancing toward the bed.

'Daddy, you've become a puritanical dodderer,' Hisvet said sharply, almost primly, 'to indulge in antique tantrums on this night of your great conquest. Your day is done. I must take your place on the Council. Tell him so, Skwee. Daddy darling, I think you're just madly jealous of Grig because you're not where he is.'

Hisvin screamed, 'O dirt that was my daughter!' and snatching with youthful speed a stiletto from his waist, drove it at Hisvet's neck betwixt violet mask and coverlet – except that Frix, lunging suddenly on her knees, swung her open left hand hard between, as one bats a ball.

The needle-like blade drove through her palm to the slim dagger's hilt and was wrenched from Hisvin's grasp.

Still on one knee, the bright blade transfixing her outstretched left palm and dripping red a little, Frix turned toward Hisvin and advancing her other hand graciously, she said in clear, winning tones, 'Govern your rage for all our sakes, dear my dear mistress's father. These matters can be composed by quiet reason, surely. You must not quarrel together on this night of all nights.'

Hisvin paled and retreated a step, daunted most likely by Frix's preternatural composure, which indeed was enough to send shivers up a man's or even a rat's spine.

The Mouser's fumbling hand closed around Scalpel's hilt. He prepared to spring out and dash back to Grig's apartment, snatching up his bundle of clothes on the way. At some point during the last score or so heartbeats, his great undying love for Hisvet had quietly perished and was now beginning to stink in his nostrils.

But at that instant the violent drapes were torn apart and there rushed from the Mouser's chosen escape route the rat Hreest in his gold-embellished black garb and brandishing rapier and dirk. He was followed by three guardsmen-rats in green uniforms, each with a like naked sword. The Mouser recognized the dirk Hreest held – it was his own Cat's Claw.

Frix moved swiftly behind the head of the bed to the post she'd earlier taken between viper and scorpion cage, the stiletto still transfixing her left hand like a great pin. The Mouser heard her murmur rapidly, 'The plot thickens. Enter armed rats at all portals. A climax nears.'

Hreest came to a sudden halt and cried ringingly at Skwee and Hisvin, 'The dismembered remains of councillor Grig have been discovered lodged against the Fifth Level sewer's exit-grille! The human spy is impersonating him in Grig's own clothes!'

Not at the moment, except for the mask, the Mouser thought, and making one last effort cried out, 'Nonthenthe! Thithe ith midthummer madneth! I am Grig! It wath thome other white rat got tho foully thlain!'

Holding up Cat's Claw and eyeing the Mouser, Hreest continued, 'I discovered this dagger of human device in Grig's apartment. The spy is clearly here.'

'Kill him in the bed,' Skwee commanded harshly, but the Mouser, anticipating a little the inevitable, had rolled out from under his sheets and now took up guard position naked, the white mask cast aside, Scalpel gleaming long and deadly in his right hand, while his left, in lieu of his dirk, held his belt and Scalpel's limp scabbard, both doubled.

With a weird laugh Hreest lunged at him, rapier a-flicker, while Skwee drew sword and came leaping across the foot of the bed, his boot crunching glass against tray beneath the coverlet.

Hreest got a bind on Scalpel, carrying both long swords out to the side, and stepping in close stabbed with Cat's Claw. The Mouser struck his own dirk aside with his doubled belt and drove his left shoulder into Hreest's chest, slamming him back against two of his green-uniformed sword rats, who were thereby forced to give ground too.

At almost the same instant the Mouser parried high to the side with Scalpel, deflecting Skwee's rapier when its point was inches from his neck. Then swiftly changing fronts, he fenced a moment with Skwee, beat the rat's blade aside, and lunged strongly. The white-clad rat was already in retreat across the foot of the bed, from the head of which Hisvet, now unmasked, watched critically, albeit a little sulkily, but the Mouser's point nevertheless reached Skwee's sword-wrist and pinked it halfway through.

By this time the third green-clad rat, a giant relatively seven feet tall, who had to duck through the doorway, came lunging fiercely, though a little slowly. Meanwhile Hreest was picking himself up from the floor, while Skwee dropped his dagger and switched his rapier to his unwounded hand.

The Mouser parried the giant's lunge, a hair's-breadth from his naked chest, and riposted. The giant counter-parried in time, but the Mouser dropped Scalpel's tip under the other's blade and continuing his riposte, skewered him through the heart.

The giant's jaw gaped, showing his great incisors. His eyes filmed. Even his fur seemed to dull. His weapons dropped from his nerveless hands and he stood dead on his feet for a moment before starting to fall. In that moment the Mouser, squatting a little on his right leg, kicked out forcefully with his left. His heel took the giant in the breastbone, pushing his corpse off Scalpel and sending it careening back against Hreest and his two green-clad sword-rats.

One of the pike-rats leveled his weapon for a run at the Mouser, but at that moment Skwee commanded loudly, 'No more single attacks! Form me a circle around him!'

The others were swift to obey, but in that brief pause Frix dropped open the silver-barred door that was one end of the scorpion's cage, and despite her dagger-transfixed hand lifted the cage and heaved it sharply, sending its fearsome occupant flying to land on the foot of the bed, where it jigged about, big by comparison as a large cat, clashing its claws, rattling its chelicerae, and menacing with its sting over its head.

Most of the rats directed their weapons at it. Snatching up her dagger, Hisvet crouched at the opposite corner from it, preparing to defend herself from her pet. Hisvin dodged in back of Skwee.

At the same time Frix dropped her good hand to the medallions on the glow-worm tank. The painting of man and leopardess rose. The Mouser didn't need the prompting of her wild smile and over-bright eyes. Snatching up the gray bundle of his clothes, he dashed up the dark steep stairs three at a time. Something hissed past his head and struck with a *zing* the riser of a stone step above and clattered down. It was Hisvet's long dagger and it had struck point-first. The stairway grew dark and he began taking its steps only two at a time, crouching low as he could and peering wide-eyed ahead. Faintly he heard Skwee's shrill command, 'After him!'

Frix with a grimace drew Hisvin's stiletto from her palm, lightly kissed the bleeding wound, and with a curtsy presented the weapon to its owner.

The bedroom was empty save for those two and Hisvet, who was drawing her violet robe around her, and Skwee, who was knotting with spade teeth and good hand a bandage round his injured wrist.

Pierced by a dozen thrusts and oozing dark blood on the violet carpet, the scorpion still writhed on its back, its walking legs and great claws a-tremble, its sting sliding a little back and forth.

Hreest, the two green sword-rats, and the three pike-rats had gone in pursuit of the Mouser and the clatter of their boots up the step stairs had died away.

Frowning darkly, Hisvin said to Hisvet, 'I still should slay you.'

'Oh, Daddy dear, you don't understand at all what happened,' Hisvet said tremulously. 'The Gray Mouser forced me at sword's point. It was a rape. And at sword's point under the coverlet he compelled me to say those dreadful things to you. You saw I did my best to kill him at the end.'

'Pah!' Hisvin spat, turning half aside.

'*She's* the one should be slain,' Skwee asserted, indicating Frix. 'She worked the spy's escape.'

'Most true, oh mighty councillor,' Frix agreed. 'Else he would have killed at least half of you, and your brains are greatly needed – in fact, indispensable, are they not? – to direct tonight's grand assault on Lankhmar Above?' She held out her red-dripping palm to Hisvin and said softly, 'That's twice, dear mistress.'

'For that you shall be rewarded,' Hisvet said, setting her lips primly. 'And for helping the spy escape – and not preventing my rape! – you shall be whipped until you can no longer scream – tomorrow.'

'Right joyfully, milady – tomorrow,' Frix responded with a return of something of her merry tones. 'But tonight there is work must be done. At Glipkerio's palace in the Blue Audience Chamber. Work for all three of us. And at once, I believe, milord,' she added deferentially, turning to Hisvin.

'That's true,' Hisvin said with a start. He scowled back and forth between his daughter and her maid three times, then with a shrug, said, 'Come.'

'How can you trust them?' Skwee demanded.

'I must,' Hisvin said. 'They're needful if I am properly to control Glipkerio. Meanwhile your place is that of supreme command, at the council table. Siss will be needing you. Come!' he repeated to the two girls. Frix worked the medallions. The second painting rose. They went all three up the stairs.

Skwee paced the bed-chamber alone, head bowed in angry thought, automatically overstepping the corpse of the giant sword-rat and circling the still-writhing scorpion. When he at last stopped and lifted his gaze, it was to rest it on the vanity table bearing the black and white bottles of the size-change magic. He approached the table with the gait of a sleepwalker or one who walks through water. For a space he played aimlessly with the vials, rolling them this way and that. Then he said aloud to himself, 'Oh, why is it that one can be wise and command a vast host and strive unceasingly and reason with diamond brilliance, and still be low as a silverfish, blind as a cutworm? The obvious is in front of our toothy muzzles and we never see it – because we rats have accepted our littleness, hypnotized ourselves with our dwarfishness, our incapacity, and our inability to burst from our cramping prison-tunnels, to leap from the shallow but deadly jail-rut, whose low walls lead us only to the stinking rubbish heap or narrow burial crypt.'

He lifted his ice-blue eyes and glared coldly at his silver-furred image in the silver mirror. 'For all your greatness, Skwee,' he told himself, 'you have thought small all your rat's life. Now for once, Skwee, think big!' And with that fierce self-command, he picked up one of the white vials and pouched it, hesitated, swept all the white vials into his pouch, hesitated again, then with a shrug and a sardonic grimace swept the black vials after them and hurried from the room.

On its back on the violet carpet, the scorpion still vibrated its legs feebly.

14

Fafhrd swiftly climbed, by the low moonlight, the high Marsh Wall of Lankhmar at the point to which Sheelba had delivered him, a good bowshot south of the Marsh Gate. 'At the gate you might run into your black pursuers,' Sheelba had told him. Fafhrd had doubted it. True, the black riders had been moving like a storm wind, but Sheelba's hut had raced across the sea-grass like a low-scudding pocket hurricane; surely he had arrived ahead of them. Yet he had put up no argument. Wizards were above all else persuasive salesmen, whether they flooded you off your feet with words like Ningauble, or manipulated you with meaningful silences, like Sheelba. For the swamp wizard had otherwise maintained his cranky quiet throughout the entire rocking, pitching, swift-skidding trip, from which Fafhrd's stomach was still queasy.

He found plenty of good holds for hand and foot in the ancient wall. Climbing it was truly child's play to one who had scaled in his youth Obelisk Polaris in the frosty Mountains of the Giants. He was far more concerned with what he might meet at the top of the wall, where he would be briefly helpless against a foe footed above him.

But more than all else – and increasingly so – he was puzzled by the darkness and silence with which the city was wrapped. Where was the battle-din; where were the flames? Or if Lankh-mar had already been subdued, which despite Ningauble's optimism seemed most likely from the fifty-to-one odds against her, where were the screams of the tortured, the shrieks of the raped, and all the gleeful clatter and shout of the victors?

He reached the wall's top and suddenly drew himself up and vaulted through a wide embrasure down onto the wide parapet, ready to draw Graywand and his ax. But the parapet was empty as far as he could see in either direction.

Wall Street below was dark, and empty too as far as he could tell. Cash Street, stretching west and flooded with pale moonlight from behind him, was visibly bare of figures. While the silence was even more marked than when he'd been climbing. It seemed to fill the great, walled city, like water brimming a cup.

Fafhrd felt spooked. Had the conquerors of Lankhmar already departed? – carrying off all its treasure and inhabitants in some unimaginably huge fleet or caravan? Had they shut up themselves and their gagged victims in the silent houses for some rite of mass torture in darkness? Was it a demon, not human army which had beset the city and vanished its inhabitants? Had the very earth gaped for victor and vanquished alike and then shut again? Or was Ningauble's whole tale wizardly flimflam? – yet even that least unlikely explanation still left unexplained the city's ghostly desolation.

Or was there a fierce battle going on under his eyes at this very moment, and he by some spell of Ningauble or Sheelba unable to see, hear, or even scent it? – until, perchance, he had fulfilled the geas of the bells which Ningauble had laid on him.

He still did not like the idea of his bells-mission. His imagination pictured the Gods *of* Lankhmar resting in their brown mummy-wrappings and their rotted black togas, their bright black eyes peeping from between resin-impregnated bandages and their deadly black staves of office beside them, waiting another call from the city that forgot yet feared them and which they in turn hated yet guarded. Waking with naked hand a clutch of spiders in a hole in desert rocks seemed wiser than waking such. Yet a geas was a geas and must be fulfilled.

He hurried down the nearest dark stone stairs three steps at a time and headed west on Cash Street, which paralleled Crafts Street a block to the south. He half imagined he brushed unseen figures. Crossing curvy Cheap Street, dark and untenanted as the others, he thought he heard a murmuring and chanting from the north, so faint that it must come from at least as far away as the Street of Gods. But he held to his predetermined course, which was to follow Cash Street to Nun Street, then three blocks north to the accursed bell-tower.

Whore Street, which was even more twisty than Cheap Street, looked tenantless too, but he was hardly half a block beyond it when he heard the tramp of boots and the clink of armor behind him. Ducking into the narrow shadows, he watched a double squad of guardsmen cross hurriedly through the moonlight, going south on Whore Street in the direction of the South Barracks. They were crowded close together, watched every way, and carried their weapons at the ready, despite the apparent absence of foe. This seemed to confirm Fafhrd's notion of an army of invisibles. Feeling more spooked than ever, he continued rapidly on his way.

And now he began to note, here and there, light leaking out from around the edges of a shuttered upper window. These dim-drawn oblongs only increased his feeling of supernatural dread. Anything, he told himself, would be better than this locked-in silence now broken only by the faint echoing tread of his own boots on the moonlit cobbles. And at the end of his trip: mummies!

Somewhere, faintly, muffled, eleven o'clock knelled. Then of a sudden, crossing narrow, black-brimming Silver Street, he heard a multitudinous pattering, like rain – save that the stars were bright overhead except for the moon's dimming of them, and he felt no drops. He began to run.

Aboard *Squid*, the kitten, as if he had received a call which he might not disregard despite all dreads, made the long leap from the scuppers to the dock, clawed his way up onto the latter and hurried off into the dark, his black hair on end and his eyes emerald bright with fear and danger-readiness.

Glipkerio and Samanda sat in his Whip Room, reminiscing and getting a tipsy glow on, to put them in the right mood for Reetha's thrashing. The fat palace mistress had swilled tankards of dark wine of Tovilyis until her black wool dress was soaked with sweat and salty beads stood on each hair of her ghostly black moustache. While her overlord sipped violet wine of Kiraay, which she had fetched from the upper pantry when no butler or page answered the ring of the silver and even the brazen summoning bell. She'd said, 'They're scared to stir since your guardsmen went off. I'll welt them properly – but only when you've had your special fun, little master.'

Now, for the nonce neglecting all the rare and begemmed instruments of pain around them and blessedly forgetting the rodent menace to Lankhmar, their thoughts had returned to simpler and happier days. Glipkerio, his pansy wreath awry and somewhat wilted, was saying with a tittering eagerness, 'Do you recall when I brought you my first kitten to throw in the kitchen fire?'

'Do I?' Samanda retorted with affectionate scorn. 'Why, little master, I remember when you brought me your first fly, to show me how neatly you could pluck off his wings and legs. You were only a toddler, but already skinny-tall.'

'Yes, but about that kitten,' Glipkerio persisted, violet wine dribbling down his chin as he took a hasty and tremble-handed swallow. 'It was black with blue eyes newly unfilmed. Radomix was trying to stop me – he lived at the palace then – but you sent him away bawling.'

'I did indeed,' Samanda concurred. 'The cotton-hearted brat! And I remember how the kitten screamed and frizzled, and how you cried afterwards because you hadn't him to throw in again. To divert your mind and cheer you, I stripped and whipped an apprentice maid as skinny-tall as yourself and with long blonde braids. That was before you got your things about hairs' – she wiped her moustache – 'and had all the girls and boys shaved. I thought it was time you graduated to manlier pleasures, and sure enough you showed your excitement in no uncertain fashion!' And with a whoop of laughter she reached across and thumbed him indelicately.

Excited by this tickling and his thoughts, Lankhmar's over-lord stood up cypress-tall-and-black in his toga, though no cypress ever twitched as he did, except perhaps in an earthquake or under most potent witchcraft. 'Come,' he cried. 'Eleven's struck. We've barely time before I must haste me to the Blue Audience Chamber to meet with Hisvin and save the city.'

'Right,' Samanda affirmed, levering herself up with her brawny forearms pulling at her knees and then pushing the pinching armchair off her large rear. 'Which whips was it you'd picked now for the naughty and traitorous minx?'

'None, none,' Glipkerio cried with impatient glee. 'In the end that well-oiled old black dog-whip hanging from your belt always seems best. Hurry we, dear Samanda, hurry!'

Reetha shot up in crispy-linened bed as she heard things creak. Shaking nightmares from her smooth-shaven head, she fumbled frantically about for the bottle whose draining would bring her protective oblivion.

She put it to her lips, but paused a moment before upending it. The door still hadn't opened and the creaking had been strangely tiny and shrill. Glancing over the edge of the bed, she saw that another door not quite a foot high had opened outward at floor level in the seamless-seeming wood paneling. Through it there stepped swiftly and silently, ducking his head a trifle, a well-formed and leanly muscular little man, carrying in one hand a gray bundle and in the other what seemed to be a long toy sword as naked as himself.

He closed the door behind him, so that it once more seemed not to be there, and gazed about piercingly.

'Gray Mouser!' Reetha yelled, springing from bed and throwing herself down on her knees beside him. 'You've come back to me!'

He winced, lifting his burdened tiny hands to his ears.

'Reetha,' he begged, 'don't shout like that again. It blasts my brain.' He spoke slowly and as deep-pitched as he could, but to her his voice was shrill and rapid, though intelligible.

'I'm sorry,' she whispered contritely, restraining the impulse to pick him up and cuddle him to her bosom.

'You'd better be,' he told her brusquely. 'Now find something heavy and put it against this door. There's those coming after, whom you wouldn't want to meet. Quick about it, girl!'

She didn't stir from her knees, but eagerly suggested, 'Why not work your magic and make yourself big again?'

'I haven't the stuff to work that magic,' he told her exasperatedly. 'I had a chance at a vial of it and like any other sex-besotted fool didn't think to swipe it. Now jump to it, Reetha!'

Suddenly realizing the strength of her bargaining position, she merely leaned closer to him and smiling archly though lovingly, asked, 'With what doll-tiny bitch have you been consorting now? No, you needn't answer that, but before I stir me to help you, you must give me six hairs from your darling head. I have good reason for my request.'

The Mouser started to argue insanely with her, then thought better of it and snicked off with Scalpel a small switch of his locks and laid them in her huge, crisscross furrowed, gleaming palm, where they were fine as baby hairs, though slightly longer and darker than most.

She stood up briskly, marched to the night table, and dropped them in Glipkerio's night draught. Then dusting off her hands above the goblet, she looked around. The most suitable object she could see for the Mouser's purpose was the golden casket of unset jewels. She lugged it into place against the small door, taking the Mouser's word as to where the small door exactly was.

'That should hold them for a bit,' he said, greedily noting for future reference the rainbow gems bigger than his fists, 'but 'twere best you also fetch—'

Dropping to her knees, she asked somewhat wistfully, 'Aren't you ever going to be big again?'

'Don't boom the floor! Yes, of course! In an hour or less, if I can trust my tricksy, treacherous wizard. Now, Reetha, while I dress me, please fetch—'

A key clinked dulcetly and a bolt thudded softly in its channel. The Mouser felt himself whirled through the air by and with Reetha onto the soft springy white bed, and a white translucent sheet whirled over them.

He heard the big door open.

At that moment a hand on his head pressed him firmly down into a squat and as he was about to protest, Reetha whispered – it was a growl like light surf – 'Don't make a bump in the sheet. Whatever happens, hold still and hide for your dear life's sake.'

A voice like battle trumpets blared then, making the Mouser glad of what shielding the sheet gave his ears. 'The nasty girl's crawled in my bed! Oh, the disgust of it! I feel faint. Wine! Ah! *Aaarrrggghhh!*' There came ear-shaking chokings, spewings, and spittings, and then the battle trumpets again, somewhat muffled, as if stuffed with flannel, though even more enraged: 'The filthy and demonic slut has put hairs in my drink! Oh, whip her, Samanda, until she's everywhere welted like a bamboo screen! Lash her until she licks my feet and kisses each toe for mercy!'

Then another voice, this one like a dozen huge kettledrums, thundering through the sheet and pounding the Mouser's tinied goldleaf-thin eardrums. 'That will I, little master. Nor heed you, if you ask I desist. Come out of there, girl, or must I whip you out?'

Reetha scrambled toward the head of the bed, away from that voice. The Mouser followed, crouching after her, though the mattress heaved like a white-decked ship in a storm, the sheet figuring as an almost deck-low ceiling of fog. Then suddenly that fog was whirled away, as if by a supernal wind, and there glared down the gigantic double red-and-black sun of Samanda's face, inflamed by liquor and anger, and of her globe-dressed, pin-transfixed black hair. And the sun had a black tail – Samanda's raised whip.

The Mouser bounded toward her across the disordered bed, brandishing Scalpel and still lugging under his other arm the gray bundle of his clothes.

The whip, which had been aimed at Reetha, changed direction and came whistling toward him. He sprang straight up with all his strength and it passed just under his naked feet like a black dragon's tail, the whistling abruptly lowering in pitch. By good luck keeping his footing as he came down, he leaped again toward Samanda, stabbed her with Scalpel in her black-wool-draped huge kneecap, and sprang down to the parquet floor.

Like a browned-iron thunderbolt, a great ax-head bit into the wood close by him, jarring him to his teeth. Glipkerio had snatched a light battle-ax from his weapon-rack with surprising speed and wielded it with unlikely accuracy.

The Mouser darted under the bed, raced across that – to him – low-ceilinged dark wide portico, emerged on the other side and doubled swiftly back around the foot of the bed to slash at the back of Glipkerio's ankle.

But this ham-stringing stroke failed when Glipkerio turned around. Samanda, limping just a little, came to her overlord's side. Gigantic ax and whip were again lifted at the Mouser.

With a rather happy hysterical scream that almost ruined the

Mouser's eardrums for good, Reetha hurled her crystal wine-flagon. It passed close between Samanda's and Glipkerio's heads, hitting neither of them, but staying their strokes at the Mouser.

All this while, unnoticed in the racket and turmoil, the golden jewel-box had been moving away, jolt by tiny jolt, from the wall. Now the door behind it was open wide enough for a rat to get through, and Hreest emerged followed by his armed band – three masked sword-rats in all, the other two green-uniformed, and three naked-faced pike-rats in browned-iron helmets and mail.

Utterly terrified by this eruption, Glipkerio raced from the room, followed only less slowly by Samanda, whose heavy treadings shook the wooden floor like earthquake shocks.

Mad for battle and also greatly relieved to face foes his own size, the Mouser went on guard, using his clothes bundle as a sort of shield and crying out fearsomely, 'Come and be killed, Hreest!'

But at that instant he felt himself snatched up with stomach-wrenching speed to Reetha's breasts.

'Put me down! Put me down!' he yelled, still in a battle-rage, but futilely, for the drunken girl carried him reelingly out the door and slammed it behind her – once more the Mouser's eardrums were assaulted – slammed it on a rat-pike.

Samanda and Glipkerio were running toward a distant, wide, blue curtain, but Reetha ran the other way, toward the kitchen and the servants' quarters, and the Mouser was perforce carried with her – his gray bundle bouncing about, his pin-sword useless, and despite his shrill protests and tears of wrath.

The rats everywhere launched their grand assault on Lankhmar Above a half hour before midnight, striking chiefly by way of golden ratholes. There were a few premature sorties, as on Silver Street, and elsewhere a few delays, as at ratholes discovered and blocked by humans at the last moment, but on the whole the attack was simultaneous.

First to emerge from Lankhmar Below were wild troops of four-foot goers, a fierce riderless cavalry, savage rats from the stinking tunnels and warrens under the slums of Lankhmar, rodents knowing few if any civilized amenities and speaking at most, a pidgin-Lankhmarese helped out with chitters and squeals. Some fought only with tooth and claw like the veriest primitives. Among them went berserkers and special-mission groups.

Then came the assassins and the incendiaries with their torches, resins, and oils – for the weapon of fire, hitherto unused, was part of the grand plan, even though the rats' upper-level tunnels were menaced thereby. It was calculated that victory would be gained swiftly enough for the humans to be enforced to put out the blazes.

Finally came the armed and armored rats, all going biped except for those packing extra missiles and parts of light-artillery pieces to be assembled above ground.

Previous forays had been made almost entirely through rat-holes in cellars and ground floors and by way of street-drains and the like. But tonight's grand assault was delivered whenever possible through ratholes on upper floors and through rat-ways that emerged in attics, surprising the humans in the supposedly safe chambers in which they had shut themselves and driving them in panic into the streets.

It was turn-about from previous nights and days, when the rats had risen in black waves and streams. Now they dropped like a black indoor rain and leaked in rat-big gushes from walls thought sound, bringing turmoil and terror. Here and there, chiefly under eaves, flames began to flicker.

The rats emerged inside almost every temple and cultish hovel lining the Street of the Gods, driving out the worshipers until that wide avenue was milling with humans too terrified to dare the dark side streets or create more than a few pockets of organized resistance.

In the high-windowed assembly hall of the South Barracks, Olegnya Mingolsbane loudly sputter-quavered to a weary audience which following custom had left their weapons outside – the soldiers of Lankhmar had been known to use them on irritating or merely boresome speakers. As he perorated, 'You who have fought the black behemoth and leviathan, you who have stood firm against Mingol and Mirphian, you who have broken the spear-squares of King Krimaxius and routed his fortressed elephants, that *you* should be daunted by dirty vermin—' eight large ratholes opened high in the back wall and from these sinister orifices a masked battery of crossbow artillery launched their whirring missiles at the aged and impassioned general. Five struck home, one down his gullet, and gargling horridly he fell from the rostrum.

Then the fire of the crossbows was turned on the startled yet lethargic audience, some of whom had been applauding Olegnya's demise as if it had been a carnival turn. From other high ratholes actual fire was tossed down in the forms of white phosphorus and flaming, oil-soaked, resin-hearted bundles of rags, while from various low golden ratholes, noxious vapors brewed in the sewers were bellows-driven.

Groups of soldiers and constables broke for the doors and found them barred from the outside – one of the most striking achievements of the special-missions groups, made possible by Lankhmar having things arranged so that she could massacre her own soldiers in times of mutiny. With smuggled weapons and those of officers, a counter-fire was turned on the ratholes, but they were difficult targets and for the most part the men of war milled about as helplessly as the worshipers in the Street of the Gods, coughing and crying out, more troubled for the present by the stinking vapors and the choking fumes of little flames here and there than by the larger fire-danger.

Meanwhile the black kitten was flattening himself on top of a cask in the granaries area while a party of armed rats trooped by. The small beast shivered with fear, yet was drawn on deeper and deeper into the city by a mysterious urging which he did not understand, yet could not ignore.

Hisvin's house had in its top floor a small room, the door and window shutters of which were all tightly barred from the inside so that a witness, if there could have been one, would have wondered how this barring had been accomplished in such fashion as to leave the room empty.

A single thick, blue-burning candle, which had somewhat fouled the air, revealed no furniture whatsoever in the room. It showed six wide, shallow basins that were part of the tiled floor. Three of these basins were filled with a thick pinkish liquid across which ever and anon a slow quivering ran. Each pink pool had a border of black dust with which it did not commingle. Along one wall were shelves of small vials, the white ones near the floor, the black ones higher.

A tiny door opened at floor level. Hisvin, Hisvet, and Frix filed silently out. Each took a white vial and walked to a pink pool and then unhesitatingly down into it. The dark dust and pinkish liquid slowed but did not stop their steps. It moved out in sluggish ripples from their knees. Soon each stood thigh-deep at a pool's center. Then each drained his vial.

For a long instant there was no change, only the ripples intersecting and dying by the candle's feeble gleam.

Then each figure began to grow while soon the pools were visibly diminished. In a dozen heartbeats they were empty of liquid and dust alike, while in them Hisvin, Hisvet, and Frix stood human-high, dry-shod, and clad all in black.

Hisvin unbarred a window opening on the Street of the Gods, threw wide the shutters, drew a deep breath, stooped to peer out briefly and cautiously, then turned crouching to the girls.

'It has begun,' he said somberly. 'Haste we now to the Blue Audience Chamber. Time presses. I will alert our Mingols to assemble and follow us.' He scuttled past them to the door. 'Come!'

Fafhrd drew himself up onto the roof of the temple of the Gods *of* Lankhmar and paused for a backward and downward look before tackling the belfry, although so far this climb had been easier even than that of the city's wall.

He wanted to know what all the screaming was about.

Across the street were several dark houses, first among them Hisvin's, while beyond them rose Glipkerio's Rainbow Palace with its moonlit, pastel-hued minarets, tallest of them the blue, like a troupe of tall, slender dancing girls behind a phalanx of black-robed squat priests.

Immediately below him was the temple's unroofed yet dark front porch and the low, wide steps leading up to it from the Street. Fafhrd had not even tried the verdigrised, copper-bound, worm-eaten doors below him. He had had no mind to go stumbling around hunting for a stairs in the inner dark and dust, where his groping hands might touch mummy-wrapped, black-togaed forms which might not lie still like other dead earth, but stir with crotchety limitless anger, like ancient yet not quite senile kings who did not relish their sleep disturbed at midnight. On both counts, an outside climb had seemed healthier and likewise the awakening of the Gods *of* Lankhmar, if they were to be wakened, better by a distant bell than by a touch on a skeletal shoulder wrapped in crumbling linen or on a bony foot.

When Fafhrd had begun his short climb, the Street of the Gods had been empty at this end, though from the open doors of its gorgeous temples – the temples of the Gods *in* Lankhmar – had spilled yellow light and come the mournful sound of many litanies, mixed with the sharper accents of impromptu prayers and beseechings.

But now the street was churning with white-faced folk, while others were still rushing screaming from temple doorways. Fafhrd still couldn't see what they were running from, and once more he thought of an army of invisibles – after all, he had only to imagine Ghouls with invisible bones – but then he noted that most of the shriekers and churners were looking downward toward their feet and the cobbles. He recollected the eerie pattering which had sent him running away from Silver Street. He remembered what Ningauble had asserted about the huge numbers and hidden source of the army besieging Lankhmar. And he recalled that *Clam* had been sunk and *Squid* captured by rats working chiefly alone. A wild suspicion swiftly bloomed in him.

Meanwhile some of the temple refugees had thrown themselves to their knees in front of the dingy fane on which he stood, and were bumping their heads on the cobbles and lower steps and uttering frenzied petitions for aid. As usual, Lankhmar was appealing to her own grim, private gods only in a moment of direst need, when all else failed. While a bold few directly below Fafhrd had mounted the dark porch and were beating on and dragging at the ancient portals.

There came a loud creaking and groaning and a sound of rending. For a moment Fafhrd thought that those below him, having broken in, were going to rush inside. But then he saw them hurrying back down the steps in attitudes of dread and prostrating themselves like the others.

The great doors opened until there was a hand's breadth between them. Then through that narrow gap there issued from the temple a torchlit procession of tiny figures which advanced and ranged themselves along the forward edge of the porch.

They were two score or so of large rats walking erect and wearing black togas. Four of them carried lance-tall torches flaming brightly white-blue at their tips. The others each carried something that Fafhrd, staring down eagle-eyed, could not quite discern – a little black staff? There were three whites among them, the rest black.

A hush fell on the Street of the Gods, as if at some secret signal the humans' tormenters had ceased their persecutions.

The black-togaed rats cried out shrilly in unison, so that even Fafhrd heard them clearly, 'We have slain your gods, O Lankhmarts! We are your gods now, O folk of Lankhmar. Submit yourselves to our worldly brothers and you will not be harmed. Hark to their commands. Your gods are dead, O Lankhmarts! We are your gods!'

The humans who had abased themselves continued to do so and to bump their heads. Others of the crowd imitated them.

Fafhrd thought for a moment of seeking something to hurl down on that dreadful little black-clad line which had cowed humanity. But the nasty notion came to him that if the Mouser had been reduced to a fraction of himself and able to live far under the deepest cellar, what could it mean but that the Mouser had been transformed into a rat by wicked magic, Hisvin's most likely? In slaying any rat, he might slay his comrade.

He decided to stick to Ningauble's instructions. He began to climb the belfry with great reaches and pulls of his long arms and doublings and straightenings of his still longer legs.

The black kitten, coming around a far corner of the same temple, bugged his little eyes at the horrid tableau of black-togaed rats. He was tempted to flee, yet moved never a muscle, as a soldier who knows he has a duty to perform, though he has forgotten or not yet learned the nature of that duty.

15

Glipkerio sat fidgeting on the edge of his seashell-shaped couch of gold. His light battle-ax lay forgot on the blue floor beside him. From a low table he took up a delicate silver wand of authority tipped with a bronze starfish – it was one of several dozen lying there – and sought to play with it nervously. But he was too nervous for that. Within moments it shot out of his hands and clattered musically on the blue floor-tiles a dozen feet away. He knotted his wand-long fingers together tightly, and rocked in agitation.

The Blue Audience Chamber was lit only by a few guttering, soot-runneled candles. The central curtains had been raised, but this doubling of the room's length only added to its gloom. The stairway going up into the blue minaret was a spiral of shadows. Beyond the dark archways leading to the porch, the great gray spindle balancing atop the copper chute gleamed mysteriously in the moonlight. A narrow silver ladder led up to its manhole, which stood open.

The candles cast on the blue-tiled inner wall several monstrous shadows of a bulbous figure seeming to bear two heads, the one atop the other. It was made by Samanda, who stood watching Glipkerio with stolid intentness, as one watches a lunatic up to tricks.

Finally Glipkerio, whose own gaze never ceased to twitch about at floor level, especially at the foot of the blue curtains masking arched blue doorways, began to mumble, softly at first, then louder and louder, 'I can't stand it any more. Armed rats loose in the palace. Guardsmen gone. Hairs in my throat. That horrid girl. That indecent hairy jumping jack with the Mouser's face. No butler or maid to answer my bell. Not even a page to trim the candles. And Hisvin hasn't come. Hisvin's not coming! I've no one. All's lost! *I can't stand it. I'm leaving! World, adieu! Nehwon, goodbye! I seek a happier universe!*'

And with that warning, he dashed toward the porch – a streak of black toga from which a lone last pansy petal fluttered down.

Samanda, clumping after him heavily, caught him before he could climb the silver ladder, largely because he couldn't get his hands unknotted to grip the rungs. She grasped him round with a huge arm and led him back toward the audience couch, meanwhile straightening and unslipping his fingers for him and saying, 'Now, now, no boat trips tonight, little master. It's on dry land we stay, your own dear palace. Only think: tomorrow, when this nonsense is past, we'll have such lovely whippings. Meanwhile to guard you, pet, you've me, who am worth a regiment. Stick to Samanda!'

As if taking her at her literal word, Glipkerio, who had been confusedly pulling away, suddenly threw his arms around her neck and almost managed to seat himself upon her great belly.

A blue curtain had billowed wide, but it was only Glipkerio's niece Elakeria in a gray silk dress that threatened momently to burst at the seams. The plump and lascivious girl had grown fatter than ever the past few days from stuffing herself with sweets to assuage her grief at her mother's broken neck and the crucifixion of her pet marmoset, and even more to still her fears for herself. But at the moment a weak anger seemed to be doing the work of honey and sugar.

'Uncle!' she cried. 'You must do something at once! The guardsmen are gone. Neither my maid nor page answered my bell, and when I went to fetch them, I found that insolent Reetha – wasn't she to be whipped? – inciting all the pages and maids to revolt against you, or do something equally violent. And in the crook of her left arm sat a living gray-clad doll waving a cruel little sword – surely it was he who crucified Kwe-Kwe! – urging further enormities. I stole away unseen.'

'Revolt, eh?' Samanda growled, setting Glipkerio aside and unsnapping whip and truncheon from her belt. 'Elakeria, look out for Uncle here. You know, boat trips,' she added in a hoarse whisper, tapping her temple significantly. 'Meanwhile I'll give those naked sluts and minions a counter-revolution they'll not forget.'

'Don't leave me!' Glipkerio implored, throwing himself at her neck and lap again. 'Now that Hisvin's forgot me, you're my only protection.'

A clock struck the quarter hour. Blue drapes parted and Hisvin came in with measured steps instead of his customary scuttling. 'For good or ill, I come upon my instant,' he said. He wore his black cap and toga and over the latter a belt from which hung ink-pot, quill-case, and a pouch of scrolls. Hisvet and Frix came close after him, in sober silken black robes and stoles. The blue drapes closed behind them. All three black-framed faces were grave.

Hisvin paced toward Glipkerio, who somewhat shamed into composure by the orderly behavior of the newcomers was standing beanpole tall on his own two gold-sandaled feet, had adjusted a little the disordered folds of his toga, and straightened around his golden ringlets the string of limp vegetable matter which was all that was left of his pansy wreath.

'Oh most glorious overlord,' Hisvin intoned solemnly, 'I bring you the worst news' – Glipkerio paled and began again to shake – 'and the best.' Glipkerio recovered somewhat. 'The worst first. The star whose coming made the heavens right has winked out, like a candle puffed on by a black demon, its fires extinguished by the black swells of the ocean of the sky. In short, she's sunk without a trace and so I cannot speak my spell against the rats. Furthermore, it is my sad duty to inform you that the rats have already, for all practical purposes, conquered Lankhmar. All your soldiery is being decimated in the South Barracks. All the temples have been invaded and the very Gods *of* Lankhmar slain without warning in their dry, spicy beds. The rats only pause, out of a certain courtesy which I will explain, before capturing your palace over your head.'

'Then all's lost,' Glipkerio quavered chalk-pale and turning his head added peevishly, 'I *told* you so, Samanda! Naught remains for me but the last voyage. World, adieu! Nehwon, farewell! I seek a happier—'

But this time his lunge toward the porch was stopped at once by his plump niece and stout palace mistress, hemming him close on either side.

'Now hear the best,' Hisvin continued in livelier accents. 'At great personal peril I have put myself in touch with the rats. It transpires that they have an excellent civilization, finer in many respects than man's – in fact, they have been secretly guiding the interests and growth of man for some time – oh, 'tis a cozy, sweet civilization these wise rodents enjoy and 'twill delight your sense of fitness when you know it better! At all events the rats, now loving me well – ah, what rare diplomacies I've worked for you, dear master! – have entrusted me with their surrender terms, which are unexpectedly generous!'

He snatched from his pouch one of the scrolls in it, and saying, 'I'll summarize,' read: '. . . hostilities to cease at once . . . by Glipkerio's command transmitted by his agents bearing his wands of authority . . . Fires to be extinguished and damage to Lankhmar repaired by Lankhmarts under direction of . . . et cetera. Damage to ratly tunnels, arcades, pleasances, privies, and other rooms to be repaired by humans. "Suitably reduced in size" should go in there. All soldiers disarmed, bound, confined . . . and so forth. All cats, dogs, ferrets, and other vermin . . . well, naturally. All ships and all Lankhmarts abroad . . . that's clear enough. Ah, here's the spot! Listen now. Thereafter each Lankhmart to go about his customary business, free in all his actions and possessions – *free*, you hear that? – subject only to the commands of his personal rat or rats, who shall crouch upon his shoulder or otherwise dispose themselves on or within his clothing, as they shall see fit, and share his bed. But *your* rats,' he went on swiftly, pointing to Glipkerio, who had gone very pale and whose body and limbs had begun again their twitchings and his features their tics, '*your* rats shall, out of deference to your high position, not be rats at all! – but rather my daughter Hisvet and, temporarily, her maid Frix, who shall attend you day and night, watch and watch, granting your every wish on the trifling condition that you obey their every command. What could be fairer, my dear master?'

But Glipkerio had already gone once more into his, 'World, adieu! Nehwon, farewell! I seek a—' meanwhile straining toward the porch and convulsing up and down in his efforts to be free of Samanda's and Elakeria's restraining arms. Of a sudden, however, he stopped still, cried, 'Of course I'll sign!' and grabbed for the parchment. Hisvin eagerly led him to his audience couch and table, meanwhile readying his writing equipment.

But here a difficulty developed. Glipkerio was shaking so that he could hardly hold pen, let alone write. His first effort with the quill sent a comet's tail in inkdrops across the clothing of those around him and Hisvin's leathery face. All efforts to guide his hand, first by gentleness, then by main force, failed.

Hisvin snapped his fingers in desperate impatience, then pointed a sudden finger at his daughter. She produced a flute from her black silken robe and began to pipe a sweet yet drowsy melody. Samanda and Elakeria held Glipkerio face down on his couch, the one at his shoulders, the other at his ankles, while Frix, kneeling with one knee on the small of his back began with her fingertips to stroke his spine from skull to tail in time to Hisvet's music, favoring her left hand with its bandaged palm.

Glipkerio continued to convulse upward at regular intervals, but gradually the violence of these earthquakes of the body decreased and Frix was able to transfer some of her rhythmic strokings to his flailing arms.

Hisvin, hard a-pace and snapping his fingers again, his shadows marching like those of giant rats moving confusedly and size-changingly against each other across the blue tiles, demanded suddenly on noting the wands of authority, 'Where are your pages you promised to have here?'

Glipkerio responded dully, 'In their quarters. In revolt. You stole my guards who would have controlled them. Where are your Mingols?'

Hisvin stopped dead in his pacing and frowned. His gaze went questioningly toward the unmoving blue doordrapes through which he had entered.

Fafhrd, breathing a little heavily, drew himself up into one of the belfry's eight windows and sat on its sill and scanned the bells.

There were eight in all and all large: five of bronze, three of browned-iron, coated with the sea-pale verdigris and the earth-dark rust of eons. Any ropes had rotted away, centuries ago for all he knew. Below them was dark emptiness spanned by four narrow flat-topped stone arches. He tried one of them with his foot. It held.

He set the smallest bell, a bronze one, swinging. There was no sound except for a dismal creaking.

He first peered, then felt up inside the bell. The clapper was gone, its supporting link rusted away.

All the other bells' clappers were likewise gone, presumably fallen to the bottom of the tower.

He prepared to use his ax to beat out the alarum, but then he saw one of the fallen clappers lying on a stone arch.

He lifted it with both hands, like a somewhat ponderous club, and moving about recklessly on the arches, struck each bell in turn. Rust showered him from the iron ones.

Their massed clangor sounded louder than mountainside thunder when lightning strikes from a cloud close by. The bells were the least musical Fafhrd had ever heard. Some made swelling beats together, which periodically tortured the ear. They must have been shaped and cast by a master of discord. The brazen bells shrieked, clanged, clashed, roared, twanged, jangled, and screamingly wrangled. The iron bells groaned rusty-throated, sobbed like leviathan, throbbed as the heart of universal death, and rolled like a black swell striking a smooth rock coast. They exactly suited the Gods *of* Lankhmar, from what Fafhrd had heard of the latter.

The metallic uproar began to fade somewhat and he realized that he was becoming deafened. Nevertheless he kept on until he had struck each bell three times. Then he peered out the window by which he had entered.

His first impression was that half the human crowd was looking straight at *him*. Then he realized it must be the noise of the bells which had turned upward those moonlit faces.

There were many more kneelers before the temple now. Other Lankhmarts were pouring up the Street of the Gods from the east, as if being driven.

The erect, black-togaed rats still stood in the same tiny line below him, auraed by grim authority despite their size, and now they were flanked by two squads of armoured rats, each bearing a small weapon which puzzled Fafhrd, straining his eyes, until he recalled the tiny crossbows which had been used aboard *Squid*.

The reverberations of the bells had died away, or sunk too low for his deafened ears to note, but then he began to hear, faintly at first, murmurings and cries of hopeless horror from below.

Gazing across the crowd again, he saw black rats climbing

unresisting up some of the kneeling figures, while many of the others already had something black squatting on their right shoulders.

There came from directly below a creaking and groaning and rending. The ancient doors of the temple of the Gods *of* Lankhmar were thrust wide open.

The white faces that had been gazing upward now stared at the porch.

The black-togaed rats and their soldiery faced around.

There strode four abreast from the wide-open doorway a company of fearfully thin brown figures, black-togaed too. Each bore a black staff. The brown was of three sorts: aged linen mummy-banding, brittle parchment-like skin stretched tight over naught but skeleton, and naked old brown bones themselves.

The crossbow-rats loosed a volly. The skeletal brown striders came on without pause. The black-togaed rats stood their ground, squeaking imperiously. Another useless volley from the tiny crossbows. Then, like so many rapiers, black staffs thrust out. Each rat they touched shriveled where he stood, nor moved again. Other rats came scurrying in from the crowd and were similarly slain. The brown company advanced at an even pace, like doom on the march.

There were screams then and the human crowd before the temple began to melt, racing down side streets and even dashing back into the temples from which they had fled. Predictably, the folk of Lankhmar were more afraid of their own gods come to their rescue than of their foes.

Himself somewhat aghast at what his ringing had roused, Fafhrd climbed down the belfry, telling himself that he must dodge the eerie battle below and seek out the Mouser in Glipkerio's vast palace.

At the corner of the temple's foot, the black kitten became aware of the climber high above, recognized him as the huge man he had scratched and loved, and realized that the force holding him here had something to do with that man.

The Gray Mouser loped purposefully out of the palace kitchen and up a corridor leading toward the royal dwelling quarters.

Though still tiny, he was at last dressed. Beside him strode Reetha, armed with a long and needle-pointed skewer for broiling cutlets in a row. Close behind them marched a disorderly-ranked host of pages armed with cleavers and mallets, and maids with knives and toasting forks.

The Mouser had insisted that Reetha not carry him on this foray and the girl had let him have his way. And truly it made him feel more manly again to be going on his own two feet and from time to time swishing Scalpel menacingly through the air.

Still, he had to admit, he would feel a lot better were he his rightful size again, and Fafhrd at his side. Sheelba had told him the effects of the black potion would last for nine hours. He had drunk it a few minutes at most past three. So he should regain his true size a little after midnight, if Sheelba had not lied.

He glanced up at Reetha, more huge than any giantess and bearing a gleaming steel weapon tall as a catboat's mast, and felt further reassured.

'Onward!' he squeaked to his naked army, though he tried to pitch his voice as low as possible. 'Onward to save Lankhmar and her overlord from the rats!'

Fafhrd dropped the last few feet to the temple's roof and faced around. The situation below had altered considerably.

The human folk were gone – that is, the living human folk.

The skeletal brown striders had all emerged through the door below and were marching west down the Street of the Gods – a procession of ugly ghosts, except these wraiths were opaque and their bony feet clicked harshly on the cobbles. The moonlit porch, steps, and flagstones behind them were blackly freckled with dead rats.

But the striders were moving more slowly now and were surrounded by shadows blacker than the moon could throw – a veritable sea of black rats lapping the striders and being augmented faster from all sides than the deadly staves could strike them down.

From the two areas ahead, to either side of the Street of the Gods, flaming darts came arching and struck in the foreranks of the striders. These missiles, unlike the crossbow darts, took effect. Wherever they struck, old linen and resin-impregnated skin began to flicker and flame. The striders came to a halt, ceased slaying rats, and devoted themselves to plucking out the flaming darts sticking in them and beating out the flames on their persons.

Another wave of rats came racing down the Street of Gods from the Marsh Gate end, and behind them on three great horses three riders leaning low in their saddles and sword-slashing at the small beasts. The horses and the cloaks and hoods of the riders were inky black. Fafhrd, who thought himself incapable of more shivers, felt another. It was as if Death itself, in three persons, had entered the scene.

The rodent fire-artillery, slewed partly around, let off at the black riders a few flaming darts which missed.

In return the black riders charged hoof-stamping and sword-slashing into the two artillery areas. Then they face toward the brown skeletal striders, several of whom still smoldered and flickered, and doffed their black hoods and mantles.

Fafhrd's face broke into a grin that would have seemed most inappropriate to one knowing he feared an apparition of Death, but not knowing his experiences of the last few days.

Seated on the three black horses were three tall skeletons gleaming white in the moonlight, and with a lover's certainty he recognized the first as being Kreeshkra's.

She might, of course, be seeking him out to slay him for his faithlessness. Nevertheless, as almost any other lover in like circumstances – though seldom, true, near the midst of a natural-supernatural battle – he grinned a rather egotistic grin.

He lost not a moment in beginning his descent.

Meanwhile Kreeshkra, for it was indeed she, was thinking as she gazed at the Gods *of* Lankhmar. *Well, I suppose brown bones are better than none at all. Still, they seem a poor fire risk. Ho, here come more rats! What a filthy city! And where oh where is my abominable Mud Man?*

The black kitten mewed anxiously at the temple's foot where he awaited Fafhrd's arrival.

Glipkerio, calm as a cushion now, completely soothed by Frix's massage and Hisvet's piping, was halfway through signing his name, forming the letters more ornately and surely than he ever had in his life, when the blue drapes in the largest archway were torn down and there pressed into the great chamber on silent naked feet the Mouser's and Reetha's forces.

Glipkerio gave a great twitch, upsetting the ink bottle on the parchment of the surrender terms, and sending his quill winging off like an arrow.

Hisvin, Hisvet, and even Samanda backed away from him toward the porch, daunted at least momentarily by the new-comers – and indeed there was something dire about that naked, shaven, youthful army be-weaponed with kitchen tools, their eyes wild, their lips a-snarl or pressed tightly together. Hisvin had been expecting his Mingols at last and so got a double shock.

Elakeria hurried after them, crying, 'They've come to slay us all! It's the revolution!'

Frix held her ground, smiling excitedly.

The Mouser raced across the blue-tiled floor, sprang up on Glipkerio's couch and balanced himself on its golden back. Reetha followed rapidly and stood beside him, menacing around with her skewer.

Unmindful that Glipkerio was flinching away, pale yellow eyes peering affrightedly from a coarse fabric of crisscrossed fingers, the Mouser squeaked loudly, 'Oh mighty overlord, no revolution this! Instead, we have come to save you from your enemies! That one' – he pointed at Hisvin – 'is in league with the rats. Under his toga you'll find a tail. I saw him in the tunnels below, member of the Rat Council of Thirteen, plotting your overthrow. It is he—'

Meanwhile Samanda had been regaining her courage. Now she charged her underlings like a black rhinoceros, her globe-shaped, pin-skewered coiffure more than enough horn. Laying about with her black whip, she roared fearsomely, 'Revolt, will you? On your knees, scullions and sluts! Say your prayers!'

Taken by surprise and readily falling back into an ingrained habit, their fiery hopes quenched by familiar abuse, the naked slim figures flinched away from her to either side.

Reetha, however, grew pink with anger. Forgetting the Mouser and all else but her rage, envenomed by many injuries, she ran after Samanda, crying to her fellow-slaves, 'Up and at her, you cowards! We're fifty to one against her!' And with that she thrust out mightily with her skewer and jabbed Samanda from behind.

The palace mistress leaped ponderously forward, her keys and chains swinging wildly from her black leather belt. She lashed the last maids out of her way and pounded on at a thumping run toward the servants' quarters.

Reetha cried over shoulder, 'After her, all! – before she rouses the cooks and barbers to her aid!' and was off in sprinting pursuit.

The maids and pages hardly hesitated at all. Reetha had refired their hot hatreds as readily as Samanda had quenched them. To play heroes and heroines rescuing Lankhmar was moonshine. To have vengeance on their old tormenter was blazing sunlight. They all raced after Reetha.

The Mouser, still balancing on the fluted golden back of Glipkerio's couch and mouthing his dramatic oration, realized somewhat belatedly that he had lost his army and was still only doll size. Hisvin and Hisvet, drawing long knives from under their black togas, rapidly circled between him and the doorway through which his forces had fled. Hisvin looked vicious and Hisvet unpleasantly like her father – the Mouser had never before noted the striking family resemblance. They began to close in.

To his left Elakeria snatched up a handful of the wands of office and raised them threateningly. To the Mouser, even those flimsy rods were huge as pikes.

To his right Glipkerio, still cringing away, reached down surreptitiously for his light battle-ax. Evidently the Mouser's loyal squeaks had gone unheard, or not been believed.

The Mouser wondered which way to jump.

Behind him Frix murmured softly, though to the Mouser's ears still somewhat boomingly, 'Exit kitchen tyrant pursued by pages unclad and maids in a state of nature, leaving our hero beset by an ogre and two – or is it three? – ogresses.'

16

Fafhrd, although he came down the temple's wall fast, found the battle once more considerably changed when he reached the bottom.

The Gods *of* Lankhmar, though not exactly in panicky rout, were withdrawing toward the open door of their temple, thrusting their staves from time to time at the horde of rats which still beset them. Wisps of smoke still trailed from a few of them – ghostly moonlit pennons. They were coughing, or more likely cursing and it sounded like coughs. Their brown skull-faces were dire – the expression of elders defeated and trying to cloak their impotent, gibbering rage with dignity.

Fafhrd moved rapidly out of their way.

Kreeshkra and her two male Ghouls were slashing and stabbing from their saddles at another flood of rats in front of Hisvin's house, while their black horses crunched rats under their hooves.

Fafhrd made toward them, but at that moment there was a rush of rats at him and he had to unsheathe Graywand. Using the great sword as a scythe, he cleared a space around him with three strokes, then started again toward the Ghouls.

The doors of Hisvin's house burst open and there fled out down the short steps a crowd of Mingol slaves. Their faces grimaced with terror, but even more striking was the fact that they were thin almost beyond emaciation. Their once-tight black liveries hung loosely on them. Their hands were skeletal. Their faces were skulls covered with yellow skin.

Three groups of skeletons: brown, ivory, and yellow – *It is a prodigy of prodigies*, Fafhrd thought, *the beginning of a dark spectrum of bones.*

Behind the Mingols and driving them, not so much to kill them as to get them out of the way, came a company of crouchy but stalwart masked men, some wearing armor, all brandishing weapons – swords and crossbows. There was something horribly familiar about their scuttling, hobble-legged gait. Then came some with pikes and helmets, but without masks. The faces, or muzzles rather, were those of rats. All the

216

newcomers, masked or nakedly fur-faced, made for the three Ghoulish riders.

Fafhrd sprang forward. Graywand singing about his head, unmindful of the new surge of ordinary rats coming against him – and came to a skidding halt.

The man-sized and man-armed rats were still pouring from Hisvin's house. Hero or no, he couldn't kill *that* many of them.

At that instant he felt claws sink into his leg. He raised his crook-fingered big left hand to sweep away from him whatever now attacked him . . . and saw climbing his thigh the black kitten from *Squid*.

That scatterbrain mustn't be in this dread battle, he thought . . . and opened his empty pouch to thrust in the kitten . . . and saw gleaming dully at its bottom the tin whistle . . . and realized that here was a metal straw to cling to.

He snatched it out and set it to his lips and blew it.

When one taps with idle finger a toy drum, one does not expect a peal of thunder. Fafhrd gasped and almost swallowed the whistle. Then he made to hurl it away from him. Instead he set it to his lips once more, put his hands to his ears, for some reason closed his eyes tight, and once more blew it.

Once again the horrendous noise went shuddering up toward the moon and down the shadowed streets of Lankhmar.

Imagine the scream of a leopard, the snarl of a tiger, and the roaring of a lion commingled, and one will have some faint suggestion of the sound the tin whistle produced.

Everywhere the little rats held still in their hordes. The skeletal Mingols paused in their shaking, staggering flight. The big armed rats, masked or helmeted, halted in their attack upon the Ghouls. Even the Ghouls and their horses held still. The fur on the black kitten fluffed out as it still clung to Fafhrd's crouching thigh, and its green eyes became enormous.

Then the awesome sound had died away, a distant bell was tolling midnight, and all the battlers fell to action again.

But black shapes were forming in the moonlight around Fafhrd. Shapes that were at first no more than shadows with a sheen to them. Then darker, like translucent polished black horn. Then solid and velvet black, their pads resting on the moonlit flagstones. They had the slender, long-legged forms of cheetahs, but the mass of tigers or lions. They stood almost as high at the shoulder as horses. Their somewhat small and prick-eared heads swayed slowly, as did their long tails. Their fangs were like needles of faintly green ice. Their eyes, which were like frozen emeralds, stared all twenty-six at Fafhrd – for there were thirteen of the beasts.

Then Fafhrd realized that they were staring not at his head but at his waist.

The black kitten there gave a shrill, wailing cry that was at once a young cat's first battle call and also a greeting.

With a screaming, snarling roar, like thirteen of the tin whistles blown at once, the War Cats bounded outward. With preternatural agility, the black kitten leaped after a group of four of them.

The small rats fled toward walls and gutters and doors – wherever holes might be. The Mingols threw themselves down. The half-splintered doors of the temple of the Gods *of* Lankh-mar could be heard to screech shut rather rapidly.

The four War Cats to whom the kitten had attached himself raced toward the man-size rats coming from Hisvin's house. Two of the Ghouls had been struck from their saddles by pikes or swords. The third – it was Kreeshkra – parried a blow from a rapier, then kicked her horse into a gallop past Hisvin's house toward the Rainbow Palace. The two riderless black horses fol-lowed her.

Fafhrd prepared to follow her, but at that instant a black parrot swooped down in front of him, beating its wings, and a small skinny boy with a puckered scar under his left eye was tugging at his wrist.

'Mouser-Mouser!' the parrot squawked. 'Danger-danger! Blue-Blue-Blue Blue Audience Chamber!'

'Same message, big man,' the urchin rasped with a grin.

So Fafhrd, running around the battle of armed rats and War Cats – a whirling melee of silvery swords and flashing claws, of cold green and hot red eyes – set out after Kreeshkra anyhow, since she had been going in the same direction.

Long pikes struck down a War Cat, but the kitten sprang like a shining black comet at the face of the foremost of the giant rodent pike-wielders as the other three War Cats closed in beside him.

The Gray Mouser lightly dropped off the back of the golden couch the instant Hisvin and Hisvet got within stabbing distance. Then, since they were both coming around the couch, he ran under it and from thence under the low table. During his short passage through the open, Glipkerio's ax crashed on the tiles to one side of him, while Elakeria's bundle of wands smashed clatteringly down on the other. He paused under the center of the table, plotting his next action.

Glipkerio darted prudently away, leaving his ax where he had let go of it from the sting of the blow. Plump Elakeria, however, slipped and fell with the force of her clumsy thwack and for the moment both her sprawled form and the ax were quite close to the Mouser.

Then – well, one moment the table was a roof a comfortable rat's-span or so above the Mouser's head. The next moment he had, without moving, bumped his head on it and very shortly afterward somehow overturned it to one side without touching it with his hands and despite the fact that he had sat down rather hard on the floor.

While Elakeria was no longer an obese wanton bulging out a gray dress, but a slender nymph totally unclad. And the head of Glipkerio's ax, which Scalpel's slim blade now touched, had shrunk to a ragged sliver of metal, as if eaten away by invisible acid.

The Mouser realized that he had regained his original size, even as Sheelba had foretold. The thought flashed through his mind that, since nothing can come of nothing, the atomies shed from Scalpel in the cellar had now been made up from those in the ax-head, while to replace his flesh and clothing he had stolen somewhat of that of Elakeria. She certainly had benefited from the transaction, he decided.

But this was not the time for metaphysics or for moralizing, he told himself. He scrambled to his feet and advanced on his shrunken-seeming tormenters, menacing with Scalpel.

'Drop your weapons!' he commanded.

Neither Glipkerio, Elakeria, or Frix held any. Hisvet let go of her long dagger at once, probably recalling that the Mouser knew she had some skill in hurling it. But Hisvin, foaming now with rage and frustration, held onto his. The Mouser advanced Scalpel flickeringly toward his scrawny throat.

'Call off your rats, Lord Null,' he ordered, 'or you die!'

'Shan't!' Hisvin spat at him, stabbing futilely at Scalpel. Then, reason returning to him a little, he added, 'And even if I wished to, I couldn't!'

The Mouser, knowing from his session at the Council of Thirteen that this was the truth, hesitated.

Elakeria, seeing her nakedness, snatched a light coverlet from the golden couch and huddled it around her, then immediately drew it aside again to admire her slender new body.

Frix continued to smile excitedly but somehow composedly, as if all this were a play and she its audience.

Glipkerio, although seeking to firm himself by tightly embracing a spirally fluted pillar between candlelit chamber and moonlit porch, clearly had the grand, rather than merely the petty twitches again. His narrow face, between its periodic convulsions, was a study in consternation and nervous exhaustion.

Hisvet called out, 'Gray lover, kill the old fool my father! Slay Glip and the rest too, unless you desire Frix as a concubine. Then rule all Lankhmar Above and Below with my willingest aid. You've won the game, dear one. I confess myself beaten. I'll be your humblest slave-girl, my only hope that some day I'll be your most favorite too.'

And so ringingly sincere was her voice and so dulcet-sweet in making its promises, that despite his experiences of her treacheries and cruelties and despite the cold murderousness of some of her words, the Mouser was truly tempted. He looked toward her – her expression was that of a gambler playing for the highest stakes – and in that instant Hisvin lunged.

The Mouser beat the dagger aside and retreated a double step, cursing only himself for the wavering of his attention. Hisvin continued to lunge desperately, only desisting when Scalpel pricked his throat swollen with curses.

'Keep your promise and show your courage,' Hisvet cried to the Mouser. 'Kill him!'

Hisvin began to gabble his curses at her too.

The Mouser was never afterwards quite certain as to what he would have done next, for the nearest blue curtains were jerked away to either side and there stood Skwee and Hreest, both mansize, both unmasked and with rapiers drawn, both of lordly, cool assured, and dire mien – the white and the black of rat aristocracy.

Without a word Skwee advanced a pace and pointed his sword at the Mouser. Hreest copied him so swiftly it was impossible to be sure it was a copy. The two green-uniformed sword-rats moved out from behind them and went on guard to either side. From behind *them*, the three pike-rats, mansize like the rest, moved out still farther on the flank, two toward the far end of the room, one toward the golden couch, beside which Hisvet now stood near Frix.

His hand clutching his scrawny throat, Hisvin mastered his astonishment and pointing at his daughter, croaked commandingly, 'Kill her too!'

The lone pike-rat obediently leveled his weapon and ran with it. As the great wavy blade passed close by her, Frix cast herself at the weapon, hugging its pole. The blade missed Hisvet by a finger's breadth and Frix fell. The pike-rat jerked back his weapon and raised it to skewer Frix to the floor, but, 'Stop!' Skwee cried. 'Kill none – as yet – except the one in gray. All now, advance!'

The pike-rat obediently swiveled round, re-leveling his weapon at the Mouser.

Frix picked herself up and casually murmuring in Hisvet's ear, 'That's three times, dear mistress,' turned to watch the rest of the drama.

The Mouser thought of diving off the porch, but instead broke for the far end of the room. It was perhaps a mistake. The two pike-rats were at the far door ahead of him, while the sword-rats at his heels gave him no time to feint around the pike-blades, kill the pike-rats and get around them. He dodged behind a heavy table and turning abruptly, managed to wound lightly in the thigh a green-uniformed rat who had run a bit ahead of the rest. But that rat dodged back and the Mouser found himself faced by four rapiers and two pikes – and just conceivably by death too, he had to admit to himself as he noted the sureness with which Skwee was directing and controlling the attack. So – slash, jump, slash, thrust, parry, kick the table – he must attack Skwee – thrust, parry, riposte, counter-riposte, retreat – but Skwee had anticipated that, so – slash, jump, thrust, jump, jump again, bump the wall, thrust – whatever he was going to do, he'd have to do it very soon!

A rat's head, detached from its rat, spun across the edge of his field of vision and he heard a happy, familiar shout.

Fafhrd had just entered the room, beheaded from behind the third pike-rat, who had been acting as a sort of reserve, and was rushing the others from behind.

At Skwee's swift signal, the lesser sword-rats and the two remaining pike-rats turned. The latter were slow in shifting their long weapons. Fafhrd beheaded the blade of one pike and then its owner, parried the second pike and thrust home through the throat of the rat wielding it, then met the attack of the two lesser sword-rats, while Skwee and Hreest redoubled their assault on the Mouser. Their snarl-twisted bristles, snarl-bared incisors, long flat furry faces and huge eyes blue and black were almost as daunting as their swift swords, while Fafhrd found equal menace in his pair.

At Fafhrd's entry, Glipkerio had said very softly to himself, 'No, I cannot bear it longer,' run out onto the porch and up the silver ladder, and sprung down through the manhole of the spindle-shaped gray vehicle. His weight overbalanced it, so that it slowly nosed down in the copper chute. He called out, somewhat more loudly, 'World adieu! Nehwon, goodbye! I go to seek a happier universe. Oh, you'll regret me, Lankhmar! Weep, oh City!' Then the gray vehicle was sliding down the chute faster and faster. He dropped inside and jerked shut the hatch after him. With a small, sullen splash the vehicle vanished beneath the dark, moon-fretted waters.

Only Elakeria and Frix, whose eyes and ears missed nothing, saw Glipkerio go or heard his valedictory.

With a sudden concerted effort Skwee and Hreest rammed the table, across which they'd been fencing, against the Mouser, to pin him to the wall. Barely in time, he sprang atop it, dodged Skwee's thrust, parried Hreest's, and on a lucky riposte sent

Scalpel's tip into Hreest's right eye and brain, whipping his sword out just soon enough to parry Skwee's next thrust.

Skwee retreated a double step. By virtue of the almost panoramic vision of his wide-spaced blue eyes, he noted that Fafhrd was finishing off the second of his two sword-rats, beating through by brute force the parries of their lighter swords, and himself suffering only a few scratches and minor pricks in the process.

Skwee turned and ran. The Mouser leaped from the table after him. Midway down the room something was falling in blue folds from the ceiling. Hisvet, midway along the wall, had slashed with her dagger the cords supporting the curtains that could divide the room in two. Skwee ran a-crouch under them, but the Mouser almost ran into them, dodging swiftly back as Skwee's rapier thrust through the heavy fabric inches from his throat.

Moments later the Mouser and Fafhrd located the central split in the drapes and suddenly parted them with the tips of their swords, closely a-watch for another rapier-thrust or even a thrown dagger.

Instead they saw Hisvin, Hisvet, and Skwee standing in front of the audience couch in attitudes of defiance, but grown small as children – if that can be said of a rat. The Mouser started toward them, but before he was halfway there, they became small as rats and swiftly tumbled down a tile-size trapdoor. Skwee, who went last, turned for one more angry chitter at the Mouser, one more shake of toy-size rapier, before he pulled the tile shut over his head.

The Mouser cursed, then burst into laughter. Fafhrd joined him, but his eyes were warily on Frix, still standing human-size behind the couch. Nor did he miss Elakeria on the couch, peering with one affrighted eye from under the coverlet while also thrusting out, inadvertently or no, one slender leg.

Still laughing wildly, the Mouser reeled over to Fafhrd, threw an arm up around his shoulders, and pummeled him playfully in the chest, demanding, 'Why did you have to turn up, you great lout? I was about to die heroically, or else slay in mass combat the seven greatest sword-rats in Lankhmar Below! You're a scene-stealer!'

Eyes still on Frix, Fafhrd roughed the Mouser's chin affectionately with his fist, then gave him an elbow-dig sharp enough to take half his breath away and stop his laughter. 'Three of them were only pikemen, or pike-rats, as I suppose you call them,' he corrected, then complained gruffly, 'I gallop two nights and a day – halfway around the Inner Sea – to save your undersized hide. And do so! Only to be told I'm an actor.'

The Mouser gasped out, still with a snickering whoop, 'You don't know how undersized! Halfway around the Inner Sea, you say . . . and nevertheless time your entrance perfectly! Why, you're the greatest actor of them all!' He dropped to his knees in front of the tile that had served as trapdoor and said in tones compounded equally of philosophy, humor, and hysteria, 'While I must lose – for ever, I suppose – the greatest love of my life.' He rapped the tile – it sounded very solid – and thrusting down his face called out softly, 'Yoo-hoo! Hisvet!' Fafhrd jerked him to his feet.

Frix raised a hand. The Mouser looked at her, while Fafhrd had never taken his eyes off her.

'Here, little man, catch!' Smiling she called to the Mouser and tossed him a small black vial, which he caught and goggled at foolishly. 'Use it if you are ever again so silly as to wish to seek out my late mistress. I have no need of it. I have worked out my bondage in this world. I have done the diabolic Demoiselle her three services. I am free!'

As she said that last word, her eyes lit up like lamps. She threw back her black hood and took a breath so deep it seemed almost to lift her from the floor. Her eyes fixed on infinity. Her dark hair lifted on her head. Lightning crackled in her hair, formed itself in a blue nimbus, and streamed like a blue cloak down her body, over and through her black silk dress.

She turned and ran swiftly out onto the porch, Fafhrd and the Mouser after her. Glowing still more bluely and crying, 'Free! Free! *Free!* Back to Arilia! Back to the World of Air,' she dove off the edge.

She did not seem to enter the waves, but skimmed just along their crests like a small faint blue comet and then mounting toward the sky, higher and higher, became a faint blue star and vanished.

'Where is Arilia?' the Mouser asked.

'I thought this was the World of Air,' Fafhrd mused.

17

The rats all over Lankhmar, after suffering huge losses, dove back everywhere into their holes and pulled tight shut the doors of such as had them. This happened also in the rooms of pink pools in the third floor of Hisvin's house, where the War Cats had driven back the last of the rats who had gained their human size by drinking the white vials there and at the expense of the flesh of Hisvin's Mingols. Now they guzzled the black vials even more eagerly, to escape back into their tunnels.

The rats also suffered total defeat in the South Barracks, where the War Cats ravaged after clawing and crashing open the doors with preternatural strength.

Their work done, the War cats regathered at the place where Fafhrd had summoned them and there faded away even as they had earlier materialized. They were still thirteen, although they had lost one of their company, for the black kitten faded away with them, comporting himself like an apprentice member of their company. It was ever afterwards believed, by most Lankhmarts, that the War Cats and the white skeletons as well had been summoned by the Gods *of* Lankhmar, whose reputation for horrid powers and dire activities was thereby bolstered, despite some guilty recollections of their temporary defeat by the rats.

By twos and threes and sixes, the people of Lankhmar emerged from their places of hiding, learned that the Rat Plague was over, and wept, prayed, and rejoiced. Gentle Radomix Kistomerces-Null was plucked from his retreat in the slums and with his seventeen cats carried in triumph to the Rainbow Palace.

Glipkerio, his leaden craft tightly collapsed around him by weight of water, until it had become a second leaden skin molded to his form – truly a handsome coffin – continued to sink in the Lankhmar Deep, but whether to reach a solid bottom, or only a balancing place between world bubbles in the waters of infinity, who may say?

The Gray Mouser recovered Cat's Claw from Hreest's belt, marveling somewhat that all the rat-corpses were yet human size. Likely enough death froze all magics.

Fafhrd noted with distaste the three pools of pink slime in front of the gold audience couch and looked for something to throw over them. Elakeria coyly clutched her coverlet around her. He dragged from a corner a colorful rug that was a duke's ransom and made that do.

There was the noise of hooves on tiles. In the high, wide archway from which the drapes had been torn there appeared Kreeshkra, still on horseback and leading the other two Ghoulish mounts, empty saddled. Fafhrd swung the skeleton girl down and embraced her heartily, somewhat to the Mouser's and Elakeria's shock, but soon said, 'Dearest love, I think it best you put on again your black cloak and hood. Your naked bones are to me the acme of beauty but here come others they may disturb.'

'Already ashamed of me, aren't you? Oh, you dirty-minded puritanical Mud Folk!' Kreeshkra commented with a sour laugh, yet complied, while the rainbows in her eye sockets twinkled.

The others Fafhrd had referred to consisted of the councillors, soldiers, and various relatives of the late overlord, including the gentle Radomix Kistomerces-Null and his seventeen cats, each now carried and cosseted by some noble hoping to gain favor from Lankhmar's most likely next overlord.

Not all the new arrivals were so commonplace. One, heralded by more hoof-cloppings on tile, was Fafhrd's Mingol mare, her tether bitten through. She stopped by Fafhrd and glared her bloodshot eyes at him as if to say, 'I am not so easily got rid of. Why did you cheat me of a battle?'

Kreeshkra patted the grim beast's nose and observed to Fafhrd, 'You are clearly a man who awakens deep loyalty in others. I trust you have the same quality yourself.'

'Never doubt me, dearest,' Fafhrd answered with fond sincerity.

Also among the newcomers and returners was Reetha, looking suavely happy as a cat who has licked cream, or a panther some even more vital fluid, and naked as ever except for three broad leather loops around her waist. She threw her arms about the Mouser. 'You're big again!' she rejoiced. 'And you beat them all!'

The Mouser accepted her embrace, though he purposely put on a dissatisfied face and said sourly, 'You were a big help! – you and your naked army, deserting me when I most needed help. I suppose you finished off Samanda?'

'Indeed we did!' Reetha smirked like a sated leopardess. 'What a sizzling she made! Look, doll, her belt of office *does* go three times round my waist. Oh, yes, we cornered her in the kitchen and brought her down. Each of us took a pin from her hair. Then—'

'Spare me the details, darling,' the Mouser cut her short. 'This night for nine hours I've been a rat, with all of a rat's nasty feelings, and that's quite long enough. Come with me, pet; there's something we must attend to ere the crowd gets too thick.'

When they returned after a short space, the Mouser was carrying a box wrapped in his cloak, while Reetha wore a violet robe, around which was still triply looped, however, Samanda's belt. And the crowd had thickened indeed. Radomix Kisto-merces-no-longer-Null had already been informally vested with Lankhmar's overlordship and was sitting somewhat bemused on the golden seashell audience couch along with his seventeen cats and also a smiling Elakeria, who had wrapped her coverlet like a sari around her sylphlike figure.

The Mouser drew Fafhrd aside. 'That's quite a girl you've got,' he remarked, rather inadequately, of Kreeshkra.

'Yes, isn't she,' Fafhrd agreed blandly.

'You should have seen mine,' the Mouser boasted. 'I don't mean Reetha there, I mean my *weird* one. She had—'

'Don't let Kreeshkra hear you use that word,' Fafhrd warned sharply though *sub voce*.

'Well, anyhow, whenever I want to see her again,' the Mouser continued conspiratorially, 'I have only to swallow the contents of this black vial and—'

'I'll take charge of that' Reetha announced crisply, snatching it out of his hand from behind him. She glanced at it, then expertly pitched it through a window into the Inner Sea.

The Mouser started a glare at her which turned into an ingratiating smile.

Flapping her black robe to cool her, Kreeshkra came up behind Fafhrd. 'Introduce me to your friends, dear,' she directed.

Meanwhile around the golden couch was an ever-thickening press of courtiers, nobles, councillors, and officers. New titles were being awarded by the dozen to all firstcomers. Sentences of perpetual banishment and confiscation of property were being laid on Hisvin and all others absent, guilty or guiltless. Reports were coming in of the successful fighting of all fires in the city and the complete vanishment of rats from its streets. Plans were being laid for the complete extirpation from under the city of the entire rat-metropolis of Lankhmar Below – subtle and complex plans which did not sound to the Mouser entirely practical. It was becoming clear that under the saintly Radomix Kistomerces, Lankhmar would more than ever be ruled by foolish fantasy and shameless greed. At moments like these it was easy to understand why the Gods *of* Lankhmar were so furiously exasperated by their city.

Various lukewarm thanks were extended to the Mouser and Fafhrd, although most of the newcomers seemed not at all clear as to what part the two heroes had played in conquering the rats, despite Elakeria's repeated accounts of the final fighting and of Glipkerio's sea-plunge. Soon, clearly, seeds would be planted against the Mouser and Fafhrd in Radomix's saintly-vague mind, and their bright heroic roles imperceptibly darkened to blackest villainy.

At the same time it became evident that the new court was disturbed by the restless tramping of the four ominous war-horses, three Ghoulish and one Mingol, and that the presence of an animated skeleton was becoming more and more disquieting, for Kreeshkra continued to wear her black robe and hood like a loose garment. Fafhrd and the Mouser looked at one another, and then at Kreeshkra and Reetha, and they realized that there was agreement between them. The Northerner mounted the

Mingol mare, and the Mouser and Reetha the two leftover Ghoulish horses, and they all four made their way out of the Rainbow Palace as quietly as is possible when hooves clop on tile.

Thereafter there swiftly grew in Lankhmar a new legend of the Gray Mouser and Fafhrd: how as rat-small midget and bell-tower giant they had saved Lankhmar from the rats, but at the price of being personally summoned and escorted to the After-world by Death himself, for the black-robed ivory skeleton was remembered as male, which would doubtless have irked Kreeshkra greatly.

However, as next morning the four rode under the fading stars toward the paling east along the twisty causeway across the Great Salt Marsh, they were all merry enough in their own fashions. They had commandeered three donkeys and laden them with the box of jewels the Mouser had abstracted from Glipkerio's bed-chamber and with food and drink for a long journey, though exactly where that journey would lead they had not yet agreed. Fafhrd argued for a trip to his beloved Cold Waste, with a long stopover on the way at the City of Ghouls. The Mouser was equally enthusiastic for the Eastern Lands, slyly pointing out to Reetha what an ideal place it would be for sunbathing unclad.

Yanking up her violet robe to make herself more comfortable, Reetha nodded her agreement. 'Clothes are so itchy,' she said. 'I can hardly bear them. I like to ride bareback – my back, not the horse's. While hair is even itchier – I can feel mine growing. You will have to shave me every day, dear,' she added to the Mouser.

He agreed to take on that chore, but added, 'However, I can't concur with you altogether, sweet. Besides protecting from brambles and dust, clothes give one a certain dignity.'

Reetha retorted tartly, 'I think there's far more dignity in the naked body.'

'Pish, girl,' Kreeshkra told her, 'what can compare with the dignity of naked bones?' But glancing toward Fafhrd's red beard and red, curled chest, she added, 'However, there is something to be said for hair.'

SWORDS AND
ICE MAGIC

CONTENTS

otherwise occupied. A surfeit of gander-sauce. Where least expected, a qualified consolation.

I
THE SADNESS OF
THE EXECUTIONER

There was a sky that was always gray.
There was a place that was always far away.
There was a being who was always sad.

Sitting on his dark-cushioned, modest throne in his low, rambling castle in the heart of the Shadowland, Death shook his pale head and pommeled a little his opalescent temples and slightly pursed his lips, which were the color of violet grapes with the silvery bloom still on, above his slender figure armored in chain mail and his black belt, studded with silver skulls tarnished almost as black, from which hung his naked, irresistible sword.

He was a relatively minor death, only the Death of the World of Nehwon, but he had his problems. Tenscore flickering or flaring human lives to have their wicks pinched in the next twenty heartbeats. And although the heartbeats of Death resound like a leaden bell far underground and each has a little of eternity in it, yet they do finally pass. Only nineteen left now. And the Lords of Necessity, who outrank Death, still to be satisfied.

Let's see, thought Death with a vast coolness that yet had a tiny seething in it, one hundred sixty peasants and savages, twenty nomads, ten warriors, two beggars, a whore, a merchant, a priest, an aristocrat, a craftsman, a king, and two heroes. That would keep his books straight.

Within three heartbeats he had chosen one hundred and ninety-six of the tenscore and unleashed their banes upon them: chiefly invisible, poisonous creatures within their flesh which suddenly gan multiply into resistless hordes, here a dark and bulky bloodclot set loose with feather touch to glide through a vein and block a vital portal, there a long-eroded artery wall tunneled through at last; sometimes slippery slime oozing purposefully onto the next footrest of a climber, sometimes an adder told where to wriggle and when to strike, or a spider where to lurk.

Death, by his own strict code known only to himself, had cheated just a little on the king. For some time in one of the deepest and darkest corners of his mind he had been fashioning the doom of the current overlord of Lankhmar, chiefest city and land in the World of Nehwon. This overlord was a gentle and tenderhearted scholar, who truly loved only his seventeen cats, yet wished no other being in Nehwon ill, and who was forever making things difficult for Death by pardoning felons, reconciling battling brothers and feuding families, hurrying barges or wains of grain to regions of starvation, rescuing distressed small animals, feeding pigeons, fostering the study of medicine and kindred arts, and most simply of all by always having about him, like finest fountain spray on hottest day, an atmosphere of sweet and wise calm which kept swords in scabbards, brows unknotted, and teeth unclenched. But now, at this very instant, by Death's crooked, dark-alleyed plotting hidden almost but not quite from himself, the thin wrists of the benign monarch of Lankhmar were being pricked in innocent play by his favoritest cat's needle-sharp claws, which had by a jealous, thin-nosed nephew of the royal ailurophile been late last night envenomed with the wind-swift poison of the rare emperor snake of tropical Klesh.

Yet on the remaining four and especially the two heroes – Death assured himself a shade guiltily – he would work solely by improvisation. In no time at all he had a vision of Lithquil, the Mad Duke of Ool Hrusp, watching from high balcony by torchlight three northern berserks wielding saw-edged scimitars joined in mortal combat with four transparent-fleshed, pink-skeletoned ghouls armed with poniards and battle-axes. It was the sort of heavy experiment Lithquil never tired of setting up and witnessing to the slaughterhouse end, and incidentally it was getting rid of the majority of the ten warriors Death had ticketed for destruction.

Death felt a less than momentary qualm recalling how well Lithquil had served him for many years. Even the best of servants must some day be pensioned off and put to grass, and in none of the worlds Death had heard of, certainly not Nehwon, was there a dearth of willing executioners, including passionately devoted, incredibly untiring, and exquisitely fantastic-minded ones. So even as the vision came to Death, he sent his thought at it and the rearmost ghoul looked up with his invisible eyes, so that his pink-broidered black skull-sockets rested upon Lithquil, and before the two guards flanking the Mad Duke could quite swing in their ponderous shields to protect their master, the ghoul's short-handled ax, already posed overshoulder, had flown through the narrowing gap and buried itself in Lithquil's nose and forehead.

Before Lithquil could gin crumple, before any of the watchers around him could nock an arrow to dispatch or menace the assassin, before the naked slavegirl who was the promised but seldom-delivered prize for the surviving gladiator could start to draw breath for a squealing scream, Death's magic gaze was fixed on Horborixen, citadel-city of the King of Kings. But not on the interior of the Great Golden Palace, though Death got a fleeting glimpse of that, but on the inwardness of a dingy workshop where a very old man looked straight up from his rude pallet and truly wished that the cool dawn light, which was glimmering through window- and louver-crack, would never more trouble the cobwebs that made ghostly arches and buttresses overhead.

This ancient, who bore the name of Gorex, was Horborixen's and perhaps all Nehwon's skillfulest worker in precious and military metals and deviser of cunningest engines, but he had lost all zest in his work or any other aspect of life for the last weary twelve-month, in fact ever since his great-granddaughter Eesafem, who was his last surviving kin and most gifted apprentice in his difficult craft, a slim, beauteous, and barely nubile girl with almond eyes sharp as needles, had been summarily abducted by the harem scouts of the King of Kings. His furnace was ice cold, his tools gathered dust, he had given himself up entirely to sorrow.

He was so sad in fact that Death had but to add a drop of his own melancholy humor to the black bile coursing slowly and miserably through the tired veins of Gorex, and the latter painlessly and instantly expired, becoming one with his cobwebs.

So! – the aristocrat and the craftsman were disposed of in no more than two snaps of Death's long, slender, pearly mid-finger and thumb, leaving only the two heroes.

Twelve heartbeats to go.

Death most strongly felt that, if only for artistry's sake, heroes should be made to make their exits from the stage of life in the highest melodramatic style, with only one in fifty score let to die of old age and in the bed of sleep for the object of irony. This necessity was incidentally so great that it permitted, he believed as part of his self-set rules, the use of outwardly perceptible and testifiable magic and need not be puttied over with realism, as in the case of more humdrum beings. So now for two whole heartbeats he listened only to the faint simmer of his cool mind, while lightly massaging his temples again with nacreous knuckles. Then his thoughts shot toward one Fafhrd, a largely couth and most romantical barbarian, the soles of whose feet and mind were nonetheless firmly set in fact, particularly when he was either very sober, or very drunk, and toward this one's lifelong comrade, the Gray Mouser, perhaps the cleverest and wittiest thief in all Nehwon and certainly the one with either the bonniest or bitterest self-conceit.

The still less than momentary qualm which Death experienced at this point was far deeper and stronger than that which he had felt in the case of Lithquil. Fafhrd and the Mouser had served him well and in vastly more varied fashion than the Mad Duke, whose eyes had been fixed on death to the point of crossedness, making his particular form of ax-dispatch most appropriate. Yes, the large vagabond Northerner and the small, wry-smiling, eyebrowarching cutpurse had been most useful pawns in some of Death's finest games.

Yet without exception every pawn must eventually be snapped up and tossed in box in the course of the greatest game, even if it has advanced to the ultimate rank and become king or queen. So Death reminded himself, who knew that even he himself must ultimately die, and so he set to his intuitively creative task relentlessly and swifter than ever arrow or rocket or falling star flew.

After the fleetingest glance southwest toward the vast, dawn-pink city of Lankhmar, to reassure himself that Fafhrd and the Mouser still occupied a rickety penthouse atop an inn which catered to the poorer sort of merchants and faced on Wall Street near the Marsh Gate, Death looked back at the late Lithquil's slaughter pen. In his improvisations he regularly made a practice of using materials closest at hand, as any good artist will.

Lithquil was in mid-crumple. The slavegirl was screaming. The mightiest of the berserks, his big face contorted by a fighting fury that would never fade till sheer exhaustion forced it, had just slashed off the bonily pink, invisibly fleshed head of Lithquil's assassin. And quite unjustly and even idiotically – but most of Death's lesser banes outwardly appear to work in such wise – a halfscore arrows were winging from the gallery toward Lithquil's avenger.

Death magicked and the berserk was no longer there. The ten arrows transfixed empty air, but by that time Death, again following the practice of economy in materials, was peering once more at Horborixen and into a rather large cell lit by high, barred windows in the midst of the harem of the King of Kings. Rather oddly, there was a small furnace in the cell, a quenching bath, two small anvils, several hammers, many other tools for working metals, as well as a small store of precious and worka-day metals themselves.

In the center of the cell, examining herself in a burnished silver mirror with almond eyes sharp as needles and now also quite as mad as the berserk's, there stood a deliciously slender girl of no more than sixteen, unclad save for four ornaments of silver filigree. She was, in fact, unclad in extremest degree, since except for her eyelashes, her every last hair had been removed and wherever such hair had been she was now tattooed in fine patterns of green and blue.

For seven moons now Eesafem had suffered solitary confine-ment for mutilating in a harem fight the faces of the King of King's favoritest concubines, twin Ilthmarts. Secretly the King of Kings had not been at all displeased by this event. Truth to tell, the facial mutilations of his special darlings slightly increased their attractiveness to his jaded appetite. Still, harem discipline had to be kept, hence Eesafem's confinement, loss of all hairs – most carefully one at a time – and tattooing.

The King of Kings was a thrifty soul and unlike many monarchs expected all his wives and concubines to perform useful work rather than be forever lolling, bathing, gossiping and brawling. So, it being the work she was so uncontestably best trained for and the one most apt to bring profit, Eesafem had been permitted her forge and her metals.

But despite her regular working of these and her consequent production of numerous beauteous and ingenious objects, Eesafem's young mind had been viciously unhinged from her twelve harem moons, seven of those in lonely cell, and from the galling fact that the King of Kings had yet to visit her once for amorous or any other reason, even despite the charming metal gifts she had fashioned for him. Nor had any other man visited her, except eunuchs who lectured her on the erotic arts – while she was securely trussed up, else she would have flown at their pudgy faces like a wildcat, and even at that she spat at them whenever able – and gave her detailed and patronizing advice on her metalworking, which she ignored as haughtily as she did their other fluting words.

Instead, her creativity, now fired by insane jealousies as well as racklike aches for freedom, had taken a new and secret turn.

Scanning the silver mirror, she carefully inspected the four ornaments adorning her slender yet wirey-strong figure. They were two breast cups and two shin-greaves, all chiefly of a delicate silver filigree, which set off nicely her green and blue tattooing.

Once her gaze in the mirror wandered over shoulder, past her naked pate with its finely patterned, fantastical skullcap, to a silver cage in which perched a green and blue parrot with eye as icily malevolent as her own – perpetual reminder of her own imprisonment.

The only oddity about the filigree ornaments was that the breast cups, jutting outward over the nipples, ended in short spikes trained straight forward, while the greaves were topped, just at the knee, with vertical ebony lozenges about as big as a man's thumb.

These bits of decor were not very obtrusive, the spikes being stained a greenish blue, as though to match her tattooing.

So Eesafem gazed at herself with a crafty, approving smile. And so Death gazed at her with a more crafty one, and one far more coldly approving than any eunuch's. And so she vanished in a flash from her cell. And before the blue-green parrot could gin squawk his startlement, Death's eyes and ears were elsewhere also.

Only seven heartbeats left.

Now it may be that in the world of Nehwon there are gods of whom even Death does not know and who from time to time take pleasure in putting obstacles in his path. Or it may be that Chance is quite as great a power as Necessity. At any rate, on this particular morning Fafhrd the Northerner, who customarily snoozed till noon, waked with the first dull silvery shaft of dawn and took up his dear weapon Graywand, naked as he, and blearily made his way from the penthouse pallet out onto the roof, where he gan practice all manner of swordstrokes, stamping his feet in his advances and from time to time uttering battleshouts, unmindful of the weary merchants he waked below him into groaning, cursing, or fright-quivering life. He shivered at first from the chill, fishy dawnmist from the Great Salt Marsh, but soon was sweating from his exercise, while his thrusts and parries, perfunctory to begin with, grew lightning-swift and most authoritative.

Except for Fafhrd, it was a quiet morning in Lankhmar. The bells had not yet begun to toll, nor the deep-throated gongs resound for the passage of the city's gentle overlord, nor the news been bruited about of his seventeen cats netted and hustled to the Great Gaol, there in separate cages to await trial.

It also happened that on this same day the Gray Mouser had waked till dawn, which usually found him an hour or so asleep. He curled in penthouse corner on a pile of pillows behind a low table, chin in hand, a woolly gray robe huddled around him. From time to time he wryly sipped sour wine and thought even sourer thoughts, chiefly about the evil and untrustworthy folk he had known during his mazily crooked lifetime. He ignored Fafhrd's exit and shut his ears to his noisy prancings, but the more he wooed sleep, the further she drew away.

The foamy-mouthed, red-eyed berserk materialized in front of Fafhrd just as the latter assumed the guard of low tierce, swordhand thrust forward, down, and a little to the right, sword slanting upward. He was astounded by the apparition, who, untroubled by sanity's strictures, instantly aimed at the naked Northerner's neck a great swipe with his saw-edged scimitar, which looked rather like a row of short broad-bladed daggers forged side to side and freshly dipped in blood – so that it was pure automatism made Fafhrd shift his guard to a well-braced high carte which deflected the berserk's sword so that it whished over Fafhrd's head with something of the sound of a steel rod very swiftly dragged along a fence of steel pickets, as each razor-edged tooth in turn met the Northerner's blade.

Then reason took a hand in the game and before the berserk could begin a back-handed return swipe, Graywand's tip made a neat, swift counter-clockwise circle and flicked upward at the berserk's sword-wrist, so that his weapon and hand went flying harmlessly off. Far safer, Fafhrd knew, to disarm – or dishand? – such a frenziedly fell opponent before thrusting him through the heart, something Fafhrd now proceeded to do.

Meantime the Mouser was likewise astounded by the abrupt, entirely non sequitur appearance of Eesafem in the center of the penthouse. It was as if one of his more lurid erotic dreams had suddenly come to solid life. He could only goggle as she took a smiling step toward him, knelt a little, carefully faced her front at him, and then drew her upper arms close to her side so that the filigree band which supported her breast cups was compressed. Her almond eyes flashed sinister green.

What saved the Mouser then was simply his lifelong antipathy to having anything sharp pointed at him, be it only the tiniest needle – or the playfully menacing spikes on exquisite silver breast cups doubtless enclosing exquisite breasts. He hurled himself to one side just as with simultaneous *zings* small but powerful springs loosed the envenomed spikes as though they were crossbow quarrels and buried them with twin *zaps* in the wall against which he had but now been resting.

He was scrambling to his feet in an instant and hurled himself at the girl. Now reason, or perhaps intuition, told him the significance of her grasping toward the two black lozenges topping her silver greaves. Tackling her, he managed to get to them before her, withdraw the twin, black-handled stilettos, and toss them beyond Fafhrd's tousled pallet.

Thereafter, twining his legs about hers in such a fashion that she could not knee him in the groin, and holding her snapping, spitting head in the crook of his left arm and by an ear – after futilely grasping for hair – and finally mastering with his right hand the wrists of her two sharp-nailed, flailing ones, he proceeded by gradual and not unnecessarily brutal steps to ravage her. As she ran out of spit, she quieted. Her breasts proved to be very small, but doubly delicious.

Fafhrd, returning mightily puzzled from the roof, goggled in turn at what he saw. How the devil had the Mouser managed to smuggle in that winsome bit? Oh, well, no business of his. With a courteous 'Pardon me. Pray continue,' he shut the door behind him and tackled the problem of disposing of the berserk's corpse. This was readily achieved by heaving him up and dropping him four storeys onto the vast garbage heap that almost blocked Specter Alley. Next Fafhrd picked up the saw-edged scimitar, pried from it the still-clenched hand, and tossed that after. Then frowning down at the encrimsoned weapon, which he intended to keep as a souvenir, he futilely wondered, 'Whose blood?'

(Disposing of Eesafem was hardly a problem capable of any such instant, hand-brushing solution. Suffice it that she gradually lost much of her madness and a little of her hatred of humanity, learned to speak Lankhmarese fluently, and ended up quite happily running a tiny smithy of her own on Copper Court behind Silver Street, where she made beautiful jewelry and sold under the counter such oddments as the finest poison-fanged rings in all Nehwon.)

Meanwhile, Death, for whom time moves in a somewhat different fashion than for men, recognized that there remained to him only two heartbeats in which to fill his quota. The extremely faint thrill of excitement he had felt at seeing his two chosen heroes foil his brilliant improvisations – and at the thought that there *might* be powers in the universe unknown to him and subtler even than his – was replaced by a wry disgust at the realization that there was no longer time enough left for artistry and for indirection and that he must personally take a hand in the business – something he thoroughly detested, since the deus ex machina had always struck him as fiction's – or life's – feeblest device.

Should he slay Fafhrd and the Mouser direct? No, they had somehow outwitted him, which ought in all justice (if there be any such thing) give them immunity for a space. Besides, it would smack now almost of anger, or even resentment. And after his fashion and despite his occasional and almost unavoidable cheating, Death was a sportsman.

With the faintest yet weariest of sighs, Death magicked himself into the royal guardroom in the Great Golden Palace in Horborixen, where with two almost sightlessly swift, mercifully near-instantaneous thrusts, he let the life out of two most noble and blameless heroes whom he had barely glimpsed there earlier, yet ticketed in his boundless and infallible memory, two brothers sworn to perpetual celibacy and also to the rescue of at least one damsel in distress per moon. And so now they were released from this difficult destiny and Death returned to brood sadly on his low throne in his modest castle in the Shadowland and to await his next mission.

The twentieth heartbeat knelled.

II
BEAUTY AND
THE BEASTS

She was undoubtedly the most beautiful girl in Lankhmar, or all Nehwon, or any other world. So Fafhrd, the red-haired Northerner, and the Gray Mouser, that swarthy, cat-faced Southerner, were naturally following her.

Her name, most strangely, was Slenya Akkiba Magus, the most witching brunette in all the worlds, and also, most oddly, the most sorcerous blonde. They knew Slenya Akkiba Magus was her name because someone had called it out as she glided ahead of them up Pinchbeck Alley, which parallels Gold Street, and she hesitated for an instant in that drawing-together fashion one only does when one's name is unexpectedly called out, before gliding on without looking around.

They never saw who called. Perhaps someone on a roof. They looked into Sequin Court as they passed, but it was empty. So was Fools Gold Court.

Slenya was two inches taller than the Gray Mouser and ten shorter than Fafhrd – a nice height for a girl.

'She's mine,' the Gray Mouser whispered with great authority.

'No, she's mine,' Fafhrd murmured back with crushing casualness.

'We *could* split her,' the Mouser hissed judiciously.

There was a zany logic to this suggestion for, quite amazingly, she was completely black on the right side and completely fair on the left side. You could see the dividing line down her back very distinctly. This was because of the extreme thinness of the dress of beige silk she was wearing. Her two colors split exactly at her buttocks.

On the fair side her hair was completely blonde. On the black side it was all brunette.

At this moment an ebony-black warrior appeared from nowhere and attacked Fafhrd with a brass scimitar.

Drawing his sword Graywand in a rush, Fafhrd parried at a square angle. The scimitar shattered, and the brazen fragments flew about. Fafhrd's wrist whipped Graywand in a circle and struck off his foe's head.

Meanwhile the Mouser was suddenly faced by an ivory-white warrior sprung from another nowhere and armed with a steel rapier, silver-plated. The Mouser whisked out Scalpel, laid a bind on the other's blade, and thrust him through the heart.

The two friends congratulated each other.

Then they looked around. Save for the corpses, Pinchbeck Alley was empty.

Slenya Akkiba Magus had disappeared.

The twain pondered this for five heartbeats and two inhalations. Then Fafhrd's frown vanished and his eyes widened.

'Mouser,' he said, 'the girl divided into the two villains! That explains all. They came from the same nowhere.'

'The same somewhere, you mean,' the Mouser quibbled. 'A most exotic mode of reproduction, or fission rather.'

'And one with a sex alternation,' Fafhrd added. 'Perhaps if we examined the corpses—'

They looked down to find Pinchbeck Alley emptier still. The two liches had vanished from the cobbles. Even the chopped-off head was gone from the foot of the wall against which it had rolled.

'An excellent way of disposing of bodies,' Fafhrd said with approval. His ears had caught the tramp and brazen clank of the approaching watch.

'They might have lingered long enough for us to search their pouches and seams for jewels and precious metal,' the Mouser demurred.

'But what was behind it all?' Fafhrd puzzled. 'A black-and-white magician—?'

'It's bootless to make bricks without straw,' said the Mouser, cutting him short. 'Let us hie to the Golden Lamphrey and there drink a health to the girl, who was surely a stunner.'

'Agreed. And we will drink to her appropriately in blackest stout laced with the palest bubbly wine of Ilthmar.'

III
TRAPPED IN THE
SHADOWLAND

Fafhrd and the Gray Mouser were almost dead from thirst. Their horses had died from the same Hell-throated ailment at the last waterhole, which had proved dry. Even the last contents of their waterbags, augmented by water of their own bodies, had not been enough to keep alive the dear dumb equine beasts. As all men know, camels are the only creatures who can carry men for more than a day or two across the almost supernaturally hot arid deserts of the World of Nehwon.

They tramped on southwestward under the blinding sun and over the burning sand. Despite their desperate plight and heat-fevered minds and bodies, they were steering a canny course. Too far south and they would fall into the cruel hands of the emperor of the Eastern Lands, who would find rare delight in torturing them before killing them. Too far east and they would encounter the merciless Mingols of the Steppes and other horrors. West and northwest were those who were pursuing them now. While north and northeast lay the Shadowland, the home of Death himself. So much they well knew of the geography of Nehwon.

Meanwhile, Death grinned faintly in his low castle in the heart of the Shadowland, certain that he had at last got the two elusive heroes in his bony grip. They had years ago had the nerve to enter his domain, visiting their first loves, Ivrian and Vlana, and even stealing from his very castle Death's favorite mask. Now they would pay for their temerity.

Death had the appearance of a tall, handsome young man, though somewhat cadaverous and of opalescent complexion. He was staring now at a large map of the Shadowland and its environs set in a dark wall of his dwelling. On this map Fafhrd and the Mouser were a gleaming speck, like an errant star or fire beetle, south of the Shadowland.

Death writhed his thin, smiling lips and moved his bony fingertips in tiny, cabalistic curves, as he worked a small but difficult magic.

His incantation done, he noted with approval that on the map a southern tongue of the Shadowland was visibly extending itself in pursuit of the dazzling speck that was his victims.

Fafhrd and the Mouser tramped on south, staggering and reeling now, their feet and minds aflame, their faces a-drip with precious sweat. They had been seeking, near the Sea of Monsters and the City of Ghouls, their strayed newest girls, Mouser's Reetha and Fafhrd's Kreeshkra, the latter a Ghoul herself, all her blood and flesh invisible, which made her bonny pink bones stand out the more, while Reetha believed in going naked and shaven from head to toe, a taste which gave the girls a mutual similarity and sympathy.

But the Mouser and Fafhrd had found nothing but a horde of fierce male Ghouls, mounted on equally skeletal horses, who had chased them east and south, either to slay them, or to cause them to die of thirst in the desert or of torture in the dungeons of the King of Kings.

It was high noon and the sun was hottest. Fafhrd's left hand touched in the dry heat a cool fence about two feet high, invisible at first though not for long.

'Escape to damp coolth,' he said in a cracked voice.

They eagerly clambered over the fence and threw themselves down on a blessed thick turf or dark grass two inches high, over which a fine mist was falling. They slept about ten hours.

In his castle Death permitted himself a thin grin, as on his map the south-trending tongue of the Shadowland touched the diamond spark and dimmed it.

Nehwon's greatest star, Astorian, was mounting the eastern sky, precursor of the moon, as the two adventurers awoke, greatly refreshed by their long nap. The mist had almost ceased, but the only star visible was the vast Astorian.

The Mouser sprang up agitatedly in his gray hood, tunic, and ratskin shoes. 'We must escape backward to hot dryth,' he said, 'for this is the Shadowland, Death's homeland.'

'A very comfortable place,' Fafhrd replied, stretching his huge muscles luxuriously on the thick greensward. 'Return to the briny, granular, rasping, fiery land-sea? Not I.'

'But if we stay here,' the Mouser countered, 'we will be will-lessly drawn by devilish and delusive will-o'-the-wisps to the low-walled Castle of Death, whom we defied by stealing his mask and giving its two halves to our wizards Sheelba and Ningauble, an action for which Death is not likely to love us. Besides, here we might well meet our two first girls, Ivrian and Vlana, now concubines of Death, and that would not be a pleasant experience.'

Fafhrd winced, yet stubbornly repeated, 'But it is comfortable here.' Rather self-consciously he writhed his great shoulders and restretched his seven feet on the deliciously damp turf. (The 'seven feet' refers to his height. He was by no means an octopus missing one limb, but a handsome, red-bearded, very tall barbarian.)

The Mouser persisted. 'But what *if* your Vlana should appear, blue-faced and unloving? Or my Ivrian in like state, for that matter?'

That dire image did it. Fafhrd sprang up, grabbing for the low fence. But – low and behold – there was no fence at hand. In all directions stretched out the damp, dark green turf of the Shadowland. While the soft drizzle had thickened again, hiding Astorian. There was no way to tell directions.

The Mouser searched in his ratskin pouch and drew out a blue bone needle. He pricked himself finding it, and cursed. It was wickedly sharp at one end, round and pierced at the other.

'We need a pool or puddle,' he said.

'Where did you get that toy?' Fafhrd quizzed. 'Magic, eh?'

'From Nattick Nimblefingers the Tailor in vasty Lankhmar,' the Mouser responded. 'Magic, nay! Hast heard of compass needles, oh wise one?'

Not far off they found a shallow puddle atop the turf. The Mouser carefully floated his needle on the small mirror of clear, placid water. It spun about slowly and eventually settled itself.

'We go that way,' Fafhrd said, pointing out from the pierced end of the needle. 'South.' For he realized the pricking end must point toward the heart of the Shadowland – Nehwon's Death

Pole, one might call it. For an instant he wondered if there were another such pole at the antipodes – perhaps a Life Pole.

'And we'll still need the needle,' the Mouser added, pricking himself again and cursing as he pouched it, 'for future guidance.'

'Hah! Wah-wah-wah-*wah*!' yelled three berserks, emerging like fleet statues from the mist. They had been long marooned in the skirts of the Shadowland, reluctant either to advance to the Castle of Death or find their Hell or Valhalla, or to seek escape, but always ready for a fight. They rushed at Fafhrd and the Mouser, bareskinned and naked-bladed.

It took the Twain ten heartbeats of clashing sword-fight to kill them, though killing in the domain of Death must be at least a misdemeanor, it occurred to the Mouser – like poaching. Fafhrd got a shallow slash wound across his biceps, which the Mouser carefully bound up.

'Wow!' said Fafhrd. 'Where did the needle point? I've got turned around.'

They located the same or another puddle-mirror, floated the needle, again found South, and then took up their trek.

They twice tried to escape from the Shadowland by changing course, once east, once west. It was no use. Whatever way they went, they found only soft-turfed earth and bemisted sky. So they kept on south, trusting Nattick's needle.

For food they cut out black lambs from the black flocks they encountered, slew, bled, skinned, dressed, and roasted the tender meat over fires from wood of the squat black trees and bushes here and there. The young flesh was succulent. They drank dew.

Death in his low-walled keep continued to grin from time to time at his map, as the dark tongue of his territory kept magically extending southwest, the dimmed spark of his doomed victims in its margin.

He noted that the Ghoulish cavalry originally pursuing the Twain had halted at the boundary of his marchland.

But now there was the faintest trace of anxiety in Death's smile. And now and again a tiny vertical frown creased his opalescent, unwrinkled forehead, as he exerted his faculties to keep his geographical sorcery going.

The black tongue kept on down the map, past Sarheenmar

and thievish Ilthmar to the Sinking Land. Both cities on the shore of the Inner Sea were scared unto death by the dark invasion of damp turf and misty sky, and they thanked their degenerate gods that it narrowly bypassed them.

And now the black tongue crossed the Sinking Lane, moving due west. The little frown in Death's forehead had become quite deep. At the Swamp Gate of Lankhmar the Mouser and Fafhrd found their magical mentors waiting, Sheelba of the Eyeless Face and Ningauble of the Seven Eyes.

'What have you been up to?' Sheelba sternly asked the Mouser.

'And what have *you* been doing?' Ningauble demanded of Fafhrd.

The Mouser and Fafhrd were still in the Shadowland, and the two wizards outside it, with the boundary midway between. So their conversation was like that of two pairs of people on opposite sides of a narrow street, on the one side of which it is raining cats and dogs, the other side dry and sunny, though in this instance stinking with the smog of Lankhmar.

'Seeking Reetha,' the Mouser replied, honestly for once.

'Seeking Kreeshkra,' Fafhrd said boldly, 'but a mounted Ghoul troop harried us back.'

From his hood Ningauble writhed out six of his seven eyes and regarded Fafhrd searchingly. He said severely, 'Kreeshkra, tired of your untameable waywardness, has gone back to the Ghouls for good, taking Reetha with her. I would advise you instead to seek Frix,' naming a remarkable female who had played no small part in the adventure of the rat-hordes, the same affair in which Kreeshkra the Ghoul girl had been involved.

'Frix is a brave, handsome, remarkably cool woman,' Fafhrd temporized, 'but how to reach her? She's in another world, a world of air.'

'While I counsel that *you* seek Hisvet,' Sheelba of the Eyeless Face told the Mouser grimly. The unfeatured blackness in *his* hood grew yet blacker (with concentration) if that were possible. He was referring to yet another female involved in the rat-adventure, in which Reetha also had been a leading character.

'A great idea, Father,' responded the Mouser, who made no bones about preferring Hisvet to all other girls, particularly since he had never once enjoyed her favours, though on the verge of doing so several times. 'But she is likely deep in the earth and in her rat-size persona. How would I do it? How, how?'

If Sheel and Ning could have smiled, they would have.

However, Sheelba said only, 'It is bothersome to see you both bemisted, like heroes in smoke.'

He and Ning, without conference, collaborated in working a small but very difficult magic. After resisting most tenaciously, the Shadowland and its drizzle retreated east, leaving the Twain in the same sunshine as their mentors. Though two invisible patches of dark mist remained, entering into the flesh of the Mouser and Fafhrd and closing forever around their hearts.

Far eastaways, Death permitted himself a small curse which would have scandalized the high gods, had they heard it. He looked daggers at his map and its shortening black tongue. For Death, he was in a most bitter temper. Foiled again!

Ning and Sheel worked another diminutive wizardry.

Without warning, Fafhrd shot upwards in the air, growing tinier and tinier, until at last he was lost to sight.

Without moving from where he stood, the Mouser also grew tiny, until he was somewhat less than a foot high, of a size to cope with Hisvet, in or out of bed. He dove into the nearest rathole.

Neither feat was as remarkable as it sounds, since Nehwon is only a bubble rising through the waters of infinity.

The two heroes each spent a delightful weekend with his lady of the week.

'I don't know why I do things like this,' Hisvet said, lisping faintly and touching the Mouser intimately as they lay side by side supine on silken sheets. 'It must be because I loathe you.'

'A pleasant and even worthy encounter,' Frix confessed to Fafhrd in similar situation. 'It is my hang-up to enjoy playing, now and then, with the lower animals. Which some would say is a weakness in a queen of the air.'

Their weekend done, Fafhrd and the Mouser were automatically magicked back to Lankhmar, encountering one another in Cheap Street near Nattick Nimblefinger's narrow and dirty-looking dwelling. The Mouser was his right size again.

'You looked sunburned,' he observed to his comrade.

'Space-burned, it is,' Fafhrd corrected. 'Frix lives in a remarkably distant land. But you, old friend, look paler than your wont.'

'Shows what three days underground will do to a man's complexion,' the Mouser responded. 'Come, let's have a drink at the Silver Eel.'

Ningauble in his cave near Ilthmar and Sheelba in his mobile hut in the Great Salt Marsh each smiled, though lacking the equipment for that facial expression. They knew they had laid one more obligation on their protégés.

IV
THE BAIT

Fafhrd the Northerner was dreaming of a great mound of gold.

The Gray Mouser the Southerner, ever cleverer in his forever competitive fashion, was dreaming of a heap of diamonds. He hadn't tossed out all of the yellowish ones yet, but he guessed that already his glistening pile must be worth more than Fafhrd's glowing one.

How he knew in his dream what Fafhrd was dreaming was a mystery to all beings in Nehwon, except perhaps Sheelba of the Eyeless Face and Ningauble of the Seven Eyes, respectively Mouser's and Fafhrd's sorcerer-mentors. Maybe, a vast, black basement mind shared by the two was involved.

Simultaneously they awoke, Fafhrd a shade more slowly, and sat up in bed.

Standing midway between the feet of their cots was an object that fixed their attention. It weighed about eighty pounds, was about four feet eight inches tall, had long straight black hair pendant from head, had ivory-white skin, and was as exquisitely formed as a single chesspiece of the King of Kings carved from a single moonstone. It looked thirteen, but the lips smiled a cool self-infatuated seventeen, while the gleaming deep eye-pools were first blue melt of the Ice Age. Naturally, she was naked.

'She's mine!' the Gray Mouser said, always quick from the scabbard.

'No, she's mine!' Fafhrd said almost simultaneously, but conceding by that initial 'No' that the Mouser had been first, or at least he had expected the Mouser to be first.

'I belong to myself and to no one else, save two or three virile demidevils,' the small naked girl said, though giving them each in turn a most nymphish lascivious look.

'I'll fight you for her,' the Mouser proposed.

'And I you,' Fafhrd confirmed, slowly drawing Graywand from its sheath beside his cot.

The Mouser likewise slipped Scalpel from its ratskin container.

The two heroes rose from their cots.

At this moment, two personages appeared a little behind the girl – from thin air, to all appearances. Both were at least nine feet tall. They had to bend, not to bump the ceiling. Cobwebs tickled their pointed ears. The one on the Mouser's side was black as wrought iron. He swiftly drew a sword that looked forged from the same material.

At the same time, the other newcomer – bone-white, this one – produced a silver-seeming sword, likely steel plated with tin.

The nine-footer opposing the Mouser aimed a skull-splitting blow at the top of his head. The Mouser parried in prime and his opponent's weapon shrieked off to the left. Whereupon, smartly swinging his rapier widdershins, the Mouser slashed off the black fiend's head, which struck the floor with a horrid clank.

The white afreet opposing Fafhrd trusted to a downward thrust. But the Northerner, catching his blade in a counter-clockwise bind, thrust him through, the silvery sword missing Fafhrd's right temple by the thinness of a hair.

With a petulant stamp of her naked heel, the nymphet vanished into thin air, or perhaps Limbo.

The Mouser made to wipe off his blade on the cotclothes, but discovered there was no need. He shrugged. 'What a misfortune for you, comrade,' he said in a voice of mocking woe. 'Now you will not be able to enjoy the delicious chit as she disports herself on your heap of gold.'

Fafhrd moved to cleanse Graywand on *his* sheets, only to note that it too was altogether unbloodied. He frowned. 'Too bad for you, best of friends,' he sympathized. 'Now you won't be able to possess her as she writhes with girlish abandon on your couch of diamonds, their glitter striking opalescent tones from her pale flesh.'

'Mauger that effeminate artistic garbage, how did you know that I was dreaming of diamonds?' the Mouser demanded.

'How did I?' Fafhrd asked himself wonderingly. At last he

begged the question with, 'The same way, I suppose, that you knew I was dreaming of gold.'

The two excessively long corpses chose that moment to vanish, and the severed head with them.

Fafhrd said sagely, 'Mouser, I begin to believe that supernatural forces were involved in this morning's haps.'

'Or else hallucinations, oh great philosopher,' the Mouser countered somewhat peevishly.

'Not so,' Fafhrd corrected, 'for see, they've left their weapons behind.'

'True enough,' the Mouser conceded, rapaciously eyeing the wrought-iron and tin-plated blades on the floor. 'Those will fetch a fancy price on Curio Court.'

The Great Gong of Lankhmar, sounding distantly through the walls, boomed out the twelve funereal strokes of noon, when burial parties plunge spade into earth.

'An after-omen,' Fafhrd pronounced. 'Now we know the source of the supernal force. The Shadowland, terminus of all funerals.'

'Yes,' the Mouser agreed. 'Prince Death, that cager boy, has had another go at us.'

Fafhrd splashed cool water onto his face from a great bowl set against the wall. 'Ah well,' he spoke through the splashes, 'Twas a pretty bait at least. Truly, there's nothing like a nubile girl, enjoyed or merely glimpsed naked, to give one an appetite for breakfast.'

'Indeed, yes,' the Mouser replied, as he tightly shut his eyes and briskly rubbed his face with a palm full of white brandy. 'She was just the sort of immature dish to kindle your satyrish taste for maids newly budded.'

In the silence that came as the splashing stopped, Fafhrd inquired innocently, '*Whose* satyrish taste?'

V
UNDER THE THUMBS
OF THE GODS

Drinking strong drink one night at the Silver Eel, the Gray Mouser and Fafhrd became complacently, even luxuriously, nostalgic about their past loves and amorous exploits. They even boasted a little to each other about their most recent erotic solacings (although it is always very unwise to boast of such matters, especially out loud; one never knows who may be listening).

'Despite her vast talent for evil,' the Mouser said, 'Hisvet remains always a child. Why should that surprise me? – evil comes naturally to children, it is a game to them, they feel no shame. Her breasts are no bigger than walnuts, or limes, or at most small tangerines topped by hazelnuts – all eight of them.'

Fafhrd said, 'Frix is the very soul of the dramatic. You should have seen her poised on the battlement later that night, her eyes raptly agleam, seeking the stars. Naked save for some ornaments of copper fresh as rosy dawn. She looked as if she were about to fly – which she can do, as you know.'

In the Land of the Gods, in short in Godsland and near Nehwon's Life Pole there, which lies in the southern hemisphere at the antipodes from the Shadowland (abode of Death), three gods sitting together cross-legged in a circle picked out Fafhrd's and the Mouser's voices from the general mutter of their worshipers, both loyal and lapsed, which resounds eternally in any god's ear, as if he held a seashell to it.

One of the three gods was Issek, whom Fafhrd had once faithfully served as acolyte for three months. Issek had the appearance of a delicate youth with wrists and ankles broken, or rather permanently bent at right angles. During his Passion he had been severely racked. Another was Kos, whom Fafhrd had revered during his childhood in the Cold Waste, rather a squat, brawny god bundled up in furs, with a grim, not to say surly, heavily bearded visage.

The third god was Mog, who resembled a four-limbed spider with a quite handsome, though not entirely human face. Once the girl Ivrian, the Mouser's first love, had taken a fancy to a jet statuette of Mog he had stolen for her and decided, perhaps roguishly, that Mog and the Mouser looked alike.

Now the Gray Mouser is generally believed to be and has always been complete atheist, but this is not true. Partly to humor Ivrian, whom he spoiled fantastically, but partly because it tickled his vanity that a god should choose to look like him, he made a game for several weeks of firmly believing in Mog.

So the Mouser and Fafhrd were clearly worshipers, though lapsed, and the three gods singled out their voices because of that and because they were the most noteworthy worshipers these three gods had ever had and because they were boasting. For the gods have very sharp ears for boasts, or for declarations of happiness and self-satisfaction, or for assertions of a firm intention to do this or that, or for statements that this or that must surely happen, or any other words hinting that a man is in the slightest control of his own destiny. And the gods are jealous, easily angered, perverse, and swift to thwart.

'It's them, all right – the haughty bastards!' Kos grunted, sweating under his furs – for Godsland is paradisial.

'They haven't called on me for years – the ingrates!' Issek said with a toss of his delicate chin. 'We'd be dead for all they care, except we've our other worshipers. But they don't know that – they're heartless.'

'They have not even taken our names in vain,' said Mog. 'I believe, gentlemen, it is time they suffered the divine displeasure. Agreed?'

In the meanwhile, by speaking privily of Frix and Hisvet, the Mouser and Fafhrd had aroused certain immediate desires in themselves without seriously disturbing their mood of complacent nostalgia.

'What say you, Mouser,' Fafhrd mused lazily, 'should we now seek excitement? The night is young.'

His comrade replied grandly, 'We have but to stir a little, to signify our interest, and excitement will seek us. We've loved and been forever adored by so many girls that we're bound to run into a pair of 'em. Or even two pair. They'll catch our present thoughts on the wing and come running. We will hunt girls – ourselves the bait!'

'So let's be on our way,' said Fafhrd, drinking up and rising with a lurch.

'Ach, the lewd dogs!' Kos growled, shaking sweat from his brow, for Godsland is balmy (and quite crowded). 'But how to punish 'em?'

Mog said, smiling lopsidedly because of his partially arachnid jaw structure, 'They seem to have chosen their punishment.'

'The torture of hope!' Issek chimed eagerly, catching on. 'We grant them their wishes—'

'—and then leave the rest to the girls,' Mog finished.

'You can't trust women,' Kos asserted darkly.

'On the contrary, my dear fellow,' Mog said, 'when a god's in good form, he can safely trust his worshipers, female and male alike, to do all the work. And now, gentlemen, on with our thinking caps!'

Kos scratched his thickly matted head vigorously, dislodging a louse or two.

Whimsically, and perhaps to put a few obstacles between themselves and the girls presumably now rushing toward them, Fafhrd and the Gray Mouser chose to leave the Silver Eel by its kitchen door, something they'd never done once before in all their years of patronage.

The door was low and heavily bolted, and when those were shot still wouldn't budge. And the new cook, who was deaf and dumb, left off his stuffing of a calf's stomach and came over to make gobbling noises and flap his arms in gestures of protest or warning. But the Mouser pressed two bronze agols into his greasy palm while Fafhrd kicked the door open. They prepared to stride out into the dismal lot covered by the eroded ashes of the tenement where the Mouser had dwelt with Ivrian (and she and Fafhrd's equally dear Vlana had burned) and also the ashes of the wooden garden house of mad Duke Danius, which they'd once stolen and occupied for a space – the dismal and ill-omened lot which they'd never heard of anyone building on since.

But when they'd ducked their heads and gone through the doorway, they discovered that construction of a sort *had* been going on (or else that they'd always seriously underestimated the depth of the Silver Eel) for instead of on empty ground open to sky, they found themselves in a corridor lit by torches held in brazen hands along each wall.

Undaunted, they strode forward past two closed doors.

'That's Lankhmar City for you,' the Mouser observed. 'You turn your back and they've put up a new secret temple.'

'Good ventilation, though,' Fafhrd commented on the absence of smoke.

They followed the corridor around a sharp turn . . . and stopped dead. The split-level chamber facing them had surprising features. The sunken half was close-ceilinged and otherwise gave the impression of being far underground, as if its floor were not eight finger-joints deeper than the raised section but eighty yards. Its furniture was a bed with a coverlet of violet silk. A thick yellow silk cord hung through a hole in the low ceiling.

The chamber's raised half seemed the balcony or battlement of a tower thrust high above Lankhmar's smog, for stars were visible in the black upper background and ceiling.

On the bed, silver-blonde head to its foot, slim Hisvet lay prone but upthrust on her straightened arms. Her robe of fine silk, yellow as desert sunlight, was outdented by her pair of small high breasts, but depended freely from the nipples of those, leaving unanswered the question of whether there were three more pairs arranged symmetrically below.

While against starry night (or its counterfeit), her dark hair braided with scrubbed copper wire, Frix stood magnificently tall and light-footed (though motionless) in her silken robe violet as a desert's twilight before dawn.

Fafhrd was about to say, 'You know, we were just talking about you,' and the Mouser was about to tread on his instep for being so guileless, when Hisvet cried to the latter, 'You again! – intemperate dirksman. I told you never even to *think* of another rendezvous with me for two years' space.'

Frix said to Fafhrd, 'Beast! I told you I played with a member of the lower orders only on *rare* occasions.'

Hisvet tugged sharply on the silken cord. A heavy door dropped down in the men's faces from above and struck its sill with a great conclusive jar.

Fafhrd lifted a finger to his nose, explaining ruefully, 'I thought the door had taken off the tip. Not exactly a loving reception.'

The Mouser said bravely, 'I'm glad they turned us off. Truly, it would have been too soon, and so a bore. On with our girl hunt!'

They returned past the mute flames held in bronze hands to the second of the two closed doors. It opened at a touch to reveal another dual chamber and in it their loves Reetha and Kreeshkra, whom only short months ago they'd been seeking near the Sea of Monsters, until they were trapped in the Shadowland and barely escaped back to Lankhmar. To the left, in muted sunlight on a couch of exquisitely smoothed dark wood, Reetha reclined quite naked. Indeed, extremely naked, for as the Mouser noted, she'd kept up her habit, inculcated when she'd been slave of a finicky overlord, of regularly shaving all of herself, even her eyebrows. Her totally bare head, held at a pert angle, was perfectly shaped and the Mouser felt a surge of sweet desire. She was cuddling to her tender bosom a very emaciated-seeming but tranquil animal, which the Mouser suddenly realized was a cat, hairless save for its score of whiskers bristling from its mask.

To the right, in dark night a-dance with the light of camp-fire and on a smooth shale shore of what Fafhrd recognized to be, by the large white-bearded serpents sporting in it, the Sea of Monsters, sat his beloved Kreeshkra, more naked even than Reetha. She might have been a disquieting sight to some (naught but an aristocratically handsome skeleton), except that the flames near which she sat struck dark blue gleams from the sweetly curved surfaces of her transparent flesh casing her distinguished bones.

'Mouser, why have you come?' Reetha cried out somewhat reproachfully. 'I'm happy here in Eevamarensee, where all men are as hairless by nature (our household animals too) as I am by my daily industry. I love you dearly still, but we can't live together and must not meet again. This is my proper place.'

Likewise, bold Kreeshkra challenged Fafhrd with, 'Mud Man, avaunt! I loved you once. Now I'm a Ghoul again. Perhaps in future time . . . But now, begone!'

It was well neither Fafhrd nor Mouser had stepped across the threshold, for at those words this door slammed in their faces too, and this time stuck fast. Fafhrd forbore to kick it.

'You know, Mouser,' he said thoughtfully, 'We've been enamored of some strange ones in our time. But always most intensely interesting,' he hastened to add.

'Come on, come on,' the Mouser enjoined gruffly. 'There are other fish in the sea.'

The remaining door opened easily too, though Fafhrd pushed it somewhat gingerly. Nothing startling, however, came into view this time, only a long dark room, empty of persons and furniture, with a second door at the other end. Its only novel feature was that the right-hand wall glowed green. They walked in with returning confidence. After a few steps they became aware that the glowing wall was thick crystal enclosing pale green, faintly clouded water. As they watched, continuing to stroll, there swam into view with lazy undulations two beautiful mermaids, the one with long golden hair trailing behind her and a sheathlike garb of wide-meshed golden fishnet, the other with short dark hair parted by a ridgy and serrated silver crest. They came close enough for one to see the slowly pulsing gills scoring their necks where they merged into their sloping, faintly scaled shoulders, and farther down their bodies those discrete organs which contradict the contention, subject of many a crude jest, that a man is unable fully to enjoy the unbifurcated woman (though any pair of snakes in love tell us otherwise). They swam closer still, their dreamy eyes now wide and peering, and the Mouser and Fafhrd recognized the two queens of the sea they had embraced some years past while deep diving from their sloop *Black Treasurer*.

What the wide-peering fishy eyes saw evidently did not please the mermaids, for they made faces and with powerful flirts of their long finny tails retreated away from the crystal wall through the greenish water, whose cloudiness was increased by their rapid movements, until they could no longer be seen.

Turning to the Mouser, Fafhrd inquired, eyebrows alift, 'You mentioned other fish in the sea?'

With a quick frown the Mouser strode on. Trailing him, Fafhrd mused puzzledly, 'You said this might be a secret temple, friend. But if so, where are its porters, priests, and patrons other than ourselves?'

'More like a museum – scenes of distant life. And a piscesium, or piscatorium,' his comrade answered curtly over shoulder.

'I've been thinking,' Fafhrd continued, quickening his steps, 'there's too much space here we've been walking through for the lot behind the Silver Eel to hold. What *has* been builded here? – or there?'

The Mouser went through the far door. Fafhrd was close behind.

In Godsland Kos snarled, 'The rogues are taking it too easily. Oh, for a thunderbolt!'

Mog told him rapidly, 'Never you fear, my friend, we have them on the run. They're only putting up appearances. We'll wear them down by slow degrees until they pray to us for mercy, groveling on their knees. That way our pleasure's greater.'

'Quieter, you two,' Issek shrilled, waving his bent wrists, 'I'm getting another girl pair!'

It was clear from these and other quick gesticulations and injunctions – and from their rapt yet tense expressions – that the three gods in close inward-facing circle were busy with something interesting. From all around other divinities large and small, baroque and classical, noisome and beautiful, came drifting up to comment and observe. Godsland *is* overcrowded, a veritable slum, all because of man's perverse thirst for variety. There are rumors among the packed gods there of other and (perish the thought!) superior gods, perhaps invisible, who enjoy roomier quarters on another and (oh woe!) higher level and who (abysmal deviltry!) even hear thoughts, but nothing certain.

Issek cried out in ecstasy, 'There, there, the stage is set! Now to search out the next teasing pair. Kos and Mog, help me. Do your rightful share.'

*

The Gray Mouser and Fafhrd felt they'd been transported to the mysterious realm of Quarmall, where they'd had one of the most fantastic adventures. For the next chamber seemed a cave in solid rock, given room-shape by laborious chipping. And behind a table piled with parchments and scrolls, inkwells and quills, sat the two saucy, seductive slavegirls they'd rescued from the cavern-world's monotonies and tortures: slender Ivivis, supple as a snake, and pleasantly plump Friska, light of foot. The two men felt relief and joy that they'd come home to the familiar and beloved.

Then they saw the room had windows, with sunlight suddenly striking in (as if a cloud had lifted), and was not solid rock but morticed stone, and that the girls wore not the scanty garb of slaves but rich and sober robes, while their faces were grave and self-reliant.

Ivivis looked up at the Mouser with inquiry but instant disapproval. 'What dost here, figment of my servile past? Tis true, you rescued me from Quarmall foul. For which I paid you with my body's love. Which ended at Tovilysis when we split. We're quits, dear Mouser, yes, by Mog, we are!' (She wondered why she used that particular oath.)

Likewise Friska looked at Fafhrd and said, 'That goes for you too, bold barbarian. You also killed my lover Hovis, you'll recall – as Mouser did Ivivis' Klevis. We are no longer simple-minded slaves, playthings of men, but subtile secretary and present treasurer of the Guild of Free Women at Tovilysis. We'll never love again unless I choose – which I do not today! And so, by Kos and Issek, now begone!' (She wondered likewise why she invoked those particular deities, for whom she had no respect whatever.)

These rebuffs hurt the two heroes sorely, so that they had not the spirit to respond with denials, jests, or patient gallantries. Their tongues clove to their hard palates, their hearts and privates grew chilly, they almost cringed – and they rather swiftly stole from that chamber by the open door ahead . . . into a large room shaped of bluish ice, or rock of the same hue and translucence and as cold, so that the flames dancing in the large fireplace were welcome. Before this was spread a rug looking wondrously thick and soft, about which were set scattered jars of unguents, small bottles of perfume (which made themselves known by their ranging scents), and other cosmetic containers and tools. Furthermore, the invitingly textured rug showed indentations as if made by two recumbent human forms, while about a cubit above it floated two living masks as thin as silk or paper or more thin, holding the form of wickedly pretty, pert girl faces, the one rosy mauvette, the other turquoise green.

Others would have deemed it a prodigy, but the Mouser and Fafhrd at once recognized Keyaira and Hirriwi, the invisible frost princesses with whom they'd once been separately paired for one long, long night in Stardock, tallest of Nehwon's northron peaks, and knew that the two gaysome girls were reclining unclad in front of the fire and had been playfully anointing each other's faces with pigmented salves.

Then the turquoise mask leapt up betwixt Fafhrd and the fire, so that dancing orange flames only shone through its staring eye holes and between its now cruel and amused lips as it spoke to him, saying, 'In what frowsty bed are you now dead asleep, gross one-time lover, that your squeaking soul can be blown halfway across the world to gape at me? Some day again climb Stardock and in your solid form importune me. I might hark. But now, phantom, depart!'

The mallow mask likewise spoke scornfully to the Mouser, saying in tones as stinging and impelling as the flames seen through its facial orifices, 'And you remove too, wraith most pitiful. By Khahkht of the Black Ice and Gara of the Blue – and e'en Kos of the Green – I enjoin it! Blow winds! and out lights all!'

Fafhrd and the Mouser were hurt even more sorely by these new rebuffs. Their very souls were shriveled by the feeling that they were indeed the phantoms, and the speaking masks the solid reality. Nevertheless, they might have summoned the courage to attempt to answer the challenge (though 'tis doubtful), except that at Keyaira's last commands they were plunged into darkness absolute and manhandled by great winds and then dumped in a lighted area. A wind-slammed door crashed shut behind them.

They saw with considerable relief that they were not

confronting yet another pair of girls (*that* would have been unendurable) but were in another stretch of corridor lit by clear-flaming torches held in brazen wall brackets in the form of gripping bird-talons, coiling squid-tentacles, and pinching crabclaws. Grateful for the respite, they took deep breaths.

Then Fafhrd frowned deeply and said, 'Mark me, Mouser, there's magic somewhere in all this. Or else the hand of a god.'

The Mouser commented bitterly, 'If it's a god, he's a thumb-fingered one, the way he sets us up to be turned down.'

Fafhrd's thoughts took a new tack, as shown by the changing furrows in his forehead. 'Mouser, I never squeaked,' he protested. 'Hirriwi said I squeaked.'

'Manner of speaking only, I suppose,' his comrade consoled. 'But gods! what misery I felt myself, as if I were no longer man at all, and *this* no more than broomstick.' He indicated his sword Scalpel at his side and gazed with a shake of his head at Fafhrd's scabbarded Graywand.

'Perchance we dream—' Fafhrd began doubtfully.

'Well, if we're dreaming, let's get on with it,' the Mouser said and, clapping his friend around the shoulders, started them down the corridor. Yet despite these cheerful words and actions, both men felt they were getting more and more into the toils of nightmare, drawing them on will-lessly.

They rounded a turn. For some yards the right-hand wall became a row of slender dark pillars, irregularly spaced, and between them they could see more random dusky slim shafts and at middle distance a long altar on which light showered softly down, revealing a tall, naked woman stretched on it, and by her a priestess in purple robes with dagger bared in one hand and large silver chalice in the other, who was intoning a litany.

Fafhrd whispered, 'Mouser! the sacrifice is the courtesan Lessnya, with whom I had some dealings when I was acolyte of Issek, years ago.'

'While the other is Ilala, priestess of the like-named goddess, with whom I had some commerce when I was lieutenant to Pulg the extortioner,' the Mouser whispered back.

Fafhrd protested, 'But we *can't* have already come all the way to the temple of Ilala, though this looks like it. It's halfway across Lankhmar from the Eel,' while the Mouser recalled tales he'd heard of secret passages in Lankhmar that connected points by distances shorter than the shortest distance between.

Ilala turned toward them in her purple robes and said with eyebrows raised, 'Quiet back there! You are committing sacrilege, trespassing on most holy ritual of the great goddess of all shes. Impious intruders, depart!' While Lessnya lifted on an elbow and looked at them haughtily. Then she lay back again and regarded the ceiling while Ilala plunged her dagger deep into her chalice and then with it flicked sprinkles of wine (or whatever other fluid the chalice held) on Lessnya's naked shape, wielding the blade as if it were as aspergillum. She aspersed her thrice – on bosom, loins, and knees – and then resumed her muttered litany, while Lessnya echoed her (or else snored) and the Mouser and Fafhrd stole on along the torchlit corridor.

But they had little time to ponder on the strange geometries and stranger religiosities of their nightmare progress, for now the left-hand wall gave way for a space to a fabulously decorated, large, dim chamber, which they recognized as the official residence room of the Grandmaster of the Thieves' Guild in Thieves' House, half Lankhmar City back again from Ilala's fane. The foreground was filled with figures kneeling away from them in devout supplication toward a thick-topped ebony table, behind which there stood queenly tall a handsome red-haired woman dressed in jewels and behind her a trim second female in maid's black tunic collared and cuffed with white.

''Tis Ivlis in her beauty from the past, for whom I stole Ohmphal's erubescent fingertips,' the Mouser whispered in stupefaction. 'And now she's got herself a peck more gems.'

'And that is Freg, her maid, looking no older,' Fafhrd whispered back hoarsely in dream-drugged wonderment.

'But what's she doing here in Thieves' House?' the Mouser pressed, his whisper feverish, 'where women are forbidden and contemned. As if *she* were grandmaster of the Guild . . . grandmistress . . . goddess . . . worshiped . . . Is Thieves' Guild upside down? . . . all Nehwon turvy-topsy . . .?'

Ivlis looked up at them across the heads of her kneeling followers. Her green eyes narrowed. She casually lifted her fingers to her lips, then flicked them sideways twice, indicating

267

to the Mouser that he should silently keep going in that direction and not return.

With a slow unloving smile, Freg made exactly the same
gesture to Fafhrd, but even more idly seeming, as if humming a
chorus. The two men obeyed, but their gazes trailing behind
them, so that it was with complete surprise, almost with starts of
fear, that they found they had walked blindly into a room of rare
woods embellished with intricate carvings, with a door before
them and doors to either side, and in the one of the latter nearest
the Mouser a freshly nubile girl with wicked eyes, in a green
robe of shaggy toweling cloth, her black hair moist, and in the
one nearest Fafhrd two slim blondes a-smile with dubious
merriment and wearing loosely the black hoods and robes of
nuns of Lankhmar. In nightmare's fullest grip they realized that
this was the very same garden house of Duke Danius, haunted
by their earliest deepest loves, impiously reconstituted from the
ashes to which the sorcerer Sheelba had burned it and profanely
refurbished with all the trinkets wizard Ningauble had magicked from it and scattered to the four winds; and that these
three nightfillies were Ivmiss Ovartamortes, niece of Karstak
like-named, Lankhmar's then overlord, and Fralek and Fro,
mirror-twin daughters of the death-crazed duke, the three she-
colts of the dark to whom they'd madly turned after losing even
the ghosts of their true loves in Shadowland. Fafhrd was wildly
thinking in unvoiced sound, 'Fafhrd and Fro, and Freg, Friska
and Frix – what is this Fr'-charm on me?' while through the
Mouser's mind was skipping likewise, 'Ivlis, Ivmiss, Ivivis (*two*
Iv's – and there's e'en an Iv in Hisvet) – who are these girl-lets of
the Iv . . . ?'

(Near the Life Pole, the gods Mog, Issek, and Kos were
working at the top of their bent, crying out to each other new
girl-discoveries with which to torment their lapsed worshipers. The crowd of spectator gods around them was now
large.)

And then the Mouser bethought him with a shiver that he had
not listed amongst his girl-lings of the Iv the archgirl of them
all, fair Ivrian, forever lost in Death's demesne. And Fafhrd
likewise shook. And the nightfillies flanking them pouted and
made moues at them, and they were fairly catapulted into the

midst of a pavilion of wine-dark silk, beyond whose unstirring folds showed the flat black horizons of the Shadowland.

Beauteous, slate-visaged Vlana spat full in Fafhrd's face, saying, 'I told you I'd do that if you came back,' but fair Ivrian only eyed the Mouser with never a sign or word.

And then they were back in the betorched corridor, more hurried along it than hurrying, and the Mouser envied Fafhrd death's spittle inching down his cheek. And girls were flashing by like ghosts, unheedingly – Mara of Fafhrd's youth, Atya who worshiped Tyaa, bovine-eyed Hrenlet, Ahura of Seleucia, and many many more – until they were feeling the utter despair that comes with being rejected not by one or a few loves, but by all. The unfairness of it alone was enough to make a man die.

Then in the rush one scene lingered awhile: Alyx the Picklock garbed in the scarlet robes and golden tiara a-swarm with rubies of the archpriest of an eastern faith, and kneeling before her costumed as clerk Lilyblack, the Mouser's girlish leman from his criminous days, intoning, 'Papa, the heathen rage, the civilized decay,' and the transvestite archpriestess pronouncing, 'All men are enemies . . .'

Almost Fafhrd and the Mouser dropped to their knees and prayed to whatever gods may be for surcease from their torment. But somehow they didn't, and of a sudden they found themselves on Cheap Street near where it crosses Crafts and turning in at a drab doorway after two females, whose backs were teasingly familiar, and following them up a narrow flight of stairs that stretched up so far in one flight that its crazy warpage was magnified.

In Godsland Mog threw himself back, blowing out his breath and saying, 'There! that gets them all,' while Issek likewise stretched himself out (so far as his permanently bent ankles and wrists would permit), observing, 'Lord, people don't appreciate how we gods work, what toil in sparrow-watching!' and the spectator gods began to disperse.

But Kos, still frowningly immersed in his task to such a degree that he wasn't aware of the pain in his short burly thighs from sitting cross-legged so long, cried out, 'Hold on! here's another pair: to wit, one Nemia of the Dusk, one Eyes of Ogo, women of lax morals and, to boot, receivers of stolen property – oh, that's vile!'

Issek laughed wearily and said, 'Quit now, dear Kos. I crossed those two off at the very start. They're our men's dearest enemies, swindled them out of a precious loot of jewels, as almost any god around could tell you. Sooner than seek them out (to be rebuffed in any case, of course) our boys would rot in hell,' while Mog yawned and added, 'Don't you ever know, dear Kos, when the game's done?'

So the befurred short god shrugged and gave over, cursing as he tried to straighten his legs.

Meanwhile, the Eyes of Ogo and Nemia of the Dusk reached the summit of the endless stairs and tiredly entered their pad, eyeing it with disfavor. (It *was* an impoverished, dingy, even noisome place – the two best thieves in Lankhmar had fallen on hard times, as even the best of thieves and receivers will in the course of long careers.)

Nemia turned round and said, 'Look what the cat dragged in.' Hardship had drastically straightened her lush curves. Her comrade Ogo-Eyes still looked somewhat like a child, but a very old and ill-used one. 'Wow,' she said wearily, 'you two look miserable, as if you'd just 'scaped death and sorry you had. Do yourselves a favor – fall down the stairs, breaking your necks.'

When Fafhrd and the Mouser didn't move, or change their woebegone expressions, she laughed shortly, dropped into a broken-seated chair, poked out a leg at the Mouser, and said, 'Well, if you're not leaving, make yourself useful. Remove my sandals, wash my feet,' while Nemia sat down before a rickety dressing table and, while surveying herself in the broken mirror, held out a broken-toothed instrument in Fafhrd's direction saying, 'Comb my hair, barbarian. Watch out for snarls and knots.'

Fafhrd and the Mouser (the latter preparing and fetching warm water) began solemn-faced to do those very things most carefully.

After quite a long time (and several other menial services rendered, or servile penances done) the two women could no longer keep from smiling. Misery, *after* it's comforted, loves company. 'That's enough for now,' Eyes told the Mouser.

'Come, make yourself comfortable.' Nemia spoke likewise to Fafhrd, adding, 'Later you men can make the dinner and go out for wine.'

After a while the Mouser said, 'By Mog, this is more like it.' Fafhrd agreed. 'By Issek, yes. Kos damn all spooked adventures.'

The three gods, hearing their names were taken in vain as they rested in paradise from their toils, were content.

VI
TRAPPED IN THE
SEA OF STARS

Fafhrd the educated barbarian and his constant comrade the Gray (Grey?) Mouser, city-born but wizard-tutored in the wilds, had in their leopard-boat *Black Racer* sailed farther south in the Outer Sea along the Quarmallian or west coast of Lankhmar continent than they had ever ventured before, or any other honest mariner they knew.

They were lured on by a pair of shimmer-sprights, as they were called, a breed of will-o'-the-wisps which men deem infallible guides to lodgements of precious metals, if only one have a master hunter's patience and craft to track them down, by reason of which they are also called treasure-flies, silver-moths, and gold-bugs. This pair had a coppery pink seeming by day and a silvery black gleam by night, promising by those hues a trove of elektrum and still dearer, because massier, white gold. They most resembled restlessly flowing, small bedsheets of gossamer. They fluttered ceaselessly about the single mast, darting ahead, drifting behind. Sometimes they were almost invisible, faintest heat-blurs in the pelting fire of the near vertical sun, ghostliest shimmers in the dark of night and easily mistaken for reflections of the White Huntress's light on sea and sail, the moon now being near full. Sometimes they moved as sprightly as their name, sometimes they drooped and lagged, but ever moved on. At such times they seemed sad (or melancholy, Fafhrd said, one of his favorite moods). On other occasions they became (if ears could be trusted) vocal with joy, filling the air about the leopard-boat with faint sweet jargonings, whispers 'twixt wind and speech, and long ecstatic purrs.

By the Gray Mouser's and Fafhrd's calculations, *Black Racer* had now left behind Lankhmar continent to loadside, and the hypothetical Western continent far, far to steerside, and struck out due south into the Great Equatorial Ocean (sometimes called – but why? – the Sea of Stars) that girdles Nehwon and is deemed wholly dire and quite uncrossable by Lankhmarts and Easterners alike, who in their sailings hug the southern coasts of the northern continents, so that one would have thought the doughtiest sailors would have ere this turned back.

But there was, you see, another reason beside the hope of vast riches – and not chiefly their great courage either, by any means – that Fafhrd and the Mouser kept sailing on in the face of unknown perils and horrid legendry of monsters that crunched ships, and currents swifter than the hurricane, and craterous maelstroms that swallowed vastest vessels in one gulp and even sucked down venturesome islands. It was a reason they spoke of seldom to each other and then only most guardedly, in low tones after long silence in the long silent watches of the night. It was this: that on the edge of darkest sleep, or sluggishly rousing from sail-shadowed nap by day, they briefly saw the shimmer-sprights as beautiful, slim, translucent girls, mirror-image twins, with loving faces and great, glimmering wings. Girls with fine hair like gold or silver clouds and distant eyes that yet brimmed with thought and witchery, girls slim almost beyond belief yet not too slim for the act of love, if only they might wax sufficiently substantial, which was something their smiles and gazes seemed to promise might come to pass. And the two adventurers felt a yearning for these shimmer-girls such as they had never felt for mortal woman, so that they could no more turn back than men wholly ensorceled or stark lockjawed mad.

That morning as their treasure-sprights led them on, looking like rays of rainbow in the sun, the Mouser and Fafhrd were each lost in his secret thoughts of girls and gold, so that neither noted the subtle changes in the ocean surface ahead, from ripply to half smooth with odd little long lines of foam racing east. Suddenly the gold-bugs darted east and the next instant something seized the leopard-boat's keel so that she veered strongly east with a bound like that of the lithe beast for which her class of craft was named. The tall mast was almost snapped and the two heroes were nearly thrown to the deck, and by the time they had recovered from their surprise the *Black Racer* was speeding east, the twin shimmer-sprights winging ahead exultantly, and the two heroes knew that they were in the grip of the Great Eastward Equatorial Current and that it was no fable.

Momentarily forgetting their aerial maybe-girls, they moved to steer north out of it, Fafhrd leaning on the tiller while the Mouser saw to the large single sail, but at that moment a northwest wind struck from astern with gale force, almost driving the *Black Racer* under as it drove her deeper and deeper south into the current. This wind was no mere gust but steadily mounted to storm force, so that it would infallibly have torn their sail away ere they could furl it save that the current below was carrying them east almost as fast as the wind harried them on above.

Then a league to the south they saw three waterspouts travelling east together, gray pillars stretching halfway from earth to sky, at thrice *Black Racer*'s speed at least, indicating that the current was still swifter there. As the two still-astonished sailormen perforce accepted their plight – helpless in the twin grasp of furiously speeding water and air as if their craft were frozen to the sea – the Gray Mouser cried out, 'O Fafhrd, now I can well believe that metaphysical fancy that the whole universe is water and our world but one wind-haunted bubble in it.'

From where white-knuckled he gripped the tiller, Fafhrd replied, 'I'll grant, what with those 'spouts and all this flying foam, it seems right now there's water everywhere. Yet still I can't believe that philosopher's dream of Nehwon-world a bubble, when any fool can see the sun and moon are massy orbs like Nehwon thousands of leagues distant in the high air, which must be very thin out there, by the by.

'But, man, this is no time for sophistries. I'll tie the tiller, and while this weird calm lasts (born of near equal speeds of current and wind, and as if the air were cut away before and closing in behind) let's triple-reef the sail and make all snug.'

As they worked, the three waterspouts vanished in the distance ahead, to be replaced by a group of five more coming up fast from astern – somewhat nearer this time, for all the while *Black Racer* was being driven gradually but relentlessly south. From almost overhead the midday sun beat down fiercely, for the storm wind blowing near hurricane force had brought no clouds or opaque air with it – in itself a prodigy unparalleled in the recollection of the Mouser or even Fafhrd, a widely sailed man. After several futile efforts to steer north out of the mighty current (which resulted only in the following storm wind shifting perversely north a point or two, driving them deeper south) the two men gave over, thereby admitting their complete inability at present to influence their leopard boat's course.

'At this rate,' Fafhrd opined, 'we'll cross the Great Equatorial Ocean in a matter of month or two. Lucky we're well provisioned.'

The Mouser replied dolefully, 'If *Racer* holds together a day amidst those 'spouts and speeds, I'll be surprised.'

'She's a stout craft,' Fafhrd said lightly. 'Just think, Small Gloomy One, the southern continents unknown to man! We'll be the first to visit 'em!'

'If there are any such. And our planks don't split. Continents? – I'd give my soul for one small isle.'

'The first to reach Nehwon's south pole!' Fafhrd daydreamed on. 'The first to climb the southern Stardocks! The first to loot the treasures of the south! The first to find what land lies at antipodes from Shadowland, realm of Death! The first—'

The Mouser quietly removed himself to the other side of the shortened sail from Fafhrd and cautiously made his way to the prow, where he wearily threw himself down in a narrow angle of shadow. He was dazed by wind, spray, exertion, the needling sun, and sheer velocity. He dully watched the coppery pinkish shimmer-sprights, which were holding position with remarkable steadiness for them at mast height a ship's length ahead.

After a while he slept and dreamed that one of them detached itself from the other, and came down and hovered above him like a long rosy spectrum and then became a fond- and narrow-visaged green-eyed girl in his arms, who loosened his clothing with slim fingers cool as milk kept in a well, so that looking down closely he saw the nipples of her dainty breasts pressing like fresh-scoured copper thimbles into the curly dark hair on his chest. And she was saying softly and sweetly, head bent forward like his, lips and tongue brushing his ear, 'Press on, press on. This is the only way to Life and immortality and paradise.' And he replied, 'My dearest love, I will.'

He woke to Fafhrd's shout and to a fugitive but clear, though almost blinding vision of a female face that was narrow and beautiful, but otherwise totally unlike that of the douce girl of his dream. A sharp, imperious face, wildly alive, made all of red-gold light, the irises of her wide eyes vermilion.

He lifted up sluggishly. His jerkin was unlaced to his waist and pushed back off his shoulders.

'Mouser,' Fafhrd said urgently, 'when I first glimpsed you but now, you were all bathed in fire!'

Gazing stupidly down, the Mouser saw twin threads of smoke rising from his matted chest where the nipples of his dream had pressed into it. And as he stared at the gray threads, they died. He smelled the stink of burning hair.

He shook his head, blinked, and pushed himself to his feet. 'What a strange fancy,' he said to Fafhrd. 'The sun must have got in your eye. Say, look there!'

The five waterspouts had drawn far ahead and had been replaced by two groups (of three and four respectively) swiftly overtaking *Black Racer* from astern, the four rather distant, the three appallingly close, so that they could see clearly the structure of each: pillars of wild gray water almost a ship's length thick and towering up to thrice mast height, where each broke off abruptly.

And in the farther distance they could now see still more groups of speeding spouts, and most distant-dim yet speediest of all a gigantic single one that looked leagues thick. A-prow the twin shimmer-sprights led on.

' 'Tis passing strange,' Fafhrd averred.

'Does one speak of a covey of waterspouts?' the Mouser wanted to know. 'Or a pride? A congeries? A fountain? Or – yes! – a tower! A tower of waterspouts!'

The day passed and half the night, and their weird situation of eastward speeding held – and *Black Racer* held together. The sea was slick and moving in long low swells across which blew thin, long, pale lines of foam. The wind was hurricane force at very least, but the velocity of the Great Equatorial Current had increased to match it.

Overhead, nearly at mast-top, the full moon shone down, scantily scattered about with stars. Her white Huntress light showed the smooth surface of the racing sea to be outdinted near and far by towers of waterspouts racing by in majestical array and yet with fantastical celerity, as if they somehow profited far more from the speed of the current than did *Black Racer*. At mast height and ship's length ahead, the twin shimmer-sprights flew on like flags of silver lace against the dark. All almost silently.

'Fafhrd,' the Gray Mouser spoke very softly, as if reluctant to break the silver moonlight's spectral spell, 'Tonight I clearly see that Nehwon *is* a vast bubble rising through waters of eternity, with continents and isles afloat inside.'

'Yes, and they'd move around – the continents, I mean – and bump each other,' Fafhrd said, softly too, albeit a little gruffly. 'That is, providing they'd float at all. Which I most strongly doubt.'

'They move all orderly, in pre-established harmony,' the Mouser replied. 'And as for buoyancy, think of the Sinking Land.'

'But then where'd be the sun and moon and stars and planets nine?' Fafhrd objected. 'All in a jumble in the bubble's midst? That's quite impossible – and ridiculous.'

'I'm getting to the stars,' the Mouser said. 'They're all afloat in even stricter pre-established harmony in the Great Equatorial Ocean, which as we've seen this day and night, speeds around Nehwon's waist once each day – that is, in its effects on the waterspouts, not on *Black Racer*. Why else, I ask you, is it called the Sea of Stars?'

Fafhrd blinked, momentarily impressed against his will. Then he grinned. 'But if this ocean's all afloat with stars,' he demanded, 'why can't we see 'em all about our ship? Riddle me that, O Sage!'

The Mouser smiled back at him, very composedly. 'They're all of 'em inside the waterspouts,' he said, 'which are gray tubes of water pointing toward heaven – by which I mean, of course, the antipodes of Nehwon. Look up, bold comrade mine, at arching sky and heaven's top. You're looking at the same Great Equatorial Ocean we're afloat in, only halfway around Nehwon from *Black Racer*. You're looking *down* (or *up*, what skills it?) the tubes of the waterspouts there, so you can see the star at bottom of each.'

'I'm looking at the full moon too,' Fafhrd said. 'Don't try to tell me *that's* at the bottom of a waterspout!'

'But I will,' the Mouser responded gently. 'Recall the gigantic spout like speeding mesa we briefly saw far south of us last noon? That was the moonspout, to invent a word. And now it's raced to sky ahead of us, in half day since.'

'Fry me for a sardine!' Fafhrd said with great feeling. Then he sought to collect his comprehension. 'And those folk on Nehwon's other side – up *there* – they're seeing a star at the bottom of each waterspout now around us here?'

'Of course not,' the Mouser said patiently. 'Sunlight drowns out their twinkles for those folk. It's *day* up there, you see.' He pointed at the dark near the moon. 'Up there, you see, they're bathed in highest noon, drenched in the light of the sun, which now is somewhere near us, but hid from us by the thick walls of his sunspout, to coin a word wholly analogous to moon-spout.'

'Oh, monstrous!' Fafhrd cried. 'For if it's day up there, you little fool, why can't we see it here? Why can't we see up there Nehwon lands bathed in light with bright blue sea around 'em? Answer me that!'

'Because there are two different kinds of light,' the Mouser said with an almost celestial tranquility. 'Seeming the same by every local test, yet utterly diverse. First, there's *direct* light, such as we're getting now from moon and stars up there. Second, there is *reflected* light, which cannot make the really longer journeys, and certainly can't recross – not one faint ray of it – Nehwon's central space to reach us here.'

'Mouser,' Fafhrd said in a very small voice, but with great certainty, 'you're not just inventing words, you're inventing the whole business – on the spur of the moment as you go along.'

'Invent the Laws of Nature?' the Mouser asked with a certain horror. 'That were far worse than darkest blasphemy.'

'Then in the name of all the gods at once!' Fafhrd demanded in a very large voice, 'how can the sun be in a waterspout and not boil it all away in an instant in an explosion vast? Tell me at once.'

'There are some things man was not meant to know,' the Mouser said in a most portentous voice. Then, swiftly switching to the familiar, 'or rather, since I am in no way superstitious, there are some things which have not yielded yet to our philosophy. An omission which in this instance I will remedy at once. There are, you see, two different kinds of *energy*, the one pure heat, the other purest light, which cannot boil the tiniest waterdrop – the direct light I've already told you of, which changes almost entirely to heat where e'er it hits, which in turn tells us why reflected light can't make the long trip back through Nehwon's midst. There, have I answered you?'

'Oh damn, damn, damn,' Fafhrd said weakly. Then managing to rally himself, if only desperately for a last time, he asked somewhat sardonically, 'All right, all right! But just where then is this floating sun you keep invoking, tucked in his vast adamantine-walled waterspout?'

'Look there,' the Mouser said, pointing due south, steerside abeam.

Across the moon-silvered gray field of the sea pricked out with speeding towers of waterspouts, almost at the dim distant horizon, Fafhrd saw a solitary gigantic waterspout huge as an island, taller than tallest mesa, moving east at least as swiftly as the rest and as ponderous-relentlessly as a juggernaut of the Emperor of the Eastern Lands. The hair rose on the back of Fafhrd's neck, he was harrowed with fear and wonder, and he said not a word, but only stared and stared as the horrendous thing forged ahead in its immensity.

After a while he began also to feel a great weariness. He looked ahead and a little up at the stiffly flapping silver lace of the twin shimmer-sprights before the prow, taking comfort from their nearness and steadiness as if they were *Black Racer*'s flags. He slowly lowered himself until he lay prone on the narrow, snugly abutting planks of the deck, his head toward the prow, his chin propped on his hands, still observing the night-sprights.

'You know how groups of stars sometimes wink out mysteriously on clearest Nehwon nights?' the Mouser said lightly and bemusedly.

'That's true enough, they do,' Fafhrd agreed, somewhat sleepily.

'That must be because the tubes of their waterspout-walls are bent enough, by a strong gale perchance, to hide their light, keep it from getting out.'

Fafhrd mumbled, 'If you say so.'

After a considerable pause the Mouser asked in the same tones, 'Is it not passing strange to think that in the heart of each dark, gray 'spout out there dotting the main, there burns (without any heat) a jewel of blinding, purest diamond light?'

Fafhrd managed what might have been a weighty sigh of agreement.

After another long pause the Mouser said reflectively, as one who tidies up loose ends, 'It's easy now to see, isn't it, that the 'spouts small and great must all be tubes? For if they were solid water by some strange chance, they'd suck the oceans dry and fill the heavens with heaviest clouds – nay, with the sea! You get my point?'

But Fafhrd had gone to sleep. In his sleep he dreamed and in that dream he rolled over on his back and one of the shimmer-sprights parted from her sister and winged down to flutter close above him: a long and slender, black-haired form, moon pale, appareled in finest silver-shot black lace that witchingly enhanced her nakedness. She was gazing down at him tenderly yet appraisingly, with eyes that would have been violet had there been more light. He smiled at her. She slightly shook her head, her face grew grave, and she flowed down against him head to heel, her wraithlike fingers busy at the great bronze buckle of his heavy belt, while with long, night-cool cheek pressed 'gainst his fevered one, she whispered softly and yet most clearly in his ear, each word a symbol finely drawn in blackest ink on moon-white paper, 'Turn back, turn back, my dearest man, to Shadowland and Death, for that's the only way to stay alive. Trust only in the moon. Suspect all other prophecies but mine. So now, steer north, steer strongly strongly north.'

In his dream Fafhrd replied, 'I can't steer north, I've tried. Love me, my dearest girl,' and she answered huskily, 'That's as may hap, my love. Seek Death to 'scape from him. Suspect all flaming youth and scarlet shes. Beware the sun. Trust in the moon. Wait for her certain sign.'

At that instant Fafhrd's dream was snatched from him and he roused numbly to the Mouser's sharp cries and to the chilling fugitive glimpse of a face narrow, beauteous, and of most melancholy mien, pale violet-blue of hue and with eyes like black holes. This above wraithlike, like-complected figure, and all receding swift as though amidst a beating of black wings.

Then the Mouser was shaking him by the shoulders and crying out, 'Wake up, wake up! Speak to me, man!'

Fafhrd brushed his face with the back of his hand and mumbled, 'Wha' happ'n?'

Crouched beside him, the Mouser narrated rapidly and somewhat breathlessly, 'The shimmer-sprights grew restless and 'gan play about the mast like corposants. One buzzed around me shrilly like a wasp, and when I'd driven it off, I saw the other nosing you from toe to waist to head, then nuzzling your neck. Your flesh grew silver-white, as white as death, the whiles the corposant became your glowing shroud. I greatly feared for you and drove it off.'

Fafhrd's muddied eyes cleared somewhat whilst the Mouser spoke and when the latter was done, he nodded and said knowingly, 'That would be right. She spoke me much of death and at the end she looked like it, poor sibyl.'

'Who spoke?' the Mouser asked. 'What sibyl?'

'The shimmer-girl, of course,' Fafhrd told him. 'You know what I mean.'

He stood up. His belt began to slip. He stared down wide-eyes at the undone buckle, then drew it up and hooked it together swiftly.

'Fafhrd, I don't know what you're talking of,' the Mouser denied, his expression suddenly hooded. 'Girl? What girl? Art seeing mirages? Has lack of erotic exercise addled your wits? Have you turned moon-mad lunatic?'

At this point Fafhrd had to speak most sharply and shrewdly to the Mouser to get him to admit that he – the Mouser – had suspected for days that the shimmer-sprights were girls, albeit girls with a strong admixture of the supernatural, insofar as any admixture of anything is able to affect the essential girlness of any such being, which isn't much.

But the Mouser did eventually make the admission although his mind had not the edge-of-sleep honesty of Fafhrd's and tended to drift off to musings on his bubble-cosmos. Yet under strong prompting by Fafhrd he even confessed to his encounter with the sun-red vermilion-eyed shimmer-girl last noon, when he'd looked afire, and upon Fafhrd's insistence recalled the exact words she'd said to him in dream.

'Your red girl spoke of Life and pressing on south to immortality and paradise,' Fafhrd summed up thoughtfully, 'whilst my dark dear talked of Death and turning back north toward Shadowland and Lankhmar and Cold Waste.' Then, with swift-growing excitement and utter amazement at his own insight, 'Mouser, I see it all! There are two different pairs of shimmer-girls! The daytime ones (you spoke with one of those) are children of the sun and messengers from the fabled Land of Gods at Nehwon's Life Pole. While the nighttimers, replacing them from dusk to dawn, are minions of the moon, White Huntress's daughters, owing allegiance to the Shadowland, which lies across the world from the Life Pole.'

'Fafhrd, hast thou thought,' the Mouser spoke from a brown study, 'how nicely calculated must be the height and diameter of each waterspout-tube, so that the star at its bottom is seen from every spot in other half of Nehwon (up there, when it's night there) but from no spot in our half down here? – which incidentally explains why stars are brightest at zenith, you see all of each, not just a lens or biconvex meniscus. It seems to argue that some divinity must—' At that point the impact of Fafhrd's words at last sank in and he said in tones less dreamy, 'Two different sets of girls? Four girls in all? Fafhrd, I think you're overcomplicating things. By Ildritch's Scimitar—'

'There are two sets of twin girls,' Fafhrd overrode him. 'That much is certain though all else be lies. And mark you this, Small Man, your sun-girls mean us ill though seeming to promise good, for how reach immortality and paradise except by dying? How reach Godsland except by perishing? The whiles the sun, pure light or no, is baleful, hot, and deadly. But my moon-girls, seeming to mean us ill, intend good only – being at once as cool and lovely as the moon. She said to me in dream, "Turn back to Death," which sounds dire. But you and I have lived with Death a dozen years and ta'en no lasting hurt – just as she said herself, "for that's the only way to stay alive. Seek Death to 'scape from him!" So steer we north at once! – as she directed. For if we keep on south, deeper and deeper into torrid realm of sun ("Beware the sun," she said!) we'll die for sure, betrayed by your false, lying girls of fire. Recall, her merest touch made your chest smoke. While my girl said, "Suspect all flaming youth and scarlet shes," capping my argument.'

'I don't see that at all,' the Mouser said. 'I *like* the sun myself, I always have. His searching warmth is best of medicines. It's you who love the cold and clammy dark, you Cold Waste savage! My girl was sweet and fiery pink with life, while yours was gloomy-spoken and as livid as a corpse, on your own admission. Take her words for things? Not I. Besides, by Ildritch's Scimitar – to get back to that – the simplest explanation is always the best as well as the most elegant. There are *two* shimmer-girls only, the one I spoke in dream and the one you spoke – not four buzzing about bewilderingly and changing guard at dawn and dusk, to our confusion. The two girls – only two! – look the same in outward seeming – copper by day, silver by night – but inwardly mine is angel, yours deadly valkyr. As was revealed in dream, your surest guide.'

'Now you are quibbling,' Fafhrd said decisively, 'and are making my head spin, to boot, with 'wildering words. This much is clear to me: We now get ready, and ready *Black Racer*, to steer north, as my poor lovely moon-girl strongly advised me more than once.'

'But Fafhrd,' the Mouser protested, 'we tried again and again to steer north yesterday and failed each time. What reason have you to suppose, you big lug—'

Fafhrd cut in with, ' "Trust only in the moon," she said. "Wait for her certain sign." So wait we, for the nonce, and watch. Look at the sea and sky, idiot boy, and be amazed.'

The Mouser was indeed. While they had been disputing, intent only on the cuts and thrusts and parries and ripostes of their word-duel, the smooth surface of the racing Sea of Stars had changed from sleek and slick to mat yet ripply. Great vibrations were speeding across it, making the leopard-boat quiver. The moon-silvered lines of foam were blowing over it less predictably – the hurricane itself, though diminished no whit, was getting flukey, the wind now hot, now cold about their necks. While in the sky were clouds at last, coming in swiftly from northwest and east at once and mounting toward the moon. All of nature seemed to cringe apprehensively, as if in anticipation of some dire event about to hap, heralding war in heaven. The two silvery shimmer-sprights appeared to share this foreboding or presentiment, for they 'gan fly about most erractically, their lace wildly aflow, uttering high cheeping cries and whistlings of alarm against the unnatural silence and at last parting so that one hovered agitatedly to the southeast above the prow, the other near the stern to the northwest.

The rapidly thickening clouds had blotted out most of the stars and mounted almost to the moon. The wind held still, exactly equalling the current's speed. *Black Racer* poised, as if at crest of a gigantic wave. For an instant the sea seemed to freeze. Silence was absolute.

The Mouser looked straight up and uttered from the back of his throat a half choked, high pitched, little scream that froze his comrade's blood. After mastering that shock, Fafhrd looked up too – at just which instant it grew very dark. The hungry clouds had blotted out the moon.

'Why did you so cry out?' he demanded angrily.

The Mouser answered with difficulty, his teeth chattering, 'Just before the clouds closed on her, *the moon moved*.'

'How could you know that, you little fool, when the clouds were moving? – which always makes the moon seem to move.'

'I don't know, but as sure as I stand firm-footed here, I saw it! *The moon began to move*.'

'Well, if the moon be in a waterspout, as you claim, she's subject to all whims of wind and wave. So what's so blood-curdling strange in her moving?' Fafhrd's frantic voice belied the reasonableness of his question.

'I don't know,' the Mouser repeated in a curiously small, strained voice, his teeth still clinking together, '*but I didn't like it*.'

The shimmer-spright at the stern whistled thrice. Her nervously twisting, lacy, silver luminescence stood out plainly in the black night, as did her sister's at the prow.

'It is the sign!' Fafhrd cried hoarsely. 'Ready to go about!' And he threw his full weight against the tiller, driving it steerside and so the rudder loadside, to steer them north. *Black Racer* responded most sluggishly, but did break the grip of current and wind to the extent of swinging north a point or two, no more.

A long flat lightning flash split the sky and showed the gray sea to the horizon's rim, where they now saw *two* giant waterspouts, the one due south, the other rushing in from the west. Thunder crashed like armies or armadas meeting at an iron-sonorous Armageddon.

Then all was wildfire and chaos in the night, great crashing waves, and winds that fought like giants whose heads scraped heaven. Whilst round about the ship the shimmer-sprights fought too, now two, now seeming four of them at least as they circled and dipped at and about each other. The frozen sea was ripped, great rags of it thrown skyward, pits opening that seemed to go down to the black, mucky seabottom unknown to man. Lightning and deafening thunderclaps became almost continuous, revealing all. And through that all, *Black Racer* somehow lived, a chip in chaos, Fafhrd and Mouser performing prodigies of seamanship.

And now from the southwest the second giant waterspout drove in like a moving mountain, sending great swells before it that mightily aided Fafhrd's tillering, driving them north, and north again, and again still north. While from the south the first giant 'spout turned back, or so it seemed, and those two (moonspout and sunspout?) battled.

And then of a sudden it was as if *Black Racer* had struck a wall. Fafhrd and Mouser were thrown to the deck and when they had madly struggled to their feet they found to their utter astonishment that their leopard-boat was floating in calm water, while in the distance lightning and thunder played, almost inaudible and unseen to their numbed ears and half-blinded eyes. There were no stars and moon, only thick night. There were no shimmer-sprights. Their sail was split to ribbons, the faint lightning showed. Under his hand Fafhrd felt a looseness in the tiller, as if the whole steering assemblage had been strained to breaking point and only survived by a miracle.

The Mouser said, 'She lists a little to stern and steerside, don't you think? She's taking water, I trow. Perhaps there's stuff shifted below. Man we the pump. Later we can bend on a new sail.'

So they fell to and for some hours worked together silently as in many old times, nursing the leopard-boat and making all new, by light of two lanterns Fafhrd rigged from the mast that burned purest leviathan-oil, for the storm had entirely gone with its lightnings and the dark clouds pressed down.

As the cloud ceiling did, indeed, over all Nehwon that night (and day on other side). Over the subsequent months and years reports drifted in of the Great Dark, as it came mostly to be called, that had shrouded all Nehwon for a space of hours, so that it was never truly known whether the moon had monstrously traveled halfway round the world that time to battle with the sun and then back again to her appointed spot, or no, though there were scattered but persistent disquieting rumors of such a dread journeying glimpsed through fugitive gaps in the cloud-cover, and even that the sun himself had briefly moved to war with her.

After long while Fafhrd said quietly as they took a break from their labors, 'It's lonely without the shimmer-sprights, don't you think?'

The Mouser said, 'Agreed. I wonder if they'd ever have led us to treasure, or ever so intended? Or would have led us, or one of us, somewhere, either your spright, or mine?'

'I still firmly believe there were four sprights,' Fafhrd said. 'So either pair of twins might have led us somewhere together without parting us.'

'No, there were only two sprights,' the Mouser said, 'and they were set on leading us in very different directions, antipodean, off from each other.' And when Fafhrd did not reply he said after a time, 'Part of me wishes I'd gone with my fiery girl to find what's like to dwell in paradise bathed by the splendid sun.'

Fafhrd said, 'Part of me wishes I'd followed my melancholy maid to dwell in the pale moon, spending the summer months mayhap in Shadowland.' Then after a silent space, 'But man was not meant for paradise, I trow, whether of warmth or coolth. No, never, never, never, never.'

'Never shares a big bed with once,' the Mouser said.

While they were speaking it had grown light. The clouds had

all lifted. The new sail shone. The leviathan lamps burned wanly, their clear beam almost invisible against the paling sky. Then in the farthest distance north the two adventurers made out the loom of a great aurochs couchant, unmistakable sign of the southernmost headland of the Eastern Lands.

'We've weathered Lankhmar continent in a single day and night,' the Mouser said.

A breeze sprang up from the south, stirring the still air. They set course north up the long Sea of the East.

VII
THE FROST
MONSTREME

'I am tired, Gray Mouser, of these little brushes with Death,' Fafhrd the Northerner said, lifting his dinted, livid goblet and taking a measured sup of sweet ferment of grape laced with bitter brandy.

'Want a big one?' his comrade scoffed, drinking likewise.

Fafhrd considered that, while his gaze traveled slowly yet without stop all the way round the tavern, whose sign was a tarnished and serpentine silver fish. 'Perhaps,' he said.

'It's a dull night,' the other agreed.

True indeed, the interior of the Silver Eel presented a tavern visage as leaden-hued as its wine cups. The hour was halfway between midnight and dawn, the light dim without being murky, the air dank yet not chill, the other drinkers like moody statues, the faces of the barkeep and his bully and servers paralyzed in expressions of petulant discontent, as if Time herself had stopped.

Outside, the city of Lankhmar was silent as a necropolis, while beyond that the world of Nehwon had been at peace – unwar, rather – for a full year. Even the Mingols of the vasty Steppes weren't raiding south on their small, tough horses.

Yet the effect of all this was not calm, but an unfocused uneasiness, a restlessness that had not yet resulted in the least movement, as if it were the prelude to an excruciating flash of cold lightning transfixing every tiniest detail of life.

This atmosphere affected the feelings and thoughts of the tall, brown-tunicked barbarian and his short, gray-clad friend.

'Dull indeed,' Fafhrd said. 'I long for some grand emprise!'

'Those are the dreams of untutored youth. Is that why you've shaved your beard? – to match your dreams? Both bare-faced lies!' the Mouser asked, and answered.

'Why have you let yours grow these three days?' Fafhrd countered.

'I am but resting the skin of my face for a full tweaking of its hairs. And you've lost weight. A wistfully youthful fever?'

'Not that, or any ill or care. Of late you're lighter, too. We are changing the luxuriant musculature of young manhood for a suppler, hardier, more enduring structure suited to great mid-life trials and venturings.'

'We've had enough of those,' the Mouser asserted. 'Thrice around Nehwon at the least.'

Fafhrd shook his head morosely. 'We've never really lived. We've not owned land. We've not led men.'

'Fafhrd, you're gloomy-drunk!' the Mouser chortled. 'Would you be a farmer? Have you forgot a captain is the prisoner of his command? Here, drink yourself sober, or at least glad.'

The Northerner let his cup be refilled from two jars, but did not change his mood. Staring unhappily, he continued, 'We've neither homes nor wives.'

'Fafhrd, you need a wench!'

'Who spoke of wenches?' the other protested. 'I mean women. I had brave Kreeshkra, but she's gone back to her beloved Ghouls. While your pet Reetha prefers the hairless land of Eevamarensee.'

The Mouser interjected *sotto voce*, 'I also had imperious, insolent Hisvet, and you her brave, dramatic queen-slave Frix.'

Fafhrd went on, 'Once, long ago, there were Friska and Ivivis, but they were Quarmall's slaves and then became free women at Tovilysis. Before them were Keyaira, Hirriwi, but they were princesses, invisibles, loves of one long, long night, daughters of dread Oomforafor and sib of murderous Faroomfar. Long before all of those, in Land of Youth, there were fair Ivrian and slender Vlana. But they were girls, those lovely in-betweens (or actresses, those mysteries), and now they dwell with Death in Shadowland. So I'm but half a man. I need a *mate*. And so do you, perchance.'

'Fafhrd, you're mad! You prate of world-spanning wild adventures and then babble of what would make them impossible: wife, home, henchmen, duties. One dull night without girl or fight, and your brains go soft. Repeat, you're mad.'

Fafhrd reinspected the tavern, and its stodgy inmates. 'It stays dull, doesn't it,' he remarked, 'as if not one nostril had twitched or ear wiggled since I last looked. And yet it is a calm I do not trust. I feel an icy chill. Mouser—'

That one was looking past him. With little sound, or none at all, two slender persons had just entered the Silver Eel and paused appraisingly inside the lead-weighted iron-woven curtains that kept out fog and could turn sword thrusts. The one was tall and rangy as a man, blue-eyed, thin-cheeked, wide-mouthed, clad in jerkin and trousers of blue and long cloak of gray. The other was wiry and supple-seeming as a cat, green-eyed, compact of feature, short thick lips compressed, clothed similarly save the hues were rust red and brown. They were neither young nor yet near middle age. Their smooth unridged brows, tranquil eyes, evenly curving jaws, and long cheek-molding hair – here silvery yellow, there black shot with darkest brown (in turn gold-shotten, or were those golden wires braided in?) – proclaimed them feminine.

That last attribute broke the congealed midnight trances of the assembled dullards, a half dozen of whom converged on the newcomers, calling low invitations and trailing throaty laughs. The two moved forward as if to hasten the encounter, with gaze unwaveringly ahead.

And then – without an instant's pause or any collision, except someone recoiled slightly as if his instep had been trod on and someone else gasped faintly as if his short ribs had encountered a firm elbow – the two were past the six. It was as if they had simply walked through them, as a man would walk through smoke with no more fuss than the wrinkling of a nostril. Behind them, the ignored smoke fumed and wove a bit.

Now there were in their way the Gray Mouser and Fafhrd, who had both risen and whose hands still indicated the hilts of their scabbarded swords without touching them.

'Ladies—' the Mouser began.

'Will you take wine—?' Fafhrd continued.

'Strengthened against night's chill,' the Mouser concluded, sketching a bow, while Fafhrd courteously indicated the four-chaired table from which they'd just risen.

The slender women halted and surveyed them without haste.

'We might—' the smaller purred.

'Provided you let Rime Isle pay for the drinks,' the taller concluded in tones bright and swift as running snow water.

At the words 'Rime Isle', the faces of the two men grew thoughtful and wondering, as if in another universe someone had said Atlantis or El Dorado or Ultima Thule. Nevertheless they nodded agreement and drew back chairs for the women.

'Rime Isle,' Fafhrd repeated conjuringly, as the Mouser did the honors with cups and jars. 'As a child in the Cold Waste and later in my adolescent piratings, I've heard it and Salthaven City whispered of. Legend says the Claws point at it – those thin, stony peninsulas that tip Nehwonland's last northwest corner.'

'For once legend speaks true,' the electrum-haired woman in blue and gray said softly yet crisply. 'Rime Isle exists today. Salthaven, too.'

'Come,' said the Mouser with a smile, ceremoniously handing her her cup, 'it's said Rime Isle's no more real than Simorgya.'

'And is Simorgya unreal?' she asked, accepting it.

'No,' he admitted with a somewhat startled, reminiscent look. 'I once watched it from a very small ship when it was briefly risen from the deeps of the Outer Sea. My more venturesome friend' – he nodded towards Fafhrd – 'trod its wet shale for a short space to see some madmen dance with devilfish which had the aspect of black fur cloaks awrithe.'

'North of Simorgya, westward from the Claws,' briskly said the red- and brown-clad woman with black hair shot with glistening dark bronze and gold. Her right hand holding steady in the air her brimming wine cup where she'd just received it, she dipped her left beneath the table and swiftly slapped it down on the arabesquery of circle-stained oak, then lifted it abruptly to reveal four small rounds gleaming pale as moons. 'You agreed Rime Isle would pay.'

With nods abstracted yet polite, the Mouser and Fafhrd each took up one of the coins and closely studied it.

'By the teats of Titchubi,' the former breathed, 'this is no *sou marque*, black dog, no *chien noir*.'

'Rime Isle silver?' Fafhrd asked softly, lifting his gaze, eyebrows a-rise, from the face of the coin toward that of the taller woman.

Her gaze met his squarely. There was the hint of a smile at the ends of her long lips, back in her cheeks. She said sincerely yet banteringly, 'Which never tarnishes.'

He said, 'The obverse shows a vast sea monster menacing out of the depths.'

She said, 'Only a great whale blowing after a deep sound.'

The Mouser said to the other woman, 'Whilst the reverse depicts a ship-shaped, league-long square rock rising from miles-long swells.'

She said, 'Only an iceberg hardly half that size.'

Fafhrd said, 'Well, drink we what this bright, alien coinage has bought. I am Fafhrd, the Gray Mouser he.'

The tall woman said, 'And I Afreyt, my comrade Cif.'

After deep draughts, they put down their cups, Afreyt with a sharp double tap of pewter on oak. 'And now to business,' she said cliptly, with the faintest of frowns at Fafhrd (it was arguable if there was any frown at all) as he reached for the wine jars. 'We speak with the voice of Rime Isle—'

'And dispurse her golden monies,' Cif added, her green eyes glinting with yellow flecks. Then, flatly, 'Rime Isle is straitly menaced.'

Her voice going low, Afreyt asked, 'Hast ever heard of the Sea Mingols?' and, when Fafhrd nodded, shifted her gaze to the Mouser, saying, 'Most Southrons misdoubt their sheer existence, deeming every Mingol a lubber when off his horse, whether on land or sea.'

'Not I,' he answered. 'I've sailed with Mingol crew. There's one, now old, named Ourph—'

'And I've met Mingol pirates,' Fafhrd said. 'Their ships are few, each dire. Arrow-toothed water rats – Sea Mingols, as you say.'

'That's good,' Cif told them both. 'Then you'll more like believe me when I tell you that in response to the eldritch prophecy, "Who seizes Nehwon's crown, shall win her all—"'

'For crown, read north polar coasts,' Afreyt interjected.

'And supremely abetted by the Wizard of Ice, Khahkht, whose very name's a frozen cough—'

'Perchance the evilest being ever to exist—' Afreyt supplemented, her eyes a sapphire moon shining frosty through two narrowed, crosswise window slits.

'The Mingols have ta'en ship to harry Nehwon's northmost coasts in two great fleets, one following the sun, the other – the Widdershin Mongols – going against it—'

'For a few dire ships, believe armadas,' Afreyt put in, still gazing chiefly at Fafhrd (just as Cif favored the Mouser), and then took up the main tale with, 'Till Sunwise and Widdershins meet at Rime Isle, overwhelm her, and fan out south to rape the world!'

'A dismal prospect,' Fafhrd commented, setting down the brandy jar with which he'd laced the wine he'd poured for all.

'At least an overlively one,' the Mouser chimed in. 'Mingols are tireless raptors.'

Cif leaned forward, chin up. Her green eyes flamed. 'So Rime Isle is the chosen battleground. Chosen by Fate, by cold Khahkht, and the Gods. The place to stop the Steppe horde turned sea raiders.'

Without moving, Afreyt grew taller in her chair, her blue gaze flashing back and forth between Fafhrd and his comrade. 'So Rime Isle arms, and musters men, and hires mercenaries. The last's my work and Cif's. We need two heroes, each to find twelve men like himself and bring them to Rime Isle in the space of three short moons. You are the twain!'

'You mean there's any other one man in Nehwon like me – let alone a dozen?' the Mouser asked incredulously.

'It's an expensive task, at very least,' Fafhrd said judiciously.

Her biceps swelling slightly under the close-fitting rust-red cloth, Cif brought up from beneath the table two tight-packed pouches as big as oranges and set one down before each man. The small thuds and swiftly damped chinkings were most satisfying sounds.

'Here are your funds!'

The Mouser's eyes widened, though he did not yet touch his globular sack. 'Rime Isle must need heroes sorely. And heroines? – if I might make suggestion.'

'That has been taken care of,' Cif said firmly.

Fafhrd's middle finger feather-brushed his bag and came away.

Afreyt said, 'Drink we.'

As the goblets lifted, there came from all around a tiny tinkling as of faery bells; a minute draft, icy chill, stole past from the door; and the air itself grew very faintly translucent, very slightly softening and pearling all things seen – all of which portents grew light-swift by incredible tiger leaps into a stunning, sense-raping clangor of bells big as temple domes and thick as battlements, an ear-splittingly roaring and whining polar wind that robbed away all heat in a trice and blew out flat the iron-and-lead-weighted door drapes and sent the inhabitants of the Silver Eel sailing and tumbling, and an ice fog thick as milk, through which Cif could be heard to cry, ''Tis icy breath of Khahkht!' and Afreyt, 'It's tracked us down!' before pandemonium drowned out all else.

Fafhrd and the Mouser each desperately gripped money bag with one hand and with the other, table, glad it was bolted down to stop its use in brawls.

The gale and the tumult died and the fog faded, not quite as swiftly as it all had come. They unclenched their hands, wiped ice crystals from brows and eyes, lit lamps, and looked around.

The place was a bloodless shambles, silent too as death until the frightened moaning began, the cries of pain and wonder. They scanned the long room, first from their tables, then afoot. Their slender tablemates were not among the slowly recovering victims.

The Mouser intoned, somewhat airily, 'We're such folk here as we've been searching for? Or have we drunk some drug that—'

He broke off. Fafhrd had taken up his fat little moneybag and headed for the door. 'Where away?' Mouser called.

Fafhrd stopped and turned. He called back unsmiling, 'North of the Trollsteps, to hire my twelve berserks. Doubtless you'll find your dozen swordsmen-thieves in warmer clime. In three moons less three days, we rendezvous at sea midway between Simorgya and Rime Isle. Till then, fare well.'

The Mouser watched him out, shrugged, rummaged up a cup and the brandy jar overset but unbroken, bedewed by the magic blast. The liquor that hadn't spilled made a gratifyingly large slug. He fingered his moneybag a moment, then teased open the hard knot in its thong. Inside, the leather had a faint amber glow. 'A golden orange indeed,' he said happily, unmindful of the forms mewling and crawling and otherwise crippling around him, and plucked out one of the packed yellow coins. Reverse, a smoking volcano, possibly snow-clad; obverse, a great cliff rising from the sea and looking not quite like ice or any ordinary rock. What drollery! He gazed again at the iron-curtained doorway. What a huge fool, he thought, to take seriously a quite impossible task set by vanished females most likely dead or at best sorceled beyond reach! Or to make rendezvous at distant date in uncharted ocean betwixt a sunken land and a fabulous one – Fafhrd's geography was even more hopeful than his usual highly imaginative wont.

And just think what rare delights – nay, what whole sets of ecstasies and blisses – this much gold would buy. How fortunate that metal was mindless slave of the man who held it!

He returned the coin, thonged shut the gold and its glow, stood up decisively, then looked back at the table top, near an edge of which the four silver coins still lay cozily flat.

While he regarded them, the grubby hand of a fat server who'd been wedged under the table by the indoor blizzard reached up and whisked them down.

With another shrug, the Mouser ambled rather grandly toward the door, whistling between his teeth a Mingol march.

Inside a sphere half again as tall as a man, a skinny old being was busy. On the interior of the sphere was depicted a world map of Nehwon, the seas in blackest blues, the lands in blackest greens and browns, yet all darkly agleam like blued, greened, and browned iron, creating the illusion that the sphere was a giant bubble rising forever through infinite murky, oily waters – as some Lankhmar philosophers assert is veriest truth about Nehwon-world itself. South of the Eastern Lands in the Great Equatorial Ocean there was even depicted a ring-shaped water wall a span across and three fingers high, such as those same philosophers say hides the sun from the half of Nehwon it is floating across, though no blinding solar disk now lay in the bottom of the liquid crater, but only a pale glow sufficient to light the sphere's interior.

Where they were not hid by a loose, light robe, the old being's four long, ever-active limbs were covered by short, stiff black hairs either grizzled or filmed with ice, while Its narrow face was nasty as a spider's. Now It lifted Its leathery lips and nervously questing long-nailed fingers toward an area of the map where a tiny, gleaming black blotch south of blue and amidst brown signified Lankhmar City on the southron coast of the Inner Sea. Was it Its breath that showed frosty, or did Its will conjure up the white wisp that streaked across the black blotch? Whichever, the vapor vanished.

It muttered high-pitched in Mingolish, 'They're gone, the bitches. Khahkht sees each fly die, and sends Its shriveling breath where'er It will. Mingols harry, world unwary. Harlots fumble, heroes stumble. And now 'tis time, 'tis time, 'tis time to gin to build the frost monstreme.'

It opened a circular trap door in the South Polar Regions and lowered Itself out on a thin line.

Three days short of three moons later, the Mouser was thoroughly disgusted, bone weary, and very cold. His feet and toes were very, very cold inside fine, fur-lined boots, which slowly rose and fell under his soles as the frosty deck lifted and sank with the long, low swell. He stood by the short mainmast, from the long yard of which (longer than the boom) the loosely furled mainsail hung in frozen festoons. Beyond dimly discerned low prow and stern and mainyard top, vision was utterly blotted out by a fog of tiniest ice crystals, like cirrus cloud come down from Stardock heights, through which the light of an unseen gibbous moon, still almost full swollen, seeped out dark pearl gray. The windlessness and general stillness, contrary to all experience, seemed to make the cold bite deeper.

Yet the silence was not absolute. There was the faint wash and drip – perhaps even tiniest crackling of thinnest ice film – as the hull yielded to the swell. There were the resultant small creakings of the timbers and rigging of *Flotsam*. And beneath or beyond these, still fainter sounds lurked in the fringes of the inaudible. A part of the Mouser's mind that worked without being paid attention strained ceaselessly to hear those last. He was of no mind to be surprised by a Mingol flotilla, or single craft even. *Flotsam* was transport, not warship, he repeatedly warned himself. Very strange some of those last real or fancied sounds were that came out of the frigid fog – shatterings of massive ice leagues away, the thump and splash of mighty oars even farther off, distant doleful shriekings, still more distant deep minatory growlings, and a laughter as of fiends beyond the rim of Nehwon. He thought of the invisible fliers that had troubled the snowy air halfway up Stardock when Fafhrd and he had climbed her, Nehwon's loftiest peak.

The cold snapped that thought chain. The Mouser longed to stamp his feet, flail his hands cross-front against his sides, or – best! – warm himself with a great burst of anger, but he perversely held off, perhaps so ultimate relief would be greater, and set to analyze his disgusted weariness.

First off, there'd been the work of finding, winning, and mastering twelve fighter-thieves – a rare breed to begin with. And training 'em! – half of 'em had to be taught the art of the sling, and two (Mog help him!) swordsmanship. And the choosing of the likeliest two for corporals – Pshawri and Mikkidu, who were now sleeping snug below with their double squad, damn their hides!

Concurrent with that, there'd been the searching out of Old Ourph and gathering of his Mingol crew of four. A calculated risk, that. Would Mingol mariners fight fiercely 'gainst their own in the pinch? Mingols were ever deemed treacherous. Yet 'twas always good to have some of the enemy on your side, the better to understand 'em. And from them he might even get wider insight into the motives behind the present Mingol excursions naval.

Concurrent with *that*, the selection, hire, patching, and provisioning of *Flotsam* for its voyage.

And then the study needed! Beginning with poring over ancient charts filched from the library of the Lankhmar Starsmen and Navigators Guild, the refreshing of his knowledge of wind, waves, and celestial bodies. And the responsibility!! for no fewer than seventeen men, with no Fafhrd to share it and spell him while he slept – to lick 'em into shape, doctor their scurvies, probe under water for 'em with boathook when they tumbled overboard (he'd almost lost thumb-footed Mikkidu that way the first day out), keep 'em in good spirits but in their places too, discipline 'em as required. (Come to think of it, that last was sometimes delight as well as duty. How quaintly Pshawri squealed when shrewdly thwacked with Cat's-Claw's scabbard! – and soon would again, by Mog!)

Lastly, the near moon-long perilous voyage itself!!! Northwest from Lankhmar across the Inner Sea. Through a treacherous gap in the Curtain Wall (where Fafhrd had once sought sequined sea-queens) into the Outer Sea. Then a swift, broad reach north with the wind on their load-side until they sighted the black ramparts of No-Ombrulsk, which shared the latitude of sunken Simorgya. There he had nosed *Flotsam* due west, away from all land and almost into the teeth of the west wind, which blew a little on their steer-side. After four days of that weary, close reach, they had arrived at the undistinguished patch of troubled ocean that marked Simorgya's grave, according to the independent cipherings of the Mouser and Ourph, the one working from his stolen chart, the other counting knots in grimy Mingol calculating cords. Then a swift two-day broad reach north again, while air and sea grew rapidly colder, until by their reckonings they were half-journey to the latitude of the Claws. And now two days of dismal beating about in one place await for Fafhrd, with the cold increasing steadily until, this midnight, clear skies had given way to the ice fog in which *Flotsam* lay becalmed. Two days in which to wonder if Fafhrd would manage to find this spot, or even come at all. Two days in which to get bored with and maddened by his scared, rebellious crew and dozen soldier-thieves – all snoring warm below, Mog flog 'em! Two days to wonder *why* in Mog's name he'd spent all but four of his Rime Isle doubloons on this insane voyage, on *work* for himself, instead of on wine and women, rare books and art objects, in short on sweet bread and circuses for himself alone.

And finally, superlastly, the suspicion growing toward conviction that Fafhrd had never started out from Lankhmar at all!!!! that he'd strode so nobly, so carkingly high-minded, out of the Silver Eel with his bag of gold – and instantly begun to spend it on those very same delights which the Mouser (inspired by Fafhrd's seeming-good example) had denied himself.

In a pinnacle of exasperation, a mountaintop of rage, the Mouser seized the padded striker from its mainmast hook and smote the ship's gong a blow mighty enough to shatter the gelid bronze. In fact, he was mildly surprised that *Flotsam*'s frosty deck wasn't showered with sharp-edged frozen shards of brown metal. Whereupon he smote it again and again and again, so that the gong swung like a signboard in a hurricane, and meanwhile he jumped up and down, adding to the general alarm the resounding thuds of his feet (and haply warming them).

The forward hatch was flung back from below and Pshawri shot up out of it like a jack-in-the-box, to scurry to the Mouser and stand before him mad-eyed. The corporal major was followed in a pouring rush by Mikkidu and the rest of the two squads, most of them half-naked. After them – and far more leisurely – came Gavs and the other Mingol crewman off watch, thonging their black hoods closely under their yellow chins, while Ourph came ghosting up behind his captain, though the two other Mingols properly kept to their stations at tiller and prow. The Mouser was vastly surprised. So his scabbard thwackings had actually done some good!

Measuredly beating the padded striker's head in the cupped palm of his right hand, the Mouser observed, 'Well, my small stealers' – (all of the thieves were in fact at least a finger-breadth shorter than the Gray One) – 'it appears you've missed a beating, *barely*,' his face in a hideous grin as he closely surveyed the large areas of bare flesh exposed to the icy air.

He went on, 'But now we must keep you warm – a sailorly necessity in this clime, for which each of you is responsible on pain of flogging, I'll have you know.' His grin became more hideous still. 'To evade night ramming attack, *man the sweeps*!'

The ragged dozen poured past him to snatch up the long, slender oars from their rack between mainmast and mizzen, and drop their looms into the ten proper locks, and stand facing prow at the ready, feet braced against sweeping studs, oar handles against chests, blades poised overside in the fog. Pshawri's squad was stationed steer-side, Mikkidu's load-side, while major and minor corporals supervised fore and aft.

After a quick glance at Pshawri, to assure himself every man was at his station, the Mouser cried, 'Flotsamers! One, two, three – sweep!' and tapped the gong, which he steadied and damped by its edge gripped in his right hand. The ten sweepsmen dipped blades into the unseen salt water and thrust heavily forward against the tholes.

'Recover!' the Mouser growled slowly, then gave the gong another tap. The ship began to move forward and the wash of the swell became tiny slaps against the hull.

'And now keep to it, you clownish, ill-clad cutpurses!' he cried. 'Master Mikkidu! Relieve me at the gong! Sir Pshawri, keep 'em sweepin' evener!' And as he handed the striker to the gasping corporal minor, he dipped his lips toward the cryptic wrinkled face of Ourph and whispered, 'Send Trenchi and Gib below to fetch 'em their warm duds on deck.'

Then he allowed himself a sigh, generally pleased yet perversely dissatisfied because Pshawri hadn't given him excuse to thwack him. Well, one couldn't have everything. Odd to think of a Lankhmar second-story man and Thieves Guild malcontent turned promising soldier-sailor. Yet natural enough – there wasn't that much difference between climbing walls and rigging.

Feeling warmer now, he thought more kindly of Fafhrd. Truly, the Northerner had not yet missed rendezvous; it was *Flotsam*, rather, that'd been early. Now was the time appointed. His face grew somber as he permitted himself the coldly realistic thought (of the sort no one likes) that it would indeed be miracle if he and Fafhrd did find each other in this watery waste, not to mention the icy fog. Still, Fafhrd was resourceful.

The ship grew silent again except for the brush and drip of the sweeps, the clink of the gong, and the small commotions as Pshawri briefly relieved oarsmen hurrying into the clothes the Mingols had fetched. The Mouser turned his attention to the part of his mind that kept watch on the fog's hiddenmost sounds. Almost at once he turned questioningly toward Old Ourph. The dwarfish Mingol flapped his arms slowly up and down. Straining his ears, the Mouser nodded. Then the beat of approaching wings became generally audible. Something struck the icy rigging overhead and a white shape hurtled down. The Mouser threw up his right arm to fend it off and felt his wrist and forearm strongly gripped by something that heaved and twisted. After a moment of breathless fear, in which his left hand

300

snatched at his dirk, he reached it out instead and touched the horny talons tight as gyves around his wrist, and found rolled around a scaly leg a small parchment, the threads of which he cut with sharpened thumbnail. Whereupon the large white hawk left his wrist and perched on the short, round rod from which the ship's gong hung.

Then by flame of fat candle a Mingol crewman fetched after lighting it from the firebox, the Mouser read in Fafhrd's huge script writ very small:

Ahoy, Little Man! – for 'tis unlike there's vessel closer in this wavy wilderness. Burn a red flare and I'll be there.

F.

And then in blacker but sloppier letters suggesting hurried afterthought:

Let's feign mutual attack when we meet, to train our crews. Agreed!

The white flame, burning steady and bright in the still air, showed the Mouser's delighted grin and also the added expression of incredulous outrage as he read the postscript. Northerners as a breed were battle-mad, and Fafhrd the feyest.

'Gib, get quill and squid ink,' he commanded. 'Sir Pshawri, take slow-fire and a red flare to the mainmast top and burn it there. Yarely! But if you fire *Flotsam*, I'll nail you to the burning deck!'

Some moments later, as the Mouser-enlisted small cat-burglar steadily mounted the rigging, though additionally encumbered by a boathook, his captain reversed the small parchment, spread it flat against the mast, and neatly inscribed on its back by light of candle, which Gib held along with the inkhorn:

Madman Most Welcome! – I'll burn them one each bell. I do *not* agree. *My* crew is trained already.

M.

He shook the note to dry it, then gingerly wrapped it closely around the glaring hawk's leg, just above talons, and threaded it tight. As his fingers came away, the bird bated with a shriek and winged off into the fog without command. Fafhrd had at least his avian messengers well trained.

A red glare, surprisingly bright, sprang forth from the fog at the masthead and rose mysteriously a full ten cubits above the top. Then the Mouser saw that, for safety's sake, his own and his ship's, the little corporal major had fixed the flare to the boathook's end and thrust it aloft, thereby also increasing the distance at which it could be seen – by at least a Lankhmar league, the Mouser hurriedly calculated. A sound thought, he had to admit, almost a brilliancy. He had Mikkidu reverse *Flotsam*'s course for practice, the steerside sweepsmen pulling water to swing the ship their way. He went to the prow to assure himself that the heavily muffled Mingol there was steadily scanning the fog ahead, next he returned to the stern, where Ourph stood by his tillerman, both equally thick-cloaked against the cold.

Then, as the red flare glowed on and the relative quiet of steady sweeping returned, the Mouser's ears unwilled resumed their work of searching the fog for strange sounds, and he said softly to Ourph without looking at him, 'Tell me now, Old One, what you really think about your restless nomad brotheren and why they've ta'en to ship instead of horse.'

'They rush like lemmings, seeking death . . . for others,' the ancient croaked reflectively. 'Gallop the waves instead of flinty steppes. To strike down cities is their chiefest urge, whether by land or sea. Perhaps they flee the People of the Ax.'

'I've heard of those,' the Mouser responded doubtfully. 'Think you they'd league with Stardock's viewless fliers, who ride the icy airs above the world?'

'I do not know. They'll follow their clan wizards anywhere.'

The red flare died. Pshawri came down rather jauntily from the top and reported to his dread captain, who dismissed him with a glare which was unexpectedly terminated by a broad wink and the command to burn another flare at the next bell, or demihour. Then turning once more to Ourph, the Mouser spoke low: 'Talking of wizards, do you know of Khahkht?'

The ancient let five heartbeats go by, then croaked, 'Khahkht is Khahkht. It is no tribal sorcerer, 'tis sure. It dwells in farthest north within a dome – some say a floating globe – of blackest ice, from whence It watches the least deeds of men, devising evil every chance It gets, as when the stars are right – better say wrong – and all the Gods asleep. Mingols dread Khahkht and yet . . . whene'er they reach a grand climacteric they turn to It, beseech It ride ahead before their greatest, bloodiest centaurings. Ice is Its favored quarter, ice Its tool, and icy breath Its surest sign save blink.'

'Blink?' the Mouser asked uneasily.

'Sunlight or moonlight shining back from ice,' the Mingol replied. 'Ice blink.'

A soft white flash paled for an instant the dark, pearly fog, and through it the Mouser heard the sound of oars – mightier strokes than those of *Flotsam*'s sweeps and set in a more ponderous rhythm, yet oars or sweeps indubitably, and swiftly growing louder. The Mouser's face grew gladsome. He peered about uncertainly. Ourph's pointing finger stabbed dead ahead. The Mouser nodded, and pitching his voice trumpet-shrill to carry, he hailed forward, 'Fafhrd! Ahoy!'

There was a brief silence, broken only by the beat of *Flotsam*'s sweeps and of the oncoming oars, and then there came out of the fog the heart-quickening though still eerie cry, 'Ahoy, small man! Mouser, well met in wildering waters! And now – on guard!'

The Mouser's glad grin grew frantic. Did Fafhrd seriously intend to carry out *in fog* his fey suggestion of a feigned ships-battle? He looked with a wild questioning at Ourph, who shrugged hugely for one so small.

A brighter white blink momentarily lightened the fog ahead. Without pausing an instant for thought, the Mouser shouted his commands. 'Load-side sweeps! pull water! Yarely! Steer-side, push hard!' And unmindful of the Mingol manning it, he threw himself at the tiller and drove it steer-side so that *Flotsam*'s rudder would strengthen the turning power of the load-side sweeps.

It was well he acted as swiftly as he did. From out the fog ahead thrust a low, thick, sharp-tipped, glittering shaft that

303

would otherwise have rammed *Flotsam*'s bow and split her twain. As it was, the ram grazed *Flotsam*'s side with shuddering rasp as the small ship veered abruptly load-side in response to the desperate sweeping of its soldier-thieves.

And now, following its ram, the white, sharp prow of Fafhrd's ship parted the gleam-shot fog. Almost incredibly lofty that prow was, high as a house and betokening ship as huge, so that *Flotsam*'s men had to crane necks up at it and even the Mouser gasped in fear and wonder. Fortunately it was yards to steerward as *Flotsam* continued to veer loadward, or else the smaller ship had been battered in.

Out of the fog dead ahead there appeared a flatness travelling sideways. A yard above the deck, it struck the mast, which might have snapped except that the flatness broke off first and there dropped with a clash at the Mouser's feet something which further widened his eyes: the great ice-crusted blade and some of the loom of an oar twice the size of *Flotsam*'s sweeps, and looking for all the world like a dead giant's fingernail.

The next huge oar missed the mast, but struck Pshawri a glancing blow and sent him sprawling. The rest missed *Flotsam* by widening margins. From the vast and towering, white, glittering bulk already vanishing in the fog there came a mighty cry: 'Oh, coward! To turn aside from battle challenge! Oh, crafty coward! But go on guard again! I'll get you yet, small one, howe'er you dodge!'

Those huge, mad words were followed by an equally insane laughter. It was the sort of laughter the Mouser had heard before from Fafhrd in perilous battle plights, now madder than ever, fiendish even, but it was loud as if there were a dozen Fafhrds voicing it in unison. Had he trained his berserks to echo him?

A clawlike hand gripped the Mouser's elbow hard. Then Ourph was pointing at the big, broken oar end on the deck. 'It's nought but ice.' The old Mingol's voice resonated with super-stitious awe. 'Ice forged in Khahkht's chill smithy.' He let go Mouser and, swiftly stooping, raised the thing in black-mitted hands widely spaced, as one might a wounded deadly serpent, and of a sudden hurled it overboard.

Beyond him, Mikkidu had lifted Pshawri's shoulders and

bloodied head from the deck. But now he was peering up at his captain over his still, senseless comrade. In his wild eyes was a desperate questioning.

The Mouser hardened his face. 'Sweep on, you sluggards,' he commanded measuredly. 'Push strongly. Mikkidu, let crewmen see to Pshawri, you chink gong for the sweeps. Swiftest beat! Ourph, arm your crew. Send down for arrows and your bows of horn – and for my soldiers their slings and ammunition. Leaden ball, not rock. Gavs, keep close watch astern, Trenchi at prow. Yarely all!'

The Gray One looked grimly dangerous and was thinking thoughts he hated. A thousand years ago in the Silver Eel, Fafhrd had announced he'd hire twelve berserks, madmen in battle. But had his dear friend, now demon-possessed, guessed then just how mad his dozen dements would be, and that their craziness would be catching? and infect himself?

Above the ice fog, the stars glittered like frost candles, dimmed only by the competing light of the gibbous moon low in the southwest, where in the distance the front of an approaching gale was rolling up the thick carpet of ice crystals floating in air.

Not far above the pearly white surface, which stretched to all horizons save the southwest, the messenger hawk the Mouser had released was winging east. As far as eye could see, no other living thing shared its vast-arched loneliness, yet the bird suddenly veered as if attacked, then frantically beat its wings and came to a twisting stop in mid-air, as if it had been seized and held helpless. Only there was nothing to be seen sharing the clear air with the thrashing bird.

The scrap of parchment around its leg unrolled like magic, lay flat in the air for a space, then rolled itself around the scaly leg again. The white hawk shot off desperately to the east, zigzagging as if to dodge pursuit and flying very close to the white floor, as if ready at any moment to dive into it.

A voice came out of the empty air at the point where the bird had been released, soliloquizing, 'There's profit enow and more in this league of Oomforafor of Stardock and the Khahkht of the Black Ice, if my ruse works – and it will! Dear devilish sisters, weep! – your lovers who defiled you are dead men already, though they still breathe and walk awhile. Delayed revenge savored and denied is sweeter than swift. And sweetest of all when the ones you hate love, but are forced to kill, each other. For if my notes effect not that mebliss, my name's not Faroomfar! And now, wing sound-swift! my flat steed of air, my viewless magic rug.'

The strange, low fog stayed thick and bitter cold, but Fafhrd's garb of reversed snow-fawn fur was snug. Gauntleted hand on the low figurehead – a hissing snow serpent – he gazed back with satisfaction from *Sea Hawk*'s prow at his oarsmen, still rowing as strongly as when he'd first commanded them on sighting Mouser's red flare from the masthead. They were staunch lads, when kept busy and battered as needed. Nine of them tall as he, and three taller – his corporals Skullick and Mannimark and sergeant Skor, the last two hid by the fog where Skor clinked time at the stern. Each petty officer immediately commanded a squad of three men.

And *Sea Hawk* was a staunch sailing galley! – a little longer and narrower of beam and with much taller mast, rigged fore and aft, than the Gray Mouser's ship (though Fafhrd could not know that, never having seen *Flotsam*).

Yet he frowned slightly. Pelly should be back by now, provided Mouser had sent a return message, and the little gray man never lost a chance to talk, whether by tongue or pen. It was time he visited the top anyhow – the Mouser might burn another flare, and Skullick wake-dream on watch. But as he neared the mast, a seven-foot ghost loomed up – a ghost in turned gray otter's fur.

'How now, Skullick?' Fafhrd rasped, looking up their half span's difference in height. 'Why have you left your station? Speak swiftly, scum!' And without other warning or preparation, he struck his corporal major a short-traveling jolt in the midriff that jarred him back a step and (rather illogically) robbed him of most of the breath he had to speak with.

'It's cold . . . as witch's womb . . . up there,' Skullick gasped with pain and difficulty. 'And my relief's . . . o'erdue.'

'From now on you'll wait on station for your relief until Hell freezes over, and haply you too. But you're relieved.' And Fafhrd struck him again in the same crucial spot. 'Now water the rowers, four measures of water to one of usquebaugh – and if you take more than two gulps of the last, I'll surely know!'

He tuned away abruptly, reached the mast in two strides, and climbed it rhythmically by the pins of its bronze collars, past the mainyard, to which the big sail was snugly furled, past the peak, until his gloved hands gripped the short, horizontal bar of the crow's-perch. As he drew himself up by it, it was a wonder how the fog gave way without gradation to star-ceilinged air, as though a fine film, impalpable yet tough, confined the ice motes, held them down. When he stood on the bar and straightened himself, he was waist-deep in fog so thick he could barely see his feet. He and the mast top were scudding through a pearly sea, strongly propelled by the invisible rowers below. The stars told him *Sea Hawk* was still headed due west. His sense of direction had worked truly in the fog below. Good!

Also, the feckless Skullick had spoken true. It was cold indeed as a she-demon's privies, yet wonderfully bracing. He noted the new wind sweeping up the fog in the southwest, and north of that the spot where he'd picked up the Mouser's flare on the horizon's brim. The deformed fat moon was there now, almost touching it, yet still most bright. If the Mouser burned another flare, it ought to be higher, because Fafhrd's rowing should be bringing the ships together. He searched the west closely to make sure another red spark wasn't being drowned by Nehwon's strong moonlight.

He saw a black speck against the lopsided, bright pearl orb. As he watched, it rapidly increased in size, grew wings, and with a white beat of them landed with jolting twin-talon grip on Fafhrd's gauntleted wrist.

'You're ruffled, Pelly. Who has troubled you?' he asked as he snapped threads and unrolled from leg the parchment scrap. He recognized the start of his own note, flipped it over, and by the flat moonlight read the Mouser's.

Madman Most Welcome! – I'll burn them one each bell. I do *not* agree. *My* crew is trained already.

M.

No feigned attack, you cur once my friend, but earnest
deadly. I want no less than your destruction, dog. To the
death!

Fafhrd read the salutation and first sentence with great relief
and joy. The next two sentences made him frown in puzzlement.
But with the dire postscript, his face fell, and his expression
became one of deep dread and utter dolefulness. He hurriedly
rescanned the script to see how the letters and words were
formed. They were the Mouser's unquestionably, the postscript
slightly scrawled 'cause writ more swift. Something he'd missed
nagged briefly at his mind, then was forgot. He crumpled the
parchment and thrust it deep in his pouch.

He said to himself in the naked, low tones of a man plunged
into nightmare, 'I can't believe and yet cannot deny. I know
when Mouser jests and when speaks true. There must be swift-
striking madness in these polar seas, perhaps loosed by that
warlock Afreyt named . . . Ice Wizard . . . It . . . Khahkht. And
yet . . . and yet I must ready *Sea Hawk* for total war, howe'er it
grieve me. A man must be prepared for *all* events, no matter how
they chill and tear his heart.'

He gave the west a final glance. The front of the southwest
gale was close now, sweeping up the ice crystals ahead of it. It
was a chord that cut off a whole sector of the circular white fog-
sea, replacing it with naked black ocean. From that came a
fleeting white glow that made Fafhrd mutter, 'Ice blink.'

Then closer still, hardly a half-score bowshots away, still in
the fog yet near its wind-smitten edge, a redness flared bright,
then died.

Fafhrd sank swiftly into the fog, going down the mast in swift
hand-over-hand drops, his boots hardly touching the bronze
collar pins.

Inside the dark-mapped globular vacuity, It ceased Its dartings,
held Itself rigidly erect, facing away from the water-walled
equatorial sun disk, and intoned in voice like grinding ice floes,
'Heed me, smallest atomies, that in rime seas seethe and freeze.
Hear me, spirits of the cold, then do straightway what you're
told. Ships are meeting, heroes greeting; gift to each, from each,

of death. Monstreme lurk, in icy murk, picket of the Mingol work 'gainst each city, hearth, and kirk. If they 'scape the Viewless's ruse, make yourself of direst use. Vessels shatter! Manbones scatter! Bloody flesh, bones darkness splatter! – every splinter, every tatter! Deeds of darkness, darkness merit – so, till's done, put out the sun!'

And with reptilian swiftness It whipped around and clapped a blacked-iron lid over the softly flaring, walled solar disk, which plunged the spherical cavity into an absolute blackness, wherein It whispered grindingly and chucklesome, ' . . .and the Ghouls conjured the sun out of Heaven, quotha! Ghouls, indeed! – ever o'er-boastful. Khahkht never boasts, but does!'

At the foot of *Flotsam*'s mainmast the Gray Mouser gripped Pshawri by the throat, but forbore to shake him. Beneath bloody head-circling bandage, his corporal major's white-circled pupils stared at him defiantly from bloodless face.

'Was one light battle-tap enough to make a crack for all your brains to leak out?' the Mouser demanded. '*Why did you fire that flare*, and so reveal us to our enemy?'

Pshawri winced but continued to oppose his gaze to the captain's glare. 'You ordered it – and did not countermand,' he stated stubbornly.

The Mouser sputtered, but had to allow the truth of that. The fool had been obedient, even if utterly lacking in judgment. Soldiers and their blind devotion to duty! especially spoken order! Most odd to think that his faithful idiot was yesterday a burglar-thief, child of treachery and lies and blinkered self-ishness. The Mouser had also guiltily to admit he could have countermanded his command, paying lip service to logic and making allowance for stupidity, and particularly have noted what the fool was up to when he mounted the mast a second time. Pshawri was clearly still shaken from his head blow, poor devil, and at least he had been quick enough in casting boathook and flare into the sea when the Mouser'd roared at him from below.

'Very well,' he said gruffly, releasing his grip. 'Next time think too – if there's time – and there was! – as well as act. Ask Ourph for a noggin of white brandy. Then be forward lookout with Gavs – I'm doubling them bow and stern.'

And with that, the Mouser himself took up the general work of trying to pierce the stilly fog with eyes and ears, wondering the while unhappy and uneasy about the nature of Fafhrd's madness and of the vast, fell vessel he'd built, bought, commandeered, or perchance got from Ningauble or other sorcerer. Or sorcerers? – it had surely been big and weird enough to be the chattel of several archimages! Conceivably a refitted prison hulk from rimy No-Ombrulsk. Or, illest thought of all (stemming from Ouirph's fears 'bout the vanished oar shard), was the sorcerer Khahkht? – and some link 'twixt that warlock and mad Fafhrd?

Flotsam ghosted on, the sweepsmen pushing only enough to keep her under way. Mouser had early ordered slowest beat to conserve their strength.

'Three bells,' Ourph softly called.

Dawn nighs, the Mouser thought.

Pshawri could not have been long at the bow when his cry came back, 'Clear sea ahead! And wind!'

The fog thinned to wisps torn and tossed aft by the eddying, frosty air. The gibbous moon was firmly bedded on the western horizon, yet still sent an eerie white glare, while south of her a few lonely stars hung in the sky. That was uncanny, the Mouser thought, for the imminent dawn should already have extinguished them. He faced east – and almost gasped. Above the low, moonlit fog bank, the heavens were darker than ever, the night was starless, while due east on the fog bank rested a sliver of blackness blacker than any night could be, as if a black sun were rising that shot out beams of a darkness powerful and active as light – not light's absence, but its enemy-opposite. And from that same thickening sliver, along with potent darkness, there seemed to come a cold more intense and different in kind from that of the bitter southwest wind striking behind his right ear.

'Ship on our loadside beam!' Pshawri cried shrilly.

At once the Mouser dropped his gaze and sighted the stranger vessel, about three bowshots distant, just emerged from the fog bank and equally illumined by the moon glare, and headed straight at *Flotsam*. At first he took it for Fafhrd's icy leviathan come again, then saw it was small as his own ship, maybe narrower of beam. His thoughts zigzagged wildly – did mad Fafhrd command a fleet? was it a Sea Mingol warcraft? or still other pirate? or from Rime Isle? He forced himself to think more to the purpose.

His heart pulsed twice. Then, 'Make sail, my Mingols all!' he commanded. 'Odd-numbered sweepsmen! rack your long tools, then arm! Pshawri! command 'em!' And he grasped the tiller as the steersman let it go.

Aboard *Sea Hawk*, Fafhrd saw *Flotsam*'s low hull and short masts and long, slantwise main and mizzen yards blackly silhouetted against the spectrally white, misshapen moon awash in the west. In the same instant he at last realized what it was that had nagged his mind at the mast top. He whipped gauntlet from his right hand, plunged the latter into his pouch, plucked out the parchment scrap, and this time reread his own note – and saw below it the damning postscript he knew he'd never written. Clearly both postscripts, penned in deceptive scrawls, were cunning forgeries, however done o'erhead in birds' realm.

So even as he felt the wind and commanded, 'Skor! Take your squad. Prepare to make sail!' he drew a favorite arrow from the quiver ready beside him on the deck, threaded the note around it in studied haste, swiftly uncased and strung his great bow, and with a curt prayer to Kos bent it to its muscle-cracking extreme and sent the pet arrow winging high into the black sky toward the moon and the black two-master.

Aboard *Flotsam*, the Mouser felt a shiver of superadded apprehension which mounted while he watched his Mingols purposefully struggling with frozen lines and ties in the freshening chilly wind, until it culminated in the *chunk* of an arrow almost vertically into the deck scarce a cubit from his foot. So the small, moonlit sailing galley (for he had meanwhile identified it as such a craft) was signaling attack! Yet the range was still so great that he knew of only one bowman in Nehwon who could have made that miraculous shot. Not letting go the tiller, he stooped and severed the threads of the pale parchment wrapped tightly just behind the arrow's half-buried head, and read (or rather mostly reread) the two notes, his with the devilish postscript he'd never seen before. Even as he finished, the characters became unreadable from the black beams of antisun fighting down the moon rays and beginning to darken that orb. Yet he made the same deduction as had Fafhrd, and hot tears of joy were squeezed from his chilled eye sockets as he realized that whatever impossible-seeming sleights of ink and voice had been worked this night, his friend was sane and true.

There was a protracted sharp crackling as the last ties of the sails were loosed and wind filled them, breaking their frozen folds and festoons. The Mouser bore on the tiller, heading *Flotsam* into what was now a strengthening gale. But at the same time he sharply commanded, 'Mikkidu! burn three flares, two red, one white!'

Aboard *Sea Hawk*, Fafhrd saw the blessed treble sign flare up in gathering unnatural murk, even as his reefed sails filled and he turned his craft into the wind. He ordered, 'Mannimark! answer those flares with like. Skullick, you dolt! slack your squad's bows. Those to the west are friends!' Then he said to Skor beside him, 'Take the helm. My friend's ship is on close-hauled southron course like ours. Work over to her. Lay us alongside.'

Aboard *Flotsam*, the Mouser was giving like directions to Ourph. He was cheered by sight of Fafhrd's flares matching his own, though he did not need their testimony. Now he longed for talk with Fafhrd. Which would be soon. The gap of black water between ships was narrowing rapidly. He wasted a moment musing whether mere chance or else some goddess had steered his comrade's arrow aside from his heart. He thought of Cif.

Aboard both ships, almost in unison, Pshawri and Mannimark cried out fearfully, 'Ship close astern!'

Out of the torn and darkening fog bank, driving with preternatural rapidity into the teeth of the gale on a course to smash them both, there had silently come a craft monstrous in size and aspect. It might well have remained unseen until collision, save that the weird rays of the rising black sun striking its load side engendered there a horrid, pale reflection, not natural white light at all, but a loathy, colorless luminescence – a white to make the flesh crawl, a cave-toad, fish-belly white. And if the substance making the reflection had any texture at all, it was that of ridged and crinkled gray horn – dead men's fingernails.

The leprous Hel-glow showed the demonic craft to have thrice the freeboard of any natural ship. Its towering prow and sides were craggy and jagged, as if it were cast entire of ice in a titanic rough mold left over from the Age of Chaos, or else hacked by jinn into crude ship-likeness from a giant berg broken off from glacier vast. And it was driven by banks of oars long and twitchy as insect legs or limbs of myriapod, yet big as jointed yards or masts, as they sent it scuttling monstrously across black ocean vast. And from its lofty deck, as if hurled by demon ballistas, catapults, and mangonels, there now came hurtling down around *Flotsam* and *Sea Hawk* great blocks of ice which sent up black, watery volcanoes. While from the jagged top of its foremast – pale, big, and twisted as a thunder-blasted pine long dead – there shot out two thin beams of blackest black, like rays of antisun but more intense, which smote the Gray Mouser and Fafhrd each in the chest with deep-striking chill and sick, spreading dizziness and weakening of will.

Nevertheless they each managed to give rapid, stinging commands, and the two ships turned away in time's nick from each other and the oared deathberg striking between them. *Flotsam* had had only to turn further into the wind and so come round smoothly and swiftly. But *Sea Hawk* perforce must jibe. Its sail shivered a space, then filled abruptly on the other side with noise like thunder crack, but the stout Ool Krut canvas did not split. Both ships scudded north before the gale.

Behind them the eldritch bergship slowed and turned with supernatural celerity, spider-walked by its strange oars, and came in monstrous pursuit, gigantically oared on. And although no word was voiced or sign given by the pursued – almost as if by taking no notice of it, the menacing tangle of ghostly white evil astern could be made not to be – a collective shudder nevertheless went through the crews and captains of the sailing galley and the long-yarded two-master.

With that began a time of trial and tension, a Reign of Terror, an Eternal Night, such as no one amongst them had ever known before. First, there was the darkness, which grew greater the higher the antisun climbed in the black heavens. Even candle flames below and the cook fires sheltered from the blast grew blue and dim. While the pustulant white glow hunting them had this quality: that its light illumined nothing it fell on, but rather darkened it, as if it carried the essence of the antilight along with it, as if it existed solely to make visible the terror of the bergship. Although the bergship was real as death and ever inching nearer, that eerie light sometimes seemed to Fafhrd and the Mouser most akin to the glows seen crawling on the inside of closed eyelids in darkness absolute.

Second, there was the cold that was a part of the antisunlight and struck deep with it, that penetrated every cranny of *Sea Hawk* and *Flotsam*, that had to be fought with both protective huddlings and violent movement, and also with drink and food warmed very slowly and with difficulty over the enfeebled flames – a cold that could paralyze both mind and body, and then kill.

Third, there was the potent silence that came with the unnatural dark and cold, the silence that made almost inaudible the constant creakings of rigging and wood, that muffled all foot-stampings and sideflailings against the cold, that turned all speech to whispers and changed the pandemonium of the great gale itself driving them north to the soft roaring of a seashell held forever to the ear.

And then there was that great gale itself, no whit weaker that it had no great noise – the gale that blew icy spume over the stern, the murderous gale that had always to be struggled against and kept watch on (gripping with fingers and thumbs like gyves to hopefully firm handholds when a man was any-where on deck above), the gale near hurricane force that was driving them ever north at an unprecedented pace. None of them had ever before sailed before such a wind, even in the Mouser's and Fafhrd's and Ourph's first passage of the Outer Sea. Any of them would have long since hove to with bare masts and likely sea anchor, save for the menace of the bergship behind.

Last, there was that monstrous craft itself, deathberg or bergship, ever gaining on them, its leggy oars ever more strongly plied. Rarely, a jagged ice block crashed in black sea beside them. Rarely, a black ray teased at hero's heart. But those were but cackling reminders. The monster craft's main menace: it did nothing (save close the distance to its fleeting foes). The monster craft's intent: grapple and board! (or so it seemed).

Each on his ship, Fafhrd and Mouser fought weariness and chill; insane desire to sleep; strange, fleeting dreads. Once Fafhrd fancied unseen fliers battling overhead, as if in fabulous aerial extension of the sea war of his and Mouser's craft 'gainst iceship huge. Once Mouser seemed to see black sails of two great fleets. Both masters cheered their men, kept them alive.

Sometimes *Sea Hawk* and *Flotsam* were far apart in their parallel flight north, quite out of sight and hail. Sometimes they came together enough to see glints of each other. And once so close their captains could trade words.

Fafhrd hailed in bursts (they were whispers in Mouser's ears), 'Ho, Small One! Heard you Stardock's fliers? Our mountain princesses . . . fighting with Faroomfar?'

The Mouser shouted back, 'My ears are frostbit. Have you sighted . . . other foe ships . . . besides monstreme?'

Fafhrd: Monstreme? What's that?

Mouser: That ill astern. My word's analogous . . . to bireme . . . quadrireme. Monstreme! – rowed by monsters.

Fafhrd: A monstreme in full gale. An awful thought! (He looked astern at it.)

Mouser: Monstreme in monsoon . . . would be awfuler.

Fafhrd: Let's not waste breath. When will we raise Rime Isle?

Mouser: I had forgot we had a destination. What time think you?

Fafhrd: First bell in second dogwatch. Sunset season.

Mouser: It should get lighter . . . when this black sun sets.

Fafhrd: It ought to. Damn the double dark!

Mouser: Damn the dimidiate halved white astern! What's its game?

Fafhrd: Freeze fast to us, I wot. Then kill by cold, else board us.

Mouser: That's great, I must say. They should hire you.

So their shouts trailed off – a joy at first, but soon a tiredness. And they had their men to care for. Besides, it was too risky, ships so close.

There passed a weary and nightmarish time. Then to the

north, where nought had changed all the black day of plunging into it, Fafhrd marked a dark red glow. Long while he doubted it, deemed it some fever in his frozen skull. He noted Afreyt's slender face bobbing among his thoughts. At his side Skor asked him, 'Captain, is that a distant fire dead ahead? Our lost sun about to rise in north?' At last Fafhrd believed in the red glow.

Aboard *Flotsam*, the Mouser, racked by the poisons of exhaustion and barely aware, heard Fafhrd whisper, 'Mouser, ahoy. Look ahead. What do you see?' He realized it was a mighty shout diminished by black silence and the gale, and that *Sea Hawk* had come close again. He could see glints from the shields affixed along her side, while astern the monstreme was close too, looming like a leprously opalescent cliff arock. Then he looked ahead.

After a bit, 'A red light,' he wheezed, then forced himself to bellow the same words alee, adding, 'Tell me what is it. And then let me sleep.'

'Rime Isle, I trow,' Fafhrd replied across the gap.

'Are they burning her down?' the Mouser asked.

The answer came back faintly and eerily, 'Remember . . . on the gold pieces . . . a volcano?'

The Mouser didn't believe he'd heard aright his comrade's next cry after that one, until he'd made him repeat it. Then, 'Sir Pshawri!' he called sharply, and when that one came limping up, hand to bandaged head, he ordered, 'Heave bucket overside on line and haul it up. I want waves' sample. Swiftly, you repulsive cripple!'

Somewhat later, Pshawri's eyebrows rose as his captain took the sloshing bucket he proffered and set it to his lips and uptilted it, next handed it back to Pshawri, swished around his teeth the sample he'd taken into his mouth, made a face, and spat to lee.

The fluid was far less icy than the Mouser had expected, almost tepid – and saltier than the water of the Sea of Monsters, which lies just west of the Parched Mountains that hide the Shadowland. He wondered for a mad moment if they'd been magicked to that vast, dead lake. 'Twould fit with monstreme. He thought of Cif.

There was impact. The deck tilted and did not rock back. Pshawri dropped the bucket and screamed.

The monstreme had thrust between the smaller ships and instantly frozen to them with its figurehead (living or dead?) of sea monster hacked or born of ice, its jaws agape betwixt their masts, while from the lofty deck high overhead there pealed down Fafhrd's laughter, monstrously multiplied.

The monstreme visibly shrank.

At one stride went the dark. From the low west the true sun burst forth, warmly lighting the bay in which they lay and striking an infinitude of golden gleams from the great, white, crystalline cliff to steerside, down which streaming water rushed in a thousand streams and runnels. A league or so beyond it rose a conical mountain down whose sides flowed glaring scarlet and from whose jaggedly truncated summit brilliant vermilion flames streamed toward the zenith, their dark smoke carried off northeastward by the wind.

Pointing at it with outthrown arm, Fafhrd called, 'See, Mouser, the red glow.'

Straight ahead, nearer than the cliff and drifting steadily still nearer, was a town or small unwalled city of low buildings hugging gentle hills, its waterfront one long low wharf, where a few ships were docked and a small crowd was assembled quietly. While to the west, rounding out the bay, there were more cliffs, the nearer bare dark rock, the farther robed in snow.

Facing the city, Fafhrd said, 'Salthaven.'

Studying the steaming, streaming, glittering white cliff and fiery peak beyond, the Mouser remembered the two scenes on his golden coins, all spent. This reminded him of the four silver coins he'd not been able to spend because they'd been snatched from his table at the Eel by the battered server, and of the two scenes on *their* faces: an iceberg and a monster. He turned round.

The monstreme was gone. Or rather, its last dissolving shards were sinking into the tranquil waters of the bay without sound or commotion, save that a little steam was rising.

Half-hurled, half-self-magicked from the monstreme's bridge, where It had been gazing out in triumph over the welter of dire, frigid forms on the decks below, Its mind obsessed with evil, back into Its cramped black sphere, Khahkht cursed in voice like Fafhrd's which midway became again a croak, 'Damn to the depths of Hell Rime Isle's strange gods! Their day will come, their dooms! Which now devise I whilst I snugly sleep . . .' It whipped the lid off the water-walled sun and spoke a spell that rotated the sphere until the sun was topmost, the Great Subequatorial Desert nethermost. It briefly fanned the former hot and then curled up in the latter and closed Its eyes, muttering, ' . . . for even Khahkht is cold.'

While on tall Stardock, Great Oomforafor listened to the news of the defeat, or setback rather, and of his dear daughters' further treacheries, as told him by his furious, bedraggled son Prince Faroomfar, who'd been hurled back much as Khahkht.

As the Mouser turned back to the great white cliff, he realized that it must be made entire of salt – hence the seaport's name – and that the hot, volcanic waters coursing down it were dissolving it, which did much to account for the warm saltiness of ocean hereabouts and the swift melting of the frost monstreme. The last made all of magic ice, he mused, both stronger and weaker than the ordinary – as magic itself than life.

Fafhrd and he, looking toward the long wharf as they experienced sweetest relief and their ships drew steadily closer to it, saw two slender figures of different heights standing somewhat apart from the other seaside welcomers, who by that token and their proud attitudes and quietly rich garb – blue-gray the one, rust-red the other – must be individuals high in the councils of Rime Isle.

VIII
RIME ISLE

Fafhrd and the Gray Mouser supervised the mooring of *Sea Hawk* and *Flotsam* by bow and stern lines made fast round great wooden bollards, then sprang nimbly ashore, feeling unutterably weary, yet knowing that as captains they should not show it. They made their way to each other, embraced, then turned to face the crowd of Rime Isle men who had witnessed their dramatic arrival standing in a semicircle around the length of dock where their battered and salt-crusted ships were now moored.

Beyond the crowd stretched the houses of Salthaven port – small, stout and earth-hugging, as befitted this most northerly clime – in hues of weathered blue and green and a violet that was almost gray, except for those in the immediate neighborhood, which seemed rather squalid, where they were all angry reds and plague yellow.

Beyond Salthaven the low rolling land went off, gray-green with moss and heather, until it met the gray-white wall of a great glacier, and beyond that the old ice stretched until it met in turn the abrupt slopes of an active and erupting volcano, although the red glow of its lava and the black volume of its flamy smoke seemed to have diminished since they first glimpsed it from their ships.

The foremost of the crowd were all large, burly, quiet-faced men, booted, trousered, and smocked as fishers. Most of them bore quarterstaves, handling them as if they knew well how to use these formidable weapons. They curiously yet composedly eyed the Twain and their ships, the Mouser's broad-beamed and somewhat lubberly trader *Flotsam* with its small Mingol crew and squad of disciplined (a wonder!) thieves, Fafhrd's trimmer galley *Sea Hawk* with its contingent of disciplined (if that can be imagined at all) berserkers. On the dock near the bollards where they'd made fast were Fafhrd's lieutenant Skor, the Mouser's – Pshawri – and two other crew members.

It was the quietness and composure of the crowd that puzzled and now began even to nettle the Mouser and Fafhrd. Here they'd sailed all the distance and survived almost unimaginable black hurricane-dangers to help save Rime Isle from a vast invasion of maddened and piratical Sea-Mingols bent on world-conquest, and there was no gladness to be seen anywhere, only stolidly appraising looks. There should be cheering and dancing and some northerly equivalent of maidens throwing flowers! True, the two steaming cauldrons of chowder borne on a shoulder-yoke by one of the fishermen seemed to betoken thoughtful welcome – but they hadn't yet been offered any!

The mouth-watering aroma of the fish-stew now reached the nostrils of the crewmen lining the sides of the two vessels in various attitudes of extreme weariness and dejection – for they were at least half as spent as their captains and had no urge to conceal it – and their eyes slowly brightened and their jaws began to work sympathetically. Behind them the sun-dancing snug harbor, so recently black-skyed, was full of small ships riding at anchor, local fishing craft chiefly with the lovely lines of porpoises, but near at hand several that were clearly from afar, including a small trading galleon of the Eastern Lands and (wonder!) a Keshite junk, and one or two modest yet unfamiliar craft that had the disquieting look of coming from seas beyond Nehwon's. (Just as there was a scatter of sailors from far-off ports in the crowd, peering here and there from between the tall Rime Islanders.)

And now the Rime Isler nearest the Twain walked silently toward them, flanked a pace behind by two others. He stopped a bare yard away, but still did not speak. In fact, he still did not seem so much to be looking at them as past them at their ships and crews, while working out some abstruse reckoning in his head. All three men were quite as tall as Fafhrd and his berserkers.

Fafhrd and the Mouser retained their dignity with some difficulty. Never did to speak first when the other man was supposed to be your debtor.

Finally the other seemed to terminate his calculations and he spoke, using the Low Lankhmarese that is the trade jargon of the northern world.

'I am Groniger, harbor master of Salthaven. I estimate your ships will be a good week repairing and revictualling. We will feed and board your crew ashore in the traders' quarters.' He gestured toward the squalid red and yellow buildings.

'Thank you,' Fafhrd said gravely, while the Mouser echoed coolly, 'Indeed, yes.' Hardly an enthusiastic welcome, but still one.

Groniger thrust out his hand, palm uppermost. 'The charge,' he said loudly, 'will be five gold pieces for the galley, seven for the tub. Payment in advance.'

Fafhrd's and the Mouser's jaws dropped. The latter could not contain his indignation, captain's dignity or no.

'But we're your sworn allies,' he protested, 'come here as promised, through perils manifold, to be your mercenaries and help save you from the locust-swarm invasion of the raptorial Sea-Mingols counseled and led by evilest Khahkht, the Wizard of Ice.'

Groniger's eyebrows lifted. 'What invasion?' he queried. 'The Sea-Mingols are our friends. They buy our fish. They may be pirates to others, but never to Rime Isle ships. Khahkht is an old wives' tale, not to be credited by men of sense.'

'Old wives' tale?' the Mouser exploded. 'When we were but now three endless nights harried by Khahkht's monstrous galley and sank it at last on your very doorstep. His invasion came that close to success. Did you not observe the universal blackness and hell-wind when he conjured the sun out of heaven three days running?'

'We saw some dark clouds blowing up from the south,' Groniger said, 'under whose cover you approached Salthaven. They vanished when they touched Rime Isle – as all things superstitious are like to do. As for invasion, there were rumors of such an eruption some months back, but our council sifted 'em and found 'em idle gossip. Have any of you heard aught of a Sea-Mingol invasion since?' he asked loudly, looking from side to side at his fellow Rime Islers. They all shook their heads.

'So pay up!' he repeated, jogging his outthrust palm, while

those behind him wagged their quarterstaves, firming their grips.

'Shameless ingratitude!' the Mouser rebuked, taking a moral tone as a leader of men. 'What gods do you worship here on Rime Isle, to be so hard-hearted?'

Groniger's answer rang out distinct and cool. 'We worship no gods at all, but do our business in the world clearheadedly, no misty dreams. We leave such fancies to the so-called civilized people – decadent cultures of the hothouse south. Pay up, I say.'

At that moment Fafhrd, whose height permitted him to see over the crowd, cried out, 'Here are those coming who hired us, harbor master, and will give the lie to your disclaimers.'

The crowd parted respectfully to let through two slender, trousered women with long knives at their belts in jeweled scabbards. The taller was clad all in blue, with like eyes, and fair hair. Her comrade was garmented in dark red, with green eyes and black hair that seemed to have gold wires braided in it. Skor and Pshawri, still stupid with fatigue, took note of them and it was impossible to mistake the message in the seadogs' kindling eyes: Here were the northern angels come at last!

'The eminent councilwomen Afreyt and Cif,' Groniger intoned. 'We are honored by their presence.'

They approached with queenly smiles and looks of amiable curiosity.

'Tell them, Lady Afreyt,' said Fafhrd courteously to the one in blue, 'how you commissioned me to bring Rime Isle twelve—' Suppressing the word 'berserk', he smoothly made it, '—stout northern fighters of the fiercest temper.'

'And I twelve . . . nimble and dextrous Lankhmar sworders and slingers, sweet Lady Cif,' the Mouser chimed in airily, avoiding the word 'thief'.

Afreyt and Cif looked at them blankly. Then their gazes became at once anxious and solicitous.

Afreyt commented, 'They've been tempest-tossed, poor lads, and doubtless it has disordered their memories. Our little northern gales come as a surprise to southerners. They seem gentle. Use them well, Groniger.' Looking intently at Fafhrd, she lifted her hand to adjust her hair and in lowering it hesitated a finger for a moment crosswise to her tightly shut long lips.

Cif added, 'Doubtless privation has temporarily addled their wits. Their ships have seen hard use. But what a tale! I wonder who they are? Nourish them with hot soup – after they've paid, of course.' And she winked at the Mouser a green dark-lashed eye on the side away from Groniger. Then the two ladies wandered on.

It is a testimony to the fundamental levelheadedness and growing self-control of the Mouser and Fafhrd (now having, as captains, to control others) that they did not expostulate at this astounding and barely-tempered rebuff, but actually each dug a hand into his purse – though they did look after the two strolling females somewhat wonderingly. So they saw Skor and Pshawri, who had been dazedly following the two apparitions of northernly delight, now approach these houris with the clear intent of establishing some sort of polite amorous familiarity.

Afreyt struck Skor aside in no uncertain fashion, but only after leaning her face close enough to his head to hiss a word or two into his ear and grasp his wrist in a way that would have permitted her to slip a token or note into his palm. Cif treated Pshawari's advances likewise.

Groniger, pleased at the way the two captains were now dragging gold pieces from their purses, nevertheless admonished them, 'And see to it that your crewmen offer no affront to our Salthaven women, nor stray one step beyond the bounds of the traders' quarter.'

Paying up took the last of the Rime Isle gold that Cif had given them back at the Silver Eel in Lankhmar, while the Mouser had to piece out his seven with two Lankhmar rilks and a Sarheenmar dubloon.

Groniger's eyebrows rose as he scanned the take. 'Rime Isle coinage! So you'd touched here before and knew our harbor rules and were only seeking to bargain? But what made you invent such an unbelievable story?'

Fafhrd shrugged and said shortly, 'Not so. Had 'em off an Eastern trading galley in these waters,' while the Mouser only laughed.

Nevertheless, a thought struck Groniger, and he looked after the two Rime Isle councilwomen speculatively as he said shortly, 'Now you may feed your men.'

The Mouser called toward *Flotsam*, 'Ho, lads! Fetch your bowls, cups, and spoons. These most hostful Rime Islanders have provided a feast for you. Orderly now! Pshawri, attend me.'

While Fafhrd commanded likewise, adding, 'Forget not they're our friends. Do 'em courtesies. A word with you, Skor.' Never do to show resentment, though that 'tub' still rankled with the Mouser, despite it being a very fair description of the broad-beamed, sweep-propelled *Flotsam*.

When the Mouser and Fafhrd had seen all their men eating and served a measure of grog to celebrate safe arrival, they turned to their somewhat doleful lieutenants, who with only a show of reluctance yielded up the notes they'd been slipped – as the Twain had surmised – along with the words, 'For your master!'

Unfolded, Afreyt's read, 'Another faction controls the Rime Isle council, temporarily. You do not know me. At dusk tomorrow seek me at the Hill of the Eight-Legged Horse,' while Cif's message was, 'Cold Khahkht has sowed dissension in our council. We never met – play it that way. You'll find me tomorrow night at the Flame Den if you come alone.'

'So she does not speak with the voice of Rime Isle after all,' Fafhrd commented softly. 'To what fiery female politicians have we joined our destinies?'

'Her gold was good,' the Mouser answered gruffly. 'And now we've two new riddles to solve.'

'Flame Den and Eight-Legged Horse,' Fafhrd echoed.

'Tub, he called her,' the Mouser mused bitterly, his mind veering. 'What godless literal-minded philosophers are we now supposed to succor in spite of themselves?'

'You're a godless man too,' Fafhrd reminded him.

'Not so, there was once Mog,' the Mouser protested with a touch of his old playful plaintiveness, referring to a youthful credulity, when he had briefly believed in the spider god to please a lover.

'Such questions can wait, along with the two riddles,' Fafhrd decided. 'Now let's curry favor with the atheist fishermen while we can.'

And accompanied by the Mouser, he proceeded ceremoniously to offer Groniger white brandy fetched from *Flotsam* by old Ourph the renegade Mingol. The harbor master was prevailed upon to accept a drink, which he took in slow sips, and by way of talk of repair docks, watering, crew dormitories ashore, and the price of salt fish, the conversation became somewhat more general. With difficulty Fafhrd and the Mouser won license to venture outside the traders' quarter, but only by day, and not their men. Groniger refused a second drink.

Inside Its icy sphere, which would have cramped a taller being, Khahkht roused, muttering, 'Rime Isle's new gods are treacherous – betray and re-betray – yet stronger than I guessed.'

It began to study the dark map of the world of Nehwon depicted on the sphere's interior. Its attention moved to the northern tongue of the Outer Sea, where a long peninsula of the Western Continent reached toward the Cold Waste, with Rime Isle midway between. Leaning Its spidery face close to the tip of that peninsula, It made out on the northern side tiny specks in the dark blue waters.

'The armada of the Widdershins Sea-Mingols invests Sayend,' It chuckled, referring to the easternmost city of the ancient Empire of Eevamarensee. 'To work!'

It wove Its thickly black-bristled hands incantingly above the gathered specks and droned, 'Harken to me, slaves of death. Hear my word and feel my breath. Every least instruction learn. First of all, Sayend must burn! Again Nehwon your horde be hurled, next Rime Isle and then the world.' One spider-hand drifted sideways toward the small green island in ocean's midst. 'Round Rime Isle let fishes swarm, provisioning my Mingol storm.' The hand drifted back and the passes became swifter. 'Blackness seize on Mingol mind, bend it 'gainst humankind. Madness redden Mingol ire, out of cold come death by fire!'

It blew strongly as if on cold ashes and a tiny spot on the peninsula tip glowed dark red like an uncovered ember.

'By will of Khahkht these weirds be locked!' It grated, sealing the incantment.

The ships of the Widdershins Sea-Mingols rode at anchor in Sayend harbor, packed close together as fish in a barrel, and as silvery white. Their sails were furled. Their midships decks, abutting abeam, made a rude roadway from the precipitous shore to the flagship, where Edumir, their chief paramount, sat enthroned on the poop, quaffing the mushroom wine of Quarmall that fosters visions. Cold light from the full moon south in the wintry sky revealed the narrow horse-cage that was the forecastle of each ship and picked out the mad eyes and rawboned head of the ship's horse, a gaunt Steppe-stallion, thrust forward through the wide-set irregular bars and all confronting the east.

The taken town, its sea-gate thrown wide, was dark. Before its walls and in its sea-street its small scatter of defenders sprawled as they'd fallen, soaked in their own blood and scurried over by the looting Sea-Mingols, who did not, however, bother the chief doors behind which the remaining inhabitants had locked and barred themselves. They'd already captured the five maidens ritual called for and dispatched them to the flagship, and now they sought oil of whale, porpoise, and scaly fish. Puzzlingly, they did not bring most of this treasure-trove down to their ships, but wasted it, breaking the casks with axes and smashing the jars, gushing the precious stuff over doors and wooden walls and down the cobbled street.

The lofty poop of the great flagship was dark as the town in the pouring moonlight. Beside Edumir his witchdoctor stood above a brazier of tinder, holding aloft a flint and a horseshoe in either hand, his eyes wild as those of the ship-horses. Next him crouched a wiry-thewed warrior naked to the waist, bearing the Mingol bow of melded horn that is Nehwon's most feared, and five long arrows winged with oily rags. While to the other side was an ax-man with five casks of the captured oil.

On the next level below, the five Sayend maidens cowered wide-eyed and silent, their pallor set off by their long dark braided hair, each in the close charge of two grim she-Mingols who flashed naked knives.

While on the main deck below that, there were ranked five young Mingol horsemen, chosen for this honor because of proven courage, each mounted on an iron-disciplined Steppe-mare, whose hoofs struck random low drum-notes from the hollow deck.

Edumir cast his wine cup into the sea and very deliberately

turned his long-jawed, impassive face toward his witchdoctor and nodded once. The latter brought down horseshoe and flint, clashing them just above the brazier, and then nurtured the sparks so engendered until the tinder was all aflame.

The bowman laid his five arrows across the brazier and then, as they came alight, plucked them out and sent them winging successively toward Sayend with such miraculous swiftness that the fifth was painting its narrow orange curve upon the mid-night air before the first had struck.

They lodged each in wood and with a preternatural rapidity the oil-drenched town flared up like a single torch, and the muffled, despairing cries of its trapped inhabitants rose like those of Hell's prisoners.

Meanwhile the she-Mingols guarding her had slashed the garments from the first maiden, their knives moving like streaks of silver fire, and thrust her naked toward the first horseman. He seized her by her dark braids and swung her across his saddle, clasping her slim, naked back to his leather-cuirassed chest. Simultaneously the ax-man struck in the head of the first cask and upended it above horse, rider, and maiden, drenching them all with gleaming oil. Then the rider twitched reins and dug in his spurs and set his mare galloping across the close-moored decks towards the flaming town. As the maiden became aware of the destination of the wild ride, she began to scream, and her screams rose higher and higher, accompanied by the rhythmic, growling shouts of the rider and the drumbeat of the mare's hoofs.

All these actions were repeated once, twice, thrice, quarce – the third horse slipped sideways in the oil, stumbled, recovered – so that the fifth rider was away before the first had reached his goal. The mares had been schooled from colthood to face and o'erlap walls of flame. The riders had drunk deep of the same mushroom wine as Edumir. The maidens had their screams.

One by one they were briefly silhouetted against the red gateway, then joined with it. Five times the flame of Sayend rose higher still, redly illuminating the small bay and the packed ship and the staring Mingol faces and glazed Mingol eyes, and Sayend expired in one unending scream and shout of agony.

When it was done, Edumir rose up tall in his fur robes and

cried in trumpet voice, 'East away now. Over ocean. To Rime Isle!'

Next day the Mouser and Fafhrd got their ships pumped out, warped to the docks assigned them, and work began on them early. Their men, refreshed by a long night's sleep ashore, set to work at repairs after a little initial grumbling, the Mouser's thieves under the direction of his chief lieutenant Pshawri and small Mingol crew. Presently there was the muffled thud of mallets driving in tow, and the stench of tar, as the loosened seams of *Flotsam* were caulked from within, while from the deck of *Sea Hawk* came the brighter music of hammers and saws, as Fafhrd's vikings mended upper works damaged by the icy projectiles of Khahkht's frost monstreme. Others reaved new rigging where needed and replaced frayed stays.

The traders' quarter, where they'd been berthed, duplicated in small the sailors' quarter of any Nehwon port, its three taverns, two brothels, several stores and shrines loosely administered by a small permanent population of ill-assorted foreigners, their unofficial mayor a close-mouthed, scarred captain named Bomar, from the Eight Cities, and their chief banker a dour black Keshite. It was borne in on Fafhrd and the Mouser that one of these fisherfolks' chief concerns, and that of the traders too, was to keep Rime Isle a valuable secret from the rest of Nehwon. Or else they had caught the habit of impassivity from their fisher-hosts, who tolerated, profited from them, and seldom omitted to enforce a bluff discipline. The foreign population had heard nothing of a Sea-Mingol eruption, either, or so they claimed.

The Rime Islanders seemed to live up to first impressions: a large-bodied, sober-clad, quiet, supremely practical and supremely confident people, without eccentricities or crochets or even superstitions, who drank little and lived by the rule of 'Mind your own business.' They played chess a good deal in their spare time and practiced with their quarterstaves, but otherwise they appeared to take little notice of each other and none at all of foreigners; though their eyes were not sleepy.

And today they had become even more inaccessible, ever since an early-sailing fishing boat had returned almost immediately to harbor with news that had sent the entire fleet of them hurrying out. And when the first of these came creaming back soon after noon with hold full of new-caught fish, swiftly salted them down (there was abundance of salt – the great eastern cliff, which no longer ran with hot volcanic waters), and put out to sea again, clapping on all sail, it became apparent that there must be a prodigious run of food fish just outside the harbor mouth – and the thrifty fishers determined to take full advantage of it. Even Groniger was seen to captain a boat out.

Individually busy with their supervisings and various errands (since only they could go outside the traders' quarter), the Mouser and Fafhrd met each other by a stretch of seawall north of the docks and paused to exchange news and catch a breather.

'I've found the Flame Den,' the former said. 'At least I think I have. It's an inner room in the Salt Herring tavern. The Ilthmart owner admitted he sometimes rents it out of a night – that is, if I interpreted his wink aright.'

Fafhrd nodded and said, 'I just now walked to the north edge of town and asked a grandad if he ever heard of the Hill of the Eight-Legged Horse. He gave a damned unpleasant sort of laugh and pointed across the moor. The air was very clear (you've noticed the volcano's ceased to smoke? I wonder that the Islers take so little note of it), and when I'd located the one heathered hill of many that was his finger's target (about a league northwest), I made out what looked like a gallows atop it.'

The Mouser grunted feeling fully at that grim disclosure and rested his elbows on the seawall, surveying the ships left in the harbor, 'foreigners' all. After a while he said softly, 'There's all manner of slightly strange things here in Salthaven, I trow. Things slightly off-key. That Ool Plerns sailing-dory now – saw you ever one with so low a prow at Ool Plerns? Or a cap so oddly-visored as that of the sailor we saw come off the Gnampf Nor cutter? Or that silver coin with an owl on it Groniger gave me in change for my dubloon? It's as if Rime Isle were on the edge of other worlds with other ships and other men and other gods – a sort of rim . . .'

Gazing out likewise, Fafhrd nodded slowly and started to

speak when there came angry voices from the direction of the docks, followed by a full-throated bellow.

'That's Skullick, I'll be bound!' Fafhrd averred. 'Got into what sort of idiot trouble, the gods know.' And without further word he raced off.

'Likely just broken bounds and got a drubbing,' the Mouser called out, trotting after. 'Mikkidu got a touch of the quarter-staff this morn for trying to pick an Isler's pouch – and serve him right! I could not have whacked him more shrewdly myself.'

That evening Fafhrd strode north from Salthaven toward Gallows Hill (it was an honester name), resolutely not looking back at the town. The sun, set in the far southwest a short while ago, gave a soft violet tone to the clear sky and the pale knee-high heather through which he trod and even to the black slopes of the volcano Darkfire where yesterday's lava had cooled. A chill breeze, barely perceptible, came from the glacier ahead. Nature was hushed. There was a feeling of immensity.

Gradually the cares of the day dropped away and his thoughts turned to the days of his youth, spent in similar clime – to Cold Corner with its tented slopes and great pines, its snow serpents and wolves, its witchwomen and ghosts. He remembered Nalgron his father and his mother Mor and even Mara, his first love. Nalgron had been an enemy of the gods, somewhat like these Rime Isle men (he was called the Legend Breaker) but more adventurous – he had been a great mountain climber, and in climbing one named White Fang had got his death. Fafhrd remembered an evening when his father had walked with him to the lip of Cold Canyon and named to him the stars as they winked on in a sky similarly violet.

A small sound close by, perhaps that of a lemming moving off through the heather, broke his reverie. He was already mount-ing the gentle slope of the hill he sought. After a moment he continued to the top, stepping softly and keeping his distance from the gibbet and the area that lay immediately beneath its beam. He had a feeling of something uncanny close at hand and he scanned around in the silence.

On the northern slope of the hill there was a thick grove of gorse more than man-high, or bower rather, since there was a narrow avenue leading in, a door of shadows. The feeling of an uncanny presence deepened and he mastered a shiver.

As his eyes came away from the gorse, he saw Afreyt standing just uphill and to one side of the grove and looking at him steadily without greeting. The darkening violet of the sky gave its tone to her blue garb. For some reason he did not call out to her and now she lifted her narrow hand crosswise to her lips, enjoining silence. Then she looked toward the grove.

Slowly emerging from the shadow door were three slender girls barely past childhood. They seemed to be leading and looking up at someone Fafhrd could not make out at first. He blinked twice, widening his eyes, and saw it was the figure of a tall, pale-bearded man wearing a wide-brimmed hat that shadowed his eyes, and either very old or else enfeebled by sickness, for he took halting steps and though his back was straight he rested his hands heavily on the shoulders of two of the girls.

And then Fafhrd felt an icy chill, for the suspicion came to him that this was Nalgron, whose ghost he had not seen since he had left Cold Corner. And either the figure's skin, beard and robe were alike strangely mottled, or else he was seeing the pale needle-clumps of the gorse through them.

But if it were a ghost, Nalgron's or another's, the girls showed no fear of it, rather a dutiful tenderness, and their shoulders bowed under its hands as they supported it along, as if its weight were real.

They slowly mounted the short distance to the hilltop, Afreyt silently following a few paces behind, until the figure stood directly beneath the end of the gallow's beam.

There the old man or ghost seemed to gain strength (and perhaps greater substantiality too) for he took his hands from the girls' shoulders and they retreated a little toward Afreyt, still looking up at him, and he lifted his face toward the sky, and Fafhrd saw that although he was a gaunt man at the end of middle age with strong and noble features not unlike Nalgron's, he had thinner lips, their ends downturning like a knowing schoolmaster's, and he wore a patch on his left eye.

He scanned around uncertainly, o'erpassing Fafhrd, who stood motionless and afraid, and then the old man turned north and lifted an arm in that direction and said in a hoarse voice that was like the soughing of the wind in thick branches, 'The Widder-Mingol fleet comes on from the west. Two raiders harry ahead, make for Cold Harbor.' Then he rapidly turned back his head through what seemed an impossibly great angle, as though his neck were broken yet somehow still serviceable, so that he looked straight at Fafhrd with his single eye, and said, 'You must destroy them!'

Then he seemed to lose interest, and weakness seized him again, or perhaps a sort of sensuous languor after task completed, for he stepped a little more swiftly as he returned toward the bower, and when the girls came in around him, his resting hands seemed to fondle their young necks lasciviously as well as take support from their slim shoulders until the shadow door, darker now, swallowed them.

Fafhrd was so struck with this circumstance, despite his fear, that when Afreyt now came stepping toward him saying in a low but businesslike voice, 'Didst mark that? Cold Harbor is Rime Isle's other town, but far smaller, easy prey for even a single Mingol ship that takes it by surprise. It's on the north coast, a day's journey away, ice-locked save for these summer months. You must—' his interrupting reply was 'Think you the girl'll be safe with him?'

She broke off, then answered shortly, 'As with any man. Or male ghost. Or god.'

At that last word, Fafhrd looked at her sharply. She nodded and continued, 'They'll feed him and give him drink and bed him down. Doubtless he'll play with their breasts a little and then sleep. He's an old god and far from home, I think, and wearies easily, which is perhaps a blessing. In any case, they serve Rime Isle too and must run risks.'

Fafhrd considered that and then, clearing his throat, said, 'Your pardon, Lady Afreyt, but your Rime Isle men, judging not only from Groniger but from others I've met, some of them councilmen, do not believe in any gods at all.'

She frowned. 'That's true enough. The old gods deserted Rime Isle long years ago and our folk have had to learn to fend for themselves in the cruel world – in this clime merciless. It's bred hard-headedness.'

'Yet,' Fafhrd said, recalling something, 'my gray friend judged Rime Isle to be a sort of rim-spot, where one might meet all manner of strange ships and men and gods from very far places.'

'That's true also,' she said hurriedly. 'And perhaps it's favored the same hard-headedness: how, where there are so many ghosts about, to take account only of what the hand can firmly grasp and can be weighed in scales. Money and fish. It's one way to go. But Cif and I have gone another – where phantoms throng, to learn to pick the useful and trustworthy ones from the flibbertigibbets and flimflammers – which is well for Rime Isle. For these two gods we've found—'

'*Two* gods?' Fafhrd questioned, raising his eyebrows. 'Cif found one too? Or is another in the bower?'

'It's a long story,' she said impatiently. 'Much too long to tell now, when dire events press upon us thick and fast. We must be practical. Cold Harbor's in dismal peril and—'

'Again your pardon, Lady Afreyt,' Fafhrd broke in, raising his voice a little. 'But your mention of practicality reminds me of another matter upon which you and Cif appear to differ most sharply with your fellow councilmen. They know of no Mingol invasion, they say, and certainly nothing of you and Cif hiring us to help repel it – and you've asked us in your notes to keep that secret. Now, I've brought you the twelve berserkers you wanted—'

'I know, I know,' she said sharply, 'and I'm pleased. But you were paid for that – and shall get further pay in Rime Isle gold as services are rendered. As for the council, the wizardries of Khahkht have lulled their suspicions – I doubt not that today's fish-run is his work, tempting their cupidity.'

'And my comrade and I have suffered from his wizardries too, I trow,' Fafhrd said. 'Nevertheless, you told us at the Silver Eel in Lankhmar that you spoke with the voice of Rime Isle, and now it appears that you speak only for Cif and yourself in a council of – what is it, twelve?'

'Did you expect your task to be all easy sailing?' she flared at him. 'Art unacquainted with set-backs and adverse gales in quests? Moreover, we *do* speak with the voice of Rime Isle, for Cif and I are the only councilpersons who have the old glory of

Rime Isle at heart – and we are both full council members, I assure you, only-daughters inheriting house, farms and council membership from fathers after (in Cif's case) sons died. We played together as children in these hills, she and I, reviving Rime Isle's greatness in our games. Or sometimes we'd be pirate queens and rape the Isle. But chiefly we'd imagine ourselves seizing power in the council, forcibly putting down all the other members—'

'So much violence in little girls?' Fafhrd couldn't help putting in. 'I think of little girls as gathering flowers and weaving garlands whilst fancying themselves little wives and mothers—'

'—and put them all to the sword and cut their wives' throats!' Afreyt finished. 'Oh, we gathered flowers too, sometimes.'

Fafhrd chuckled, then his voice grew grave. 'And so you've inherited full council membership – Groniger always mentions you with respect, though I think he has suspicions of something between us – and now you've somehow discovered a stray old god or two whom you think you can trust not to betray you, or delude you with senile ravings, and he's told you of a great two-pronged Mingol invasion of Rime Isle preparatory to world conquest, and on the strength of that you went to Lankhmar and hired the Mouser and me to be your mercenary captains, using your own fortunes for the purpose, I fancy—'

'Cif is the council treasurer,' she assured him with a meaningful crook of her lips. 'She's very good at figures and accounts – as I am with the pen and words, the council's secretary.'

'And yet you trust this god,' Fafhrd pressed on, 'this old god who loves gallows and seems to draw strength from them. Myself, I'm very suspicious of all old men and gods. In my experience they're full of lechery and avarice – and have a long lifetime's experience of evil to draw on in their twisty machinations.'

'Agreed,' Afreyt said. 'But when all's said and done a god's a god. Whatever nasty itches his old heart may have, whatever wicked thoughts of death and doom, he must first be true to his god's nature: which is, to hear what we say and hold us to it, to speak truth to man about what's going on in distant places, and to prophecy honestly – though he may try to trick us with words if we don't listen to him very carefully.'

'That does agree with my experience of the breed,' Fafhrd admitted. 'Tell me, why is this called the Hill of the Eight-Legged Horse?'

Without a blink at the change of subject, Afreyt replied, 'Because it takes four men to carry a coffin or the laid-out corpse of one who's been hanged – or died any other way. Four men – eight legs. You might have guessed.'

'And what is this god's name?'

Afreyt said: 'Odin.'

Fafhrd had the strangest feeling at the gong-beat sound of that simple name – as if he were on the verge of recalling memories of another lifetime. Also, it had something of the tone of the gibberish spoken by Karl Treuherz, that strange other-worlder who had briefly come into the lives of Fafhrd and the Mouser astride the neck of a two-headed sea serpent whilst they were in the midst of their great adventure-war with the sapient rats of Lankhmar Below-Ground. Only a name – yet there was the feeling of walls between worlds disturbed.

At the same time he was looking into Afreyt's wide eyes and noting that the irises were violet, rather than blue as they had seemed in the yellow torchlight of the Eel – and then wondering how he could see any violet at all in anything when that tone had some time ago faded entirely from the sky, which was now full night except that the moon a day past full had just now lifted above the eastern highland.

From beyond Afreyt a light voice called tranquilly, attuned to the night, 'The god sleeps.'

One of the girls was standing before the mouth of the bower, a slim white shape in the moonlight, clad only in simple frock that was hardly more than a shift and left one shoulder bare. Fafhrd marvelled that she was not shivering in the chill night air. Her two companions were dimmer shapes behind her.

'Did he give any trouble, Mara?' Afreyt called. (Fafhrd felt a strange feeling at that name, too.)

'Nothing new,' the girl responded.

Afreyt said, 'Well, put on your boots and hooded cloak – May and Gale, you also – and follow me and the foreign gentleman, out of earshot, to Salthaven. You'll be able to visit the god at dawn, May, to bring him milk?'

'I will.'

'Your children?' Fafhrd asked in a whisper.

Afreyt shook her head. 'Cousins. Meanwhile,' she said in a voice that was likewise low, but businesslike, 'you and I will discuss your instant expedition with the berserks to Cold Harbor.'

Fafhrd nodded, although his eyebrows rose a little. There was a fugitive movement in the air overhead and he found himself thinking of his and the Mouser's one-time loves, the invisible mountain-princesses Hirriwi and Keyaira, and of their night-riding brother, Prince Faroomfar.

The Gray Mouser saw his men fed and bedded down for the night in their dormitory ashore, not without some fatherly admonitions as to the desirability of prudent behavior in the home port of one's employers. He briefly discussed the morrow's work with Ourph and Pshawri. Then, with a final enigmatic scowl all around, he threw his cloak over his left shoulder, withdrew into the chilly evening, and strolled toward the Salt Herring.

Although he and Fafhrd had had a long refreshing sleep aboard the *Flotsam* (declining the shore quarters Gronigen had offered them, though accepting for their men), it had been a long, exactingly busy, and so presumably tiring day – yet now, somewhat to his surprise, he felt new life stirring in him. But this new life invading him did not concern itself with his and Fafhrd's many current problems and sage plans for future contingencies, but rather with a sense of just how preposterous it was that for the past three moons he should have been solemnly playing at being captain of men, fire-breathing disciplinarian, prodigious navigator, and the outlandishly heroic rest of it. He, a thief, captaining thieves, drilling them into sailorly and warlike skills that would be of no use to them whatever when they went back to their old professions – ridiculous! All because a small woman with golden glints in her dark hair and in her green eyes had set him an unheard-of task. Really, most droll.

Moonlight striking almost horizontally left the narrow street in shadow but revealed the cross-set beams above the Salt Herring's door. Where did they get so much wood in an island so far north? That question at least was answered for him when he pressed on inside. The tavern was built of the gray beams and planks of wrecked or dismantled ships – one wall still had a whaleback curve and he noted in another the borings and embedded shells of sea creatures.

A slow eyesweep around showed a half dozen oddly sorted mariners quietly drinking and two youngish Islers even more quietly playing chess with chunky stone pieces. He recalled having seen this morning with Groniger the one playing the black.

Without a word he marched toward the inner room, the low doorway to which was now half occupied by a brawny and warty old hag sitting bowed over on a low stool, who looked the witch-mother of all unnatural giants and other monsters.

His Ilthmart host came up beside him, wiping his hands on the towel that was his apron and saying softly, 'Flame Den's taken for tonight – a private party. You'd only be courting trouble with Mother Grum. What's your pleasure?'

The Mouser gave him a hard, silent look and marched on. Mother Grum glowered at him from under tangled brows. He glowered back. The Ilthmart shrugged.

Mother Grum moved back from her stool, bowing him into the inner room. He briefly turned his head, favoring the Ilthmart with a cold superior smile as he moved after her. One of the Islers, lifting a black rook to move it, swung his eyes motionless and bent over the board as if in deepest thought.

The inner room had a small fire in it, at any rate, to provide movement to entertain the eye. The large hearth was in the center of the room, a stone slab set almost waist high. A great copper flue (the Mouser wondered what ship's bottom it had helped cover) came down to within a yard of it from out of the low ceiling, and into this flue the scant smoke twistingly flowed. Elsewhere in the room were a few small, scarred tables, chairs for them, and another doorway.

Sidewise together on the edge of the hearth sat two women who looked personable, but used by life. The Mouser had seen one of *them* earlier in the day (the late afternoon) and judged her a whore. Their somewhat provocative attire now, and the red stockings of one, were consonant with his theory.

The Mouser went to a table a quarter way around the fire from them, cast his cape over one chair and sat down in another, which commanded both doorways. He knit his fingers together and studied the flames impassively.

Mother Grum returned to her stool in the doorway, presenting her back to all three of them.

One of the two whorish-looking women stared into the fire and from time to time fed it with driftwood that sang and sometimes tinged the flames with green and blue and with thorny black twigs that spat and crackled and burned hot orange. The other wove cat's cradles between the spread fingers of her outheld hands on a long loop of black twine. Now and then the Mouser looked aside from the fire at her severe angular creation.

Neither of the women took notice of the Mouser, but after a while the one feeding the fire stood up, brought a wine jar and two small tankards to his table, poured into one, and stood regarding him.

He took up the tankard, tasted a small mouthful, swallowed it, set down the tankard, and nodded curtly without looking at her.

She went back to her former occupation. Thereafter the Mouser took an occasional swallow of wine while studying and listening to the flames. What with their combination of crackling and singing, they were really quite vocal in that rather small, silent room – resembling an eager, rapid, youthful voice, by turns merry and malicious. Sometimes the Mouser could have sworn he heard words and phrases.

While in the flames, continually renewed, he began to see faces, or rather one face which changed expression a good deal – a youthful handsome face with very mobile lips, sometimes open and amiable, sometimes convulsed by hatreds and envies (the flames shone green a while), sometimes almost impossibly distorted, like a face seen through hot air above a very hot fire. Indeed once or twice he had the fancy that it was the face of an actual person sitting on the opposite side of the fire from him, sometimes half rising to regard him through the flames, sometimes crouching back. He was almost tempted to get up and walk around the fire to check on that, but not quite.

The strangest thing about the face was that it seemed familiar to the Mouser, though he could not place it. He gave up racking his brains over that and settled back, listening more closely to the flame-voice and trying to attune its fancied words to the movements of the flame-face's lip.

Mother Grum got up again and moved back, bowing. There entered without stooping a lady whose russet cloak was drawn across the lower half of her face, but the Mouser recognized the gold-shot green eyes and he stood up. Cif nodded to Mother Grum and the two harlots, walked to the Mouser's table, cast her cloak atop his, and sat down in the third chair. He poured for her, refilled his own tankard, and sat down also. They drank. She studied him for some time.

Then, 'You've seen the face in the fire and heard its voice?' she asked.

His eyes widened and he nodded, watching her intently now.

'But have you guessed why it seems familiar?'

He shook his head rapidly sitting forward, his expression a most curious and expectant frown.

'It resembles you,' she said flatly.

His eyebrows went up and his jaw dropped, just a little. That was true! It did remind him of himself – only when he was younger, quite a bit younger. Or as he saw himself in mirror these days only when in a most self-infatuated and vain mood, so that he saw himself as unmarked by age.

'But do you know why?' she asked him, herself intent now.

He shook his head.

She relaxed. 'Neither do I,' she said. 'I thought you might know. I marked it when I first saw you in the Eel, but as to why – it is a mystery within mysteries, beyond our present ken.'

'I find Rime Isle a nest of mysteries,' he said meaningfully, 'not the least your disapproval of myself and Fafhrd.'

She nodded, sat up straighter, and said, 'So now I think it's high time I told you why Afreyt and I are so sure of a Mingol invasion of Rime Isle while the rest of the council disbelieves it altogether. Don't you?'

He nodded emphatically, smiling.

'Almost a year ago to the day,' she said, 'Afreyt and I were walking alone upon the moor north of town, as has been our habit since childhood. We were lamenting Rime Isle's lost glories and lost (or man-renounced) gods and wishing for their return, so that the Isle might have surer guidance and fore-knowledge of perils. It was a day of changeable winds and weather, the end of spring, not quite yet summer, all the air alive, now bright, now gloomed-over, as clouds raced past the sun. We had just topped a gentle rise when we came upon the form of a youth sprawled on his back in the heather with eyes closed and head thrown back, looking as if he were dying or in the last stages of exhaustion – as though he had been cast ashore by the last great waves of some unimaginably great storm on high.

'He wore a simple tunic of homespun, very worn, and the plainest sandals, worn thin, with frayed thongs, and a very old belt dimly pricked out with monsters, yet from first sight I was almost certain that he was a god.

'I knew it in three ways. From his insubstantiality – though he was there to the touch, I could almost see the crushed heather through his pale flesh. From his supernal beauty – it was . . . the flame-face, though tranquil-featured, almost as if in death. And from the adoration I felt swelling in my heart.

'I also knew it from the way Afreyt acted, kneeling at once like myself beside him across from me – though there was something unnatural in her behavior, betokening an amazing development when we understood it aright, which we did not then. (More of that later.)

'You know how they say a god dies when his believers utterly fail him? Well, it was as if this one's last worshiper were dying in Nehwon. Or as if – this is closer to it – all his worshipers had died in his own proper world and he whirled out into the wild spaces between the worlds, to sink or swim, survive or perish according to the reception he got in whatever new world whereon chance cast him ashore. I think it's within the power of gods to travel between the worlds, don't you? – both involuntarily and also by their own design. And who knows what unpredictable tempests they might encounter in dark mid-journey?

'But I was not wasting time in speculations on that day of miracles a year ago. No, I was chafing his wrist and chest, pressing my warm cheek against his cold one, prising open his lips with my tongue (his jaw was slack) and with my open lips clamped upon his (and his nostrils clipped between my finger and thumb) sending my fresh, new-drawn breaths deep into his lungs, the meanwhile fervently praying to him in my mind, though I know they say the gods hear only our words, no thoughts. A stranger, happening upon us, might have judged us in the second or third act of lovemaking, I the more feverish seeking to rekindle his ardor.

'Meanwhile Afreyt (again here's that unnatural thing I mentioned) seemed to be as busy as I across from me – and yet somehow I was doing all the work. The explanation of that came somewhat later.

'My god showed signs of life. His eyelids quivered, I felt his chest stir, while his lips began to return my kisses.

'I uncapped my silver flask and dribbled brandy between his lips, alternating the drops with further kisses and words of comfort and endearment.

'At last he opened his eyes (brown shot with gold, like yours) and with my help raised up his head, meanwhile muttering words in a strange tongue. I answered in what languages I know, but he only frowned, shaking his head. That's how I knew he was not a Nehwon god – it's natural, don't you think, that a god, all-knowing in his own world, would be at a loss at first, plunged into another? He'd have to take it in.

'Finally he smiled and lifted his hand to my bosom, looking at me questioningly. I spoke my name. He nodded and shaped his lips, repeated it. Then he touched his own chest and spoke the name "Loki".'

At that word the Mouser knew feelings and thoughts similar to those of Fafhrd hearing 'Odin' – of other lives and worlds, and of Karl Treuherz's tongue and his little Lankhmarese-German, German-Lankhmarese dictionary that he'd given Fafhrd. At the same moment, though for that moment only, he saw the fire-face so like his own in the flames, seeming to wink at him. He frowned wonderingly.

Cif continued, 'Thereafter I fed him crumbs of meat from my script, which he accepted from my fingers, eating sparingly and sipping more brandy, the whiles I taught him words, pointing to this and that. That day Darkfire was smoking thick and showing flames, which interested him mightily when I named it. So I took flint and iron from my script and struck them together, naming "fire". He was delighted, seeming to gather strength from the sparks and smoldering straws and the very word. He'd stroke the little flames without seeming to take hurt. That frightened me.

'So passed the day – I utterly lost in him, unaware of all else, save what struck his fancy moment by moment. He was a wondrously apt scholar. I named objects both in our Rime tongue and Low Lankhmarese, thinking it'd be useful to him as he got his vision for lands beyond the Isle.

'Evening drew in. I helped the god to his feet. The wan light washing over him seemed to dissolve a little his pale flesh.

'I indicated Salthaven, that we should walk there. He assented eagerly (I think he was attracted by its evening smokes, being drawn to fire, his trumps) and we set out, he leaning on me lightly.

'And now the mystery of Afreyt was made clear. She would by no means go with us! And then I saw, though only very dimly, the figure *she* had been succoring, tending and teaching all day long, as I had Loki – the figure of a frail old man (god, rather), bearded and one-eyed, who'd been lying close alongside Loki at the first, and I empowered to see only the one and she the other!'

'A most marvelous circumstance indeed,' the Mouser commented. 'Perhaps like drew to like and so revealed itself. Say, did the other god by any chance resemble Fafhrd? – but for being one-eyed, of course.'

She nodded eagerly. 'An older Fafhrd, as 'twere his father. Afreyt marked it. Oh, you must know something of this mystery?'

The Mouser shook his head, 'Just guessing,' and asked, 'What was *his* name – the older god's?'

(She told him.)

'Well, what happened next?'

'We parted company. I walked the god Loki to Salthaven, he leaning on my arm. He was still most delicate. It seems one worshiper is barely enough at best to keep a god alive and visible, no matter how active his mind – for by now he was pointing out things to me (and indicating actions and states) and naming them in Rimic, Low Lankhmarese – and High as well! – before I named them, sure indication of his god's intellect.

'At the same time he was, despite his weakness, beginning to give me indications of a growing interest in me (I mean, my person) and I was fast losing all doubts as to how I'd be expected to entertain him when I got him home. Now, I was very happy to have got, hopefully, a new god for Rime Isle. And I must needs adore him, if only to keep him alive. But as for making him free of my bed, I had a certain reluctance, no matter how ghostly-insubstantial his flesh turned out to be in closest contact (and if it stayed that way)!

'Oh, I supppose I'd have submitted if it had come to that; still, there's something about sleeping with a god – a great honor, to be sure, but (to name only one thing) one surely couldn't expect faithfulness (if one wanted that) – certainly not from the whimsical, merry and mischievous god this Loki was showing himself to be! Besides, I wanted to be able to weigh clearhead-edly the predictions and warnings for Rime Isle I hoped to get from him – not with a mind dreamy with lovemaking and swayed by all the little fancies and fears that come with full infatuation.

'As things fell out, I never had to make the decision. Passing this tavern, he was attracted by a flickering red glow and slipped inside without attracting notice (he was still invisible to all but me). I followed (that got me a look or two, I being a respectable councilwoman) and pressed on after him as he followed the pulsing fire-glow into this inner room, where a great bawdy party was going on and the hearth was ablaze. Before my eyes he melted into the flames and joined with them!

'The revelers were somewhat taken aback by my intrusion, but after looking them over with a smile I merely turned and went out, waving my hand at them and saying, "Enjoy!" – that was for Loki too. I'd guessed he'd got where he wanted to be.'

And she waved now at the dancing flames, then turned back to the Mouser with a smile. He smiled back, shaking his head in wonder.

She continued, 'So I went home, well content, but not before I'd reserved the Flame Den (as I then learned this place is called) for the following night.

'Next day I hired two harlots for the evening (so there'd be entertainment for Loki) and Mother Grum to be our doorwoman and ensure our privacy.

'That night went as I guessed it would. Loki had indeed taken up permanent residence in the fire here and after a while I was able to talk with him and get some answers to questions, though nothing of profit to Rime Isle as yet. I made arrangements with the Ilthmart for the Flame Den to be reserved one night each week, and like bargains with Hilsa and Rill to come on those nights and entertain the god and keep him happy. Hilsa, has the god been with you tonight?' she called to the woman feeding the fire, the one with red stockings.

'Twice,' that one replied matter-of-factly in a husky voice. 'Slipped from the fire invisibly and back again. He's content.'

'Your pardon, Lady Cif,' the Mouser interposed, 'but how do these professional women find such close commerce with an invisible god to be? What's it like? I'm curious.'

Cif looked toward them where they sat by the fire.

'Like having a mouse up your skirt,' Hilsa replied with a short chuckle, swinging a red leg.

'Or a toad,' her companion amended. 'Although he dwells in the flames, his person is cold.' Rill had laid aside her cat's cradle and joined her hands, fingers interweaving, to make shadowfaces on the wall, of prick-eared gigantic werewolves, great sea serpents, dragons, and long-nosed, long-chinned witches. 'He likes these hobgoblins,' she commented.

The Mouser nodded thoughtfully, watching them for a while, and then back to the fire.

Cif continued, 'Soon the god, I could tell, was beginning to get the feel of Nehwon, fitting his mind to her, stretching it out to her farthest bounds, and his oracles became more to the point. Meantime Afreyt, with whom I conferred daily, was caring for old Odin out on the moor in much the same way (though using girls to comfort and appease him 'stead of full-grown women, he being an older god), eliciting prophecies of import.

'Loki it was who first warned us that the Mingols were on the move, mustering horse-ships against Rime Isle, mounting under Khahkht's urgings toward a grand climacteric of madness and rapine. Afreyt put independent question to Odin and he confirmed it – they were together in the tale at every point.

'When asked what we must do, they both advised – again independently – that we seek out two certain heroes in Lankhmar and have them bring their bands to the Isle's defence. They were most circumstantial, giving your names and haunts, saying you were their men, whether or not you knew it in this life, and they did not change their stories under repeated questioning. Tell me, Gray Mouser, have you not known the god Loki before? Speak true.'

'Upon my word, I haven't, Lady Cif,' he averred, 'and am no more able than you to explain the mystery of our resemblance. Though there is a certain weird familiarity about the name, and Odin's too, as if I'd heard them in dreams or nightmares. But however I rack my brains, it comes no clearer.'

'Well,' she resumed after a pause, 'the two gods kept up their urgings that we seek you out and so half a year ago Afreyt and I took ship for Lankhmar on Hlal – with what results you know.'

'Tell me, Lady Cif,' the Mouser interjected, rousing himself from his fire-peerings, 'how did you and tall Afreyt get back to Rime Isle after Khahkht's wizardrous blizzard snatched you out of the Silver Eel?'

'It transpired as swiftly as our journey there was long,' she said. 'One moment we were in his cold clutch, battered and blinded by wind-driven ice, our ears assaulted by a booming laughter. The next we had been taken in charge by two feminine flying creatures who whirled us at dizzying speed through darkness to a warm cave where they left us breathless. They said they were a mountain king's two daughters.'

'Hirriwi and Keyaira, I'll be bound!' the Mouser exclaimed. 'They must be on our side.'

'Who are those?' Cif inquired.

'Mountain princesses Fafhrd and I have known in our day. Invisibles like our revered fire-dweller here.' He nodded toward the flames. 'Their father rules in lofty Stardock.'

'I've heard of that peak and dread Oomforafor, its king, whom some say is with his son Faroomfar an ally of Khahkht. Daughters against father and brother – that would be natural. Well, Afreyt and I after we'd recovered our breath made our way to the cavern's mouth – and found ourselves looking down on Rime Isle and Salthaven from a point midway up Darkfire. With some difficulty we made our way home across rock and glacier.'

'The volcano,' the Mouser mused. 'Again Loki's link with fire.' His attention had been drawn back to the hypnotic flames.

Cif nodded. 'Thereafter Loki and Odin kept us informed of the Mingols' progress toward Rime Isle – and your own. Then four days ago Loki began a running account of your encounters with Khahkht's frost monstreme. He made it most vivid – sometimes you'd have sworn he was piloting one of the ships himself. I managed to reserve the Flame Den the succeeding nights (and have it now for the next three days and nights also), so we were able to follow the details of the long flight or long pursuit – which, truth to tell, became a bit monotonous.'

'You should have been there,' the Mouser murmured.

'Loki made me feel I was.'

'Incidentally,' the Mouser said casually, 'I'd think you'd have rented the Flame Den every night once you'd got your god here.'

'I'm not made of gold,' she informed him without rancor. 'Besides, Loki likes variety. The brawls that others hold here amuse him – were what attracted him in the first place. Furthermore, it would have made the council even more suspicious of my activities.'

The Mouser nodded. 'I thought I recognized a crony of Groniger's playing chess out there.'

'Hush,' she counseled him. 'I must now consult the god.' Her voice had grown a little singsong in the later stages of her narrative and it became more so as, without transition, she invoked, 'And now, O Loki god, tell us about our enemies across the seas and in the realms of ice. Tell us of cruel, cold Khahkht, of Edumir of the Widdershin Mingols and Gonov of the Sunwise. Hilsa and Rill, sing with me to the god.' And her voice became a somnolent two-toned, wordless chant in which the other women joined: Hilsa's husky voice, Rill's slightly shrill one, and a soft growling that after a bit the Mouser realized came from Mother Grum – all tuned to the fire and its flame-voice.

The Mouser lost himself in this strange medley of notes and

all at once, the crackling flame-voice, as if by some dream magic, became fully articulate, murmuring rapidly in Low Lankhmarese with occasional words slipped in that were as hauntingly strange as the god's own name.

'Storm clouds thicken round Rime Isle. Nature brews her blackest bile. Monsters quicken, nightmares foal, niss and nicor, drow and troll.' (Those last four nouns were all strange ones to the Mouser, specially the bell-toll sound of 'troll'.) 'Sound alarms and strike the drum – in three days the Mingols come, Sunwise Mingols from the east, horse-head ship and human beast. Trick them all most cunningly – lead them to the spinning sea, to down-swirling dizzy bowl. Trust the whirlpool, 'ware the troll! Mingols to their deaths must go, down to weedy hell below, never draw an easy breath, suffer an unending death, everlasting pain and strife, everlasting death in life. Mingol madness ever burn! Never peace again return!'

And the flame-voice broke off in a flurry of explosive crackles that shattered the dream-magic and brought the Mouser to his feet with a great start, his sleepy mood all gone. He stared at the fire, walked rapidly around it, peered at it closely from the other side, then swiftly scanned the entire room. Nothing! He glared at Hilsa and Rill. They eyed him blandly and said in unison, 'The god has spoken,' but the sense of a presence was gone from the fire and the room as well, leaving behind not even a black hole into which it might have retired – unless perchance (it occurred to the Mouser) it had retired into *him*, accounting for the feeling of restless energy and flaming thought which now possessed him, while the litany of Mingol doom kept repeating itself over and over in his memory. 'Can such things be?' he asked himself and answered himself with an instant and resounding 'Yes!'

He paced back to Cif, who had risen likewise. 'We have three days,' she said.

'So it appears,' he said, then, 'Know you aught of trolls? What are they?'

'I was about to ask you that,' she replied. 'The word's as strange to me as it appears to be to you.'

'Whirlpools, then,' he queried, his thoughts racing. 'Any of them about the isle? Any sailors' tales—?'

'Oh, yes – the Great Maelstrom off the isle's rock-fanged east coast with its treacherous swift currents and tricky tides, the Great Maelstrom from whence the island gets what wood it owns, after it's cast up on the Beach of Bleached Bones. It forms regularly each day. Our sailors know it well and avoid it like no other peril.'

'Good! I must put to sea and seek it out and learn its every trick and how it comes and goes. I'll need a small sailing craft for that while *Flotsam*'s laid up for repairs – there's little time. Aye, and I'll need more money too – shore silver for my men.'

'Wherefore to sea?' her breath catching, she asked. 'Wherefore must you dash yourself at such a maw of danger?' – but in her widening eyes he thought he could see the dawning of the answer to that.

'Why, to put down your foes,' he said ringingly. 'Heard you not Loki's prophecy? We'll expedite it. We'll drown at least one branch of the Mingols e'er ever they set foot on Rimeland! And if, with Odin's aid, Fafhrd and Afreyt can scupper the Widder-Mingols half as handily, our task is done!'

The triumphant look flared up in her eyes to match that in his own.

The waning moon rode high in the southwest and the brightest stars still shone, but in the east the sky had begun to pale with the dawn, as Fafhrd led his twelve berserks north out of Salthaven. Each was warmly clad against the ice ahead and bore longbow, quiver, extra arrow-pack, belted ax, and bag of provender. Skor brought up the rear, keen to enforce Fafhrd's rule of utter silence while they traversed the town, so that this breach of port regulations might go unnoticed. And for a wonder they had not been challenged. Perhaps the Rimelanders slept extra sound because so many of them had been up to all hours salting down the monster fish-catch, the last boatloads of which had come in after nightfall.

With the berserks tripped along the girls May and Mara in their soft boots and hooded cloaks, the former with a jar of fresh-drawn milk for the god Odin, the latter to be the expedition's guide across central Rime Isle to Cold Harbor, at

Afreyt's insistence – 'for she was born on a Cold Harbor farm and knows the way – and can keep up with any man.'

Fafhrd had nodded dubiously on hearing that. He had not liked accepting responsibility for a girl with his childhood sweetheart's name. Nor had he liked leaving the management of everything in Salthaven to the Mouser and the two women, now that there was so much to do, and besides all else the new task of investigating the Grand Maelstrom and spying out its ways, which would occupy the Mouser for a day at least, and which more befitted Fafhrd as the more experienced ship-conner. But the four of them had conferred together at midnight in *Flotsam*'s cabin behind shrouded portholes, pooling their knowledge and counsels and the two gods' prophecies, and it had been so decided.

The Mouser would take Ourph with him, for his ancient sea-wisdom, and Mikkidu, to discipline him, using a small fishing craft belonging to the women. Meanwhile, Pshawri would be left in sole charge of the repairs on *Flotsam* and *Sea Hawk* (subject to the advisements of the three remaining Mingols), trying to keep up the illusion that Fafhrd's berserks were still aboard the latter. Cif and Afreyt would take turns in standing by at the docks to head off inquiries by Groniger and deal with any other matters that might arise unexpectedly.

Well, it should work, Fafhrd told himself, the Rime Islers being such blunt, unsubtle types, hardy and simple. Certainly the Mouser had seemed confident enough – restless and driving, eyes flashing, humming a tune under his breath.

Onwinging dawn pinkened the low sky to the east as Fafhrd tramped ahead through the heather, lengthening his stride, an ear attuned to the low voices of the men behind and the lighter ones of the girls. A glance over shoulder told him they were keeping close order, with Mara and May immediately behind him.

As Gallows Hill showed up to the left, he heard the men mark it with grim exclamations. A couple spat to ward off ill omen.

'Bear the god my greeting, May,' he heard Mara say.

'If he wakes enough to attend to aught but drink his milk and sleep again,' May replied as she branched off from the expedition and headed for the hill with her jar through the dissipating shadows of night.

Some of the men exclaimed gloomily at that, too, and Skor called for silence.

Mara said softly to Fafhrd, 'We bear left here a little, so as to miss Darkfire's icefall, which we skirt through the Isle's center until it joins the glacier of Mount Hellglow.'

Fafhrd thought, what cheerful names they favor, and scanned ahead. Heather and gorse were becoming scantier and stretches of lichened, shaly rock beginning to show.

'What do they call this part of Rime Isle?' he asked her.

'The Deathlands,' she answered.

More of the same, he thought. Well, at any rate the name fits the mad, death-bent Mingols and this gallows-favoring Odin god too.

The Mouser was tallest of the four short, wiry men waiting at the edge of the public dock. Pshawri close beside him looked resolute and attentive, though still somewhat pale. A neat bandage went across his forehead. Ourph and Mikkidu rather resembled two monkeys, the one wizened and wise, the other young and somewhat woebegone.

The salt cliff to the east barely hid the rising sun, which glittered along its crystalline summit and poured light on the farther half of the harbor and on the fishing fleet putting out to sea. The Mouser gazed speculatively after the small vessels – you'd have thought the Islanders would have been satisfied with yesterday's monster catch, but no, they seemed even more in a hurry today, as if they were fishing for all Nehwon or as if some impatient chant were beating in their heads, driving them on, such as was beating in the Mouser's now: *Mingols to their deaths must go, down to weedy hell below* – yes, to hell they must go indeed! and time was wasting and where was Cif?

That question was answered when a skiff came sculling quietly along very close to the dock, propelled by Mother Grum sitting in the stern and wagging a single oar from side to side like a fish's tail. When Cif stood up in the boat's midst her head was level with the dock. She caught hold of the hand the Mouser reached down and came up in two long steps.

'Few words,' she said. 'Mother Grum will scull you to *Sprite*,' and she passed the Mouser a purse.

'Silver only,' she said with a wrinkle of her nose as he made to glance into it.

He handed it to Pshawri. 'Two pieces to each man at nightfall, if I'm not returned,' he directed. 'Keep them hard at work. 'Twere well *Flotsam* were seaworthy by noon tomorrow at latest. Go.'

Pshawri saluted and made off.

The Mouser turned to the others. 'Down into the skiff with you.'

They obeyed, Ourph impassive-faced, Mikkidu with an apprehensive sidewise look at their grim boatwoman. Cif touched the Mouser's arm. He turned back.

She looked him evenly in the eye. 'The Maelstrom is danger-ous,' she said. 'Here's what perhaps can quell it, if it should trap you. If needs must, hurl it into the pool's exact midst. Guard it well and keep it secret.'

Surprised at the weight of the small cubical object she pressed into his hand, he glanced down at it surreptitiously. 'Gold?' he breathed, a little wonderingly. It was in the form of a skeleton cube, twelve short thick gold-gleaming edges conjoined squarely.

'Yes,' she replied flatly. 'Lives are more valuable.'

'And there's some superstition—?'

'Yes,' she cut him short.

He nodded, pouched it carefully, and without other word descended lightly into the skiff. Mother Grum worked her oar back and forth, sending them toward the one small fishing craft remaining in the harbor.

Cif watched after them as their skiff emerged into full sunlight. After a while she felt the same sunlight on her head and knew it was striking golden highlights from her dark hair. The Mouser never looked around. She did not really want him to. The skiff reached *Sprite* and the three men climbed nimbly aboard.

She could have sworn there'd been no one near, but next she heard the sound of a throat being cleared behind her. She waited a few moments, then turned around.

'Master Groniger,' she greeted.

'Mistress Cif,' he responded in equally mild tones. He did not look like a man who had been sneaking about.

'You send the strangers on a mission?' he remarked after a bit.

She shook her head slowly. 'I rent them a ship, the lady Afreyt's and mine. Perhaps they go fishing.' She shrugged. 'Like any Isler, I turn a dollar when I can and fishing's not the only road to profit. Not captaining your craft today, master?'

He shook his head in turn. 'A harbor chief first has the responsibilities of his office, mistress. The other stranger's not been seen yet today. Nor his men either . . .'

'So?' she asked when he'd paused a while.

'. . . though there's a great racket of work below deck in his sailing galley.'

She nodded and turned to watch *Sprite* making for the harbor mouth under sail and the skiff sculling off with its lone shaggy haired, squat figure.

'A meeting of the council has been called for tonight,' Groniger said as if in afterthought. She nodded without turning around. He added in explanation, casually, 'An audit has been asked for, Lady Treasurer, of all gold coin and Rimic treasures in your keeping – the golden arrow of truth, the gold circles of unity, the gold cube of square-dealing . . .'

She nodded again, then lifted her hand to her mouth. He heard the sigh of a yawn. The sun was bright on her hair.

By midafternoon Fafhrd's band was high in the Deathlands, here a boulder-studded expanse of barren, dark rock between low glacial walls a bowshot off to the left, closer than that on the right – a sort of broad pass. The westering sun beat down hotly, but the breeze was chill. The blue sky seemed close.

First went the youngest of his berserks, unarmed, as point. (An unarmed man really scans for the foe and does not engage them.) Twoscore yards behind him went Mannimark as cover-point and behind *him* the main party led by Fafhrd with Mara beside him, Skor still bringing up the rear.

A large white hare broke cover ahead and raced away past them the way they had come, taking fantastic bounds, seemingly terrified. Fafhrd waved in the men ahead and arranged two-thirds of his force in an ambush where the stony cover was good, putting Skor in charge of them with orders to hold that position and engage any enemy on sight with heavy arrow fire but on no account to charge. Then he rapidly led the rest by a circuitous and shielded route up onto the nearest glacier. Skullick, Mara, and three others were with them. Thus far the girl had lived up to Afreyt's claims for her, making no trouble.

As he cautiously led them out onto the ice, the silence of the heights was broken by the faint twang of bowstrings and by sharp cries from the direction of the ambush and ahead.

From his point of vantage Fafhrd could see his ambush and, almost a bowshot ahead of it in the pass, a party of some forty men. Mingols by their fur smocks and hats and curvy bows. The men of his ambush and some dozen of the Mingols were exchanging high-arching arrow fire. One of the Mingols was down and their leaders seemed in dispute. Fafhrd quickly strung his bow, ordering the four men with him to do the same, and they sent off a volley of arrows from his flanking position. Another Mingol was hit – one of the disputants. A half dozen returned their fire, but Fafhrd's position had the advantage of height. The rest took cover. One danced up and down, as if in rage, but was dragged behind rocks by companions. After a bit the whole Mingol party, so far as Fafhrd could tell, began to move off the way they'd come, bearing their wounded with them.

'And now charge and destroy 'em?' Skullick ventured, grinning fiendishly. Mara looked eagerly.

'And show 'em we're but a dozen? I forgive you your youth,' Fafhrd retorted, halting Skor's fire with a downward wave of his arm. 'No, we'll escort 'em watchfully back to their ship, or Cold Harbor, or whatever. Best foe is one in flight,' and he sent a runner to Skor to convey his plan, meanwhile thinking how the fur-clad Steppe-men seemed less furiously hell-bent on rapine than he'd anticipated. He must watch for Mingol ruses. He wondered what old god Odin (who'd said 'destroy') would think of his decision. Perhaps Mara's eyes, fixed upon him with what looked very much like disappointment, provided an answer.

The Mouser sat on the decked prow of *Sprite*, his back to the mast, his feet resting on the root of the bowsprit, as they re-approached Rime Isle, running down on the island from the northeast. Some distance ahead should lie the spot where the maelstrom would form and now, with the tide ebbing, getting toward the time – if he'd calculated aright and could trust information got earlier from Cif and Ourph. Behind him in the stern the old Mingol managed tiller and triangular fore-and-aft mainsail handily while Mikkidu, closer, watched the single narrow jib.

The Mouser unstrapped the flap of the small deep pouch at his belt and gazed down at the compact dully gold-gleaming 'whirlpool-queller' (to give a name to the object Cif had given him) nested inside. Again it occurred to him how magnificently spendthrift (but also how bone-stupid) it was to make such a necessarily expendable object of gold. Well, you couldn't dictate prudence to superstition . . . Or perhaps you could.

'Mikkidu!' he called sharply.

'Yes, sir?' came the answer – immediate, dutiful and a shade apprehensive.

'You noted the long coil of thin line hanging inside the hatch? The sort of slender yet stout stuff you'd use to lower loot to an accomplice outside a high window or trust your own weight to in a pinch? The sort some stranglers use?'

'Yes, sir!'

'Good. Fetch it for me.'

It proved to be as he'd described it and at least a hundred yards long, he judged. A sardonic smile quirked his lips as he knotted one end of it securely to the whirlpool-queller and the other end to a ring bolt in the deck, checked that the rest of the coil lay running free, and returned the queller to his pouch.

They'd been half a day sailing here. First a swift run to the east with wind abeam as soon as they'd got out of Salthaven harbor, leaving the Rimic fishing fleet very busy to the south-west, where the sea seemed to boil with fish, until they were well past the white salt headland. Then a long slow beat north into the wind, taking them gradually away from the Isle's dark craggy east coast, which, replacing the glittering salt, trended toward the west. Finally, now, a swift return, running before the wind, to that same coast where a shallow bay guarded by twin crags lured the unwary mariner. The sail sang and the small waves, advancing in ranked array, slapped the creaming prow. The sunlight was bright everywhere.

The Mouser stood up, closely scanning the sea immediately ahead for submerged rocks and signs of tides at work. The speed of *Sprite* seemed to increase beyond that given it by the wind, as though a current had ripped it. He noted an eddying ahead, sudden curves in the wave-topping lines of foam. Now was the time! – if there was to be. He called to Ourph to be ready to go about.

Despite all these anticipations he was taken by surprise when (it seemed it must be) an unseen giant hand gripped *Sprite* from below, turned it instantly sideways and jerked it ahead in a curve, tilting it sharply inward. He saw Mikkidu standing in the air over the water a yard from the deck. As he involuntarily moved to join the dumbfounded thief, his left hand automatically seized the mast while his right, stretching out mightily, grabbed Mikkidu by the collar. The Mouser's muscles cracked but took the strain. He deposited Mikkidu on the deck, putting a foot on him to keep him there, then crouched into the wind that was rattling the sails, and managed to look around.

Where ranked waves had been moments before, *Sprite* at prodigious speed was circling a deepening saucer of spinning black water almost two hundred yards across. Dimly past the wildly flapping mainsail the Mouser glimpsed Ourph clinging with both hands to the tiller. Looking again at the whirlpool he saw that *Sprite* was appreciably closer to its deepening center, whence jagged rocks now protruded like a monster's blackened and broken fangs. Without pause he dug in his pouch for the queller and, trying to allow for wind and *Sprite*'s speed, he hurled it at the watery pit's center. For a space it seemed to hang glinting golden-yellow in the sunlight, then fell true.

This time it was as if a hundred giant invisible hands had smote the whirlpool flat. *Sprite* seemed to hit a wall. There was a sudden welter of cross-chopping waves that generated so much foam that it piled up on the deck and one would have sworn the water was filled with soap.

The Mouser reassured himself that Ourph and Mikkidu were there and in an upright position so that, given time, they might recover. Next he ascertained that the sky and sea appeared to be in their proper places. Then he checked on the tiller and sails. His eye falling away from the bedraggled jib lit on the ringbolt in the prow. He reeled in the line attached to it (not very hopefully – surely it would have snagged or snapped in the chaos they'd just endured) but for a wonder it came out with the queller still tightly knotted to the end of it, more golden-bright than ever from its tumbling it had got in the rocks. As he pouched it and laced tight the soggy flap, he felt remarkably self-satisfied.

By now the waves and wind had resumed something like their normal flow and Ourph and Mikkidu were stirring. The Mouser set them back at their duties (refusing to discuss at all the whirlpool's appearance and vanishment) and he cockily had them sail *Sprite* close inshore, where he noted a beach of jagged rocks with considerable gray timber amongst them, bones of dead ships.

Time for the Rime-men to pick up another load, he thought breezily. Have to tell Groniger. Or perhaps best wait for the next wrecks – Mingol ones! – which should provide a prodigious harvest.

Smiling, the Mouser set course for Salthaven, an easy sail now with the favoring wind. Under his breath he hummed, 'Mingols to their deaths must go, down to weedy hell below.' Aye, and their ships to rock-fanged doom.

Somewhere between cloud layers north of Rime Isle there floated miraculously the sphere of black ice that was Khahkht's home and most-times prison. Snow falling steadily between the layers gave the black sphere a white cap. The falling snow also accumulated on and so whitely outlined the mighty wings, back, neck, and crest of the invisible being poised beside the sphere. This being must have been clutching the sphere in some fashion, for whenever it shook its head and shoulders to dislodge the snow, the sphere jogged in the thin air.

Three quarters of the way down the sphere, a trapdoor had been flung open and from it Khahkht had thrust Its head, shoulders, and one arm, like a peculiarly nasty god looking sidewise down and out of the floor of heaven.

The two beings conversed together.

Khahkt: *Fretful monster! Why do you trouble my celestial privacy, rappings on my sphere? Soon I'll be sorry that I gave you wings.*

Faroomfar: *I'd as soon shift back to a flying invisible ray-fish. It had advantages.*

Khahkht: *For two black dogs, I'd—!*

Faroomfar: *Contain your ugly self, granddad. I've good reason to knock you up. The Mingols seem to lessen in their frenzy. Gonov of the Sunwise descending on Rime Isle has ordered his ships double-reef for a mere gale. While the Widder-raiders coming down across the Isle have turned back from a force less than a third their size. Have your incantments weakened?*

Khahkht: *Content you. I have been seeking to assess the two new gods who aid Rime Isle: how powerful, whence they come, their final purpose, and whether they may be suborned. My tentative conclusion: They're a treacherous pair, none too strong – rogue gods from a minor universe. We'd best ignore 'em.*

The snow had re-gathered on the flier, a fine dust of it revealing even somewhat of his thin, cruel, patrician features. He shook it off.

Faroomfar: *So, what to do?*

Khahkht: *I'll refire the Mingols where (and if) they flinch back, never you fear. Do you, meanwhile, evade your wicked sisters if you're able and work what devilish mischief you can on Fafhrd (it's he that's cowed the Widder-raiders, right?) and his band. Aim at the girl. To work!*

And he drew back into his black, snow-capped sphere and slammed the trapdoor, like a reverse jack-in-the-box. The falling snow was disturbed in a broad downward sweep as Faroomfar spread wings and began his descent from the heights.

Most commendably, Mother Grum was waiting in the skiff at the anchorage when Ourph and Mikkidu brought *Sprite* breezing in neatly to make fast to the buoy and furl the sail under the Mouser's watchful, approving eye. He was still in a marvelously good mood of self-satisfaction and had even unbent to make a few benign remarks to Mikkidu (which puzzled the latter mightily) and discourse sagely by whimsical fits and starts with the wise, if somewhat taciturn, old Mingol.

Now sharing the skiff's mid thwart with Ourph, while

Mikkidu huddled in the prow, the Mouser airily asked the hag as she sculled them in, 'How went the day, Mother? Any word for me from your mistress?' When she answered him only with a grunt that might mean anything or nothing, he merely remarked with mild sententiousness, 'Bless your loyal old bones,' and let his attention wander idly about the harbor.

Night had fallen. The last of the fishing fleet had just come in, low in the water with another record-breaking catch. His attention fixed on the nearest pier, where a ship on the other side was unloading by torchlight and four Rime-men, going in single file, were bearing ashore what were undoubtedly the prizes of their monster (and monstrous) haul.

Yesterday the Rimelanders had impressed him as very solid and sober folk, but now more and more he was finding something oafish and loutish about them, especially these four as they went galumphing along, smirking and gaping and with eyes starting out of their heads beneath their considerable burdens.

First went a bent-over, bearded fellow, bearing upon his back by its finny tail a great silver tunny as long-bodied as he and even thicker.

Next a rangy chap carrying by neck and tail, wound round and over his shoulders, the largest eel the Mouser had ever seen. Its bearer gave the impression that he was wrestling with it as he hobbled – it writhed ponderously, still alive. *Lucky it's not twined about his neck*, the Mouser thought.

The man after the eel-carrier had, by a wicked handhook through its shell, a giant green crab on his back, its ten legs working persistently in the air, its great claws opening and closing. And it was hard to tell which of the two's eyes goggled out the farthest, the shellfish's or the man's.

Finally a fisherman bearing over shoulder by its bound-together tentacles an octopus still turning rainbow colours in its death-spasms, its great sunken eyes filming above its monstrous beak.

Monsters bearing monsters, the Mouser epitomized with a happy chuckle. *Lord, what grotesques we mortals be!*

And now the dock should be coming up. The Mouser turned round in his seat to look that way and saw . . . not Cif, he decided regretfully after a moment . . . but at any rate (and a little to his initial surprise) Hilsa and Rill at the dock's edge, the latter bearing a torch that flamed most merrily, both of them smiling warm welcomes and looking truly most brave in their fresh paint and whore's finery, Hilsa in her red stockings, Rill in a bright yellow pair, both in short gaudy smocks cut low at the neck. Really, they looked younger this way, or at least a little less shopworn, he thought as he leaped up and joined them on the dock. How nice of Loki to have sent his priestesses . . . well, not priestesses exactly, but professional ladies, nurses and playmates of the god . . . to welcome home the god's faithful servant.

But no sooner had he bowed to them in turn than they put aside their smiles and Hilsa said to him urgently in a low voice, 'There's ill news, captain. Lady Cif's sent us to tell you that she and the Lady Afreyt have been impeached by the other council members. She's accused of using coined gold she had the keeping of and other Rimic treasures to fee you and the tall captain and your men. She expects you with your famed cleverness, she told me, to concoct some tale to counter all this.'

The Mouser's smile hardly faltered. He was struck rather with how gayly Rill's torch flickered and flared as Hilsa's doleful words poured over him. When Rimic treasures were mentioned he touched his pouch where the queller reposed on its snipped-off length of cord. He had no doubt that it was one of them, yet somehow he was not troubled.

'Is that all?' he asked when Hilsa had done. 'I thought at least you'd tell me the trolls had come, against whom the god has warned us. Lead on, my dears, to the council hall! Ourph and Mikkidu, attend us! Take courage, Mother Grum—' (he called down to the skiff) '—doubt not your mistress's safety.'

And linking arms with Hilsa and Rill he set out briskly, telling himself that in reverses of fortune such as this, the all-important thing was to behave with vast self-confidence, flame like Rill's torch with it! That was the secret. What matter that he hadn't the faintest idea of what tale he would tell the council? Only maintain the appearance of self-confidence and at the moment when needed, inspiration would come!

What with the late arrival of the fishing fleet the narrow streets were quite crowded as they footed it along. Perhaps it was market night as well, and maybe the council meeting had something to do with it. At any rate there were a lot of 'foreigners' out and Rime Islers too, and for a wonder the latter looked stranger and more drolly grotesque than the former. Here came trudging those four fishers again with their monstrous burdens! A fat boy gaped at them. The Mouser patted his head in passing. Oh, what a show was life!

Hilsa and Rill, infected by the Mouser's lightheartedness, put on their smiles again. He must be a grand sight, he thought, strolling along with two fine whores as if he owned the town.

The blue front of the council hall appeared, its door framed by some gone galleon's massive stern and flanked by two glum louts with quarterstaves. The Mouser felt Hilsa and Rill hesitate, but crying in a loud voice, 'All honor to the council!' he swept them inside with him, Ourph and Mikkidu ducking in after.

The room inside was larger and somewhat more lofty than the one at the Salt Herring, but was gray-timbered like it, built of wrecks. And it had no fireplace, but was inadequately warmed by two smoking braziers and lit by torches that burned blue and sad (perhaps there were bronze nails in them), not merrily golden-yellow like Rill's. The main article of furniture was a long heavy table, at one end of which Cif and Afreyt sat, looking their haughtiest. Drawn away from them toward the other end were seated ten large sober Isle-men of middle years, Groniger in their midst, with such doleful, gloomily indignant, outraged looks on their faces that the Mouser burst out laughing. Other Islers crowded the walls, some women among them. All turned on the newcomers faces of mingled puzzlement and disapproval.

Groniger reared up and thundered at him, 'You dare to laugh at the gathered authority of Rime Isle? You, who come bursting in accompanied by women of the streets and your own trespassing crewmen?'

The Mouser managed to control his laughter and listen with the most open, honest expression imaginable, injured innocence incarnate.

Groniger went on, shaking his finger at the other, 'Well, there he stands, councilors, a chief receiver of the misappropriated gold, perchance even of the gold cube of honest dealing. The man who came to us out of the south with tales of magic storms and day turned night and vanished hostile vessels and a purported Mingol invasion – he who has, as you perceive, Mingols amongst his crew – the man who paid for his dockage in Rime Isle gold!'

Cif stood up at that, her eyes blazing, and said, 'Let him speak, at least, and answer this outrageous charge, since you won't take my word.'

A councilman rose beside Groniger. 'Why should we listen to a stranger's lies?'

Groniger said, 'I thank you, Dwone.'

Afreyt got to her feet. 'No, let him speak. Will you hear nothing but your own voices?'

Another councilman got up.

Groniger said, 'Yes, Zwaakin?'

That one said, 'No harm to hear what he has to say. He may convict himself out of his own mouth.'

Cif glared at Zwaakin and said loudly, 'Tell them, Mouser!'

At that moment the Mouser, glancing at Rill's torch (which seemed to wink at him) felt a godlike power invading and possessing him to the tips of his fingers and toes – nay, to the end of his every hair. Without warning – in fact, without knowing he was going to do it at all – he ran forward across the room and sprang atop the table where its sides were clear toward Cif's end.

He looked around compellingly at all (a sea of cold and hostile faces, mostly), gave them a searching stare, and then – well, as the godlike force possessed every part of him utterly, his mind was perforce driven completely out of himself, the scene swiftly darkened, he heard himself *beginning* to say something in a mighty voice, but then he (his mind) fell irretrievably into an inner darkness deeper and blacker than any sleep or swound.

Then (for the Mouser) no time at all passed . . . or an eternity.

His return to awareness (or rebirth, rather – it seemed that massive a transition) began with whirling yellow lights and grinning, open-mouthed, exalted faces mottling the inner darkness, and the sense of a great noise on the edge of the audible and of a resonant voice speaking words of power, and then without other warning the whole bright and deafening scene materialized with a rush and a roar and he was standing insolently tall on the massive council table, with what felt like a wild (or even demented) smile on his lips, while his left fist rested jauntily on his hip and his right was whirling around his head the golden queller (or cube of square dealing, he reminded himself) on its cord. And all around him every last Rimelander – councilmen, guards, common fishers, women (and Cif, Afreyt, Rill, Hilsa, Mikkidu, needless to say) – was staring at him with rapturous adoration (as if he were a god or legendary hero at least) and standing on their feet (some jumping up and down) and cheering him to the echo! Fists pounded the table, quarter-staves thudded the stony floor resoundingly. While torchmen whirled their sad flambeaux until they flamed as yellow-bright as Rill's.

Now in the name of all the gods at once, the Mouser asked himself, continuing however to grin, *whatever* did I tell or promise them to put them all in such a state? In the fiend's name, *what*?

Groniger swiftly mounted the other end of the table, boosted by those beside him, waved for silence, and as soon as he'd got a little of that commodity assured the Mouser in a great feelingful voice, advancing to make himself heard, 'We'll do it – oh, we'll do it! I myself will lead out the Rimic contingent, half our armed citizenry, across the Deathlands to Fafhrd's aid against the Widdershins, while Dwone and Zwaaken will man the armed fishing fleet with the other half and follow you in *Flotsam* against the Sunwise Mingols. Victory!'

And with that the hall resounded with cries of 'Death to the Mingols!' 'Victory!' and other cheers the Mouser couldn't quite make out. As the noise passed its peak, Groniger shouted, 'Wine! Let's pledge our allegiance!' while Zwaaken cried to the Mouser, 'Summon your crewmen to celebrate with us – they've the freedom of Rime Isle now and for ever!' (Mikkidu was soon dispatched.)

The Mouser looked helplessly at Cif – though still maintaining his grin (by now he must look quite glassy-eyed, he thought) – but she only stretched her hand toward him, crying, flush-cheeked, 'I'll sail with you!' while Afreyt beside her proclaimed,

'I'll go ahead across the Deathlands to join Fafhrd, bringing god Odin with me!'

Groniger heard that and called to her, 'I and my men will give you whatever help with that you need, honored council-lady,' which told the Mouser that besides all else he'd got the atheistical fishermen believing in gods – Odin and Loki, at any rate. *What* had he told them?

He let Cif and Afreyt draw him down, but before he would begin to question them, Cif had thrown her arms around him, hugged him tight, and was kissing him full on the lips. This was wonderful, something he'd been dreaming of for three months and more (even though he'd pictured it happening in somewhat more private circumstances) and when she at last drew back, starry-eyed, it was another sort of question he was of a mind to ask her, but at that moment tall Afreyt grabbed him and soon was kissing him as soundly.

This was undeniably pleasant, but it took away from Cif's kiss, made it less personal, more a sign of congratulations and expression of overflowing enthusiasm than a mark of special affection. His Cif-dream faded down. And when Afreyt was done with him, he was at once surrounded by a press of well-wishers, some of whom wanted to embrace him also. From the corner of his eye he noted Hilsa and Rill bussing all and sundry – really, all these kisses had no meaning at all, including Cif's of course, he'd been a fool to think differently – and at one point he could have sworn he saw Groniger dancing a jig. Only old Ourph, for some reason, did not join in the merriment. Once he caught the old Mingol looking at him sadly.

And so the celebration began that lasted half the night and involved much drinking and eating and impromptu cheering and dancing and parading round and about and in and out. And the longer it went on, the more grotesque the cavorting and footstamping marches got, and all of it to the rhythm of the vindictive little rhyme that still went on resounding deep in the Mouser's mind, the tune to which everything was beginning to dance: 'Storm clouds thicken round Rime Isle. Nature brews her blackest bile. Monsters quicken, nightmares foal, niss and nicor, drow and troll.' Those lines in particular seemed to the

Mouser to describe what was happening just now – a birth of monsters. (But where were the trolls?) And so on (the rhyme) until its doomful and monstrously compelling end: 'Mingols to their deaths must go, down to weedy hell below, never draw an easy breath, suffer an unending death, everlasting pain and strife, everlasting death in life. Mingol madness ever burn! Never peace again return!'

And through it all the Mouser maintained his perhaps glassy-eyed smile and jaunty, insolent air of supreme self-confidence, he answered one repeated question with, 'No, I'm no orator – never had any training – though I've always liked to talk,' but inwardly he seethed with curiosity. As soon as he got a chance, he asked Cif, 'Whatever did I say to bring them around, to change their minds so utterly?'

'Why, you should know,' she told him.

'But tell me in your own words,' he said.

She deliberated. 'You appealed entirely to their feelings, to their emotions,' she said at last, simply. 'It was wonderful.'

'Yes, but what exactly did I say? What were my words?'

'Oh, I can't tell you *that*,' she protested. 'It was so all of a piece that no one thing stood out – I've quite forgotten the details. Content you, it was perfect.'

Later on he ventured to inquire of Groniger, 'At what point did my arguments begin to persuade you?'

'How can you ask that?' the grizzled Rimelander rejoined, a frown of honest puzzlement furrowing his brow. 'It was all so supremely logical, clearly and coldly reasoned. Like two and two makes four. How can one point to one part of arithmetic as being more compelling than another?'

'True, true,' the Mouser echoed reluctantly, and ventured to add, 'I suppose it was the same sort of rigorous logic that persuaded you to accept the gods Odin and Loki?'

'Precisely,' Groniger confirmed.

The Mouser nodded, though he shrugged in spirit. Oh, he knew what had happened all right, he even checked it out a little later with Rill.

'Where did you light your torch?' he asked.

'At the god's fire, of course,' she answered. 'At the god's fire in the Flame Den.' And then she kissed him. (She wasn't too bad at that either, even though there was nothing to the whole kissing business.)

Yes, he knew that the god Loki had come out of the flames and possessed him for a while (as Fafhrd had perhaps once been possessed by the god Issek back in Lankhmar) and spoken through his lips the sort of arguments that are so convincing when voiced by a god or delivered in time of war or comparable crisis – and so empty when proclaimed by a mere mortal on any ordinary occasion.

And really there was no time for speculation about the mystery of what he'd said, now that there was so much to be done, so many life-and-death decisions to be made, so many eventful trains of action to be guided to their conclusions – once these folk had got through celebrating and taken a little rest.

Still, it would be nice to know just a little of what he'd actually said, he thought wistfully. Some of it might even have been clever. Why in heaven's name, for instance, and to illustrate what, had he taken the queller out of his pouch and whirled it around his head?

He had to admit it was rather pleasant being possessed by a god (or would be if one could remember any of it) but it did leave one feeling empty, that is, except for the ever-present Mingols-to-their-deaths jingle – that he'd never get shut of, it seemed.

Next morning Fafhrd's band got their first sight of Cold Harbor, the sea, and the entire Mingol advance force all at once. The sun and west wind had dissipated the coastal fog and blew it from the glacier, on the edge of which they were now all making their way. It was a much smaller and vastly more primitive settlement than Salthaven. To the north rose the dark crater-summit of Mount Hellglow, so lofty and near that its eastern foothills still cast their shadows on the ice. A wisp of smoke rose from it, trailing off east. At the snowline a shadow on the dark rock seemed to mark the mouth of a cavern leading into the mountain's heart. Its lower slopes were thickly crusted with snow, leading back to the glacier which, narrow at this point, stretched ahead of them north to the glittering gray sea, surprisingly near. From the glacier's not-very-lofty foot, rolling grassy turf with occasional clumps of small northern cedars deformed by the wind stretched off to the southwest and its own now-distant snowy heights, wisps of white fog blowing eastways and vanishing across the rolling sunlit land between.

Glimpses of a few devastated and deserted hill farms late yesterday and early this morning, while they'd been trailing and chivvying the retreating Mingol marauders, had prepared them for what they saw now. Those farmhoues and byres had been of turf or sod solely, with grass and flowers growing on their narrow roofs, smokeholes instead of chimneys. Mara, dry-eyed, pointed out the one she'd dwelt in. Cold Harbor was simply a dozen such dwellings atop a rather steep hill or large mound backed against the glacier and turf-walled – a sort of retreat for the country-dwellers in times of peril. A short distance beyond it, a sandy beach fronted the harbor itself and on it three Mingol galleys had been drawn ashore, identified by the fantastic horse cages that were the above-deck portion of their prows.

Ranged round the mound of Cold Harbor at a fairly respectable distance were some fourscore Mingols, their leaders seemingly in conference with those of the twoscore who'd gone raiding ahead and but now returned. One of these latter was pointing back toward the Deathlands and then up at the glacier, as if describing the force that had pursued them. Beyond them the three Steppe stallions free from their cages were cropping turf. A peaceful scene, yet even as Fafhrd watched, keeping his band mostly hid (he hoped) by a fold in the ice (he did not trust too far Mingol aversion to ice) a spear came arching out of the tranquil-seeming mound and (it was a prodigious cast) struck down a Mingol. There were angry cries and a dozen Mingols returned the fire. Fafhrd judged that the besiegers, now reinforced, would surely try soon a determined assault. Without hesitation he gave orders.

'Skullick, here's action for you. Take your best bowman, oil, and a firepot. Race ahead for your life to where the glacier is nearest their beached ships and drop fire arrows in them, or attempt to. Run!

'Mara, follow them as far as the mound and when you see the ship's smoke, but not before, run down and join your friends if the way is clear. Careful! – Afreyt will have my head if aught befalls you. Tell them the truth about our numbers. Tell them to hold out and to feint a sortie if they see good chance.

'Mannimark! Keep one man of your squad and maintain watch here. Warn us of Mingol advances.

'Skor and the rest, follow me. We'll descend in their rear and briefly counterfeit a pursuing army. Come!'

And he was off at a run with eight berserks lumbering after, arrow-quivers banging against their backs. He'd already picked the stand of stunted cedars from the cover of which he planned to make his demonstration. As he ran, he sought to run in his mind with Skullick and his mate, and with Mara, trying to make the timing right.

He arrived at the cedars and saw Mannimark signaling that the Mingol assault had begun. 'Now howl like wolves,' he told his hard-breathing men, 'and really scream, each of you enough for two. Then we'll pour arrows toward 'em, longest range and fast as you can. Then, when I give command, back on the glacier again! as fast as we came down.'

When all this was done (and without much marking of consequences – there was not time) and he had rejoined Mannimark, followed by his panting band, he saw with delight a thin column of black smoke ascending from the beached galley nearest the glaciers. Mingols began to run in that direction from the slopes of the beleaguered mound, abandoning their assault. Midway he saw the small figure of Mara running down the glacier to Cold Harbor, her red cloak standing out behind her. A woman with a spear had appeared on the earth wall nearest the child, waving her on encouragingly. Then of a sudden Mara appeared to take a fantastically long stride, part of her form was obscured, as if there were a blur in Fafhrd's vision there, and then she seemed to – no, did! – rise in the air, higher and higher, as though clutched by an invisible eagle, or other sightless predatory flier. He kept his eyes on the red cloak, which suddenly grew brighter as the invisible flier mounted from shadow into sunlight with his captive. He heard a muttered exclamation of sympathy and wonder close beside him, spared a sidewise glance, and knew that Skor also had seen the prodigy.

'Keep her in sight, man,' he breathed. 'Don't lose the red

cloak for one moment. Mark where she goes through the trackless air.'

The gaze of the two men went upward, then west, then steadily east toward the dark mountain. From time to time Fafhrd looked down to assure himself that there were no untoward developments requiring his attention of the situations at the ships and at Cold Harbor. Each time he feared his eyes would never catch sight of the flying cloak again, but each time they did. The red patch grew smaller, tinier. They almost lost it as it dipped into the shadow again. Finally Skor straightened up.

'Where did it go?' Fafhrd asked.

'To the mouth of the cave at the snowline,' Skor replied. 'The girl was drawn there through the air by what magic I know not. I lost it there.'

Fafhrd nodded. 'Magic of a most special sort,' he said rapidly. 'She was carried there, I must believe, by an invisible flier, ghoul-related, an old enemy of mine, Prince Faroomfar of lofty Stardock. Only I among us have the knowledge to deal with him.'

He felt, in a way, that he was seeing Skor for the first time: a man an inch taller than himself and some five years younger, but with receding hairline and a rather scanty straggling russet beard. His nose had been broken at some time. He looked a thoughtful villain.

Fafhrd said, 'In the Cold Waste near Illek-Ving I hired you. At No-Ombrulsk I named you my chief lieutenant and you swore with the rest to obey me for *Sea Hawk*'s voyage and return.' He locked eyes with the man. 'Now it comes to the test, for you must take command while I seek Mara. Continue to harry the Mingols but avoid a full engagement. Those of Cold Harbor are our friends, but do not join with them in their fort unless no other course is open. Remember we serve the lady Afreyt. Understood?'

Skor frowned, keeping his eyes locked with Fafhrd's, then nodded once.

'Good!' Fafhrd said, not sure at all that it was so, but knowing he was doing what he had to. The smoke from the burning ship was less – the Mingols seemed to have saved her. Skullick and his fellow came running back with their bows, grinning.

'Mannimark!' Fafhrd called. 'Give me two torches. Skullick! – the tinder-pouch.' He unbuckled the belt holding his long-sword Graywand. He retained his ax.

'Men!' he addressed them. 'I must be absent for a space. Command goes to Skor by this token.' He buckled Graywand to that one's side. 'Obey him faithfully. Keep yourselves whole. See that I'm given no cause to rebuke you when I return.'

And without more ado he made off across the glacier toward Mount Hellglow.

The Mouser forced himself to rise soon as he woke and to take a cold bath before his single cup of hot gahveh (he was in that sort of mood). He set his entire crew to work, Mingols and thieves alike, completing *Flotsam*'s repairs, warning them that she must be ready to sail by the morrow's morn at least, in line with Loki god's promise: 'In three days the Mingols come.' He took considerable pleasure in noting that several of them seemed to be suffering from worse hangovers than his own. 'Work them hard, Pshawri,' he commanded. 'No mercy to slug-a-beds and shirkers!'

By then it was time to join with Cif in seeing off Afreyt's and Groniger's overland expedition. He found the Rime-landers offensively bright-eyed, noisy, and energetic, and the way that Groniger bustled about, marshalling them, was a caution.

Cif and Afreyt were clear-eyed and smiling also in their brave russets and blues, but that was easier to take. He and Cif walked a ways with the overland marchers. He noted with some amusement and approval that Afreyt had four of Groniger's men carrying a curtained litter, though she did not occupy it as yet. So she was making the man pay for yesternight's false (or at least, tactless) accusation, and would cross the Deathlands in luxurious ease. That was more in his own style.

He was in an odd state of mind, almost feeling himself a spectator rather than a participant in great events. The incident of the stirring speech he had made last night (or rather the oration that the god Loki had delivered through his lips while he was blacked out) and didn't remember (and couldn't dis-cover) a word of still rankled. He felt the sort of unimportant servant, or errand boy, who's never allowed to know the contents of the sealed messages he's given to deliver.

In this role of observer and critic he was struck by how grotesque was the weaponry of the high-stepping and ebullient Rimelanders. There were the quarterstaves, of course, and heavy single-bladed spears, but also slim fishing spears and great pitchforks and wickedly hooked and notched pikes, and long flails with curious heavy swiples and swingles a-dangle from their ends. A couple even carried long narrow-bladed and sharp-looking spades. He remarked on it to Cif and she asked him how he armed his own thief-band. Afreyt had gone on a little ahead. They were nearing Gallows Hill.

'Why, with slings,' he told Cif. 'They're as good as bows and a lot less trouble to carry. Like this one,' and he showed her the leather sling hanging from his belt. 'See that old gibbet ahead? Now mark.'

He selected a lead ball from his pouch, centered it in the strap and, sighting quickly but carefully, whirled it twice round his head and loosed. The *thunk* as it struck square on was unexpectedly loud and resounding. Some Rimelanders applauded.

Afreyt came hurring back to tell him not to do that again – it might offend god Odin. Can't do anything right this morning, the Mouser told himself sourly.

But the incident had given him a thought. He said to Cif, 'Say, maybe I was demonstrating the sling in my speech last night when I whirled the cube of square dealing around on its cord. Do you recall? Sometimes I get drunk on my own words and don't remember too well.'

She shook her head. 'Perhaps you were,' she said. 'Or perhaps you were dramatizing the Great Maelstrom which will swallow the Sun Mingols. Oh, that wondrous speech!'

Meanwhile they had come abreast of Gallows Hill and Afreyt had halted the march. He strolled over with Cif to find out why and for farewells – this was about as far as they'd planned to come.

To his surprise he discovered that Afreyt had set the two men with spades and several others to digging up the gallows, to unrooting it entire, and also had had its bearers set down the litter in front of the little grove of gorse on the north side of the hill, and part its curtains. While he watched puzzledly, he saw the girls May and Gale emerge from the grove, walking slowly and carefully and going through the motions of assisting someone – only there was no one there.

Except for the men trying to rock the gallows loose, everyone had grown silent, watchfully attentive.

In low undertones Cif told the Mouser the girls' names and what was going on.

'You mean to say that's Odin god they're helping and they're able to see him?' he whispered back. 'I remember now, Afreyt said she was taking him along, but – Can *you* see him at all?'

'Not very distinctly in this sunlight,' she admitted. 'But I have done so, by twilight. Afreyt says Fafhrd saw Odin most clearly in the dusk, evening before last. It's given only to Afreyt and the girls to see him clearly.'

The strange slow pantomime was soon concluded. Afreyt cut a few spiny branches of gorse and put them in the litter ('So he'll feel at home,' Cif explained to the Mouser) and started to draw the curtains, but, 'He wants *me* inside with him,' Gale announced in her shrill childish voice. Afreyt nodded, the little girl climbed in with a shrug of resignation, the curtains were drawn at last, and the general hush broke.

Lord, what idiocy! the Mouser thought. We two-footed fantasies will believe anything. And yet it occurred to him uneasily that he was a fine one to talk, who'd heard a god speak out of a fire and had his own body usurped by one. Inconsiderate creatures, gods were.

With a rush and a shout the gallows came down and its base up out of the earth, spraying dirt around, and a half dozen stalwart Rimelanders lifted it onto their shoulders and prepared to carry it so, marching single file after the litter.

'Well, they *could* use it as a battering ram, I suppose,' the Mouser muttered. Cif gave him a look.

Final farewells were said then and last messages for Fafhrd given and mutual assurances of courage until victory and death to the invader, and then the expedition went marching off in great swinging strides, rhythmically. The Mouser, standing with

Cif as he watched them go toward the Deathlands, got the impression they were humming under their breaths, 'Mingols to their deaths must go,' and so on, and stepping to its tune. He wondered if he'd begun to say those verses aloud, so that they'd picked it up from him. He shook his head.

But then he and Cif turned back alone, and he saw it was a bright day, pleasantly cool, with the breeze ruffling the heather and wildflowers waving on their delicate stems, and his spirits began to rise. Cif wore her russets in the shape of a short gown, rather than her customary trousers, and her dark golden-glinting hair was loose, and her movements were unforced and impulsive. She still had reserve, but it was not that of a councilman, and the Mouser remembered how thrilling last night's kiss had been, before he'd decided it didn't mean anything. Two fat lemmings popped out just ahead of them and stood on their hind legs, inspecting them, before ducking behind a bush. In stopping so as not to overrun them, Cif stumbled and he caught her and after a moment drew her to him. She yielded for a moment before she drew away, smiling at him troubledly.

'Gray Mouser,' she said softly, 'I am attracted to you, but I have told you how you resemble the god Loki – and last night when you swayed the Isle with your great oratory that resemblance was even more marked. I have also told you of my reluctance to take the god home with me (making me hire Hilsa and Rill, two familiar devils, to take care of him). Now I find, doubtless because of the resemblance, a kindred hesitation with respect to you, so that perhaps it is best we remain captain and councilwoman until the defense of Rime Isle is accomplished and I can sort you out from the god.'

The Mouser took a long breath and said slowly that he supposed that was best, thinking meanwhile that gods surely interfered with one's private life. He was mightily tempted to ask her whether she expected *him* to turn to Hilsa and Rill (devils or no) to be comforted, but doubted she would be inclined to allow him a god's liberties to that degree (granted he desired such), no matter how great the resemblance between them.

In this impasse, he was rather relieved to see beyond Cif's

372

shoulder that which allowed him to say, 'Speaking of the she-demons, who are these that are coming from Salthaven?'

Cif turned at that, and there true enough were Rill and Hilsa hurrying toward them through the heather, with Mother Grum plodding along behind, dark figure to their colorful ones. And although it was bright day three hours and more, Rill carried a lit torch. It was hard to see the flame in the sunlight, but they could mark by the way its shimmer made the heather wave beyond. And as the two harlots drew closer, it was evident that their faces were brimming with excitement and a story to tell, which was poured forth on their arrival and on the Mouser asking dryly: 'Why are you trying to light up the day, Rill?'

'The god spoke to us but now, most clearly from the Flame Den fire,' she began, 'saying "Darkfire, Darkfire, take me to Darkfire. Follow the flame—"' Hilsa broke in, '"—go as it bends," the god said crackingly, "turn as it wends, all in my name."'

Rill took up again, 'So I lit a fresh torch from the Flame Den blaze for him to travel in, and we carefully marked the flame and followed as it leaned, and it has led us to you!'

'And look,' Hilsa broke in as Mother Grum came up, 'now the flame would have us go to the mountain. It points toward her!' And she waved with her other hand north toward the icefall and the silent black scoriac peak beyond with its smoke-plume blowing west.

Cif and the Mouser dutifully looked at the torch's ghostly flame, narrowing their eyes. After a bit, 'The flame *does* lean over,' the Mouser said, 'but I think that's just because it's burning unevenly. Something in the grain of the wood or its oils and resins—'

'No, indubitably it motions us toward Darkfire,' Cif cried excitedly. 'Lead on, Rill,' and the women all turned sharply north, making for the glacier.

'But, ladies, we have hardly time for a trip upmountain,' the Mouser called after protestingly, 'what with preparations to be made for the Isle's defense and tomorow's sailing against the Mingols.'

'The god has commanded,' Cif told him over shoulder. 'He knows best.'

Mother Grum said in her growly voice, 'I doubt not he intends us to make a closer journey than mountaintop. Round-about is nearer than straight, I ween.'

And with that mystifying remark the women went on, and the Mouser shrugged and perforce followed after, thinking what fools these women were to be scurrying after a burning bush or branch as if it were the very god, even if the flame *did* bend most puzzlingly. (And he *had* heard fire speak, night before last.) Well, at any rate, he wasn't really needed for today's repairs on *Flotsam*; Pshawri could boss the crew as well as he, or at least well enough. Best keep an eye on Cif while this odd fit was on her and see she – or her three strangely sorted god-servants – came to no harm.

Such a sweet, strong, sensible, ravishing woman, Cif, when not godstruck. Lord, what troublesome, demanding and cap-tious employers gods were, never a-quiet. (It was safe to think such thoughts, he told himself, gods couldn't read your thoughts – everyone had *that* privacy – though they could overhear your slightest word spoken in undertone – and doubt-less make deductions from your starts and grimaces.)

Up from the depths of his skull came the wearisome compulsive chant, 'Mingols to their deaths must go,' and he was almost grateful to the malicious little jingle for occupying his mind troubled by the vagaries of gods and women.

The air grew chilly and soon they were at the icefall and in front of it a dead scrubby tree and a mounded upthrust of dark purplish rock, almost black, and in its midst a still blacker opening wide and tall as a door.

Cif said, 'This was not here last year,' and Mother Grum growled, 'The glacier, receding, has uncovered it,' and Rill cried, 'The flame leans toward the cave!' and Cif said, 'Go we down,' and Hilsa quavered, 'It's dark,' and Mother Grum rumbled, 'Have no fear. Dark is sometimes best light, and down best way go up.'

The Mouser wasted no time on words, but broke three branches from the dead tree (Loki-torch might not last for ever) and shouldering them, followed swiftly after the women into the rock.

*

Fafhrd doggedly climbed the last, seemingly endless slope of icy stone below Mount Hellglow's snowline. Orange light from the sun near setting beat on his back without warmth, and bathed the mountainside and the dark peak above with its wispy smoke blowing east. The rock was tough as diamond with frequent hand-holds – made for climbing – but he was weary and beginning to condemn himself for having abandoned his men in peril (it amounted to that) to come on a wild romantical goose-chase. Wind blew from the west, crosswise to his climb.

This was what came of taking a girl on a dangerous expedition and listening to women – or one woman, rather. Afreyt had been so sure of herself, so queenly-commanding – that he'd gone along with her against his better judgment. Why, he was chasing after Mara now mostly for fear of what Afreyt would think of him if aught befell the girl. Oh, he knew all right how he'd justified himself this morning in giving himself this job rather than sending a couple of his men. He'd jumped to the conclusion it was Prince Faroomfar had kidnapped Mara and he'd had the hope (in view of what Afreyt and Cif had told about being rescued from Khahkht's wizardry by flying mountain-princesses) that Princess Hirriwi, his beloved of one glorious night long gone, would come swimming along sightlessly on her invisible fish-of-air to offer him her aid against her hated brother.

That was another trouble with women, they were never there when you wanted or really needed them. They helped each other, all right, but they expected men to do all sorts of impossible feats of derring-do to prove themselves worthy of the great gift of their love (and what was that when you got down to it? – a fleeting clench-and-wriggle in the dark, illuminated only by the mute, incomprehensible perfection of a dainty breast, that left you bewildered and sad).

The way grew steeper, the light redder, and his muscles smarted. The way it was going, darkness would catch him on the rock-face, and then for two hours at least the mountain would hide the rising moon.

Was it solely on Afreyt's account that he was seeking Mara? Wasn't it also because she had the same name as his first young sweetheart whom he'd abandoned with his unborn child when he'd left Cold Corner as a youth to go off with yet another woman, whom he'd in turn abandoned – or led unwittingly to her death, really the same thing? Wasn't he seeking to appease that earlier Mara by rescuing this child one? That was yet another trouble with women, or at least the women you loved or had loved once – they kept on making you feel guilty, even beyond their deaths. Whether you loved them or not, you were invisibly chained to every woman who'd ever kindled you.

And was even *that* the deepest truth about himself going after the girl Mara? – he asked himself, forcing his analysis into the next devious cranny, even as he forced his numbing hands to seek out the next holds on the still steepening face in the dirty red light. Didn't he really quicken at thought of her, just as god Odin did in his senile lubricity? Wasn't he and no other chasing after Faroomfar because he thought of the prince as a lecherous rival for this delicate tidbit of girl flesh?

For that matter, wasn't Afreyt's girlishness – her slenderness despite her height, her small and promising breasts, her tales of childhood make-believe maraudings with Cif, her violet-eyed romancing, her madcap bravado – that had attracted him even in far-off Lankhmar? That and her Rime Isle silver had chained him, and set him on the whole unsuitable course of becoming a responsible captain of men – he who had been all his days a lone wolf – with lone-leopard comrade Mouser. Now he'd reverted back to it, abandoning his men. (Gods grant Skor keep his head and that some at least of his disciplines and preachments of prudence had taken effect!) But oh, this lifelong servitude to girls – whimsical, fleeting, tripping little demons! White, slim-necked, sharp-toothed, restlessly bobbing weasels with the soulful eyes of lemurs!

His blindly reaching hand closed on emptiness and he realized that in his furious self-upbraiding he'd reached the apex of the slope without knowing it. With belated caution he lifted his head until his eyes looked just over the edge. The sun's last dark red beams showed him a shale-scattered ledge some ten feet wide and then the mountain going up again precipitous and snowless. Opposite him in that new face was a great recess or cavern-mouth as wide as the ledge and twice that height. It was very dark inside that great door but he could make out the bright red of Mara's cloak, its hood raised, and within the hood, shadowed by it, her small face, very pale-cheeked, very dark-eyed – really a smudge in darkness – staring toward him.

He scrambled up, peering around suspiciously, then moved toward her, softly calling her name. She did not reply with word or sign though continuing to stare. There was a warm, faintly sulfurous breeze blowing out of the mountain and it ruffled her cloak. Fafhrd's steps quickened and with a swift-growing anticipation of unknown horror whirled the cloak aside to reveal a small grinning skull set atop a narrow-shouldered wooden cross about four feet high.

Fafhrd moved backwards to the ledge, breathing heavily. The sun had set and the gray sky seemed wider and more palely bright without its rays. The silence was deep. He looked along the ledge in both directions, fruitlessly. Then he stared into the cave again and his jaw tightened. He took flint and iron, opened the tinder-pouch, and kindled a torch. Then holding it high in his left hand and his unbelted ax gently a-swing in his right, he walked forward into the cave and toward the mountain's heart, past the eerie diminutive scarecrow, his foot avoiding its stripped-away red cloak, along the strangely smooth-walled passageway wide and tall enough for a giant, or a winged man.

The Mouser hardly knew how long he'd been closely following the four godstruck females through the strangely tunnel-like cave that was leading them deeper and deeper under the glacier toward the heart of the volcanic mountain Darkfire. Long enough, at any rate, for him to have split and slivered the larger ends of the three dead branches he was carrying, so they would kindle readily. And certainly long enough to become very weary of the Mingols death-chant, or Mingol jingle, that was now not only resounding in his mind but being spoken aloud by the four rapt women as if it were a marching, or rather scurrying song, just as Groniger's men had seemed to do. Of course in this case he didn't have to ask himself where they'd got it, for they'd all originally heard it with him night before last in the Flame Den, when Loki god had seemed to speak from the fire, but that didn't make it any easier to endure or one whit less boresome.

At first he'd tried to reason with Cif as she hurried along with the others like a mad maenad, arguing the wisdom of venturing so recklessly into an uncharted cavern, but she'd only pointed at Rill's torch and said, 'See how it strains ahead. The god commands us,' and gone back to her chanting.

Well, there was no denying that the flame was bending forward most unnaturally when it should have been streaming back with their rapid advance – and also lasting longer than any torch should. So the Mouser had had to go back to memorizing as well as he could their route through the rock which, chill at first, as one would expect from the ice above, was now perceptibly warmer, while the heating air carried a faint brimstone stench.

But at all events, he told himself he didn't have to *like* this sense of being the tool and sport of mysterious forces vastly more powerful than himself, forces that didn't even deign to tell him the words they spoke through him (that business of the speech he'd given but not heard one word of bothered him more and more). Above all he didn't have to celebrate this bondage to the inscrutable, as the women were doing, by mindlessly repeating words of death and doom.

Also he didn't like the feeling of being in bondage to women and absorbed more and more into their affairs, such as he'd felt ever since accepting Cif's commission three months ago in Lankhmar, and which had put him in bondage, in turn, to Pshawri and Mikkidu and all his men, and to his ambitions and self-esteem.

Above all, he didn't like being in bondage to the idea of himself being a monstrous clever fellow who could walk widdershins round all the gods and godlets, from whom everyone expected godlike performance. Why couldn't he admit to Cif at least that he'd not heard a word of his supposedly great speech? And if he could do that walk-widdershins bit, why didn't he?

The cavernous tunnel they'd been following so long debouched into what seemed a far vaster space steaming with vapors, and then they were suddenly brought up short against a great wall that seemed to extend indefinitely upward and to either side.

The women broke off their doom-song and Rill cried,

'Whither now, Loki?' and Hilsa echoed her tremulously. Mother Grum rumbled, 'Tell us, wall,' and Cif intoned strongly, 'Speak, O god.'

And while the women were saying these things, the Mouser stole forward rapidly and laid his hand on the wall. It was so hot he almost snatched back his hand, but did not, and through his palm and outspread fingers he felt a steady strong pulsation, a rhythm in the rock, exactly as if it were itself sounding the women's song.

And then as if in answer to the women's entreaty, the Loki torch, which had burnt down to little more than a stub, flared up into a great seven-branched flame, almost intolerably bright – it was a wonder Rill could hold it – showing the frighteningly vast extent of the rock face. Even as it flared, the rock seemed to heave under the Mouser's hand monstrously with each pulsation of its song and the floor began to rock with it. Then the great rock face bulged, and the heat became monstrous too, and the brimstone stench intensified so they were all set a-gagging and a-coughing even as their imaginations envisioned instant earthquake and cave-brimming floods of red-hot lava exploding from the mountain's heart.

It says much for the Mouser's prudence that in that short period of panic and terrified wonder it occurred to him to thrust one of his frayed branches into the blinding flame. And it was well he did so, for the great god-flame now died down as swiftly as it had flared up, leaving only the feeble illumination of the burning branch of ordinary dead wood afire in his hands. Rill dropped the dead stub of her burnt-out torch with a cry of pain, as if only now feeling how it had burned her, while Hilsa whimpered and all the women groped about dazedly.

And as if command had questionless passed to the Mouser with the torch, he now began to shepherd them back the way they had come, away from the strangling fumes, through the now-bewilderingly shadowy passageways that only he had conned and that still resounded with the dreadful rock music aping their own, a symphony of doom-song monstrously reverberated by solid tone – away toward the blessed outer light and air and sky, and fields and blessed seas.

Nor was that the full measure of the Mouser's far-sighted

prudence (so far-sighted that he sometimes couldn't tell what was its aim), for in the moment of greatest panic, when the stub of Loki-torch had fallen from Rill's hand, he had thought to snatch it up from the rocky floor and thrust it, hardly more than a hot black cinder, deep into his pouch. It burnt his fingers a little, he discovered afterwards, but luckily it was not so hot that his pouch caught fire.

Afreyt sat on a lichened rock outside the litter on the broad summit-pass of the Deathlands (near where Fafhrd had first encountered the Mingols, though she didn't know that) with her gray cloak huddled about her, resting. Now and again a wind from the east, whose chilliness seemed that of the violet sky, ruffled the litter's closed curtains. Its bearers had joined the other men at one of the small fires to the fore and rear, built with carried wood to heat chowder during this evening pause in their march. The gallows had been set down by Afreyt's direction and its base and beam-end wedged in rock, so that it rested like a fallen-over 'L', its angle lifting above the litter like a crooked roof, or like a rooftree with one king-post.

There was still enough sunset light in the west for her to wonder if that was smoke she saw moving east above the narrow crater of Mount Hellglow, while in the cold east there was sufficient night for her to see, she was almost sure, a faint glow rising from that of Mount Darkfire. The eastwind blew again and she hunched her shoulders and drew the hood of her cloak more closely against her cheeks.

The curtains of the litter parted for a moment and May slipped out and came and stood in front of Afreyt.

'What's that you've got around your neck?' she asked the girl.

'It's a noose,' the latter explained eagerly, but with a certain solemnity. 'I braided it, Odin showed me how to make the knot. We're all going to belong to the Order of the Noose, which is something Odin and I invented this afternoon while Gale was taking a nap.'

Afreyt hesitatingly reached her hand to the girl's slender throat and inspected the loop of heavy braid with uneasy fascination. There, surely enough, was the cruel hangman's knot drawn rather close, and tucked into it a nosegay of small mountain flowers, somewhat wilted, gathered this morning on the lower slopes.

'I made one for Gale,' the girl said. 'She didn't want to wear it at first because I'd helped invent it. She was jealous.'

Afreyt shook her head reprovingly, though her mind wasn't on that.

'Here,' May continued, lifting her hand which had been hanging close to her side under the cloak. 'I've made one for you, a little bigger. See, it's got flowers too. Put back your hood. You wear it under your hair, of course.'

For a long moment Afreyt looked into the girl's unblinking eyes. Then she drew back her hood, bent down her head, and helped lift her hair through. Using both hands, May drew the knot together at the base of Afreyt's throat. 'There,' she said, 'that's the way you wear it, snug but not tight.'

While this was happening, Groniger had come up, carrying three bowls and a small covered pail of chowder. When the nooses had been explained to him, 'A capital conceit!' he said with a great grin, his eyebrows lifting. 'That'll show the Mingols something, let them know what they're in for. It's a grand chant the Little Captain gave us, isn't it?'

Afreyt nodded, looking sideways a moment at Groniger. 'Yes,' she said, 'his wonderful words.'

Groniger glanced back at her in similar fashion. 'Yes, his wonderful words.'

May said, 'I wish I'd heard him.'

Groniger handed them the bowls and swiftly poured the thick, steaming soup.

May said, 'I'll take Gale hers.'

Groniger said gruffly to Afreyt, 'Sup it while it's hot. Then get some rest. We go on at moonrise, agreed?' and when Afreyt nodded, strode off rather bumptiously, cheerily rumble-humming the chant to which they'd marched all day, the Mouser's – or Loki's, rather.

Afreyt narrowed her brows. Normally Groniger was such a sober man, dull-spirited she'd once thought, but now he was almost like a buffoon. Was 'monstrously comical' too strong an expression? She shook her head slowly. All the Rime-men were getting like that, loutish and grotesque and somehow bigger.

Perhaps it was her weariness made her see things askew and magnified, she told herself.

May came back and they got out their spoons and fell to. 'Gale wanted to eat hers inside,' the girl volunteered after a bit. 'I think she and Odin are cooking up something.' She shrugged and went back to her spooning. After another while: 'I'm going to make nooses for Mara and Captain Fafhrd.' Finally she scraped her bowl, set it aside, and said, 'Cousin Afreyt, do you think Groniger's a troll?'

'What's that?' Afreyt asked.

'A word Odin uses. He says Groniger's a troll.'

Gale came excitedly out of the litter with her empty bowl, but remembering to draw the curtains behind her.

'Odin and I have invented a marching song for us!' she announced, stacking her bowl in May's. 'He says the other god's song is all right, but he should have one of his own. Listen, I'll chant it for you. It's shorter and faster than the other.' She screwed up her face. 'It's like a drum,' she explained earnestly. Then, stamping with a foot: 'March, march, over the Death-lands. Go, go, over the Doomlands. Doom! – kill the Mingols. Doom! – die the heroes. Doom! Doom! Glorious doom!' Her voice had grown quite loud by the time she was done.

'Glorious doom?' Afreyt repeated.

'Yes. Come on, May, chant it with me.'

'I don't know that I want to.'

'Oh, come on. I'm wearing your noose, aren't I? Odin says we should all chant it.'

As the two girls repeated the chant in their shrill voices with mounting enthusiasm, Groniger and another Rime-man came up.

'That's good,' he said, collecting the bowls. 'Glorious doom is good.'

'I like that one,' the other man agreed. 'Doom! – kill the Mingols!' he repeated appreciatively.

They went off chanting it in low voices.

The night darkened. The wind blew. The girls grew quiet.

May said, 'It's cold. The god'll be getting chilly. Gale, we'd better go inside. Will you be all right, cousin Afreyt?'

'I'll be all right.'

A while after the curtains closed behind them, May stuck her head out.

'The god invites you to come inside with us,' she called to Afreyt.

Afreyt caught her breath. Then she said as evenly as she could, 'Thank the god, but tell him I will remain here . . . on guard.'

'Very well,' May said and the curtains closed again.

Afreyt clenched her hands under her cloak. She hadn't admitted to anyone, even Cif, that for some time now, Odin had been fading. She could hardly see even a wispy outline any more. She could still hear his voice, but it had begun to grow faint, lost in wind-moaning. The god had been very real at first on that spring day when she and Cif had found him, and found that there were two gods. He'd seemed so near death then, and she'd labored so hard to save him. She'd been filled with such adoration, as if he were some ancient hero-saint, or her own dear, dead father. And when he had caressed her fumblingly and muttered in disappointment (it sounded), 'You're older than I thought,' and drifted off to sleep, her adoration had been contaminated by horror and rejection. She'd got the idea of bringing in the girls (Did that make her a monster? Well, perhaps) and after that she'd managed very well, keeping it all at a distance.

And then there'd been the excitement of the journey to Lankhmar and the perils of Khahkht's ice-magic and the Mingols and the renewed excitement of the arrival of the Mouser and Fafhrd and the realization that Fafhrd did indeed resemble a younger Odin – was *that* what had made god Odin fade and grow whisper-voiced? She didn't know, but she knew it helped make everything torturesome and confusing – and she couldn't have borne to enter the litter tonight. (Yes, she was a monster.)

She felt a sharp pain in her neck and realized that in her agitation she'd been tugging at the pendant end of the noose beneath her cloak. She loosened it and forced herself to sit quietly. It was full dark now. There *were* faint flames flickering from Darkfire and Hellglow too. She heard snatches of talk from the campfires and bits of the new chant and laughter as the story of that went round. It was very cold, but she did not move. The east grew silvery-pale, the milky effulgence domed up, and at last the white moon edged into view.

The camp stirred then and after a while the bearers came up and unwedged Odin's gallows and lifted it up and the litter too, and Afreyt arose, unkinking her stiff joints and stamping her numbed feet, and they all marched off west across the moon-silvered rock, shouldering their grotesque weapons and the two larger burdens. Some of them limped a bit (after all, they were sailors, their feet unused to marching) but they all went on briskly to the new Odin-chant, hunching their backs against the east wind, which now blew strong and steadily.

Fafhrd had just kindled his second torch from the ember-end of the first and his surroundings had grown warmer, when the lofty passageway he was following debouched into a cavern so vast that the light he bore seemed lost in it. The sound of the cast-away torch-stub hitting rock awakened distant faint echoes and he came to a stop, peering up and around. Then he began to see multitudinous points of light as stars, where flakes of mica in the fire-born stone reflected his torch, and in the middle distance an irregular pillar of mica-flecked rock and on its top a small pale bundle that drew his eye. Then from above he heard the beat of great wings, a pause, then another beat – as though a great vulture were circling in the cavernous dark.

He called, 'Mara!' toward the pillar and the echoes came back and amongst them shrill and faint, his own name called and the echoes of that. Then he realized that the wing-beat had ceased and that one of the high mica-stars was getting rapidly brighter, as though it were swiftly traveling straight down toward him, and he heard a rush in the air as of a great hawk stooping.

He jerked his whole body aside from the bright sword darting at him and simultaneously struck with his ax just behind it. The torch was torn from his grasp, what seemed like a leather sail struck him to his knees, and then there was a great wing-beat, very close, and another, and then the shrill bellow of a man in agony that despite its extremity held a note of outrage.

As he scrambled to his feet, he saw his torch flaring wide on the rocky floor and transfixing it the bright sword that had struck it from his grasp. Wing-beat and bellowing were going off from him now. He set his boot on the torch handle, preparatory to withdrawing the sword from it, but as he went to take hold of the latter, his fingers encountered a scaly hand, slenderer than his own, gripping it tightly, and (his groping fingers ascertained) warmly wet at the wrist, where it had been chopped off. Both hand and blood alike were invisible, so that although his fingers touched and felt, his eyes saw only the sword's hilt, the silver cross-guard, the pear-shaped silver pommel, and the black leather grip wrapped with braided silver wire.

He heard his name spoken falteringly close behind him and turning saw Mara standing there in her white smock looking woebegone and confused, as if she'd just been lifted from the pillar's top and set down there. As he spoke her name in answer, a voice came out of the air beside Mara and a little above her, speaking in the chilling and confounding tones of a familiar and beloved voice turned hateful in nightmare.

The sightless mountain princess Hirriwi said, 'Woe to you, barbarian, for having come north again without first paying your respects at Stardock. Woe to you for coming at another woman's call, although we favor her cause. Woe for deserting your men to chase this girl-chit, whom we would have (and have) saved without you. Woe for meddling with demons and gods. And woe upon woe for lifting your hand to maim a prince of Stardock, to whom we are joined, though he is our dearest enemy, by bonds stronger than love and hate. A head for a head and a hand for a hand, think on that. Quintuple woe!'

During this recital, Mara had moved to Fafhrd, where he knelt upright, his face working as he stared at and hearkened to emptiness. He had put his arm about her shoulders and together they stared at the speaking gloom.

Hirriwi continued, her voice less ritually passionate, but every whit as cold, 'Keyaira heals and comforts our brother, and I go to join them. At dawn we will return you, journeying upon our fish of air, to your people, where you will know your weird. Until then, rest in the warmth of Hellfire, which is not yet a danger to you.'

With that she broke off and there was the sound of her going away. The torch flickered low, almost consumed, and great weariness took hold of Fafhrd and Mara and they lay down side by side and sleep was drawn up over them from their toes to their eyes. Fafhrd, at last thought, wondered why it should move him so strangely that Mara clutched his left hand, bent up beside his shoulder, in both of hers.

Next day Salthaven was a-bustle so early and so wildly – so fantastically – with preparations for the great sailing that it was hard to tell where the inspirations of nightmare and worry-dream ended and those of (hopefully) wide-eyed day began. Even the 'foreigners' were infected, as if they too had been hearing the Mingols-to-the-deaths chant in their dreams, so that the Mouser had been impelled against his better judgment to man Fafhrd's *Sea Hawk* with the most eager of them under Bomar their 'mayor' and the Ilthmart tavern-owner. He made Pshawri their captain with half the thieves to support his authority and two of the Mingols, Trenchi and Gavs, to help him con the ship.

'Remember you are boss,' he told Pshawri. 'Make them like it or lump it – and keep to windward of me.'

Pshawri, his new-healed forehead wound still pink, nodded fiercely and went to take up his command. Above the salt cliff the eastern sky was ominously red with sunrise, while glooms of night still lingered in the west. The east wind blew strongly.

From *Flotsam*'s stern the Mouser surveyed the busy harbor and his fleet of fishing boats turned warships. Truly, they were a weird sight, their decks which had so recently been piled with fish now bristling with pikes and various impromptu weapons such as he'd seen Groniger's men shoulder yesterday. Some of them had lashed huge ceremonial spears (bronze-pointed timbers, really) to their bowsprits – for use as rams, he supposed, the Fates be kind to 'em! While others had bent on red and black sails, to indicate bloody and baleful intentions, he guessed – the soberest fisherman was a potential pirate, that was sure. Three were half wreathed in fishnets – protection against arrow fire? The two largest craft were commanded by Dwone and Zwaakin, his sub-admirals, if that could be credited. He shook his head.

If only he had time to get his thoughts straight! But ever since he'd awakened events (and his own unpredictable impulses) had been rushing, nay, stampeding him. Yesterday, he'd managed to lead Cif and the other three women safely out of the quaking and stinking cave-tunnels (he glanced toward Darkfire – it was still venting into the red sky a thick column of black smoke, which the east wind blew west) only to discover that they'd spent an unconscionable time underground and it was already evening. After seeing to Rill's hand, badly burned by the Loki-torch, they'd had to hurry back to Salthaven for conferences with all and sundry – hardly time to compare notes with Cif on the whole cavern experience . . .

And now he had to break off to help Mikkidu instruct the six Rimeland replacements for the thieves they'd lost to *Sea Hawk* – how to man the sweeps and so forth.

And *that* was no sooner done (matter of a few low-voiced instructions to Mikkidu, chiefly) than here came Cif climbing aboard, followed by Rill, Hilsa, and Mother Grum – all of them save for the last in sailorly trousers and jackets with knives at their belts. Rill's right arm was in a sling.

'Here we are, yours to command, captain,' Cif said brightly.

'Dear . . . councilwoman,' the Mouser answered, his heart sinking, '*Flotsam* can't sail into possible battle with women aboard, especially—' He let a meaningful look serve for '—whores and witches.'

'Then we'll man *Sprite* and follow you after,' she told him, not at all downcast. 'Or rather range ahead to be the first to sight the Sunwise Mingols – you know *Sprite*'s a fast sailer. Yes, perhaps that's best, a women's fighting-ship for soldieresses.'

The Mouser submitted to the inevitable with what grace he could muster. Rill and Hilsa beamed. Cif touched his arm commiseratingly.

'I'm glad you agreed,' she said. 'I'd already loaned *Sprite* to three other women.' But then her face grew serious as she lowered her voice to say, 'There is a matter that troubles me you should know. We were going to bring god Loki aboard in a firepot, as yesterday he traveled in Rill's torch—'

'Can't have fire aboard a ship going into battle,' the Mouser responded automatically. 'Besides, look how Rill got burned.'

'But this morning, for the first time in over a year, we found the fire in the Flame Den unaccountably gone out,' Cif finished. 'We sifted the ashes. There was not a spark.'

'Well,' said the Mouser thoughtfully, 'perhaps yesterday at the great rock face after he flamed so high the god temporarily shifted his dwelling to the mountain's fiery heart. See how she smokes!' And he pointed toward Darkfire, where the black column going off westward was thicker.

'Yes, but we don't have him at hand that way,' Cif objected troubledly.

'Well, at any rate he's still on the island,' the Mouser told her. 'And in a sense, I'm sure, on *Flotsam* too,' he added, remembering (it made his fire-stung fingers smart anew) the black torch-end he still had in his pouch. That was another thing, he told himself, that wanted thinking about . . .

But just then Dwone came sailing close by to report the Rime fleet ready for action and hardly to be held back. The Mouser had perforce to get *Flotsam* under way, hoisting what sail she could carry for the beat against the wind, and setting his thieves and their green replacements to sweeping while Ourph beat time, so that she'd be able to keep ahead of the handier fishing craft.

There were cheers from the shore and the other ships and for a short while the Mouser was able to bask in self-satisfaction at *Flotsam* moving out so bravely at the head of the fleet, and his crew so well disciplined, and (he could see) Pshawri handling *Sea Hawk* nicely enough, and Cif standing beside him glowing-eyed – and himself a veritable admiral, no less, by Mog!

But then the thoughts which he hadn't had time to straighten all day began to cark him again. Above all else he realized that there was something altogether foolhardy, in fact utterly ridiculous, about them all setting sail so confidently with only one hairbrained plan of action, on nothing more than the crackling word of a fire, the whisper of burning twigs. Still he **had a compelling feeling** in his bones that they were doing the **right thing and nothing** could harm them, and he would **peradventure find the** Mingol fleet and that another wonderful inspiration would come to him at the last minute . . .

At that moment his eye lit on Mikkidu sweeping with

considerable style in the bowmost steerside position and he came to a decision.

'Ourph, take the tiller and take her out,' he directed. 'Call time to the sweeps.

'My dear, I must leave you for a brief space,' he told Cif. Then taking the last Mingol with him, he went forward and said in a gruff voice to Mikkidu, 'Come with me to my cabin. A conference. Gib will replace you here,' and then hurried below with his now apprehensive-eyed lieutenant past the wondering glances of the women.

Facing Mikkidu acros the table in the low-ceilinged cabin (*one* good thing about having a short captain and still shorter crew, it occurred to him) he eyed his subordinate mercilessly and said, 'Lieutenant, I made a speech to the Rime Islers in their council hall night before last that had them cheering me at the end. You were there. *What did I say?*'

Mikkidu writhed. 'Oh, captain,' he protested, blushing, 'how can you expect—'

'Now none of that stuff about it being so wonderful you can't remember – or other weaseling out,' the Mouser cut him short. 'Pretend the ship's in a tempest and her safety depends on you giving me a square answer. Gods, haven't I taught you yet that no man of mine ever got hurt from me by telling me the truth?'

Mikkidu digested that with a great gulp and then surrendered. 'Oh, captain,' he said, 'I did a terrible thing. That night when I was following you from the docks to the council hall and you were with the two ladies, I bought a drink from a street vendor and gulped it down while you weren't looking. It didn't taste strong at all, I swear it, but it must have had a tremendous delayed kick, for when you jumped on the table and started to talk, I blacked out – my word upon it! When I came to you were saying somthing about Groniger and Afreyt leading out half the Rimelanders to reinforce Captain Fafhrd and the rest of us sailing out to entice the Sun Mingols into a great whirlpool, and everybody was cheering like mad – and so of course I cheered too, just as if I'd heard everything that they had.'

'You can swear to the truth of that?' the Mouser asked in a terrible voice.

Mikkidu nodded miserably.

The Mouser came swiftly around the table and embraced him and kissed him on his quivering cheek. 'There's a good lieutenant,' he said most warmly, clapping him on the back. 'Now go, good Mikkidu, and invite the lady Cif attend me here. Then make yourself useful on deck in any way your shrewdness may suggest. Don't stand now in a daze. Get at it, man.'

By the time Cif arrived (not long) he had decided on his approach to her.

'Dear Cif,' he said without preamble, coming to her, 'I have a confession to make to you,' and then he told her humbly but clearly and succinctly the truth about his 'wonderful words' – that he simply hadn't heard one of them. When he was done he added, 'So you can see not even my vanity is involved – whatever it was, it was Loki's speech, not mine . . . so do you now tell me truth about it, sparing me nothing.'

She looked at him with a wondering smile and said, 'Well, I was puzzled as to what you could have said to Mikkidu to make him so head-in-the-clouds happy – and am not sure I understand that even now. But, yes, my experience was, I now confess, identical with his – and not even the taking of an unknown drink to excuse it. My mind went blank, time passed me by, and I heard not a word you said, except those last directions about Afreyt's expedition and the whirlpool. But everyone was cheering and so I pretended to have heard, not wanting to injure your feelings or feel myself a fool. Oh, I was a sheep! Once I was minded to confess my lapse to Afreyt, and now I wish I had, for she had a strange look on her then – But I didn't. You think, as I do now, that she also—?'

The Mouser nodded decisively. 'I think that not one soul of them heard a word to remember of the main body of my – or, rather, Loki's talk, but later they all pretended to have done so, just like so many sheep indeed – and I the black goat leading them on. So only Loki knows what Loki said and we sail out upon an unknown course against the Mingols, taking all on trust.'

'What to do now?' she asked wonderingly.

Looking into her eyes with a tentative smile and a slight shrug that was at once acquiescent and comical, he said, 'Why, we go on, for it is your course and I am committed to it.'

Flotsam gave a long lurch then, with a wave striking along her side, and it nudged Cif against him, and their arms went round each other, and their lips met thrillingly – but not for long, for he must hurry on deck, and she too, to discover (or rather confirm) what had befallen.

Flotsam progressed out of Salthaven harbor and the salt cliff's lee to the Outer Sea where the east wind smote them more urgently and the swells and the sunlight struck their canvas and deck. The Mouser took the tiller from sad-faced Ourph and that old one and Gib and Mikkidu set sail for the first eastward tack. And one by one *Sea Hawk* and the weirdly accoutered fishing boats repeated their maneuver, following *Flotsam* out.

That selfsame east wind which blew west across the southern half of Rime Isle, and against which *Flotsam* labored, farther out at sea was hurrying on the horse-ships of the Sunwise Mingols. The grim galleys, each with its bellying square sail, made a great drove of ships, and now and again a stallion screamed in its bow-cage as they plunged ahead through the waves, which cascaded spray through the black, crazily-angled bars. All eyes strained west-ahead, and it would have been hard to say which eyes glared the more madly, those of the furclad grinningly white-toothed men, or those of long-faced, grimacingly white-toothed beasts.

On the poop of the flagship this frenzy looked in a more philosophical direction, where Gonov discoursed with his witch-doctor and attendant sages propounding such questions as, 'Is it sufficient to burn a city to the ground, or must it also be trampled to rubble?' and contemplating such answers as, 'Most meritorious is to pound it to sand, aye, to fine loam, without burning at all.'

While the strong westwind that blew east across the northern half of the island (with a belt of squalls and fierce eddies between the two winds) was hurrying on from the west across trackless ocean the like fleet of the Widdershins Mingols, where Edumir had proposed this query to his philosophers: 'Is death by suicide in the first charge, hurling oneself upon the foeman's virgin spear, to be preferred to death by self-administered poison in the last charge?'

He hearkened to their closely-reasoned answers and to the counter-question: 'Since death is so much to be desired, surpassing the delights of love and mushroom wine, how did our all-noble and revered ancestors ever survive to procreate us?' and at last observed, his white-rimmed eyes gazing east yearningly, 'That is all theory. On Rime Isle we will once more put these recondite matters to the test of practice.'

While high above all winds Khahkht in his icy sphere ceaselessly studied the map lining it, whereon he moved counters for ships and men, horses and women – aye, even gods – bending his bristly face close, so that no unlawful piece might escape his fierce scrutiny.

By early morning sunlight and against the nipping wind, Afreyt hurried on alone through the heather dotted by stunted cedars past the last silent hill farm, with its sagging gray-green turf roofs, before Cold Harbor. She was footsore and weary (even Odin's noose around her neck seemed a heavy weight) for they'd marched all night with only two short rest-stops and midway they'd been buffeted by changing winds reaching tornadic strength as they'd passed through the transition belt between the southeastern, Salthaven half of Rime Isle, which the east wind presently ruled, and the northwestern, Cold Harbor half, where the equally strong west wind now held sway. Yet she forced herself to scan carefully ahead for friend or foe, for she had constituted herself vanguard for Groniger and his gro-tesquely burdened trampers. A while ago in the twilight before dawn she'd gone from litter-side up to the head of the column and pointed out to Groniger the need of having a guard ahead now that they were nearing their journey's end and should be wary of ambushes. He had seemed unconcerned and heedless, unable to grasp the danger, almost as if he (and all the other Rime men, for that matter) were intent only on marching on and on, glaze-eyed, growling Gale's doom-chant, like so many monstrous automatons, until they met the Mingols, or Fafhrd's force. Failing those, she believed, they would stride into the chilly western ocean with never a halt or waver, as did the lemming hordes in their climacteric. But neither had Groniger voiced any objection to her spying on ahead – nor even concern for her safety. Where *was* the man's one-time clear-headedness and prudence?

Afreyt was not unversed in island woodcraft and she now spotted Skor peering toward Cold Harbor from the grove of dwarf cedars whence Fafhrd had launched yestermorning's brief arrow-fusillade. She called Skor's name, and he whipped around nocking an arrow to his bow, then came up swiftly when he saw her familiar blues.

'Lady Afreyt, what do you here? You look weary,' he greeted her succinctly. He looked weary himself and hollow-eyed, his cheeks and forehead smudged with soot above his straggly russet beard, perhaps against the glare of glacial ice.

She quickly told him about the Rimeland reinforcements approaching behind her.

His weariness seemed to lift from him as she spoke. 'That's brave news,' he said when she had done. 'We joined our lines (I'm now making the rounds of them) with those of the Cold Harbor defenders before sunset yesterday and have the Mingol fore-raiders penned on the beach – and all by bluff! The mere sight of the forces you describe, strategically deployed, will cause 'em to take ship and sail away, I think – and we not lift a finger.'

'Your pardon, lieutenant,' she rejoined, her own weariness lifting at his optimism, 'but I have heard you and your fellows named berserker – and have always thought it was the way of such to charge the enemy at the first chance, charge wolf-howling and bounding, mother-naked?'

'To tell the truth, that was once my own understanding of it,' he replied, thoughtfully rubbing his broken nose with the back of his hand, 'but the captain's changed my mind for me. He's a great one for sleights and deceits, the captain is! Makes the foe imagine things, sets their own minds to work against 'em, never fights when there's an easier way – and some of his wisdom has rubbed off on us.'

'Why are you wearing Fafhrd's sword?' she asked, seeing it suddenly.

'Oh, he went off yestermorning to Hellglow after the girl, leaving me in command, and he's not yet returned,' Skor answered readily, though a crease of concern appeared between

393

his brows, and he went on briefly to tell Afreyt about Mara's strange abduction.

'I wonder at him leaving you all so long to shift without him, merely for that,' Afreyt commented, frowning.

'Truth to tell, I wondered at it myself, yestermorning,' Skor admitted. 'But as events came on us, I asked myself what the captain would do in each case, and did that, and it's worked out – so far.' He hooked a middle-finger over a fore-one.

There came a faint tramping and the whispers of a hoarse chant and turning they saw the front of the Rime column coming downhill.

'Well, they look fearsome enough,' Skor said, after a moment. 'Strange, too,' he added, as the litter and gallows hove into view. The girls in their red cloaks were walking beside the former.

'Yes, they are that,' Afreyt said.

'How are they armed?' he asked her. 'I mean, besides the pikes and spears and quarterstaves and such?'

She told him those were their only weapons, as far as she knew.

'They'd not stand up to Mingols, then, not if they had to cover any distance to attack,' he judged. 'Still, if we showed 'em under the right conditions, and put a few bowmen amongst 'em . . .'

'The problem, I think, will be to keep them from charging,' Afreyt told him. 'Or, at any rate, to get them to stop marching.'

'Oh, so it's that way,' he said, raising an eyebrow.

'Cousin Afreyt! Cousin Afreyt!' May and Gale were crying shrilly while they waved at her. But then the girls were pointing overhead and calling, 'Look! Look!' and next they were running downhill alongside the column, still waving and calling and pointing at the sky.

Afreyt and Skor looked up and saw, at least a hundred yards above them, the figures of a man and a small girl (Mara by her red cloak) stretched out flat on their faces and clinging to each other and to something invisible that was swiftly swooping toward Cold Harbor. They came around in a great curve, getting lower all the time, and headed straight for Skor and Afreyt. She saw it was Fafhrd and Mara, all right, and she realized that she and Cif must have looked just so when they were being rescued from Khahkht's blizzard by the invisible mountain princesses. She clutched Skor, saying rapidly and somewhat breathlessly, 'They're all right. They're hanging onto a fish-of-the-air, which is like a thick flying carpet that's alive, but invisible. It's guided by an invisible woman.'

'It would be,' he retorted obscurely. Then they were buffeted by a great gust of air as Fafhrd and Mara sped past close overhead and still flat out – both of them grinning excitedly, Afreyt was able to note as she cringed down, at least Fafhrd's lips were drawn back from his teeth. They came to rest midway between her and Groniger at the head of the column, which had slowed to gawk, about a foot above the heather, which was pressed down in a large oval patch, as if Fafhrd and Mara were lying prone on an invisible mattress wide and thick enough for a king's bed.

Then the air travelers had scrambled to their feet and jumped down after an unsteady step or two. Skor and Afreyt were closing in on them from one side and May and Gale from the other, while the Rimelanders stared openmouthed. Mara was shrieking to the other girls, 'I was abducted by a very nasty demon, but Fafhrd rescued me! He chopped off its hand!' And Fafhrd had thrown his arms around Afreyt (she realized she'd invited it) and he was saying, 'Afreyt, thank Kos you're here. What's that you've got around your neck?' Next without letting Afreyt go, to Skor, 'How are the men? What's your position?' All the while the staring Rimelanders marched on slowly and almost painfully, like sleepers peering at another wonder out of a nightmare which has entrapped them.

And then all others grew suddenly silent and Fafhrd's arms dropped away from Afreyt as a voice that she had last heard in a cave on Darkfire called out like an articulate silver trumpet, 'Farewell, girl. Farewell, barbarian. Next time, think of the courtesies due between orders and of your limitations. My debt's discharged, while yours has but begun.'

And with that a wind blew out from where Fafhrd and Mara had landed (from *under* the invisible mattress, one must think), bending the heather and blowing the girls' red coats out straight from them (Afreyt felt it and got a whiff of animal stench neither fish nor fowl nor four-legged) and then it was as if something large and living were taking off into the air and swiftly away, while a silvery laughter receded.

Fafhrd threw up his hand in farewell, then brought it down in a sweeping gesture that seemed to mean, 'Let's say goodbye to all that!' His expression, which had grown bleakly troubled during Hirriwi's speaking, became grimly determined as he saw the Rime column marching slowly into them. 'Master Groniger!' he said sharply. 'Captain Fafhrd?' that one replied thickly, as one half-rousing from a dream. 'Halt your men!' Fafhrd commanded, and then turned to Skor, who made report, telling his leader in somewhat more detail matter told earlier to Afreyt, while the column slowly ground to a halt, piling up around Groniger in a disorderly array.

Meanwhile Afreyt had knelt beside Mara, assured herself that the girl wasn't outwardly injured, and was listening bemused as Mara proudly but deprecatingly told the other girls about her abduction and rescue. 'He made a scarecrow out of my cloak and the skull of the last little girl he'd eaten alive, and he kept touching me, just like Odin does, but Fafhrd cut off his hand and Princess Hirriwi got my cloak back this morning. It was neat riding through the sky. I didn't get dizzy once.'

Gale said, 'Odin and I made up a marching song. It's about killing Mingols. Everyone's chanting it.' May said, 'I made nooses with flowers in them. They're a mark of honor from Odin. We're all wearing them. I made one for you and a big one for Fafhrd. Say, I've got to give Fafhrd his noose. It's time he was wearing it, with a big battle coming.'

Fafhrd listened patiently, for he'd wanted to know what that ugly thing around Afreyt's neck was. But when Mara had asked him to bend down his head, and he looked up spying the curtained litter, and recognized the uprooted gallows beyond it, he felt a shivery revulsion and said angrily, 'No, I won't wear it. I won't mount his eight-legged horse. Get those things off your necks, all of you!'

But then he saw the hurt, distrustful look in the girls' eyes as Mara protested, 'But it's to make you strong in battle. It's an honor from Odin.' And then the look of concern in Afreyt's eyes as she gestured toward the litter, its curtains fluttering in the wind (he sensed the grim holiness that seemed to emanate from it), and the look of expectation in the eyes of Groniger and the other Rimers, made him change his mind. He said, making his voice eager, 'I'll tell you what I'll do, I'll wear it around my wrist, to strengthen it,' and he thrust his left hand through the noose and after a moment May tightened it.

'My left arm,' he explained, lying somewhat, 'has always been markedly weaker than my right in battle. This noose will help strengthen it. I'll take yours too,' he said to Afreyt with a meaningful look.

She loosened it from around her neck with feelings of relief which partly changed to apprehension as she saw it tightened around Fafhrd's wrist beside the first noose.

'And yours, and yours, and yours,' he said to the three girls. 'That way I'll be wearing a noose for each of you. Come on, you wouldn't want my left arm weak in battle, would you?'

'There!' he said when it was done, gripping the five pendant cords in his left hand and whirling them. 'We'll whip the Mingols off Rime Isle, we will!'

The girls, who had seemed a little unhappy about losing their nooses, laughed delighted, and the Rimers raised an unexpected cheer.

Then they marched on, Skor scouting ahead after remembering to give Fafhrd back his sword, and Fafhrd trying to put some order into the Rimers and keep them quiet – although the wind helpfully blew the drum-noise of their chant from the beach. The girls and Afreyt dropped back with the litter, though not as far as Fafhrd wished. The company picked up a couple of Fafhrd's men, who reported the Mingols massing on the beach around their ships. And then they mounted a slight rise where the lines extended south from the fortress-hump of Cold Harbor, Fafhrd and his men holding back the now overeager Rimers. A mounting cry of woe came from the beach beyond and they all beheld a wonderfully satisfying sight: the three Sea Mingol galleys launching into the wind, forward oars out and working frantically while small figures gave a last heave to the sterns and scrambled aboard.

Then came an arresting cry from Cold Harbor and they began to see out in the watery west a host of sails coming up over the horizon: the Widder-Mingol fleet. And with the sight of it they became aware also of a faint distant rumbling, as of the hoofbeat of innumrable war-horses charging across the steppes. But the Rimelanders recognized it as the voice of Hellfire, threatening eruption where it smoked blackly to the north. While to the south churned high-domed clouds, betokening a change of wind and weather.

The Gray Mouser fully realized that he was in one of the tighest spots he'd ever been in during the course of a danger-dappled career – with this difference, that this time the spot was shared by three hundred friendly folk (even dear, thinking of Cif beside him), along with any number of enemies (the Sun-Sea-Mingol fleet, that was, in close pursuit). He'd raised *them* (the Mingols) with the greatest of ease and was now luring them so successfully to their destruction that *Flotsam* was last, not first, of the Rime Island fleet, which was spread out disorderly before him, *Sea Hawk* nearest, and within arrow range of the pursuing Mingols, who came in endless foaming shrieking whinnying numbers, their galleys sailing faster with the wind than he. Moments ago one of the horseships had driven herself under with excess of sail, and foundered, and not a sister ship had paused to give her aid. Dead ahead some four leagues distant was the Rimic coast with the two crags and inviting bay (and blackly smoking Darkfire beyond) that marked the position of the Great Maelstrom. North, the clouds churned, promising change of weather. The problem, as always, was how to get the Mingols into the Maelstrom, while avoiding it himself (and his friends with him), but he had never *appreciated* the problem quite so well as now. The hoped-for solution was that the whirlpool would turn on just *after* the Rimers and *Sea Hawk* and he had sailed across it, and so catch at least the van of the close-crowding Mingol fleet. And the way they were all bunched now, that required perfect, indeed God-like timing, but he'd worked his hardest at it and after all the gods were supposed to be on his side, weren't they? – at least two of them.

The horse-galleys of the Mingols were so close that Mikkidu and his thieves had their slings ready, loaded with leaden ball, though under orders not to cast unless the Mingols started arrow fire. Across the waves a stallion screamed from its cage.

Thought of the Maelstrom made the Mouser look in his pouch for the golden queller. He found it, all right, but somehow the charred stub of the Loki-torch had got wedged inside it. It was really no more than a black cinder. No wonder Rill had burned herself so badly, he thought, glancing at her bandaged hand – when Cif had stayed on deck, the harlots, and Mother Grum, had insisted on the same privilege and it seemed to cheer the men.

The Mouser started to unwedge the black god-brand, but then the odd thought occurred to him that Loki, being a god (and in some senses this cinder was Loki), deserved a golden house or carapace, so on a whim he wrapped the length of stout cord attached to it tightly round and round the weighty golden cube and knotted it, so that the two objects – queller and god-brand – were inextricably conjoined.

Cif nudged him. Her gold-flecked green eyes were dancing, as if to say, 'Isn't this exciting!'

He nodded a somewhat temperate agreement. Oh, it was exciting, all right, but it was also damnably uncertain – everything had to work out just so – why, he could still only guess at the directions god Loki had given them in the speech he had forgotten and none else had heard . . .

He looked around the deck, surveying faces. It was strange, but everyone's eyes seemed to flash with the same eager juvend excitement as was in Cif's . . . it was even in Gavs', Trenchi's, and Gib's (the Mingols) . . . even in Mother Grum's, bright as black beads . . .

In all eyes, that is, except the wrinkle-netted ones of old Ourph helping Gavs with the tiller. They seemed to express a sad and patient resignation, as though contemplating tranquilly from some distance a great and universal woe. On an impulse the Mouser took him from his task and drew him to the lee rail.

'Old man,' he said, 'you were at the council hall the night before last when I spoke to them all and they cheered me. I take it that, like the rest, you heard not one word of what I said, or at best only a few – the directives for Groniger's party and our sailing today?'

For the space of perhaps two breaths the old Mingol stared at him curiously, then he slowly shook his bald dome, saying, 'No, captain, I heard every last word you spoke (my eyes begin to fail me a little, but my ears not) and they greatly saddened me (your words) for they expressed the same philosopohy as seizes upon my steppe-folk at their climacterics (and often otherwhen), the malign philosophy that caused me to part company with them in early years and make my life among the heathen.'

'What do you mean?' the Mouser demanded. 'A favor – be brief as possible.'

'Why, you spoke – most winningly indeed (even I was tempted) – of the glories of death and of what a grand thing it was to go down joyfully to destruction carrying your enemies with you (and as many as possible of your friends also), how this was the law of life and its crowning beauty and grandeur, its supreme satisfaction. And as you told them all that they soon must die and how, they all cheered you as heartily as would have my own Mingols in their climacteric and with the selfsame gleam in their eyes. I well know that gleam. And, as I say, it greatly saddened me (to find you so fervent a death-lover) but since you are my captain, I accepted it.'

The Mouser turned his head and looked straight into the astonished eyes of Cif, who had followed close behind him and heard every word old Ourph had spoken, and looking into each other's eyes they saw the same identical understanding.

At that very instant the Mouser felt *Flotsam* beneath his feet slammed to a stop, spun sideways to her course, and sent off circling at prodigious speed just as had happened to *Sprite* day before yesterday, but with a greater force proportionate to her larger size. The heaven reeled, the sea went black. He and Cif were brought up against the taffrail along with a clutter of thieves, whores, witches (well, one witch), and Mingol sailors. He bid Cif cling to it for dearest life, then found his footing on the tilted deck, and raced past the rattling whipping mainsail (and past young Mikkidu embracing the mainmast with eyes tight shut in ultimate terror or perhaps in rapture) to where his own vision was unimpeded.

Flotsam, *Sea Hawk*, and the whole Rime fleet were circling at dizzying velocity more than halfway down the sides of a whirl-pool at least two leagues wide, whose wide-spinning upper reaches held what looked like the entire Mingol fleet, the galleys near the edge tiny as toys against the churning sky, while at the maelstrom's still-distant center the fanged rocks protruding through the white welter there were like a field of death.

Next below *Flotsam* in the vast wheel of doom spun Dwone's fishing smack, so close he could see faces. The Rimers clutching their weird weapons and each other looked monstrously happy, like drunken and lopsided giants bound for a ball. Of course, he told himself, these were the monsters whose quickening Loki had envisioned, these were the trolls or whatever. And that reminded him of what, by Ourph's irrefutable testimony, Loki intended for them all and peradventure for Fafhrd and Afreyt also, and all the universe of seas and stars.

He snatched the golden queller from his pouch and seeing the black cinder at its heart thought, 'Good! – rid of two evils at one stroke.' Aye, but he must pitch it to the whirlpool's midst, and how to get it there, so far away? There was some simple solution, he was sure, it was on the tip of his unseen thoughts, but there were really so many distractions at the moment . . .

Cif nudged him in the waist – one more distraction. As he might have expected, she had followed him close against his strictest bidding and now with a wicked grin was pointing at . . . of course, his sling!

He centered the precious missile in the strap and motioning Cif to the mast to give him room, tried out his footing on the tilted deck, taking short dancing steps, and measuring out distance, speed, windage, and various imponderables with eyes and brain. And as he did those things, whirling the queller-brand about his head, dancing out as it were the prelude to what must be his life's longest and supremest cast, there danced up from his mind's darkest deep words that must have been brewing there for days, words that matched Loki's final four evil couplets in every particular, even the rhymes (almost), but that totally reversed their meaning. And as the words came bobbing to the surface of his awareness he spoke them out, softly he thought, though in a very clear voice – until he saw that Cif was listening to him with unmistakable delight at each turn of phrase, and Mikkidu had his shut eyes open and was hearing, and the monstrous Rimers on Dwone's smack had all their sobering faces turned his way. He somehow had the conviction that in the midst of that monstrous tumult of the elements his words were nevertheless being heard to the whirlpool's league-distant rim – aye, and beyond that, he knew not how far. And this is what he spoke: 'Mingols to their deaths must go? Oh, not so, not so, not so! Mingols, draw an easy breath. Leave to wanton after death. Let there be an end to strife – even Mingols relish life. Mingol madness cease to burn. Gods to proper worlds return.'

And with that he spun dancingly across the deck, as though he were hurling the discus, the queller-brand at the end of his sling a gold-glinting circlet above his head, and loosed. The queller-brand sped up gleaming toward the whirlpool's midst until it was too small for sight.

And then . . . the vasty whirlpool was struck flat. Black water foamed white. Sea and sky churned as one. And through that hell of the winds' howling and the waves' crash there came a rumbling earth-shaking thunder and the red flash of huge distant flames as Darkfire erupted, compounding pandemonium, adding the strokes of earth and fire to those of water and air, completing the uproar and riot of the four elements. All ships were chips in chaos, glimpsed dimly if at all, to which men clung like ants. Squalls blew from every compass-point, it seemed, warring together. Foam covered decks, mounded to mast tops.

But before that had transpired quite in *Flotsam*'s case, the Mouser and some others too, gripping rail or mast, eyes stinging with salt sea, had seen, mounting for a few brief moments to the sky, from the whirlpool's very midst as it was smitten flat, what looked like the end of a black rainbow (or a skinny and curving black waterspout impossibly tall, some said afterwards) that left a hole behind it in the dark clouds, through which *something* maddening and powerful had vanished for ever from their minds, their beings, and from all Nehwon.

And then the Mouser and his crew and the women with them were all fighting to save themselves and *Flotsam* in the midst of an ocean that was all cross chop and in the teeth of a gale that had reversed direction completely and now blew from the west, carrying the thick black smoke from Darkfire out toward them. Around them other ships fought the same fight in a great roiling confusion covering several square leagues that gradually sorted itself out. The Rime fishing boats and smacks (somewhat larger) with their handier rigs (and *Flotsam* and *Sea Hawk* too) were able to tack southwest against the wind and set slow courses for Salthaven. The Mingol galleys with their square sails could only run before it (the heavy seas preventing the use of oars) away from the sobering chaos of the dreadful isle whose black smoke pursued them and their dreary drenched stallions. Some of the horse-ships may have sunk, for *Flotsam* fished two Mingols out of the waves, but these were unclear as to whether they had been swept overboard or their ships lost, and far too miserable to seem like foes. Ourph, smiling serenely, later brought them hot chowder, while the west wind cleared the sky. (Regarding the winds, at the moment of decision the west wind had spilled south, blowing out all along the east coast of Rime Isle, and the east wind had spilled north, driving away from the whole west coast of the island, while the belt of storm between had rotated clockwise somewhat, causing wild, veering whirlwinds in the Deathlands.)

At the same instant as the Mouser slung the queller-brand, Fafhrd was standing on the seaward turf-wall of Cold Harbor, confronting the Widder-Mingol fleet as it neared the beach and brandishing his sword. This was no mere barbarian gesture of defiance, but part of a carefully thought-out demonstration done in the hope of awing the Sea-Mingols, even though Fafhrd admitted (to himself only) that the hope was a forlorn one. Earlier, when the three Mingol advance-raiders had departed the beach, they had made no move to join with or await their fleet, although they surely must have sighted its sails, but had instead rowed steadily away south as long as eye followed. This had made Fafhrd wonder whether they had not taken some fright on the isle which they had not wanted to face again, even with the backing of their main force. In this connection he had particularly remembered the cries of woe and dread that had come from the Mingols as Groniger's Rime Islers had topped the rise and hove into their view. Afreyt had confided to him how during the long march overland those same countrymen of hers had come to seem monstrous to her and somehow bigger, and he had had to admit that they made the same strange impression on him. And if they seemed bigger (and monstrous) to him and her, how much bigger might they not appear to Mingols?

And so they had taken thought together, Fafhrd and Afreyt, and had made suggestions and given commands (supplemented by bullyings and blandishments as needed) and as a result Groniger's relief-force was posted at intervals of twenty paces in a long line that began far up on the glacier and continued along the ramparts of Cold Harbor and along the rise and stretched off for almost a league south of the settlement, each Isler brandishing his pike or other weapon. While betwixt and between them all along were stationed the defenders of Cold Harbor (their countrymen, though lacking their aura of monstrousness) and Fafhrd's berserks, to swell their sheer numbers and also to keep the Salthaven Islers at their posts, from which they still had a dreamy, automatonlike tendency to go marching off. Midmost on the broad ramparts of Cold Harbor, widely flanked by Groniger and another pike-waver, rested Odin's litter with the gallows propped over it as in the Deathlands, while around it were stationed Fafhrd, Afreyt, and the three girls, the last waving their red cloaks on long rakes like flags. (Anything for effect, Fafhrd had said, and the girls were eager to play their part in the demonstration.) Afreyt had a borrowed spear while Fafhrd alternately shook his sword and the cords of the five nooses drawn around his left hand – shook them at the massed Mingol ships nearing the harbor. Groniger and the other Islers were shouting Gale's (or Odin's) doom-chant: 'Doom! Kill the Mingols! Doom! Die the heroes.'

And then (just as, on the other side of Rime Isle, the Mouser hurled his queller-brand, as has been said) the whirlwinds betokening the reversal of gales moved across them northward, whipping the red flags, and the heavens were darkened and there came the thunder of Hellfire erupting in sympathy with Darkfire. The sea was troubled and soon pocked to the north by the ejecta of Hellglow, great rocks that fell into the waves like the shouted 'Doom! Doom!' of the chant in a great cannonading. And the Widder-Mingol fleet was retreating out to sea under the urging of the wind that now blew off the shore – away, away from that dreadful burning coast that appeared to be guarded by a wall of giants taller than trees and by all the powers of the four elements. And Hellfire's smoke stretched out above them like a pall.

But before that had all transpired (in fact, at the same instant as, a hundred leagues east, a black rainbow or waterspout shot up to the sky from the whirlpool's center) Odin's litter began to rock and toss on the ramparts, and the heavy gallows to twitch and strain upward like a straw or like a compass needle responding to an unknown upward magnetism. Afreyt screamed as she saw Fafhrd's left hand turn black before her eyes. And Fafhrd bellowed with sudden agony as he felt the nooses May had braided (and decorated with flowers) tighten restlessly about his wrist as so many steel wires, contracting deeper and deeper between arm bones and wrist bones, cutting skin and flesh, parting gristle and tendons and all tenderer stuff, while that hand was restlessly dragged upward. And then the curtains of the litter all shot up vertically and the gallows stood up on its beam end and vibrated. Suddenly something black and gleaming shot up to the sky, holing the clouds, and Fafhrd's black severed hand and all the nooses went with it.

Then the curtains fell back and the gallows crashed from the wall and Fafhrd stared stupidly at the blood pouring from the stump that ended his left arm. Mastering her horror, Afreyt clamped her fingers on the spouting arteries and bid May, who was nearest at hand, take knife and slash up the skirt of her white smock for bandages. The girl acted quickly, and with these folded in wads and also used as ties, Afreyt bound up Fafhrd's great wound in its own blood and staunched the flow of that while he watched blank-faced. When it was done, he muttered, ' "A head for a head and a hand for a hand," she said,' and Afreyt retorted sharply, 'Better a hand than a head – or five.'

In Its cramping sphere Khahkht of the Black Ice smote the sharply curving walls in Its fury and tried to scratch Rime Isle off the map. It ground together the pieces representing Fafhrd and the Mouser and the rest between Its opposed horny black palms and scrabbled frantically for the pieces standing for the two intrusive gods – but those two pieces were gone. While in far Stardock, maimed Prince Faroomfar slept more easily, knowing himself avenged.

A full two months after the events before-narrated, Afreyt had a modest fish-dinner in her low-eaved, violet-tinted house on the north edge of Salthaven, to which were invited Groniger, Skor, Pshawri, Rill, old Ourph, and of course Cif, the Gray Mouser, and Fafhrd – the largest number her table would accommodate without undue crowding. The occasion was the Mouser's sailing on the morrow in *Sea Hawk* with Skor, the Mingols, Mikkidu, and three others of his original crew on a trading venture to No-Ombrulsk with goods selected (purchased and otherwise accumulated) chiefly by Cif and himself. He and Fafhrd were sorely in need of money to pay for dockage on their vessels, crew-wages, and many another expenses, while the two ladies were no better off, owing yet-to-be-finally-determined sums to the council – of which, however, they were still members, as yet. Fafhrd had to travel no distance at all to get to the feast, for he was guesting with Afreyt while he convalesced from his maiming – just as the Mouser was staying at Cif's place on no particular excuse at all. There had been raised eyebrows at these arrangements from the rather straight-laced Islers, which the four principals had handled by firmly overlooking them.

During the course of the dinner, which consisted of oyster chowder, salmon baked with Island leeks and herbs, corn cakes made of costly Lankhmar grain, and light wine of Ilthmar, conversation had ranged around the recent volcanic eruptions and attendant and merely coincidental events, and their consequences, particularly the general shortage of money. Salthaven had suffered some damage from the earthquake and more from the resultant fire. The council hall had survived but the Salt Herring tavern had been burned to the ground with its Flame Den. ('Loki was a conspicuously destructive god,' the Mouser observed, 'especially where his métier, fire, was involved.' 'It was an unsavory haunt,' Groniger opined.) In Cold Harbor, three turf roofs had collapsed, unoccupied of course because everyone had been taking part in the defensive demonstration at the time. The Salthaven Islers had begun their homeward journey next day, the litter being used to carry

Fafhrd. 'So some mortal got some use of it besides the girls,' Afreyt remarked. 'It was a haunted-seeming conveyance,' Fafhrd allowed, 'but I was feverish.'

But it was the short store of cash, and the contrivances adopted to increase that, which they chiefly talked about. Skor had found work for himself and the other berserks for a while helping the Islers harvest drift-timber from the Beach of Bleached Bones, but there had not been the anticipated glut of Mingol wrecks. Fafhrd talked of manning *Flotsam* with some of his men and bringing back from Ool Plerns a cargo of natural wood. ('When you're entirely recovered, yes,' Afreyt said.) The Mouser's men had gone to work as fishermen bossed by Pshawri, and had been able to feed both crews and sometimes have a small surplus left to sell. Strangely, or perhaps not so, the monster catches made during the great run had all spoiled, despite their salting-down, and gone stinking bad, worse than dead jellyfish, and had had to be burned. (Cif said, 'I told you Khahkht magicked that run – and so they were phantom fish in some sense, tainted by his touch, no matter how solid-seeming.') She and Afreyt had sold *Sprite* to Rill and Hilsa for a tidy sum; the two professionals' adventure on *Flotsam*, amazingly, had given them a taste for the sea-life and they were now making a living as fisherwomen, though not above turning a trick at their old trade in off hours. Hilsa was out night-fishing this very evening with Mother Grum. Even the foe had fallen on hard times. Two of the three fore-raiding Sea-Mingol galleys that had rowed off south had put into Salthaven three weeks later in great distress, having been battered about by storms and then becalmed, after having fled off ill-provisioned. The crew of one had been reduced to eating their sacred bow-stallion, while that of the other had so far lost their fanatic pride along with their madness that they had sold theirs to 'Mayor' Bomar, who wanted to be the first Rime Isle man (or 'foreigner') to own a horse, but succeeded only in breaking his neck on his first attempt to ride it. (Pshawri commented, 'He was – *absit omen* – a somewhat overweening man. He tried to take away from me command of *Sea Hawk*.')

Groniger claimed that Rime Isle, meaning the council chiefly, was as badly off as anyone. The bluff harbor master, seemingly more hard-headed and skeptical than ever for his one experience of enchantment and the supernatural, made a point of taking a very hard line with Afreyt and Cif and a very dim view of the latter's irregular disbursements from the Rime treasury in the isle's defense. (Actually he was their best friend on the council, but he had his crustiness to maintain.) 'And then there's the Gold Cube of Square Dealing,' he reminded her accusingly, 'gone for ever!' She smiled. Afreyt served them hot gahveh, an innovation in Rimeland, for they'd decided to make an early evening of it what with tomorrow's sailing.

'I wouldn't be too sure of that,' Skor said. 'Working around the Beach of Bleached Bones you get the feeling that everything washes ashore there, eventually.'

'Or we could dive for it,' Pshawri proposed.

'What? – and get Loki-cinder back with it?' the Mouser asked, chuckling. He looked toward Groniger. 'Then you'd still be a cloudy-headed god's-man, you old atheist!'

'That's as may be,' the Isler retorted. 'Afreyt said I was a troll-giant for a space, too. But here I am.'

'I doubt you'd find it, dove you never so deep,' Fafhrd averred softly, his gaze on the leather stall covering his still bandaged stump. 'I think Loki-cinder vanished out of Nehwon-world entire, and many another curious thing with it – the queller (after it had done its work) that had become his home (Gods love gold) and Odin-ghost and some of his appurtenances.'

Rill, beside him, touched the stall with her burnt hand which had been almost as long as his stump in healing. It had created a certain sympathy between them.

'You'll wear a hook on it?' she asked.

He nodded. 'Or a socket for various tools, utensils, and instruments. There are possibilities.'

Old Ourph said, sipping his steaming gahveh, 'It was strange how closely the two gods were linked, so that when one departed, the other went.'

'When Cif and I first found them, we thought they were one,' Afreyt told him.

'We saved their lives,' Cif asserted. 'We were very good hosts, on the whole, to both of them.' She caught Rill's eye, who smiled.

'When you save a suicide, you take upon yourself responsibilities,' Afreyt said, her eyes drifting toward Fafhrd's stump. 'If on his next attempt, he takes others with him, it's your doing.'

'You're gloomy tonight, Lady Afreyt,' the Mouser suggested, 'and reason too curiously. When you set out in that mood there's no end to the places you can go, eh, Fafhrd? We set out to be captains, and seem in process of becoming merchants. What next? Bankers? – or pirates?'

'As much as you like of either,' Cif told him meaningly, 'as long as you remember the council holds Pshawri and your men here, hostage for you.'

'As mine will be for me, when I seek that timber,' Fafhrd said. 'The pines at Ool Plerns are very green and tall.'

THE KNIGHT AND
KNAVE OF SWORDS

ACKNOWLEDGEMENTS

To my friends who helped me editorially with this book, my thanks. They are James A. Minor, Miriam Rodstein, Anne Ross, Pamela Troy, David A. Wilson, and particularly Margo Skinner.

CONTENTS

I
SEA MAGIC

I

On the world of Nehwon and the land of Simorgya, six days fast
sailing south from Rime Isle, two handsome silvery personages
conversed intimately yet tensely in a dim and irregularly lit hall
of pillars open overhead to the darkness. Very strange was that
illumination – greenish and yellowish by turns, it seemed to
come chiefly from grotesquely shaped rugs patching the Stygian
floor and lapping the pillars' bases and also from slowly moving
globes and sinuosities that floated about at head height and
wove amongst the pillars, softly dimming and brightening like
lethargic and plague-stricken giant fireflies.

Mordroog said sharply, 'Caught you that thrill, sister? – faint
and far north away, yet unmistakably *ours*.'

Ississi replied eagerly, 'The same, brother, as we felt two days
agone – *our* mystic gold dipped deep in the sea for a space, then
out again.'

'The same indeed, sister, though this time with a certain
ambiguity as to the out – whether that or otherwise gone,'
Mordroog assented.

'Yet the now-confirmed clue is certain and bears only one
interpretation: our chiefest treasures, that were our most main
guards, raped away long ages agone – and now at long last we
know the culprits, those villainous pirates of Rime Isle!'
breathed Ississi.

'Long, long ages agone, before ever Simorgya sank (and the
fortunate island kingdom became the dark infernal realm) – and
their vanishment the hastener or very agent of that sinking. But
now we have the remedy – and who knows when our treasure's
back what long-sunken things may rise in spouting wrath to
consternate the world? Your attention, sister!' snapped Mordroog.

The abysmal scene darkened, then brightened as he dipped his hand into the pouch at his waist and brought it out again holding something big as a girl's fist. The floating globes and sinuosities moved inward inquisitively, jogging and jostling each other. Their flaring glows rebounded through the murk from a lacy yet massy small gold globe showing between his thin clawed silver fingers – its twelve thick edges like those of a hexahedron embedded in the surface of a sphere and curving conformably to that structure. He proffered it to her. The golden light gave the semblance of life to their hawklike features.

'Sister,' he breathed, 'it is now your task, and geas laid upon you, to proceed to Rime Isle and regain our treasure, taking vengeance or not as opportunity affords and prudence counsels – whilst I maintain here, unifying the forces and regathering the scattered allies against your return. You will need this last cryptic treasure for your protection and as a hound to scent out its brothers in the world above.'

Now for the first time Ississi seemed to hesitate and her eagerness to abate.

'The way is long, brother, and we are weak with waiting,' she protested, wailing. 'What was once a week's fast sailing will be for me three black moons of torturesome dark treading, press I on ever so hard. We have become the sea's slaves, brother, and carry always the sea's weight. And I have grown to abhor the daylight.'

'We have also the sea's strength,' he reminded her commandingly, 'and though we are weak as ghosts on land, preferring darkness and the deep, we also know the old ways of gaining power and facing even the sun. It is your task, sister. The geas is upon you. Salt is heavy but blood is sweet. Go, go, go!'

Wherewith she snatched the goldy ghost-globe from his grip, plunged it into her pouch, and turning with a sudden flirt made off, the living lamps scattering to make a dark northward route for her.

With the last 'Go,' a small bubble formed at the corner of Mordroog's thin, snarling, silvery lips, detached itself from them, and slowly grew in size as it mounted from these dark deeps up toward the water's distant surface.

2

Three months after the events aforenarrated, Fafhrd was at archery practice on the heath north of Salthaven City on Rime Isle's southeastern coast – one more self-imposed, self-devised, and self-taught lesson of many in learning the mechanics of life for one lacking a left hand, lost to Odin during the repulse of the Widder Sea-Mingols from the Isle's western shores. He had firmly affixed a tapering, thin, finger-long iron rod (much like a sword blade's tang) to the midst of his bow and wedged it into the corresponding deep hole in the wooden wrist heading the close-fitting leather stall, half the length of his forearm and dotted with holes for ventilation, that covered his newly-healed stump – with the result that his left arm terminated in a serviceably if somewhat unadjustably clutched bow.

Here near town the heath was grass mingled with ankle-high heather, here and there dotted with small clumps of gorse, in and out of which the occasional pair of plump lemmings played fearlessly, and man-high gray standing stones. These last had perhaps once been of religious significance to the now atheistical Rime Islers – who were atheists not in the sense that they did not believe in gods (that would have been very difficult for any dweller in the world of Nehwon) but that they did not socialize with any such gods or harken in any way to their commands, threats, and cajolings. They (the standing stones) stood about like so many mute gray grizzle bears.

Except for a few compact white clouds a-hang over the Isle, the late afternoon sky was clear, windless, and surprisingly balmy for this late in autumn, in fact on the very edge of winter and its icy, snow-laden winds.

The girl accompanied Fafhrd in his practicing. The silver-blonde thirteen-year-old now trudged about with him collecting arrows – half of them transfixing his target, which was a huge ball. To keep his bow out of the way Fafhrd carried it as if over his shoulder, maimed left arm closely bent upward.

'They ought to have an arrow that would shoot around corners,' Gale said apropos of hunting behind a standing stone.

'That way you'd get your enemy if he hid behind a house or a tree trunk.'

'It's an idea,' Fafhrd admitted.

'Maybe if the arrow had a little curve in it—' she speculated.

'No, then it would just tumble,' he told her. 'The virtue of an arrow lies in its perfect straightness, its—'

'You don't have to tell me that,' she interrupted impatiently. 'I keep hearing all about that, over and over, from Aunt Afreyt and Cousin Cif when they lecture me about the Golden Arrow of Truth and the Golden Circles of Unity and all those.' The girl was referring to the closely guarded gold ikons that had been from time immemorial the atheist-holy relics of the Rime Isle fisherfolk.

That made Fafhrd think of the Golden Cube of Square Dealing, forever lost when the Mouser had hurled it to quell the vast whirlpool which had vanquished the Mingol fleet and threatened to sink his own in the great sea battle. Did it lie now in mucky black sea bottom near the Beach of Bleached Bones or had it indeed vanished entire from Nehwon-world with the errant gods, Odin and Loki?

And that in turn made him wonder and worry a little about the Gray Mouser, who had sailed away a month ago in *Sea Hawk* on a trading expedition to No-Ombrulsk with half his thieves and *Flotsam*'s Mingol crew and Fafhrd's own chief lieutenant, Skor. The little man (Captain Mouser, now) had planned on getting back to Rime Isle before the winter blizzards.

Gale interrupted his musings. 'Did Aunt Afreyt tell you, Captain Fafhrd, about cousin Cif seeing a ghost or something last night in the council hall treasury, which only she has a key to?' The girl was holding up the big target bag clutched against her so that he could pull out the arrows and return them over shoulder to their quiver.

'I don't think so,' he temporized. Actually, he hadn't seen Afreyt today, or Cif either for that matter. For the past few nights he hadn't been sleeping at Afreyt's but with his men and the Mouser's at the dormitory they rented from Groniger, Salthaven's harbor master and chief councilman, the better to supervise the mischievous thieves in the Mouser's absence – or at least that was an explanation on which he and Afreyt could safely agree. 'What did the ghost look like?'

'It looked very mysterious,' Gale told him, her pale blue eyes widening above the bag which hid the lower part of her face. 'Sort of silvery and dark, and it vanished when Cif went closer. She called Groniger, who was around, but they couldn't find anything. She told Afreyt it looked like a princess-lady or a big thin fish.'

'How could something look like a woman and a fish?' Fafhrd asked with a short laugh, tugging out the last arrow.

'Well, there are mermaids, aren't there?' she retorted triumphantly, letting the bag fall.

'Yes,' Fafhrd admitted, 'though I don't expect Groniger would agree with us. Say,' he went on, his face losing for a bit its faintly drawn, worried look, 'put the target bag behind that rock. I've thought of a good way to shoot around corners.'

'Oh, good!' She rolled the target bag close against the back of one of the ursine, large gray stones and they walked off a couple of hundred yards. Fafhrd turned. The air was very still. A distant small cloud hid the low sun, though the sky was otherwise very blue and bright. He swiftly drew an arrow and laid it against the short wooden thumb he'd affixed to the bow near its centre just above its tang. He took a couple of shuffling steps while his frowning eyes measured the distance between him and the rock. Then he leaned suddenly back and discharged the arrow high into the air. It went up, up, then came swiftly down – close behind the rock, it looked.

'That's not around a corner,' Gale protested. 'Anybody can do that. I meant sideways.'

'You didn't say so,' he told her. 'Corners can be up or down or sideways right or left. What's the difference?'

'Up-corners you can drop things around.'

'Yes indeed you can!' he agreed and in a sudden frenzy of exercise that left him breathing hard sent the rest of the arrows winging successively after the first. All of them seemed to land close behind the standing stone – all except the last, which they heard clash faintly against rock – but when they'd walked up to where they could see, they found that all but the last arrow had missed. The feathered shafts stood upright, their points plunged into the soft earth, in an oddly regular little row that didn't quite reach the target-bag – all but the last, which had gone through an edge of the bag at an angle and hung there, tangled by its three goosefeather vanes.

'See, you missed,' Gale said, 'all but the one that glanced off the rock.'

'Yes. Well, that's enough shooting for me,' he decided, and while she pulled up the arrows and carefully teased loose the last, he loosened the bow's tang from its wood socket, using the back of his knife blade as a pry, then unstrung the bow and hung it across his back by its loose string around his chest, then fitted a wrought-iron hook into the wrist-socket, wedging it tight by driving the head of the hook against the stone. He winced as he did that last, for his stump was still tender and the dozen last shots he'd made had tried it.

3

As they walked toward the low, mostly red-roofed homes of Salthaven, the setting sun on their backs, Fafhrd studied the gray standing stones and asked Gale, 'What do you know about the old gods Rime Isle had? – before the Rime men got atheism.'

'They were a pretty wild, lawless lot, Aunt Afreyt says – sort of like Captain Mouser's men before they became soldiers, or your berserks before you tamed them down.' She went on with growing enthusiasm, 'They certainly didn't believe in any Golden Arrow of Truth, or Golden Ruler of Prudence, or Little Gold Cup of Measured Hospitality – mighty liars, whores, murderers, and pirates, I guess, all of them.'

Fafhrd nodded. 'Maybe Cif's ghost was one of them,' he said.

A tall, slender woman came toward them from a violet-toned house. When Afreyt neared them she called to Gale, 'So that's where you were. Your mother was wondering.' She looked at Fafhrd. 'How did the archery go?'

'Captain Fafhrd hit the target almost every time,' Gale announced for him. 'He even hit it shooting around corners! And I didn't help him a bit fitting his bow or anything.'

Afreyt nodded.

Fafhrd shrugged.

'I told Fafhrd about Cif's ghost,' Gale went on. 'He thought it might be one of the old Rime goddesses – Rin the Moon-runner, one of those. Or the witch queen Skeldir.'

Afreyt's narrow blonde eyebrows arched. 'You go along now, your mother wants you.'

'Can I keep the target for you?' the girl asked Fafhrd.

He nodded, lifted his left elbow, and the big ball dropped down. Gale rolled it off ahead of her. The target-bag was smoky red with dye from the snowberry root, and the last rays of the sun setting behind them gave it an angry glare. Afreyt and Fafhrd each had the thought that Gale was rolling away the sun.

When she was gone he turned to Afreyt, asking, 'What's this nonsense about Cif meeting a ghost?'

'You're getting skeptical as an Isler,' she told him unsmiling. 'Is something that robs a councilman of his wits and half his strength nonsense?'

'The ghost did that?' he asked as they began to walk slowly toward town.

She nodded. 'When Gwaan pushed into the dark treasury past Cif, he was clutched and struck senseless for an hour's space – and has since not left his bed.' Her long lips quirked. 'Or else he stumbled in the churning shadows and struck his head 'gainst the wall – there's that possibility too, since he has lost his memory for the event.'

'Tell me about it more circumstantially,' Fafhrd requested.

'The council session had lasted well after dark, for the waning gibbous moon had just risen,' she began. 'Cif and I being in attendance as treasurer and scribe. Zwaaken and Gwaan called on Cif for an inventory of the ikons of the virtues – ever since the loss of the Gold Cube of Square Dealing (though in a good cause) they've fretted about them. Cif accordingly unlocked the door to the treasury and then hesitated on the threshold. Moonlight striking in through the small barred window (she told me later) left most of the treasure chamber still in the dark, and there was something unfamiliar about the arrangement of the things she saw that sounded a warning to us. Also, there was a faint noxious marshy scent—'

'What does that window look on?' Fafhrd asked.

'The sea. Gwaan pushed past her impatiently (and *most* discourteously), and then she swears there was a faint blue smoke like muted lightning and in that trice she seemed to see a silent skinny figure of silver fog embrace Gwaan hungrily. She got the impression, she said, of a weak ghost seeking to draw strength from the living. Gwaan gave a choking cry and pitched to the floor. When torches were brought in (at Cif's behest) the chamber was otherwise empty, but the Gold Arrow of Truth had fallen from its shelf and lay beneath the window, the other ikons had been moved slightly from their places, as if they'd been feebly groped, while on the floor were narrow patches, like footprints, of stenchful black bottom muck.'

'And that was all?' Fafhrd asked as the pause lengthened. When she'd mentioned the thin silvery fog figure, he'd been reminded of someone or something he'd seen lately, but then in his mind a black curtain fell on that particular recollection-flash.

Afreyt nodded. 'All that matters, I guess. Gwaan came to after an hour, but remembered nothing, and they've put him to bed, where he stays. Cif and Groniger have set special watch on all the Rimic gold tonight.'

Suddenly Fafhrd felt bored with the whole business of Cif's ghost. His mind didn't want to move in that direction. 'Those councilmen of yours, all they ever worry about is gold – they're misers all!' he burst out at Afreyt.

'That's true enough,' she agreed with him – which annoyed Fafhrd for some reason. 'They still criticize Cif for giving the Cube to the Mouser along with the other moneys in her charge, and talk still of impeaching her and confiscating her farm – and maybe mine.'

'Ah, the ingrates! And Groniger's one of the worst – he's already dunning me for last week's rent on the men's dormitory, barely two days overdue.'

Afreyt nodded. 'He also complains your berserks caused a disturbance last week at the Sea Wrack tavern.'

'Oh he does, does he?' Fafhrd commented, quieting down.

'How are the Mouser's men behaving?' she asked.

'Pshawri keeps 'em in line well enough,' he told her. 'Not that they don't need my supervision while the Gray One's away.'

'*Sea Hawk* will have returned before the gales, I'm sure of that,' she said quietly.

'Yes,' Fafhrd said.

They had come opposite her house and now she went inside with a smiled farewell. She did not invite him to dinner, which was somehow annoying, although he would have refused; and although she had glanced once or twice toward his stump, she had not asked how it fared – which was tactful, but also somehow annoying.

Yet the irritation was momentary, for her mention of the Sea Wrack had started his mind off in a new direction which fully occupied it as he walked a little more rapidly. The past few days he had been feeling out of sorts with almost everyone around him, weary of his left-hand problems, and perversely lonely for Lankhmar with its wizards and criminous folks, its smokes (so different from this bracing northern sea air) and sleazy grandeurs. The night before last he'd wandered into the Sea Wrack, Salthaven's chief tavern since the Salt Herring had burned, and discovered a certain comfort in observing the passing scene there while sipping a pint or two of black ale.

Although called the Wrack and Ruin by its habitués (he'd learned as he was leaving), it had seemed a quiet and restful place. Certainly no disturbances, least of all by his berserks (that had been last week, he reminded himself – if it had really ever happened), and he had found pleasure in watching the slow-moving servers and listening to the yarning fishers and sailors, two low-voiced whores (a wonder in itself), and a sprinkling of eccentrics and puzzlers, such as a fat man sunk in mute misery, a skinny graybeard who peppered his ale, and a very slender silent woman in bone-gray touched with silver who sat alone at a back table and had the most tranquil (and not unhandsome) face imaginable. At first he'd thought her another whore, but no one had approached her table, none (save himself) had seemed to take any notice of her, and she hadn't even been drinking, so far as he could recall.

Last night he'd returned and found much the same crowd (and the same pleasant relief from his own boredom), and tonight he found himself looking forward to visiting the place again – after he'd been to the harbour and scanned south and east away for *Sea Hawk*.

4

At that moment Rill came around the next corner and hailed him cheerily, waving a hand that showed a red scar across the palm – memento of an injury that had created a bond between herself and Fafhrd. The dark-haired whore-turned-fisher-woman was neatly and soberly clad – a sign that she was not at the moment engaged in either of her trades.

They chatted together, at ease with each other. She told him about today's catch of cod and asked after the Mouser (when now expected) and his and Fafhrd's men and how Fafhrd's stump was holding up (she was the one person he could talk to about that) and about his general health and how he was sleeping.

'If badly,' she said, 'Mother Grum has useful herbs – or I might be of help.'

As she said that last, she chuckled, gave him an inquiring sidewise smile, and tugged his hook with her scarred forefinger, permanently crooked by the same deep burn that had left a red track across her palm. Fafhrd smiled back gratefully, shaking his head.

At that moment Pshawri came up with Skullick behind him to report on the day's work and other doings, and after a moment Rill went off. Some of Fafhrd's men had found employment on the new building going up where the Salt Herring had stood, a couple had worked on *Flotsam*, while the remainder had been cod-fishing with those men of the Mouser's who were not on *Sea Hawk*.

Pshawri made his report in a jaunty yet detailed and dutiful manner that reminded Fafhrd of the Mouser (he'd picked up some of his captain's mannerisms), which both irritated and amused Fafhrd. For that matter all the Mouser's thieves, being wiry and at least as short as he, reminded Fafhrd of his comrade. A pack of Mousers – ridiculous!

He stopped Pshawri's report with a 'Content you, you've

done well. You too, Skullick. But see that your mates stay out of the Wrack and Ruin. Here, take these.' He gave the young berserk his bow and quiver. 'No, I'll be supping out. Leave me, now.'

And so he continued on alone toward the Sea Wrack and the docks under the bright twilight, called here the violet hour. After a bit he realized with faint surprise and a shade of self-contempt why he was hurrying and why he had avoided Afreyt's bed and turned down Rill's comradely invitation – he was looking forward to another evening of watching and spinning dreams about the silent slender woman in bone-white and silver at the Wrack and Ruin, the woman with the so distant eyes and tranquil, not unhandsome face. Lord, what romantic fools men were, to overpass the known and good in order to strain and stretch after the mysterious merely unknown. Were dreams simply better than reality? Had fancy always more style? But even as he philosophized fleetingly of dreams, he was wending ever deeper into this violet-tinged one.

5

Familiar voices raised in vehemence pulled him partially out of it. Down the side lane he was crossing he saw Cif and Groniger talking excitedly together. He would have stolen onward unseen, returning entirely to his waking dream, but they spotted him.

'Captain Fafhrd, have you heard the ill news?' the grizzle-haired harbor master called as he approached with long strides. 'The treasury's been looted of its gold-things, and Zwaaken who was guarding them struck dead!'

The small russet-clad woman with golden glints in her dark brown hair who came hurrying along with him amplified, 'It happened no longer ago than sunset. We were close by in the council hall, ready to share the guard duty after dark (you've heard of last night's apparition?) when there came a cry from the vault and a blue flash from the cracks around the door. Zwaaken's face was frozen in a grimace and his clothes smoked . . . all the ikons were gone.'

It was strange, but Fafhrd barely took in what Cif was saying. Instead he was thinking of how even *she* was beginning to remind him of the Mouser and to behave like the Gray One. They said that people long in love began to resemble each other. Could that apply so soon?

'Yes, now it's not just the Gold Cube of Square Dealing we lack,' Groniger put in. 'All, all gone.'

His bringing in that roused Fafhrd again a little and nettled him. Altogether, in fact, he strangely found himself more irritated than interested or concerned by the news, though of course he would have liked to help Cif, who was the Mouser's darling.

'I've heard of your ghost,' he told her. 'All the rest is news. Is there any particular way in which I can help you now?'

They looked at him rather strangely. He realized his remark had been a somewhat cold one, so although he was most eager to get by himself again, he added, 'You can call on my men for help if you need it in your search for the thieves. They're at their dormitory.'

'On which you owe me rent,' Groniger put in automatically.

Fafhrd graciously ignored that. 'Well,' he said, 'I wish you good luck in your hunt. Gold is valuable stuff.' And with a little bow he turned and continued on his way. When he'd gone some distance he heard their voices again, but could no longer make out what they were saying – which meant their words happily weren't for him.

He reached the harbor while the violet light was still bright across the sky and realized with a throb of pleasure that that was one reason he had been in such a hurry and impatient of all else. The few folk about moved or stood quietly, unmindful of his coming. The air was still. He crossed to the dock's verge and scanned searchingly south and southeast to where violet sky met unruffled grey sea in a long horizon line, with never a cloud or smudge of haze between.

No sign of a sail or hint of a hull, not one. Mouser and *Sea Hawk* remained somewhere in the seaworld beyond.

But there was still time for sign or hint to appear before light failed. His dreamy gaze wandered to things closer. East rose the smooth salt cliffs, gray in the twilight. Between them and the low headland to the west, the harbor was empty. Off in that direction, to the right, *Flotsam* was moored close in, while to the left, nearer, was a light wooden pier that would be taken up when the winter gales arrived and to which a few ship's boats and other small harbour craft were moored. Among these was *Flotsam*'s small sailing dory, in which Fafhrd was in the habit of going out alone – more training in making do with a hook for a left hand – and also a narrow, mastless, shallow craft, little more than a shaped plank, that was new to him.

6

The violet light was draining away from the sky now and he once more scanned the southern and south eastern horizon and the long expanse of water between – a magical emptiness that drew him powerfully. Still no sign. He turned away regretfully and there, coming across the dock so as to arrive at its verge a score of feet from him, where the pier extended into the harbour, was his silent, tranquil-faced lady of the Sea Wrack. She might have been an apparition for all the notice the few dock-folk took of her; she almost brushed a sailor as she passed him by and he never moved. Behind her faint voices called to her from the town (what were they concerned about – a hunt for something? Fafhrd had forgotten) and the shadows came down from the north, driving out the last violet tones from the heavens. The silent woman had a pouch at her hip that clinked once faintly while her pale hands drew round her a silver-glinting bone-white robe that also shadowed her face. And then as she passed closest to him, she turned her head so that her black-edged green eyes looked straight into his, and she put her hand into her bosom and drew forth a short gold arrow which she showed him and then slipped into her pouch, which clinked again, and then she smiled at him for three heartbeats a smile that was at once familiar and strange, aloof and alluring, and then turned her head forward and went out onto the pier.

7

And Fafhrd followed her, not knowing behind his forehead, or really caring, whether her gaze or smile had cast an actual enchantment upon him, but only that this was the direction in which he wanted to go, away from the toils and puzzlements and responsibilities and boredoms of Salthaven and toward the vasty south and the Mouser and Lankhmar – *her* way and whatever mysteries she stood for. Another part of his mind, a part linked chiefly with his feet and hands (though one of them was only a hook), wanted also to follow her on account of the golden arrow, though he could no longer remember why that was important.

As he stepped down onto the wooden pier, she reached its end and stepped on to the narrow craft he'd noticed, and then without casting off or any other preparatory action, she lifted wide her arms as she faced the prow and the pale gray twilight, her back to him, so that her robe spread out to either side, and it bellied forward as if with an unseen wind, and she and her slight craft moved away toward the harbour mouth across the unruffled waters.

And then he felt on his right cheek a steady breeze blowing silently from the west, and he boarded the sailing dory and cast off and let down the centerboard and ran up the small sail and made it fast and then, taking its sheet in his right hand and controlling the tiller with his hook, sailed out noiselessly after her. He wondered a little (but not very much) why no one called after them or even appeared to watch them, their craft moving as if by magic and hers so strangely and with such a strange sail.

8

Exactly how long they glided on in this fashion he did not know or care, but the gray sky darkened to black night and stars came out around her hooded head, and the gibbous moon rose, dimming the stars a little, and was for a while before them and then behind (their craft must have turned in a very wide circle and headed north, it seemed), so that the moon's deathly white light no longer dazzled his eyes but was reflected softly from his dory's wind-rounded sail and made the Sea Wrack woman's bone-white silvery robes stand out ahead on her shining craft as they ever bellied forward to either side of her. Very steady was the silent wind that did that, and under its urging his craft gained upon hers so that at the last they almost seemed to touch. He wished that she would turn her head so that he could see more of her, yet at the same time he wanted them to go sailing on enchantedly for ever.

And then it seemed to him that the sea itself had tilted imperceptibly upward so that their noiselessly locked craft were mounting together toward the moon-dimmed stars. And at that point she turned around and moved slowly toward him and he likewise rose and moved effortlessly toward her, without any effect whatsoever on the dreamlike motion of their two craft as they mounted ever onward and upward. And she smiled the wondrous smile again at him and looked at him with love, and beyond her hooded head great weaving streamers of soft red and green and pale blue luminescence mounted toward the zenith (he knew them to be the northern lights) as though she stood at the altar of a great cathedral with all its stained-glass windows shedding a glory upon her. Glancing fleetingly to either side, he saw without great surprise or fear that their two craft were indeed mounting toward the stars on a great tongue of dark solid water that rose with precipice to either side, like a vast wall, from the moonlit sea far below. But all he had thought for was her proudly smiling face and daring, dancing gaze, enshrined by the aurora, that summed up for him all the allure of mystery and adventure.

She dipped then into the pouch at her waist and brought up the gold arrow and proffered it to him, holding it by either end in her dainty slim-fingered hands, and the moonlight showed him her small pearly teeth as she smiled.

Then he noted that his hook, which seemed to have a will of its own, had reached out and encircled the short shaft of the arrow between her hands and was tugging at it, while his right hand, which appeared to be operating with like independence of his bewitched mind, had shot forward, grasped the bulging pouch by its neck, and ripped it from her waist.

At that, her loving gaze grew fiercely desirous and her smile widened and grew wild and she tugged sharply back on the arrow so that it bent acutely at its midst, and the blue component of the aurora flaring behind her seemed to enter into her body and flash in her gaze and glow along her arms and hands, and the golden arrow glowed brighter still, a blue aura all around it, and Fafhrd's hook glowed equally, and there was a dazzling shower of blue sparks where hook and shaft met. Glad was Fafhrd then for the wooden wrist between his stump and his hook, for his every hair rose on end and he felt a prickling, tickling strangeness all over his skin.

But still his hook dragged blindly at the arrow, and now it came away with it, sharply bent but no longer blue-glowing. He snatched it off the hook with forefinger and thumb of his right hand, which still clutched the bag. And then as he backed away into his dory, he saw her loving countenance lengthening into a snout, her green eyes bulging and moving apart, swimming sidewise across her face, her pale skin turning to silvery scales, while her sweet mouth widened and gaped to show row upon row of razorlike triangular teeth.

She darted at him, he thrust out his left arm to fend her off, her jaws met with a great snap, while those dreadful teeth closed on his hook with a wrench and a clash.

9

And then all was tumult and swirling confusion, there was a clangour and a roaring in his ears, the solid water gave way and he and his craft plunged down, down, down, gut-wrenchingly, to the sea's surface and without check or hindrance as far again below it – until he and his dory were suddenly floating in a great tunnel of air floored, walled, and roofed by water, as far below the sea's surface as the water-wall had risen above it – and extending up to that surface just as the wall had stretched down to it. This incredible tunnel was lit silver by the misshapen moon glaring down it and greenish-yellow by a general phosphorescence in its taut, watery walls, from within which monstrous fish-faces moped and mowed at him and nuzzled the dory's hull. The other craft and the metamorphosing woman were gone.

The weirdness of the scene (together with the horrid transformation of the Sea Wrack woman) had banished his bewitchment and brought all his mind alive. He knelt in the dory's midst, peering about. And now the roaring in his ears increased and a great wind began to blow up the tunnel from the deeps, filling the dory's small sail and driving it along toward the mad moon. As this infernal gale swiftly grew to a hurricane, Fafhrd threw himself flat, anchoring himself by gripping the base of the dory's mast in the bend of his left elbow (for his hook was gone and his right hand had other employment). Silvery-green water flashed by, foam streamed back from the prow. And now a steady thunder began to resound from the deeps behind, adding itself to the tumultuous roaring, and it flashed through his frantic thoughts that such a sound might be caused by the tunnel closing up behind him, further increasing the might of the wind blowing him up this great silvery throat.

Space opened. The dory leaped like a flying fish, skiddingly struck roiled black water, righted itself, and floated flat – while from behind came a final thunderous crack.

It was as if the sea herself had spat them forth, then shut her lips.

10

In shorter space of time than he'd have thought possible without magic, before even his breathing had evened out, the sea calmed and the dory rode lonely and alone on its dark surface. South-ward the moon shone. Its rays gleamed on the fracture where his hook had been bitten off. He realized that his right hand still gripped the neck of the bag he'd grabbed from Cif's ghost (or the Sea Wrack woman, or whatever), while still clipped between his thumb and forefinger was a bent golden arrow.

Northward a ghostly aurora was glimmering, fading, dying. And in the same direction the lights of Salthaven gleamed, closer than he'd have guessed. He got out the single oar, set it across the stern, and began to scull homeward against the steady breeze, keeping wary watch on the silent black waters all around the dory.

II

Fafhrd was once more at archery practice on the heath of gray standing stones, companioned by Gale. But today a brisk north wind was singing in the heather and bending the gorse – forerunner more than likely of winter's first gale . . . and still no sign of *Sea Hawk* and the Mouser.

Fafhrd had slept late this morning and so had many another Rime Isler. It had been past midnight when he'd wearily sculled up to the docks, but the port had been awake with the theft of civic treasures and his own disappearance, and he'd been confronted at once by Cif, Groniger, and Afreyt – Rill too, and Mother Grum, and several others. It turned out that after Fafhrd's vanishment (none had noted his actual departure – an odd thing, that) a rumour had been bruited about (though hotly denied by the ladies) that *he* had made away with the gold ikons. Great was the rejoicing when he revealed that he had got them all safely back (save for the sharp bend in the Arrow of Truth) and an extra one besides – one which, as Fafhrd was quick to point out, might well be the lost Cube of Square Dealing, its edges systematically deformed to curves. Groniger was inclined to doubt this and much concerned about both deformations, but Fafhrd was philosophic.

He said, 'A crooked Arrow of Truth and a rounded-off Cube of Square Dealing strike me as about right for this world, more in line with accepted human practices.'

His account of his adventures on, above, and below the sea, and of the magic Cif's ghost had worked and her horrid last transformation, had produced reactions of wonder and amazement – and some thoughtful frowning. Afreyt had asked some difficult questions about his motives for following the Sea Wrack woman, while Rill had smiled knowingly.

As for the identity of Cif's ghost, only Mother Grum had

strong convictions. 'That'll be somewhat from sunken Simor-gya,' she'd said, 'come to repossess their pirated baubles.'

Groniger had disputed that last, claiming the ikons had always been Rime Isle's, and the old witch had shrugged.

Now Gale asked him as they collected arrows, 'And the fish-lady bit your hook off just like that?'

'Yes, indeed,' he assured her. 'I'm having Mannimark forge me a new one – of bronze. You know, that hook saved me twice – I'm getting to feel quite fond of it – once from the blue essence of lightning bolt coursing through the sea monster's extremities, and once from having another chunk of my left arm bitten off.'

Gale asked, 'What was it that made you suspicious of the fish-lady, so that you followed her?'

'Come on with those arrows, Gale,' he told her. 'I've thought of a new way to shoot around corners.'

This time he did it by aiming into the wind so that it carried his arrow in a sidewise curve behind the gray standing stone hiding the red bag. Gale said it was almost as much cheating as dropping an arrow in from above, but later they found he'd hit his target.

II
THE MER SHE

I

The ripening new-risen moon of the world of Nehwon shone yellowly down on the marching swells of the Outer Sea, flecking with gold their low lacy crests and softly gilding the taut triangular sail of the slim galley hurrying northwest. Ahead, the last sunset reds were fading while black night engulfed the craggy coast behind, shrouding its severe outlines.

At *Sea Hawk*'s stern, beside old Ourph, who had the tiller, stood the Gray Mouser with arms folded across his chest and a satisfied smile linking his cheeks, his short stalwart body swaying as the ship slowly rocked, moving from shallow trough to low crest and to trough again with the steady southwest wind on her loadside beam, her best point of sailing. Occasionally he stole a glance back at the fading lonely lights of No-Ombrulsk, but mainly he looked straight ahead where lay, five nights and days away, Rime Isle and sweet Cif, and poor one-hand Fafhrd and the most of their men and Fafhrd's Afreyt, whom the Mouser found rather austere.

Ah, by Mog and by Loki, he thought, what satisfaction equals that of captain who at last heads home with ship well ballasted with the get of monstrously clever trading? None! he'd warrant. Youth's erotic capturings and young manhood's slayings – yea, even the masterworks and life-scrolls of scholar and artist – were the merest baubles by compare, callow fevers all.

In his self-enthusiasm the Mouser couldn't resist going over in his mind each last item of merchant plunder – and also to assure himself that each was stowed to best advantage and stoutly secured, in case of storm or other ill-hap.

First, lashed to the sides, in captain's cabin beneath his feet, were the casks of wine, mostly fortified, and the small kegs of bitter brandy, Fafhrd's favourite tipple – those assuredly could not be stored elsewhere or entrusted to another's overwatching (except perhaps yellow old Ourph's here), he reminded himself as he lifted a small leather flask from his belt to his lips and took a measured sup of elixir of Ool Hruspan grape; he had strained his throat bellowing orders for *Sea Hawk*'s stowing and swift departure, and its raw membranes wanted healing before winter air came to try them further.

And amongst the wine in his cabin was also stored, in as many equally stout, tight barrels, their seams tarred, the wheaten flour – plebeian stuff to the thoughtless, but all-important for an isle that could grow no grain except a little summer barley.

Forward of captain's cabin – and now with his self-enthusiasm at glow point, the Mouser's mused listing-over turned to actual tour of inspection, he first speaking word to Ourph and then moving prow-wards catlike along the moonlit ship – forward of captain's cabin was chiefest prize, the planks and beams and mast-worthy rounds of seasoned timber such as Fafhrd had dreamed of getting at Ool Plerns, south where trees grew, when his stump was healed and could carry hook, such same timber won by cunningest bargaining maneuvers at No-Ombrulsk, where no more trees were than at Rime Isle (which got most of its gray wood from wrecks and nothing much bigger than bushes grew) and where they (the 'Brulskers) would sooner sell their wives than lumber! Yes, rounds and squares and planks of the precious stuff, all lashed down lengthwise to the rowers' benches from poop to forecastle beneath the boom of the great single sail, each layer lashed down separately and canvassed and tarred over against the salt spray and wet, with a precious long vellum-thin sheet of beaten copper between layers for further protection and firming, the layers going all the way from one side of *Sea Hawk* to the other, and all the way up, tied-down timber and thin copper alternating, until the topmost layer was a tightly lashed, canvassed deck, its seams tarred, level with the bulwarks – a miracle of stowage. (Of course, this would make rowing difficult if such became needful, but oars were rarely required on voyages such as the remainder of this one promised to be, and there were always some risks that had to be run by even the most prudent sea commander.)

Yes, it was a great timber-bounty that *Sea Hawk* was bearing to wood-starved Rime Isle, the Mouser congratulated himself as he moved slowly forward alongside the humming, moonlit sail, his softly shod feet avoiding the tarred seams of the taut canvas deck, while his nostrils twitched at an odd, faint, goaty-musky scent he caught, but it (the timber) never would have been won except for his knowledge of the great lust of Lord Logben of No-Ombrulsk for rare strange ivories to complete his White Throne. The 'Brulskers would sooner part with their girl-concubines than their timber, true enough, but the lust of Lord Logben for strange ivories was a greater desire than either of those, so that when with low drummings the Kleshite trading scow had put into 'Brulsk's black harbour and the Mouser had been among the first to board her and had spotted the behemoth tusk amongst the Kleshite trading treasures, he had bought it at once in exchange for a double-fist lump of muskodorous ambergris, common stuff in Rime Isle but more precious than rubies in Klesh, so that they were unable to resist it.

Thereafter the Kleshites had proffered their lesser ivories in vain to Lord Logben's major-domo, wailing for the mast-long giant snow serpent's white furred skin, that was *their* dearest desire, procured by Lord Logben's hunters in the frigid mountains known as the Bones of the Old Ones, and in vain had Lord Logben offered the Mouser its weight in electrum for the tusk. Only when the Kleshites had added their pleas to the Mouser's demands that the 'Brulskers sell him timber, offering for the unique snow serpent skin not only their lesser ivories but half their spices, and the Mouser had threatened to sink the tusk in the bottomless bay rather than sell it for less than wood, had the 'Brulskers been forced by their Lord to yield up a quarter shipload of seasoned straight timber, as grudgingly as the Mouser had seemed to part with the tusk – whereafter all the trading (even in timber) had gone more easily.

Ah, that had been most cunningly done, a masterstroke! the Mouser assured himself soberly.

As these most pleasant recollections were sorting themselves to best advantage within the Mouser's wide, many-shelved skull, his noiseless feet had carried him to the thick foot of the mast, where the false deck made by the timber cargo ended. Three yards farther on began the decking of the forecastle, beneath

438

which the rest of the cargo was stowed and secured: ingots of bronze and little chests of dyes and spices and a larger chest of silken fabrics and linens for Cif and Afreyt – that was to show his crew he trusted them with all things except mind-fuddling, duty-betraying wine – but mostly the forward cargo was tawny grain and white and purple beans and sun-dried fruit, all bagged in wool against the sea-damp: food for the hungry Isle. There was your real thinking man's treasure, he told himself, beside which gold and twinkling jewels were merest trinkets, or the pointy breasts of young love or words of poets or the pointed stars themselves that astrologers cherished and that made men drunk with distance and expanse.

In the three yards between false deck and true, their upper bodies in the shadow of the latter and their feet in a great patch of moonlight, on which his own body cast its supervisory shadow, his crew slept soundly while the sea cradle-rocked 'em: four wiry Mingols, three of his short, nimble sailor-thieves with their lieutenant, Mikkidu, and Fafhrd's tall lieutenant, Skor, borrowed for this voyage. Aye, they slept soundly enough! he told himself with relish (he could clearly distinguish the bird-twittering snores of ever-apprehensive Mikkidu and the lion-growling ones of Skor), for he had kept tight rein on them all the time in No-Ombrulsk and then deliberately worked them mercilessly loading and lashing the timber at the end, so that they'd fallen asleep in their tracks after the ship had sailed and they had supped (just as he'd cruelly disciplined himself and permitted himself no freedom time in port, no slightest recreation, even such as was desirable for hygienic reasons), for he knew well the appetites of sailors and the dubious, debilitating attractions of 'Brulsk's dark alleys – why, the whores had paraded daily before *Sea Hawk* to distract his crew. He remembered in particular one hardly-more-than-child among them, an insolent skinny girl in tattered tunic faded silver-gray, same shade as her precociously silver hair, who had moved a little apart from the other whores and had seemed to be forever flaunting herself and peering up at *Sea Hawk* wistfully yet somehow tauntingly, with great dark waifish eyes of deepest green.

Yes, by fiery Loki and by eight-limbed Mog, he told himself, in the discharge of his captain's duties he'd disciplined himself most rigorously of all, expending every last ounce of strength, wisdom, cunning (and voice!) and asking no reward at all except for the knowledge of responsibilities manfully shouldered – that, and gifts for his friends. Suddenly the Mouser felt nigh to bursting with his virtues and somehow a shade sorry about it, especially the 'no reward at all' bit, which now seemed manifestly unfair.

Keeping careful watch upon his wearied-out men, and with his ears attuned to catch any cessation of, or the slightest variation in their snorings, he lifted his leathern pottle to his lips and let a generous, slow, healthful swallow soothe his raw throat.

As he thrust the lightened pottle back into his belt, securely hooking it there, his gaze fastened on one item of cargo stored forward that seemed to have strayed from its appointed place – either his concentrated watching or else some faint unidentified sound had called it to his attention. (At the same instant he got another whiff of the musky, goaty, strangely attractive sea odour. Ambergris?) It was the chest of silks and thick ribbons and linens and other costly fabrics intended chiefly for his gift to Cif. It was standing out a little way from the ship's side, almost entirely in the moonlight, as if its lashings had loosened, and now as he studied it more closely he saw that it wasn't lashed at all and that its top was wedged open a finger's breadth by a twist of pale orange fabric protruding near a hinge.

What monstrous indiscipline did this signify?

He dropped noiselessly down and approached the chest, his nostrils wrinkling. Was unsold ambergris cached inside it? Then, carefully keeping his shadow off it, he gripped the top and silently threw it wide open on its hinges.

The topmost silk was a thick lustrous copper-coloured one chosen to match the glints in Cif's dark hair.

Upon this rich bedding, like a kitten stolen in to nap on fresh-laundered linens, reposed, with arms and legs somewhat drawn in but mostly on her back, and with one long-fingered hand twisting down through her tousled silvery hair so as to shadow further her lidded eyes – reposed that self-same wharf-waif he'd but now been recalling. The picture of innocence, but the odour (he knew it now) all sex. Her slender chest rose and fell gently and slowly with her sleeping inhalations, her small breasts and rather larger nipples outdenting the flimsy fabric of her ragged tunic, while her narrow lips smiled faintly. Her hair was somewhat the same shade as that of silver-blonde, thirteen-year-old Gale back on Rime Isle, who'd been one of Odin's maidens. And she was, apparently, not a great deal older.

Why, this was worse than monstrous, the Mouser told himself as he wordlessly stared. That one or two or more of all of his crew should conspire to smuggle this girl aboard for his or their hot pleasure, tempting her with silver or feeing her pimp or owner (or else kidnapping her, though that was most unlikely in view of her unbound state) was bad enough, but that they should presume to do this not only without their captain's knowledge but also in complete disregard of the fact that *he* enjoyed no such erotic solacing, but rather worked himself to the bone on their behalf and *Sea Hawk*'s, solicitous only of their health and welfare and the success of the voyage – why, this was not only wantonest indiscipline but also rankest ingratitude!

At this dark point of disillusionment with his fellow man, the Mouser's one satisfaction was his knowledge that his crew slept deeply from exhaustion he'd inflicted on them. The chorus of their unaltering snores was music to his ears, for it told him that although they'd managed to smuggle the girl aboard successfully, not one of them had yet enjoyed her (at least since the loading and business of getting under way was done). No, they'd been smote senseless by fatigue, and would not now wake for a hurricane. And that thought in turn pointed out to him the way to their most appropriate and condign punishment.

Smiling widely, he reached his left hand toward the sleeping girl, and, where it made a small peak in her worn silver-faded tunic, delicately yet somewhat sharply tweaked her right nipple. As she came shuddering awake with a suck of indrawn breath, her eyes opening and her parted lips forming an exclamation, he swooped his face toward hers, frowning most sternly and laying his finger across his now disapprovingly set lips, enjoining silence.

She shrank away, staring at him in wonder and dread and keeping obediently still. He drew back a little in turn, noting the twin reflections of the misshapen moon in her wide dark eyes and how strangely the lustrous coppery silk on which she cowered contrasted with her hair tangled upon it, fine and silver pale as a ghost's.

From around them the chorus of snores continued unchanged as the crew slept on.

From beside her slender naked feet the Mouser plucked up a black roll of thick silken ribbon, and unsheathing his dirk, Cat's Claw, proceeded to cut three hanks from it, staring broodingly at the shrinking girl all the while. Then he motioned to her and crossed his wrists to indicate what was wanted of her.

Her chest lifting in a silent sigh, and shrugging her shoulders a little, she crossed her slender wrists in front of her. He shook his head and pointed behind her.

Again divining his command, she crossed them there, turning upon her side a little to do so.

He bound her wrists together crosswise and tightly, then bound her elbows together also, noting that they met without undue strain upon her slender shoulders. He used the third hank to tie her legs together firmly just above the knees. Ah, discipline! he thought – good for one and all, but in particular the young!

In the end she lay supine upon her bound arms, gazing up at him. He noted that there seemed to be more curiosity and speculation in that gaze than dread and that the twin reflections of the gibbous moon did not waver with any eye-blinking or -watering.

How very pleasant this all was, he mused: his crew asleep, his ship driving home full-laden, the slim girl docile to his binding of her, he meting out justice as silently and secretly as does a god. The taste of undiluted power was so satisfying to him that it did not trouble him that the girl's silken-smooth flesh glowed a little more silvery pale than even moonlight would easily account for.

Without any warning or change in his own brooding expression, he flicked inside the protruding twist of fabric and closed the lid of the chest upon her.

Let the confident minx worry a bit, he thought, as to whether I intend to suffocate her or perchance cast the chest overboard, she being in it. Such incidents were common enough, he told himself, at least in myth and story.

Tiny wavelets gently slapped *Sea Hawk*'s side, the moonlit sail hummed as softly, and the crew snored on.

The Mouser wakened the two brawniest Mingols by twisting a big toe of each and silently indicated that they should take up the chest without disturbing their comrades and bear it back to his cabin. He did not want to risk waking the crew with sound of words. Also, using gestures spared his strained throat.

If the Mingols were privy to the secret of the girl, their blank expressions did not show it, although he watched them narrowly. Nor did old Ourph betray any surprise. As they came nigh him, the ancient Mingol's gaze slipped over them and roved serenely ahead and his gnarled hands rested lightly on the tiller, as though the shifting about of the chest were a matter of no consequence whatever.

The Mouser directed the younger Mingols in their setting of the chest between the lashed cases that narrowed the cabin and beneath the brass lamp that swung on a short chain from the low ceiling. Laying finger to compressed lips, he signed them to keep strict silence about the chest's midnight remove. Then he dismissed them with a curt wave. He rummaged about, found a small brass cup, filled it from a tiny keg of Fafhrd's bitter brandy, drank off half, and opened the chest.

The smuggled girl gazed up at him with a composure he told himself was creditable. She had courage, yes. He noted that she took three deep breaths, though, as if the chest had indeed been a bit stuffy. The silver glow of her pale skin and hair pleased him. He motioned her to sit up, and when she did so, set the cup against her lips, tilting it as she drank the other half. He unsheathed his dirk, inserted it carefully between her knees, and drawing it upward, cut the ribbon confining them. He turned, moved away aft, and settled himself on a low stool that stood before Fafhrd's wide bunk. Then with crooked forefinger he summoned her to him.

When she stood close before him, chin high, slender shoulders thrown back by virtue of the ribbons binding her arms, he eyed her significantly and formed the words, 'What is your name?'

'Ississi,' she responded in a lisping whisper that was like the ghosts of wavelets kissing the hull. She smiled.

2

On deck, Ourph had directed one of the younger Mingols to take the tiller, the other to heat him gahveh. He sheltered from the wind behind the false deck of the timber cargo, looking toward the cabin and shaking his head wonderingly. The rest of the crew snored in the forecastle's shadow. While on Rime Isle in her low-ceilinged yellow bedroom Cif woke with the thought that the Gray Mouser was in peril. As she tried to recollect her nightmare, moonlight creeping along the wall reminded her of the mer-ghost which had murdered Zwaaken and lured off Fafhrd from sister Afreyt for a space, and she wondered how Mouser would react to such a dangerous challenge.

3

Bright and early the next morning the Mouser threw on a short gray robe, belted it, and rapped sharply on the cabin's ceiling. Speaking in a somewhat hoarse whisper, he told the impassive Mingol thus summoned that he desired the instant presence of Master Mikkidu. He had cast a disguising drape across the transported chest that stood between the crowding casks that narrowed farther the none-too-wide cabin, and now sat behind it on the stool, as though it were a captain's flat desk. Behind him on the crosswise bunk that occupied the cabin's end Ississi reposed and either slept or shut-eyed waked, he knew not which, blanket-covered except for her streaming silver hair and un-confined save for the thick black ribbon trying one ankle securely to the bunk's foot beneath the blanket.

(*I'm no egregious fool*, he told himself, to *think that one night's love brings loyalty*.)

He nursed his throat with a cuplet of bitter brandy, gargled and slowly swallowed.

(*And yet she'd make a good maid for Cif, I do believe, when I have*

444

done with disciplining her. Or perchance I'll pass her on to poor maimed and isle-locked Fafhrd.)

He impatiently finger-drummed the shrouded chest, wondering what could be keeping Mikkidu. A guilty conscience? Very likely!

Save for a glimmer of pale dawn filtering through the curtained hatchway and the two narrow side ports glazed with mica, which the lashed casks further obscured, the oil-replenished swaying lamp still provided the only light.

4

There was a flurry of running footsteps coming closer, and then Mikkidu simultaneously rapped at the hatchway and thrust tousle-pated head and distracted eyes between the curtains. The Mouser beckoned him in, saying in a soft, brandy-smoothed voice, 'Ah, Master Mikkidu, I'm glad your duties, which no doubt must be pressing, at last permit you to visit me, because I do believe I ordered that you come at once.'

'Oh, Captain, sir,' the latter replied rapidly, 'there's a chest missing from the stowage forward. I saw that it was gone as soon as Trenchi wakened me and gave me your command. I only paused to rouse my mates and question them before I hurried here.'

(*Ah-ha*, the Mouser thought, *he knows about Ississi, I'm sure of it, he's much too agitated, he had a hand in smuggling her aboard. But he doesn't know what's happened to her now – suspects everything and everyone, no doubt – and seeks to clear himself with me of all suspicion by reporting to me the missing chest, the wretch!*)

'A chest? Which chest?' the Mouser meanwhile asked blandly. 'What did it contain? Spices? Spicy things?'

'Fabrics for Lady Cif, I do believe,' Mikkidu answered.

'Just fabrics for the Lady Cif and nothing else?' the Mouser inquired, eyeing him keenly. 'Weren't there some other things? Something of *yours*, perhaps?'

'No, sir, nothing of mine,' Mikkidu denied quickly.

'Are you sure of that?' the Mouser pressed. 'Sometimes one will tuck something of one's own inside another's chest – for safekeeping, as it were, or perchance to smuggle it across a border.'

'Nothing of mine at all,' Mikkidu maintained. 'Perhaps there were some fabrics also for the other lady . . . and, well, just fabrics, sir and – oh, yes – some rolls of ribbon.'

'Nothing but fabrics and ribbon?' the Mouser went on, prodding him. 'No fabrics made into garments, eh? – such as a short silvery tunic of some lacy stuff, for instance?'

Mikkidu shook his head, his eyebrows rising.

'Well, well,' the Mouser said smoothly, 'what's happened to this chest, do you suppose? It must be still on the ship – unless someone has dropped it overboard. Or was it perhaps stolen back in 'Brulsk?'

'I'm sure it was safe aboard when we sailed,' Mikkidu asserted. Then he frowned. 'I *think* it was, that is.' His brow cleared. 'Its lashings lay beside it, loose on the deck!'

'Well, I'm glad you found something of it,' the Mouser said. 'Where on the ship do you suppose it can be? Think, man, where can it be?' For emphasis, he pounded the muffled chest he sat at.

Mikkidu shook his head helplessly. His gaze wandered about, past the Mouser.

(*Oh-ho*, the latter thought, *does he begin to get a glimmering at last of what has happened to his smuggled girl? Whose plaything she is now? This might become rather amusing.*)

He recalled his lieutenant's attention by asking, 'What were your men able to tell you about the runaway chest?'

'Nothing, sir. They were as puzzled as I am. I'm sure they know nothing. I *think*.'

'Hmn. What did the Mingols have to say about it?'

'They're on watch, sir. Besides, they answer only to Ourph – or yourself, of course, sir.'

(*You can trust a Mingol*, the Mouser thought, *at least where it's a matter of keeping silent.*)

'What about Skor, then?' he asked. 'Did Captain Fafhrd's man know anything about the chest's vanishment?'

Mikkidu's expression became a shade sulky. 'Lieutenant Skor is not under my command,' he said. 'Besides that, he sleeps very soundly.'

There was a thuddingly loud double knock at the hatchway.

'Come in,' the Mouser called testily, 'and next time don't try to pound the ship to pieces.'

Fafhrd's chief lieutenant thrust bent head with receding reddish hair through the curtains and followed after. He had to bend both back and knees to keep from bumping his naked pate on the beams. (*So Fafhrd too would have had to go about stooping when occupying his own cabin*, the Mouser thought. *Ah, the discomforts of size.*)

Skor eyed the Mouser coolly and took note of Mikkidu's presence. He had trimmed his russet beard, which gave it a patchy appearance. Save for his broken nose, he rather resembled a Fafhrd five years younger.

'Well?' the Mouser said peremptorily.

'Your pardon, Captain Mouser,' the other replied, 'but you asked me to keep particular watch on the stowage of cargo, since I was the only one who had done any long voyaging on *Sea Hawk* before this faring, and knew her behaviour in different weathers. So I believe that I should report to you that there is a chest of fabrics – you know the one, I think – missing from the fore steerside storage. Its lashings lie all about, both those which roped it shut and those which tied it securely in place.'

(*Ah-ha*, the Mouser thought, *he's guilty too and seeks to cover it by making swift report, however late. Never trust a bland expression. The lascivious villain!*)

With his lips he said, 'Ah yes, the missing chest – we were just speaking of it. When do you suppose it became so? – I mean missing. In 'Brulsk?'

Skor shook his head. 'I saw to its lashing myself – and noted it still tied fast to the side as my eyes closed in sleep a league outside that port. I'm sure it's still on *Sea Hawk*.'

(*He admits it, the effrontrous rogue!* the Mouser thought. *I wonder he doesn't accuse Mikkidu of stealing it. Perhaps there's a little honour left 'mongst thieves and berserks.*)

Meanwhile the Mouser said, 'Unless it has been dropped overboard – that is a distinct possibility, do you not think? Or mayhap we were boarded last night by soundless and invisible pirates while you both snored, who raped the chest away and nothing else. Or perchance a crafty and shipwise octopus,

447

desirous of going richly clad and with arms skilful at tying and untying knots—'

He broke off when he noted that both tall Skor and short Mikkidu were peering wide-eyed beyond him. He turned on his stool. A little more of Ississi showed above the blanket – to wit, a small patch of pale forehead and one large green silver-lashed eye peering unwinking through her long silvery hair.

He turned back very deliberately and, after a sharp 'Well?' to get their attention, asked in his blandest voice, 'Whatever are you looking at so engrossedly?'

'Uh – nothing at all,' Mikkidu stammered, while Skor only shifted gaze to look at the Mouser steadily.

'Nothing at all?' the Mouser questioned. 'You don't perhaps see the chest somewhere in this cabin? Or perceive some clue to its present disposition?'

Mikkidu shook his head, while after a moment Skor shrugged, eyeing the Mouser strangely.

'Well, gentlemen,' the Mouser said cheerily, 'that sums it up. The chest must be aboard this ship, as you both say. So hunt for it! Scour *Sea Hawk* high and low – a chest that large can't be hid in a seaman's bag. And use your eyes, both of you!' He thumped the shrouded box once more for good measure. 'And now – dismiss!'

(*They both know all about it, I'll be bound. The deceiving dogs!* the Mouser thought. *And yet . . . I am not altogether satisfied of that.*)

5

When they were gone (after several hesitant, uncertain backward glances), the Mouser stepped back to the bunk and, planting his hands to either side of the girl, stared down at her green eye, supporting himself on stiff arms. She rocked her head up and down a little and to either side, and so worked her entire face free of the blanket and her eyes of the silken hair veiling them and stared up at him expectantly.

He put on an enquiring look and flirted his head toward the hatchway through which the men had departed, then directed the same look more particularly at her. It was strange, he mused, how he avoided speaking to her whenever he could except with pointings and gestured commands. Perhaps it was that the essence of power lay in getting your wishes gratified without ever having to speak them out, to put another through all his paces in utter silence, so that no god might overhear and know. Yes, that was part of it at least.

He formed with his lips and barely breathed the question, 'How did you *really* come aboard *Sea Hawk?*'

Her eyes widened and after a while her peachdown lips began to move, but he had to turn his head and lower it until they moistly and silkily brushed his best ear as they enunciated, before he could clearly hear what she was saying – in the same Low Lankhmarese as he and Mikkidu and Skor had spoken, but with a delicious lisping accent that was all little hisses and gasps and warblings. He recalled how her scent had seemed all sex in the chest, but now infinitely flowery, dainty, and innocent.

'I was a princess and lived with the prince Mordroog, my brother, in a far country where it was always spring,' she began. 'There a watery influence filtered all harshness from the sun's beams, so that he shone no more bright than the silvery moon, and winter's rages and summer's droughts were tamed, and the roaring winds moderated to eternal balmy breezes, and even fire was cool – in that far country.'

Every whore tells the same tale, the Mouser thought. *They were all princesses before they took to the trade*. Yet he listened on.

'We had golden treasure beyond all dreaming,' she continued, 'unicorns that flew and kittens that flowed were my pets, and we were served by nimble companies of silent servitors and guarded by soft-voiced monsters – great Slasher and vasty All-Gripper, and Deep Rusher, who was greatest of all.

'But then came ill times. One night while our guardians slept, our treasure was stolen away and our realm became lonely, farther off and more secret still. My brother and I went searching for our treasure and for allies, and in that search I was raped away by bold scoundrels and taken to vile, vile 'Brulsk, where I came to know all the evil there is under the hateful sun.'

This too is a familiar part of each harlot's story, the Mouser told

449

himself, *the raping away, the loss of innocence, instruction in every vice*. Yet he went on listening to her ticklesome whispering.

'But I knew that one day *that one* would come who would be king over me and carry me back to my realm and dwell with me in power and silvery glory, our treasures being restored. And then you came.'

Ah, now the personal appeal, the Mouser thought. *Very familiar indeed. Still, let's hear her out. I like her tongue in my ear. It's like being a flower and having a bee suck your nectar.*

'I went to your ship each day and stared at you. I could do naught else at all, however I tried. And you would never look at me for long, and yet I knew that our paths lay together. I knew you were a masterful man and that you'd visit upon me rigours and inflictions beside which those I'd suffered in dreadful 'Brulsk would be nothing, and yet I could not turn aside for an instant, or take my eyes away from you and your dark ship. And when it was clear you would not notice me, or act upon your true feelings, or any of your men provide a means for me to follow you, I stole aboard unseen while they were all stowing and lashing and you were commanding them.'

(*Lies, lies, all lies*, the Mouser thought – and continued to listen.)

'I managed to conceal myself by moving about amongst the cargo. But when at last you'd sailed from harbour and your men slept, I grew cold, the deck was hard, I suffered keenly. And yet I dared not seek your cabin yet, or otherwise disclose myself, for fear you would put back to 'Brulsk to put me off. So I gradually freed of its lashings a chest of fabrics I'd marked, working and working like a mouse or shrew – the knots were hard, but my fingers are clever and nimble, and strong whenever the need is – until I could creep inside and slumber warm and soft. And then you came for me, and here I am.'

The Mouser turned his head and looked down into her large green eyes, across which golden gleams moved rhythmically with the lamp's measured swinging. Then he briefly pressed a finger across her soft lips and drew down the blanket until her ribbon-fettered ankle was revealed and he admired her beautiful small body. It was well, he told himself, for a man to have always a beautiful young woman close by him – like a beautiful cat, yes, a young cat, independent but with kitten ways still. It was well when such a one talked, speaking lies much as any cat would *('Twas crystal clear she must have had help getting aboard – Skor and Mikkidu both, likely enough)*, but best not to talk to her too much, and wisest to keep her well bound. You could trust folk when they were secured – indeed, trussed! – and not otherwise, no, not at all. And that was the essence of power – binding all others, binding all else! Keeping his eyes hypnotically upon hers, he reached across her for the loose hanks of black ribbon. It would be well to fetter her three other limbs to foot and head of bunk, not tightly, yet not so loosely that she could reach either wrist with other hand or with her pearly teeth – so he could take a turn on deck, confident that she'd be here when he returned.

6

On Rime Isle Cif, strolling alone across the heath beyond Salthaven, plucked from the slender pouch at her girdle a small male figure of sewn cloth stuffed with lint. He was tall as her hand was long and his waist was constricted by a plain gold ring which would have fitted one of her fingers – and that was a measure of the figure's other dimensions. He was dressed in a gray tunic and gray, gray-hooded cloak. She regarded his featureless linen face and for a space she meditated the mystery of woven cloth – one set of threads or lines tying or at least restraining another such set, with a uniquely protective pervious surface the result. Then some odd hint of expression in the faintly brown, blank linen face suggested to her that the Gray Mouser might be in need of more golden protection than the ring afforded, and thrusting the doll feet-first back into her pouch, she strode back toward Salthaven, the council hall, and the recently ghost-raped treasury. The north wind coming unevenly rippled the heather.

7

His throat burning from the last swallow of bitter brandy he'd taken, the Mouser slipped through the hatchway curtains and stole silently on deck. His purpose was to check on his crew (surprise 'em if need be!) and see if they were all properly occupied with sailorly duties (tied to their tasks, as it were!), including the fool's search for the missing chest he'd sent them on in partial punishment for smuggling Ississi aboard. (She was secure below, the minx, he'd seen to that!)

The wind had freshened a little and *Sea Hawk* leaned to steerside a bit farther as she dashed ahead, lead-weighted keel balancing the straining sail. The Mingol steersman leaned on the tiller while his mate and old Ourph scanned with sailorly prudence the southwest for signs of approaching squalls. At this rate they might reach Rime Isle in three more days instead of four. The Mouser felt uneasy at that, rather than pleased. He looked over the steerside apprehensively, but the rushing white water was still safely below the oarholes, each of which had a belaying pin laid across it, around which the ropes lashing down the middle tier of the midship cargo had been passed. This reminder of the security of the ship unaccountably did not please him either.

Where was the rest of the crew? he asked himself. A-search forward below for the missing chest? Or otherwise busy? Or merely skulking? He'd see for himself! But as he strode forward across the taut canvas sheathing the timber treasure, the reason for his sudden depression struck him, and his steps slowed.

He did not like the thought of soon arrival or of the great gifts he was bringing (in fact, *Sea Hawk's* cargo had now become hateful to him) because all that represented ties binding him and his future to Cif and crippled Fafhrd and haughty Afreyt too and all his men and every last inhabitant of Rime Isle. Endless responsibility – that was what he was sailing back to. Responsibility as husband (or some equivalent) of Cif, old friend to Fafhrd (who was already tied to Afreyt, no longer comrade), captain (and guardian!) of his men, father to all. Provider and protector! – and first thing you knew they, or at least one of them, would be protecting *him*, confining and constraining him for his own good in tyranny of love or fellowship.

Oh, he'd be a hero for an hour or two, praised for his sumptuous get. But next day? Go out and do it again! Or (worse yet) stay at home and do it. And so on, *ad infinitum*. Such a future ill sorted with the sense of power he'd had since last night's sailing and which the girl-whore Ississi had strangely fed. Himself bound instead of binding others, and adventuring on to bind the universe mayhap and put it through its paces, enslave the very gods. Not free to adventure, discover, and to play with life, tame it by all-piercing knowledge and by shrewd commands and put it through its paces, search out each dizzy height and darksome depth. The Mouser *bound*? No, no, no, no!

As his feelings marched with that great repeated negation, his inching footsteps had carried him forward almost to the mast, and through the sail's augmented hum and the wind's and the water's racket against the hull, he became aware of two voices contending vehemently in strident whispers.

He instantly and silently dropped on his belly and crawled on very cautiously until the top half of his face overlooked the gap between timber cargo and forecastle.

His three sailor-thieves and the two other Mingols sprawled higgledy piggledy, lazily napping, while immediately below him Skor and Mikkidu argued in what might be called loud undertones. He could have reached down and patted their heads – or rapped them with fisted knuckles.

'There you go bringing in the chest again,' Mikkidu was whispering hotly, utterly absorbed in the point he was making. 'There *is* no longer any chest on *Sea Hawk*! We've searched every place on the ship and not found it, so it has to have been cast overboard – that's the only explanation! – but only after (most like) the rich fabrics it contained were taken out and hid deviously in any number of ways and places. And there I must, with all respect, suspect old Ourph. He was awake while we slept, you can't trust Mingols (or get a word out of them, for that matter), he's got merchant's blood and can't resist snatching any rich thing, he's also got the cunning of age, and—'

Mikkidu perforce paused to draw breath and Skor, who seemed to have been patiently waiting for just that, cut in with,

'Searched every place *except* the Captain's cabin. And we searched that pretty well with our eyes. So the chest has to be the draped oblong thing he sat behind and even thumped on. It was exactly the right size and shape—'

'That was the Captain's desk,' Mikkidu asserted in outraged tones.

'There *was* no desk,' Skor rejoined, 'when Captain Fafhrd occupied the cabin, or on our voyage down. Stick to the facts, little man. Next you'll be denying again he had a girl with him.'

'*There was no girl!*' Mikkidu exploded, using up at once all the breath he'd managed to draw, for Skor was able to continue without raising his voice, 'There was indeed a girl, as any fool could see who was not oversunk in doggish loyalty – a dainty delicate piece just the right size for him with long, long silvery hair and a great green eye casting out lustful gleams—'

'That wasn't a girl's long hair you saw, you great lewd oaf,' Mikkidu cut in, his lungs replenished at last. 'That was a large dried frond of fine silvery seaweed with a shining, sea-rounded green pebble caught up in it – such a curio as many a captain's cabin accumulates – and your woman-starved fancy transformed it to a wench, you lickerish idiot—

'Or else,' he recommenced rapidly, cutting in on himself, as it were, 'it was a lacy silver dress with a silver-set green gem at its neck – the Captain questioned me closely about just such a dress when he was quizzing me about the chest before you came.'

My, my, the Mouser thought, *I never dreamed Mikkidu had such a quick fancy or would spring to my defence so loyally. But it does now appear, I must admit, that I have falsely suspected these two men and that Ississi somehow did board* Sea Hawk *solo. Unless one of the others – no, that's unlikely. Truth from a whore – there's a puzzler for you.*

Skor said triumphantly, 'But if it was the dress you saw on's bunk and the dress had been in the chest, doesn't that prove the chest too was in the cabin? Yes, it may well have been a filmy silver dress we saw, now that I think of it, which the girl slipped teasingly and lasciviously out of before leaping between the sheets, or else your Captain Mouser ripped it off her (it looked torn), for he's as hot and lusty as a mink and ever boasting of his dirksmanship – I've heard Captain Fafhrd say so again and again, or at least imply it.'

What infamy was this now? the Mouser asked himself, suddenly indignant, glaring down at Skor's balding head from his vantage point. *It was his own place to chide Fafhrd for his womanizing, not hear himself so chidden for the same fault (and boastfulness to boot) by this bogus Fafhrd, this insolent, lofty, jumped-up underling.* He involuntarily whipped up his fist to smite.

'Yes, boastful, devious, a martinet, and mean,' Skor continued while Mikkidu spluttered. 'What think you of a captain who drives his crew hard in port, holds back their pay, puritanically forbids shore leave, denies 'em all discharge of their natural urges – and then brings a girl aboard for his own use and flaunts her in their faces? And *then* plays games with them about her, sends them on idiot's hunt. *Petty* – that's what I've heard Captain Fafhrd call it – or at least show he thought so by his looks.'

The Mouser, furious, could barely restrain himself from striking out. *Defend me, Mikkidu,* he inwardly implored. *Oh the monstrousness of it – to invoke Fafhrd. Had Fafhrd really—*

'Do you really think so?' he heard Mikkidu say, only a little doubtfully. 'You really think he's got a girl in there? Well, if that's the case I must admit he is a very devil!'

The cry of pure rage that traitorous utterance drew from the sprung-up Mouser made the two lieutenants throw back their heads and stare, and brought the nappers fully awake and almost to their feet.

He opened his mouth to utter rebuke that would skin them alive – and then paused, wondering just what form that rebuke could take. After all, there *was* a naked girl in his cabin with her legs tied wide – in fact, spread-eagled. His glance lit on the lashings of the chest of fabrics still lying loose on the deck.

'Clear up that strewage!' he roared, pointing it out. 'Use it to tie down doubly those grain sacks there.' He pointed again. 'And while you're at it—' (he took a deep breath) 'double lash the entire cargo! I am not satisfied that it won't shift if hurricane strikes.' He directed that last remark chiefly at the two lieutenants, who peered puzzledly at the blue sky as they moved to organize the work.

'Yes, double lash it all down tight as eelskin,' he averred, beginning to pace back and forth as he warmed to his task. 'Pass

455

the timber's extra ropings around belaying pins set *inside* the oarholes and then draw them tight across the deck. See that those wool sacks of grain and fruit are lashed really tight – imagine you're corseting a fat woman, put your foot in her back and really pull those laces. For I'm not convinced those bags would stay in place if we had green water aboard and dragging at them. And when all that is done, bring a gang aft to further firm the casks and barrels in my cabin, marry them indissolubly to *Sea Hawk*'s deck and sides. Remember, all of you,' he finished as he danced off aft, 'if you tie things up carefully enough – your purse, your produce, or your enemies, and eke your lights of love – nothing can ever surprise you, or escape from you, or harm you!'

8

Cif untied the massive silver key from the neck of her soft leather tunic, where it had hung warm inside, unlocked the heavy oaken door of the treasury, opened it cautiously and suspiciously, inspected the room from the threshold – she'd been uneasy about the place ever since the sea-ghost's depredations. Then she went in and relocked the door behind her. A small window with thumb-thick bars of bronze illumined not too well the wooden room. On a shelf reposed two ingots of pale silver, three short stacks of silver coins, and a single golden stack, still shorter. The walls of the room crowded in on a low circular table, in the gray surface of which a pentacle had been darkly burnt. She named over to herself the five golden objects standing at the points: the Arrow of Truth, kinked from Fafhrd's tugging of it from the demoness; the Rule of Prudence, a short rod circled by ridges; the Cup of Measured Hospitality, hardly larger than a thimble; the Circles of Unity, so linked that if any one were taken away, the other two fell apart; and the strange skeletal globe that Fafhrd had recovered with the rest and suggested might be the Cube of Square Dealing smoothly deformed (something she rather doubted). She took the Mouser doll from her pouch and laid it in their midst, at pentalpha's centre. She sighed with relief, sat down on one of the three stools there were, and gazed pensively at the doll's blank face.

9

As the Mouser approved the last cask's double lashings and then dismissed as curtly his still-baffled lieutenants and their weary work gang – fairly drove 'em from his cabin! – he felt a surge of power inside, as if he'd just stepped or been otherwise carried over an invisible boundary into a realm where each last object was plainly labelled 'Mine Alone!'

Ah, that had been sport of the best, he told himself – closely supervising the gang's toil while standing all the while in their midst atop the draped chest he'd had them hunting all day long, and while the girl Ississi lay naked and securely spread-eagled beneath the blanket spread across his bunk – and they all somehow conscious of her delectable presence yet never quite daring to refer to it. Power sport indeed!

In a transport of self-satisfaction he whipped the drape from the chest, threw back its top, and admired the expanse of coppery silk so revealed and the bolts of black ribbon. Now *there* was a bed fit for a princess's nuptials, he told himself as he filled and downed a brass cup of brandy, a couch somewhat small, but sufficient and soft all the way down to the bottom.

His mind and his feet both dancing with all manner of imaginings and impulses, he moved to the bunk and whirled off its coverings and—

The bunk's coarse gray single sheeting was covered by a veritable black snow-sprinkle of ribbon scraps and shreds. Of Ississi there was no sign.

After a long moment's searching of it with his astounded eyes, he fairly dived across the bunk and fumbled frantically all the way around the thin mattress's edges and under them, searching for the razor-keen knife or scissors that had done this or (who knew?) some sharp-toothed, ribbon-shredding small animal secretly attendant on the girl whore and obedient to her command.

A trilling sigh of blissful contentment made him switch

convulsively around. In the midst of the new-opened chest, got there by sleights he could scarce dream of, Ississi sat cross-legged facing him. Her arms were lifted while her nimble hands were swiftly braiding her long straight silvery hair, an action which showed off her slender waist and dainty small breasts to best advantage, while her green eyes flashed and her lips smiled at him, 'Am I not exceedingly clever? Surpassingly clever and wholly delightful?'

The Mouser frowned at her terribly, then sent the same expression roving to either side, as if spying for a route by which she could have got unseen from bunk to chest past the double-lashed and closely abutting casks – and mayhap for her confederates, animal, human, or demonic. Next he got off the bunk and, approaching her, edged his way around the chest and back, eyeing her up and down as though searching for concealed weapons, even so little as a sharpened fingernail, and turning his own body so that his frown was always fixed on her and he never lost sight of her for an instant, until he faced her once more.

His nostrils flared with his deep breathing, while the lamp's yellow beams and shadows swayed measuredly across his dark angry presence and her moon-pale skin.

She continued to braid her hair and to smile and to warble and trill, and after a short while her trillings and warblings became a sort of rough song of recitation, one shot with seeming improvisations, as though she were translating it into Low Lankhmarese from another language.

'Oh, the golden gifts of my land are six, And round you now they're straitly fixed. The Golden Shaft of Death and Desire, The Rod of Command whose smart's like fire, The Cup of Close Confinement and Minding, The Circles of Fate whose ways are winding. The Cubical Prison of god and of elf, The Many-Barred Globe of Simorgya and Self. Deep, oh deep is my far country, Where gold will carry us, me and thee.'

The Mouser shook his finger before her face in dark challenge and dire warning. Then he slashed lengths of ribbed black silk ribbon from a roll, twisting and tugging it to test its strength, continuing to eye her all the while, and he bound her legs together as they were, slender ankle to calf, just below the knee, and slender calf to ankle. Then he held out his hand for hers imperiously. She rapidly finished plaiting her hair, whipped the braid round her head and tucked it in, so that it became a sort of silvery coronet. Then with a sigh and a turning away of her somewhat narrow face, she held out her wrists to him close together, the palms of her hands upward.

He seized them contemptuously and drew them behind her and bound them there, as he had on the previous night, and her elbows too, drawing her shoulders backward. And then he tipped her over forward so that her face was buried in the coppery silk intended for Cif (how long ago?) and led a double ribbon from her bound wrists down her spine to her crosswise-bound lower legs, and drew it tight as he could, so that her back was perforce arched and her face lifted free of the silk.

But despite his mounting excitement, the thought nagged him that there had been something in her warbled ditty which he had not liked. Ah yes, the mention of Simorgya. What place had that sunken kingdom in a whore's never-never lands? And all her earlier babble of moist and watery influences in the imagined land where she queened, or rather princessed it – There, she was at it again!

'Come, Brother Mordroog, to royally escort us,' she warbled over the orangy silk, seemingly unmindful of her acute discomforts. 'Come with our guardians, Deep Rusher your horse – your behemoth, rather, and you in his castle. Come also with Slasher and vasty All-Gripper, to shatter our prison and ferry us home. And send all your spirits coursing before you, so our minds are engulfed—'

The shadows steadied unnaturally as the lamp's swing shortened quiveringly, then stopped.

On the deck immediately above their heads there was consternation. The wind had unaccountably faded and the sea grown oily calm. The tiller in Skor's grip was lifeless, the sheet that Mikkidu fingered slack. The sky did not appear to be overcast, yet there was a shadowed, spectral quality to the sunlight, as though an unpredicted eclipse or other ominous event impended. Then without warning the dark sea mounded up boiling scarce a spear's cast off steerside – and subsided again without any diminishment in the feeling of foreboding. The spreading wave jogged *Sea Hawk*. The two lieutenants and

Ourph stared about wonderingly and then at each other. None of them marked the trail of bubbles leading from the place of the mounding toward the becalmed sailing galley.

10

In the treasury Cif had the sudden feeling that the Mouser stood in need of more protection. The doll looked lonely there at pentagram's centre. Perhaps he was too far from the ikons. She gathered the ikons together and after a moment's hesitation thrust the doll, doubled up, into the barred globe. Then she poked the ruler and the crooked arrow in along with him, transfixing the globe (more gold close to him!), almost as an afterthought clapped the tiny cup like a helmet on the protruding doll's head, and set all down on the linked rings. Then she seated herself again, staring doubtfully at what she had done.

II

In the cabin the Grey Mouser rolled the bound Ississi over on her back and regarded the silvery girl opened up for his enjoyment. The blood pounded in his head and he felt an increasing pressure there, as if his brain had grown too large for his skull. The motionless cabin grew spectral, there was a sense of thronging presences, and then it was as if part of him only remained there while another part whirled away into a realm where he was a giant coursing through rushing darkness, uncertain of his humanity, while the pressure inside his skull grew and grew.

But the part of him in the cabin still was capable of sensation, though hardly of action, and this one watched helpless and aghast, through air that seemed to thicken and become more like water, the silvery, smiling, trussed-up Ississi writhe and writhe yet again while her skin grew more silvery still – scaly silvery – and her elfin face narrowed and her green eyes swam apart, while from her head and back and shoulders, and along the backs of her legs and her hands and arms, razor-sharp spines erected themselves in crests and, as she writhed once more again mightily, cut through all the black ribbons at once so they floated in shreds about her. Then through the curtained hatchway there swam a face like her own new one, and she came up from the coppery silk in a great forward undulation and reached the palms of her back-crested hands out toward the Mouser's cheeks lovingly on arms that seemed to grow longer and longer, saying in a strange deep voice that seemed to bubble from her, 'In moments this prison will be broken, Deep Rusher will smash it, and we will be free.'

At those words the other part of the Mouser realized that the darkness through which he was now coursing upward was the deep sea, that he was engulfed in the whale-body and great-foreheaded brain of Deep Rusher, her monster, that it was the tiny hull of *Sea Hawk* far above him that his massive forehead was aimed at, and that he could no more evade that collision than his other self in the cabin could avoid the arms of Ississi.

12

In the treasury Cif could not bear the woeful expression with which the blank linen face of the doll appeared to gaze out at her from under the jammed-down golden helmet, nor the sudden thought that the sea demoness had recently fondled all that gold hemming in the doll. She grabbed it up with its prison, withdrew it from the barred globe and snatched off its helmet, and while the ikons chinked down on the table she clutched the stuffed cloth to her bosom and bent her lips to it and cherished and kissed it, breathing it words of endearment.

13

In the cabin the Mouser was able to dodge aside from those questing silvery spined hands, which went past him, while in the dark realm his giant self was able to veer aside from *Sea Hawk's* hull at the last moment and burst out of the darkness, so that his

461

two selves were one again and both back in the cabin – which now lurched as though *Sea Hawk* were capsizing.

On deck all gaped, flinching, as a black shape thicker than *Sea Hawk* burst resoundingly from the dark water beside them, so close the ship's hull shook and they might have reached out and touched the monster. The shape erected itself like a windowless tower built all of streaming black boot leather, down which sheets of water cascaded. It shot up higher and higher, dragging their gazes skyward, then it narrowed and with a sweep of its great flukes left the water altogether, and for a long moment they watched the dark dripping underbelly of black leviathan pass over *Sea Hawk*, vast as a storm cloud, lacking lightning perhaps but not thunder, as he breached entire from the ocean. But then they were all snatching for handholds as *Sea Hawk* lurched down violently sideways, as though trying to shake them from her back. At least there was no shortage of lashings to grab onto as she slid with the collapsing waters into the great chasm left by leviathan. There came the numbing shock of that same beast smiting the sea beyond them as he returned to his element. Then salt ocean closed over them as they sank down, down, and down.

Afterward the Mouser could never determine how much of what next happened in the cabin transpired under water and how much in a great bubble of air constrained by that other element so that it became more akin to it. (No question, he was wholly under water toward the end.) There was a somewhat slow or, rather, measured dreamlike quality to all subsequent movements there – his, the transformed Ississi's, and the creature he took to be her brother – as if they were made against great pressures. It had elements both of a savage struggle – a fierce, life-and-death fight – and of a ceremonial dance with beasts. Certainly his position during it was always in the centre, beside or a little above the open chest of fabrics, and certainly the transformed Ississi and her brother circled him like sharks and darted in alternately to attack, their narrow jaws gaping to show razorlike teeth and closing like great scissors snipping. And always there was that sense of steadily increasing pressure, though not now within his skull particularly, but over his entire body and centering, if anywhere, upon his lungs.

It began, of course, with his evading of Ississi's initial loving and murderous lunge at him, and his moving past her to the chest she had just quitted. Then, as she turned back to assault him a second time (all jaws now, arms merged into her silver-scaled sides and her crested legs merged, but eyes still great and green), and as he, in turn, turned to oppose her, he was inspired to grab up with both hands from the chest the topmost fabric and, letting it unfold sequentially and spread as he did so, whirl it between him and her in a great lustrous, baffling coppery sheet, or pale rosy-orange cloud. And she was indeed distracted from her main purpose by this timely interposition, although her silvery jaws came through it more than once, shredding and shearing and altogether making sorry work of Cif's intended cloak or dress of state or treasurer's robes, or whatever.

Then, as the Mouser completed his whirling turn, he found himself confronting the in-rushing silver-crested Mordroog, and to hold *him* off snatched up and whirlingly interposed the next rich silken fabric in the chest, which happened to be a violet one, his reluctant gift for Afreyt, so now it became a great pale purple cloud-wall soon slashed to lavender streaks and streamers, through which Mordroog's silver and jaw-snapping visage showed like a monstrous moon.

This maneuver brought the Mouser back in turn to face Ississi, who was closing in again through coppery shreds, and this attack was in turn thwarted by the extensive billowing-out of a sheet of bold scarlet silk, which he had meant to present to the capable whore-turned-fisherwoman Hilsa, but now was as effectively reduced to scraps and tatters as any incarnadined sunset is by conquering night.

And so it went, each charming or at least clever fabric gift in turn sacrificed – brassy yellow satin for Hilsa's comrade Rill, a rich brown worked with gold for Fafhrd, lovely sea-green and salmon pink sheets (also for Cif), a sky blue one (still another for Afreyt – to appease Fafhrd), a royal purple one for Pshawri (in honour of his first lieutenancy), and even one for Groniger (soberest black) – but each sheet successively defeating a dire attack by silvery sea demon or demoness, until the cabin had been filled with a most expensive sort of confetti and the bottom of the chest had been reached.

But by then, mercifully, the demonic attacks had begun to lessen in speed and fury, grow weaker and weaker, until they were but surly and almost aimless switchings-about (even floppings-about, like those of fish dying), while (*most* mercifully – almost miraculously) the dreadful suffocating pressure, instead of increasing or even holding steady, had started to fall off, to lessen, and now was continuing to do so, more and more swiftly.

What had happened was that when *Sea Hawk* had slid into the hole left by leviathan, the lead in her keel (which made her seaworthy) had tended to drag her down still farther, abetted by the mass of her great cargo, especially the bronze ingots and copper sheetings in it. But on the other hand, the greater part of her cargo by far consisted of items that were *lighter than water* – the long stack of dry, well-seasoned timber, the tight barrels of flour, and the woollen sacks of grain, all of these additionally having considerable amounts of air trapped in them (the timber by virtue of the tarred canvas sheathing it, the grain because of the greasy raw wool of the sacks, so they acted as so many floats). So long as these items were above the water they tended to press the ship more deeply into it, but once they were under water, their effect was to drag *Sea Hawk* upward, toward the surface.

Now under ordinary conditions of stowage – safe, adequate stowage, even – all these items might well have broken loose and floated up to the surface individually, the timber stack emerging like a great disintegrating raft, the sacks bobbing up like so many balloons, while *Sea Hawk* continued on down to a watery grave carrying along with it those trapped below decks and any desperately clinging seamen too shocked and terror-frozen to loosen their panic-grips.

But the imaginative planning and finicky overseeing the Mouser had given the stowage of the cargo at 'Brulsk, so that Fafhrd or Cif or (Mog forbid!) Skor should never have cause to criticize him, and also in line with his determination, now he had taken up merchanting, to be the cleverest and most foresighted merchant of them all, taken in conjunction with the mildly sadistic fury with which he had driven the men at their stowage work, ensured that the wedgings and lashings-down of this cargo were something exceptional. And then when, earlier today and seemingly on an insane whim, he had insisted that all those more-than-adequate lashings be doubled, and then driven the men to that work with even greater fury, he had unknowingly guaranteed *Sea Hawk*'s survival.

To be sure, the lashings were strained, they creaked and boomed underwater (they were lifting a whole sailing galley), but not a single one of them parted, not a single air-swollen sack escaped before *Sea Hawk* reached the surface.

14

And so it was that the Mouser was able to swim through the hatchway and see untainted blue sky again and blessedly fill his lungs with their proper element and weakly congratulate Mikkidu and a Mingol paddling and gasping beside him on their most fortunate escape. True, *Sea Hawk* was water-filled and awash, but she floated upright, her tall mast and bedraggled sail were intact, the sea was calm and windless still, and (as was soon determined) her entire crew had survived, so the Mouser knew there was no insurmountable obstacle in the way of their clearing her of water first by bailing, then by pumping (the oarholes could be plugged, if need be), and continuing their voyage. And if in the course of that clearing, a few fish, even a couple of big ones, should flop overside after a desultory snap or two (best be wary of all fish!) and then dive deep into *their* proper element and return to their own rightful kingdom – why, that was all in the Nehwonian nature of things.

15

A fortnight later, being a week after *Sea Hawk*'s safe arrival in Salthaven, Fafhrd and Afreyt rented the Sea Wrack and gave Captain Mouser and his crew a party, which Cif and the Mouser had to help pay for from the profits of the latter's trading voyage. To it were invited numerous Isler friends. It coincided with the year's first blizzard, for the winter gales had held off and been providentially late coming. No matter, the salty tavern was snug and the food and drink all that could be asked for – with perhaps one exception.

'There was a faint taste of wool fat in the fruit soup,' Hilsa observed. 'Nothing particularly unpleasant, but noticeable.'

'That'll have been from the grease in the sacking,' Mikkidu enlightened her, 'which kept the sea salt out of 'em, so they buoyed us up powerfully when we sank. Captain Mouser thinks of everything.'

'Just the same,' Skor reminded him *sotto voce*, 'it turned out he did have a girl in the cabin all the while – and that damned chest of fabrics too! You can't deny he's a great liar whenever he chooses.'

'Ah, but the girl turned out to be a sea demon, and he needed the fabrics to defend himself from her, and that makes all the difference,' Mikkidu rejoined loyally.

'I never saw her as aught but a ghostly and silver-crested sea demon,' old Ourph put in. 'The first night out from No-Ombrulsk I saw her rise from the cabin through the deck and stand at the taffrail, invoking and communing with sea monsters.'

'Why didn't you report that to the Mouser?' Fafhrd asked, gesturing toward the venerable Mingol with his new bronze hook.

'One never speaks of a ghost in its presence,' the latter explained, 'or while there is a chance of its reappearance. It only gives it strength. As always, silence is silver.'

'Yes, and speech is golden,' Fafhrd maintained.

Rill boldly asked the Mouser across the table, 'But just how did you deal with the sea demoness while she was in her girl-guise? I gather you kept her tied up a lot, or tried to?'

'Yes,' Cif put in from beside him. 'You were even planning at one point to train her to be a maid for me, weren't you?' She smiled curiously. 'Just think, I lost that as well as those lovely materials.'

'I attempted a number of things that were rather beyond my powers,' the Gray One admitted manfully, the edges of his ears turning red. 'Actually, I was lucky to escape with my life.' He turned toward Cif. 'Which I couldn't have done if you hadn't snatched me from the tainted gold in the nick of time.'

466

'Never mind, it was I put you amongst the tainted gold in the first place,' she told him, laying her hand on his on the table, 'but now it's been hopefully purified.' (She had directed that ceremony of exorcism of the ikons herself, with the assistance of Mother Grum, to free them of all baleful Simorgyan influence got from their handling by the demoness. The old witch was somewhat dubious of the complete efficacy of the ceremony.)

Later Skor described leviathan arching over *Sea Hawk*. Afreyt nodded appreciatively, saying, 'I was once in a dory when a whale breached close alongside. It is not a sight to be forgotten.'

'Nor is it when viewed from the other side of the gunnel,' the Mouser observed reflectively. Then he winced. 'Mog, what a head thump that would have been!'

III
THE CURSE OF THE SMALLS
AND THE STARS

I

Late one nippy afternoon of early Rime Isle spring, Fafhrd and the Gray Mouser slumped pleasantly in a small booth in Salthaven's Sea Wrack tavern. Although they'd been on the Isle for only a year, and patronizing this tavern for an eight-month, the booth was recognized as *theirs* when either was in the place. Both men had been mildly fatigued, the former from supervising bottom repairs to *Sea Hawk* at the new moon's low tide – and then squeezing in a late round of archery practice, the latter from bossing the carpentering of their new warehouse-and-barracks – and doing some inventorying besides. But their second tankards of bitter ale had about taken care of that, and their thoughts were beginning to float free.

Around them they heard the livening talk of other recuperating labourers. At the bar they could see three of their lieutenants grousing together – Fafhrd-tall Skor, and the somewhat reformed small thieves Pshawri and Mikkidu. Behind it the keeper lit two thick wicks as the light dimmed as the sun set outside.

Frowning as he pared a thumbnail with razor-keen Cat's Claw, the Mouser said, 'I am minded of how scarce seventeen moons gone we sat just so in Silver Eel tavern in Lankhmar, deeming Rime Isle a legend. Yet here we are.'

'Lankhmar,' Fafhrd mused, drawing a wet circle with the firmly socketed iron hook that had become his left hand after the day's bow bending, 'I've heard somewhere of such a city, I do believe. 'Tis strange how oftentimes our thoughts do chime together, as if we were sundered halves of some past being, but whether hero or demon, wastrel or philosopher, harder to say.'

'Demon, I'd say,' the Mouser answered instantly, 'a demon

warrior. We've guessed at him before. Remember? We decided he always growled in battle. Perhaps a were-bear.'

After a small chuckle at that, Fafhrd went on, 'But then (that night twelve moons gone and five in Lankhmar) we'd had twelve tankards each of bitter instead of two, I ween, yes, and lacing them too with brandy, you can bet – hardly to be accounted best judges twixt phantasm and the veritable. Yes, and didn't two heroines from this fabled isle next moment stride into the Eel, as real as boots?'

Almost as if the Northerner hadn't answered, the small, gray-smocked, gray-stockinged man continued in the same thoughtful reminiscent tones as he'd first used, 'And you, liquored to the gills – agreed on that! – were ranting dolefully about how you dearly wanted work, land, office, sons, other responsibilities, and e'en a wife!'

'Yes, and didn't I get one?' Fafhrd demanded. 'You too, you equally then-drunken destiny-ungrateful lout!' His eyes grew thoughtful also. He added, 'Though perhaps comrade or co-mate were the better word – or even those plus partner.'

'Much better all three,' the Mouser agreed shortly. 'As for those other goods your drunken heart was set upon – no disagreement there! – we've got enough of those to stuff a hog! – except, of course, far as I know, for sons. Unless, that is, you count our men as our grown-up unweaned babies, which sometimes I'm inclined to.'

Fafhrd, who'd been leaning his head out of the booth to look toward the darkening doorway during the latter part of the Mouser's plaints, now stood up, saying, 'Speaking of them, shall we join the ladies? Cif and Afreyt's booth 'pears to be larger than ours.'

'To be sure. What else?' the Mouser replied, rising springily. Then, in a lower voice, 'Tell me, did the two of them just now come in? Or did we blunder blindly by them when we entered, sightless of all save thirst quench?'

Fafhrd shrugged, displaying his palm. 'Who knows? Who cares?'

'*They might*,' the other answered.

Many Lankhmar leagues east and south, and so in darkest moonless night, the archmagus Ningauble conferred with the sorceress Sheelba at the edge of the Great Salt Marsh. The seven luminous eyes of the former wove many greenish patterns within his gaping hood as he leaned his quaking bulk perilously downward from the howdah on the broad back of the forward-kneeling elephant which had borne him from his desert cave, across the Sinking Land through all adverse influences, to this appointed spot. While the latter's eyeless face strained upward likewise as she stood tall in the doorway of her small hut, which had travelled from the Marsh's noxious centre to the same dismal verge on its three long rickety (but now rigid) chicken legs. The two wizards strove mightily to outshout (outbellow or outscreech) the nameless cosmic din (inaudible to human ears) which had hitherto hindered and foiled all their earlier efforts to communicate over greater distances. And now, at last, they strove successfully!

Ningauble wheezed, 'I have discovered by certain infallible signs that the present tumult in realms magical, botching my spells, is due to the vanishment from Lankhmar of my servitor and sometimes student, Fafhrd the barbarian. All magics dim without his credulous and kindly audience, while high quests fail lacking his romantical and custard-headed idealisms.'

Sheelba shot back through the murk, 'While I have ascertained that my illspells suffer equally because the Mouser's gone with him, my protégé and surly errand boy. They will not work without the juice of his brooding and overbearing malignity. He must be summoned from that ridiculous rim-place of Rime Isle, and Fafhrd with him!'

'But how to do that when our spells won't carry? What servitor to trust with such a mission to go and fetch 'em? I know of a young demoness might undertake it, but she's in thrall to Khahkht, wizard of power in that frosty area – and he's inimical to both of us. Or should the two of us search out in noisy spirit realm to be our messenger that putative warlike ascendant of theirs and whilom forebear known as the Growler? A dismal task! Where'er I look I see naught but uncertainties and obstacles—'

'I shall send word of their whereabouts to Mog the spider god, the Gray One's tutelary deity! – this din won't hinder prayers,' Sheelba interrupted in a harsh, clipped voice. The presence of the vacillating and loquacious over-sighted wizard, who saw seven sides to every question, always roused her to her best efforts. 'Send you like advisors to Fafhrd's gods, stone-age brute Kos and the fastidious cripple Issek. Soon as they know where their lapsed worshippers are, they'll put such curses and damnations on them as shall bring them back squealing to us to have those taken off.'

'Now why didn't *I* think of that?' Ningauble protested, who was indeed sometimes called the Gossiper of the Gods. 'To work! To work!'

3

In paradisiacal Godsland, which lies at the antipodes of Nehwon's death pole and Shadowland, in the southernmost reach of that world's southernmost continent, distanced and guarded from the tumultuous northern lands by the Great eastward-rushing Equatorial Current (where some say swim the stars), sub-equatorial deserts, and the Rampant Mountains, the gods Kos, Issek, and Mog sat somewhat apart from the mass of more couth and civilized Nehwonian deities, who objected to Kos's lice, fleas, and crabs, and a little to Issek's effeminacy – though Mog had contacts among these, as he sarcastically called 'em, 'higher beings'.

Sunk in divine somnolent broodings, not to say almost deathlike trances, for prayers, petitions, and even blasphemous nametakings had been scanty of late, the three mismatched godlings reacted at once and enthusiastically to the instant-aneously-transmitted wizard missives.

'Those two ungodly swording rogues!' Mog hissed softly, his long thin lips stretched slantwise in a half spider grin. 'The very thing! Here's work for all of us, my heavenly peers. A chance to curse again and to bedevil.'

'A glad inspiro that, indeed, indeed!' Issek chimed, waving his limp-wristed hands excitedly. '*I* should have thought of that! – our chiefest lapsed worshippers, hidden away in frosty and forgotten far Rime Isle, farther away than Shadowland itself, *almost* beyond our hearing and our might. Such infant cunning! Oh, but we'll make them pay!'

'The ingrate dogs!' Kos grated through his thick and populous black beard. 'Not only casting us off, their natural heavenly fathers and rightful da's, but forsaking *all* decent Nehwonian deities and running with atheist men and gone a-whoring after stranger gods beyond the pale! Yes, by my lights and spleen, we'll make 'em suffer! Where's my spiked mace?'

(On occasion Mog and Issek had been known to have to hold Kos down to keep him from rushing ill-advised out of Godsland to seek to visit personal dooms upon his more disobedient and farther-strayed worshippers.)

'What say we set their women against them, as we did last time?' Issek urged twitteringly. 'Women have power over men almost as great as gods do.'

Mog shook his humanoid cephalothorax. 'Our boys are too coarse-tasted. Did we estrange from them Afreyt and Cif, they'd doubtless fall back on amorous arrangements with the Salthaven harlots Rill and Hilsa – and so on and so on.' Now that his attention had been called to Rime Isle, he had easy knowledge of all overt things there – a divine prerogative. 'No, not the women this time, I ween.'

'A pox on all such subtleties!' Kos roared. 'I want tortures for 'em! Let's visit on 'em the strangling cough, the prick-rot, and the Bloody Melts!'

'Nor can we risk wiping them out entirely,' Mog answered swiftly. 'We haven't worshipers to spare for that, you fire-eater, as you well know. Thrift, thrift! Moreover, as you should also know, a threat is always more dreadful than its execution. I propose we subject them to some of the moods and preoccupations of old age and of old age's bosom comrade, inseparable though invisible-seeming – Death himself! Or is that too mild a fear and torment, thinkest thou?'

'I'll say not,' Kos agreed, suddenly sober. 'I know that it scares *me*. What if the gods should die? A hellish thought.'

'That infant bugaboo!' Issek told him peevishly. Then turning to Mog with quickening interest, 'So, if I read you right, old Arach, let's narrow your silky Mouser's interests in and in from the adventure-beckoning horizon to the things closest around him: the bed table, the dinner board, the privy, and the kitchen sink. Not the far-leaping highway, but the gutter. Not the ocean, but the puddle. Not the grand view outside, but the bleared windowpane. Not the thunder-blast, but the knuckle crack – or ear-pop.'

Mog narrowed his eight eyes happily. 'And for your Fafhrd, I would suggest a different old-age curse, to drive a wedge between them so they can't understand or help each other, that we put a geas upon him to count the stars. His interests in all else will fade and fail, he'll have mind only for those tiny lights in the sky.'

'So that, with his head in the clouds,' Issek pictured, catching on quick, 'he'll stumble and bruise himself again and again, and miss all opportunities of earthly delights.'

'Yes, and make him memorize their names and all their patterns!' Kos put in. 'There's busy-work for an eternity. I never could abide the things myself. There's such a senseless mess of stars, like flies or fleas. An insult to the gods to say that we created them!'

'And then, when those two have sufficiently humbled themselves to us and done suitable penance,' Issek purred, 'we will consider taking off or ameliorating their curses.'

'I say, leave 'em on always,' Kos argued. 'No leniency. Eternal damnation! – that's the stuff!'

'That question can be decided when it arises,' Mog opined. 'Come, gentlemen, to work! We've some damnations to devise in detail and deliver.'

4

Back at the Sea Wrack tavern, Fafhrd and the Gray Mouser had, despite the latter's apprehensions, been invited to join with and buy a round of bitter ale for their lady-friends Afreyt and Cif, leading and sometimes office-holding citizens of Rime Isle, spinster-matriarchs of otherwise scionless dwindling old families in that strange republic, and Fafhrd's and the Mouser's partners and co-adventurers of a good year's standing in questing, business, and (this last more recently) bed. The questing part had consisted of the almost bloodless routing from the Isle of an invading naval force of maniacal Sea-Mingols, with the help of twelve tall berserks and twelve small warrior-thieves the two heroes had brought with them, and the dubious assistance of the two universes-wandering hobo gods Odin and Loki, and (minor quest) a small expedition to recover certain civic treasures of the Isle, a set of gold artefacts called the Ikons of Reason. And they had been *hired* to do these things by Cif and Afreyt, so business had been mixed with questing in their relationship from the very start. Other business had been a merchant venture of the Mouser (Captain Mouser for this purpose) in Fafhrd's galley *Sea Hawk* with a mixed crew of berserks and thieves, and goods supplied by the ladies, to the oft frozen port of No-Ombrulsk on Nehwon mainland – that and various odd jobs done by their men and by the women and girls employed by and owing fealty to Cif and Afreyt.

As for the bed part, both couples, though not yet middle-aged, at least in looks, were veterans of amorous goings-on, wary and courteous in all such doings, entering upon any new relationships, including these, with a minimum of commitment and a maximum of reservations. Ever since the tragic deaths of their first loves, Fafhrd's and the Mouser's erotic solacing had mostly come from a very odd lot of hard-bitten if beauteous slave-girls, vagabond hoydens, and demonic princesses, folk easily come by if at all and even more easily lost, accidents rather than goals of their weird adventurings; both sensed that anything with the Rime Isle ladies would have to be a little more serious at least. While Afreyt's and Cif's love-adventures had been equally transient, either with unromantic and hard-headed Rime Islanders, who are atheistical realists even in youth, or with sea-wanderers of one sort or another, come like the rain – or thunder-squall, and as swiftly gone.

All this being considered, things did seem to be working out quite well for the two couples in the bed area.

And, truth to tell, this was a greater satisfaction and relief to the Mouser and Fafhrd than either would admit even to himself. For each was indeed beginning to find extended questing a mite tiring, especially ones like this last which, rather than being one of their usual lone-wolf forays, involved the recruitment and command of other men and the taking on of larger and divided responsibilities. It was natural for them, after such exertions, to feel that a little rest and quiet enjoyment was now owed them, a little surcease from the batterings of fate and chance and new desire. And, truth to tell, the ladies Cif and Afreyt were on the verge of admitting in their secretest hearts something of the same feelings.

So all four of them found it pleasant during this particular Rime Isle twilight to take a little bitter ale together and chat of this day's doings and tomorrow's plans and reminisce about their turning of the Mingols and ask each other gentle questions about the times before they'd all four met – and each flirt privily and cautiously with the notion that each now had two or three persons on whom they might always rely fully, rather than one like-sexed comrade only.

During the course of this gossiping Fafhrd mentioned again his and the Mouser's fantasy that they were halves – or perhaps lesser fractions, fragments only – of some noted or notorious past being, explaining why their thoughts so often chimed together.

'That's odd,' Cif interjected, 'for Afreyt and I have had like notion and for like reason: that she and I were spirit-halves of the great Rimish witch-queen Skeldir, who held off the Simorgyans again and again in ancient times when that island boasted an empire and was above the waves instead of under them. What was your hero's name – or mighty rogue's? – if that likes you better.'

'I know not, lady, perhaps he lived in times too primitive for names, when man and beast were closer. He was identified by his battle growling – a leonine cough deep in the throat whene'er he entered an encounter.'

'Another like point!' Cif noted. 'Queen Skeldir announced her presence by a short dry laugh – her invariable utterance when facing dangers, especially those of a sort to astound and confound the bravest.'

'Gusorio's my name for our beastish forebear,' the Mouser threw in. 'I know not what Fafhrd thinks. Great Gusorio. Gusorio the Growler.'

'Now he begins to sound like an animal,' Afreyt broke in. 'Tell me, have you ever been granted vision or dream of this Gusorio, or heard perhaps in darkest night his battle growl?'

But the Mouser was studying the dinted table top. He bent his head as his gaze travelled across it.

'No, milady,' Fafhrd answered for his abstracted comrade. 'At least not I. It's something we heard of a witch or fortune-teller, figment, not fact. Have you ever heard Queen Skeldir's short dry laugh, or had sight of that fabled warrior sorceress?'

'Neither I nor Cif,' Afreyt admitted, 'though she is in the Isle's history parchments.'

But even as she answered him, Fafhrd's questioning gaze strayed past her. She looked behind and saw the Sea Wrack's open doorway and the gathering night.

Cif stood up. 'So it's agreed we dine at Afreyt's in a half hour's time?'

The two men nodded somewhat abstractedly. Fafhrd leaned his head to the right as he continued to stare past Afreyt, who with a smile obligingly shifted hers in the opposite direction.

The Mouser leaned back and bent his head a little more as his gaze trailed down from the tabletop to its leg.

Fafhrd observed, 'Astarion sets soon after the sun these nights. There's little time to observe her.'

'God forbid I should stand in the evening star's way,' Afreyt murmured humorously as she too arose. 'Come, cousin.'

The Mouser left off watching the cockroach as it reached the floor. It had limped interestingly, lacking a mid leg. He and Fafhrd drank off their bitters, then slowly followed their ladies out and down the narrow street, the one's eyes thoughtfully delving in the gutter, as if there might be treasure there, the other's roving the sky as the stars winked on, naming those he knew and numbering, by altitude and direction, those he didn't.

5

Their work well launched, Sheelba retired to Marsh centre and Ningauble toward his cavern, the understorm abating, a good omen. While the three gods smiled, invigorated by their cursing. The slum corner of Heaven they occupied now seemed less chilly to Issek and less sweatily enervating to Kos, while Mog's devious spider mind stepped down more pleasant channels.

Yes, the seed was well planted, and left to germinate in silence, might have developed as intended, but some gods, and some sorcerers too, cannot resist boasting and gossiping, and so by way of talkative priests and midwives and vagabonds, word of what was intended came to the ears of the mighty, including two who considered themselves well rid of Fafhrd and the Mouser and did not want them back in Lankhmar at all. And the mighty are great worriers and spend much time preventing anything that troubles their peace of mind.

And so it was that Pulgh Arthonax, penurious and perverse overlord of Lankhmar, who hated heroes of all description – but especially fair-complected big ones like Fafhrd – and Hamomel, thrifty and ruthless grand master of the Thieves Guild there, who detested the Mouser generally as a freelance competitor and particularly as one who had lured twelve promising apprentices away from the Guild to be his henchmen – these two took counsel together and commissioned the Assassins Order, an elite within the Slayers' Brotherhood, to dispatch the Twain in Rime Isle before they should point toe toward Lankhmar. And because Arth-Pulgh and Hamomel were both most miserly magnates and insatiably greedy withal, they beat down the Order's price as far as they could and made it a condition of the commission that three-fourths of any portable booty found on or near the doomed Twain be returned to them as their lawful share.

So the Order drew up death warrants, chose by lot two of its currently unoccupied fellows, and in solemn secret ceremony attended only by the Master and the Recorder, divested these of their identities and rechristened them the Death of Fafhrd and the Death of the Gray Mouser, by which names only they should henceforth be known to each other and within the profession until the death warrants were served and their commissions fulfilled.

6

Next day repairs to *Sea Hawk* continued, the low tide repeating, Witches Moon being only one day old. During a late morning break Fafhrd moved apart from his men a little and scanned the high bright sky toward north and east, his gaze ranging. Skor ventured to follow him across the wet sand and copy his peerings. He saw nothing in the gray-blue heavens, but experience had taught him his captain had exceptionally keen eyesight.

'Sea eagles?' he asked softly.

Fafhrd looked at him thoughtfully, then smiled, shaking his head, and confided, 'I was imagining which stars would be there, were it now night.'

Skor's forehead wrinkled puzzledly. 'Stars by day?'

Fafhrd nodded. 'Yes. Where think you the stars are by day?'

'Gone,' Skor answered, his forehead clearing. 'They go away at dawn and return at evening. Their lights are extinguished – like winter campfires! For surely it must be cold where the stars are, higher than mountaintops. Until the sun comes out to warm up things, of course.'

Fafhrd shook his head. 'The stars march west across the sky each night in the same formations which we recognize year after year, dozen years after dozen, and I would guess gross after gross. They do not skitter for the horizon when day breaks or seek out lairs and earth holes, but go on marching with the sun's glare hiding their lights – under cover of day, one might express it.'

'Stars shining by day?' Skor questioned, doing a fair job of hiding his surprise and bafflement. Then he caught Fafhrd's drift, or thought he did, and a certain wonder appeared in his eyes. He knew his captain was a good general who made a fetish of keeping track of the enemy's position especially in terrain affording concealment, as forest on land or fog at sea. So by his very nature his captain had applied the same rule to the stars and studied 'em as closely as he'd traced the movements of the Mingol scouts fleeing across Rime Isle.

Though it was strange thinking of the stars as enemies. His captain was a deep one! Perhaps he did have foes among the stars. Skor had heard rumour that he'd bedded a queen of the air.

7

That night as the Gray Mouser and Cif leisurely prepared for bed in her low-eaved house tinted a sooty red on the north-western edge of Salthaven City, and whilst that lady busied herself at her mirrored dressing table, the Mouser himself sitting on bed's edge set his pouch upon a low bedside table and withdrew from it a curious lot of commonplace objects – curious in part because they were so commonplace – and arranged them in a line on the table's dark surface.

Cif, made curious by the slow regularity of his movements she saw reflected cloudily in the sheets of silver she faced, took up a small flat black box and came over and sat herself beside him.

The objects included a toothed small wooden wheel as big almost as a Sarheenmar dollar with two of the teeth missing, a finch's feather, three lookalike gray round pebbles, a scrap of blue wool cloth stiff with dirt, a bent wrought-iron nail, a hazelnut, and a dinted small black round that might have been a Lankhmar *tik* or Eastern halfpenny.

Cif ran her eye along them, then looked at him questioningly.

He said, 'Coming here from the barracks at first eve, a strange mood seized me. Low in the sunset glow the new moon's faintest and daintiest silver crescent had just materialized like the ghost of a young girl – and just in the direction of this house, at that, as though to signal your presence here – but somehow I had eyes only for the gutter and the pathside. Which is where I found those. And a remarkable lot they are for a small northern seaport. You'd think Ilthmar at least . . .' He shook his head.

'But why collect 'em?' she queried. *Like an old ragpicker*, she thought.

He shrugged. 'I don't know. I think I thought I might find a use for them,' he added doubtfully.

She said, 'They do look like oddments that might be involved in casting a spell.'

He shrugged again, but added, 'They're not all what they seem. *That*, for instance—' He pointed at one of three gray spherelets. '—is not a pebble like the other two, but a lead slingshot, perhaps one of my own.'

Struck by his thrusting finger, *that* rolled off the table and hit the terrazzo floor with a little dull yet clinky thud, as if to prove his observation.

As he recovered it, he paused with his eyes close to the floor to study first the crushed black marble of the terrazzo flecked with dark red and gold, and second Cif's near foot, which he then drew up onto his lap and studied still more minutely.

'A strangely symmetric pentapod coral outcrop from sea's bottom,' he observed, and planted a slow kiss upon the base of her big toe, insinuated the tip of his tongue between it and the next.

'There's an eel nosed around in my reef,' she murmured.

Laying his cheek upon her ankle, he sighted up her leg. She was wearing a singlet of fine brown linen that tied between her legs. He said, 'Your hair has exactly the same tints as are in the flooring.'

She said, 'You think I didn't select the marble for crushing with that in mind? Or add in the gold flakes? Here's a present of sorts for you.' And she pushed the small flat black box down her leg toward him from her groin to her knee.

He sat up to inspect it, though keeping her foot in his lap.

On the black fabric lining it, there lay like a delicate mist cloud the slender translucent bladder of a fish.

Cif said, 'I am minded to experience your love fully tonight. Yet not as fully, mind you, as to wish that we fashion a daughter together.'

The Mouser said, 'I've seen the like of this made of thinnest leather well oiled.'

She said, 'Not as effectual, I believe.'

He said, 'To be sure, here, it would be something from a fish, this being Rime Isle. Tell me, did harbor master Groniger fashion this, as thrifty with the Isle's sperm as with its coins?' Then he nodded.

He reached over and drew her other foot up on his lap also. After saluting it similarly, he rested the side of his face on both her ankles and sighted up the narrow trough between her legs. 'I am minded,' he said dreamily but with a little growl in his voice, 'to embark on another slow and intensely watchful journey, mindful of every step, such as that by which I arrived at this house this evening.'

She nodded, wondering idly if the growl were Gusorio's, but it seemed too faint for that.

8

In the bow of a laden grainship sailing north from Lankhmar across the Inner Sea to the land of the Eight Cities, the Death of Fafhrd, who was tall and lank, dire as a steel scarecrow, said to his fellow passenger, 'This incarnation likes me and likes me not. 'Tis a balmy journey now but it'll be long and by all accounts cold as witchcunt at the end, albeit summer. Arth-Pulgh's a mean employer, and unlucky. Hand me a medlar from the sack.'

The Death of the Gray Mouser, lithe as a weasel and forever smiling, replied, 'No meaner nor no curster than Hamomel. Working for whom, however, is the pits. I've not yet shaken down to this persona, know not its likings. Reach your own apples.'

9

A week later, the evening being unseasonably balmy and Witches Moon at first quarter near the top of the sky, a hemispherical silver goblet brimful of stars and scattering them dimmed by moonwine all over the sky as it descended toward the lips of the west, drawn down by the same goddess who had lifted it, Afreyt and Fafhrd after supping alone at her violet-tinted pale house on Salthaven's northern edge were minded to wander across the great meadow in the direction of Elvenhold, a northward slanting slim rock spire two bowshots high, chimneyed and narrowly terraced, that thrust from the rolling fields almost a league away to the west.

'See how her tilt,' Fafhrd observed of that slender mountainlet, 'directs her at the dark boss of the Targe—' (naming the northernmost constellation in the Lankhmar heavens) '—as if she were granite arrow aimed at skytop by the gods of the underworld.'

'Tonight the earth is full of the heat of these gods' forges, pressing summer scents from spring flowers and grasses. Let's rest awhile,' Afreyt answered, and truly although it was not yet May Eve, the heavy air was more like Midsummer's. She touched his shoulder and sank to the herby sward.

After a stare around the horizon for any sky wanderer on verge of rise or set, Fafhrd seated himself by her right side. A low lurhorn sounded faintly from the town behind them or the sea beyond that.

'Night fishers summoning the finny ones,' he hazarded.

'I dreamed last night,' she said, 'that a beast thing came out of the sea and followed me dripping salt drops as I wandered through a dark wood. I could see its silver scales between the dark boles in the gloom. But I was not afeared, and it in turn seemed to respond to this cue, for the longer it followed me the less it became like a beast and the more like a seaperson, and come not to work a hurt on me but to warn me.'

'Of what?' and when she was silent, 'Its sex?'

'Why, female—' she answered at once, but then becoming doubtful '—I think. Had it sex? I wonder why I did not wait for it to catch up, or perhaps turn sudden and walk toward it? I think I felt, did I so, and although I feared it not, it would turn to a beast again, a deep-voiced beast.'

'I too dreamed strangely last night, and my dream strangely chimed with yours, or was it by day I dreamed? For I have begun to do that,' Fafhrd announced, dropping himself back at full length on the springy sward, the better to observe the seven spiralled stars of the Targe. 'I dreamt I was pent in the greatest of castles with a million dark rooms in it, and that I searched for Gusorio (for that old legend between the Mouser and me is sometimes more than a joke) because I'd been solemnly told, perchance in a dream within the dream, that he had a message for me.'

She turned and leaned over him, her eyes staring deep into his as she listened. Her palely golden hair fell forward in two sweeping smooth cascades over her shoulders. He readjusted his position slightly so that five of the stars of Targe rose in a semicircle from her forehead (his eyes straying now and again toward her shadowed throat and the silver cord lacing together the sides of her violet bodice) and he continued, 'In the twelve times twelve times twelfth room there stood at the far door a figure clad all in silver-scale mail (there's our dreams chiming) but its back was toward me and the longer I looked at it, the taller and skinnier it seemed than Gusorio should be. Nevertheless I cried out to it aloud and in the very instant of my calling knew that I'd made an irreparable mistake and that my voice would work a hideous change in it and to my harm. See, our dreams clink again? But then, as it started to turn, I awoke. Dearest princess, did you know that the Targe crowns you?' And his right hand moved toward the silver bow drooping below her throat as she bent down to kiss him.

But as he enjoyed those pleasures and their continuations and proliferations while the moon sank, which pleasures were greatly enhanced by their starry background, the far ecstasies complementing the near, he marvelled how these nights he seemed to be walking at once toward brightest life and darkest death, while through it all Elvenhold loomed in the low distance.

10

'No question on it, Captain Mouser's changed,' Pshawri said with certainty, yet also amazedly and apprehensively, to his fellow lieutenant Mikkidu as they tippled together two evenings later in a small booth of the Sea Wrack. 'Here's yet another example if 't be needed. You know the care he has for our grub, to see that cookie doesn't poison us. Normally he'll taste a spoon of stew, say what it lacks or not, even order it dumped (that happened once, remember?) and go dancing off. Yet this very afternoon I spied him standing before the roiling soup kettle and staring into it for as long as it takes to stow *Flotsam's* mainsail and then rig it again, watching it bubble and seethe with greatest interest, the beans and fish flakes bobbing and the turnips and carrots turning over, as though he were reading there auguries and prognostics on the fate of the world!'

Mikkidu nodded. 'Or else he's trotting about bent over like Mother Grum, seeing things even an ant ignores. He had me stooping about after him over a route that could have been the plan of a maze, pointing out in turn a tangle of hair combings, a penny, a pebble, a parchment scrap scribbled with runic, mouse droppings, and a dead cockroach.'

'Did he make you eat it?' asked Pshawri.

Mikkidu shook his head wonderingly. 'No chewings . . . and no chewings out either. He only said at the end, when my legs had started to cramp, "I want you to keep these matters in mind in the future."'

'And meantime Captain Fafhrd—'

The two semi-rehabilitated thieves looked up. Skor from the next booth had thrust over his balding head, worry-wrinkled, which now loomed above them. '—is so busy keeping watch on the stars by night – and by day too, somehow – that it's a wonder he can navigate Salthaven without breaking his neck. Think you some evil wight has put a spell on both?'

Normally the Mouser's and Fafhrd's men were mutually rivalrous, suspicious, and disparaging of each other. It was a measure of their present concern for their captains that they pooled their knowledge and took frank counsel together.

Pshawri shrugged as hugely as one so small was able. 'Who knows? 'Tis such footling matters, and yet . . .'

'Chill ills abound here,' Mikkidu intoned. 'Khahkht the Wizard of Ice, Stardock's ghost fliers, sunken Simorgya . . .'

II

At the same moment Cif and Afreyt, in the former's sauna, chatted together with even greater but more playful freedom. Afreyt confided with mock grandeur, 'I'll have you know that Fafhrd compared my niplets to stars.'

Cif chortled midst the steam and answered coarsely with mock pride, 'The Mouser likened my arse hole to one. *And* to the stem dimple of a pome. And his own intrusive member to a stiletto! Whate'er ails them doesn't show in bed.'

'Or does it?' Afreyt questioned laughingly. 'In my case, stars. In yours, fruits and cutlery too.'

12

As the Deaths of Fafhrd and the Mouser jounced on donkeyback at the tail of a small merchant troop to which they'd attached themselves travelling through the forested land of the Eight Cities from Kvarch Nar to Illik Ving, Witches Moon being full, the former observed, 'The trouble with these long incarnations as the death of another is that one begins to forget one's own proper persona and best interests, especially if one be a dedicated actor.'

'Not so, necessarily,' the other responded. 'Rather, it gives one a clear head (What head clearer than Death's?) to observe oneself dispassionately and examine without bias the terms of the contract under which one operates.'

'That's true enough,' Fafhrd's Death said, stroking his lean jaw while his donkey stepped along evenly for a change. 'Why think you this one talks so much of booty we may find?'

'Why else but that Arth-Pulgh and Hamomel expect there will be treasure on our intendeds or about them? There's a thought to warm the cold nights coming!'

'Yes, and raises a nice question in our order's law, whether we're being hired principally as assassins or robbers.'

'No matter that,' Death of the Mouser summed up. 'We know at least we must not hit the Twain until they've shown us where their treasure is.'

'Or treasures are, more like,' the other amended, 'if they distrust each other, as all sane men do.'

13

Coming in opposite directions around a corner behind Salt-haven's council hall after a sharp rain shower, the Mouser and Fafhrd bumped into each other because the one was bending down to inspect a new puddle while the other studied the clouds retreating from arrows of sunshine. After grappling together briefly with sharp growls that turned to sudden laughter, Fafhrd was shaken enough from his current preoccupations by this small surprise to note the look of puzzled and wondrous brooding that instantly replaced the sharp friendly grin on the Mouser's face – a look that was undersurfaced by a pervasive sadness.

His heart was touched and he asked, 'Where've you been keeping yourself, comrade? I never seem to see you to talk to these past days.'

''Tis true,' the Mouser replied with a sharp grimace, 'we do seem to be operating on different *levels*, you and I, in our movings around Salthaven this last moon-wax.'

'Yes, but where are your *feelings* keeping?' Fafhrd prompted.

Heart-touched in turn and momentarily impelled to seek to share deepest and least definable difficulties, the Mouser drew Fafhrd to the lane side and launched out, 'If you said I were homesick for Lankhmar, I'd call you a liar! Our jolly comrades and grand almost-friends there, yes, even those good not to be trusted female troopers in memory revered, and all their perfumed and painted blazonry of ruby (or mayhap emerald?) lips, delectable tits, exquisite genitalia, they draw me not a whit! Not even Sheelba with her deep diggings into my psyche, nor your spicedly garrulous Ning. Nor all the gorgeous palaces, piers, pyramids, and fanes, all that marble and cloud-capped biggery! But oh . . .' and the underlook of sadness and wonder became keen in his face as he drew Fafhrd closer, dropping his voice, ' . . . the *small things* – those, I tell you honest, *do* make me homesick, aye, yearningly so. The little street braziers, the lovely litter, as though each scrap were sequinned and bore hieroglyphs. The hennaed and the diamond-dusted footprints. I knew those things, yet I never looked at them closely enough, savoured the *details*. Oh, the thought of going back and counting the cobblestones in the Street of the Gods and fixing for ever in my memory the shape of each and tracing the course of the rivulets of rainy trickle between them! I'd want to be rat size again to do it properly, yes even ant size, oh, there is no end to this fascination with the small, the universe written in a pebble!'

And he stared desperately deep into Fafhrd's eyes to ascertain if that one had caught at least some shred of his meaning, but the big man whose questions had stirred him to speak from his inmost being had apparently lost the track himself somewhere, for his long face had gone blank again, blank with a faint touch of melancholia and eyes wandering doubtfully upward.

'Homesick for Lankhmar?' the big man was saying. 'Well, I do miss her stars, I must confess, her southern stars we cannot see from here. But oh . . .' And now *his* face and eyes fired for the brief span it took him to say the following words, '. . . the thought of the still more southern stars we've never seen! The untravelled southern continent below the Middle Sea. Godsland and Nehwon's life pole, and over 'em the stars a world of men have died and never seen. Yes, I am homesick for those lands indeed!'

The Mouser saw the flare in him dim and die. The Northerner shook his head. 'My mind wanders,' he said. 'There are a many of good enough stars here. Why carry worries afar? Their sorting is sufficient.'

'Yes, there are good pickings now here along Hurricane Street and Salt, and leave the gods to worry over themselves,' the Mouser heard himself say as his gaze dropped to the nearest puddle. He felt *his* flare die – if it had ever been. 'Things will shake down, get done, sort themselves out, and feelings too.'

Fafhrd nodded and they went their separate ways.

14

And so time passed on Rime Isle. Witches Moon grew full and waned and gave way to Ghosts Moon, which lived its wraith-short life in turn, and Midsummer Moon was born, sometimes called Murderers Moon because its full runs low and is the latest to rise and earliest to set of all full moons, not high and long like the full moons of winter.

And with the passage of time things did shake down and some of them got done and sorted out after a fashion, meaning mostly that the out of the way became the commonplace with repetition, as it has a way of doing.

Sea Hawk got fully repaired, even refitted, but Fafhrd's and Afreyt's plan to sail her to Ool Plerns and fell timber there for wood-poor Rime Isle got pushed into the future. No one said, 'Next summer,' but the thought was there.

And the barracks and warehouse got built, including a fine drainage system and a cesspool of which the Mouser was inordinately proud, but repairs to *Flotsam*, though hardly languishing, went slow, and Cif's and his plan to cruise her east and trade with the Ice Gnomes north of No-Ombrulsk even more visionary.

Mog, Kos, and Issek's peculiar curses continued to shape much of the Twain's behaviour (to the coarse-grained amusement of those small-time gods), but not so extremely as to interfere seriously with their ability to boss their men effectively or be sufficiently amusing, gallant, and intelligent with their female co-mates. Most of their men soon catalogued it under the heading 'captains' eccentricities', to be griped at or boasted of equally but no further thought of. Skor, Pshawri, and Mikkidu did not accept it quite so easily and continued to worry and wonder now and then and entertain dark suspicions as befitted lieutenants, men who are supposedly learning to be as imaginatively responsible as captains. While on the other hand the Rime Islers, including the crusty and measuredly friendly Groniger, found it a good thing, indicative that these wild allies and would-be neighbours, questionable protégés of those head-strong freewomen Cif and Afreyt, were settling down nicely into law-abiding and hardheaded island ways. The Gray Mouser's concern with small material details particularly impressed them, according with their proverb: rock, wood, and flesh; all else a lie, or, more simply still: Mineral, Vegetable, Animal.

Afreyt and Cif knew there had been a change in the two men, all right, and so did our two heroes too, for that matter. But they were inclined to put it down to the weather or some deep upheaval of mood as had once turned Fafhrd religious and the Mouser calculatedly avaricious. Or else – who knows? – these might be the sort of things that happened to anyone who settled down. Oddly, neither considered the possibility of a curse, whether by god or sorcerer or witch. Curses were violent things that led men to cast themselves off mountaintops or dash their children's brains out against rocks, and women to castrate their bed partners and set fire to their own hair if there wasn't a handy volcano to dive into. The triviality and low intensity of the curses misled them.

When all four were together they talked once or twice of supernatural influences on human lives, speaking on the whole more lightly than each felt at heart.

'Why don't you ask augury of Great Gusorio?' Cif suggested. 'Since you are shards of him, he should know all about both of you.'

'He's more a joke than a true presence one might address a prayer to,' the Mouser parried, and then riposted, 'Why don't you or Afreyt appeal for enlightenment to that witch, or warrior-queen of yours, Skeldir, she of the silver-scale mail and the short dry laugh?'

'We're not on such intimate terms as that with her, though claiming her as ancestor,' Cif answered, looking down diffidently. 'I'd hardly know how to go about it.'

Yet that dialogue led Afreyt and Fafhrd to recount the dreams they'd previously shared only with each other. Whereupon all four indulged in inconclusive speculations and guesses. The Mouser and Fafhrd promptly forgot those, but Cif and Afreyt stored them away in memory.

And although the curses on the Twain were of low intensity, the divine vituperations worked steadily and consumingly. Examples: Fafhrd became much interested in a dim hairy star low in the west that seemed to be slowly growing in brightness and luxuriance of mane and to be moving east against the current, and he made a point of observing it early each eve. While it was noticed that the busily peering Captain Mouser had a favourite route for checking things out that led from the Sea Wrack, where he'd have a morning nip, to the low point in the lane outside, to the windy corner behind the council hall where he'd collided with Fafhrd, to his men's barracks, and by way of the dormitory's closet, which he'd open and check for mouseholes, to his own room and shelved closet and to the kitchen and pantry, and so to the cesspool behind them of which he was so proud.

So life went on tranquilly, busily, unenterprisingly in and around Salthaven as spring gave way to Rime Isle's short sharp summer. Their existence was rather like that of industrious lotus eaters, the others taking their cues from the bemused and somewhat absentminded Twain. The only exception to this most regular existence promised to be the day of Midsummer Eve, a traditional Isle holiday, when at the two women's suggestion they planned a feast for all hands (and special Isle friends and associates) in the Great Meadow at Elvenhold's foot, a sort of picnic with dancing and games and athletic competitions.

15

If any could be said to have spent an unpleasant or unsatisfactory time during this period, it was the wizards Sheelba and Ningauble. The cosmic din had quieted down sufficiently for them to be able to communicate pretty well between the one's swamp hut and the other's cave and get some confused inkling of what Fafhrd and the Mouser and their gods were up to, but none of that inkling sounded very logical to them or favorable to their plot. The stupid provincial gods had put some unintelligible sort of curse on their two pet errand boys, and it was working after a fashion, but Mouser and Fafhrd hadn't left Rime Isle, nothing was working out according to the two wizards' wishes, while a disquieting adverse influence they could not identify was moving northwest across the Cold Waste north of the Land of the Eight Cities and the Trollstep Mountains. All very baffling and unsatisfactory.

16

At Illik Ving the Death of the Twain joined a caravan bound for No-Ombrulsk, changing their mounts for shaggy Mingol ponies inured to frost, and spent all of Ghosts Moon on that long traverse. Although early summer, there was sufficient chill in the Trollsteps and the foothills of the Bones of the Old Ones and in the plateau of the Cold Waste that lies between these ranges for them to refer frequently to the seed bags of brazen apes and the tits of witches, and hug the cookfire while it lasted, and warm their sleep with dreams of the treasures their intendeds had laid up.

'I see this Fafhrd as a gold-guarding dragon in a mountain cave,' his Death averred. 'I'm into his character fully now, I feel. And on to it too.'

'While I dream the Mouser as a fat gray spider,' the other echoed, 'with silver, amber, and leviathan ivory cached in a score of nooks, crannies, and corners he scuttles between. Yes, I can play him now. And play with him too. Odd, isn't it, how like we get to our intendeds at the end?'

Arriving at last at the stone-towered seaport, they took lodgings at an inn where badges of the Slayers' Brotherhood were recognized, and they slept for two nights and a day, recuperating. Then Mouser's Death went for a stroll down by the docks, and when he returned, announced, 'I've taken passage for us in an Ool Krut trader. Sails with the tide day after morrow.'

'Murderers Moon begins well,' his wraith-thin comrade observed from where he still lay abed.

'At first the captain pretended not to know of Rime Isle, called it a legend, but when I showed him the badge and other things, he gave up that shipmasters' conspiracy of keeping Salthaven and western ports beyond a trade secret. By the by, our ship's called the *Good News*.'

491

'An auspicious name,' the other, smiling, responded. 'Oh Mouser, and oh Fafhrd, dear, your twin brothers are hastening toward you.'

17

After the long morning twilight that ended Midsummer Eve's short night, Midsummer Day dawned chill and misty in Salthaven. Nevertheless, there was an early bustling around the kitchen of the barracks, where the Mouser and Fafhrd had taken their repose, and likewise at Afreyt's house, where Cif and their nieces May, Mara, and Gale had stayed overnight.

Soon the fiery sun, shooting his rays from the northeast as he began his longest loop south around the sky, had burnt the milky mist off all Rime Isle and showed her clear from the low roofs of Salthaven to the central hills, with the leaning tower of Elvenhold in the near middle distance and the Great Meadow rising gently toward it.

And soon after that an irregular procession set out from the barracks. It wandered crookedly and leisurely through town to pick up the men's women, chiefly by trade, at least in their spare time, sailorwives, and other island guests. The men took turns dragging a cart piled with hampers of barley cakes, sweetbreads, cheese, roast mutton and kid, fruit conserves and other Island delicacies, while at its bottom, packed in snow, were casks of the Isle's dark bitter ale. A few men blew woodflutes and strummed small harps.

At the docks Groniger, festive in holiday black, joined them with the news. 'The *Northern Star* out of Ool Plerns came in last even to No-Ombrulsk. I spoke with her master and he said the *Good News* out of Ool Krut was at last report sailing for Rime Isle one or two mornings after him.'

At this point Ourph the Mingol begged off from the party, protesting that the walk to Elvenhold would be too much for his old bones and a new crick in his left ankle, he'd rest them in the sun here, and they left him squatting his skinny frame on the warming stone and peering steadily out to sea past where *Sea*

Hawk, *Flotsam*, *Northern Star*, and other ships rode at anchor among the Island fishing sloops.

Fafhrd said to Groniger, 'I've been here a year and more and it still wonders me that Salthaven is such a busy port while the rest of Nehwon goes on thinking Rime Isle is a legend. I know *I* did for a half lifetime.'

'Legends travel on rainbow wings and sport gaudy colours,' the harbormaster answered him, 'while truth plods on in sober garb.'

'Like yourself?'

'Aye,' Groniger grunted happily.

'And 'tis not a legend to the captains, guild masters, and kings who profit by it,' the Mouser put in. 'Such do most to keep legends alive.' The little man (though not little at all among his corps of thieves) was in a merry mood, moving from group to group and cracking wise and gay to all and sundry.

Skullick, Skor's sub-lieutenant, struck up a berserk battle chant and Fafhrd found himself singing an Ilthmar sea chanty to it. At their next pickup point tankards of ale were passed out to them. Things grew jollier.

A little ways out into the Great Meadow, where the thoroughfare led between fields of early ripening Island barley, they were joined by the feminine procession from Afreyt's. These had packed their contribution of toothsome edibles and tastesome potables in two small red carts drawn by stocky white bearhounds big as small men but gentle as lambs. And they had been augmented by the sailorwives and fisherwomen Hilsa and Rill, whose gift to the feast was jars of sweet-pickled fish. Also by the witch-woman Mother Grum, as old as Ourph but hobbling along stalwartly, never known to have missed a feast in her life's long history.

They were greeted with cries and new singings, while the three girls ran to play with the children the larger procession had inevitably accumulated on its way through town.

Fafhrd went back for a bit to quizzing Groniger about the ships that called at Salthaven port, flourishing for emphasis the hook that was his left hand. 'I've heard it said, and seen some evidence for it too, myself, that some of them hail from ports that are nowhere on Nehwon seas I know of.'

'Ah, you're becoming a convert to the legends,' the black-clad man told him. Then, mischievously, 'Why don't you try casting the ships' horoscopes with all you've learned of stars of late, naked and hairy ones?' He frowned. 'Though there was a black cutter with a white line that watered here three days ago whose home port I wish I could be surer of. Her master put me off from going below, and her sails didn't look enough for her hull. He said she hailed from Sayend, but that's a seaport we've had reliable word that the Sea-Mingols burned to ash less than two years agone. He knew of that, he claimed. Said it was much exaggerated. But I couldn't place his accent.'

'You see?' Fafhrd told him. 'As for horoscopes, I have neither skill nor belief in astrology. My sole concern is with the stars themselves and the patterns they make. The hairy star's most interesting! He grows each night. At first I thought him a rover, but he keeps his place. I'll point him out to you come dark.'

'Or some other evening when there's less drinking,' the other allowed grudgingly. 'A wise man is suspicious of his interests other than the most necessary. They breed illusions.'

The groupings kept changing as they walked, sang, and danced – and played – their way up through the rustling grass. Cif took advantage of this mixing to seek out Pshawri and Mikkidu. The Mouser's two lieutenants had at first been suspicious of her interest in and influence over their captain – a touch of jealousy, no doubt – but honest dealing and speaking, the evident genuineness of her concern, and some furtherance of Pshawri's suit to an Island woman had won them over, so that the three thought of themselves in a limited way as confederates.

'How's Captain Mouser these days?' she asked them lightly. 'Still running his little morning checkup route?'

'He didn't today,' Mikkidu told her.

'While yesterday he ran it in the afternoon,' Pshawri amplified. 'And the day before that he missed.'

Mikkidu nodded.

'I don't fret about him o'er much,' she smiled at them, 'knowing he's under watchful and sympathetic eyes.'

And so with mutual buttering up and with singing and dancing the augmented holiday band arrived at the spot just south of Elvenhold that they'd selected for their picnic. A

494

portion of the food was laid out on white sheeted trestles, the drink was broached, and the competitions and games that comprised an important part of the day's programme were begun. These were chiefly trials of strength and skill, not of endurance, and one trial only, so that a reasonable or even somewhat unreasonable amount of eating and drinking didn't tend to interfere with performance too much.

Between the contests were somewhat less impromptu dancings than had been footed earlier: Island stamps and flings, old-fashioned Lankhmar sways, and kicking and bouncing dances copied from the Mingols.

Knife-throwing came early – 'so none will be mad drunk as yet, a sensible precaution,' Groniger approved.

The target was a yard section of mainland tree trunk almost two yards thick, lugged up the previous day. The distance was fifteen long paces, which meant two revolutions of the knife, the way most contestants threw. The Mouser waited until last and then threw underhand as a sort of handicap, or at least seeming handicap, against himself, and his knife embedded deeply in or near the centre, clearly a better shot than any of the earlier successful ones, whose points of impact were marked with red chalk.

A flurry of applause started, but then it was announced that Cif had still to throw; she'd entered at the last possible minute. There was no surprise at a woman entering; that sort of equality was accepted on the Isle.

'You didn't tell me beforehand you were going to,' the Mouser said to her.

She shook her head at him, concentrating on her aim. 'No, leave his dagger in,' she called to the judges. 'It won't distract me.'

She threw overhand and her knife impacted itself so close to his that there was a *klir* of metal against metal along with the woody *thud*. Groniger measured the distances carefully with his beechwood ruler and proclaimed Cif the winner.

'And the measures on this ruler are copied from those on the golden Rule of Prudence in the Island treasury,' he added impressively, but later qualified this by saying, 'Actually, my ruler's more accurate than that ikon; doesn't expand with heat and contract with cold as metals do. But some people don't like to keep hearing me say that.'

'Do you think her besting the Captain is good for discipline and all?' Mikkidu asked Pshawri in an undertone, his new trust in Cif wavering.

'Yes, I do!' that one whispered back. 'Do the Captain good to be shook up a little, what with all this old-man scurrying and worrying and prying and pointing out he's going in for.' *There*, he thought, *I've spoken it out to someone at last, and I'm glad I did!*

Cif smiled at the Mouser. 'No, I didn't tell you ahead of time,' she said sweetly, 'but I've been practicing – privately. Would it have made a difference?'

'No,' he said slowly, 'though I might have had second thoughts about throwing underhand. Are you planning to enter the slinging contest too?'

'No, never a thought of it,' she answered. 'Whatever made you think I might?'

Later the Mouser won that one, both for distance and accuracy, making the latter cast so powerful that it not only holed the centre of the bull's-eye into the padded target box but went through the heavier back of the latter as well. Cif begged for the battered slug as a souvenir, and he presented it to her with elaborate flourishes.

''Twould have pierced the cuirass of Mingsward!' Mikkidu fervently averred.

The archery contests were beginning, and Fafhrd was fitting the iron tang in the middle of his bow into the hardwood heading of the leather stall that covered half his left forearm, when he noted Afreyt approaching. She'd doffed her jacket, for the sun was beating down hotly, and was wearing a short-sleeved violet blouse, blue trousers wide-belted with a gold buckle, and purple-dyed short holiday boots. A violet hand-kerchief confined a little her pale gold hair. A worn quiver with one arrow in it hung from her shoulder, and she was carrying a big longbow.

Fafhrd's eyes narrowed a bit at those, recalling Cif and the knife throwing. But 'You look like a pirate queen,' he greeted her, and then only inquired, 'You're entering one of the contests?'

'I don't know,' she said with a shrug. 'I'll watch along through the first.'

'That bow,' he said casually, 'looks to me to have a very heavy pull, and tall as you are, to be a touch long for you.'

'Right on both counts,' she agreed, nodding. 'It belonged to my father. You'd be truly startled, I think, to see how I managed to draw it as a stripling girl. My father would doubtless have spanked me soundly if he'd ever caught me at it, or rather lived long enough to do that.'

Fafhrd lifted his eyebrows inquiringly, but the pirate queen vouchsafed no more. He won the distance shot handily but lost the target shot (through which Afreyt also watched) by a finger's breadth to Skor's other sub-lieutenant, Mannimark.

Then came the high shot, which was something special to Midsummer Day on Rime Isle and generally involved the loss of the contestant's arrow, for the target was a grassy, nearly vertical stretch on the upper half of the south face of Elvenhold. The north face of the slanting rock tower actually overhung the ground a little and was utterly barren, but the south face, though very steep, sloped enough to hold soil to support herbage, rather miraculously. The contest honoured the sun, which reached this day his highest point in the heavens, while the contesting arrows, identified by coloured rags of thinnest silk attached to their necks, emulated him in their efforts.

Then Afreyt stepped forward, kicked off her purple boots and rolled up her blue trousers above her knees. She plucked her arrow, which bore a violet silk, from her quiver and threw that aside. 'Now I'll reveal to you the secret of my girlish technique,' she said to Fafhrd.

Quite rapidly she sat down facing the dizzy slope, set the bow to her bare feet, laying the arrow between her big toes and holding it and the string with both hands, rolled back onto her shoulders, straightened her legs smoothly, and loosed her shot.

It was seen to strike the slope near Fafhrd's yellow, skid a few yards higher, and then lie there, a violet taunt.

Afreyt, bending her legs again, removed the bow from her feet, and rolling sharply forward, stood up in the same motion.

'You practiced that,' Fafhrd said, hardly accusingly, as he finished screwing the hook back in the stall on his left arm.

She nodded. 'Yes, but only for half a lifetime.'

'The lady Afreyt's arrow didn't stick in,' Skullick pointed out. 'Is that fair? A breath of wind might dislodge it.'

'Yes, but there is no wind and it somehow got highest,' Groniger pointed out to him. 'Actually, it's accounted lucky in the high shot if your arrow doesn't embed itself. Those that don't sometimes are blown down. Those that do stay up there are never recovered.'

'Doesn't someone go up and collect the arrows?' Skullick asked.

'Scale Elvenhold? Have you wings?'

Skullick eyed the rock tower and shook his head sheepishly. Fafhrd overheard Groniger's remarks and gave the harbormaster an odd look but made no other comment at the time.

Afreyt invited both of them over to the red dogcarts and produced a jug of Ilthmar brandy, and they toasted her and Fafhrd's victories – the Mouser's too, and Cif's, who happened along.

'This'll put feathers in your wings!' Fafhrd told Groniger, who eyed him thoughtfully.

The children were playing with the white bear-hounds. Gale had won the girls' archery contest and May the short race.

Some of the younger children were becoming fretful, however, and shadows were lengthening. The games and contests were all over now, and partly as a consequence of that the drinking was heavying up as the last scraps of food were being eaten. Among the whole picnic group there seemed to be a feeling of weariness, but also (for those no longer very young but not yet old) new jollity, as though one party were ending and another beginning. Cif's and Afreyt's eyes were especially bright. Everyone seemed ready to go home, though whether to their own places or the Sea Wrack was a matter of age and temperament. There was a chill breath in the air.

Gazing east and down a little toward Salthaven and the harbour beyond, the Mouser opined that he could already see low mist gathering around the bare masts there, and Groniger confirmed that. But what was the small lone dark figure trudging up-meadow toward them in the face of the last low sunlight?

'Ourph, I'll be bound,' said Fafhrd. 'What's led him to make the hike after all?'

But it was hard to be sure the big Northerner was right; the figure was still far off. Yet the signal for leaving had been given, things were gathered, the carts repacked, and all set out, most staying near the carts, from which drinks continued to be forthcoming. And perhaps these were responsible for a resumption of the morning's impromptu singing and dancing, though now it was not Fafhrd and the Mouser but others who took the lead in this. The Twain, after a whole day of behaving like old times, were slipping back under the curses they knew not of, the one's eyes forever on the ground, with the effect of old age unsure of its footing, the other's on the sky, indicative of old age's absentmindedness.

Fafhrd turned out to be right about the up-meadow trudger, but it was few words they got from Ourph as to why he'd made the hike he'd earlier begged off from.

The old Mingol said only to them, and to Groniger, who happed to be by, 'The *Good News* is in.' Then, eyeing the Twain more particularly, 'Tonight stay away from the Sea Wrack.'

But he would answer nothing more to their puzzled queries save 'I know what I know and I've told it,' and two cups of brandy did not loosen his Mingol tongue one whit.

The encounter put them behind the main party, but they did not try to catch up. The sun had set some time back, and now their feet and legs were lapped by the ground mist that already covered Salthaven and into which the picnic party was vanishing, its singing and strumming already sounding tiny and far off.

'You see,' Groniger said to Fafhrd, eyeing the twilit but yet starless sky while the mist lapped higher around them, 'you won't be able to show me your bearded star tonight in any case.'

Fafhrd nodded vaguely but made no answer save to pass the brandy jug as they footed it along: four men walking deeper and deeper, as it were, into a white silence.

18

Cif and Afreyt, very much caught up in the gaiety of the evening party, and bright-eyed drunk besides, were among the first to enter the Sea Wrack and encounter arresting silence of another sort, and almost instantly come under the strange, hushing spell of the scene there.

Fafhrd and the Mouser sat at their pet table in the low-walled booth playing backgammon, and the whole tavern frightenedly watched them while pretending not to. Fear was in the air.

That was the first impression. Then, almost at once, Cif and Afreyt saw that Fafhrd couldn't be Fafhrd, he was much too thin; nor the Mouser the Mouser, much too plump (though every bit as agile and supple-looking, paradoxically).

Nor were the faces and clothing and accouterments of the two strangers anything really like the Twain's. It was more their expressions and mannerisms, postures and general manner, self-confident manner, those and the fact of *being at that table*. The sublime impression the two of them made that they were who they were and that they were in their rightful place.

And the fear that radiated from them with the small sounds of their gaming: the muted rattle of shaken bone dice in one or the other's palm-closed leather cup, the muted clatter as the dice were spilled into one or other of the two low-walled felt-lined compartments of the backgammon box, the sharp little clicks of the bone counters as they were shifted by ones and twos from point to point. The fear that riveted the attention of everyone else in the place no matter how much they pretended to be understanding the conversations they made, or tasting the drinks they swallowed, or busying themselves with little tavern chores. The fear that seized upon and recruited each picnic newcomer. Oh yes, this night something deadly was coiling here at the Sea Wrack, make no mistake about it.

So paralysing was the fear that it cost Cif and Afreyt a great effort to sidle slowly from the doorway to the bar, their eyes never leaving that one little table that was for now the world's hub, until they were as close as they could get to the Sea

Wrack's owner, who with downcast and averted eye was polishing the same mug over and over.

'Keeper, what gives?' Cif whispered to him softly but most distinctly. 'Nay, sull not up. Speak, I charge you!'

Eagerly that one, as though grateful Cif's whiplash command had given him opportunity to discharge some of the weight of dread crushing him, whispered them back his tale in short, almost breathless bursts, though without raising an eye or ceasing to circle his rag.

'I was alone here when they came in, minutes after the *Good News* docked. They spoke no word, but as though the fat one were the lean one's hunting ferret, they *scented out* our two captains' table, sat themselves down at it as though they owned it, then spoke at last to call for drink.

'I took it them, and as they got out their box and dice cups and set up their game, they plied me with harmless-seeming and friendly questions mostly about the Twain, as if they knew them well. Such as: How fared they in Rime Isle? Enjoyed they good health? Seemed they happy? How often came they in? Their tastes in drink and food and the fair sex? What other interests had they? What did they like to talk of? As though the two of them were courtiers of some great foreign empire come hither our captains to please and to solicit about some affair of state.

'And yet, you know, so *dire* somehow were the tones in which those innocent questions were asked that I doubt I could have refused them if they'd asked me for the Twain's heart's blood or my own.

'This too: The more questions they asked about the Twain and the more I answered them as best I might, the more they came to look like . . . to resemble our . . . you know what I'm trying to say?'

'Yes, yes!' Afreyt hissed. 'Go on.'

'In short, I felt I was their slave. So too, I think, have felt all those who came into the Sea Wrack after them, save for old Mingol Ourph, who shortly stayed, somehow then parted.

'At last they sucked me dry, bent to their game, asked for more drink. I sent the girl with that. Since then it's been as you see now.'

There was a stir at the doorway through which mist was curling. Four men stood there, for a moment bemused. Then Fafhrd and the Mouser strode toward their table, while old Ourph settled down on his hams, his gaze unwavering, and Groniger almost totteringly sidled toward the bar, like a man surprised at midday by a sleepwalking fit and thoroughly astounded at it.

Fafhrd and the Mouser leaned over and looked down at the table and open backgammon box over which the two strangers were bent, surveying their positions. After a bit Fafhrd said rather loudly, 'A good rilk against two silver smerduke on the lean one! His stones are poised to fleet swiftly home.'

'You're on!' the Mouser cried back. 'You've underestimated the fat one's back game.'

Turning his chill blue eyes and flat-nosed skull-like face straight up at Fafhrd with an almost impossible twist of his neck, the skinny one said, 'Did the stars tell you to wager at such odds on my success?'

Fafhrd's whole manner changed. 'You're interested in the stars?' he asked with an incredulous hopefulness.

'Mightily so,' the other answered him, nodding emphatically.

'Then you must come with me,' Fafhrd informed him, almost lifting him from his stool with one fell swoop of his good hand and arm that at once assisted and guided, while his hook indicated the mist-filled doorway. 'Leave off this footling game. Abandon it. We've much to talk of, you and I.' By now he had a brotherly arm – the hooked one, this time – around the thin one's shoulders and was leading him back along the path he'd entered by. 'Oh, there are wonders and treasures un-dreamed amongst the stars, are there not?'

'Treasures?' the other asked coolly, pricking an ear but holding back a little.

'Aye, indeed! There's one in particular under the silvery asterism of the Black Panther that I lust to show you,' Fafhrd replied with great enthusiasm, at which the other went more willingly.

All watched astonishedly, but the only one who managed to speak out was Groniger, who asked, 'Where are you going, Fafhrd?' in rather outraged tones.

The big man paused for a moment, winked at Groniger, and smiling said, 'Flying.'

Then with a 'Come, comrade astronome,' and another great arm-sweep, he wafted the skinny one with him into the bulging white mist, where both men shortly vanished.

Back at the table the plump stranger said in loud but winning tones, 'Gentle sir! Would you care to take over my friend's game, continue it with me?' Then in tones less formal, 'And have you noticed that these mug dints on your table together with the platter burn make up the figure of a giant sloth?'

'Oh, so you've already seen that, have you?' the Mouser answered the second question, returning his gaze from the door. Then, to the first, 'Why, yes, I will, sir, and double the bet! – it being my die cast. Although your friend did not stay long enough even to arrange a chouette.'

'*Your* friend was most insistent,' the other replied. 'Sir, I take your bet.'

Whereupon the Mouser sat down and proceeded to shake a masterly sequence of double fours and double threes so that the skinny man's stones, now his own, fleeted more swiftly to victory than ever Fafhrd had predicted. The Mouser grinned fiendishly, and as they set up the stones for another game, he pointed out to his more thinly smiling adversary in the table-top's dints and stains the figure of a leopard stalking the giant sloth.

All eyes were now back on the table again save those of Afreyt. And of Fafhrd's lieutenant, Skor. Those four orbs were still fixed on the mist-bulging doorway through which Fafhrd had vanished with his strangely unlike doublegoer. Since babyhood Afreyt had heard of those doleful nightwalkers whose appearance, like the banshee's, generally betokened death or near mortal injury to the one whose shape they mocked.

Now while she agonized over what to do, invoking the witch queen Skeldir and lesser of her own and (in her extremity) others' private deities, there was a strange growling in her ears – perhaps her rushing blood. Fafhrd's last word to Groniger kindled in her memory the recollection of an exchange of words between those two earlier today, which in turn gave her a bright inkling of Fafhrd's present destination in the viewless fog. This in turn inspired her to break the grip upon her of fear's and indecision's paralysis. Her first two or three steps were short and effortful ones, but by the time she went through the doorway, she was taking swift giant strides.

Her example broke the dread-duty deadlock in Skor, and the lean, red-haired, balding giant followed her in a rush.

But few in the Sea Wrack except Ourph and perhaps Groniger noted either departure, for all gazes were fixed again on the one small table where now Captain Mouser in person contested with his dread were-brother, battling the Islanders' and his men's fears for them as it were. And whether by smashing attack, tortuous back game, or swift running one like the first, the Mouser kept winning again and again and again.

And still the games went on, as though the series might well outlast the night. The stranger's smile kept thinning. That was all, or almost all.

The only fly in this ointment of unending success was a nagging doubt, perhaps deriving from a growing languor on the Mouser's part, a lessening of his taunting joy at each new win, that destinies in the larger world would jump with those worked out in the little world of the backgammon box.

19

'We have reached the point in this night's little journey I'm taking you on where we must abandon the horizontal and embrace the vertical,' Fafhrd informed his comrade astronomer, clasping him familiarly about the shoulders with left arm, and wagging right forefinger before that cadaver face, while the white mist hugged them both.

The Death of Fafhrd fought down the impulse to squirm away with a hawking growl of disgust close to vomiting. He abominated being touched except by outstandingly beautiful females under circumstances entirely of his own commanding. And now for a full half-hour he had been following his drunken and crazy victim (sometimes much too closely for comfort, but that wasn't his own choosing, Arth forbid) through a blind fog, and mostly trusting the same madman to keep them from breaking their necks in holes and pits and bogs, and putting up with being touched and arm-gripped and back-slapped (often by that doubly disgusting hook that felt so like a weapon), and listening to a farrago of wild talk about long-haired asterisms and bearded stars and barley fields and sheep's grazing ground and hills and masts and trees and the mysterious southern continent until Arth himself couldn't have held it, so that it was only the madman's occasional remention of a treasure or treasures he was leading his Death to that kept the latter tagging along without plunging exasperated knife into his victim's vitals.

And at least the loathsome cleavings and enwrappings expressive of brotherly affection that he had made himself submit to had allowed him to ascertain in turn that his intended wore no undergarment of chain mail or plate or scale to interfere with the proper course of things when knife time came. So the Death of Fafhrd consoled himself as he broke away from the taller and heavier man under the legitimate and friendly excuse of more closely inspecting the rock wall they now faced at a distance of no more than four or five yards. Farther off the fog would have hid it.

'You say we're to climb this to view your treasure?' He couldn't quite keep his incredulity out of his voice.

'Aye,' Fafhrd told him.

'How high?' his Death asked him.

Fafhrd shrugged. 'Just high enough to get there. A short distance, truly.' He waved an arm a little sideways, as though dispensing with a trifle.

'There's not much light to climb by,' his Death said somewhat tentatively.

Fafhrd replied, 'What think you makes the mist whitely luminous an hour after sunset? There's enough light to climb by, never fear, and it'll get brighter as we go aloft. You're a climber, aren't you?'

'Oh, yes,' the other admitted diffidently, not saying that his experience had been gained chiefly in scaling impregnable towers and cyclopean poisoned walls behind which the wealthier and more powerful assassin's targets tended to hide themselves – difficult climbs, some of them, truly, but rather artificial ones, and all of them done in the line of business.

Touching the rough rock and seeing it inches in front of his somewhat blunted nose, the Death of Fafhrd felt a measurable repugnance to setting foot or serious hand on it. For a moment he was mightily minded to whip out dagger and end it instanter here with the swift upward jerk under the breastbone, or the shrewd thrust from behind at the base of the skull, or the well-known slash under the ear in the angle of the jaw. He'd never have his victim more lulled, that was certain.

Two things prevented him. One, he'd never had the feeling of having an audience so completely under his control as he'd had this afternoon and evening at the Sea Wrack. Or a victim so completely eating out of his hand, so walking to his own destruction, as they said in the trade. It gave him a feeling of being intoxicated while utterly sober, it put him into an 'I can do anything, I am God' mood, and he wanted to prolong that wonderful thrill as far as possible.

Two, Fafhrd's talk perpetually returning to treasure, and the way the invitation now to climb some small cliff to view it so fitted with his Cold Waste dreams of Fafhrd as a dragon guarding gold in a mountain cavern – these combined to persuade him that the Fates were taking a hand in tonight's happening, the youngest of them drawing aside veil and baring her ruby lips to him and soon the more private jewellery of her person.

'You don't have to worry about the rock, it's sound enough, just follow in my footsteps and my handholds,' Fafhrd said impatiently as he advanced to the cliff's face and mounted it, the hook making harsh metallic clashes.

His Death doffed the short cloak and hood he wore, took a deep breath and, thinking in a small corner of his mind, 'Well, at least this madman won't be able to fondle me more while we're climbing – I hope!' went up after him like a giant spider.

It was as well for Fafhrd that his Death (and the Mouser's too) had neglected to make close survey of the landscape and geography of Rime Isle during this afternoon's sail in. (They'd been down in their cabin mostly, getting into their parts.) Otherwise he might have known that he was now climbing Elvenhold.

20

Back in the Sea Wrack the Mouser threw a double six, the only cast that would allow him to bear off his last four stones and leave his opponent's sole remaining man stranded one point from home. He threw up the back of a hand to mask a mighty yawn and over it politely raised an inquiring eyebrow at his adversary.

The Death of the Mouser nodded amiably enough, though his smile had grown very thin-lipped indeed, and said, 'Yes, it's as well we write finished to my strivings. Was it eight games, or seven? No matter. I'll seek my revenge some other time. Fate is your girl tonight, cunt and arse hole, that much is proven.'

A collective sigh of relief from the onlookers ended the general silence. They felt the relaxation of tension as much as the two players, and to most of them it seemed that the Mouser in vanquishing the stranger had also dispersed all the strange fears that had been loose in the tavern earlier and running along their nerves.

'A drink to toast your victory, salve my defeat?' the Mouser's Death asked smoothly. 'Hot gahveh perhaps? With brandy in't?'

'Nay, sir,' the Mouser said with a bright smile, collecting together his several small stacks of gold and silver pieces and funnelling them into his pouch, 'I must take these bright fellows home and introduce 'em to their cellmates. Coins prosper best in prison, as my friend Groniger tells me. But, sir, would you not accompany me on that journey, help me escort 'em? We can drink there.' A brightness came into his eyes that had nothing whatever in common with a miser's glee. He continued, 'Friend who discerned the tree sloth and saw the black panther, we both know that there are mysterious treasures and matters of interest compared to which these clinking counters are no more than that. I yearn to show you some. You'll be intrigued.'

At the mention of 'treasure', his Death pricked up his ears much as his fellow assassin had at Fafhrd's speaking the word. Mouser's would-be nemesis had had his Cold Waste dreams too, his appetites whetted by the privations of long drear journeying, and by the infuriating losses he'd had to put up with tonight as well. And he too had the conviction that the Fates must be on his side tonight by now, though for the opposite reason. A man who'd been so incredibly lucky at backgammon was bound to be hit by a great bolt of unluck at whatever feat he next attempted.

'I'll come with you gladly,' he said softly, rising with the Mouser and moving with him toward the door.

'You'll not collect your dice and stones?' the one queried. ''Tis a most handsome box.'

'Let the tavern have it as a memorial of your masterly victory,' his Death replied negligently, with a sort of muted grandi-loquence. He tossed aside an imaginary blossom.

Ordinarily *that* would have been too much to the Mouser, arousing all his worst suspicions. Only rogues pretended to be *that* carelessly munificent. But the madness with which Mog had cursed him was fully upon him again, and he forgot the matter with a smile and a shrug.

'Trifles all,' he agreed.

In fact the manner of the two of them was so lightly casual for the moment, not to say la-di-da, that they might well have gotten out of the Sea Wrack and lost in the fog without anyone noticing, except of course for old Ourph, whose head turned slowly to watch the Mouser out the door, shook itself sadly, and then resumed its meditations or cogitations or whatever.

Fortunately there were those in the tavern deeply and intelligently concerned for the Mouser, and not bound by Mingolly fatalisms. Cif had no impulse to rush up to the Mouser upon his win. She'd had too strong a sense of something more than backgammon being at stake tonight, too lingering a conviction of something positively unholy about his were-adversary, and doubtless others in the tavern had shared those feelings. Unlike most of those, however, any relief she felt did not take her attention away from the Mouser for an instant. As he and his unwholesome doublegoer exited the doorway, she hurried to it.

Pshawri and Mikkidu were at her heels.

They saw the two ahead of them as dim blobs, shadows in the white mist, as it were, and followed only swiftly enough to keep them barely in sight. The shadows moved across and down the lane a bit, paused briefly, then went on until they were traveling along back of the building, made of gray timbers from wrecked ships, that was the council hall.

Their pursuers encountered no other fog venturers. The silence was profound, broken only by the occasional *drip-drip* of condensing mist and a few very brief murmurs of conversation from ahead, too soft and fleeting to make out. It was eerie.

At the next corner the shadows paused another while, then turned it.

'He's following his regular morning route,' Mikkidu whispered softly.

Cif nodded, but Pshawri gripped Mik's arm in warning, setting a finger to his lips.

But true enough to the second lieutenant's guess, they followed their quarry to the new-built barracks and saw the Mouser bow his doublegoer in. Pshawri and Mikkidu waited a bit, then took off their boots and entered in stocking feet most cautiously.

Cif had another idea. She stole along the side of the building, heading for the kitchen door.

Inside, the Mouser, who had uttered hardly a dozen words since leaving the Sea Wrack, pointed out various items to his guest and watched for his reactions.

Which threw his Death into a state of great puzzlement. His intended victim had spoken some words about a treasure or treasures, then taken him outside and with a mysterious look pointed out to him a low point in a lane. What could that mean? True, sunken ground sometimes indicated something buried there – a murdered body, generally. But who'd bury a treasure in the lane of a dinky northern seaport, or a corpse, for that matter? It didn't make sense.

Next the gray-clad baffler had gone through the same rigmarole at a corner behind a building of strangely weathered, heavy-looking wood. That had for a moment seemed to lead somewhere, for there'd been an opalescent something lodged in one of the big beams, its hue speaking of pearls and treasure. But when he'd stooped to study it, it had turned out to be only a worthless seashell, worked into the grey wood Arth knew how!

And now the riddlesome fellow, holding a lamp he'd lit, was standing in a bunkroom beside a closet he'd just opened. There didn't seem to be much of anything in it.

'Treasure?' the Mouser's Death breathed doubtfully, leaning forward to look more closely.

The Mouser smiled and shook his head. 'No. Mice holes,' he breathed back.

The other recoiled incredulously. Had the brains of the masterly backgammon player turned to mush? Had something in the fog stolen away his wits? Just what *was* happening here? Maybe he'd best out knife and slay at once, before the situation became too confusing.

But the Mouser, still smiling gleefully, as if in anticipation of wonders to behold, was beckoning with his free hand into a short hall and then a smaller room with two bunks only, while the lamp he held beside his head made shadows crawl around them and slip along the walls.

Facing his Death, he threw open the door of a wider closet, stretched himself to his fullest height and thrust his lamp aloft, as if to say, 'Lo!'

The closet contained at least a dozen shallow shelves smoothly surfaced with black cloth, and on them were very neatly arranged somewhere between a thousand and a myriad tiny objects, as if they were so many rare coins and precious gems. As if, yes . . . but as to what these objects really were . . . recall the nine oddments the Mouser had laid out on Cif's bed table three months past . . . imagine them multiplied by ten hundred . . . the booty of three months of ground peering . . . the loot of ninety days of floor delving . . . you'd have a picture of the strange collection the Mouser was displaying to his Death.

And as his Death leaned closer, running his gaze incredulously back and forth along the shelves, the triumphant smile faded from the Mouser's face and was replaced by the same look of desperate wondering he'd had on it when he told Fafhrd of yearning for the small things of Lankhmar.

21

'We've reached our picnic ground,' Afreyt told Skor as they strode through the mist. 'See how the sward is trampled. Now cast we about for Elvenhold.'

''Tis done, lady,' he replied as she moved off to the left, he to the right, 'but why are you so sure Captain Fafhrd went there?'

'Because he told Groniger he was going flying,' she called to him. 'Earlier Groniger had said that none could climb Elvenhold without wings.'

'But the Captain could,' Skor, taking her meaning, called back, 'for he's scaled Stardock,' thinking, though not saying aloud, *But that was before he lost a hand.*

Moments later he sighted vertical solidity and was calling out that he'd found what they were seeking. When Afreyt caught up with him by the rock wall, he added, 'I've also found proof that Fafhrd and the stranger did indeed come this way, as you deduced they would.'

And he held up to her the hooded cloak of Fafhrd's Death.

22

Fafhrd, followed closely by his Death, climbed out of the fog into a world of bone-white clarity. He faced away from the rock to survey it.

The top of the mist was a flat white floor stretching east and south to the horizon, unbroken by treetop, chimney or spire of Salthaven, or mast top in the harbour beyond. Overhead the night shone with stars somewhat dimmed by the light of the round moon, which seemed to rest on the mist in the southeast.

'The full of Murderers Moon,' he remarked oratorically, 'the shortest and the lowest running full of the year, and come pat on Midsummer's Day Night. I told you there'd be light enough to climb by.'

His Death below him savoured the appropriateness of the lunar situation but didn't care much for the light. He'd felt securer climbing in the fog with the height all hid. He was still enjoying himself, but now he wanted to get the killing done as soon as Fafhrd revealed where the cave or other treasure spot was.

Fafhrd faced around to the tower again. Soon they were edging up past the grassy stretch. He noted his white-flagged arrow and left it where it was, but when he came to Afreyt's he reached over precariously, snagged it with his hook, and tucked it in his belt.

'How much farther?' his Death called up.

'Just to the end of the grass,' Fafhrd called down. 'Then we traverse to the opposite edge of Elvenhold, where there's a shallow cave will give our feet good support as we view the treasure. Ah, but I'm glad you came with me tonight! I only hope the moon doesn't dim it too much.'

'How's that?' the other asked, a little puzzled, though considerably enheartened by the mention of a cave.

'Some jewels shine best by their own light alone,' Fafhrd replied somewhat cryptically. Clashing into the next hold, his hook struck a shower of white sparks. 'Must be flint in the rock hereabouts,' he observed. 'See, friend, minerals have many ways of making light. On Stardock the Mouser and I found diamonds of so clear a water they revealed their shape only in the dark. And there are beasts that shine, in particular glow wasps, diamondflies, firebeetles, and nightbees. I know, I've been stung by them. While in the jungles of Klesh I have encountered luminous flying spiders. Ah, we arrive at the traverse.' And he began to move sideways, taking long steps.

His Death copied him, hastening after. Footholds and handholds both seemed surer here, while back at the grass he'd twice almost missed a hold. Beyond Fafhrd he could see what he took to be the dark cave mouth at the end of this face of the rock pylon they'd mounted. Things seemed to be happening more quickly while simultaneously time stretched out for him – sure sign of climax approaching. He wanted no more talk – in particular, lectures on natural history! He loosened his long knife in its scabbard. Soon! Soon!

Fafhrd was preparing to take the step that would put him squarely in front of the shallow depression that looked at first sight like a cave mouth. He was aware that his comrade astronomer was crowding him. At that moment although the two of them were clearly alone on the face, he heard a short dry laugh, not in the voice of either of them, that nevertheless sounded as if it came from somewhere very close by. And somehow that laugh inspired or stung him into taking, instead of the step he'd planned, a much longer one that took him just past the seeming cave mouth and put his left foot on the end of the ledge, while his right hand reached for a hold beyond the shallow depression so that his whole body would swing out past the end of this face and he would hopefully see the bearded star which was currently his dearest treasure and which until this moment tonight Elvenhold itself had hid from him.

At the same moment his Death struck, who had perfectly anticipated his victim's every movement except the last inspired one. His dagger, instead of burying itself in Fafhrd's back, struck rock in the shallow depression and its blade snapped. Staggered by that and vastly surprised, he fought for balance.

Fafhrd, glancing back, perceived the treacherous attack and rather casually booted his threatener in the thigh with a free foot. By the bone-white light of Murderers Moon, the Death of Fafhrd fell off Elvenhold and, glancingly striking the very steep grassy slope once or twice, was silhouetted momentarily, long limbs writhing, against the floor of white fog before the latter swallowed him up and the scream he'd started. There was a distant *thud* that nevertheless had a satisfying finality to it.

Fafhrd swung out again around the end of the cliff. Yes, his bearded star, though dimmed by the moonlight, was definitely discernible. He enjoyed it. The pleasure was, somewhat re- motely, akin to that of watching a beautiful girl undress in almost dark.

'Fafhrd!' Then again, 'Fafhrd!'

Skor's shout, by Kos, he told himself. And Afreyt's! He pulled himself back on the ledge and, securely footed there, called, 'Ahoy! Ahoy below!'

Back at the barracks things were moving fast and very nervously, notably on the part of the Mouser's Death. He almost dirked the vaunting idiot on sheer impulse in overpowering disgust at being shown that incredible mouse's museum of trash as though it were a treasure of some sort. Almost, but then he heard a faint shuffling noise that seemed to originate in the building they were in, and it never did to slay when witnesses might be nigh, were there another course to take.

He watched the Mouser, who looked somewhat disappointed now (had the idiot expected to be praised for his junk display?), shut the closet door and beckon him back into the short hall and through a third door. He followed, listening intently for any repetition of the shuffling noise or other sound. The moving shadows the lamp cast were a little unnerving now; they suggested lurkers, hidden observers. Well, at least the idiot hadn't deposited in his trash closet the gold and silver coins he'd won this night, so presumably there was still hope of seeing their 'cell mates' and some real treasure.

Now the Mouser was pointing out, but in a somewhat perfunctory way, the features of what appeared to be a rather well-appointed kitchen: fireplaces, ovens, and so forth. He rapped a couple of large iron kettles, but without any great enthusiasm, sounding their dull, sepulchral tones.

His manner quickened a little, however, and the ghost at least of a gleeful smile returned to his lips as he opened the back door and went out into the mist, signing for his Death to follow him. That one did so, outwardly seeming relaxed, inwardly alert as a drawn knife, poised for any action.

Almost immediately the Mouser stooped, grasped a ring, and heaved up a small circular trapdoor, meanwhile holding his lamp aloft, its beams reflecting whitely from the fog but not helping vision much. The Mouser's Death, his nerves tortured beyond endurance, whipped out his dirk and next fell dead across the cesspool mouth with Cif's dagger in his ear, thrown from where she stood against the wall hardly a dozen feet away.

And somewhere, along with these actions, there were a brief

growl and a short dry laugh. But those were things Cif and the Mouser claimed afterward to have heard. At the present moment there was only the Mouser still holding his lamp and peering down at the corpse and saying as Cif and Pshawri and Mikkidu rushed up to him, 'Well, he'll never get his revenge for tonight's gaming, that's for certain. Or do ghosts ever play backgammon, I wonder? I've heard of them contesting parties at chess with living mortals, by Mog.'

24

Next day at the council hall Groniger presided over a brief but well-attended inquest into the demise of the two passengers on the *Good News*. Badges and other insignia about their persons suggested they were members not only of the Lankhmar Slayers Brotherhood, but also of the even more cosmopolitan Assassins Order. Under close questioning, the captain of the *Good News* admitted knowing of this circumstance and was fined for not reporting it to the Rime Isle harbormaster immediately on making port. A bit later Groniger found that they were murderous rogues, doubtless hired by foreign parties unknown, and that they had been rightly slain on their first attempts to practise their nefarious trade on Rime Isle.

But afterward he told Cif, 'It's as well that you slew him, and with his dagger in his hand. That way, none can say it was a feuding of newcomers to the Isle with foreigners their presence attracted here. And that you, Afreyt, were close witness to the other's death.'

'I'll say I was!' that lady averred. 'He came down not a yard from us – eh, Skor? – almost braining us. And with his hand death-gripping his broken dagger. Fafhrd, in future you should be more careful of how you dispose of your corpses.'

When questioned about the cryptic warning he'd brought the Mouser and Fafhrd, old Ourph vouched, 'The moment I heard the name *Good News* I knew it was an ill-omened ship, bearing watching. And when the two strangers came off and went into the Sea Wrack, I perceived them as dressed up, slightly luminous skeletons only, with bony hands and eyeless sockets.'

'Did you see their corpses at the inquest so?' Groniger asked him.

'No, then they were but dead meat, such as all living become.'

25

In Godsland the three concerned deities, somewhat shocked by the final turn of events and horrified to see how close they'd come to losing their chief remaining worshippers, lifted their curses from them as rapidly as they were able. Other concerned parties were slower to get the news and to believe it. The Assassins Order posted the two Deaths as 'delayed' rather than 'missing', but prepared to make what compensation might be unavoidable to Arth-Pulgh and Hamomel. While Sheelba and Ningauble, considerably irked, set about devising new strategems to procure the return of their favourite errand boys and living touchstones.

26

The instant the gods lifted their curses, the Mouser's and Fafhrd's strange obsessions vanished. It happened while they were together with Afreyt and Cif, the four of them lunching al fresco at Cif's. The only outward sign was that the Twain's eyes widened incredulously as they stared and then smiled at nothing.

'What deliciously outrageous idea has occurred to you two?' Afreyt demanded, while Cif echoed, 'You're right! And it has to be something like that. We know you two of yore!'

'Is it that obvious?' the Mouser inquired, while Fafhrd fumbled out, 'No, it's nothing like that. It's . . . No, you've all got to hear this. You know that thing about stars I've been having? Well, it's gone!' He lifted his eyes. 'By Issek, I can look at the blue sky now without having it covered with the black flyspecks of the stars that would be there now if it were dark!'

'By Mog!' the Mouser exploded. 'I had no idea, Fafhrd, that your little madness was so like mine in the tightness of its grip.

For I no longer feel the compulsion to try to peer closely at every tiny object within fifty yards of me. It's like being a slave who's set free.'

'No more ragpicking, eh?' Cif said. 'No more bent-over inspection tours?'

'No, by Mog,' the Mouser asserted, then qualified that with a 'Though of course little things can be quite as interesting as big things; in fact, there's a whole tiny world of—'

'Uh-uh, you better watch out,' Cif interrupted, holding up a finger.

'And the stars too are of considerable interest, my unnatural infatuation with 'em aside,' Fafhrd said stubbornly.

Afreyt asked, 'What do you think it was, though? Do you think some wizard cast a spell on you? Perchance that Ningauble you told me of, Fafhrd?'

Cif said, 'Yes, or that Sheelba you talk of in your sleep, Mouser, and tell me isn't an old lover?'

The two men had to admit that those explanations were distant possibilities.

'Or other mysterious or even otherworldly beings may have had a hand in it,' Afreyt proposed. 'We know Queen Skeldir's involved, bless her, from the warning laughter you heard. And, for all you make light of him, Gusorio. Cif and I did hear those growlings.'

Cif said, the look in her eyes half wicked, half serious, 'And has it occurred to any of you that, since Skeldir's warnings went to you two men, that *you* may be transmigrations of her? And we – Skeldir help us! – of Great Gusorio? Or does that shock you?'

'By no means,' Fafhrd answered. 'Since transmigration would be such a wonder, able to send the spirit of woman or man into animal, or vice versa, a mere change of sex should not surprise us at all.'

27

The backgammon box of the two Deaths was kept at the Sea Wrack as a curiosity of sorts, but it was noted that few used it to play with, or got good games when they did.

IV
THE MOUSER GOES BELOW

I

It is an old saw in the world of Nehwon that the fate of heroes who seek to retire, or of adventurers who decide to settle down, so cheating their audience of honest admirers – that the fate of such can be far more excruciatingly doleful than that of a Lankhmar princess royal shanghaied as cabin girl aboard an Ilthmar trader embarked on the carkingly long voyage to tropic Klesh or frosty No-Ombrulsk. And let such heroes merely whisper a hint about a 'last adventure' and their noisiest partisans and most ardent adherents alike will be demanding that it end at the very least in spectacular death and doom, endured while battling insurmountable odds and enjoying the enmity of the evilest archgods.

So when those two humorous dark-side heroes the Gray Mouser and Fafhrd not only left Lankhmar City (where it's said more than half the action of Nehwon world is) to serve the obscure freewomen Cif and Afreyt of lonely Rime Isle on the northern rim of things, but also protracted their stay there for two years and then three, wiseacres and trusty gossips alike began to say that the Twain were flirting with just such a fate.

True, their polar expedition had seemed to begin well enough, even showily, with reports filtering back of them gathering and training (or taming) small bands of adventurers mad as themselves to serve them, and then word of a great victory where they turned back from the frigid island of philosophic fishermen a two-pronged invasion of suicidal Sea-Mingols, during which they enforced the service of two weird outlander gods outlandishly named Loki and Odin, and also played fast and loose with the five gold Ikons of Reason, which were atheist Rime Isle's chiefest treasure, and otherwise made fools of the Isle's gruff and slow-moving and -speaking dwellers.

But then, especially when they stayed on and on in the chilly north, second reports began to undercut and diminish all these feisty achievements. It was said that their victory had been a trivial psychological one, got by delaying maneuvers – what in a more familiar world would have been called Fabian tactics – and that in the end it never would have been won except for an unexpected unseasonal change in the winds, the simultaneous but fortuitous eruption of Rime Isle's volcanos Hellglow and Darkfire, and the coincidental surging of the Island's notorious Great Maelstrom, which sucked under a few leading galleys in the Mingols' advance squadron and so discouraged the rest.

That (so these second reports went) far from playing tricks on the Islanders, the Mouser and Fafhrd were making friends with them, copying their sober ways, and forcing their henchmen to do likewise – transforming these cutpurses and berserks into law-abiding sailors, fishermen, mechanics, even carpenters who'd built for themselves and their two masters a year-round barracks.

That instead of playing ducks and drakes with the gold Ikons, Fafhrd had actually rescued four of them from a thievish sea-demoness from the sunken empire of Simorgya, whom the Mouser had additionally thwarted in the course of a trading voyage to No-Ombrulsk to get timber and grain for the wood-poor, corn-hungry, sea-girt republic.

Furthermore, that he (the Mouser) had used the fifth Ikon, the Skeleton Cube of Square Dealing, enwedged with a cinder sacred to the stranger fire-god Loki and containing the essence of that alien god's being, to sling into the centre of the Great Maelstrom after it had pulled under the Mingol picket ships and magically still for ever its spinning whorls before they scuppered the rickety Rime fleet also. There the cube lay snuggled in sand and slickly slimed at whirlpool-maw's centre seventeen fathoms down, a precious heavy handful, kernel for legends and bait for treasure seekers, locking the Maelstrom tight and prisoning a god.

Finally, that in place of swindling and abandoning Cif and Afreyt, as they'd been known to serve some earlier employers and lovers alike, the two disgustingly reformed rascals and rakes were busily courting the two freewomen, clearly with lasting relationships of mutual benefit in mind.

These disquieting – nay, shocking – secondary rumours were what caused many to at last give credence to a widely-disbelieved early report: that in the almost bloodless final battle with the Mingols, Fafhrd had somehow lost his left hand, eventually replacing it with a leather socket for his bow, fork, knife – a whole kit of tools. This was seen now as part of the working out of the old Nehwonian saw about the woes that afflict heroes who try to step down from their glorious and entertaining destinies. The luck of Fafhrd and the Gray Mouser had turned at last, it was said, and they were on the road to oblivion.

The ones who believed this – and they were many – were also quick to accept the report that the wizardly mentors of the Twain, Sheelba of the Eyeless Face and Ningauble of the Seven Eyes, had turned against them in disappointment and disgust and moved their no-account gods – spiderish Mog, limp-wristed Issek, and lousy Kos – to inflict upon them the curse of old age, turning them into cranky old men before their time. Likewise the secret news that figures no less illustrious and powerful than the Overlord of Lankhmar and the Grandmaster of its Thieves Guild had sent assassins to Rime Isle to wipe them out. Even when word came drifting southward that the two tarnished heroes had somehow thwarted their assassins at the last moment and wriggled out from under the old-age curse, detractors were quick to point out that this was not to their credit since it could hardly have been managed without a lot of help from Cif, Afreyt, and those two ladies' Moon Goddess.

No, these detractors maintained, Fafhrd and Mouser were on the skids (as good as dead) for disdaining their proper hero-villain roles and seeking a snug harbour for their declining years, and as soon as some proper gods (Kos, Mog, and Issek were nobodies!) got the ear of Death in his low castle in the Shadowland and spoke a word into it, they were for ever done for.

Now, if these criticisms and dire forecasts had been referred to the two heroes at whom they were directed, Fafhrd might well have replied that he'd come north on a dare and great challenge, and that since then problems and menaces had been coming at him hot and heavy, and as for his hand, he'd lost that saving the necks of his mistress Afreyt and her three girl acolytes of the Moon Goddess and he was trying to make the best of his deficiency, so why the criticism? While the Gray Mouser might well have answered, 'What did the fools expect?' *He'd* never worked as hard in his life at being a hero as he had up here in the shivery inclement arctic clime, taking responsibility not only for his twelve witless apprentice hero-thieves under their barely less imbecilic lieutenants Mikkidu and Pshawri *and* for his lady Cif and her dependents as well, but *also* from time to time for Fafhrd's berserks too, and half the dwellers of Rime Isle besides.

Yet despite these protests each of the Twain felt a gloomy shiver stiffen his short hairs now and again, for both knew well how cruelly and unreasonably demanding audiences can be and how unendingly bitter the enmity of gods as the two of them fumbled with their twisted, slowly unravelling destinies in a world that from time to time imitates that of fancy and romance most cunningly, so as to keep its creatures concerned and moving to prevent their sinking into black despair or bored inaction.

2

Pshawri, the Gray Mouser's slender young lieutenant, sat with head bowed and taking slow deep breaths on the aft thwart of the sailing dory *Kringle*, anchored in a dead calm two Lankhmar leagues east of Rime Isle above the dark centre of the Great Maelstrom, quiescent now for an unprecedented seventeen moons, though when a-spin, a ridgy, ship-devouring, roaring water monster.

The noonday sun of late summer's Satyrs Moon beat down on his wiry nakedness as he studied the five smooth leadstone boulders, each big as his head, lying firm on the dory's bottom. From a snug thong low around his middle hung a scabbarded and well-greased dirk and a bag of stout fishnet, its mouth marked and held open by a circlet of reed. With each belly-bulging inhalation the thong indented his slim side just above where three grayish moles made an inconspicuous equilateral triangle on his left hip.

Against the gunnel opposite him sprawled his sworn-to-secrecy sailing comrade, Fafhrd's seven-foot second sergeant, Skullick. This lean yet comically hulking one left off staring lazily yet doubtfully at Pshawri to turn half on his side and scan down through the near pellucid saltwater at the sea floor seventeen fathoms below. It was mostly pale sand, green-tinged by depth. He could see *Kringle*'s tiny shadow and her anchor line going down almost vertically toward the dark cluster of savage rocks marking the whirlpool's maw, and around that the dim shapes of gnawed wrecks waiting a long, long time now for storms and the whirlpool's own action to break them up and drive their waterlogged timbers ashore on the Beach of Bleached Bones, there to be salvaged by the wood-starved Rimers.

'All clear, as yet,' he called softly over shoulder. 'Nary a tiger ray nor black hog-nose showing. No fish of size at all.

'None the less,' he added, 'if you take my reed, you'll try to spot and snag the gift you intend Captain Mouser on your first dive, before you've roiled the fine sand or roused a man-eater. Foot-steer for the likeliest wreck, scanning carefully ahead for treasure-glints, then swiftly snatch, were the best way. Anything metal'd be a fine memento for him of his scuppering the Sunwise Mingol fleet whilst saving the Rimer ships. Don't set your heart on finding the golden Whirlpool Queller itself—' His voice grew loving '—the twelve-edged skeleton cube small as a girl's fist, with the cindery black torch end wedged within it that holds all that's left in Nehwon of the stranger god Loki who maddened us Rimers a year and five moons ago when Maelstrom last time spumed and spun. Small swift profits are surest, as I've more than once heard your captain tell mine when he thinks Fafhrd's dreaming too big.'

Pshawri replied to this glib palaver with never a word or sign, nor did aught else to break his measuredly deep breathing, his surfeit-feast of air. Finally he lifted his face to gaze tranquilly beyond Skullick at the Rime Isle coast, mostly low-lying, except to the north, where the volcano Darkfire faintly fumed and dimmer ice-streaked crags loomed beyond.

His gaze went up and south from the volcano to where five neat shapely clouds had come coursing out of the west like a small fleet of snowy-sailed, high-castled galleons.

Skullick, who'd been copying Pshawri's peerings, burst out with, 'I'll swear I've seen those same five clouds before.'

Pshawri used the breath in one of his slow exhalations to say somewhat dreamily, 'You think clouds have beings and souls, like men and ships?'

'Why not?' responded Skullick. 'I think that all things do bigger than lice. In any case, these five presage a change in weather.'

But Pshawri's gaze had dropped to the Isle's south corner, where the White Crystal Cliffs sheltered the low red and yellow roofs of Salthaven; beyond them, the low hump of Gallows Hill and the lofty leaning rock needle of Elvenhold. His expression hardly changed, yet a shrewd searcher might have seen, added to his tranquillity, the solemnity of one who perhaps looks on cosy shores for the last time.

Without breaking the rhythm of his breathing, he rummaged in the small pile of his clothes beside him, found a moleskin belt-pouch, withdrew a somewhat grimy folded sheet with broken seal of green wax with writing in violet ink, unfolded and perused it swiftly – as one who reads not for the first time.

He refolded the sheet, remarking evenly to Skullick, 'If, against all likelihood, aught should befall me now, I'd like Captain Mouser to see *this*.' He touched the broken seal before returning the item to the moleskin pouch.

Skullick frowned, but then bethought himself and simply nodded.

Hoisting the nearest small leadstone boulder and clasping it to his waist, Pshawri slowly stood up. Skullick rose too, still forbearing to speak.

Then Lieutenant Pshawri, serene-visaged, stepped over *Kringle*'s side with no more fuss than one who goes into the next room.

Before his swift and almost splashless transition from the realm of the winds to that of the cold currents, Skullick remembered to call after him merrily, 'Sneeze and choke, burst a blood vessel!'

As the water took them, Pshawri felt the boulder grow lighter, so that his right hand alone was enough to hug it close. Opening his eyes to the rushing fluid, he looped his left arm loosely round the anchor line beside him, directing his descent toward the rock cluster.

He looked down. The bottom seemed still far away. Then as the water tightened its grip on him, he saw the rock cluster slowly open into a five-petalled dark flower with a circle of pale sand at its heart.

The wrecks around came plainer into view so that he could make out the green weed-furred skull of the bow-stallion of the nearest, but disregarding Skullick's advice, Pshawri directed his descent toward the centre of the circle of virgin sand, where he discerned *something*, a slightly darker point.

As the water squeezed him tight, then tighter yet, and there began a pulsing in his ears, and he felt the first urge to blow out his breath, he unhooked his arm from the anchor line and coasted down between the huge jagged rocks, let go the stone, and thrusting down both hands before him, seized on the central *something*.

It felt smoothly cubical in form, yet with something grainy and rough-wedged inside its twelve edges. It was surprisingly massy for its size, resisting movement. He rubbed an edge along his thigh. Just before the cloud of loamy sand raised by his feet and the stone's plunge engulfed it, he saw along the rubbed edge a yellowish gleam. He brought it against his waist, found the mouth of the fishnet bag by the feel of the reed circlet, and thrust in his trophy.

At the same time a dry voice seemed to say in his ear, 'You shouldn't have done that,' and he felt a sharp pang of guilt, as if he'd just committed a theft or rape.

Fighting down a surge of panic, he straightened his body, thrusting his hands high above his head, and with a threshing of his legs and a powerful downward sweep of his palms, drove upward out of the sand cloud, between the savage rocks, and toward the light.

At the same moment Skullick, who'd been following all this as best he might from seventeen fathoms above, saw fully a half-dozen similar sand puffs erupt from the quiescent green-tinged sand plain of wrecks all around and a like number of black hog-nosed sharks, each about as big as *Kringle*'s shadow, streak toward the rock cluster and the tiny swimming figure above it.

Pshawri stroked upward alongside the anchor line, feeling he climbed a cliff, his gaze fixed on *Kringle*'s small spindle shape. Blood pounded in his ears and to hold his breath was pain. Yet as the spindle shape grew larger, he thought to stroke so as to rotate his body for a cautionary scan around and down.

He had not completed a half turn when he saw a black shape driving up toward him head-on.

It speaks well for Pshawri's presence of mind that he completed his rotation, making sure there was no nearer attacker to deal with, before facing the hog-nose.

Continuing to coast upward, threshing his legs a little, he drew his dirk. There was yet barely time to thrust his right hand through the loop of the pommel thong before he gripped it.

The scene darkened. He aimed the dirk, his arm bent just a little, at the up-rushing mask which somewhat resembled that of a great black boar.

His shoulder was jolted, his arm wrenched, a *long* black shape was hurtling past, rough hide scraped his hip and side, then he was driving upward again with strong palm-sweeps toward *Kringle*'s hull, very large now though the scene remained strangely darkened.

He felt a blessed surge of relief as he broke surface close alongside and grasped for the gunnel. But in the same instant he felt himself strongly gripped under the shoulders and powerfully heaved upward, his legs flying, and he heard the clash of jaws.

Skullick, his rescuer, saw a red line start out on the mallet snout of the black shark as the beast breached, bit air, then sneezed before falling back – and also the red points that began to fleck his comrade's side as he lowered him to the deck.

Pshawri's spent legs were wobbly yet he managed to stand. He saw that the first of the five fish-shaped clouds hid the sun. It had veered north, as though curious about the Maelstrom and determined to inspect it, and the other four had followed it in line. A strong breeze from the southwest explained this and chilled Pshawri, so he was glad for the large rough towel Skullick tossed his way.

'A goodly tickle you gave him in the nose, my boyo,' that one congratulated. 'He'll sneeze longer than you bleed where he scraped you, never you fear. But, by Kos, Pshawri, how they all came after you! You'd no sooner raised sand than they were up and streaking in from far and near. Like lean black watchdogs!' He appealed incredulously, 'Think you they *felt* your stone-abetted impact through the sand so far? By Kos, they must have!'

'There was more than one?' Pshawri asked, shivering as he spoke for the first time since his dive.

'More? I counted full five blacks at the end, besides two tiger rays. I told you it was more dangerous than you dreamed, and now events have proved me sevenfold right. You're lucky to have got out with your life, lucky you found no treasure to delay you. A few moments more and you'd not have been facing one shark, but three or four!'

Pshawri had been about to display his golden find for his comrade's admiration when Skullick's words not only told him the latter hadn't seen him make it, but also reawakened the strange pang of guilt and foreboding he'd felt below.

While hurrying into his clothes, a process in which he was speeded by the quickening breeze and absence of sun, he managed to switch the slimy cube from the uneasy revealment of the net bag to the revealing concealment of his moleskin belt pouch, while Skullick scanned the sky.

'See how the weather shifts,' that one called. 'What witch has whistled up this frigid wind? Cold from the south, at any rate southwest – unnatural. Mark how that line of clouds that hides the sun veers widdershins. Lucky you did *not* find the whirlpool-queller, or else we'd have the spinning of that element to deal with. As it is, I fear our presence irks the Maelstrom. Up anchor, cully, hoist sail and away! We'll find your captain's gift another day!'

Pshawri was happy to spring to with a will. Relentless action left less time for feeling strange guilts and thinking crazy thoughts about clouds. And the calm waters, though wind-ruffled, showed no other signs of movement.

3

In jam-packed Godsland, which lies lofty and mountaingirt near Nehwon's south pole, a handsome young god, who had been drawing crowds in the stranger's pavilion by sleeping entranced for seventeen months, woke with an enraged shout that seemed loud enough to reach the Shadowland at Godsland's antipodes, and that momentarily deafened half the divinities and all the demi-divinities in his heavenly audience.

Among the latter were Fafhrd's and the Gray Mouser's three particular godlings – brutal Kos, spiderish Mog, and the limp-wristed Issek – who had been teased to come witness the feat of supernal hibernation not only out of sheer curiosity, but also from intimations that the handsome young sleeping stranger and his record-breaking trance were somehow involved with their two most illustrious (though often backsliding) worshipers. The three reacted variously to the ear-splitting cry. Issek covered his while Kos dug a little finger into one.

And now it became apparent that Loki's piercing shout had indeed reached the Shadowland, for the slender, seemingly youthful, opalescent-fleshed figure of Death, or its simulacrum, appeared at the foot of the silken bier on which the angry young god crouched, and the two were seen by the deafened divinities to hold converse together, Loki fiercely commanding, Death raising objections, placating, temporizing, though nodding repeatedly and smiling winningly at the same time.

Yet despite the latter's amiable behavior there were shrinkings back among the members of the motley heavenly host, for even in Godsland Death is not a popular figure nor widely trusted.

Fafhrd's and Mouser's three oddly matched godlings, who had earlier wormed their way quite close to the red-draped bier, regained their audition in time to hear Loki's last summary command.

'So be it then, sirrah! So soon as all the essential formalities of your paltry world are satisfied and necessary niggling conditions met – so soon and not one instant later! – I want the impious mortal who consigned me to deep watery oblivion to be sent a like distance underground. It is commanded!'

With a final bow and strange obsequious look, Nehwon's Death (or its simulacrum) said softly, 'Harkening in obedience,' and vanished.

'I like that!' quick-witted Mog remarked in an indignant ironic undertone to his two cronies. 'Out of sheer spite toward the Gray Mouser for his dunking, this vagabond Loki proposes to rob us of one of our chief worshipers.'

After a face-saving haughty glare around (for Death's departure had been snubbingly abrupt), Loki slid off the bier to confer in urgent whispers with another stranger god, dignified but elderly to the point of doddering, who responded with rather senile-seeming nods and shrugs.

'Yes,' Issek replied venomously to Mog. 'And now, see, he's trying to persuade his comrade, old Odin, to demand of Death a like doom for Fafhrd.'

'No, I doubt that,' Kos protested. 'The dodderer has already revenged himself on Fafhrd by taking his left hand. And he's had no indignities visited on him to reawaken his ire. He's hung on here while his comrade slept because he has nowhere better to go.'

'I'd not count on that,' Mog said morosely. 'Meanwhile, what's to do about the clear threat to the Mouser? Protest to Death this wanton raid by a *foreign* god on our dwindling congregation?'

'I'd want to think twice before going that far,' Issek responded dubiously. 'Appeals to him have been known to backfire on their makers.'

'I don't like dealing with him myself, and that's a fact,' Kos seconded. 'He gives me the cold shivers. Truth to tell, I don't think you can trust the Powers any further than you can trust foreign gods!'

'He didn't seem too happy about Loki's arrogance toward him,' Issek put in hopefully. 'Perhaps things will work out well without our meddling.' He smiled a somewhat sickish smile.

Mog frowned but spoke no more.

Back in one of the long corridors of his mist-robed mazy low castle under the sunless moist gray skies of the Shadowland,

Death thought coolly with half his mind (the other half was busy as always with his eternal work everywhere in Nehwon) of what a stridently impudent god this young stranger Loki was and what a pleasure it would be to break the rules, spit in the face of the other Powers, and carry him off before his last worshiper died.

But as always good taste and sportsmanship prevailed.

A Power must obey the most whimsical and unreasonable command of the least god, insofar as it could be reconciled with conflicting orders from other gods and provided the proprieties were satisfied – that was one of the things that kept Necessity working.

And so although the Gray Mouser was a good tool he would have liked to decide when to discard, Death began with half his mind to plan the doom and demise of that one. Let's see, a day and a half would be a reasonable period for preparation, consultations, and warnings. And while he was at it, why not strengthen the Gray One for his coming ordeal? There were no rules against that. It would help him if he were heavier, massier in body and mind. Where get the heaviness? Why, from his comrade Fafhrd, of course, nearest at hand. It would leave Fafhrd light-headed and -bodied for a while, but that couldn't be helped. And then there were the proper and required warnings to think about . . .

While half Death's mind was busy with these matters, he saw his Sister Pain slinking toward him from the corridor's end on bare silent feet, her avid red eyes fixed on his pale slate cool-gray ones. She was slender as he and like complected, except that here and there her opalescence was streaked with blue – and to his great distaste she padded about, as was her wont, in steamy nakedness, rather than decently robed and slippered like himself.

He prepared to stride past her with never a word.

She smiled at him knowingly and said with languorous hisses in her voice, 'You've a choice morsel for me, haven't you?'

4

While these ominous Nehwonal and supernal events were transpiring that so concerned them, Fafhrd and the Gray Mouser were relaxedly and unsuspectingly sipping dark brandy by the cool white light, which Rime Islers call bistory, of a leviathan-oil lamp in the root-and-wine cellar of Cif's snug Salthaven abode while that lady and Afreyt were briefly gone to the lunar temple at the arctic port-town's inland outskirts on some business involving the girl acolytes of the moon goddess, whose priestesses Cif and Afreyt were, and the girl acolytes their nieces.

Since their slaying of their would-be killers and the lifting of the old-age curse, the two captains had been enjoying to the full their considerable relief, leaving the overseeing of their men to their lieutenants, visiting their barracks but once a day (and taking turns even at that – or even having their lieutenants make report to them, a practice to which they'd sunk once or twice lately), spending most of their time at their ladies' cosier and more comfortable abodes and pleasuring themselves with the sportive activities (including picnicking) which such companionship made possible and to which their recent stints as grumpy and unjoyous old men also inclined them, abetted by the balmy weather of Thunder and Satyrs Moon.

Indeed, today the last had got a bit too much for them. Hence their retreat to the deep, cool, flagstoned cellar, where they were assuaging the melancholy that unbridled self-indulgence is strangely apt to induce in heroes by rehearsing to each other anecdotes of ghosts and horrors.

'Hast ever heard,' the tall Northerner intoned, 'of those sinuous earth-hued tropical Kleshite ghouls with hands like spades that burrow beneath cemeteries and their environs, silently emerge behind you, then seize you and drag you down before you can gather your wits to oppose it, digging more swiftly than the armadillo? One such, it's said, subterraneously pursued a man whose house lay by a lich-field and took him in his own cellar, which doubtless had a feature much like *that*.' And he directed his comrade's attention to an unflagged area, just behind the bench on which they sat, that showed dark sandy loam and was large enough to have taken the passage of a broad-shouldered man.

'Afreyt tells me,' he explained, 'it's been left that way to let the cellar breathe – a most necessary ventilation in this clime.'

The Mouser regarded the gap in the flagging with considerable distaste, arching his brows and wrinkling his nostrils, then recovered his mug from the stout central table before them and took a gut-shivering slug. He shrugged. 'Well, tropic ghouls are unlikely here in polar clime. But now I'm reminded – hast ever heard tell? – of that Ool Hrusp prince who so feared his grave, abhorring earth, that he lived his whole life (what there was of it) in the topmost room of a lofty tower twice the height of the mightiest trees of the Great Forest where Ool Hrusp is situated?'

'What happened to him in the end?' Fafhrd duly inquired.

'Why, although he dwelt secure two thousand leagues from the edge of the desert southeast of the Inner Sea and with all that water between to distance him, a monstrously dense sandstorm borne on a typhoon wind sought him out, turned the green canopy of the forest umber, sifted his stone eyrie full, and suffocated him.'

From upstairs came a smothered cry.

'My story must have carried,' the Mouser observed. 'The girls seem to have returned.'

He and Fafhrd looked at each other with widening eyes.

'We promised we'd watch the roast,' the latter said.

'And when we came down here,' the other continued, 'we told ourselves we'd go up and check and baste it after a space.'

Then both together, chiming darkly, 'But *you* forgot.'

There was a swift patter of footsteps – more than one pair – on the cellar stairs. Somehow five slender girls came down into the cool bistoric glow without tripping or colliding. The first four wore sandals of white bearhide, near identical knee-length tunics of fine white linen and yashmaks of the same material, hiding most of their hair and all of their faces below their eyes, whose merry flashing nevertheless showed they were all grinning.

The fifth, who was the slenderest, went barefoot in a shorter white-belted white tunic of coarser weave and wore a yashmak of reversed white unshorn lamb's hide and, despite the weather, gloves of the same material. Her gaze seemed grave.

All but she tore off their yashmaks together, showing them to be Afreyt's flaxen-haired nieces May, Mara, and Gale, and Cif's niece Klute, who was raven-tressed.

But Fafhrd and Mouser knew that already. The two had risen. May danced toward them excitedly. 'Uncle Fafhrd! We've had an adventure!'

Following at her heels, Mara cut in, 'We were almost kidnapped aboard an Ilthmar trader that was a secret slaver!'

'Anything could have happened to us!' Gale exulted, taking her turn. 'Imagine! They say Eastern princes will pay fortunes for twelve-year-old blonde virgins!'

'Only, our new friend escaped from the trader and warned Aunts Cif and Afreyt,' black-haired Klute topped her triumphantly, looking back toward the fifth girl, who hadn't come forward or unyashmaked. 'She'd been kidnapped herself at Tovilyis and been a prisoner on *Weasel* all Satyrs Moon!'

Gale grabbed back the news-telling with, 'But she's a novice of Skama just like us. Tovilyis coven. Her mother was a priestess of the moon.'

'And she's a princess herself too!' May topped them all. 'A really-truly princess of south Lankhmar land!'

'You can tell she's a princess,' Mara fairly shrieked, 'because she always wears gloves!'

'Don't squeal like a piglet, Mara,' May reproved, seeing a surer way to hog attention, and for a longer time. 'Girls, we have omitted to introduce our new friend and rescuer.' And when that one still hung back, dropping her eyes demurely, May placed herself beside her and gently impelled her forward.

'Uncle Fafhrd,' she said gravely, 'may I introduce you to my new friend and rescuer of all of us, the Princess Fingers of Tovilyis? And, dear Princess, my friend, may I tender your hand to our most honoured guest Captain Fafhrd, a great hero of Rime Isle, my Aunt Afreyt's lover, and my own dearest uncle!'

The strangely yashmaked girl dropped her eyes still farther and seemed to shiver slightly all over, yet let her left hand be drawn forward.

Fafhrd took it and, bowing ceremoniously low and looking straight into the hooded and half-averted face, said, 'Any friend of May's is a friend of mine, most honoured Princess Fingers, while as the rescuer of her and all my other friends here, I owe you eternal gratitude. My sword is yours.' And he kissed the lamb's hide for three heartbeats. Her head tipped up a trifle and her eyelashes fluttered.

All the other girls ooh'ed and aah'ed, though there was a hard expression on Klute's face, while the Mouser's gaze grew somewhat sardonic.

May repossessed herself of the gloved hand and swung it toward the Mouser.

'Dear Uncle Mouser,' she intoned, her voice speeding up just a little because of the repetition, despite her efforts to vary her speech, 'could I introduce you to my new friend and benefactress of all us girls, the Princess Fingers of south Lankhmar land? Princess dear, my friend, could I entrust your precious hand to our honoured guest Captain Mouser, Klute's Aunt Cif's lover and my own good, beloved, honorary uncle – and hero of Rime Isle second only to Fafhrd?'

The Mouser's eyebrows lifted formidably. 'Her left hand? No, you may not,' he dismissed May harshly, setting his fists upon his hips and standing as tall as possible, which involved leaning back a little. Then, looking sneeringly down his nose at the scrawny figure cowered before him, he made a fearsome face and barked commandingly, 'Manners, child! – for it is a child you are, an ill-bred and conceited snit of a girl-child, whatever else you may be.'

The other girls gasped in consternation at this turn of talk, while Fafhrd gave his comrade an unfriendly glare, but the one addressed swiftly drew off her gloves and unyashmaked, revealing a piquant face blushing almost the same hue as her close-cropped hair as she tucked the three lambskin items inside her belt.

Lifting her eyes to the Mouser, she said in a low clear voice, 'You rebuke me well, sir. I most humbly apologize.' She spoke (though with a strange lisping accent) the same Low Lankhmarese the others all had used, which was the common trade language of most of Nehwon. Then she extended up toward him palm down a slender pale right hand.

He took it without gripping, resting it on his spread fingers as he observed it thoughtfully. 'Fingers,' he said slowly, as though savouring the word. 'Now that's an odd name for a princess.'

'I am no princess, sir,' she responded instantly. 'That's but something I told the priestess when I came off *Weasel*, to be sure my warning would be listened to.'

The other girls stared at her as though betrayed, but the Gray Mouser only nodded ruminatively, hefting her hand as though appraising it. 'That fits better with what I find here,' he said, 'much as your speech says Ilthmar to my ears and not Tovilyis. Observe,' he continued, as if lecturing, 'though narrow, this is a strong and efficient working hand, has done much gripping and squeezing, rubbing and slapping, twisting and prodding, tapping and stroking, finger dancing, et cetera.' He turned it over, so her palm lay upward, and rubbed that testingly with his thumb in a circle. 'And yet despite the work it's done, it's moist and most pleasingly soft. That's from the oil in the lambswool of the gloves. I doubt not that her uncommon yashmak equally benefits her cheeks, lips, and winsome chin, making them all luxuriously smooth.' He sighed thoughtfully. Then, 'May, approach us! Hold out your hand.' The blonde girl obeyed wonderingly. He dropped the hand he'd been supporting into it and turned toward Klute, who was grinning wickedly.

'How does my favourite niece?'

The other girls appeared to be hunting furiously for something to say. Fafhrd swung toward the Mouser, Fingers looked tranquil, when all of a sudden Afreyt called briskly from the top of the stairs, 'That's enough games in the cellar and skulking in the forecastle! On deck all of you and earn your dinners!'

Klute and the Mouser led the way, gossiping airily, he making much of her, Mara and Gale followed somewhat glumly. Fafhrd deftly caught up May and Fingers where the Mouser had left them standing bemusedly hand in hand and, holding them comfortably in either arm, brought up the rear.

'My co-captain has somewhat crabbed ways,' he explained to them lightly. 'Would question the credentials of the Queen of Heaven, yet be jealous of a chipmunk that won attention. He treasures an insult above all else.'

534

5

Cif's kitchen was wide and low-ceilinged, ventilated and somewhat cooled by an early evening breeze sweeping through opposite open doors, although the low rays of the setting sun still struck in.

Tall silver-blonde Afreyt and lithe green-eyed Cif were still in their long white priestess tunics, though both had unyashmaked. After embracing the Mouser, the latter directed him and Fafhrd as to carrying the two tables and some benches outdoors on the room's shadeside. The girls were gathered about Afreyt, May and Gale eagerly addressing her in low voices while gazing around from time to time over their shoulders.

When the two men returned from their task, they found the two moon priestesses standing side by side and changed to gayer scoop-necked tunics of yellow-striped violet and green spotted with brown. The girls, apparently already given their directions, set to carrying tablecloths and trays of condiments and dining utensils outside.

Cif said, 'I gather you've already been acquainted with our new guest?'

'And told of the signal service she did our nieces and all Rime Isle, for that matter?' Afreyt added.

'We have indeed,' Fafhrd affirmed. 'And I assume you've already taken measures against the miscreants captaining and crewing *Weasel*?'

'That we have,' Afreyt affirmed. 'The Council was convened in jig time and swiftly persuaded to deal with the matter Rime Isle fashion – they imposed a considerable fine (on other charges than intended kidnapping: that *Weasel*'s woodwork showed holes suspiciously like those of the boreworm that swiftly infests other craft) and sent the infamous trader packing posthaste.'

'We invited harbormaster Groniger home to dinner with us,' Cif took up, 'but he's gone by way of the headland to check that that pestilent *Weasel* has dock-parted as sworn to and is on her way.'

'So what's all this, most dear Gray Mouser,' Afreyt demanded quietly, 'about your badgering the poor child and ignoring she's a novice of the goddess and even refusing to grip hands with her?'

Straightening himself and folding his arms across his chest and looking her in the eye, even doing the leaning back bit, the Mouser retorted loudly, 'Poor child, forsooth! She is no princess, as she swift confessed, nor any kidnapped moon novice from Tovilyis, I'll be sworn. What her game is I do not know, though I could guess at it, but here's the truth: She's nothing but a cabin-girl from Ilthmar where the rat is worshiped, the lowest of the low, beneath recognition, a common child ship-whore hired on for the erotic solacing of all aboard, unfit to share your roof, Lady Afreyt, or company with your innocent nieces or with Cif's except to corrupt them. All signs point to it! Her name alone is proof. As Fafhrd here would instantly confirm, were he not lost in romancing, fondly willing to play knight-and-princess games for a child audience whatever the risk. Which is his chief weakness, you may be sure!'

The others tried to hush or answer him, the girls all listened wide-eyed, slowing in their chores, but he doggedly maintained his tirade to its end, whereupon silver-blonde Afreyt, her blue eyes flashing lightning, spoke arrow-swift, 'One thing's confirmed beyond question, mean-minded man, she is a true novice of the goddess: she knows the cryptic words and secret signs.'

To which Cif swiftly added, 'She knows the colour. She wears the garment and the yashmak.'

'And gloves?' the Mouser inquired blandly. 'I never knew you and Afreyt wear gloves of any hue in summertime. Even in winter it is mittens only. The girls the same, goes without saying.'

Cif shot back, 'We at Rime Isle are but one twig of the sisterhood. Doubtless they have different local customs in Tovilyis.'

The Mouser smiled. 'Dear lady, you are far too innocent, and limited in your knowledge by your island life. There's more evil in gloves than you ever dreamed, more uses for a yashmak than a badge of purity or advertisement of a man's possession, or for a mask. Amongst the more knowing Ilthmar cabingirls (and this one is no novice, I'll be bound!) it is the practice to wear such things to keep their hands soft, also their lips and faces, while as for their privities, you may be sure they enjoy the close covering of oily wool, being tweaked shamelessly hairless besides. For, hark you, on Ilthmar ships the cabingirl delights the crewmen by her hands alone, the short knowing dance of her most pliant fingers; there'd be too much risk of damage to her otherwise, and fresh cabingirls do not grow on sea trees, as they say. *That*, by the by, is why her name is proof. The mates and lesser officers have the freedom of her face and teats, all above waist, while what's below is reserved for his eminence the captain alone, besides all else he wants. But he, the wisest aboard, can be trusted to see she doesn't conceive. The arrangement is swift, efficient, and practical – helps maintain discipline and status both.'

By this time the girls were all gathered close around, four of them goggle-eyed, Fingers respectfully attentive.

'But is this true he says?' Afreyt asked Fafhrd with some indignation. 'Are there such cabingirls and naughty practices?'

'I'd like to lie to spite him for his boorishness,' the Northerner averred, 'but I must agree there are such practices and cabingirls, and not alone on Ilthmar ships. Mostly their parents sell them to the trade. Some grow up to become hardy sailors themselves, or wed a passenger, though that is rare.'

'All men are beasts,' Cif said darkly. 'New proofs keep coming in.'

'And women beastesses,' the Mouser added *sotto voce*. 'Or animalesses?'

Afreyt shook her head, then looked at Fingers, who did, alas, appear to have been hearing all these enormities with remarkable coolness.

'What say you to all this, child?' she asked, straight out.

'All Captain Mouser said is mostly true,' Fingers replied simply, making a little grimace suiting her piquant mien, 'about cabingirls and such, I mean, although I only know what I learned serving aboard *Weasel*. Unwillingly. But on the first legs of our voyage there was a two-years-older cabingirl, jumped ship at Ool Plerns, who taught me much. And my parent did not hire or sell me into the trade. I was stolen from her – that much is true of "kidnapped". But I did not tell you about these matters, Lady Afreyt and Lady Cif, when I escaped and brought you my warning, singling out you two because you wore the colour and the yashmak, because I did not think that they were vital.'

The Mouser butted in complacently with, 'So much for the story of *Weasel* being a slaver. Her tale is fishy.'

'She never told us *Weasel* was a slaver!' Afreyt snapped.

'She lost one cabingirl at Ool Plerns,' Cif put in eagerly. 'What more natural than that the brutes should plot to steal a replacement here? – where are none such for hire, I'll be bound. All Rime Isle women serving sailors must be full-grown.'

The Mouser launched in again satisfiedly with, 'But surely, Lady Afreyt, you and Cif cannot have taken this tale of multiple slavings and kidnappings very seriously. Else you'd not now be letting *Weasel* sail free away without thorough search of every space aboard might harbour prisoners?'

'Again, you're wrong,' the tall woman told him angrily. 'The two men sent aboard to discover boreworm holes searched her most thoroughly before they found them!'

'No other girls aboard *Weasel*?' the Mouser inquired ingenuously. 'No females at all?' Both women nodded, glaring at him. 'So, no evidence at all for kidnap theories,' he concluded blandly.

'But Cif's suggestion about their lusting after a second cabingirl – or maybe four—' Afreyt began exasperatedly.

'Your pardon, my dear,' Fafhrd interrupted without heat yet commandingly, 'but would it not be best if we do our guest Fingers the courtesy of listening to her full story without any more interruptions? – especially sly, argumentative ones!' And he gave the Mouser a very hard look. 'She tells it well, speaking concisely.' He smiled at her.

'That's sensible,' Afreyt admitted graciously. 'But before we do, since it's oppressive here, let's go outside where she can speak and we can listen comfortably. We'll delay serving dinner. It will not spoil. Yes, girls, you may come along,' she added, seeing their expressions, 'and place yourselves at the same table. Chores can wait, but no chattering.'

6

Outside, Rime Isle's treeless summer verdure stretched out to the sea and to the nearby headland, which was still in sunshine, broken only by a few low juts of rock and fewer grazing sheep, and, like a giant's round shield cast down close by on the turf, the dark bronze flatness of a large moondial that marked a white-witch dwelling and traced the wanderings of Nehwon's moon through the constellations of Nehwon's broad zodiac; the several bright star pairs of the Lovers, the dim stars of the Ghosts, and the skinny long triangle of the Knife, with the bright tipstar red as blood. The ghostly moon herself, on the verge of full, hung low above the watery eastern horizon, from behind which she'd emerged within the quarter hour. The cooling eve breeze rippled around them gently. The house they'd just left hid them from the sun (soon to plunge into the western sea) save where its flat red rays gleamed from the open kitchen door and windows behind them.

The four adults took seat with Fingers in their midst. The four other girls leaned into the four spaces between.

She began, 'I was born at Tovilyis, where my mother was an officer in the Guild of Free Women and a moon priestess besides. I never knew my father. Quite a few Guild children didn't. I became a moon novice there, where truly white gloves are worn, though not of lamb's hide.' She touched those under her belt. 'The Guild falling into hard times, I journeyed with my mother for a space, settling in Ilthmar, where we worked as weavers, from my dexterity at which occupation and at the flute and small drum and the games cat's cradle and shadow shape, I got the nickname Fingers, which later proved to be most ominous indeed. We got Ilthmar accents. Mother says, fit in! We even paid lip service to the Rat and made sacrifice on his holidays at his dockside temple on the Inner Sea. Beneath the dark low portico of which I was one night sandbagged, as I later deduced, awakening to find myself aboard *Weasel*, choppy gray Inner Sea all around, feeling dizzy and headachy. I was more than naked, being shorn and shaved of all hair save my eyelashes and brows. And I was being instructed by one of her officers and this two-year-older cabingirl called Hothand in the latter's arts, which are by no means always exercised in cabins.

'When I balked at some of their directions and demands, they set boreworms to me.'

'Monstrous!' Fafhrd exclaimed. Afreyt frowned at him and flirted an admonitory hand for silence while the Mouser laid a remindful finger across his blandly smiling lips.

Fingers continued, 'As you may know, those bristly grey caterpillars, though feeding solely on wood, will flee the light if brought outside their tunnels by wriggling into the nearest crevice or small orifice, whether it be in inert material or living flesh, thereafter writhing deeper and deeper until they starve for lack of dead wood or proper food. My instructress told me they're sometimes used to break in or discipline new whores, young or older, since they mostly do no lasting damage, only excruciate.'

'So there *were* boreworms—' the Mouser began, instantly clapping his hand over his mouth.

'So I complied, recalling my mother's rule, Fit in! – and learned another sort of finger-work and other skills besides, until I earned the grudging praise of my young instructress. I did not seek to excel her, since I needed friends and she was my chief watchdog when we were in ports. I did not, for example, copy her signature, which also accounted for her nickname, and which was to blow into her hand before she used it in her work. I walked my fingers upon the bodies of those I serviced, keeping up a glib patter as I approached the target area, about my hand being a lost and ensorcelled princess, conjured tiny, who marvelled innocently at all the items she encountered in her little world and the actions that she was moved to perform upon them. The sailors relished that. It fed their fancy.

'So occupied, and under Hothand's hard and watchful eye, I first saw the docks of Lankhmar, forest-girt Kvarch Nar, Ool Hrusp, and other cities on the Inner Sea.

'I also early came to the conclusion that my period of sandbagged unconsciousness had been prolonged with drugs, not for hours but days at least. For as soon as I'd been able to examine myself at leisure, I'd discovered that my head hair had grown and my skin paled as much as it had during my fortnight's seclusion before my novice's initiation, while all my body hairs had been tweaked out. But what else had happened during this period, and if I'd been prisoned at one place or carried about before being taken aboard *Weasel*, I could never learn, nor would (or perhaps could) Hothand tell me. There was in my mind only a weltering sea of dark nightmarish impressions I couldn't decipher.

'Hothand became my friend, but not to the point where she invited me to desert with her at Ool Plerns. I think she might have, except she knew that losing both cabingirls would be a sure way to ensure a desperately determined pursuit. In fact, before she left she tied me up most securely (she was expert at that) and gagged me, saying mysteriously, before she kissed me goodbye, "I am doing this for your own good, little Fingers. It may save you a beating."

'And indeed I was not beaten, but when *Weasel* next docked, at No-Ombrulsk before our long reach here, I was confined below, tethered to timber by a chain and an iron-studded locked collar to which the captain alone held the key. It had previously chained his pursuit hound until the bitch died on *Weasel*'s last voyage but this.

'I've never felt lonelier than I did on the long wearisome sail that next came. At the worst moments I'd comfort myself by remembering Hothand's last kiss, though hating her madly at the same time. I also determined to escape ship at Rime Isle (which I'd always before thought a fable) no matter how strange and savage its inhabitants.' She looked around at them all and her eyes twinkled. 'I knew that my first step must be to do all in my power to ensure I was not again chained below. So, no longer having to fear Hothand's resentment, I devoted all my ingenuity and imagination to heightening and prolonging the ecstasies of all I serviced, though not long enough, of course, in the case of crewmen, to offend captain or officers if such were about. And sympathize with them all, goes without saying, in a motherly way, working to increase the area of familiarity and trust among us.

'With the result that when we finally raised Rime Isle and docked in Salthaven, I was allowed on deck for a short look and a breath, though under guard. I soon decided the shorefolk were civil and humane, but I pretended fear and distaste of all I saw, which helped persuade my captors there was little risk of my sneaking off.

'When you, May and Gale, joined those peering at the newly-arrived ship, I soon was hearing indecently lustful whispers from all the *Weasel*'s crew around me.'

'Really?'

'Truly?'

She nodded solemnly at the two girls and went on, 'I pretended to be angry with them, wanting barbarian girls when they had me, but that night I confessed to the captain how much I would enjoy teaching you with his aid the arts in which Hothand had instructed me and disciplining you when you turned balky, complaining I'd had no one to humiliate since becoming chief cabingirl. He said he'd like to please me but that kidnapping you would be too risky. I kept on wheedling him, however, and he finally told me it would be another matter if I went ashore and lured you to come aboard secretly without telling anyone. I pretended to be terrified of setting foot on savage Rime Isle, but in the end I let him persuade me.

'So that's how I was able to escape from *Weasel* and warn you, dear Lady Afreyt and Lady Cif,' Fingers concluded with a doubtful smile.

'You see?' the Mouser broke his enforced silence almost gleefully. 'She planned the whole kidnapping herself! Or at least forced the *Weasel*'s captain to sharpen his plans. It's the old saw, "A devious plot? Some woman wove it!"'

'But she only did it in order to—' Cif began furiously.

Afreyt said simultaneously, 'Captain Mouser, with all respect, you are impossible!'

Cif rebegan, 'She only employed the tricksy guile you would yourself in like situation.'

'That's pure truth,' Fafhrd confirmed. 'Guest Fingers, you are the Princess of Plotters. I never heard a braver tale.' Then, *sotto voce* to Afreyt, 'I declare, Mouser gets more stubborn-cranky every day. He can't have shaken the old-age curse. That would explain it.'

Mara piped up, 'You wouldn't really have enjoyed beating us, would you, Fingers?'

KLUTE: I bet she would. With a dogwhip! The pursuit hound's.

GALE: No, she wouldn't, she'd think of something worse, like putting boreworms up our noses.

MAY: Or in our ears!

KLUTE: Or maybe in our salad.

GALE: Or up our—

AFREYT: Children! That's quite enough. Go and fetch out our dinners, all of you. Quickly. Fingers, please help them.

They trooped off excitedly, beginning to whisper as they reached the kitchen.

7

Afreyt said, 'And while we're eating our dinners, Mouser, I hope you won't—'

But he interrupted, 'Oh, I know well enough when you're all against me. I'll be wordless willingly. Let me tell you, it's hard work being the voice of prudence and good sense when you're all being noble and generous and riding your liberal hobby horses recklessly.'

Cif smiled with a shrug and one eye toward heaven. 'Just the same, I'd feel better if you'd go a little further than just being quiet and—'

'Why not?' he demanded hugely with the ghost of a growl. 'Break one, break all. Princess Fingers,' he called, 'would your majesty please approach me?'

The girl put down the covered tray of hotcakes she'd just carried in and turned toward him with eyes lowered respectfully. 'Yes, sir?'

He said, 'My friends here tell me I should take your right hand.' She extended hers. He took it, saying, 'Princess, I admire your courage and cunning, in which latter quality they tell me you resemble myself. Good guesting and all that!' and he squeezed. She hid a wince as she smiled up at him. He held on. 'But hear this, royalty: no matter how clever you are, you're not as clever as I am. And if, through you, any of these girls, or any of my other friends, should come to harm, remember you will have me to answer to.'

She replied, 'That's a proviso I'll accept and abide by most happily, sir,' and with a little bow she hurried back to the kitchen.

'Bring out four more settings,' Afreyt called after her. 'I see Groniger coming in company from the headland. Who are those who walk beside him, Fafhrd?'

'Skullick and Pshawri,' he told her, scanning the group moving down toward them out of the last sunset gleam, 'come to make report to us of the day's accomplishments. And old Ourph – these days the ancient Mingol often suns his old bones up there where he can scan both the harbour to the south and the sleepy Maelstrom to the east beyond.'

The last sun patch upon the headland darkened and the misty moon at once seemed to grow brighter above the four oncomers.

'They hurry on apace,' Cif commented. 'Old Ourph as well, who commonly lags behind.'

Afreyt assured herself the girl's task was done and extra places set. 'Then fall to, all of you, with the goddess' blessing. Else we'll never start feeding.'

They had sampled the pickles and spices and nibbled garden-fresh radishes and were chomping roast lamb and sweet mint conserves by the time the four striders drew nigh. Simultaneously the cloud ceiling swiftly went lemon pale with reflected light from the setting or set sun, like a soft sustained trumpet peal of welcome. Their faces showed sudden clear in the afterglow, as if they'd all been unmasked.

Groniger said laconically, '*Weasel* left harbour. Dappled sky to the north presages a wind to speed her on her way. And there's news of a rather greater interest,' he added, glancing down toward bent and wrinkle-visaged Ourph.

When that one didn't speak at once, or anyone immediately ask, 'What is it?' Pshawri launched out with, 'Before *Weasel* got off, Captain Mouser, I traded deer pelts and a sable for seven nice planks, two slabs of oak, and peppercorns Cook wanted. We harvested the field of ear-corn and whitewashed the barn. Gilgy seems healed of his sunstroke.'

544

'The wood was seasoned?' Mouser asked testily. Pshawri nodded. 'Then next time say so. I like conciseness, but not at the expense of precision.'

Skullick took up. 'Skor had us careen *Sea Hawk*, Captain Fafhrd, it being Satyrs' lowest tide, what with moon's full tomorrow night, and we finished copper-sheathing her steer-side. There was a wildfowl hunt. I took *Klingle* fishing. We caught naught.'

'Enough,' Fafhrd said, waving him silent. 'What's this news of import, Ourph?'

Afreyt arose, saying, 'It can wait on courtesy. Gentlemen, join us. There are places set.'

The three others nodded thanks and moved to the well to rinse up, but the ancient Mingol held his ground, bending on Fafhrd a gaze black as his long-skirted tunic and saying portentously, 'Captain, as I did take my watch upon the headland, in mid-afternoon, the sun being halfway descended to the west, I looked toward the great Maelstrom that for this year and half year, this last six seasons, has been still as mountain lake, unnaturally so, and I saw it 'gin to stir and keep on stirring, slowly, slowly, slowly, as though the sea were thick as witch's brew.'

To everyone's surprise, the Mouser cried out a long loud '*What?*' rising to his feet and glaring direly. 'What's that you say, you dismal dodderer? You black spider of ill omen! You dried up skeleton!'

'No, Mouser, he speaks true,' Groniger reproved him, returning to take his place prepared next to the women. 'I saw it with my own eyes! The currents have come right again at last and Rime Isle's whirlpool is spinning sluggishly. With any luck – and help of northern storm that's gathering – she'll spin ashore the rest of the Mingol wrecks for us to salvage, along with other ships have sunken since. Cheer up, friend.'

The Mouser glowered at him. 'You calculating miser greedy for gray driftwood gain! No, there are things sea-buried there I would not have fished up again. Hark ye, old Ourph! Ere the 'pool 'gan spin, saw ye any ill-doers sniffing about? I smell wizard's work.'

'No wizards, Captain Mou, no one at all,' the ancient Mingol averred. 'Pshawri and Skullick—' He waved toward the two taking places farther down the table. '—took *Kringle* there earlier and anchored for a while. They will confirm my statement.'

'*What!*' Again that low-shrieking, long-drawn-out accusatory word sped from the Mouser's lips as he swung glaring toward the two Ourph had mentioned. 'You took out *Kringle?* Meddled in the Maelstrom?'

'What matter?' Skullick retorted boldly. 'I told you we went fishing. We anchored for a while. And Pshawri did one dive.' Old Ourph nodded. 'Nothing at all.'

'Fafhrd can deal with you,' the Mouser told him dismissingly. Then, focusing on his own man, 'What mischief were you up to, Pshawri? What were you diving for? What did you hope to find? Plunging in Maelstrom's midst without my order or permission? *What did you bring up with you from the dive?*'

Flushing darkly, 'Captain, you do me wrong,' Pshawri replied, looking him straight in the eye. 'Skullick can answer for me. He was there.'

'He brought up nothing,' Skullick said flatly. 'And whatever he might have brought up, I'm sure he would have saved to give to you.'

'I do not believe you,' the Mouser said. 'You're insubordinate, both of you. With you, Lieutenant Pshawri, I can deal. For the rest of this moon you are demoted to common seaman. At new moon I will reconsider your case. Until then the matter is closed. I wish to hear no more of it.'

Fafhrd spoke from mouth's corner to Afreyt beside him. 'Two temper tantrums in one evening! No question, the old-age curse still grips him.'

Afreyt whispered back, 'I think he's taking out on Pshawri what's left of his strange anger at the Fingers girl.'

PSHAWRI: Captain, you wrong me.

MOUSER: I said, 'No more!'

OURPH: Cap Mou, I singled out your lieutenant and Fafhrd's sergeant to bear me witness, not accuse 'em of aught.

GRONIGER: We of Rime Isle abhor wizardry, superstition, and ill-speaking all. Life's bad enough without them.

SKULLICK: There have been some accusations made this eve and ill words spoken—

546

FAFHRD: An' so let's have no more of them. Pipe down, Sergeant!

During these interchanges the Mouser sat scowling straight ahead and, save for his curt admonition, with lips pressed tightly together.

Afreyt got to her feet, drawing Cif up with her, who sat on her other side. 'Gentlemen,' she said quietly, 'this evening you would all gratify me by following Captain Mouser's wise advice, which as you can see he follows himself; setting us good example, of no more words on this perplexing matter.' She looked the table around with a particularly asking eye toward Pshawri.

Cif said, 'And after all, it is Full Moon Day Eve.'

'So please eat up your dinner,' Afreyt went on, smiling, 'or I shall think you do not like our cooking.'

'And replenish your mugs,' Cif added. 'In wine's best wisdom.'

As they sat down, Fafhrd and Groniger applauded lightly in approval and the girls all clapped imitatively.

Old Ourph croaked, 'It's true, silence is silver.'

Sitting beside Fingers, May told her, 'I've an extra white tunic I can lend you for tomorrow night.'

On her other side Gale said, 'And I have a spare yashmak. And I believe Klute has—'

'Unless, of course,' May interrupted, 'you'd want to wear your own things.'

'No,' Fingers hastened to say, 'now I'm on Rime Isle, I want to look like you.' She smiled.

Cif whispered to Afreyt, 'It's a strange thing. I know the Mouser's behaved like a monster tonight, and yet I can't help feeling that in some way he's *right* about Fingers and Pshawri, that they both lied to us in some way, maybe different ways. She was so cool about it all, almost the way a sleepwalker would talk.

'And Pshawri – he's always trying to impress the Mouser and win his praise, which rubs Mouser the wrong way. But a fortnight back, when the last Lankhmar trader came in – the *Comet*, she was – she carried a letter with a green seal for Pshawri, and since then there's been something new about his clashes with Mouser, something new and heavy.'

Afreyt said, 'I've sensed a different mood in Pshawri myself. Any idea what was in the letter?'

'Of course not.'

'Then tell me this: This strange feeling you have about the Mouser and the other two, does it come from your own thinking and imaginings, or from the goddess?'

'I wish I were sure,' Cif said as the two of them looked out together at the misted and ghastly bare gibbous moon.

AFREYT: Perchance at tomorrow night's ceremony she'll provide an answer.

CIF: We must press her.

8

That night Rime Isle most unaccountably grew wondrous cold and colder still, a blizzardly north wind blowing until the massive driftwood chimes in the leviathan-jaw arch of the Moon Temple clanked together dolefully and all sleepers suffered heavy sense-drugging nightmares, some toilsome and shivery heaving ones. When dawn at last came glimmering through swirls of powder snow, it was revealed that Fafhrd in ill nightcrawler's grip had somehow worked his way, dragging the covers after, up the maze of silver and brazen rods heading Cif's grand guest bed until the back of his head pressed the ceiling and he hung as one crucified asleep, while she below, hugging his ankles, dreamt they wandered a wintry waste embraced until a frigid gust parted them and whirled the Northerner high into the ice-gray sky until he seemed no bigger than a struggling gull, and that a like Morphean bondage had drawn the Gray Mouser, naked save for hauled-with sheet, out of and then under the second-best guest bed whereon he and Cif had gone excitingly to their slumbers, and she dreamed that they endlessly traversed shadowy subterranean corridors, their only light an eerie glow emanating from the Mouser's upper face, as if he wore a narrow glowing mask in which his eyes were horrid pits of darkness, until the Gray One slipped away from her through a trapdoor whereon was writ in phosphorescent Lankhmarese script, 'The Underworld'.

But all such personal plights and predicaments, ominous nightsights and sleepwalks, were soon almost forgot, became hazy in memory, as the extent of the general calamity was realized and a desperate rush to correct it began.

There were loved ones to be chafed, lost sheep to be succored – aye, and half-frozen shepherds too and other sleepers-out – cold ovens to be cleared of summer stowage and fired, kindling cut and seacoal shovelled, winter clothes dug from the bottoms of chests, strained moorings doubled and trebled of ships tossing at their docks and anchors, hatches battened in roofs and decks, lone dwellers visited.

When there was time for talk and wondering, some guessed that Khahkht the Wizard of Ice was on a rampage, others that the invisible winged Princes of lofty Stardock were out raiding, or – alarmist! – that the freezing glacial streams had at last tunnelled through Nehwon's crust and dowsed her inner fires. Cif and Afreyt looked to find answers at the full moon ceremony, and when Mother Grum and the Senior Council cancelled it on grounds of inclement weather (it being held outdoors), went on with their preparations anyway. Mother Grum raised no objections, believing in freedom of worship, but the Council refused it formal sanction.

So, it was no great wonder that the congregation that gathered before the chimes-arch of the open Moon Temple, with its twelve stone columns marking the year's twelve moons, was such a small one: in the main, exactly those who had dined at Afreyt's the previous evening and been pressed to attend by her and Cif. Those two were there, of course, being ringleaders of the outlaw rite, snug in their winter-priestess garb of white fur-hooded robes, mittens, and wool-lined ramskin boots. The five girls came as obedient novices, though it would have been hard to keep them away from what they considered a prize adventure. They wore like gear, only with shorter capes, so that from time to time their rosy knees showed, and the weird weather made Fingers' lamb's hide yashmak and gloves highly appropriate. Fafhrd and Mouser came as their ladies' lovers, although they'd spent a hard day working, first at Afreyt's, then at their barracks. Both looked a little distant-minded, as though each had begun to remember the nightmares that had accompanied their strange nightcrawlings. Skullick and Pshawri turned up with them. Presumably their captains had reinforced with commands the entreaties of their captains' mistresses, though Pshawri had an oddly intent look, and even the carefree Skullick a concerned one.

Ourph had not been pressed by anyone to attend, in view of his great age, but he was there nevertheless, close-wrapped in dark Mingol furs, with conical black-fur cap and sealskin boots to which small Mingol snowshoes were affixed.

Harbor master Groniger too, whose atheism might have been expected to keep him away. He said in explanation, 'Witchery is always my business. Though arrant superstition, three out of four times it's associated with crime – piracy and mutiny at sea, all manner of ill-workings on land. And don't tell me about you moon priestesses being white witches, not black. I know what I know.'

And in the end Mother Grum showed up herself, fur-bundled to the ears and waddling on snowshoes larger than Ourph's. 'It's my duty as coven mistress,' she grumbled, 'to get you out of any scrapes your wild behavior gets you into and to see that in any case no one tries to stop you.' She glared amiably at Groniger.

With her came Rill the Harlot, also a moon priestess, whose maimed left hand gave her a curious sympathy (unmixed with lechery, or so 'twas thought) with Fafhrd, who'd lost his entirely.

These fifteen, irregularly grouped, stood looking east across the sharp-serrated snow-shedding gables of the small, low, close-set houses of Salthaven, awaiting moonrise. They rapidly shuffled their feet from time to time to warm them. And whenever they did, the massy grey slabs of the sacred wind chime chain-hung from the lofty single-bone leviathan-jaw arch seemed to vibrate faintly yet profoundly in sympathy, or in memory of their earlier hollow clanking when the gale had blown, or perhaps in anticipation of the goddess's near apparition.

When the low glow of that approach intensified toward a central area above the toothed roofs, the nine females drew somewhat apart from the six males, turning their backs on them and crowding together closely, so that the invocatory words Afreyt whispered might not be overheard by the men, nor the holy objects Cif drew from under her wide cloak and showed around be glimpsed by them.

Then, when a dazzlingly white fingernail clipping of the orb's self, serrated by the teeth of the central-most roof, showed, there was a general sigh of recognition and fulfillment which was echoed inanimately by an intensification of the chimes' real or imagined low vibrations, and the groups broke up and intermingled and joined hands in one long line, the girls leading with May at their head, the rest linked at random, and the whole company began a slow rhythmic circling of the Temple, twice all the way around, then interweaving the carven stone moon pillars – that of the Snow, the Wolf, the Seed, the Witch, the Ghost, the Murderer, the Thunder, the Satyr, the Harvest, the Second Witch, the Frost, and the Lovers – by sixes, by fours, by threes, by two, and individually.

The girls wove their way one after the other, linked hand to hand, gracefully as in a dream. Old Ourph footed it agilely, stamping out the time, while Mother Grum moved briskly for all her fat and with a surprisingly sure rhythm. Rill brought up the rear, swinging a leviathan oil lamp, unlit, from her maimed hand.

As the moonlight slowly strengthened, Fingers marvelled somewhat fearfully at the strange Rimish runes and savage scenes carved in the thick moon pillars. Gale squeezed her hand reassuringly and told her in whispered snatches how they represented the adventures of the legendary witch queen Skeldir when she descended into the Underworld to get the help that enabled her to turn back the three dire Simorgyan invasions in the Isle's olden days.

When the seven slow mystic circlings had been completed and the glaringly white orb of Skama (the goddess's holiest name) fully arisen, so that sky-black hugged her all around, May led the weaving line out across the great meadow to the west, moving forward confidently in the full moonshine. For a short way the shadows of the twelve pillars and the jaw-hung chime accompanied them, then they launched out one by one across the trackless moonlit expanse, the frozen and snow-dusted grass crackling under their feet. May followed a serpentine course; veering now left, now right, that copied their last pillar-weaving, but went straight west, their shadows preceding them.

And then Afreyt called out in vibrant tones the sacred name, 'Skama!' and they all began to chant, in time to their dancing advance, the first song to the Goddess:

'Twelve faces has our Lady of the Dark
As she walks nightly cross her starry park:
Snow, Wolf, and Seed Moon, Witches, Ghosts, and Knife,
The Murderer's badge; six more of dark and light:
Thunder, Lust, Harvest, Witches second life;
Then end the year with Frost and Lovers bright;
Queen of the Night and Mistress of the Dark
In your black veils and clinging silver sark.'

Their voices fell silent for five beats, Afreyt again called, 'Skama!' and they began Her second song, their steps becoming longer and more gliding to suit the changed rhythm:

'These be your signets, dread Mistress of Mystery:
Rainbow and bubble, the flame and the star,
Night bee and glow wasp, volcano, cool history,
Things that are hintings of wonders afar;
Comet and hailstone and strange turns of history,
Queen of the Darkness and Lamp of the Night,
Lover of Terror, cruel and sisterly—
Crone, Girl, and Mother, arise in your white!'

A four-beat pause, once more 'Skama!' from Afreyt, and now their dance became a rapid and stamping one, as though they advanced to the pounding of a drum:

'Snow Moon, Wolf Moon, Seed Moon, Witch Moon;
Ghost Moon, Knife Moon, Blast Moon, Lust Moon;
Sickle, Witch Two, Frost Moon, Fuck Moon.
Skama beckons, Skeldir goes down
By the lightless narrow stoneway,
Buried Rimish fashion feet first,

Bravely facing poison monsters,
Treading serpents with her bare feet;
Through dry earth and solid rock;
Sinks like ghost into the granite;
Skeldir's courage fails, she falters—
When she spies the moon below her,
In the heart of darkness, light!'

This time Afreyt let twenty beats go by before giving her invocation, and the hand-linked linear company began a repetition of the three songs while they continued their curving and countercurving westward advance. A little toward the north Elvenhold loomed, a pale stout needle of rock and scrub heather to whose square top the strongest bow could not loft arrow. Two moons ago, on fateful Midsummer Day, all of them save Fingers and Ourph had picnicked there. While toward the south began a series of low rolling hills, at first mere swells in the sea of moonlit grass. And toward these hills May now began to lead their way, an overall southward veering of the dancing line.

By the songs' second repetition islands of gorse and furze were appearing in the grassy ocean. May led between them toward a somewhat higher hill.

'Our destination?' Fingers asked Gale, softly singing the question into the song they were on.

'Yes,' Gale replied in murmured snatches while swaying to the song. 'In old times it had a gallows. Then 'twas the ghost god Odin's hill when he counselled Aunt Afreyt. I was one of his handmaids.'

FINGERS: What did you have to do?

GALE: For one thing, I was his cabingirl, you could say.

FINGERS: You were? You said he was a ghost. Was he solid enough for such things?

GALE: Enough. He wanted all sorts of touching, both do and be done by.

FINGERS: Gods are just like men. Your aunt let you?

GALE: It was very important information she was getting from him. Helped save Rime Isle. Also, I braided nooses for him. He made us wear them around our necks.

FINGERS: That sounds scary. Dangerous.

GALE: It was. That's how Uncle Fafhrd lost his left hand. He was wearing them all around his left wrist in that battle I told you about. When Odin and the gallows vanished up into the sky, the nooses all tightened to nothing and shot up after – and Uncle Fafhrd's hand with them.

FINGERS: Really scary. If you'd kept them round your necks—

GALE: Yes. Later, when Aunt Cif and Mother Grum purified the hill and cut down the bower where May and Mara and I had loved up the old god, they changed its name from Gallows to Goddess's Hill, and we've been holding the summer full-moon rites on it.

MARA: Whatever are you two whispering about? I can see Aunt Afreyt frowning at you.

They instantly took up the song, which by now was another. 'The little demons!' Afreyt whispered to Fafhrd in a not particularly angry voice.

He turned back toward her and nodded, though even less concerned than she, just as he'd sometimes been chanting tonight and sometimes not, as the mood took him.

The chill air was very still and fantastically clear. It occurred to Fafhrd that he had never in his life seen the full moon shine so bright, not even from Stardock. At that instant, as though some hidden cord of weakness deep in his vitals had been shrewdly plucked, he felt a spasm of unmanning faintness flurry through him, a feeling of insubstantiality, as if the world were about to fade away from him, or he from the world. It was all he could do to stand upright and not shake.

As the weird qualm receded somewhat, he looked along the curving line of brightly lit moonlit faces to learn if it were something others had felt. Halfway up the hill the five girls moved on slowly in line, chanting raptly. Fingers, nearest of them but for Gale, looked toward him, but tranquilly, as though she'd simply sensed his gaze upon her. Next closest after the girls, Pshawri, dutifully chanting, or at least moving his lips. Finally, not five feet away, the Mouser, making not even pretence of chanting, seemingly lost in a brown study, but very much at ease, hood thrown back to bare his close-cropped head to the frosty air, while Fafhrd's covered his ears.

Looking on his other side he saw, in orderly succession and

554

absorbed in the ceremony: Afreyt, Groniger, Skullick, old Ourph the Mingol, Cif, fat Mother Grum the Witch, and Rill the Harlot.

And then Fafhrd looked at Cif again (she must have started) and saw that she was now staring past him, her pale face of a sudden contorted with an expression of incredulous horror.

He whipped around and saw, on his side, one face fewer than there'd been before. While he'd been looking in the other direction, the Mouser had gone away somewhere and his fingers dropped away unfelt from the hook that was the Northerner's left hand.

And then he noticed that Pshawri, with an expression on his face not unlike that of Cif's, was staring at the Northerner's knees as if the Gray Mouser's young lieutenant were stupefiedly witnessing some horrifying miracle. Fafhrd looked down and saw that the Mouser had indeed dropped away! Straight down feet first into the frozen earth so he was buried upright to his waist and was no taller than a dwarf. Impossible! But there it was.

Just then, as if some subterranean being gripping the Mouser's ankles had given another mighty yank, Fafhrd's comrade swiftly sank another half yard so he was buried to the chin like a Mingol traitor whom vengeful mates will leisurely dispatch by bowling rocks at his head and leaden-weighted skulls, though only after his concubines have been allowed (or forced) to kiss him one time each full on the lips.

And then the Mouser looked up at Fafhrd with moonlit eyes widening, as if in full realization of his horrid plight, and gasped in piteous appeal, 'Help me!' And his tall comrade could only quake and stare.

Fafhrd heard from behind the sound of onrunning footsteps, boots ringing on frozen earth. And for a moment it seemed to him that he could see the moonlit ground through the Mouser's head, as if the little man were becoming attenuated, insubstantial. Or was that only his strange qualm returning? His own swimming eyes?

And then, as if those subterranean hands were giving another tug, the Mouser began to move downward once again rapidly.

From behind him Cif cast herself full length on the frozen

ground, her outstretched hands snatching at the disappearing head.

Fafhrd regained his power of movement and swiftly scanned around in case the Mouser's ghost were floating off in some other direction. The air seemed full of movement, but nothing substantial when he looked closely.

With three exceptions everyone was staring at Cif or else hurrying toward her, who was now scrabbling through the scant frozen grass, as though frenziedly hunting for a jewel she'd dropped there. Afreyt and Groniger were looking off intently toward Elvenhold. The tall woman pointed at something and the deliberate man nodded in agreement.

While Fingers was staring straight at Fafhrd in cool accusal, as if asking, 'Why didn't you save your friend?'

9

From the Gray Mouser's point of view, what had happened was this:

He'd been staring toward the moon, quite unmindful of the cold and the ceremony, lost in puzzlement as to how he could at once feel so heavy – as though wearied to death and barely able to stay erect, victim of some heatless fever – and yet at the same time so listless-light and insubstantial, as if he were thinning out to become a ghost whom the slightest breeze might blow away. The two feelings didn't agree at all, yet both were there.

Without warning, he experienced a spasm of strange faintness, like Fafhrd's but more intense, so that he blacked out completely. It was as if the ground had been taken out from under his feet. When he came to his senses again, he was looking up at his northern comrade, who had never before seemed quite so tall.

He must have simply keeled over, he told himself, and fallen flat. But when he tried to get up, he found he could move neither hand nor foot, bend waist or knee. Was he paralysed? Everywhere below his neck something gripped him closely, and when he moved his fingers and thumbs against each other (both hands being imprisoned down by his sides so he couldn't spread fingers or make a fist), that *something* felt suspiciously grainy, like raw earth.

In the most horrifying reorientation he'd ever experienced in the course of an eventful life, flat-on-my-back became buried-to-my-neck. Oh dismal! And so incredible that he couldn't really say whether it was the world, or he, that had moved to effect the dreadful exchange.

Something terribly swift in his mind scanned almost instantaneously the pressures all over his body. Were they slightly greater around his ankles? As if he wore gyves, as if something or *someone* gripped both his legs – such as the quicksand nixies Sheelba had warned him against in the Great Salt Marsh. Oh Mog, no!

His gaze traveled up Fafhrd, who seemed tall as a pine, and he gasped out his agonized plea – *and the great lout would only goggle and grimace at him, mop and mow in the moonlight, not only withholding help, but also seeming utterly unmindful of the priceless privilege he enjoyed of standing free atop the ground rather than being immured in it!*

Beyond Fafhrd he saw Cif running straight at him. If she kept on, she'd boot his face, the mad maenad! He instinctively tried to duck aside and only succeeded in wrenching his neck. And then he felt the grip on his ankles tighten and cold earth mount his chin, as his whole being was drawn downward. He clapped his lips tightly together to keep dirt out, drew one swift breath, then tried to narrow his nostrils, finally closed tight his eyes as his engulfment continued. Last thing he saw was the moon. As the gray glow of it transmitted through his eyelids vanished upward, he felt his pate scratched and his topknot sharply tweaked. Then even that was gone and there remained only a grainy coldness sliding up his cheeks. Strangely, then, it seemed to grow a little warmer and – a very little – looser, so he could puff some of the air trapped in his mouth out into his cheeks. The texture of the stuff scraping his cheeks changed from earth to wool to earth again. He realized his cowl had been dragged upward from around his neck and left buried above him. And then the rough sliding seemed to stop. One other thing he had to admit: the feeling of heaviness that had so long dogged him was completely gone. However closely confined, he seemed now rather to be floating.

The swift something in his mind produced for his consideration a list of the beings who might hate him enough to wish him such a horrid doom and also conceivably have the magical power to effect it on him. The wizards Quarmal of Quarmall, Khakht the Ice Wizard, Great Oomforafor, Hisvin the Rat King, his own mentor Sheelba turned against him, dear diabolic Hisvet, the gods Loki and Mog. It went on and on.

One thing stood out: any world in which a man could be twitched into his grave by the legerdemain of some mad principality or power was *monstrously* unfair!

10

Aboveground, Cif rose to her knees, from where she'd been crouched, breaking her fingernails scrabbling at the frosty ground, and stretched her arms around the girls, who had been crowding in close and all trying to touch her, more for their own comfort and reassurance than for hers. She tried to touch them all in turn and draw them to her, hushing their clamours, though as much for her own comfort as for theirs. They felt cold.

Dumbstruck, Fafhrd turned back to ask Afreyt exactly what she'd seen when Mouser had seemed to sink into the ground impossibly. To his confusion he saw that she and Groniger were already a dozen yards away, hurrying toward Elvenhold, while Rill was sprinting after them at an angle from where she'd been at the end of the ritual line, the unlit lamp still streaming out behind her.

With a slow, puzzled headshake he turned forward again and saw, beyond the huddled backs of Cif and the girls, Pshawri convulsed in an agony, his features grimaced, his eyes squeezed half shut, his taut body rocking forward and back, and literally tearing his hair. By Kos, did the knave think it was mourning time already?

Then the tortured eyes of the Mouser's young lieutenant fixed upon Cif. They widened, his body ceased to rock, he left off tearing his hair and he threw out both arms to her in mute appeal.

She responded immediately, pushing fully to her feet to go to him. But at that moment Fafhrd found his voice.

'Don't move a step!' he called commandingly in carefully enunciated battle tones. 'Stay where you are exactly – or we will lose the spot where Mouser disappeared into the ground.'

And he moved toward her deliberately, his sound right hand working to free his double-headed hand ax from the case where it hung at his side, its short helve pendant.

'The spot where we must dig,' he amplified, going to his knees close behind her.

She turned around, and seeing him bringing out his ax and thinking he meant to chop into the ground with it, cried in alarm, 'Oh, don't do that, you might hurt *him*.'

He shook his head reassuringly, and grasping the axe at the juncture of its head and helve, scraped with it strongly inward toward his knees, feeling with his hook through the earth he uncovered. He scraped three like swaths behind the first, baring a space about as big as a trapdoor, and then repeated the process, going an inch deeper.

Meanwhile Pshawri was approaching Cif, fumbling in his pouch and babbling, 'Sweet Lady, I am responsible for this dire mishap to my captain. I alone am guilty. Here, let me show you . . .'

Without ceasing his work, Fafhrd called sharply, 'Forget that, Pshawri, and come here. I have an errand for you.'

But when that one did not seem to hear his words, only continuing to stare desperately at Cif and now groping at her arms to draw her attention, Fafhrd signed to her to draw the madman aside and hear his mouthings, meanwhile commanding, 'You, Skullick, then! Come here!'

When his young sergeant swiftly obeyed, though not without an uneasy glance toward Pshawri, Fafhrd instructed him tersely, while keeping on with his scrapings, 'Skullick, run like the wind back to the barracks. Find Skor and Mikkidu. Bid them haste here with one or two men apiece bringing heavy work gloves, scoops, shovels, pails, lanterns, and ropes. Don't try to explain anything – here, take my ring. Then do you choose a man each of the Mouser's men and mine – and a Mingol – and come on after with planks and the instruments needful for shoring a shaft, more ropes, pulleys, food, fuel, water, a keg of brandy, blankets, the medicine case. Come as soon as these can be gathered. Use the dogcarts. Mannimark to remain in command at the barracks. Any questions? No? Then go!'

Skullick went. Instantly Rill took his place.

'Fafhrd,' she said urgently, 'Afreyt and Groniger bid me tell you that whatever you believe we saw, or think we saw, deceived perhaps by a phantom, the Mouser, at the end, raced with preternatural speed toward Elvenhold and then took cover. They go to hunt him. They urge you join them, after sending for lanterns, the dogs Racer and Gripper, and an unwashed piece of the Mouser's intimate clothing.'

Fafhrd left off scraping out the square hole, which was five or six inches deep, to look around questioningly at those who had been listening.

'Captain, he sank into the ground where you are digging,' said Ourph the Mingol. 'I saw.'

'It's true,' growled Mother Grum, 'though he grew somewhat insubstantial at the end.'

Cif broke away from the importunate Pshawri to aver with great certitude, 'He went down there. I touched his pate and top hair before he sank away.'

Pshawri followed behind her, crying, 'Here, Lady, I've found it. Here is the proof I lied to the Captain when I told him yesternight I brought up nothing from my Maelstrom dive.'

It was a skeleton cube of smooth metal big as an infant's fist with something dark wedged inside. The metal looked like silver in the moonlight, but Cif knew that without question it was gold – the Rimish ikon that the Mouser had slung into the Great Maelstrom's centre to quieten it after the wrecking of the Sea-Mingol armada.

'My taking of this from the whirlpool's maw,' mad-eyed Pshawri proclaimed, 'though meant to please him, has been the means of my captain's doom. As he himself feared might hap. Gods, was ever man so cruelly self-deceived?'

'Why did you lie to him, then?' Fafhrd asked. 'And why did you so desire to possess it?'

'I may not tell you,' Pshawri said miserably. 'That is a private matter between myself and the Captain. Gods, what's to do? What is to do?'

'We keep on digging here,' Fafhrd decided, suiting action to word. 'Rill, tell Afreyt and Groniger of my decision.'

'First let me make your work here easier,' that one said, bringing the leviathan lantern from behind her and planting it on the ground next the square hole Fafhrd was digging, then snapping the fingers of her right hand thrice.

'Burn without heat,' she said simultaneously.

The simple magic worked.

Leviathan light white as new-fallen snow, pure bistory, sprang into being and illumined the surroundings like a piece of the full moon brought down to earth, so that every dirt grain inside the new-digged square seemed individually visible.

Fafhrd thanked her duly and Rill made off briskly toward Elvenhold.

Fafhrd turned back and said, 'Pshawri, sit across the hole from me and feel through the new dirt uncovered by each of my axe scrapes. Two hands work faster than a hook. Gale! You – and Fingers here – come and kneel beside me and clear off to either side the earth my axe scrapes up. Now I'm through the frozen turf, I can take deeper swaths. Pshawri, while you are feeling for the Mouser's head, tell us, coolly and clearly, all that your conscience will allow about your Maelstrom dive.'

'You think he may yet survive?' Cif asked falteringly, as though doubting her own wild hopes.

'Madam,' said Fafhrd, 'I've known the Gray One for some time. It never does to underestimate his resourcefulness under adversity or coolth in peril.'

II

Tight-packed upright in dirt, as if he had been honoured with a Rimish pit burial, the Mouser became aware of a lump in his throat which, as he observed it, slowly grew larger and harder and began to involve or elicit twitching sensations in his cheeks and his mouth's roof, and like painful feelings or impulses

561

toward movement, deep in his chest. A tension grew in that whole area and there began the faintest buzzing in his ears. All these sensations continued to increase without respite.

He recalled that his last breath had been drawn while he still saw the moon.

With a tremendous effort of will he fought down the urge to gulp in a great breath (which could fill his mouth with dust, set him coughing and gasping – not to be thought of!). He began very slowly (almost experimentally, you might say, except it had to be done – and soon!) to inhale, at first through his nostrils but swiftly switching to his barely parted lips, where his tongue could wet them and, moving from side to side, push back intrusive particles of earth, keep them at bay – somewhat like the approved technique for smoking hashish whereby one draws in thin whifflets of air on either side of the pipe to dilute the rich fumes. (Ah, mused the Mouser, the wondrous freedom of the tongue inside the mouth! No matter how the body were confined. Folk appreciated it insufficiently.)

And all the while he was drawing cold sips of precious life-giving air that had been stored between the particles of solid ground, and while letting no more dirt grains pass his lips than he could easily swallow. Why, in this fashion, he speculated, he might eventually move through the ground, taking in earth at his anterior end, perhaps – who knows? – extracting nutriment from it and then excreting it in a faecal trail.

But then the lump in his throat caught his attention again. He blew out *that* breath (it took an appreciable time, there was resistance) and slowly (remember, always slowly! he told himself) took in a second breath.

He decided after several repetitions of this process that if he worked at it industriously, losing no time but never letting himself be tempted to rush things, he could keep the lump in his throat (and the impulse to gasp) down to a tolerable size.

So for the present, understandably, everything not connected with breathing became of secondary importance to the Mouser – nay, tertiary!

He told himself that if he kept up the process long enough, it would become habitual, and then there would be room in his mind to think of other things, or at least of other aspects of his current predicament.

A question then would be: Would he care to do so when the time came? Would there be profit or comfort in such speculation?

As the Mouser did indeed slowly become able to attend to other matters, he noted a faint reddish glow within his eyelids. A few breaths later he told himself that could not be, it took sunlight to do that and here he had not even the moon. (He would have permitted himself a small sob, except under his present circumstances the slightest breathing irregularity was not to be thought of.)

But curiosity, once roused, persisted (' . . . even to the grave,' he told himself with sententious melodrama), and after a few more breaths he parted his eyelids the narrowest slit, hedged by his lashes.

Nothing attacked him, not the tiniest grain of sand, and there was indeed yellow light.

After a bit he parted his lids still farther, while dutifully keeping up his breathing, of course, and surveyed the little scene.

Judging by the way the view was brightly yellow-rimmed, the illumination appeared to be coming from his own face. He remembered the strange dream or night incident Cif had told him of, in which she'd seen him wearing a phosphorescent half-mask with ovals of blackness where his eyes would be. Perhaps she had indeed foreseen the future, for he now appeared to be wearing just such a mask.

What the light revealed was this: He was facing into a brown wall, so close it was blurred, but not close enough to touch in any way his bared optics.

Yet as he studied it, he seemed increasingly able to see into it, so that about a finger's length beyond the frontal blur, individual grains of earth were sharply defined, as if some occult power of vision were mixed in with the natural sort, the former merging into and extending the latter.

By this means, whatever it might be, he saw a black pebble buried in the earth about six inches away, and beside that a dark green one as big as his thumb, and next to *that* the ringed black reddish face of an earthworm with small central circular mouth working, pointing almost directly at him so that its segments, seen in sharp perspective, nearly merged.

And then for the first time the element of hallucination or pure fantasy entered his vision, for it seemed to him that the worm addressed him in a high piping voice, saying, 'O Mortal Man, what guards you? Why cannot I approach you to gnaw your eyeballs?'

Yet at the same time it so convinced the Mouser that he was beguiled into replying in soft gruff tones, 'Ho, Fellow Prisoner—'

He got no further. His own voice, however diminished, made such a clamour in the confined space, reverberating back and forth within his skull and jaw, like wind chimes in a hurricane, that both his ears felt deep pain and he almost forgot to breathe.

The unexpectedly powerful vibrations raised by his incautious speaking also appeared to have upset the delicate equilibrium with which he hung in the sea of soil around him, for he noted that the two pebbles and the worm had begun to move upward all together, although he felt no corresponding downward pull upon his ankles. Clearly, he had prematurely attempted too much.

He carefully closed his eyes and reconcentrated all his attention on his slowly breathing in and breathing out, resolutely ignoring the deepening of his entombment.

12

Aboveground notable progress had been made in the Mouser search. It had got more organized. Both parties from the barracks had arrived and there was the reassuring presence of young men busily at work. Fafhrd's big, lean ex-berserks, Northerners like him, and the Mouser's reformed thieves, compact and wiry. The two dogcarts that had brought water, food, and lumber had been unloaded and the two-bearhound team of one had been unharnessed and ranged about watchfully. A small hot fire had been built and there were the heavy rich odours of mutton soup warming and gravy brewing. Mother Grum and old Ourph huddled beside the blaze.

Fafhrd's square hole, widened by a foot on each side, had gone deep enough so that the heads of those digging it and feeling through the dirt were below ground level. Fafhrd had given over his job to his trusty lieutenant Skor, a prematurely balding redhead, while Pshawri continued at the same task, assisted now by Mara and Klute. A Northerner stood on the rim and every minute or so drew up a big pail of earth and emptied it to the side in one sweeping throw. The Mouser's other lieutenant, Mikkidu, and another thief had started to put in the first tier of shoring from above, hammering eight-foot planks side by side with wooden mallets. Two leviathan-oil lanterns in the dark side of the hole glowed upward on their three faces. The full moon was three hours higher than when Skama had been honoured by the dance across the Great Meadow.

Fafhrd and Cif stood by the fire, sipping hot gahveh with the two oldsters. It was the first rest he'd taken. Behind him were Gale and Fingers, not drawing attention to themselves, partly for fear of being sent back to Salthaven by the next dogcart as May had been, to reassure their families all the girls were safe. Also in the fireside gahvehing group were Afreyt, Groniger, and Rill, the last having run to Elvenhold to summon the other two for conference and, as it turned out, argument.

Afreyt said to Fafhrd, without heat, 'Dear man, I deeply admire and respect your loyalty to and regard for your old friend that makes you search for him with such stubborn singlemindedness along one trail only, a trail where your greatest success can hardly be more than the digging up of a corpse. But I question your logic. Since there are other trails – and Groniger and I both attest to that – trails promising a more useful sort of success, if any, why not expend at least half our efforts on those? Nay, why not all?'

'That appears to me to be most closely reasoned,' Groniger put in, seconding.

'You think I was guided by logic and reason in what I did?' Fafhrd asked with a shade of impatience, even contempt, shaking his hook at them. '*I saw him sink*, I tell you. So did others. Cif *felt* him go straight down.'

565

'I too,' from Ourph. 'We saw one miracle, why not expect another?'

Afreyt took up, 'Yet all of you who saw him sink have admitted, at one time or another since, that he grew insubstantial toward the end. And so did he to Gron and I, I freely admit, in his flight toward Elvenhold. But does not that equality argue for us giving an equal weight to both possibilities?'

Fafhrd replied, a little tiredly, 'I'm bothered myself by those impressions of the Mouser fading. In view of them, the idea of also searching for him elsewhere on Rime Isle seems sensible, and when I sent Gib the Mingol back with the second dogcart for more lumber, you heard me tell him to fetch some rag of the Mouser's and the two scent dogs if available.'

Cif spoke up. 'I keep wondering if there's not some way to use, in hunting Mou, the golden queller Pshawri brought up from the Maelstrom. It's enwedged with the black cinder of god Loki, whom I'm convinced is responsible for Mou's present plight. A most treacherous and madly malevolent deity, as I learned in my dealings with him.'

'You're right about that last,' Mother Grum agreed darkly, but before she could say more, Skor yelled up from the hole, 'Captain, I've uncovered something buried seven feet deep you'll want to see. Will send it up.'

Fafhrd moved quickly to the rim, took something off the top of the next bucketload drawn up, shook it out and then closely inspected it.

'It's the Mouser's cowl which he wore tonight,' he announced to them all triumphantly. 'Now tell me he didn't sink straight down into the ground here!'

Cif snatched it from him and confirmed the identification.

Afreyt called 'Snowtreader!', knelt by the shoulder of the white bearhound who came up, working her fingers deep in his great ruff and speaking earnestly in his shaggy ear. He took a thoughtful snuff of the dirt-steeped garment and began to move about questioningly, muzzle to the ground. He came to the hole, gazed down into it searchingly for a long moment, his eyes green in the lampglow, then sat down on the rim, lifted his muzzle to the moon and howled long and dolorously like a trumpet summoning mourners to a hero's funeral.

13

It was well that the Gray Mouser had the lifelong habit, whenever he woke from slumber, of assessing his situation as fully as possible before making the least move. After all, there might always be murderous enemies lurking about waiting for him to betray his exact location by an unguarded movement or exclamation, so as to slay him before he had his wits about him.

And it attests to his presence of mind that when he discovered himself to be everywhere confined by grainy dirt and simultaneously recalled the stages by which he had arrived at this dismal predicament, he did not waste energy and invite inquiry by frantic reactions, he simply continued to pursue his thoughts and explore his surroundings, so far as the latter was possible.

To the best of his recollection his second downward slide or glide through the ground had not lasted long, and after coming to rest a second time, he had concentrated so exclusively on the task of breathing a sufficiency of earth-trapped air to stay alive and hold at bay the impulse to gasp that the dark monotony of his occupation had by gradual stages hypnotized him into sleep.

And now, awake again and feeling somewhat refreshed, though perceptibly chilled, he was still breathing regularly, shallowly, slowly – no impulse to pant – with his tongue busy at intervals, keeping his barely parted lips moist and fending off intrusive dirt. Why, this was good! It showed that the whole operation had become sufficiently automatic for him safely to gain the rest he might well need if his incarceration underground proved overlong – which might well be the case, he must admit.

He noticed now that although his arms lay flat against his sides, they had during his second descent – each bent at the elbow and his hands pushed upward by the sandy soil through which he'd descended – crawled up the front of his body toward his waist, so the fingers of his right now rested against the scabbard of his dagger Cat's Claw, a contact he found reassuring. He set himself to working his fingers up the scabbard, pausing to regularize his breathing whenever it became the least bit laboured. When his fingers finally reached their goal, he was surprised to discover they touched, not the dagger's crosspiece and grip, but a section of the sharp narrow blade near the tip. The sandy soil encasing him, rubbing upward against his body as he'd descended, had also almost carried the dagger entirely out of its sheath.

He pondered this new circumstance, wondering if he should attempt to return the strayed weapon to its scabbard by drawing it down a little at a time by its blade pinched between his forefinger and thumb, lest some further sliding on his part separate him from it altogether, a prospect that alarmed him. Or should he try to work his hand up farther still and grip its hilt so as to have it ready for action should unforeseen change in his situation ever permit him to use it? This line of operation appealed to him most, though promising to involve more work.

During the course of this self-debate he thoughtlessly asked himself aloud, 'Which or which?' and instantly winced in anticipation of heavy pain. But he had spoken in quite soft tones, and although the words thundered a bit in his ears, there were no other dolorous consequences. He was enheartened to discover that he could enjoy his own conversational companionship underground, provided he spoke not much louder than a whisper, for truth to tell, he was becoming quite lonely. But after trying it out two or three times, he desisted; he found that every time he spoke he felt ridiculously terrified of being overheard and so betraying his presence and being taken at a disadvantage, though what or whom he had to fear deep in the dirty bosom of this scantily populated polar island he could not say. Not carnivorous Kleshite ghouls, surely? But likely the gods, if such rogue beings exist, who are said to hear our faintest spoken words, even our whispers.

After a time he decided to let the problem of Cat's Claw rest a while and once again risk a visual inspection of his surroundings, since the persistent reddish glow within his eyelids told him that he carried his own peculiar illumination to this deeper spot. He had not done this earlier for two reasons. First, it seemed wise to attend only to one thing at a time besides his breathing; to attempt more would invite exhaustion and a confusion that might well lead to panic and loss of the control that he had with difficulty won. Second, he had so few activities open to him in his constricted circumstance that he would do well to hoard them and dole them out like a miser, lest he fall victim to a boredom that might well become literally maddening, a suicidal tedium.

Taking the same precautions as he had before, he got his eyes open without incident and once again found himself facing a blurred grainy wall, only this time streaked with white and dull blue, as though there were an admixture of chalk and slate in the soil hereabouts. And once again he discovered that the longer he stared at it, to the accompaniment only of his measured silent ex- and inhalations, the deeper he was able to see into it by some power of occult vision.

For a while this time there were no definite objects to be seen, such as the worm and the pebbles, yet there were fugitive glimmerings and tiny marching movements such as the eyes see when there is no light, making it hard to determine whether they were happening inside his eyes or out in the reaches of cold ground.

Eventually, at a distance, he judged, of eight or ten feet out from him, the blue-shadowed white streaks began to organize themselves into a slender female figure, upright as he was and facing him, as pale as death, with eyes and lips serenely shut as though she were asleep. A strange quality in the blue-shadowed whiteness seemed familiar to him and this daunted him, though where and when he had encountered it before he could not tell.

His intimate yet somehow mystic view of this quiescent figure seemed not so much obscured by the three intervening yards of solid dirt as softened by them, as though he were viewing it (her?) through several of the finest imaginable veils, such as might grace some ethereal princess's boudoir rather than these cruel cemetery confines.

At first he thought he was imagining the whole vision and told himself how apt the human eye is to see definite shapes of things in smoke, expanses of vegetation, old tapestries, simmering stews, slow fires, and similars – and especially apt to interpret pale indistinct shapes as human bodies. But the longer he looked at it, the more distinct it got. Looking away and then back didn't banish it, nor did consciously trying to make it seem something else.

All this while the figure remained in the same attitude with visage serene, never changing as a creation of the imagination might be expected to do, so in the end he decided she must be an actual piece of statuary buried by some strange chance at just this spot, though the style seemed to him not at all Rimish. While her glimmering whiteness still seemed unpleasantly familiar. Where? When? He racked his brains.

Then there came a flurry of those small glimmering marching forms that were so hard to pin down as to location. They resolved themselves into a number of fine-beaded white lines connected to points on the quiescent naked female form – its eyes, ears, nostrils, mouth, and privacies. As he studied them they grew more distinct and he saw that the individual beads were creeping along in single file, toward the figure in about half the lines and away from it in the others. The word 'maggots' came into his mind and stayed despite his efforts to banish it. And the finely beaded busy lines became more real, no matter how vehement his self-assertion that they were but strayed figments of his imagination.

But then it occurred to him that if he truly were watching maggots devour dead buried flesh, there would inevitably be diminutions and other changes for the worse in the latter, whereas the slim blue-shadowed she-figure now appeared more attractive, if anything, than when he had first glimpsed her, in particular the small, saucy, unsagging breasts, medallions of supreme artistry, whose large azure nipplets implored kisses. Were the situation otherwise he would surely be feeling desire despite their unromanitc and highly constrictive surroundings. He coldly imagined hand-capturing her dainty tits and torment-ingly teasing them to their utmost erection, tonguing them avidly – gods! Could nothing break his constant awareness of the dreadful Mouser-shaped *mould* encasing him? (But to not get too far afield, wit-worshipping dolt, he told himself – recall to breathe!) Old legends said Death had a skinny sister denominated Pain, passionately devoted to the loathsome torture that often was Death's prelude.

But she was only a statue, he reminded himself desperately.

Her lips parted and a lissome blue tongue ran around them hungrily.

Her eyes opened and she fixed her red-glinting gaze upon him.

She smiled.

Suddenly he knew where he had seen her opalescently white complexion before. In the Shadowland! Upon the slender face and neck and hands and wrists of Death himself, whom he had twice beheld there. And she resembled Death facially and in her slenderness.

Then she puckered her lips and, through all the dirt that buried them both, he heard the thrilling soft seductive whistle with which a Lankhmar streetgirl invites trade. He felt the hair lift on the back of his neck while an icy chill went through him.

And then, to his extremest horror, this pale ghoulwaif, Sister of Death, seemingly without effort extended both her glimmering narrow hands toward him, blue palms turned invitingly upward and opalescent fingers rippling tremulously, and then gathering those same fingers together cuppingly and kicking back her left and right legs successively, began slowly to swim toward him through the harsh earth everywhere closely encasing them both as if it offered no more resistance to her blue-shadowed starkly naked form than it did to his occult vision.

Despite all his good resolutions to avoid panicky overexertion while buried, he strained convulsively backward, away from the dirt swimmer, in a spasm like to burst his heart. Then, just as his effort reached an excruciating peak he abandoned it, he felt emptiness behind him and launched himself into it – with an instant spurt of reverse fear: that he might fall for ever into a bottomless pit.

He could have spared himself that last terror. He had barely retreated a half yard, no more than one short step, when he felt himself everywhere backed again from head to heel with cold grainy earth.

But now there was an emptiness in front of him, the space from which he'd just withdrawn his trunk, head, and one leg. And there was time to draw a deep, big, glorious breath – one worth twenty of his cautious air sips – and to retreat the other leg before the forward dirt caught up with him again, brutally slapping his face in its eagerness to mould itself exactly to his central facade, as if matter or its gods and goddesses indeed possessed that abhorrence of vacua which some philosophers attribute to it, or to them.

Neither his startlement at all this totally unexpected occurrence nor his wonderment as to the natural laws or miracles by which it had been effected were great enough, despite the monster breath, to cause him to interrupt his regimen of slow small inhalations through barely parted lips, nor his watchful forward-spying between equally constricted eyelids.

The latter showed his deathly slim pursuer fully a yard closer to him and with her orientation changed almost completely from the vertical to the horizontal by her powerful swimming motions as she chased him head-on, so that he found himself staring aghast straight into her voracious red-glinting eyes.

This sight was so she-wolfishly dire to him that it inspired him to another gut-bursting effort to back away, with just at its peak the new hope that the strange miracle he'd just experienced might repeat itself. And rather to his surprise, it did: the dizzying emptiness behind, the half-yard backward lurch, the emptiness before, the glorious deep breath, the stinging impact against his whole front, but most tellingly upon his naked face, of cold grainy earth angrily reestablishing its total hold on him.

This time, assessing the effects of his two short retreats, he saw that he'd lost Cat's Claw, which now lay itself midway between him and his pursuer, its point directed straight at him. Evidently the ground embedding its hilt had torn it away from him at his first backward step, but his finger and thumb on its tip had held on as long as they were able, which had changed the dagger's attitude from vertical to horizontal, while his second backward step had completed the divorcement between him and his weapon. Squinting down with difficulty, he saw the finger and thumb in question beaded with blood where the sharp blade had cut them. Poor digits, wounded in parting, they had done their best!

He wondered if the fell form following hard upon him would knock the abandoned weapon out of her way, for she was headed straight toward it, or perhaps snatch it up to use against him, but he was already into his third soul-wrenching miracle-provoking effort and must concentrate all of his being on that. And when he was congratulating himself on his third half-yard gain (only it seemed more like a yard this time) and giant breath, he saw looking back that his pale pursuer had stroked herself a little higher in the earth-sea so that she overpassed Cat's Claw by a finger's breadth where it lay now midway between the stalactite buds of her downward-jutting small breasts, its keen tip still directed straight at him like a compass needle pointing him out, while her smooth belly traversed the blade.

He noted that Cat's Claw's scabbard had worked loose from his belt and lay in the ground's grip a little way behind him in the same attitude – pointing toward him – as its parent weapon did, now lying beyond his pursuer.

But now he was making his fourth – no, fifth! – bobbing retreat, face pommelled by invisible earth. Damn it! It was all so demeaning – curtseying away from Death's skinny, shameless sister!

The thought occurred to him that her and his means of progression through solid earth were both so strange and yet so grossly different that he might well be in the grip of some powerful hallucination or mighty dream in deathly sleep, rather than that of reality.

Do not believe that! he told himself. Banish the thought! For if you did, you might relax your efforts to breathe, both the tiny air sips and, where circumstances permitted, the deep gulps, for those, he knew at some level far below reason, were vital – nay, fundamental! – to his survival in this dark realm.

And yet as he strongly kept up those breathings small and large, piling repetition upon repetition, and maintained or even seemed to lengthen his lead upon his fell fair follower (who was now overpassing closely his dagger's scabbard as she had the dagger), the scene surrounding him grew gloomier by slow stages, the mind-light by which he saw it dimmed, his movements manifested a reptilian heaviness along with power, a chthonic scaliness and hairiness, and sleep enshrouded him like blindness, leaving him only an awareness of profound laboured progression through grainy blackness.

14

The impression aboveground that the Mouser search had slacked off was misleading. It had simply grown somewhat more routinized and realistic. What it had lost in dash had been more than made up in dogged efficiency. In most of the participants concerned excitement boiled underneath, or at least simmered.

The moon halfway down the western sky was glaringly bright. Her white light shadowed the face and front of another of Fafhrd's men standing with wide-braced feet on the lip of the hole, intermittently busy drawing up and emptying the earth bucket. His sidewise castings now made a wide low mound more than a foot high toward its centre. The drawings-up took longer and the glow on his shadowed chest and under face from the lamps inside the shaft at its working foot was much less – both measures of the shaft's increasing depth. In fact, other workers were at the same time lowering down into it planks for a second tier of shorings, the first having been firmly fixed in place by nailed crosspieces, small forged wrought-iron spikes joining the varying lengths of wood so precious on Rime Isle.

The monstrous winterchange of the weather had not moderated, but grown worse, for a strong steady north breeze had set in, redoubling the night's bitter chill. A half tent had been set up, just north of the cookfire and facing it, to give shelter to the latter and radiant heat to the former. Here, among others, Klute and Mara slumbered, quite worn out by their spell of work in the hole, for as Skor had pointed out, 'To dig for coal and tubers, even gold and treasure, is one thing; for human flesh you hope alive (somehow!) quite another and most wearying!'

The discovery of the Mouser's cowl seven feet down had led Fafhrd and Cif to take over the digging and sifting work from Skor and the girls in their eagerness to speed the small Gray One's rescue. But after two hours' furious labour they had relinquished their places, this time to Skor again and to Gale, whose girl-size was an especial advantage when the hole was crowded with those putting in the second tier of shorings beneath the first.

After climbing up the shaft by the big pegs set like a ladder in its sides, and feeling the north breeze's bite as they emerged into the cold moonshine, Cif and Fafhrd had headed for the cookfire where hot black gahveh and soup were available, whereafter Cif had gone to join the small group conferring just beyond the blaze, while Fafhrd, professing no taste for talk, had moved back under the half tent's shelter and, nursing a steaming black mug laced with brandy, carefully seated himself on the foot of the cot where Klute and Mara slept embracing each other for warmth.

On the far side of the fire they were discussing a matter on which Cif had strong opinions – the proper present use (if any) and ultimate disposal of the trophy Pshawri had brought up from the Maelstrom, the skeletal gold cube enwedged with black iron-tough torch cinder and known as the Whirlpool Queller from the magical use the Gray Mouser had made of it in turning back the Sunwise Sea-Mingol fleet, now almost two years by.

Afreyt believed it should be enshrined in the Moon Temple as a memorial of Rime Isle's most recent victory over her enemies.

With Islish materialism crusty Groniger argued that, freed of its disfiguring cinder – a dubious item which the moon priest-esses could have if they wished – it should be returned to the treasury house to take again its rightful place among the golden Ikons of Reasons, as the Sextuple Square or Cube of Square Dealing.

But Mother Grum averred that the addition of the cinder had transformed the Cube into a magical weapon of might to be entrusted to the witchy coven she headed, which happened to include several moon priestesses.

Rill seconded her, saying, 'I held the cinder when it was yet a torch lit at Loki's fire, and its flame bent sideways, pointing us out the path that led us to the god's new lair in the flame wall at the back of the caverns fronting the root of the volcano Darkfire. Might there not be a like virtue in the cinder to show us the way to Captain Mouser now he is underground?'

Cif broke in eagerly, 'Let's dowse for him with it! Suspend the Queller on a cord and move it about the hole and watch what happens. This should tell us if he has deviated from straight-down sinking like the shaft, in which direction he is going. What think you all?'

'I'll tell you this, Lady,' Pshawri said rapidly, 'when Captain Mouser rebuked me yesternight for meddling with the Maelstrom, I felt the cube vibrate through my pouch against my leg, as though there were some occult link between the Queller and the captain, though neither he nor anyone knew then I had recovered it.'

The faint tintinnabulation of tiny harness bells shaken briskly drew all Cif's listeners' and finally her own gaze east, away from the moon, to where a bobbing cart lamp told of the imminent arrival of a dogteam from the barracks.

But neither the jingling bells nor the earlier talk penetrated very deeply into the vast melancholy reverie into which Fafhrd had slowly sunk as he nursed his chilling brandied gahveh and rested his aching bones in the half tent's shadows.

It had begun just as he'd gingerly seated himself on the foot of Mara's and Klute's cot with the sudden vivid memory – startling in its power – of another occasion, almost two decades gone, when he'd had to work furiously for seeming hours to rescue the Mouser from death's closest grip and in the end had had to drag the Gray One screaming and kicking from his intended coffin. It had all happened in the sorcery-built magic emporium of those cosmic pedlars of filth, the Devourers, and there had been no rest periods on that occasion either. Fafhrd had first endlessly and most resourcefully to argue with their two cantankerous and elephant-brained wizardly mentor-masters Sheelba of the Eyeless Face and Ningauble of the Seven Eyes just to get the all-essential means and information to achieve the rescue and then battle interminably and with brilliantly-devised instant stratagems against a tireless iron statue, a devilish two-handed longsword of blued steel – not to mention gaudy giant spiders whom his obscenely ensorceled comrade saw as beauteous supple girls in scanty velvet dresses.

But that time the Mouser had been present all the while, playing the fool, calling out zany comments to the battlers, and even slain the statue in the end by splitting its massive head with Fafhrd's axe, thinking the weapon was a jester's bladder, while he, Fafhrd, had been the one being buried under the double weight of wizards' words and crushing iron blows. But this time the Mouser simply vanished without frills or fanfare, swallowed by earth in fashion most conclusive without warning, without shroud or coffin to shield him from the ground's cruel cold grip, and without words, foolish or otherwise, except that piteous, gasped-out 'Help me, Fafhrd,' before his mouth was stopped by hungry upward-gliding clay. And now that he was gone, there was no fighting to be done to get him back, no mighty battling with sword or words, but only very slow, laborious scraping and digging, careful, methodical, and which seemed to make sense and hold out hope only so long as one was doing it. As soon as you stopped digging, you realized what a last-chance, forlorn-hope, desperate rescue attempt it really was – to believe a man could somehow breathe long enough underground, like a Kleshite ghoul or Eastern Lands fakir, for you to tunnel your way to him. Pitiful! Why, Fafhrd'd only been able to persuade himself and the others to it because no one had a better idea – and because they all (some of 'em, anyway) needed busy-work to keep at bay the sickening sense of loss and of fear for self lest a like fate befall.

Fafhrd balled his good fist and almost in his gust of frustration smote the cot beside his thigh, but recalled in time the sleeping girls. He'd thought the next cot was empty, but now saw that its dark green blanket hid a single sleeper, whose slight form and short shock of flame-red hair showed her to be the self-styled Ilthmar princess and cabingirl Fingers, who'd been following him around all night gazing at him reproachfully for not somehow saving the Mouser before he sank or else sinking into the ground beside him like a staunch comrade should. He felt a sudden spurt of sharp anger at the minx – what cause had she to criticize him so?

Yet it was true, he upbraided himself as another flood of melancholy memories engulfed him, that he and his gray comrade had often behaved like death-seekers, as when they'd sailed in stony-faced silence side by side forever westward in the Outer Sea, seeking that coast of doom called the Bleak Shore, or lured by shimmersprites, steered their craft south into the great Equatorial Current whence no ships return, or when they'd surmounted Stardock, Nehwon's mightiest peak, or dared Quarmall's cavern and twice encountered Death himself in the sunless Shadowland; yet on this last occasion, when Nehwon had swallowed the Mouser, whatever the rationale, he had held back.

With a silvery jangle of harness bells the laden dogcart drew up beyond the fire. As he got down from the driver's seat, Skullick gave out the news, the words tumbling from his mouth, that the Great Maelstrom had been observed to be turning more swiftly, heaving and churning as it swirled round and round in the cold moonshine. Cif and Pshawri came to their feet.

The noise broke into Fafhrd's reverie just enough as to make him aware of what his entranced gaze had been unseeingly resting on. The girl Fingers had turned over in her sleep so that her face was visible and one bare arm had emerged to lie atop the coarse blanket like a pale serpent. Of whom did her face remind him? he asked himself. He had loved those features once, he was suddenly certain. What sweet and yielding female . . . ?

And then as he studied her face more closely, he saw that her eyes were open and watching him and that her lips were curved in a sleepy smile. The tip of her tongue came out at a corner and licked them around. Fafhrd felt his sharp anger return, if it were just that. The saucy baggage! What call had she to look at him as though they shared a secret? Why was she spying on him? What was her game? He flashed that when she'd first appeared simpering and posing to him and the Gray Mouser in the cellar, they had just been speaking of men snatched under the ground or pursued on high by vengeful earth. Why had that been? What had that synchronicity presaged? Had she aught to do with the Mouser's vanishment downward, this tainted witch-child from the rat city of Ilthmar? He rose up fast and silently, moved as swiftly to her cot and stood bent over her and glaring down, as though to strip her of her secrets by his gaze's force, and with his hand upraised, he knew not to do what, while she smiled up at him with perfect confidence.

'Captain!' Skor's urgent bellow came hollowly out of the hole and boomed around.

Forgetting all else, Fafhrd dodged from under the shelter tent and was the first to reach the mouth of the shaft, over which there was now set a stout man-high ironwood tripod, from which depended a pair of pulleys to halve the effort needed to raise the dirt.

Steadying himself by two of its legs, the Northerner leaned out and looked straight down. The planks of the second tier of shorings were in place, securely braced with crosspieces and tied to the first tier – and the excavating had gone a couple of feet below them. From the pulley by his cheek two lines went down to the second pulley atop the handle of the bucket, which was set half filled 'gainst a side of the shaft. Against two other sides Skor and Gale were pressed back, upturned faces large and small, in shadow, the one framed by scanty red locks, the other by profuse blond tresses. By the fourth side were two leviathan-oil lamps. Their white light fell strongly on the slender object lying flat in the centre of the shaft's bottom. Fafhrd would have recognized it anywhere.

'It's Captain Mouser's dirk, Captain,' Skor called up, 'lying just as we uncovered it.'

'I didn't move it the least bit as I brushed and worked the earth away,' Gale confirmed in her piping tones.

'That's a wise girl,' Fafhrd called down. 'Leave it so. And don't move from where you are, either of you. I'm coming down.'

Which he accomplished swiftly by way of the ladder of thick pegs jutting from the shoring, going down hand over hook. When he reached the crowded bottom, he knelt at once over Cat's Claw, bending down his head to inspect it closely.

'We didn't find the scabbard anywhere,' Gale explained somewhat unnecessarily.

He nodded. 'The ground gets chalky here,' he observed. 'Did either of you find a chunk of the stuff?'

'No,' Gale responded quickly, 'but I've a lump of yellow umber.'

'That'll do fine,' he said, holding out his hand. When she'd dug it from her pouch and handed it to him, he sighted carefully along the dagger's blade and rubbed a big gold mark on the foot of the shoring to show which way the weapon pointed.

'That's something we may want to remember,' he explained shortly. He lifted the wicked knife from its site, turning it over and reinspecting it from blade tip to pommel, but he could discern no special markings, no message of any sort, on that side either.

'What have you found, Fafhrd?' Cif called down.

'It's Cat's Claw, all right. I'll send it up to you,' he called back. He handed the knife to Skor. 'I'll take over for a space down here. You get some rest.' He accepted from his lieutenant the short-handled square spade that had replaced his axe as chief digging and scraping tool. 'You're a good man, Skor.' That one nodded and mounted by the pegs.

'I'm coming down, Fafhrd. My turn to help,' Afreyt announced from above.

Fafhrd looked at Gale. At close range the golden strands were sweaty and the fair complexion streaked with dirt. Pallor and tired smudges around the blue eyes belied the air of smiling readiness the girl put on. 'You need a rest too. And sleep, you hear? But only after you've had a mug of hot soup.' He took from her her scoop and handbroom. 'You've done well, child.'

While she wearily yet reluctantly mounted the pegs, with Afreyt urging her to greater speed from above, Fafhrd drove the spade into the earth near the hole's edge, continuing the excavation straight down.

After Afreyt had climbed into the hole to join Fafhrd in his task, the harlot Rill led the exhausted Gale back to the cookfire beyond the shelter tent. Cif followed them, somewhat like a sleepwalker, staring at the knife she held, which Skor had handed her, and after a bit the others gravitated back too. Standing in the cold to watch folk dig is of no lasting profit.

Rill was pressing Gale to finish the mug of soup she'd poured her.

'Drink it all down while there's some heat in it. That's a good girl. Why, you still feel like ice! You need to be under blankets. And get a sleep, you're groggy. Come on now, no arguments.'

And she led her off willingly enough to the shelter tent.

Cif was still staring bemusedly at the Mouser's knife, slowly turning it over and over, so that its bright blade periodically reflected the low firelight.

Old Ourph said ruminatively, 'When Khahkht the Conqueror was buried bound and beweaponed alive for treason, but later cleared and dug up, it was found his daggers had worked their way yards from his corpse in opposite directions, so strong and wide were his hatreds.'

Pshawri said, 'I thought Khahkht was a Rimish ice devil, not a Mingol warchief paramount.'

After a while Ourph replied, 'Great conquerors live on as their enemies' devils.'

'Or their own folk's, sometimes,' Groniger put in.

Skullick said, 'If dead old Khahkht could make his daggers travel through solid earth, why didn't he have them cut his bonds?'

Rill returned with an armful of girls' clothes which she hung by the fire and then sat down beside Cif, saying, 'I stripped her down to the buff and bundled her into a warmed nook beside the drowsy Ilthmar kid, who'd half waked but was bound again for slumberland.'

After a courteous pause, Ourph explained, 'Khahkht's bonds were chains of adamant.'

Groniger said speculatively, 'I can see how the Mouser's hood would be stripped away upward as he was dragged down, since it had no ties to his other clothing. And I suppose the up-sliding earth, pressing against the dagger's grip and crosspiece, might effect the same result, though taking longer, as he was dragged still farther down by . . . whatever it was.'

'But wouldn't the knife have been left point down, vertical in the earth, then?' Skullick argued.

Mother Grum interrupted, 'Black magic of some breed took him. That's why the knife got left. Iron doesn't obey devil power.'

Skullick went on to Groniger, 'But the dagger was uncovered lying flat, horizontal. Which would mean by your theory he was being dragged sideways at that point, in the direction Cat's Claw pointed. In which case we're digging the shaft the wrong way, keeping on straight down.'

'Gods! I wish we knew exactly what happened to him down there,' Pshawri averred, some of his earlier agony coming back into his voice and aspect. 'Did he draw Cat's Claw to do battle with the monster dragging him under, free himself of it? Or was he more actively attacked down there and drew the knife in self-defence?'

'How could he do either of those things when closely cased in hard earth?' Groniger objected.

'He'd manage somehow!' Pshawri shot back. 'But then how came the dagger to be left behind? He'd never been parted from Cat's Claw willingly, of that I'm sure.'

'Perhaps he lost consciousness then,' Rill interposed.

'Or perhaps they were both attacked, the dragger and the dragged, by some third party,' Skullick hazarded. 'How much do any of us know what may go on down there?'

A look of sheer horror had been growing in Cif's visage as she eyed the knife. She burst out, 'Stop breaking our minds and hearts, all of you, with all these guesses!' She took the Mouser's cowl out of her pouch and rapidly wrapped up the dagger in it, folding in the ends. 'I cannot think while looking at that thing.' She handed the small gray package to Mother Grum. 'There, keep it safe and hid,' she said, 'while we get on to efforts more constructive.'

A change came over the small white-clad woman, who'd seemed consumed moments before with nervous grief. She rose lithely from her seat by the fire, saying to Pshawri, 'Follow me, Lieutenant. We'll dowse for your captain with his Whirl-pool Queller you rescued from the Maelstrom, beginning at the shaft head, and so determine whether and how he's deviated from the straight down in his strange journey through solid earth.' She wet two fingers in her mouth and held them high a space. 'While we were talking, feeding our woes with horror, the north breeze died – which'll make the dowsing easier for us, its results surer. And you must do the dowsing, Pshawri, because although it galls me somewhat to admit it, you seem the one most sensitive to the Gray Mouser's presence.'

Although looking puzzled and taken aback at first by her words, it was with a seeming sense of relief and a growing eagerness that the skinny ex-thief came to his feet. 'I'm with you, Lady, of course, in any effort to regain the Captain. What do I do?'

As she explained, they started toward the shaft head. The eyes of the others followed them. After a bit Skullick and Rill got up and strolled after and, several moments later, Groniger. But old Ourph and Mother Grum – and Snowtreader and the other

582

cartdog, both of whom had been unharnessed – stayed warm by the fire.

A bucket was coming up from the hole, heaping full. When its earth had been scattered, Pshawri positioned himself by the hole, knees bent and spread a little, head bent forward, looking down earnestly at the black-gold cinder cube suspended on a cubit's length of sailor's twine he'd found in his pouch and held at the top between the thumb and ring finger of his left hand.

Cif stood north of him, spreading her cloak to ward off any remnants of the north breeze, though there seemed no need. The cold air had become quite still.

But although the contraption looked like a pendulum, it did not act like one, neither beginning to swing back and forth in any direction nor yet around in a circle or ellipse.

'And there's no vibration either,' Pshawri reported in a low voice.

Cif extended a slender forefinger and laid it very lightly and carefully atop the pinching juncture of his finger and thumb. After a space of three heartbeats she nodded in confirmation and said, 'Let's try on the opposite of the hole.'

'Why do you use the ring finger and left hand?' Rill asked curiously.

'I don't know,' Pshawri said puzzledly. 'Maybe because that finger feels the touchiest of the lot. And left hand seems right for magic.'

At that last word Groniger growled a sceptical 'Hmmph!'

Fafhrd and Afreyt seemed to be digging and sifting strenuously yet still carefully at the bottom of the hole, which had gotten as much as a foot deeper. Cif called down to them an explanation of what she and Pshawri were doing, ending with, '. . . and then we'll spiral out from here in wider and wider circles, dowsing every few feet. When we get a strong reading – *if* we do – I'll signal you.'

Fafhrd waved that he understood and returned to his digging.

The second reading showed the same results. Pshawri and Cif moved out four yards and began their first methodical circling of the hole, dowsing every few steps. One by one their small company of observers returned to the fire, wearied by sameness. A full bucket came up from the hole.

And after a while, another.

Slowly the white-glowing lantern with which Cif had provided herself grew more distant from the hole. Slowly the pile of dug earth beside it grew. Fingers and Gale slept in each other's arms. While the full moon inched down the western sky.

Time passed.

15

The yellowing moon was no more than two fists above the western horizon of Rime Isle's central hills when Fafhrd's probing spade encountered stone. They'd deepened the hole by about a woman's height below the second tier of shoring. At first Fafhrd thought the obstruction a small boulder and tried to dig around it. Afreyt warned him against overspeed but he persisted. The boulder grew larger and larger. Soon the whole bottom of the shaft was a flat floor of solid rock.

He lifted his eyes to Afreyt's. 'What's to do now?'

She shook her head.

A spear's cast southeast of the hole the two dowsers began to get results.

The twine-and-cube pendulum suspended from Pshawri's left hand instead of hanging straight down dead, as it had done over a hundred successive times by count, slowly began to swing forth and back, away from the hole and toward it. They both stared down at it wonderingly, suspicious.

'Are you making it do that, Pshawri?' Cif whispered.

'I don't think so,' he answered doubtfully.

And then the wonder happened. The swings of the cube toward the hole began to get shorter and shorter, and those away longer and longer, until they stopped altogether and the cube hung straining away from the hole, perceptibly out of the vertical.

'How are you doing that, Pshawri?' Her voice was small, respectful.

'I don't know,' he replied shakily. 'It pulls. And I'm getting a vibration.'

She touched his hand with her forefinger, as before. Almost immediately she nodded, looking at him with awe.

'I'll call Afreyt and Fafhrd. Don't you move.'

She rummaged a metal whistle from her pouch and blew it. The note was shrill and piercing in the cold still air.

Down in the hole they heard it. 'Cif's signal,' Afreyt said, but Fafhrd had already chinned himself on the lowest peg and was hauling himself up the rest hand over hook. She hung one of the lanterns on one arm and followed him up, using both hands and feet.

Fafhrd scanned around and saw a small white glow out in the frozen meadow across the hole from where he stood. It moved back and forth to call attention to itself. He looked down the wood-lined shaft and spotted at its foot the yellow ochre mark he'd made to show the direction Cat's Claw had pointed when it was found. It was in line with the distant lamp. He sucked in his breath, took from Afreyt the lit lamp she'd brought up with her, held it aloft, and moved it twice from side to side in answering signal. The one in the meadow was immediately lowered.

'That tears it,' he told Afreyt, lowering the lamp. 'The dagger and the dowsing agree. The shaft must now be dug in that direction, footed upon the rock we've just uncovered and lined and roofed with wood to shield it from collapse.'

She nodded and said swiftly, 'Skullick suggested earlier that was the message the horizontal attitude and pointing of Cat's Claw were intended by the Gray Mouser to convey.'

Idlers crowded around them to hear what new was up. The Northerner at the pulley gazed at Fafhrd intently.

He continued raptly, 'The side passage should be narrow and low to conserve wood. The shoring planks can be sawed in three to make its walls. We should be able to dig faster sideways, yet great care must still be exercised in breaking earth.'

Afreyt broke in, 'There'll be a power of digging, nevertheless, just to take the side passage out below the point where Cif and Skullick are now standing.'

'That's true,' he answered, 'and also true that Captain Mouser may have been drawn away we know not how far, judging by the swiftness and ease with which he first sank. He may be anywhere out there. And yet I feel it's vital we continue on digging from that spot, abiding by the one solid clue we have that we know is from *him*: his pointing knife! That's a more material clue than any hints and suggestions to be got from dowsing. No, the digging that we've started must go on, else we lose all drive and organization. That we're not doing it right now carks me. But I myself have grown too frantic for the nonce to do the work properly with all due precautions.' He appealed to Afreyt, 'You yourself, dear, warned me that I was overspeeding, and I was.'

He turned to the stalwart at the pulley and commanded, 'Udall, fetch Skor! Wake him if he's asleep. Ask him – with courtesy – to come to me here. Tell him he's needed.' Udall went. Fafhrd turned back to Afreyt, explaining, 'Skor has the patience for the task that I lack, at least at this moment.' His voice changed. 'And would you, my dear, not only continue with the sifting for now, but also take on for me the direction of the whole task in my absence? Here, take my signet. Wear it on your fist.' He held out his right hand to her, fingers spread. She drew the ring from off the little one. 'I want to go apart (I don't think well in company) and brood upon this matter, on ways of recovering the Gray One besides digging and dowsing. I *think* he will return here eventually, exit the underworld same place he entered it – that's why we must keep digging at this spot – yet that's at best the likeliest end. There are a thousand other possibilities to be considered. My mind's afire. The Gray One and I have been in a hundred predicaments and plights as bad as this one.

'Would you do that for me, dear?' he finished. 'The sifting you can assign to Rill or two of the girls, or even at a pinch to Mother Grum.'

'Leave it all to me, Captain,' she said, rubbing along his jaw the clenched knuckles of her right hand, which now wore his silver crossed-swords signet upon the middle finger.

Her action was playful, affectionate, but her violet eyes were anxious and her voice sober as death.

Snowtreader had responded as swiftly as Fafhrd to Cif's whistle, bounding out across the frosty meadow. He stopped before Cif, who was still signaling with her high-held lamp. Then his eyes went to bent-over Pshawri and the object hanging oddly from the lieutenant's rock-steady hand. He sniffed at it gingerly and suspiciously, gave a whine of recognition, and hurried on across the meadow a dozen more yards with his nose close to the ground, then paused to look back and bark twice.

Cif lowered her lamp at Fafhrd's answering signal from the shaft head. Pshawri appealed to her, 'Would you mark this spot here, Lady? I think we should follow Snowtreader's lead and hurry on while the scent is hot, dowsing at intervals.'

Using her dagger pommel for a hammer, she drove into the ground over which Pshawri had been hovering one of the small stakes they'd brought and tied to it a short length of gray ribbon from her pouch. She said, 'I think you're right. Though while I was signaling, I had the thought that the cinder we're dowsing with is Loki's. It might be guiding us toward him rather than Mouser, and I know from experience what wild goose hunts, what weird will-o'-the-wisp chases that god might lead us on.'

'No, Lady,' Pshawri assured her, 'it's the Captain's signals I'm getting. I know his vibes. And Snowtreader would never confuse him with that tricksy stranger god. What's more, the dog didn't howl this time, as he did so dolefully when the moon was high, but only whined – a sign he's scenting a live thing, no carrion corpse.'

Cif observed, 'You're awfully fond of the Captain, aren't you? I pray Skama you're right. Lead on, then. The others will catch up.'

She was referring to the five dark forms between her and the cookfire and the other lights around the shaft head: Rill, Skullick, Groniger, Ourph, and Mother Grum, all grown curious. Beyond them and the little lights round the shaft head, the setting moon was just touching the horizon, as though going to earth amongst Rime Isle's central hills.

Back at the now-lonely cookfire Fafhrd poured himself a half mug of simmering gahveh, tempered it with brandy, drank half of that off in one big hot swallow, and set himself to think shrewdly and systematically of the Gray Mouser's plight, as he'd told Afreyt he would.

He discovered almost at once that his whirling, plunging thoughts and fancies were not to be tamed that way.

Nor did the rest of the mug's contents, taken at a gulp, enforce tranquillity and logic upon stormy disorder.

He paced around in a circle, breaking off when he found himself beginning to twist, jerk, and stamp in a frenzy of control-seeking.

He shook his fingers in front of his face, as if trying to conjure things from empty air.

In a sudden frantic reversal of attitude he asked himself whether he really wanted to rescue the Mouser at all. Let the Gray One escape by his own devices. He'd managed it often enough in the past, by Kos!

He'd have liked to measure his wilder imaginings against Rill's practicality, Groniger's sturdy reason, Mother Grum's dogmatic witch-reasonings, or Ourph's Mingol fatalism. But they'd all traipsed off after the dowsers. He'd told Afreyt he wanted solitude, but now he asked himself how as a man to think without talking? He felt confused, light-headed, light in other ways, as if a puff of wind might knock him down.

He looked at the things around him: the fire, the soup, the piled lumber, the girls' clothes warming, the shelter tent, its cots.

He didn't need to talk to children, he told himself. Let them sleep. He wished he could.

But his strange nervousness grew. Finally, to discharge it in action, he seized a fresh brandy jug with his right hand, hooked up a lamp with his other upper extremity, set out across the meadow after the dowsers.

He walked unevenly, veering and correcting himself. He wasn't sure he wanted to catch up with the dowsers. But he had to be moving, or else explode.

16

In the cosy nest from which she'd been watching Fafhrd's every action, Fingers roused Gale by yanking the pale tuft of her fine maiden hair. 'That hurt, you fiend,' the Rimish girl protested, rubbing her eyes. 'No one else ever summoned me from slumber so.'

'It hurts most where you love most,' the cabingirl recited as by rote, continuing in livelier tones, 'I knew you'd want to be wide awake, dear demon, to hear the latest news of your hero uncle with the growly name.'

'Fafhrd?' Gale was all attention.

'The same. He's just come out of the hole, cavorted around the fire, and now taken a lamp and a jar and gone off after your dark-haired aunt who's dowsing for your other uncle. I think he's fey and wants watching over.'

'Where are our clothes?' Gale asked at once, squirming half out of the nest.

'The lady with the scarred hand set them to warm close by the fire before they all went off ahead of Fafhrd. Come on, I'll race you.'

'Someone will see us.' Gale clapped her slender forearm across her barely budded breasts.

'Not if we rush, Miss Prim and Proper.'

The two girls streaked to the fire through the frigid air and, looking around and giggling the while, hurried into their toasty clothes as swiftly as if they'd both been sailors. Then they moved out hand in hand, following Fafhrd's lamp, while the last sliver of full moon hid itself behind Rime Isle's central hills and the sky paled with the first hint of dawn.

17

The Mouser struggled awake from darkest depths. The process seemed to involve toilsome stages of marginal consciousness, but when he finally – and quite suddenly – felt himself fully master of his mind, he found his body sprawled at full length with his bent head pillowed on the crook of his left elbow and the bracing reek of salt sea filling his nostrils.

For a blessed moment he supposed himself to be abed in his trim room in the Salthaven barracks built last year by his men and Fafhrd's, and with the window open to the cool damp morning breeze.

His first attempted movements shattered that illusion. He was in the same dreadful plight he'd been when his awareness had last ebbed away to chthonic darkness while he was most effortfully fleeing Death's skinny sister Pain.

Except his plight had worsened – he'd lost the strange power of movement he'd had then, of laborious crabwise retreat. That seemed to depend, for its generation, upon extremes of terror.

And the sea stink was new. That must be coming from the grainy earth that gripped him vicelike. And that earth was now perceptibly damp. Which must in turn mean that his flight had led him to the Rime Isle coast, to the sea's fringes. Perhaps he was already under the cold, tumultuous, merciless waters of the boundless Outer Sea.

And he was no longer buried upright but lying flat. Truly it was astonishing what a difference that made. Upright, though as closely confined as a statue by its mould, one felt somehow free and on guard. Whereas lying flat, whether supine or prone, was the posture of submission. It made one feel utterly helpless. It was the very worst—

No, he interrupted himself, don't exaggerate. Worse than flat would be buried upside down, heels above head. Best leave off imagining confinements lest he think of one that was still worse.

He set himself to do the same routine things he'd done after his earlier underground lapse of consciousness – regularize and maximize his furtive breathing, assure himself of the continuing glow about his eyes and of his seeming occult power to see, albeit somewhat dimly, for some yards all around him.

The way his head was bent, he found he was looking down his body, along his legs and past his feet. He wished he had a wider range of vision, yet at least there was no blue and chalky female form pursuing him sharklike from that direction.

It was really unnerving, though, how defenceless his flat attitude made him feel, all ready to be trampled, or spat upon, or skewered with pitchfork.

He'd had previous strayings into the realm of Death without his nerve failing, he reminded himself, straining for reassurance and to keep panic at bay. There'd been that time in Lankhmar when he'd entered the magic shop of the Devourers and laid down fearlessly in a black-pillowed coffin and also walked quite eagerly into a mirror that was a vertical pool of liquid mercury held upright by mighty sorceries.

But he'd been drunk and girlstruck then, he reminded himself, though at the time the mercury had felt cool and refreshing (not grainy and suffocating like this stuff!), and he'd afterward nursed the private conviction that he'd been about to discover a secret heroes' heaven high above the one reserved for the gods when Fafhrd had jerked him out of the silver fluid.

No matter. His present friends and lovers, he told himself, must be working like beavers right now to effect his recovery, either by digging (there were enough of them surely) or by working some magic or supernal deal. Perhaps right at this moment dear Cif was manipulating the Golden Ikons of the Isle as she had last year when his mind had been trapped in the brain of a sounding whale.

Or Fafhrd might have figured out some trick to get him back. Though the great oaf had hardly looked capable of such when Mouser had last seen him, goggling down bewilderedly at his disappearing comrade.

Yet how would any of them know where to dig for him, the way he'd moved around? Or be able to dig for him at all, if he were already beneath the Outer Sea?

Which reminded him in turn that according to the most ancient legends, Simorgya had invaded Rime Isle in prehistoric times by way of long long tunnels leading under the wild waves. That was before the more southern isle sank beneath the billows and its cruel inhabitants grew gills and fins.

A fantasy, no doubt, old witches' tales. Yet if such tunnels ever had existed, he was surely in the right place to find them now, Rime Isle's south coast. Or find at least one – surely that was not hoping too much. And so as he industriously sipped air through barely parted lips from the dank earth enfolding him, exhaling in little puffs more forcibly than he inhaled, to drive back intrusive moist granules, he became aware of a pale green undulation parallel to his body some three yards out from him, as though something were moving back and forth out there, up and down a narrow corridor, while it closely regarded him. After a time it resolved itself into the dainty form of the Simorgyan demoness Ississi not more than a quarter – nay, hardly an eighth! – of the way though her girl-fish shape-change: there was the barest hint of a crest along her spine, and the merest suggestion of webs joining the roots of her slender fingers, and only the slightest green tinge to her glorious complexion, she of the large yellow green eyes and lisping seductive speech, who'd been so amenable to harshest discipline, at least for quite a while. And she seemed to be wearing a filmy rainbow robe composed of the tatters and rags of the costly, colourful, fine fabric destroyed during his final submarine bout with her when *Sea Hawk* had sunk for a space.

For a moment his dissolving skepticism reasserted itself as he asked himself how he could be so certain it was indeed Ississi in this hazy realm where any fish (or girl, for that matter) looked very much like the next (and both like phantoms woven of greenish smoke). But even as he posed that question, the vision became more real, each winsome feature more clearly defined. What's more, he realized he was in no way frightened of her despite the circumstances of their encounter. In fact, as his eyes moved slowly back and forth as they followed her to and froing, he found himself growing drowsy, the regular movement was so restful. He even found himself developing the illusion (surely it must be one?) that his entire body, not just his eyes, was moving slowly forward and back in unison with hers, as if it had unbeknownst to himself escaped into a corridor or tunnel parallel with hers and was afloat in the unresistant air!

Just at that moment he received a shock which caused him sharply to revise any opinion he may have entertained about one young female being very much like the next – or one fish, for that matter. Although he had not seen Ississi's half-smiling lips close up or pucker in any way, he heard a trilling soft seductive whistle.

Looking sharply down along his legs and beyond his feet, he saw the blue-streaked chalky form of Sister Pain advancing toward him in a tigerish rush with talons spread out to either side of her grinning narrow face and eyes aglow with red sadistic fire.

Confirming an earlier intuition of his as well as his guess about the tunnels, without any physical effort on his part, but a tremendous mental one, he began to move away from her at the same speed with which she came horrendously on, so that they both were flashing through the grainy yet utterly unresistant earth at nightmare speed, and Ississi's figure vanished behind them in a trice . . .

No, not quite. For it seemed to the Mouser that at that point his pursuer paused for an instant while her blue-pied flesh drank up the other's pale green substance, superadding Ississi's fishy furies to her own dire hungers before coming again horrifically on.

He was dearly tempted to glance forward to get some clue to where they were hastening beneath the Outer Sea, for they were trending deeper, yet dared not do so for fear that in trying to dodge some barely glimpsed seeming obstacle, he'd dash himself into the rocky walls flashing by so close. No, best trust himself to whatever mighty power gripped him. However blind, it knew more than he.

There whipped past the dark mouth of an intersecting tunnel leading southward if he'd kept his bearings, he judged. To Simorgya? In which case, whither did this branch he was careening through extend? To No-Ombrulsk? Beyond that, under land, to the Sea of Monsters? To the dread Shadowland itself, abode of Death?

What use to speculate when he had yielded up control of his movements to the whirlwind? Against all reasonable expectations, he found his great speed lulling despite the pearly flash and fleeting glow of sea fossils. Perhaps at this very moment, for all he knew, he was breathing softly back in a snug grave in Rime Isle and dreaming this dream. Even the Great God Himself must have had moments while creating the universe or 'verses when He was absolutely certain He was dreaming. All's well, he mused. He dropped off.

18

Cif insisted on repeating Pshawri's next reading as their dowsing led them back across the Great Meadow, dangling the cinder cube from her own left-hand ring finger and thumb, and when she got the same result as he had decided they should alternate taking readings thereafter. He submitted to this arrangement with proper grace, but couldn't quite conceal his nervousness whenever the magic pendulum was out of his hands, at such times watching her like a hawk.

'You're jealous of me about the Captain, aren't you?' she rallied the young lieutenant, though not teasingly.

He considered that soberly and answered with equal frankness, 'Well, yes, Lady, I am – though in no way challenging your own far greater and different claim on his concern. But I did meet him before you did, when he recruited me in Lankhmar for his band before he outfitted *Flotsam* and set sail for Rime Isle.'

'You forget,' she corrected him gently, 'that before your enlistment the Lady Afreyt and I journeyed to Lankhmar to hire him and Fafhrd in the Isle's defence, though on that occasion we were swiftly raped back to this polar clime by Khahkht's icy blast.'

'That's true,' he allowed. 'Nevertheless . . .' He seemed to think better of it.

'Nevertheless what?'

'I was going to say,' he told her somewhat haltingly, 'that I think he was aware of me before that time. After all, we were both freelance thieves, though he infinitely my superior, and that means a lot in Lankhmar, where the Guild's so strong, and there were other reasons . . . Well, anyway, I knew *his* reputation.'

Cif had just completed a reading and clutched the cinder cube in her right hand, not having yet put it in her pouch nor passed it on to him for like securing. She was about to ask Pshawri, 'What other reasons?' but instead lost herself in study of his broody features, which were just becoming visible in the gray light without help of the white glow of the lamp, which sat on the ground next where she had dowsed.

Only Astarion, Nehwon's brightest star, was still a pale dot in the dawn-violet heavens, and would soon be gone. Ahead of them but off to their left (for their dowsing was gradually turning them south of the path their party had travelled last evening) a blanket of fog risen from the ground hid all of Salthaven but the highest roofs and the pillars and wind-chime arch of the Moon Temple, tinied by distance. The fog lapped higher round those objects as they watched and, although there was no wind, advanced toward them, whitely distilled from earth. Its far edge brightened where the sun would rise, although a squadron of clouds cruising above had not yet caught its rays.

'It must be cold for the Captain down there below,' Pshawri breathed with an involuntary shudder.

'You *are* most deeply concerned about him, aren't you?' Cif observed. 'Beyond the ordinary. I've noticed it for the past fortnight. Ever since you received a missive inscribed in violet ink and sealed with green wax, carried on the last trader before *Weasel* in from Lankhmar.'

'You have sharp eyes, Lady,' he voiced.

'I saw it when Captain Mouser emptied the mail pouch. What is it, Pshawri?'

He shook his head. 'With all respect, Lady, it is a matter that concerns solely the Captain and myself – and one other. I cannot speak of it without his leave.'

'The Captain knows about it?'

'I do not think so. Yet I can't be sure.'

Cif would have continued her queries, although Pshawri's reluctance to answer more fully seemed genuine and deep-rooted – and more than a little mysterious – but at that moment the five from the fire caught up with them and the mood for exchanging confidences was lost. In fact, Cif and Pshawri felt rather on exhibition, for during the next couple of dowsings each of the newcomers had to see for themselves close up the wonder of the heavy cube cinder hanging out of true, straining away from the shaft head definitely though slightly. In the end even sceptical Groniger was convinced.

'I must believe my eyes,' he said grudgingly, 'though the temptation not to is strong.'

'It's harder to believe such things by day,' Rill pointed out. 'Much easier at night.'

Mother Grum nodded. 'Witchcraft is so.'

The sun had emerged by then, beating a yellow path to them across the top of the fog, which strangely persisted.

And both Cif and Pshawri had to answer questions about the cord's subtle variations imperceptible to sight.

'It's just there,' she said, 'a faint thrilling.'

'I can't tell you how I know it's from the Captain,' he had to admit. 'I just do.'

Groniger snorted.

'I wish I could be as sure as Pshawri,' Cif told them at that. 'For me it doesn't sign his name.'

Two more dowsings brought them within sight of Rime Isle's south coast. They prepared to dowse a third time a few paces short of where the meadow grew bare and sloped down rockily and rather sharply for some ten more paces to the narrow beach lapped by the wavelets of the Outer Sea. To the west this small palisade grew gradually steeper and approached the vertical. To the east the stubborn fog reached to within a bowshot of them. Farther off they could spy rising from its whiteness the tops of the masts of the ships riding at anchor in Salthaven's harbour or docked at its wharves.

It was Pshawri's turn to dangle the cube cinder. He seemed somewhat nervous, his movements faster, though steady enough as he locked into position with legs bent, right eye centred over the finger juncture pinching the cord.

Cif and Rill both crouched on their knees close by, so as to observe the pendulum from the side at eye level. They seemed about to make an observation, but Pshawri from his superior vantage point forestalled them.

'The bob no longer pulls southeast,' he rapped out in a quick strident voice, 'but drags down straight and true.'

There were low hisses of indrawn breaths and a 'Yes!' from Rill. Cif suggested at once that she repeat his reading, and he gave her the pendulum without demur, though his nervousness seemed to increase. He stationed himself between her and the water. The others completed a ragged circle around her. Rill still crouched close.

After a pause, 'Still straight down,' Cif said, with another 'Yes,' from Rill. 'And the vibration.'

Skullick uncorked with, 'If the bob slanting means he's moving in that direction, then straight down says that Captain Mouser is below us but not moving just now.'

Cif lifted her eyes toward the speaker. 'If it is the Captain.'

'But the *how* of all this?' Groniger asked wonderingly, shaking his head.

596

'Look,' Rill said in a strange voice. 'The bob is moving again.'

They all eyed another wonder. The bob was swinging back and forth between the direction of the shaft head and the sea, but at least five times as slowly as the period of a pendulum of that length. It crawled its swing.

There was some awe in Skullick's usually irreverent voice. 'As if he were pacing back and forth down there. Right now.'

'Maybe he's found a sea tunnel,' Mother Grum suggested.

'Those fables,' Groniger growled.

Without warning the gold-glinting dark-coloured bob jumped seaward to taut cord's length from Cif's hand. She gave a quick hiss of pain and it sped on, trailing its cord like a comet's tail and narrowly missing Rill's head.

In a diving catch Pshawri interposed the cupped palm of his right hand, which it smote audibly. He clapped his other hand across it as he himself rolled over and came to his feet with both hands tightly cupped together, as if they caged a small animal or large insect, the cord dangling from between them, and walked back to Cif while the rest watched fascinatedly.

Skullick said, almost religiously, 'As if, after pacing, the Captain shot off through solid earth under the sea like a bolt of lightning. If such can be imagined.'

Groniger just shook his head, a study in sorely tried skepticism.

Pshawri said to Cif, lifting his elbows, 'Lady, would you please unbutton my pouch for me?'

She was studying the red-scored pads of her left ring finger and thumb, where the cord had taken skin as it had jerked away from between them, but she quickly complied with his instructions, being careful not to use these two digits in the process.

He plunged his cupped hands into his pouch and went on saying, 'Now tie the cord around the button – no, through the central button hole of the pouch flap. Use a square knot. Although it is not moving now, this thing is best securely confined. I don't trust it any more, no matter what it's told us.'

Cif followed the further instructions without argument, saying, 'I thoroughly agree with you, Lieutenant Pshawri. In fact, I don't think the cinder cube has been tracing the Mouser's movements underground at all, except perhaps at first to start us off.'

The knot was firmly tied. As Pshawri withdrew his hands she closed the flap on the pouch and he buttoned its three buttons.

'Then to what power do you think it's responding?' Rill asked, getting to her feet.

'To Loki's,' Cif averred. 'I think he wants to lead us on a wild goose chase across the sea. It has all the earmarks of his handiwork: a fascinating lure, strange developments mixed with painful surprises.' She popped her injured finger and thumb into her mouth and sucked them.

'It does seem like his tricksy behaviour,' Rill agreed.

'He's an outlaw god, all right,' Mother Grum nodded. 'And vengeful. Likely the one who sent Captain Mouser down.'

'What's more,' mumbled Cif, talking around her fingers, 'I think I know the way to scotch his plots and perhaps return the Mouser to us.'

'Dowsers ahoy!' a bright new voice called out. They turned and saw Afreyt coming briskly across the Meadow carrying a hamper woven of reeds.

She went on, 'There's news from the digging I thought you all should know, but Cif especially. By the way, where's Fafhrd?'

'We haven't seen him, Lady,' Pshawri told her.

'Why should he be here?' Groniger asked blankly.

'Why, he left off digging to rest and think alone,' Afreyt explained as she reached them and set the hamper on the grass. 'But then Udall and another saw him take a jug and lamp and head out after you. They had nothing to do and watched him until he was halfway to you, Udall said.'

'We've none of us seen him,' Cif assured her.

'But then where are Gale and Fingers?' Afreyt next asked. 'Their cot in the shelter tent was empty and their clothes gone that had been warming beside the fire. I thought they must have followed after Fafhrd, like they'd been doing all night.'

'We haven't seen pelt or paws of them either,' Cif insisted. 'But what's this news you promised?'

'But then where in Nehwon . . .' Afreyt began, looking around at the others. They all shook their heads. She told herself, 'Leave it,' and Cif, 'This should please you, I think.

We've driven the sideways corridor about fifteen paces in . . . the digging went faster than straight down – it was a soft sand stretch – and the shoring was easier, despite the added task of roofing . . . when we found this embedded halfway up the face.'

And she handed Cif a grit-flecked dirk scabbard.

'Cat's Claw's?'

'The same.'

'Right!' Cif said as she examined it eagerly.

'And it was lying horizontal, point end toward us,' Afreyt went on, 'as if the earth had torn it from his belt as he was being dragged or somehow gotten along, or as though he had left it that way as a clue for us.'

'It proves that Captain Mouser's down below, all right,' Skullick voiced.

'It does give weight to the two earlier findings of the dirk and cowl,' Groniger admitted.

'And so you can understand,' Afreyt went on, 'why I wanted to tell Fafhrd about it at once. And you, of course, Cif. But what's been happening with the dowsing? What's brought you here to the coast? You surely haven't traced him this far – or have you?'

So Cif told Afreyt how the dowsing had gone and how the bob had tried to escape on the last trial of its powers and was no longer trusted, and also her guess that Loki was behind it all.

Afreyt commented at that, 'Fafhrd himself warned me the evidence from dowsing would be uncertain and ambiguous compared with the clues got from actual digging, which he thought should be kept up in any case, to hold open an exit from the underworld for the Gray One at the same point he'd entered it. And you may very well be right about Loki trying to lead us astray. He was a tricksy god, as you know better than I, loving destruction above all else. For that matter, old Odin wasn't reliable either, taking Fafhrd's hand after the loving worship we'd provided him.'

Pshawri interposed, 'Lady Cif, just before the Lady Afreyt joined us, you said you'd thought of a way to foil Loki's plots and clear the way for Captain Mouser's return.'

Cif nodded. 'Since the cube cinder is of no use to us as a talisman, I think that one of us should take it and hurl it into the flame pit, the molten lava lake of volcano Darkfire, hopefully returning god Loki to his proper element and perchance assuaging his ire against the Captain.'

'And lose for ever one of Rime Isle's ikons, the Gold Cube of Square Dealing?' Groniger protested.

'That gold's for ever tainted with the stranger god's essence,' Mother Grum informed him, 'something I cannot exorcise. Cif's rede is good.'

'A golden ikon can be refashioned and resanctified,' old Ourph pointed out. 'Not so a man.'

'I cannot muster argument against such action, though it seems to me sheerest superstition,' said Groniger wearily. 'This morn's events have taken me out of my own element of reason.'

'And if it must be done,' Cif went on, 'you, Pshawri, are the one to attempt it. You raped the cube cinder from the Maelstrom's maw. You should be the one returns it to the fire.'

'If the damned thing will let itself be hurled into the flame pit,' Skullick burst out, his irreverence at last regenerated. 'You'll hurl it and it'll take flight the gods know where.'

'I'll find a way to constrain it, never fear,' the young lieutenant assured him, an uncustomary iron in his voice. He turned to Cif. 'From my heart's depths I thank you, Lady, for that task. When I wrested that accursed object from the whirlpool, I do now believe I doomed Captain Mouser to his present plight. It is my dearest desire to wipe out that fault.'

'Now wait a moment, all of you,' Afreyt cut in. 'I am myself inclined to agree with you about the Queller and Darkfire. It strikes me as the wise thing to do. But this is a step may mean the life or death of Captain Mouser. I do not think that we should take it without the agreement of Captain Fafhrd, his lifelong comrade and forever. I wear his ring, it's true, yet in this matter would not speak for him. So I come back to it: where's Fafhrd?'

'Who are these coming toward us from Salthaven?' Rill interrupted in an arresting voice. 'If I don't mistake their identities, they may bring new bearing on that question.'

The fog blanket to the east was finally breaking up and shredding under the silent bombardment of the sun's bright beams, although the latter were losing a little of their golden strength as the orb mounted and the sky became heavy. Through the white rags and tatters two slight and white-clad figures trudged: who waved their hands and broke into a run upon seeing that they were observed. As they drew closer it was to be seen that the redhead's eyes were large in her small face but the silver-blonde's larger still.

'Aunt Afreyt!' Gale called as soon as they got near. 'We've had a great adventure and we've got the most amazing news to tell!'

'Never mind that now,' Afreyt answered somewhat shortly. 'Tell us, where's Fafhrd?'

'How did you know?' Gale's eyes grew larger still. 'Well, I was going to build up to it, but since you ask right off: Uncle Fafhrd has swum up into the sky to board a cloud ship of Arilia or flag a flier from Stardock. I think he's looking for help in finding Uncle Mouser.'

'Stop talking nonsense,' Cif burst out.

'Fafhrd can't swim through air,' Afreyt pointed out.

'Sea tunnels of Simorgya! Cloud ships of Arilia!' Groniger protested. 'That's too much nonsense for a cold summer morning.'

'But it's what happened,' the girl insisted. 'Why, Aunt Afreyt, you yourself saw Fafhrd and Mara flying high through air when the invisible princess Hirriwi of Stardock rescued them from Hellfire on her invisible fish of air. Fingers saw more than I did. She'll tell you.'

The Ilthmar cabingirl said, 'Aboard *Weasel* the sailors all assured me that the strangest sorts of vessels dock at Rime Isle, including the cloud galleons of the Queendom of the Air. And I did see Captain Fafhrd swimming strongly atop the fog toward a cloud that could have been such a vessel.'

'Arilia is a fable, child,' Groniger assured her gently. 'Sailors tell all sorts of lies. Actually Rime Isle's the least fantastic place in all of Nehwon.'

'But Uncle Fafhrd did mount up the sky,' Gale reaffirmed stubbornly. 'I don't know how. Maybe Princess Hirriwi taught him to fly and he never told us about it. He's awfully modest. But he did it. We both saw him.'

'All right, all right,' Cif told her. 'I think you'd best just tell us the whole story from the beginning.'

Afreyt said, 'But first you need a cup of wine to calm you down and also warm you. You've been long out on a chilly morning that may go down in legend.' She opened her hamper, took out a jug of fortified sweet wine and two small silver mugs, filled them halfway, and made both children drink them down. This led to serving wine to all the others.

Gale said, 'Fingers should start it. At the beginning I was asleep.'

Fingers told them, 'Captain Fafhrd came back from the diggings just after the rest of you all went off. He drank some gahveh and brandy and began to pace up and down, frowning and rubbing his wrist against his forehead as if he were trying to think out some problem. He got very nervous and fey. Finally he took up a jug, hung a lamp on his hook, and went off after you. I waked Gale and told her I thought he needed watching.'

'That's right,' Gale took over. 'So we jumped out of bed and ran to the fire and got dressed.'

'That explains it,' Afreyt interjected.

'What?' Pshawri asked.

'Why Udall kept watching Fafhrd so long. Go on, dear.'

Gale continued, 'It was easy to follow Uncle Fafhrd because of his lamp. The darkness was fading anyway, the stars going out. At first we didn't try to catch up with him or let him know we were behind him.'

'You were afraid he'd send you back,' Cif guessed.

'That's right. At first he seemed to be following you, but where you turned south he kept straight on east. It was getting quite light now, but the sun was still in hiding. Every so often he'd stop and look ahead at the fog and the rooftops and the windchime arch sticking up out of it and lift his head to scan the sky above it – that's when I saw the little fleet of clouds – and raise his hand before his face to invoke the gods and ask their help.'

'That was the hand that had the jug in it?' Afreyt asked.

'It must have been,' the girl replied, 'for I don't recall the lamp going up and down.'

'And then Uncle Fafhrd began to run in the strangest slow

way, he seemed to float and almost stop between each step. Of course, we started to run too. We were all into the fog by now, which seemed to slow him and support him at the same time, so his steps were longer.

'The fog got over our heads and hid him from us. We got to the Moon Arch and Fingers started to climb it before I could tell her that was frowned on. She got above the fog and called down . . .'

Gale stretched a hand toward Fingers, who continued, 'Truly, gentles, I saw Captain Fafhrd swimming strongly through the top of the fog, up its long white slope, while a good distance beyond him, the goal of his mighty self-sailing, there was – I know the eyes can be fooled and my mind was full of the sailors' tales, nevertheless, my word as a novice witch – there was a dense cloud that looked very much like a white ship with a high sterncastle. Sunlight flashed from its silver brightwork.

'Then that same sun got into my eyes and I stopped seeing anything clearly. I'd called some of it down to Gale and I climbed down and told her the rest.'

Gale took up again. 'We ran through Salthaven to the eastern headland. The fog was breaking up and burning off, but we couldn't see anything clearly. When we got there, the Maelstrom was seething and mists rising from it. But overhead it was clear and I could see Uncle Fafhrd, very high now, beside the white cloudship, showing only its keel. There were five gulls around him. Then the mists from below came between us. I thought you should know, Aunt Afreyt. But since it was on the way to the diggings, we decided to tell Aunt Cif first.'

Fingers added, 'I saw what she saw, gentles. But Captain Fafhrd was very far off then. It could have been a very large marine bird – a sea mandragon escorted by five sea hawks.'

The listeners looked at each other.

'This rings true,' Afreyt said quite softly. 'I feared that Fafhrd was fey when he was last down the shaft.'

'You believe what these girls tell us?' Groniger asked only somewhat incredulously.

'To be sure she does,' Mother Grum answered.

'But why would he go to air folk,' Skullick wanted to know, 'to get advice on someone lost underground?'

'You can't guess the designs of a fey one,' Rill told him.

'But what of the Gray Mouser now?' Cif addressed Afreyt. 'As Fafhrd's spokeswoman, what say you to sending Pshawri to Darkfire?'

'Let him go, of course, and luck with him. Luck and quietus to Loki,' that lady responded without hesitation. 'Here's provisions for you, Lieutenant.' From her hamper she gave him a small loaf and a hard sausage and the near empty sweet wine jug, which would do to carry cool water he'd get at Last Spring on the way.

After a quick glance to assure himself the others were otherwise occupied, Pshawri said to Afreyt in a low voice, 'Lady, would you add to your kindnesses one further favour?' and when she nodded, handed her a folded paper indited in violet ink with broken green seals. 'Keep this for me. Should I not return (such things happen), give it to Captain Fafhrd, if he's back. Otherwise read it yourself – and show it to Lady Cif at your decision.'

'I'll do that,' she said softly, and then resuming her normal voice, called, 'Cif dear, you'll take over for Fafhrd and me at the digging. I'll give you Fafhrd's ring.'

'Can you doubt it?' Cif replied, turning back from Mother Grum, with whom she'd been conferring.

Afreyt went on, 'For it's now my turn to do some thinking about a lost one – and to see that these two outwearied girls do some sound sleeping. I'll take them to your place, Cif, and see to all there. Skama, shield *me* from feyness, except it be *your* inspiration.'

So without more ceremony the three parties separated: Pshawri north toward distant, smoke-trailing Darkfire; Cif, Skullick, and Rill back to the diggings; Afreyt, Groniger, and the weary old and young pairs to Salthaven.

Trudging with the last party, and suddenly looking every bit as tired as Afreyt had described her, Fingers recited as by someone already asleep and dreaming,

> *After the dog has eaten out his heart,*
> *The cat his liver, and his secret parts*
> *Uprooted and devoured by the hog,*

He shall sleep sounder then than any log,
A shadow prince enrobed by moonlit fog.'

'Was that your brother, Princess?' Gale asked, wrinkling her nose. 'You know the nicest poems, I must say.'

After a moment Afreyt inquired thoughtfully, 'But what kind of a poem was it, dear Fingers? Where did it come from?'

Still somewhat in a sleepy singsong, the weary child responded, 'It is the augmented third stanza of a Quarmallian death spell effective only in its entirety.' She shook her head and blinked her eyes and came more awake. 'Now how did I know that?' she asked. 'My mother was born in Quarmall, that is true, but that was another of the things we weren't supposed to tell most people.'

'Yet she taught you this Quarmall death spell,' Afreyt stated.

Fingers shook her head decidedly. 'My mother never dealt in death spells, nor taught me any. She is a white witch, truly.' She looked puzzledly at Gale and then up at Afreyt and asked, 'Why does a memory wink off whenever you try to watch it closely? Is it because we cannot live for ever?'

19

As consciousness next glimmered, glowed, and then shone noontide bright in the Gray Mouser's skull, he would have been certain he was dreaming, for in his nostrils was the smell of Lankhmar earth, richly redolent of the grainfields, the Great Salt Marsh, the River Hlal, the ashes of innumerable fires, and the decay of myriad entities, a unique melange of odours, and he was ensconced in one of the secretmost rooms of all Lankhmar City, one he knew well although he had visited it only once. How could his underground journeying possibly have carried him so far, two thousand leagues or more, one tenth the way at least around all Nehwon world? – except that he had never in his life had a dream in which the furniture and actors were so clearly distinct and open to scrutiny in all their details.

But as we know, it was the Mouser's custom on waking

anywhere not to move more than an eye muscle or make the least sound, even that of a deeper breath, until he had taken in and thoroughly mastered the nature of his surroundings and his own circumstances amongst them.

He was comfortably seated cross-legged about a Lankhmar cubit (a forearm's length) behind a narrow low table beside the foot of the wide bed, sheeted in white silk curiously coarse of weave, in the combined underground bedroom and boudoir of the rat princess Hisvet, his most tormenting one-time paramour, daughter of the wealthy grain merchant Hisvin, in the buried city of Lankhmar Below. He knew it was that room and no other by its pale violet hangings, silver fittings, and a half hundred more apposite details, chiefest perhaps two painted panels in the far wall depicting an unclad maiden and crocodile erotically intertwined and a youth and leopardess similarly entangled. As had been the case some five years ago, the room was lit by narrow tanks of glow worms at the foot of the walls, but now also by silver cages hanging cornice high and imprisoning flashing firebeetles, glow wasps, nightbees, and diamondflies big as robins or starlings. While on the low table before him rested a silver waterclock with visible pool, upon the centre of which a large drop fell every third breath or dozenth heartbeat, making circular ripples, and a cut crystal carafe of pale golden wine, reminding him he was abominably thirsty.

So much for the furniture of his dream, vision, or true sighting. The actors included slim Hisvet herself wearing a violet wrap whose colour matched the hangings and her lips. She was seated on the bed's foot, looking as merry and schoolgirl innocent (and devilishly attractive) as always, her fine silver-blond hair drawn through a small ring of that metal behind her head, while standing at dutiful attention close before her were two barefoot maids with hair cropped short and wearing identical closely fitting hip-length black and white tunics. Hisvet was lecturing them, laying out rules of some sort, apparently, and they were listening most earnestly, although they showed it in different ways, the brunette nodding her head, smiling her understanding, and darting her gaze with sharp intelligence, while the blonde maintained a sober and distant, yet wide-eyed expression, as though memorizing

Hisvet's every word, inscribing each one in a compartment of her brain reserved for that purpose alone.

But although Hisvet worked her violet lips and the tip of her mottled blue and pink tongue continuously in the movements of speech and lifted an admonitory right forefinger from time to time and once touched it successively on the tips of the out-spread fingertips of her supine left hand to emphasize points one, two, three, and four, not a single word could the Gray Mouser hear. Nor did any one of the three ever look once in his direction, even the saucy dark-haired wench whose gaze went everywhere else.

Since both maids in their very short tunics were quite as attractive as their ravishing mistress, their disregard of him began to wound the Mouser's vanity not a little.

Since there seemed nothing for the moment to do but watch them, the Mouser soon developed a hankering to see their naked shapes. So far as the maids were concerned, he might get his wish simply by waiting. Hisvet had a remarkable instinct for such matters and was perfectly willing to let other women entertain for her – distribute her favours, as it were.

But as to her own secret person, it still remained a mystery to the Mouser, whether under the robes, wraps, and armour she affected there was a normal maiden form or a slender rat tail and eight tits, which his imagination pictured as converging pairs of large-nippled and large-aureoled bud-breasts, the third pair to either side of her umbilicus and the fourth close together upon her pubis.

It also was a mystery to him whether the three females and he were all now of rat size or human size – ten inches or five feet high. Certainly he'd had none of the shape-changing elixir that was used in moving between Lankhmar Above and the rat city of Lankhmar Below.

His hankerings continued. Surely he deserved some reward for all the underground perils he'd braved. Women could do men so much good so easily.

There remained the problem of the three women's perfect inaudibility.

Either, he guessed, they were engaged in an elaborate panto-mime (plotted by Hisvet to tease him?), or it *was* a dream despite its realism, or else there was some hermetic barrier (most likely magical) between his ears and them.

Supporting this last possibility was the point that while he could see the giant luminescent insects move about in their cages, striking the silver bars with wing and limb while making their bright shinings and flashes, no angry buzzings or sounds of any sort came down from them; while (most telling of all in its way) only silence accompanied the infrequent but regular plashes of the singular crystalline drops into the shimmering pool of the waterclock so close at hand.

One final circumstance suggestive of magic at work and matching the strange quiet of the scene otherwise so real: miraculously suspended in the air above the near edge of the low table, in a vertical attitude with ring-pommelled small silver grip uppermost, was a tapering whip of white snow-serpent hide scarcely a cubit long, so close at hand he could perceive its finely rugose surface, yet spy no thread or other explanation of its quiet suspension.

Well, that was the scene, he told himself. Now to decide on how to enter it, assert himself as one of the actors. He would lean suddenly forward, he told himself, reach out his right hand, seize with his three bottom fingers the neck of the carafe, un-stopper it with forefinger and thumb preparatory to putting it to his parched lips, saying meanwhile something to the effect of, 'Greetings, dearest delightful Demoiselle, do me the kindness of interrupting this charade to give an old friend notice. Don't be alarmed, girls,' that last being for the two maids, of course.

No sooner thought than done!

But, from the start, things went most grievously agley. On his first move he felt himself gripped by a general paralysis that struck like lightning. His whole front was bruised, his right hand and arm scraped, from every side dark brown grainy walls rushed in upon him, his 'Greetings' became on the first syllable a strangled growl that stabbed his ears, pained his whole skull, and changed to a fit of coughing that left him with what seemed a mouthful of raw dirt.

He was *still* in the same horrid buried predicament he'd been in ever since he'd slipped down out of the full-moon ceremony on Gallows Hill into the cold cruel ground that was at once so strangely permeable to his involuntary passage through it and so adamantly resistant to his attempts to escape it. This time he'd been fooled by the perfection of the occult vision, which let him see through solid earth for a distance around him, into thinking he was free, disregarding the evidence of all his other avenues of awareness. Evidently he *had* somehow been brought to Lankhmar's underenvirons, and nothing now remained to do but begin anew the slow game of regularizing his breathing, calming his pounding heart, and freeing his mouth grain by grain of the dirt that had entered it during his spasm, carefully working his tongue to best advantage, in order to assure bare survival. For after the pain in his skull subsided he became aware of a general weakness and a wavering of consciousness that told him he was very near the edge between being and not being and must work most cunningly to draw back from it.

During this endeavor he was assisted by the fact that he never quite altogether lost sight of a larger white and violet visual reality around him. There were patchy flashes and glimpses of it alternating with the grainy dark dirt, and he was also helped by the faint yellow glow continuing to emanate from his upper face.

When the Mouser finally re-won all the territory he'd lost by his incautious sally, he was surprised to see fair Hisvet still going through all the motions of talking, and the winsome maids through those of attending her every word, as animatedly as before. Whatever was she saying?

While carefully maintaining all underground breathing routines, he concentrated his attention on other channels of sensation than the visual, seeking to widen and deepen, and bringing to bear all his inner powers, and after a time his efforts were rewarded.

The next heavy drop fell into the pool of the waterclock with an audible dulcet *plash*! He almost, but not quite, gave a start.

Almost immediately a glow wasp *buzzed* and a diamondfly whirred its transparent wings against the wire-thin pale bars.

Hisvet leaned back on her elbows and said in silver tones, 'At ease, girls.'

They appeared to relax their attention – a little, at any rate.

609

She tapped three fingers against the ruby rondure of her lips as she yawned prettily. 'My, that was a most lengthy and boring lecture,' she commented. 'Yet you endured it most commendably, dear Threesie,' she addressed the dark-haired maid. 'And you too, Foursie,' she told the fair-haired one. She picked up from beside her a long emerald-headed pin and flourished it playfully. 'There was not once the need for me to make use of *this* upon either of you,' she said, laughing, 'to recall to attention the wilful wandering mind and wake the lazy dreamer.'

Both girls shaped their lips to appreciative smiles, while giving the pin most sour looks.

Hisvet handed it to Foursie, who bore it somewhat gingerly across the room to a drawered chest topped with cosmetics and mirrors, and inserted it into a spherical black cushion that held jewel-headed others such, compassing all the hues of the rainbow.

Meanwhile Hisvet addressed Threesie, whose eyes widened as she listened. 'During my talk I twice got the distinct impression that we were being spied on by an evil intelligence, one of the criminous sort my father deals with, or one of our own enemies, or a cast-off lover perchance.' She searched her gaze around the walls, lingering somewhat overlong, the Mouser felt, in his direction.

'I will meditate on it,' she continued. 'Dear Threesie, fetch me my silver-inlaid black opal figure of the world of Nehwon which I call the Opener of the Way.'

Threesie nodded dutifully and went to the same chest Foursie had just visited, passing her midway.

'Dear Foursie,' Hisvet greeted the blonde, 'fetch me a beaker of white wine. My throat has grown quite dry with all that stupid talking.'

Foursie bowed her fair-thatched head and came to the low table set against the wall behind which the Mouser was embedded in earth invisible to him. He studied her appreciatively as she unstoppered the carafe he'd so disastrously snatched at and neatly filled a shining glass so tall and narrow it looked like a measuring tube. Her white uniform tunic was secured down the front with large circular jet buttons.

Returning to her mistress, she went down on her knees

without bending her slender body in any other way and proffered the refreshment.

'Taste it first,' Hisvet instructed.

Getting this instruction, not uncommonly given servants by aristocrats, Foursie threw back her head and poured a short gush of the fluid between her parted lips without touching them to the glass, which she next held out to show its level was perceptibly decreased.

Hisvet accepted it, saying, 'That was well executed, Foursie. Next time don't wait for instruction. And you might lick your lips and smile to show that you enjoyed.'

Foursie bobbed her head.

'Dear Demoiselle,' Threesie called from where she knelt at the chest of drawers, 'I cannot find the Opener.'

'Have you searched carefully for it?' Hisvet called back, her voice becoming slightly thin. 'It is an oblate sphere big as two thumbs, inset with silver bounding the continents and flat diamonds for the cities and a larger amethyst and turquoise making the death and life poles.'

'Dear Demoiselle, I know the Opener,' Threesie called respectfully.

Hisvet, who was looking at Foursie again, shrugged her shoulders, then set the narrow glass to her lips and downed its contents in three swallows. 'That was refreshing.' Again the lip pats.

A rutching sound turned her attention back to Threesie. 'No, do not open the other drawers,' she directed. 'It would not be there. Just search the top one thoroughly and *find it*. Set out the contents one by one on top of the chest if necessary.'

'Yes, Demoiselle.'

Hisvet caught Foursie's eye again, rolled hers toward busy Threesie, sketched another shrug, and commented confidingly, 'This could become a tiresome annoyance, you know, a true weariness. No, girl, don't bob your head. That's all right on Threesie, but it's not your style. Incline it once, demurely.'

'Yes, mistress.' Her single nod was shy as a virgin princess's.

'How are you doing, Threesie?'

The brunette turned to face them. Her reply was barely loud

enough to cross the room. 'Demoiselle, I must confess myself defeated.'

After a rather long pause, Hisvet said reflectively, 'That could be quite bothersome for you, Threesie, you know. As senior maid present, you would be wholly responsible for any deficiencies, disappearances, or thefts. Think about it.'

After another pause, she sighed and said, holding out the empty glass, 'Foursie, fetch me the springy implement of correction.'

The blonde inclined her head, took the glass, and walking somewhat more slowly, returned to the low table, set down the glass, refilled it, and reached across to seize the magically suspended white whip, which she lifted with a little twist and bore off with the glass, thereby solving a minor mystery for the Mouser. The whip had simply been hanging on a hook on the wall. But since the wall had been and was again invisible to him, so was the hook protruding from it.

He felt a stirring of interest in the scene he spied on from his confining point of vantage, and was duly grateful to have his mind taken a little off his own troubles. He knew something of Hisvet's ways and could guess the next developments, or at least speculate rewardingly. Dark-haired Threesie seemed well cast as the villain or culprit of his triangular piece. Leaning back against the chest of drawers and scowling, she looked a bird of ill omen in her uniform black tunic, though the large circular alabaster buttons going down the front added a comic note. Foursie did her kneeling trick a second time. Hisvet accepted the whip and replenished drink, saying graciously, 'Thank you, my dear. I feel much better with these both by me. Well, Threesie?'

'I am thinking, Demoiselle,' that one said, 'and it comes to me that when I entered this room Foursie was crouched where I stand now with the drawer open I have just searched thoroughly, and she was rummaging around in it. She pushed it shut at once, but may well have taken somewhat from it, I realize now, and hid it about her person.'

'Demoiselle, that's not true!' Foursie protested, turning pale. 'The drawer was never open, nor I at it.'

'She is a vicious little liar, dear mistress,' Threesie shot back. 'Mark how she blanches!'

'Hush, girls,' Hisvet reproved. 'I have thought of a simple way to settle this most unseemly dispute. Threesie dear, had Foursie opportunity to hide the Opener elsewhere in the room after she took it, if she did? As I recall, I entered shortly after you did.'

'No, mistress, she had not.'

'Well, then,' Hisvet said, smiling. 'Threesie, come here. Foursie dear, strip off your tunic, so she may search you thoroughly.'

'Demoiselle!' the blonde uttered reproachfully. 'You would not shame me so.'

'No shame at all,' Hisvet assured her ingenuously, lifting her silver eyebrows. 'Why, child, suppose I were entertaining a lover, I might very well – probably would – have you and Threesie disrobe, so as not to embarrass him, or at all events make us both feel conspicuous. Or we might have the whim to ask one of you or both to join in our play under direction. Frix understood these things, as I hope Threesie does. Frix was incomparable. Not even Twosie comes close to matching her. But as you know, Frix managed to work out her term of service, discharge the geas my father set upon her. There's never been another Onesie, and that's why.'

Both maids nodded agreement, though somewhat grimly in their two different styles. They'd each heard somewhat too much about the Incomparable Onesie.

The Mouser was beginning to enjoy himself. Why, look, the piece was barely begun and Hisvet had managed to switch around the roles of the two other characters! He wished Fafhrd were here, he'd enjoy hearing Frix praised so. He'd been quite gone on the princess of Arilia, especially when she'd been Hisvet's imperturbable slave-maid. Though the large loon wouldn't appreciate being entombed, that was certain. Probably too big to survive by scavenging air in any case. Which reminded him, he'd best keep in mind his own breathing. And not lose sight of the ever-present possibility of the intrusion into the scene of some third force from either the under- or overworld. Talk about having to watch two ways!

In response to Hisvet's, 'And so, no nonsense, child. Strip, I said!' Foursie had been arguing, 'Have compassion, Demoiselle. To disrobe for a lover would be one thing. But to strip to be searched by a fellow servant is simply too humiliating. I couldn't bear it!'

Hisvet sprang up off the bed. 'I've quite lost patience with you, you prudish little bitch. Who are you to say what you'll bear – or bare, for that matter? Threesie, grip her arms! If she struggles, pinion them behind her.'

The dark maid, who was already back of Foursie, seized and tightly held her elbows down at her sides, meanwhile smiling somewhat evilly at her mistress across the fair maid's shoulder. Hisvet reached out a straight right arm, chucked the girl's chin up until they were looking each other straight in the eye, and then proceeded very deliberately to unbutton the top black button.

Foursie said, with as much dignity as she could muster, 'I would have submitted to you, Demoiselle, without my arms held.'

But Hisvet said only, very deliberately also, 'You are a silly schoolgirl, Foursie dear, needing considerable teaching, which you're going to get. You would submit to me? But not to my maid acting on my orders? To being with, Threesie is not your equal fellow servant. She outranks you and is empowered to correct you in my absence.'

As she spoke she went on undoing the buttons, taking her time and digging her knuckles and pressing the large buttons into the girl's flesh edgewise as she did so. At the undoing of the third button the maid's small, firm, pink-nippled breasts popped out. Hisvet continued, 'But as it is, you're getting your way, aren't you, Foursie? I am disrobing you and not dear Threesie here, though she is witnessing. In fact, I'm "maiding" you, how's that for topsy-turvy? You're getting the deluxe treatment, one might say, though I strongly doubt you will get much pleasure from it.'

She finished with the buttons, looked the girl up and down, lightly flicked her breasts with the back of her hand, and said with a cheery laugh, 'There, that wasn't so bad, was it, dear? Threesie, finish.'

Grinning, the dark maid slid the white tunic down Foursie's arms and off them.

'Why, you are blushing, Foursie,' Hisvet observed, chuckling.

'On Whore Street that's a speciality, I'm told, and ups the price. Inspect the garment carefully,' she warned Threesie. 'Feel along each seam and hem. She may have pilfered something smaller than the Opener. And now, dear child, prepare yourself to be searched from head to toe by a maid who is your superior, whilst I direct and witness.' Taking up the silver-handled whip of white snow-serpent hide from the bed and gesturing with it, she directed Foursie, 'Lift out your arms a little from your sides. There, that's enough. And stand so that your entire anatomy is more accessible. A little wider stance, please. Yes, that will do.'

The Mouser noted that all the maid's body hair had been shaven or plucked. So that practice, favoured by witless Glipkerio, the Scarecrow Overlord, was still followed in Lankhmar. A seemly and most attractive one, the Mouser thought.

'There's nothing hidden in the garment, Threesie? You're sure? Well, toss it by the far wall and then you might begin by running your fingers through Foursie's hair. Bend forward, child! Slowly and carefully, Threesie. I know her mop's quite short, but you'd be shocked to learn how much a little hair can sometimes hide. And don't forget the ears. We're looking for tiny things.'

Hisvet yawned and took a long swallow of wine. Foursie glared at her nearer tormentor. There is something peculiarly degrading about being handled by the ears, having them spread and bent this way and that. But Threesie, learning from her mistress, only smiled sweetly back.

'And now the mouth,' Hisvet directed. 'Open wide, Foursie, as for the barber-surgeon. Feel in each cheek, Threesie. I don't suppose Foursie's been playing the little squirrel, but there's no telling. And now . . . Surely you're not at a loss, Threesie? Perhaps I should have expressed it, search her from top to bottom. You may lubricate your fingers with my pomade. But use it sparingly, its basis is the essential oil with which they anoint the Emperor of the East. Don't agonize so, Foursie! Imagine it's your lover exploring you, dextrously demonstrating his tender regard. Who is your lover, Foursie? You do have one, I trust? Come to recall, I've caught the fair page Hari looking at you in that certain way. I wonder what he'd think if he could see you as you're presently occupied. Droll. I've half a mind to summon him. Well, that's half done. And now, Threesie, her darker avenue of amatory bliss. bend over, Foursie. Treat her gently, Threesie. Some of these matters appear to be quite new to our little girl, advanced subjects for our student, though I know that's hard to credit. What Foursie, tears? Cheer up, child! You're not proved guilty yet, in fact you're well on the way to being cleared. Life has all sorts of surprises.'

The Mouser smiled cynically from his weird invisible prison. Around Hisvet surprises were invariably disastrous, he knew from experience. He was thoroughly enjoying himself, so far as his limited circumstances permitted. He thought of how all of his greatest loves and infatuations had been for short and slim girls like these. Lilyblack came to mind, back when he'd bravoed and racketeered for Pulg and Fafhrd had found god in Issek. Reetha, who'd been Glipkerio's silver-chained maid. Ivivis of Quarmall, supple as a snake. Innocent, tragic Ivrian, his first love, whose princess-dreams he'd fed. Cif, of course. The nightfilly Ivmiss Ovartamortes. That made seven, counting Hisvet. And there was one other, an eighth, whose name and identity evaded him, who was also a maid by profession and particularly delectable because somehow forbidden. Who *had* she been? What *was* her name? If he could recall one more detail he'd remember all. Maddening! Of course, he'd had all manner of larger women, but this elusive memory involved all smaller than himself, his special pantheon of little darlings. You'd think a man in his grave (and that was truly his situation, face it) would be able to concentrate his mind upon one subject, but no, even here there were details to distract you, self-responsibilities that had to be taken care of, as keeping up an even rhythm of shallow breathing, pushing back intrusive dirt off his lips, keeping constant watch before and behind – It occurred to him that Foursie too must be telling herself that last thing, though much good it would do her – which reminded him to return to the enjoyment of the three-girl comedy which destiny had provided for his secret viewing.

Hisvet was saying, 'Now, Foursie, go to the far wall and stand facing it while I hear Threesie's report and confer with her. And stop blubbering, girl! Use your discarded tunic to wipe the tears and snot off your face.'

Hisvet led Threesie back to the foot of the bed, set her empty glass on the low table, and said in a voice that Mouser could barely hear, despite the advantages of nearness and occult audition, 'I take it, Threesie, you didn't find the Opener or anything else?'

'No, dear Demoiselle, I did not,' the dark maid replied, and then went on in a voice that was more like a stage whisper, 'I'm certain she's swallowed it. I suggest she be given a strong emetic, and if that fails, a powerful cathartic. Or both together, to save time.'

Foursie too heard that, the Mouser judged by the way her shoulders drew together as she faced the wall.

Hisvet shook her head and said in the same low tones as before, 'No, that won't be necessary, I think, though it could be amusing under other circumstances. Now it suits my design to have her think she's been completely cleared of any suspicion of theft.' She faced around and changed to her most ringing silver voice, 'Congratulations, Foursie, you'll be glad to hear that your fellow maid has given you a clean bill of health. Isn't that wonderful? And now come here at once. No, don't try to put on your tunic. Leave that soiled rag. You need a lot more practice in serving naked, which you ought to be able to do every bit as efficiently, coolly, and nicely without the reassurance of a frock. And perhaps practice in other activities one generally carries out best in one's skin. Beginning now.'

The Lankhmar Demoiselle in the violet wrap yawned again and stretched. 'That wretched session has quite wearied me. Foursie, you may begin your nude apprenticeship (that's a joke, girl) by fetching me a fat pillow from the head of the bed.'

When Foursie came around with her plump lemon-hued burden, her eyes asking a question, Hisvet indicated with her whip the bottom corner of the bed, and when the fair maid had placed the pillow there, gave her the whip, saying, 'Hold this for me,' and stretched herself out with her head on the pillow. But after murmuring, 'Ah, that's better,' and wriggling her toes, she lifted up on an elbow, looked toward Threesie, and pointed with her other hand down at the carpet by the foot of the bed, saying, 'Threesie, come here. I want to show you something privately.'

When the dark maid came eagerly, all agog for more secrets, Hisvet laid her silver-tressed head back again upon the pillow, whose hue contrasted nicely with her violet wrap, and said, 'Lean down, so your head is close to mine. I want this to be quite private. Foursie, stand clear.'

But when Threesie stooped down, her lips working with high excitement, Hisvet began at once to criticize. 'No, don't bend your knees! I did not bid you crouch over me like an animal. Keep your legs straight.'

By bending her waist more, pushing her buttocks back, and also throwing her arms out behind her, the dark maid managed to comply with her instructions without overbalancing. Her and her mistress's faces were upside down to each other.

'But, Demoiselle,' Threesie pointed out humbly, 'when I bend over like this in this short tunic, I expose myself behind. Especially with your rule against undergarments.'

Hisvet smiled up at her. 'That's very true,' she observed, 'and I designed them partly with that in mind, so that when told to pick up something from the floor, for instance, a maid would stoop gracefully, as in a curtsey, keeping her head and shoulders erect. It's far more seemly and civilized.'

Threesie said uncertainly, 'But when you go down like that you have to bend your knees, you squat. You told me not to bend—'

'That's quite a different matter,' Hisvet interrupted, impatience gathering in her voice. 'I told you to lean down your head.'

'But, Demoiselle—' Threesie faltered.

Hisvet reached up and caught an earlobe between forefinger and thumb, dug in the nails, twisted sharply and gave a downward tug. Threesie squealed. Hisvet let go and, patting her cheek, told her, 'That's all right. I just want to rivet your attention and make you stop your silly babble. Now, listen carefully. While you did the body search on Foursie passably well, it became frightfully obvious that you, as well as Foursie, needless to say, were in sore need of instruction in the amatory arts, which it falls on me to give you, since you're my own dear maid and no one else's.' And reaching her hand higher, she hooked her fingers around the back of Threesie's neck and pulled her head down briskly but thoughtfully, leaning her own head to the left at the last moment, so that her lips met at an angle those of Threesie, who managed to keep her balance by further and somewhat desperate rearward outthrustings.

The Mouser thought, I knew that this was coming. But one certainly cannot fault the little darlings for their occasional itch for each other, since their taste is so exactly like my own. Strange, come to think of it, that Fafhrd and I have never seemed to experience this like-sex urge. Is it a deficiency in us? I must discuss the question with him some time. And with Cif too, for that matter, ask her if she and Afreyt ever played games . . . no, maybe not ask, I could understand Afreyt lusting for Cif, but not dear Ciffy for that beanpole Venus.

Hisvet shifted her fingers behind Threesie's back to the short hairs there, lifted her head to its original position as briskly as she'd lowered it, and said, 'That was passable also. Next time, if such should be, employ your tongue somewhat more freely. Be adventurous, girl.'

Wide-eyed, Threesie gasped, 'Excuse me, Demoiselle, but was that kiss, for which I thank you most humbly, the something you said you wished to show me privately?'

'No, it was not,' Hisvet informed her, thrusting a hand deep into a side pocket of her wrap. 'That is a different matter, rather sadder for you.' Pulling Threesie's head down again, this time by the neck of her black tunic, she brought a fist out of the pocket, opened it under Threesie's eyes, displaying on her cupped palm a globular black opal travelled with silver lines and pocked here and there with small, pale, glittering dots. 'What do you suppose this is?' she asked.

'It appears to be the Opener of the Way, dear Demoiselle.' Threesie faltered. 'But how—'

'Quite right, girl. I took it earlier from the chest myself and just now remembered. So Foursie could hardly have swallowed it, could she? Or even taken it from the chest, for that matter.'

'No, Demoiselle,' the dark maid agreed reluctantly. 'But Foursie's only a servant of the lowest rank, little better than a slave. It was natural to suspect her. Moreover, you yourself must have known—'

'I told you I only now remembered!' Hisvet reminded her in dangerous tones. She raised her voice. 'Foursie!'

'Yes, Demoiselle?' came the swift reply.

'Threesie is to be punished for bearing false witness against a fellow servant. Since you're the party who would have been injured, I think it's most appropriate that you administer the chastisement. Moreover, you are conveniently at hand and have my whip. Do you know how to use it?'

'I think I do, Demoiselle,' Foursie answered evenly. 'When I was a child down on the farm I used to ride a mule.'

'That's nice to know,' Hisvet called. 'Wait for directions.'

As Threesie quite involuntarily started to move away, Hisvet rotated the fist grasping her tunic so that it tightened around Threesie's neck and Hisvet's knuckles dug into the maid's throat.

'Listen,' she hissed, 'if you so much as move a step or flex your knees during what's coming, I'll have my father put a geas on you. And not a relatively nice and easy one like Frix. She merely had to serve me faithfully and cheerfully as slave until she'd thrice saved my life at risk of her own. Straighten those knees now!'

Threesie complied. She had seen old Hisvin send a berserk cook into mortal convulsions, so he died in his tracks with mouth exuding greenish foam, merely by staring at him fixedly.

Hisvet eased her grip on the top of Threesie's tunic. She scowled in thought. Then her face broke into a smile. She called, 'Foursie, here's how. Time your blows to the plashes of the waterclock, one for one, nothing in between – don't let yourself get carried away. Start with the third plash after the next. I'll call the first of those so you get it right.'

Hisvet's hand on the neck of the black tunic became busy, undoing the three big top white buttons rapidly.

The waterclock plashed, sounding unnaturally loud. Hisvet called, 'Ready!' Tension took hold.

Though pendant, the dark maid's breasts were quite as small and firm as the fair one's, with thicker nipples the rosy hue of fresh scrubbed copper. Hisvet fondled them.

'How many blows, Demoiselle?' Threesie asked in a small, fearfully anxious voice. 'In all?'

'Hush! I haven't decided yet. You're supposed to be enjoying this. And you really are, I can tell, for your nipples are hardening despite your terrors. And your aureoles are all goose bumps. You should indicate pleasure at my squeezings and finger-dancing across your tits by sighing and moaning.'

The waterclock plashed. 'One!' Hisvet called, then ominously for Threesie's benefit, 'You've started to bend your legs again,' and taking the hand away from the maid's bosom, reached out and gave each of her knees a firm shove.

In his retreat the Mouser spared a glance for the ripples spreading and reflecting in the clock's pool. A shiver of genuine fear surprised him at the thought that he seemed to be just too well placed for watching for it all to be a matter of chance. Had Hisvet arranged it so? Did she somehow know that he, or at least some spirit, was watching invisibly? Was it all to get him off guard?

No, he told himself, I'm starting to think too tricky. This was just one of those glorious guilty visions that, it was to be hoped, lightened the last moments of buried men less fortunate or resourceful than he. His eyes feasted on Foursie as the girl positioned herself to the far side of Threesie's quivering rear, measuring distances with her eyes and the white whip, her pink-nippled breasts jouncing a bit as she danced with excitement. She was flushed all over, and not with embarrassment, he was sure.

Plash went the waterclock. 'Two!' Hisvet called. She shifted her hand to the back of Threesie's neck, pulled down until the maid's blanched tight face was a hand's breadth above her own, said rapidly, 'We're doing another kiss. It'll help you bear the pain and I want to feel you getting it, taste your reaction. Keep your knees straight,' and she pulled the maid's face down all the way, and kissed her fiercely. Her free hand played with Threesie's maiden breasts.

The third *plash* was tailed with a narrow *thwack* and muffled squeal. Threesie bucked. And all for me, the little darlings, Mouser thought. Foursie's blue eyes flashed like a fury's in ecstasy. She was breathing hard. She drew back the white whip to begin another blow, remembered in time to wait.

Hisvet let up Threesie's head to breathe. 'Lovely,' she told her. 'Your scream came down my throat. It tasted divine spice.' Then, 'Excellent, Foursie,' she called. 'Stay on your toes, girl.'

Threesie cried, 'Hesset help me,' invoking the Lankhmar moon goddess. 'Make her stop, Demoiselle, I'll do anything.'

Hisvet said, 'Hush, girl. Hesset give you courage,' and pulled down her head again, stifling her cries against her waiting lips. Her other hand pressed back on the maid's knees.

The three sounds were much the same. Threesie's buck was more of a caper. The Mouser was surprised by his arousal, felt a flicker of shame, recalled in time to breathe shallowly, et cetera.

The moment Hisvet let up Threesie's head to take a breath, the maid pleaded, 'Make her stop, she'll kill me,' then couldn't contain indignation. 'Demoiselle, you knew she hadn't stolen the jewel. You led me on.'

Hisvet's hand, busy with her breasts, seized up flesh and skin midway between them as though her thumb and forefinger knuckle were pinchers, squeezed, twisted, rubbed together, and jerked down all at once. Threesie squealed. 'Silence, you stupid slut,' her mistress hissed. 'You enjoyed making her suffer, now you're paying. You little fool! Don't you realize a maid who falsely betrays her fellow maid would just as readily betray her mistress? I expect real loyalty from my maids. Foursie, lay on hard.' And she pulled the maid's face against hers just as the drop *plashed* and the third blow fell. This time when Hisvet released her head, there were no instant words, tears spurted down instead. Hisvet shook them off, dipped her free hand again in her wide pocket.

And this time the Mouser was surprised by his impulse to shut his eyes. But nasty fascination and the urgent messages from his stiffening member were too strong.

Hisvet lectured, 'One other thing I expect of my maid: love, when the whim is on me. That's the chief reason she must always keep herself clean and attractive.' She mopped Threesie's face with a large kerchief, then held it to her nose. 'Blow,' she commanded. 'And then swallow hard. I don't want you blubbering snot on me.'

Threesie obeyed, but then the injustice of it all overwhelmed her. 'But it isn't *fair*,' she bleated woefully. 'It's not fair at *all*.'

Those words and tones had a strange and unexpected effect upon the earth-embraced Mouser. They recalled to him the name that had eluded him of the eighth little darling. A score and two or three years slipped away and he was lolling in dishabille on the wide couch in the private dining chamber of the Silver Eel tavern in Lankhmar, and Ivlis's maid Freg was pacing back and forth before him in her delicious young slim nakedness, and then she had stopped by him and turned toward him, tears spurting from her eyes, and bleated woefully those identical same trite words.

He knew the circumstances all right, knew them by heart. Barely a fortnight had passed since the fairly satisfactory ending of the affair of Omphal's jewel-crusted skull and other vengeful brown bones from the forgotten burial crypt in the great house of the Thieves Guild. The gems salvaged had been adequate, especially when there was added thereto the person of Ivlis, a lean, shifty, fox-faced glorious redhead. He'd had her the second night after, though that hadn't been easy, and it was more or less understood between Fafhrd and him that Freg was the Northerner's booty. But then the big oaf had delayed making his move, dawdled over nailing down his conquest, seemed hardly grateful at all to the Mouser for having taken on the more difficult seduction, leaving his comrade the juicier, tenderer prey, to be had for no more exertion than pushing back on to the bed (nine times out of ten the big man was incomprehensibly slower than he about such matters), so that after two or three more nights and nothing more forward, and feeling impatient and feckless and at war with all Nehwon – and with Fafhrd too, for the nonce – and opportunity presenting, he'd yielded to temptation and bedded the silly chit, which hadn't been all that easy either. And then on their third or fourth assignation she turned stormy and accused him of getting her drunk and forcing her the first time and claimed to have been deeply in love with Fafhrd and he with her, she knew, only they'd been moving slowly so as to savour fully their romance before declaring and enjoying it, and the Mouser had cut in with his nasty lust and wily ways and managed to root a child in her, she was certain of that, and so spoiled everything. And although he was still deeply infatuated with Freg, that had angered him and he'd told the little fool that he always tried out the virtue of girls who set their cap for Fafhrd and tried to romance him, to see if they were worthy of him and would stay faithful, and none of them had passed the test so far, but she'd done worst. And she had spouted tears and whimpered those nine words Threesie'd just voiced. And the next day Freg had been gone from Lankhmar, no one knew where, and Fafhrd had fallen into a melancholy fit, and Ivlis'd turned nasty, and he'd not breathed a word then or ever about the part he'd played.

All of which went to show, he told himself, how a suddenly triggered lost memory, like a ghost from the grave, could be so real as to blot out completely a poignantly interesting, nastily fascinating present, almost create another present, as it were, for several heartbeats till it had run its course inside his eyes.

They were between blows in Hisvet's boudoir. The violet wrap was undone just far enough to bare her own top pair of small, palely violet-nippled breasts, and she was holding down to them the tousled head of the dark maid, who was tonguing them industriously under instructions. She broke these off to carol, 'To force the unwilling to accept joy is so rewarding! To cause the recalcitrant to discover pleasure in pain is even more so!' The fair maid was doing a rapid little dance in place to contain her pent excitement and rotating the poised white whip in a little circle in time with her flashing toes. Hisvet called gaily to incite her on, 'Remember, Foursie, the slut had her fingers up you prying around, not gently, I'll warrant,' and the clock *plashed* and the whip whistled and *thwacked* and Threesie joined in the dance.

When Hisvet let up her head, the dark maid said rapidly, 'If you'll have her stop just for a while, Demoiselle, I'll lick your ass most lovingly, I promise,' and Hisvet replied, 'All in good time, girl,' and reaching back in an excess of arousal, caught hold with thumb and forefinger knuckle of her by the midst of her maiden mound and gave it the same sort of pincher's tweak as she had the maid's flesh midway between her breasts, where a blue bruise now showed; and the dark maid squealed muffledly.

But then, just as Foursie stayed her dance to strike and the Mouser's erection grew almost unbearably hard, Hisvet cried sharply, 'Break off the whipping, Foursie! Don't strike again!'

624

and the maid obeyed with a spasmodic effort, and Hisvet ducked her head and shoulders out from under Threesie's arched front and stared searchingly at the wall by the waterclock just where the whip had hung, her nostrils flaring and with blue-and-pink-mottled tongue showing in her open mouth. She announced raptly and anxious, 'I sense the near presence of Death or a close relative, some murderous demon lord or deadly demoness. It must have scented your ecstasy of torment, Threesie, and come hunting.'

The Mouser felt they were all staring straight at him, then noted that their gazes went in slightly different directions: His-vet's intense but cool; Foursie's shocked and terrified as she backed away, dropping the pristine white whip; Threesie's somewhat not yet grasping her good fortune, as she stood in bent position in her sagging and worked-up black tunic stretched back toward her rear, crisscrossed with red welts, and with her knees still straight.

Hisvet continued, 'Run, Foursie, and warn my father of this menace. Bid him haste here, bringing his wand and sigils. Nay, do not stay to dress or hunt a towel, as if you were a simpering virgin. Go as you are. And speed! There's *danger* here, you witlet!'

Then, turning her furious attention to Threesie, 'Quit standing there so docilely bent over with legs invitingly spread, lamebrain, all ready for the slavering hounds of death to mount you. Spring to and defend *my* rear, mind cripple!'

Just then the Mouser felt what seemed a large centipede crawl across his left thigh, somehow insinuating itself between his flesh and the grainy earth encasing him, and then march down his rigid, like-embedded cock, and settle itself in a ring round his tumescent glans. And there swung in round his head from the other side, moving through the earth effortlessly, a face like a beautiful skull tightly covered by blue-pied, chalky white skin with eyes that were intent red embers, and pressed itself against his own face closely from forehead to chin, so he felt through her blue lips mashing his her individual two ranks of teeth. He realized that the centipede was the bone tips of her skeletal hand (the other pressed the back of his neck at the base of his own skull) and those bony fingertips now moved slightly upon his

625

stiff member, inducing it to spend one drop, but one drop only, of its load, giving him a sickening, joyless jolt of heavy black pain that left him weak and gasping. But no sooner had that pain begun to fade down when the slim bone fingers moved and the second jolt came equal to the first, and after agonizing pauses the third and fourth.

The stangury! The worst pain that a man can suffer, he'd once heard, when urine must be voided drop by drop – this was the same, except it was his seed.

And it kept on.

His wavering mind confused it with the plashes of the waterclock. But Threesie had suffered only eight or nine stripes at most. How many drops would it take to discharge his heavy load? And render his member flaccid? Two score hundred?

The violet-hung boudoir and Hisvet and her crew were gone. All that remained for vision was the vermilion volume lit by Pain's hot ember eyes and his phosphorescent mask, hell in a very small place.

In a voice that was rough, rasping, infinitely dry, sardonic-tender, Death's sister whispered throatily, 'My very own dear love. My dearest one.'

As his torment continued, his wavering consciousness and gasping and trembling general weakness warned him the end was near. Despite the continuing jolts of agony, he concentrated on regulating his breathing, making it shallow, pushing back with his tongue the grains his gasps had drawn. With the roaring in his ears, it became a surf of boulders he had to keep at bay.

20

Cif was cheered to find things orderly busy at the diggings, the dogcart unloading, some men wolfing midday bread and soup by the fire, while at the shaft head the stubby wide cone of dug dirt had grown visibly higher and the brighter growl of a saw spoke of shorings and roofing for the tunnel being readied. Fafhrd's man Fren, on duty at the windlass, told her that Skor, the girl Klute, and Mikkidu were down, the first two working at the face, that last walking dirt between there and the shaft. She commented on a faint stench, coming irregularly.

'I whiffed something myself once or twice already,' Fren agreed, making a face. 'Like rotten eggs?'

At his offer, she rode the empty bucket down, standing, her small-booted feet fitting with room to spare.

At the shaft the foul odour became stronger. Looking up at Rill and Skullick, she held her nose. They copied her gesture, nodding. As she neared the bottom, Mikkidu came backing out of the tunnel's low entry lugging a full bucket and she stepped out away from him, preparatory to helping switch the hook from the empty bucket to the full one.

But as he swung it around, he pitched over it into her arms. Digging in her heels, she managed to prop the Mouser's small lieutenant, snarling at him, 'What's the matter with you, Mik? Are you drunk?'

When he answered her groggily, 'No, Lady,' his eyes weaving, she pushed him against the wall, leaving him to recover his wits and balance, and hurried into the tunnel.

Here the stink was intense and she held her breath. A few fast scurrying steps brought her to the end, where the light of a leviathan-oil lamp burning blue and dim showed her Skor on his knees slumped forward against the rough face he'd been scraping, his shoulders slack, while beside him Klute lay prone on the rock floor, evidently having passed out as she'd tried to crawl away.

Cif took her under the armpits and half dragged, half carried her out of the tunnel. Mikkidu was rubbing his forehead. She called, 'Skullick!' but he was already climbing down by the pegs. Klute was writhing a little and mewling faintly with her eyes closed. Cif slung her over an arm, stepped into the empty bucket, and signaled Fren to hoist. The pulleys creaked. In passing she told Skullick, 'Skor's collapsed at the face. Fumes and foul air, get him out fast.'

At the top she passed Klute to Rill and Fren and then stepped out herself. The girl was muttering, 'Can't find my scoop.' Rill told her, 'Wake up, Klute. Try to breathe deeply,' and remarked to Cif, 'There was such a stench in the cave toward Darkfire.'

Cif nodded and turned back to watch Skullick drag Skor out

of the tunnel. He called, 'He'll come out of it, Lady. His pulse is still there.' Mikkidu seemed recovered, for he helped Skullick get a rope around the unconscious man's chest so he could be hoisted up the shaft, and then climbed the pegs alongside to steady the dead-weight burden on its way.

When Fafhrd's lieutenant was stretched out next to the shaft head, Cif took his pulse under the jaw, didn't like its reedy feel, and directed Mikkidu to lift his shoulders and head (by its scanty red hair) while she straddled his lap, clasped him around with both arms, and fed him air from her own lips, alternating with brief tightenings of her hug.

When Skor's pulse seemed stronger, she directed he be carried to the shelter tent and delegated Rill to keep close watch and continue her nursing as needed. Then she quizzed Mikkidu sharply.

'You were going into and out of the tunnel, you must have noticed the fumes.'

'I did, Lady,' he replied, 'and warned Skor. But he made light of them, being so concentrated on speeding the digging.'

'Well, he was right about that, though imprudent,' she said with weight. 'The digging must continue at the face if we're to have a chance of saving Captain Mouser. Fresh air must be conveyed there in good supply. And speedily.'

'Aye, Lady,' Mikkidu agreed dubiously, 'but how?'

'I have had opportunity to think that matter through,' she told him. 'Mik, last autumn you were with the captains on their great snow-serpent hunt in the Death Lands that lie midway betwixt the volcanoes Darkfire and Hellglow?'

'Who of us wasn't, Lady?' that one replied. 'Aye, and busy for a fussy fortnight afterward flaying and curing the uncut hides.'

'As I recall,' she went on, 'there were some forty perfect hides got in all.'

'Two score and seven to be precise, Lady. All laid up at the barracks with camphor and cloves against the next trading voyage by one of the captains. They'd bring a fortune in Lankhmar.'

'As I too thought.' She nodded. 'The dogcart is still here. I've a mind to send you back in it to fetch out those same hides. All of them.'

He stared at her puzzledly.

'Are you aware,' she asked him, 'that each of those hides constitutes a wrist-wide, sound leather tube nine or ten cubits long? Three or four yards?'

'Yes, Lady,' he began, his brow still clouded, 'but—'

'Come on, I'll go with you,' she said with a merry grin, standing up from where they'd been sitting beside the fire. 'For you'll need someone to attend to the hides while you're busy seeing to the unshipping of the great bellows at the smith-forge preparatory to its conveyance here.'

'Lady,' Mikkidu said, his face lighting up, 'I do believe I get a glimmering of your intention.'

'And so do I!' was voiced admiringly by Skullick, who'd been listening in.

'Good!' Cif told the latter. 'Then you can take charge here whilst I'm away.'

And she dragged Fafhrd's ring off her thumb and gave it to Skullick.

21

Pshawri broke a pane of ice to free the waters of Last Spring for easy imbibing.

When he had lapped his fill he backed away, dancing his thanks in a solemn little jig such as no one had ever seen him foot. He was a secretive young man.

He ended his jig with a slow rotation widdershins, scanning his still, chill, hazy-white surroundings from right to left. Darkfire's smoke plume was a smudge in the northern milk-sky. His gaze lingered studiously on the southwest and south, as though he expected pursuers there, and from the height to which he roved it, either flying ones or else very big and tall indeed.

He was at the boundary between the Moor and barren Lava Lands, though a dusting of snow hid the blackness of the latter, blurring the distinction.

He undid one button of his pouch hanging against his belly in front and carefully wormed out the bottle Afreyt had given him, mindful of the pouch's precious contents, and drank off half the remnant of fortified sweet wine, toasting the smoke plume. Then he bore the bottle back to the spring, submerged it until it was almost full, recorked it and returned it to his pouch. After rebuttoning the latter, he felt it over with a gesture curiously reminiscent of a pregnant woman feeling for movement.

He sketched a second jig that included a stamping defiance toward the south-southwest, then turned and loped away north.

22

Toward evening the girl Fingers woke refreshed in the bed at Cif's house she'd occupied night before last. She slid herself from under the blanket without waking Gale, slipped into one of the two robes of towelling lying across the foot, belted it, and wandered down to the large kitchen, where Afreyt, similarly clad, stood beside a narrow door of gray driftwood with a row of pegs and two small windows of horn in the wall alongside it. The pegs were empty save for two, whence hung a worn robe larger than her own and an iron-studded belt bearing sheathed dirk and smallax, with boots set below.

'I bathe in steam,' the tall lady said. 'Will you join me?'

'Gratefully, Lady,' the girl replied. 'You heap me with kindnesses I can never repay.'

'My privilege,' Afreyt replied. 'In return you might tell me of Ilthmar and Tovilyis, where I've never been.' Her violet eyes twinkled. 'And scrub my back.' She hung her robe, Fingers copying her, on an empty peg and led the way into a narrow chamber consisting of four wide driftwood steps and dimly lit by four small windows, and shut the door behind them. Beside it were a long-handled dipper and two buckets, the farther one filled with water, the near with round stones glowing dark red toward their centre and toasting Fingers' calves and knees as she passed close to them. Afreyt poured two-and-a-half dippers of water into the hot rocks. There was an explosive sizzling and clouds of steam enveloped them. Afreyt seated herself on the third step, Fingers following suit, and noting or divining the girl's looks of surprise and mild alarm at the increase in the moist heat, remarked, 'It teases the heart a little, does it not? Do not fear to inhale deeply. Move down a step if it's uncomfortable,' she advised.

'It does indeed, Lady,' Fingers agreed, but held her level.

'Now tell me of foul filthy Ilthmar and its nasty rat god,' Afreyt suggested. 'In what figure is he shown or depicted?'

'In that of a man, Lady, with a rat's head and long tail. On ritual occasions his human priests wear a rat mask, carry a long snaky whip resembling a giant rat's tail, and go naked or robed according to the nature of the rite.'

'How is the relationship between humanity and the ratty kind rationalized?' Afreyt inquired.

'In olden times, when rats had their cities above-ground, they warred with and enslaved a race of giants. Ourselves, Lady, humankind. Then in the course of numerous revolts and repressions, the rats transferred their cities underground for privacy and to give them peace and quiet to perfect their culture, but maintaining secret dominion over their servant-slaves.' The girls voice was thoughtful. Her left hand played with a ridgy white seashell embedded in the gray plank on which their sweat dripped. Beside it was a boreworm hole, into which she ran her little finger back and forth. It fitted nicely. She continued, 'There's a dark magic known only to the doubly initiated (which my mother and I were not) whereby rats and their allies may switch size back and forth between rat and human. The rats' prophets and chiefest allies amongst humankind are numbered among their saints, of whom the recentest to be canonized are St Hisvin of Lankhmar and his daughter, St Hisvet, Lankhmar Below being the chiefest city of the rats, although, unlike Ilthmar, the worship of the rat god is forbidden in Lankhmar Above.'

Afreyt handed Fingers a stiff-bristled brush and presented her back, on which the girl, kneeling, got to work industriously. The tall woman said, 'Have you seen representations in Ilthmar of this female saint?'

'Aye, Lady, there's a carving at her small shrine in the Rat's dockside temple. (Rats were also the first mariners, teaching man the art.) She is depicted nude with her hair in one braid long as her slender self and with eight dainty rat dugs; two

631

centred in small high breasts, the next pair low on her rib cage, two flanking her cord scar, and two close to either side her maiden mound above the leg crease.'

'My, such a multiplicity of charms! One wonders whether to envy or despise.' Afreyt chuckled.

'Her cult's a very popular one, Lady,' the girl replied somewhat defensively as she scrubbed away. 'She commands demons, it is believed, and has enjoyed the services of Queen Frixifrax of Arilia.'

Afreyt laughed. 'Truth to tell, child, I would have been inclined to rate your whole rat tale nonsense, like half the stories fed us Rime Islers dwelling on the edge of things to awe and befool us, did it not fit so well with what Fafhrd has told me about his and Captain Mouser's greatest adventure (though there were more than one of those, to hear them talk) during the last days of Overlord Glipkerio's reign, when there was an incursion or eruption of armed rats into Lankhmar City, along with many other weird events, and involving the unscrupulous grain merchant Hisvin and his scandalous daughter, Hisvet, both the rats' allies and bearing the same names as the two saints in your own strange tale.'

'I am grateful your Ladyship believes at least partly in my truthful account,' Fingers replied a little huffily. 'I may be overcredulous, Lady, but never a liar.'

Afreyt turned around smiling. 'Don't be so formal and serious,' she chided merrily. 'Give me the brush and turn your back.'

The girl complied, facing the two high horn windows to the outside, which were now whitening with the rising moon a day past full. Afreyt scraped the brush across a lump of green soap and set to work, saying, 'During the twists and turns of that famous rat-man fracas in Lankhmar (it happened at least ten years ago – you'd have been still an infant at Tovilyis), the Gray Mouser had to pretend a great love for this Hisvet chit (so Fafhrd tells me), pursuing her through a series of magical size changes from Lankhmar Above down to Lankhmar Below and then back again. His true love then was a royal kitchen slave named Reetha, at least she was the one he ended up with. At that time Fafhrd's consort was the Ghoulish warrior-maid Kreeshkra

– a walking skeleton because Ghouls' flesh's invisible, their bones on view. Truly there are times when I don't know if I can believe half of the things Fafhrd says, while the Mouser's always a great liar – he boasts of it.'

'I was told Ghouls ate people,' Fingers observed, bracing her back against Afreyt's brisk scrubbing. 'And much later I heard about the latter-day rat war in Lankhmar. Friska told me about it in Ilthmar, after we'd moved there from Tovilyis, when she was warning me against believing everything the rat priests told us.'

'Friska?' Afreyt questioned, pausing in her scrubbing.

'My mother's name when she was a slave in Quarmall before she escaped to Tovilyis, where I was born. She hasn't always used it afterward and I don't think I've mentioned it until now.'

'I see,' Afreyt said absently, as though lost in sudden thought.

'You've stopped doing my back,' the girl observed.

'Because it's done,' the other said. 'It's pink all over. Tell me, child, did your mother Friska escape from Quarmall all by herself?'

'No, Lady, she had her friend Ivivis with her, whom I grew to calling aunt in Tovilyis,' Fingers explained, turning back so she faced the narrow gray door again, its outlines visible once more through the thinning steam. 'They were smuggled out of Quarmall by their lovers, two mercenary warriors quitting the service of Quarmall and his two sons. The cavern world of Quarmall's no easy place to escape from, Lady, deep, secret, and mysterious. Fugitives are recaptured or die strangely. In the ports that rim the Inner Sea – Lankhmar, Ilthmar, Kvarch Nar, Ool Hrusp – it's deemed as fabulous a place as this Rime Isle.'

'What happened to the two mercenaries who were your mother's and aunt's lovers and worked their escape?' Afreyt inquired.

'Ivivis quarrelled with hers, and upon reaching Tovilyis, enlisted in the Guild of Free Women. My mother was nearing her time (*my* time, it was) and elected to stay with her friend. Her lover (my father) left her money and swore to return some day, but of course never did.'

There was a flurry of knocking and the narrow gray door opened and closed, admitting Gale, who peered around eagerly through the thinning steam.

'Has Uncle Fafhrd flown back down from the sky?' she demanded. 'Why didn't you wake me? Those are his things outside, Aunty Afreyt!'

'Not yet,' that lady told her, 'but there have been messages of sorts from him, or so it seems. After you two were sleeping, May brought me Fafhrd's belt, which she'd found hanging on a berry bush as though fallen from the sky. Her words, though she'd not heard your tale. I sent her and the others hunting and went out myself, and there were soon discovered his two boots (one on a roof) and dirk and smallax, which had split the council hall's weathercock.'

'He cast them down to lighten ship when he got above the fog.' Gale rushed to conclusions.

'That's the best guess I've heard,' Afreyt said, reaching the dipper to Gale, handle first. 'Renew the steam,' she directed. 'One cup.'

The girl obeyed. There was a gentler sizzling, and warm steam came billowing up around them again.

'Maybe he's waiting for tonight's fog,' the girl suggested. 'I'm much more worried about Uncle Mouser.'

'The digging goes on and another clue's been unearthed – a sharpened iron *tik* (Lankhmar's least coin) such as the Gray One habitually carries on his person. So Cif told me when she was here early afternoon to bathe and change, while you two were still asleep. There'd been some difficulty about the air, but your aunt took care of it.'

'They'll find him,' Gale assured her.

'I share both your hopes for both the captains,' Fingers put in, returning somewhat to formality.

'Fafhrd will be all right,' Gale asserted confidently. 'You see, I think he needs the fog to buoy him up, at least until he gets started stroking well, and the fog will be back before dawn. He'll swim down then.'

'Gale thinks her uncle can do anything,' Afreyt explained, scrubbing her vigorously. 'He's her hero.'

'He certainly is,' the girl maintained aggressively. 'And

because he's my uncle, there can't be anything between us to spoil it when I'm fully grown up.'

'Truly a hero has many lady loves: whores, innocents, princesses,' Fingers observed in tones that were both earnest and worldly wise. 'That's one of the first things my mother told me.'

'Friska?' Afreyt checked.

'Friska,' Fingers confirmed, and then bethought herself of a compliment that would sustain the worldly mood which she enjoyed. 'I must say, Lady, that I greatly admire the coolness and lack of jealousy with which you regard your lover's previous attachments. For Captain Fafhrd is surely a hero – I suspected as much when he began so swiftly and resolutely to dig for his friend and set the rest of us all helping. I became completely certain when he took off so blithely into the sky on his friend's service.'

'I don't know about all that,' Afreyt replied, eyeing Fingers somewhat dubiously, 'especially my coolness toward love rivals of whatever age or condition. Though it's true Fafhrd's had an awful many sweethearts, to hear him talk (the Mouser the same), and not only from those classes you mention, but really weird ones like the Ghouless Kreeshkra and that wholly invisible snowmount Princess Hirriwi and (for Mouse) that eight-tit slinky Hisvet – everything from demonesses to mermaids and shimmersprites.' Warming to it, she continued, 'But I think Cif and I are a match for them, at least in quality if not numbers. We've bedded gods ourselves – or at least arranged for their bedding,' she added correctively and a bit guiltily, remembering.

Listening to this recital, Gale seemed to get a bit uneasy, certainly wide-eyed. Fingers put an arm around her shoulders, saying, 'So you see, little one, it *is* better to have one's hero a friend and uncle only, is it not?'

Afreyt couldn't resist saying, 'Aren't you overdoing the wise old aunt a bit?' Then, recalling Fingers' circumstances, she dropped her smile, adding, 'But I was forgetting . . . you know what.'

Fingers nodded gravely and fetched a sigh that she thought suitable for A Cabingirl Against Her Will. Then she gave a squeal. Gale had yanked her hair.

'I don't know about Uncle Fafhrd,' the Rimish girl told her, making a face, 'but I certainly want you as a friend and not an auntie!'

'And now it's time we stopped talking heroes and she-devils and got back to worrying about two real men,' Afreyt picked that moment to announce. 'Come on, I'll rinse you.'

And taking up the water container, she poured a gush each on the blond and reddish heads, then emptied it over her own head.

23

Returning back to that same eventful day's darksome beginning, we find Fafhrd trudging frantically east by leviathan light from the lamp he carried and with a feather-footedness and hectic lightheadedness that puzzled and alarmed him, across the frosty Great Meadow toward fog-blanketed Salthaven and the horizon beyond, paling with the imminent dawn. His anxiety for the Mouser in desperate plight, his selfish urge to shuck off that bondage, and his wishful hope for a miracle solution to this problem . . . these three feelings balled up unendurably within him, so that he lifted the brown brandy jug in his right hand to his teeth and fixed them around the protruding cork, biting into it, and drew the jug from off it, spat the cork aside, and downed two swallows that were like lightning brands straight down his throat.

Then yielding to an unanticipated yet imperative impulse, born perhaps of the two blazing swigs, he scanned the sky ahead above the fog.

And, lo, the miracle! For a wide stream of brightness, travelling up the pale sky from the impending sun, called his attention to a small fleet of on-cruising clouds. And as he in-spected those five pearl-gray white-edged shapes with a sharp clear vision that was like youth returned, he discerned that the midmost was shaped like a large slender pinnace with towering stern-castle driven by a single translucent sail that bellied smoothly toward him, by all signs a demigalleon of the cloud queendom of Arilia, fable no longer.

And as if there had resounded in his ear a single chime,

infinitely stirring and sweet, of the silver bell with which they'd sound the watches upon such a vessel, the knowledge came to him – a message and more – that his old comrade-mistress Frix was aboard her, captaining her crew. And the confident determination was born in him to join her there. And his concern for the Mouser and what Afreyt and his men expected of him dropped away, and he no longer worried about the girls Fingers and Gale following him, and his footsteps grew carefree and light as those of his youth on a Cold Corner hunting morn. He took a measured sup of brandy and skipped ahead.

The women whom Fafhrd loved seriously (and he rarely loved otherwise) seemed to him when he thought about it to split into the two classes of comrade-mistresses and beloved girls. The former were fearless, wise, mysterious, and sometimes cruel; the latter were timorous, adoring, cute, and mostly faithful – sometimes to the point of making too much of it. Both were – apparently had to be, alas – young and beautiful, or at least appear so. The comrade-mistresses were best at that last, on the whole.

Oddly, the beloved girls were more apt to have been actual comrades, sharing day-to-day haps, mishaps, and boredoms, than the others. What made the others seem more like comrades, then? When he asked himself that, which he did seldom, he was apt to decide it was because they were more realistic and logical, thought more like men, or at least like himself. Which was a desirable thing, except when they carried their realism and logic to the point where it became unpleasantly painful to him. Which accounted for their cruel streak to be sure.

And then the comrade-mistresses more often than not had a supernatural or at least preternatural aura about them. They partook of the demonic and divine.

Fafhrd's first beloved girl had been his childhood sweetheart, Mara, whom he'd got pregnant, only to run away with his first comrade-mistress, the wandering actress and failed thief, Vlana, one of the unsupernatural ones, her only glamours those of stage and crime.

Other super- and preternatural females had included the Ghoulish she-soldier, Kreeshkra, a transparent-fleshed beautiful

637

walking skeleton, and the wholly invisible (save when she tinted her skin or resorted to like stratagem such as wetting herself before being pelted by a lover with rose petals) Princess Hirriwi of Stardock.

Sample beloved girls were Luzy of Lankhmar, the fair swindler Nemia of the Dusk (not all of this class, too, were law-abiding), and faint-hearted and bouncing Friska, whom he'd rescued from the cruelties of Quarmall – not altogether willingly. On learning his wild plan she'd told him, 'Take me back to the torture chamber.'

But of all his lady lovers, first in his heart was Hisvet's one-time slave-maid and guardian, the tall, dark-haired, and altogether delicious Frix, now again Queen Frixifrax of Arilia, although she was almost, but not quite, *too* tall and slender. (Just as he knew that Hisvet herself, though heartless and mostly cruel, was somehow the Mouser's inmost favourite.)

Above all else, Frix's love was ever tactful, and even in scenes of extremest ecstasy and peril she had an utterly fearless and completely dispassionate overview of life, as if she saw it all as a grand melodrama, even to the point of coolly calling out stage directions to the participants of an orgy or mêlée whilst chaos whirled about them.

Of course this train of reasoning left out Afreyt, surely the best of comrade-mistresses as well as his current one, a better archer than himself, loving and wise, an altogether admirable woman – and able to get along with Mouser too.

But Afreyt, though greatly gifted, was wholly human, while the demonic and divine Frix fairly glimmered with supernatural highlights. As at this very moment, when after another and larger swig of brandy on the fly, a short but steady sighting far ahead miraculously showed her standing at the bow of her cloud-pinnace like a figurehead carved of pale ivory as she cheered and welcomed him on. This wondrous apparition of her touched off a memory flash of an assignation with her in a mountaintop castle where they'd ingeniously spied together on two of her waiting ladies tall and mantis-slender as herself while they were mutually solacing each other, and later joined them in their gentle sport.

That ivory prow-vision, together with attendant memories,

made him feel light as air and added yards to his stride, so that his next two skimming skips carried him knee-deep and waist-deep into the fog bank, while the third never ended. He drained the brandy jug of its last skimpy swallow, cast it and the lamp behind him to either side, and then swam forward up the face of the deepening fog bank, employing a powerful breaststroke while flattening his legs like a fish's tail.

Exultation suffused him as he felt himself mounting the side of a long stationary swell in an ocean of foam, but his strong sweeping strokes soon carried him above the fog. He resolutely forbore to look down, keeping his gaze upon the wondrously prowed white pinnace, concentrating all his attention and energies on flight. He felt his deltoid and pectoral muscles swell and lengthen and his arms flatten into wings. The rhythm of flight took over.

He noted that, though still mounting, he was veering to the left because of the lesser purchase his hook got on the air than the palm-paddle of his good right hand, but instead of trying to correct he kept on undauntedly, confident the motion would bring him around in a great circle in sight of his goal again and closer to it.

And so it did. He continued to mount in great spirals. He noted that along the way five snowy seagulls had appeared and were soaring up circularly too, evenly spaced around him like the points of a pentacle. It gave him a warm feeling to be so escorted.

He was well into his fifth spiral and nearing his goal, momentarily waiting for the cloud-ship to swing into his view from the left behind him, the sun's rays baking through his clothes becoming almost uncomfortable. He was selecting just the right words with which to greet his aerial paramour when he flew into shadow and something hard yet resilient struck the back of his head a shrewd blow, so that black spots and flashing diamond points danced in his eyes and all his senses wavered.

His first reaction to this unexpected assault was to look up behind him.

A dark pearl-gray wind-weathered, smoothly rounded leviathan-long shape hovered above him just out of reach – as he discovered when he grasped at it with hand and hook, his second reaction. It seemed to be drifting sideways slowly. He'd bumped into the hull of the cloud-ship he'd been seeking and then rebounded from it somewhat.

His third reaction, as the pain in his skull lessened and his vision cleared somewhat, was a mistake. He looked down.

The whole southwest corner of Rime Isle lay below him, uncomfortably small and far down: Salthaven town and harbour with its tiny red roofs and wisp-pennoned toothpick masts thrusting through its thinning coverlet of fog, the rocky coast leading off west, the narrow lofty headland to the east, and north of that the Great Maelstrom spinning furiously, an infinitely menacing foamy pinwheel.

The sight froze Fafhrd's privates. His reaction was anything but beat his wings (arms, rather), flutter his legs-tail, resuming flying, and so land lightly on the cloud-craft's deck and sketch a bow to Frix. The blow had halted all those avian rhythms as if they'd never possessed him; it had nauseated him, switched him from glorious drunkenness to near puking hangover in a trice. Instead of master of the air, he felt as if he were flimsily glued to it up here, pasted to this height by some fragile magic, so that the least wrong move, or wrong thought even, might break the flimsy bond and pitch him down, down, down!

His sailor's instinct was to lighten ship. It was the last resort when your vessel was sinking, and so presumably the wisest course when falling was the danger. With infinite caution and deliberation he began a series of slow contortions calculated to bring his manual extremities of hand and hook into successive contact with his feet, waist, neck, and so forth, so as to rid himself of all abandonable weight whatever *without* at the same time making some uncalculated movement that would cause him to come unstuck from the sky wherein he was so precariously poised.

This course of action had the added advantage of concentrating all his attention on his body and the space immediately around it, so he was not tempted to look down again and suffer the full pangs of vertigo.

He did note, as he gently cast aside his right and left boot, ax and dirk, their sheaths, finally his pouch and iron-studded belt, that they floated off slowly to about the distance of a man's length, then dropped away as if jerked down, seeming almost to vanish instantly – suggesting some magical sphere or spell of safety about him.

He didn't trust it.

So long as he confined himself to discarding such relatively ponderous and rigid items, his convoy of gulls continued to circle him evenly, but when he continued on to divest himself of all his garments (for this seemed certainly no time for half measures) they broke formation and (either attracted by the flimsy and flappable nature of his discards, or else outraged at the shameless impropriety of his action) made fierce darts and dives at and upon each piece of clothing to the accompaniment of raucous barking squawks and bore them off triumphantly in their sharp talons as if reasserting the honour of their squadron.

Fafhrd paid very little attention to these captious avian antics, concentrated as he was upon making not the least incautious or marginally violent movement.

Eventually he had divested himself of his very last implement and garment save for one.

It shows how much he had come to think of his hook together with the cork-and-leather cuff carrying it as his true left hand that he did not jettison them with the rest of the abandonable material.

But it was not until he'd stripped himself stark naked (save for hook) that he bethought himself of a final way to 'lighten ship'. He was admiring the bright golden gleam of the powerful stream of urine arching above him and then down over his head out of his vision's range (it had first hit him in the eye but he corrected); it was not until then that he realized that in the course of his emergency undressing he had passed out of the shadow of the cloud-craft's hull and was bathed in full hot sunlight (which had, coincidentally, counterbalanced nicely any chill he might otherwise have felt at abandoning his last scrap of clothing in the sharp air of early morning).

But where had the Arilian cloud-vessel got to? He looked about and finally saw its narrow deck its own ship's length *beneath* him – a score of yards at least. Meanwhile, he himself was slowly but steadily mounting to portside of its rather ghostly or at least somewhat translucent mast top and upper rigging, whereon were perched the five raptorial gulls, busily shredding with claws and beaks the clothing they'd appropriated from him and, looking more now like cormorants than gulls, staring at him from time to time disgustedly.

And now a wholly different, in fact opposite fear took sudden hold of Fafhrd – that he might continue to rise inexorably until all below became too tiny to be seen and he was lost in space, or until he reached the forever frost-capped height of mountain-tops and perished of cold – especially when chilly night came on (how stupid he'd been to discard *all* his clothes – he'd been in a dismal panic that was sure!) – or got himself devoured by the airy monsters that inhabited such altitudes such as the invisible giant fliers he'd first encountered on Stardock, or even reach the mysterious stars (if he lasted that long before dying of thirst and hunger) and be dazzled to death by them or suffer whatever other fate the Bright Ones kept in store for impudent venturers such as he must appear to them.

Unless, of course, he had the good fortune to encounter the moon first or the secret (invisible?) Queendom of Arilia, if that were anything more than a great fleet of cloud-ships.

This thought reminded him that there was such a ship close at hand, of which he'd had great hopes and expectations before the brandy had died in him.

After a moment's gloomy apprehension that it had heartlessly sailed off or perhaps vanished entire (its upper works at least had looked so very ghostly), he was relieved to see it still floated below him, though some thirty feet farther down than at last glimpse – there was at least that distance between him and the masthead with its quincunx of cormorantishly-behaving sea-gulls, who still shredded his garments vindictively, although their shrill squawkings had subsided.

He searched the vessel with his eyes for Frix, but the tall, supernally attractive beauty was nowhere to be seen, not in the bow impersonating a figurehead, or anywhere else – if she ever had been present, he added wryly, to anything but his overeager and overbrandied imagination.

He did spot, however, a sixth figure in the rigging, besides the birds, a trim young woman halfway up it on the other side of the rigging, faced away from him and leaning back against the ratlines with arms outspread as if to expose herself to sun's rays. She wore an abbreviated white lace chemise, was barefoot, and carried a small curved silver trumpet slung round her neck. She was also too short for Frix and a blonde to boot, instead of raven-tressed.

Fafhrd called down 'Ahoy!' not softly, but not unnecessarily loudly either, for although his new fear of rising indefinitely preoccupied his thoughts, he still entertained the conviction that any violent movement or speech would be unwise. Just rising a few yards did not convince him that he could not fall, especially when he surveyed the emptiness below.

The lazing maiden did not look up or give the least other indication that she had heard him.

'Ahoy!' Fafhrd repeated, quite a bit more loudly, but again with no discernible reaction from her, unless her yawn now was intended as that.

'Ahoy!' Fafhrd bellowed, forgetting his worries about the possible dire effects of loud noises.

Rather slowly, then, she turned her head and lifted her face toward him. But nothing more.

'Cloud girl,' Fafhrd called down in friendly tones but a shade peremptorily, 'summon your mistress on deck. I'm an old friend.'

She went on staring at him. Nothing more, except perhaps to lift her brows superciliously.

Fafhrd called sharply, 'I'm Captain Fafhrd, out of *Sea Hawk*,' naming his ship riding at anchor in Rime harbour. 'And as you can plainly see, I'm in distress. Inform *your* captain of these circumstances. And be assured she knows me well.'

After staring at him a while more, the cloud girl nodded moodily and descended to the deck hand over hand, taking her time, and after another look up at him, strolled toward the sterncastle.

Fafhrd was annoyed. 'Oh, hurry up, girl,' he called, 'and if it's formalities you want, tell the Queen of Arilia that an old friend respectfully craves instant audience.'

She paused in the door of the sterncastle to look up at him once more and inquire in a shrill pert voice, 'Was that the respect led you to piss on our ship?' before she flipped up the tail of her chemise and vanished inside.

Fafhrd made dignified growling noises in his throat, though there were none to hear them but the gulls, and was emboldened to try to swim down to the cloudship's mast top, getting himself positioned with head turned down toward it, body upside down, though it took an intense effort of will to make himself use full power in what persisted in seeming an attempt to come unstuck from the heights and launch a disastrous fall. He kept himself aimed at the rigging so he'd intercept it if the worst occurred.

He was breathing heavily and had fought his way down, he judged, about a quarter of the distance when the saucy cloud girl reemerged, followed (at last!) by Frix, garbed like a dashing captain of Amazon marines in tropical dress uniform of silver-trimmed white lace which strikingly set off her slender form, dark hair, and coppery complexion wonderfully, white deerskin hip boots, a wide-brimmed hat of like material, with ostrich plumes, and a silver-studded belt of snow-serpent hide from which depended a long slim sabre with silver fittings.

She glanced up at shaggy-headed, hairy, naked Fafhrd laboring down toward her with prodigious effort and spoke a word to the cloud maiden clad in her scanty lace, who lifted her silver trumpet to her lips and blew a sweet and stirring call.

Whereupon there came trooping from the sterncastle six tall willowy women akin to Frix in figure and dress-uniformed like to the soldiers in such a captain's company, except that from their unstudded belts there hung, not swords, but in each instance three objects which Fafhrd first identified as a cased small-dirk, a tiny sporran, and a small cylindrical canteen, while upon their neatly short-cropped heads were uniform caps of colours peach, lime, lemon, vermilion, lavender, and robin's egg, counting from first to last as they lined up. They were followed by a smaller she, who might have been the pert trumpeter's twin, except the silver instrument she carried was a crossbow from which depended a coil of thin silver line. Frix spoke to her, pointing upward. She dropped to a bare knee, and bending her back acutely and letting the coil fall to the deck beside her, aimed her piece at Fafhrd.

Fortunately for his composure, he divined her intent and dear Frix's purpose just as she let fly.

Her flashing missile mounted swiftly and surely. The line it carried aloft uncoiled from the deck with rippling smoothness and nary a tangle. The blunt silver quarrel reached the apex of its flight a foot from Fafhrd's face. His right hand closed upon it confidently, as if he were capturing a stingless glow wasp. The six tall and almost spidery-slender mariners took up the other end of the silvery line and began to haul. Fafhrd felt the line tighten without parting and himself drawn down perceptibly as they hauled, and at that very instant he began to experience a sweet relief such as is felt only by one who knows himself to be secure in the true hands of love.

His breathing evened out, his relaxing muscles seemed all to lengthen individually, he felt himself become as willowy (in a wholly male wise, he assured himself) as the six delightful creatures drawing him down against his natural (unnatural, rather!) buoyancy. After a final flutter or two of his lower limbs and sweep of his hook-terminated free arm, he resigned to them that small and almost frolicsome labor. He might even have closed his eyes, it felt so restful, except that he was beginning to enjoy so thoroughly using them to inspect his destination. The cloud pinnace was such a handsome vessel, and the longer he gazed at its rigging and sails the realer they got.

From time to time as he let himself be played in, like a willingly caught fish of air, came nagging remembrances of his friends on Rime Isle below, and the Mouser still deeper down, and of their likely worries over him, and their own more troublesome plights. But he wasn't gone for long, not really gone, just receiving sorely needed refreshment aloft, he told himself more than once.

Finding himself now level with the mainmast top, he gave some thought to how he appeared to his rescuers. He decided against transferring to the rigging – no one seemed to expect him to and he might well seem ridiculous, as in trying to decide whether to go down the rigging head first or feet. So he merely avoided becoming entangled in it. There wasn't much he could do about nakedness except let himself be drawn in behind the handheld quarrel with grace and easy dignity, no contortions,

645

his legs together like a fish's tail. He sketched a wave or two with his hook to the glowering cormorants (no gulls!) as he passed them by.

When his descent had begun, his rescuers had been no more than six tallish very slender like-clad females hauling in unison upon the line with easy gracefulness, but now he began to perceive their individualities. The first on the line, she of the peach cap, was a rangy blonde structured like a coursing leopard (Nehwon's swiftest four-foot beast) from the desert steppes of Evamarensee, with small breasts like firmly-bedded pomegranates, while through the white tropic lace of her uniform showed a rosy orange hue, indicating she wore an under-chemise of like tint to her cap. Withal she was of haughty mien, with jutting brow, icy-blue eyes, and hollowed cheeks, a mole on the left one near the nostrils. By Kos, it was Floy! During his last rendezvous but one with Frix and her ladies in a star-grazing Arilian pleasure palace upon a sky-scraping peak in the moon-raking mountain range which rims the northern shore of Nehwon's southern continent, facing the planet-ringing equatorial ocean, he had on a wager let himself be bound naked so securely he could move not a finger and then watched Frix and Floy erotically delight to culminating first themselves with themselves alone and then, exercising infinite slow inventiveness, each other whilst alternately Floy recited 'The Rapes of St Hisvet and Skeldir' and Frix gave a dry clinical account of her and Floy's every least action and the response thereto – until he came, which he'd bet he'd not.

But now his steady descent turned Fafhrd's attention to the approaching deck. Reaching down his left arm, he hooked a ratline, and drawing himself down strongly with both arms, he jackknifed his body without bending his knees and landed solidly on the soles of both feet at once.

Then, maintaining the downward pull with hook alone, he straightened himself erect, facing the grinning crossbow girl. She was of the small wiry acrobatic sort the Mouser favoured, fair complected, and the lace of her chemise showed through no extraneous colour. He nodded his approval and handed her upon his palm the silver quarrel by which he'd been drawn in.

She took it without demur or change of grin and gave him, as if in return, a gold bracelet of doughnut shape large enough to fit his thick wrist. It was of the solid soft metal, he judged – massy enough by itself to balance his weird buoyancy.

'Thank you, archer,' he said. She nodded and began to coil the line that the marines with caps of varying hue (should he think of them as Frix's colour guard?) had let drop.

His recognition of Floy having intensified his general awareness and brought pertinent memories close to hand, Fafhrd was able to greet the next two lady marines – the one with pale green and yellow caps and lace-revealed underthings – with an easy, 'Greetings, dear Bree, sweet Elowee.'

But although both smiled guardedly, neither ventured so much as a word in reply. Bree shook her head slightly but sharply, frowning, while demure Elowee rolled her eyes back toward the end of the line, where Frix stood, and worked her features as though to say, 'She's in one of her moods. Be careful.'

Fafhrd recalled how he'd first met those two without their knowledge while he and Frix, wine cups in hand, were on a secret spying expedition to reawaken their venereal appetites. Entering a dark apartment, the Queen of the Air had led him to where black cushions closely circled a window in the floor that let upon a closet below, brightly lit by ranks of candles. Through painted gauze they'd observed these long-legged coltish creatures erotically ministering to each other. Bree enthusiastic and masterful, sometimes giving explicit directions, Elowee coy, protesting, and somewhat overheated (those candles!), even indignant. The infatuated pair had knelt closely side by side, kissing, fondling each other's small breasts, teasing the nipples big, and oft and anon a hand would drop down for a more thrilling and intrusive caress. After a while Frix had begun to whisper in Fafhrd's ear how the kneeling lovers might vary their touches were he the partner. He'd warned her the unconscious actors might overhear, but she'd assured him their ears had been well rubbed with a salve that reduced audition. Much later he'd discovered that things had not been as secret, or the actors as unknowing, as they'd seemed.

('That little hole was hot as hell,' Bree confided at a subsequent orgy, 'but Frix insisted on them so you'd have no trouble seeing us clearly through the painted gauze. She's a fiend for detail. Oh, the things we've endured to tickle your lust and satisfy an artsy mistress – and Elowee got splashed with hot wax. It's a wonder we didn't burn down the pleasure palace.')

But now Bree's and Elowee's hidden warnings about Frix had caused Fafhrd to give thought to his own appearance and to the impression he was creating. He decided a bit more dignity and restraint were called for. He straightened himself further, slowed his stride, and let the golden torus dangle down from his hand with seeming carelessness, yet positioned so that it served somewhat as a golden fig leaf.

Yet he was hard put to maintain his unnatural gravity and not burst into laughter when he saw that the last three colour-marines were his oldest erotic pals among Frix's ladies: the boisterous redhead Chimo, wicked-eyed and black-haired Nixi, and the saintly-appearing Bibi, who was forever finding new ways to play the simpleton and innocent.

There sprang up in his mind the memory of an idyllic Arilian vacation afternoon when he lay supine with his head pillowed upon Chimo's inner thigh where she sat spread-legged while Nixi knelt beyond her knee on his side and Bibi crouched high in the equilateral triangle made by his own spread legs. And ever and anon he'd roll his head to the near side and implant a long slow nibbling kiss along the length of Chimo's carmine nether lips and then roll his head the other way to suck and tongue the faintly rugose nipples of Nixi's small upstanding breasts, now pendant, while Chimo caressed them with her right hand. Bibi busied herself variously with his own erotic gear (whilst Chimo worked on hers – employment for the left hand) until waves of pleasure rolled in over him and time came almost to a stop.

And now, by all signs there was shaping up, he told himself, the possibility of another such great moment of supernal ecstasy indefinitely prolonged, or of an even greater one, did he not blow it by some unintended rejection or piece of boorish behaviour.

Yes, indeed, he assured himself rapidly, things did seem to be working around to a grand payoff in the great game of trading heroic feats for intimate maidenly favours that all heroes lived or at least hoped by, no matter how disordered and irregular the bookkeeping.

And now, having greeted and inspected, as it were, the six slender marines of Frix's colour guard, he found himself facing the dashing captain herself, attended by her trim trumpeter, standing before the inviting hatchway of the aftercastle from which there poured warm, sweetly perfumed air. During the short tour he'd recovered a sense of his proper weight and thirst and appetites, only slightly troubled by an awareness of hairy and unwashed uncouthness.

Frix lifted a lace-gauntleted hand. 'Greetings, old friend,' she spoke. 'Welcome aboard *Soft Airs.*'

'My thanks, dear lady,' he replied according to form, 'for greatly needed and desired hospitality.'

'Then you shall accompany us below, where are greater amenities,' she responded. 'My ladies will busy themselves refreshing and arraying you, whilst you regale us, if you will, with an account of your recentest adventures, feats, and forays.'

Fafhrd inclined his head. It occurred to him that this was the largest company of ladies with whom he'd ever been entertained by Frix. Had he really become a seven-maiden hero? Or, counting the two girls, a nine?

Smiling graciously, Frix turned to lead the way. The pert girl grimaced comically.

Fafhrd followed, thinking that the resources of a pleasure pinnace might well exceed those of a palace.

As the long-legged ladies trooped up around him familiarly, he noted that the objects depending from their white belts were actually a shaving mug, a large shaving brush (the sporran), and a razor.

24

When Fingers and Gale came hurrying downstairs from dressing, they found Afreyt deep in the perusal (or reperusal) of a creased and somewhat sullied paper with broken green seal writ in violet ink.

Gale cried out reproachfully, 'Aunty Afreyt! You're reading the letter Pshawri gave you for safekeeping!'

Alfreyt looked up. 'You have sharp eyes,' she remarked.

'Know, child, it is the right – nay, duty! – of any grown-up (especially a woman) to read any document entrusted to them, so they may give testimony to its contents should it be stolen or taken forcibly from them before they are able to return or deliver it.' She folded and thrust it down her bosom. Gale eyed her dubiously, Fingers without expression. Afreyt arose. 'And now on with your cloaks and winter gear,' she directed. 'There's work for us at the diggings, I've no doubt.'

A flurry of wind stung their faces with ice needles as they entered the night pale with the chill glow of the barely gibbous moon and a faint deep melancholy note resounded from the wind chimes the other side of Salthaven. Afreyt set a fast pace for the barracks. No others were abroad. At irregular intervals the wind chimes repeated their profound reverberation, like a god muttering in his sleep.

At the barracks were lights and labor and a loaded dogcart ready to leave. Afreyt commandeered it for herself and the girls, pulling rank on Mannimark, which drew from Gale a look of further disillusion with 'grown-ups' as she clambered reluctantly aboard. Fingers took it more naturally, copying the older woman's queenly mien and manner.

'Any message for the diggings?' that one asked the mustached man as she took the long whip from its socket. 'I'll make your excuses, Sergeant. I'm sure the other cart will be back for you soon.'

'No mind, Lady,' he answered. 'We'll walk.'

'Very well, Sergeant.' And with a whip crack and jingle of bells the cart was off, making a sharp turn that headed them into the cutting wind and away from the risen low-moon. The girls ducked their faces into their hoods but Afreyt lifted hers high. The occasional boom of the chimes grew less faint as they approached the Moon Temple, and then there was added to it a still deeper clanking as a heavier beam was struck and boomed its note.

'The north blast quickens,' she commented. 'It will be bitter crossing the Meadow.'

Soon the fire facing the shelter tent became their beacon and promise of warmth. Afreyt signalled their approach with a flurry of whip cracks.

'Where's Lady Cif?' she asked the knot of soup drinkers.

'At the face, Lady,' Skullick replied.

'Unload,' she directed, and springing down, followed by the girls, made for the pit, whence rose a short pale column of white light.

Beside it the pile of dug dirt was higher and wider and Fren walked a strange short sentry-go, stepping on the forward edge of the big forge-bellows next the pit edge, mounting its slant in three short steps (which made it sink), giving its top handle an upward yank after stepping off it (which helped an interior spring expand it again), drawing in air, and so back to the pit edge and repeat the mini march.

Peering down the shaft from the opposite edge of the hole, the three females saw how the first furry snow-white serpent's hide emerged from the bellow's front and curved downward, its crested head clamping its jaws on the tail of the second, and so on downward until the fifth entered the cross corridor at the shaft's bottom, where two leviathan lamps provided illumination.

They could see the furry tube slacken and swell as each successive giant's breath of fresh air travelled down.

Afreyt explained to the girls, 'Each tail tip is clipped off short and thrust inside the jaws of the preceding snow serpent, a clear glue making the juncture airtight. Spirits of wine dissolve this, so the hides may be parted, cleaned, and restored (the tail tips are kept) to something like their original value afterward. Else all would be monstrously unthrifty.' And with a sign to the windlass man and a 'You next' to the girls, she stepped into the empty pail and travelled down beside the slowly pulsating, furry white tube, stepped out at the bottom and waited until it returned with Fingers and Gale.

The horizontal passage was a dimly lit, stone-floored, narrow, unlofty rectangle, so that Afreyt must stoop as she led the way, although the girls were able to walk upright as they followed.

'I expected it to be warmer underground,' Gale observed.

'The dragon's breath we're blowing down is chill,' the older woman reminded her. 'Look, there's a fortune in wood around us,' she told the girls.

'A hero's life is worth any expenditure,' Fingers assured her somewhat loftily.

'So it behooves those who may have to ransom or rescue them to lay up cash,' Afreyt responded. 'Luckily the lumber's all salvageable, like the hides.'

Just ahead appeared to be solid rock, and seemingly from it, but actually from around it, there materialized a short man carrying a full pail before him and another behind. It was the Mouser's other lieutenant, Mikkidu. They managed to squeeze past him and then along a short section of corridor where the left wall was stone, the right wood, until it had jogged past the obstruction into bright light, which showed their journey's end eight yards ahead.

From the ceiling's last short crossboard hung a large leviathan lamp, while beneath the as yet unroofed yard of tunnel, Cif knelt away from them and worked at the naked face with wooden trowel and gloved left hand, scraping and brushing away the stuff that was of a consistency between flaky sandstone and packed sand. While supported by an upslanted peg in the right-hand wall, the last snow-serpent puffed chill gusts that stirred the falling dust and fine debris.

So great was the small woman's concentration on her exacting task that she was unaware of their presence until Afreyt touched her shoulder.

She turned on them a blank stare, swiftly rising to her feet. Then her eyes wavered and she lurched forward into her friend's arms.

'You're out on your feet,' Afreyt protested. 'You should have been relieved at the face hours ago! Here, take a swallow of this,' she added, withdrawing a silver flask from her pouch and uncorking it with her teeth while continuing to support Cif with her other arm.

The outwearied woman grasped it and gulped the watered brandy greedily.

'Have you had any rest at all since coming out this noon?' Afreyt demanded.

'I lay in the tent awhile, but it made me nervous.'

'So you're coming up at once with me. There's a new matter we must discuss alone. Gale! Take over here at the face. Fingers can help you – it's a sort of work her deft hands should be good at.'

'Oh good!' said Gale.

Fingers: 'You honour me.'

Cif made no demur, accepting support but asking, 'What new matter?'

'All in good time.'

Just past the jog they encountered Mikkidu returning with empty pails. Afreyt addressed him, 'I'm taking the lady Cif home for long-needed rest. You're in charge now. Gale and our new friend Fingers are working the face. See that they aren't kept at it too long and are both sent to Cif's house by midnight.'

When he shot Cif a look of inquiry, she nodded and then remembered to give him Fafhrd's ring.

Aboveground the dogcart had been unloaded and Skullick was greeting Mannimark and Faf's berserk Gort as they came loping in.

Afreyt poured Cif a mouthful of hot soup and directed, 'Hitch up fresh dogs. I'm driving the Lady Cif home. She needs rest badly. No other load. Here Mikkidu has the ring.'

'Mara and May were due to go this trip,' Skullick pointed out. The blonde girls waved from where they huddled in the shelter tent.

'I'll take them, of course,' Afreyt said. 'Girls, climb aboard! And take a blanket with you. And another for Lady Cif.'

Returning to Salthaven, they all had the wind at their backs, which was some improvement. None was inclined to talk. Midway Cif asked suspiciously, 'Was there poppy dust in the watered brandy you fed me? It has a sickly, bitter aftertaste.'

'Only enough to induce tranquillity and encourage sleep, but not enforce it.'

Afreyt drove straight to Cif's and had the girls return the cart to the barracks before wending to their own homes. She warmed a solid meal while Cif got comfortable, saw it consumed, then poured them both brandy and handed Cif the letter Pshawri had entrusted to her, saying, 'I've read it, of course. Matter of import for you, certainly.'

Cif studied the broken green seal and the violet-inked address as she unfolded it. 'This sheet was in the Captain's last mail bag from Lankhmar,' she averred, 'before he distributed the letters to his men.'

Then she was silent while she read to herself the following:

Dear Son Pshawri,

I hope this finds you alive and continuing to prosper on your northern adventure in service of that notable rogue the Gray Mouser.

I am to tell you he has more reason to make you his lieutenant than even he weens.

When you were young I pointed him out to you among other noteworthy Lankhmarts. But I did not see fit to tell you (or him) that he was your father. Such tactics seldom work out to my knowledge and experience, and I would scorn to curry favour in such a way.

It happened in my salad days, before I became a professional woman, and while I was body maid to the dancer Ivrian and we were all caught up in a supernal intrigue involving the Thieves Guild, some of its jewelled relics, and the Mouser's uncouth barbarian comrade Fafhrd.

They vied with each other to seduce me. Fafhrd loved me the more, but the Mouser was tricksier and measured his drinks more carefully – and mine. The best of what I know of the uses of evil and falsity was taught me by that devil.

But now you find yourself by chance in service of the very same man, you may find the knowledge of advantage to you. Use it as you see fit. Luckily the relationship is supported by evidence. Triads of equidistant moles run in his family.

Thanks for the silver ring and seven rilks.

Prosper,
your loving mother Freg

Cif lifted her eyes to Afreyt's. 'That letter rings true to me,' she said, nodding soberly.

'You think so too?' the other replied.

'By Skama's scales, what else! It is man's nature to plant his seed where'er the soil looks good.'

'A hero's doubly so . . .' Afreyt chimed, 'whence else his deeds of daring?'

654

Cif mused, 'When we told Mou and Faf of our courting of the stranger gods Odin and Loki in Rime Isle's service and even setting sexual lures and ties for them, I recall they hinted of their own conquests among female divinities – the viewless Stardock princesses, some nixies of the sea, the rat queen Hisvet, and some princess of the air who served her as a maid.'

Afreyt pointed out, 'This woman claiming Pshawri as her son would seem to have no noble blood at all, let alone divine. How would you feel should he claim son-right of Captain Mouser?'

Cif looked up sharply. 'Pshawri has served Mou faithfully and may do more than that in this now quest! I favour Pshawri's claim. The resemblances between them run deep – Mou bears upon his hip a triad of dark moles.'

'Another question,' Afreyt went on. 'Has your Gray lover ever professed to you any out-of-way sexual tastes?'

'Has your red-haired barbarian?' Cif countered.

'I don't know if you could rightly call it out-of-way,' the other said with a wry laugh, 'but once when we were playing somewhat listlessly abed, he suggested inviting Rill to join us. I told him I'd strangle him first and indeed tried to. In the excitement of the delirium this led to, the original proposal was forgotten at the time and just how playful or serious it had been at the time of it being made.'

Cif laughed, then grew thoughtful in turn. 'I once recall the Mouser pestering me as to whether I'd ever felt an attraction to the same sex as my own. At the time I put him in his place, of course, telling I had no truck with any such filthy practices, but since I have wondered once or twice about his curiosity.'

Afreyt looked at her quizzically. 'Oh,' she said, 'so you didn't tell him about our . . .' She left her words hanging.

'But we were barely more than girls when that happened,' Cif protested.

'True indeed,' Afreyt said. 'Barely fourteen, as I recall. But you are drowsing off, I plainly see. And so, to tell the truth, am I.'

25

Next time the Gray Mouser came first to consciousness, he had forgotten not only who but what he was.

He wondered why a darkness-dwelling creature that was no more than a limp fleshy pocket not moist enough for its own comfort and occupied by two hard, smooth, pointy semicircular ridges that fit together neatly and by a sort of blind sessile snail busy exploring itself and its container endlessly and scavenging life-giving air from the dry grainy outside, should be equipped with a mighty mind capable of mastering whole worlds of life and experience.

The sentient pocket with in-dwelling restless mollusc knew of its mind's might from the variety and rapid sequence of its inscrutable mysterious thoughts and memories which threat-ened momently to burst into clarity and stain the omnipresent dark with flaring colours. It knew its dry, grainy, closely packed immediate surroundings by a dull yellow glow so dim as hardly to deserve the name of light at all. It was a sort of dim seeing locked in solidity.

Without preamble or warning there blazed up for this buried mind the moving picture of a brilliantly lamp-lit room, lined with a great map of Nehwon-world and shelves of ancient books, wherein a venerable, kingly, seated biped beast silently discoursed to a considerably smaller version of itself standing attentively before it.

Memory told the sentient pocket that the beast was man, and then in a flash of insight it realized that behind the handsome full red mobile lips known as mouth lay such a moist pocket as itself with pale pointy smooth ridges called teeth and an indwelling anchor named tongue, and that as a consequence of all this there must be attached to it a body such as that of the beast under view and itself be man also, however cabined and confined in grainy earth.

Instantly his mind began to get a host of little messages from this attached body, which turned out to be in foetal position with both hands tenderly cupping its genitals, rag-limp after their torture by stangury-style orgasm in the skeletal embrace of blue-pied Sister Pain.

Memory of that terrible triggering made him wonder for a moment if he were not simply gazing into another room in the apartments of Hisvet in Lankhmar Below, perhaps that of her sorcerer-father Hisvin, with Foursie due to burst in naked the next moment chattering out her demon alarm – and the dread blue lady once again centipede-walk her bone hand round his waist from behind as he lay trapped and confined by dirt.

But, no! The very earth that clasped him so intimately had changed profoundly in texture and in reek. The rocks from which nature had ground it had been igneous and metamorphic rather than sedimentary, he could tell. The moisture in it was not Salt Marsh and Hlal-mouth brackish, but had the icy bite of the mineralized streams riveleting from the Mountains of Hunger, a thousand Lankhmar leagues to the south of that metropolis. The commingled effluvia were not those of polyglot Lankhmar but of some more intense and secret community with a pervading mushroom odour. Toadstool wine!

A second contemplation of the new buried room and its occupants made much clear. However had he for a moment confused schoolmasterish, peevish Hisvin with this imperious figure discoursing to the crafty-looking lad who stood before him – the beaky nose, the wattled cheeks, the proud hawklike visage, but above all the ruby-red eyeballs with white irises and glittering jet pupils – those last alone should have told him (but for lingerings of his torture-wrought amnesia) that this could be none other than Quarmal, Lord of Quarmall, on numerous counts his and friend Fafhrd's dearest enemy.

As soon as this realization struck him he noted other clues to the scene's identity and locale, such as a curtain of dangling cords billowing inward at the room's far end, and behind that, dimly glimpsed, a thick-thighed, short-armed human monster walking without moving forward – one of the almost mindless slaves specially bred to work the treadmills that spun the great wooden fans that sucked down air into the many ramp-joined levels of the buried city and its low-ceilinged mushroom fields.

Unquestionably he was half again as far from Rime Isle as he'd been when overtaken by Sister Pain while spying on

Hisvet's remedy for boredom on tedious afternoons in Lankh-mar Below, the distance demi-doubled – a prodigious feat of subterranean transversing, one must admit. Unless, of course, both experiences were incidents in a lengthy nightmare dreamed while shallowly buried on Gallows Hill – which more and more seemed the explanation of choice for all this underground hugger-mugger, provided he were eventually rescued from it, to be sure.

Coming out of this reverie, the Mouser checked that his shallow breathing of earth-trapped air was still unlaboured and then scanned anew the long room lined with books and charts and philosophic instruments. How characteristic of most of his life, he told himself, was his present situation? To be on the outside in drenching rain or blasting snow or (like now) worse and looking in at a cosy abode of culture, comfort, companion-ship, and couth – what man wouldn't turn to thieving and burglary when faced at every turn with such a fate?

But back to the business at hand, he told himself, resuming his scanning of the spacious room with its two-and-one-half occupants (the half being for the monstrous treadslave, laboring behind the wavy curtain of cords at the far end).

The soundlessly lecturing Lord Quarmal perched on a high stool beside a narrow table, and the attentive lad (whose dutiful answers or replies were likewise inaudible) were like a study in old and young skinniness . . . and wariness, to judge by their expressions. He also noted a family resemblance in their features, although the lad's eyes had no sign of the old man's ruby-red balls and white irises, while the latter's long-hair tufts between his shrivelled ears and bald pate had no greenish cast such as that shown by the other's short-cropped locks.

What were they being cagey about? he asked himself. Damn it, why was this talk blocked off? Recalling he'd had the same trouble hearing Hisvet and Company at first, he focused his attention (or, rather, the occult auditory) in one effort to make it come through to him as clearly as the visual did.

Failing to achieve any results, he decided shortly he must be pressing. He relaxed his concentration and let his mind drift. A gesture of Quarmal with the long thin stiff wand or rod he carried turned his attention to the big Nehwon map, the handsome craft of which tempted the Mouser to scan it almost idly for a while. The colours were mostly naturalistic, with blues representing seas and lakes, yellow for deserts, white for snow and ice, and so forth. Close to the west edge, near the dark blue of the Outer Sea, Quarmall stood out in royal purple as clearly as if there'd been a sign reading 'You are here.'

Just north of it were several small white ovals – the peaks of the Mountains of Hunger. Then a great space of pale brown with the blue thread of the Hlal winding through it – the grainfields. Then Hlal mouth with the city of Lankhmar on its east bank, and above those the paler blue expanse of the Inner Sea.

Next above that, the dark green Land of the Eight Cities ending in the white-topped wall of the Trollstep Mountains and, everywhere north of that, the white of the Cold Waste. And, off in the Outer Sea deep blue of the top-west corner, something he'd never seen on a map before, Rime Isle. It looked very small. The Mouser shivered to see depicted the distance between his home port and Quarmall. This had all better be a nightmare dream, he told himself.

His gaze next travelling east beyond the Cold Waste, it came to the Sea of Monsters and, beyond that, another shiversome first in his experience of charts: an elliptical black blotch with a glowing sapphire blue spot at its centre that had to be the Shadowland, Abode of Death. Why, in the Empire of the East it meant execution by torture for a cartographer to limn that land.

Scattered across the map, but mostly near cities, were enigmatic glowing small purple dots, along with a lesser number of gleaming red ones, as though it had been generously arrayed with amethyst-headed pins, sparsely with ruby ones. What might they signify? The Mouser frowningly noted that one of the reds marked Rime Isle at its Salthaven corner.

At this point the Gray One became aware he had been hearing for some time a faint but steady whispering roar, like that of an array of monster seashells, and realized that it was the hollow noise of the treadslave-driven fans that kept Quarmall from suffocating. It was more than ten years since he'd been employed here bodyguarding Prince Gwaay and heard that sound, but once one heard it, one didn't forget.

Then he began to get strange hissing modulations of the soft roar corresponding with the more vigorous shapings of old Quarmal's lips. They were like the sinister whispers of vindictive ghosts. The Mouser felt a thrill of accomplishment when he provisionally identified the language as High Quarmallese and a surge of triumph when he caught the first indisputable phrase in that sibilant tongue, 'treasure caravans of Kush', while Quarmal ticked off with his long rod on the map that jungle kingdom far south of the buried city he himself ruled. Next thing the Mouser knew he was hearing the entire dialogue with perfect clarity and comprehension. It seemed like a miracle, a wondrous witchcraft, despite his high opinions of his own linguistic skills.

QUARMAL: While it is true, dearest Igwarl, son of my loins and heir of my caverns, that the taking of revenge on injurers and traducers of Quarmall is the chiefest duty of a Lord of Quarmall, it must never be achieved at risk of breaching Quarmall's secrecy. That is why the purple points on the map representing our spies and hidden allies are many more than the crimson ones, marking our assassins.

IGWARL: So the brave wielders of the knife, revered parent, must always be outnumbered by the softspeakers and double-dealers?

QUARMAL: Not many of my assassins employ the knife. Some steal away priceless life by poisons sweet as sleep or lulling deathspells fair as a dream of love.

IGWARL: Why must things never be done forthrightly, as in war?

QUARMAL: Ah, the impetuosity of youth. Quarmall tried war and lost, now works a surer way. Let me pose you a question. Whom may a Prince of Quarmall trust in furthering his designs?

IGWARL: You, sire. Not my mother. A brother, never! But he may trust his playmate concubines, if they be sisters and he has had the training and command of them.

From his close-buried coign of vantage the Mouser saw the in-blown cords part as a naked girl entered the long chamber past the toiling treadslave. She was of Igwarl's age, looked his wiry double, had the same greenish-blond hair close-cropped, and bore before her like a sword at thrust a slender two-edged knife as she advanced inexorably upon the unperceiving boy. She moved rhythmically yet with a limp, favouring her left foot. The expression on her face was that of a sleepwalker – blank, serene.

QUARMAL: What of a sister? Issa, say. She's to be trusted?

IGWARL: Better than lesser playmate concubine – since she has been like trained even more carefully.

QUARMAL: I am glad to hear so. Look behind you.

Igwarl turned. And froze.

Quarmal let him come to full realization of his plight. The old man's eyes were as intent as those of a leopard. He held the rod ready in his right hand. He shook his left hand free from its sleeve and poised it at head level a foot from his face.

The girl reached striking distance.

Swift as a snake, Igwarl drew a dagger from his belt.

His aged parent rapped his knuckles with the rod and the weapon clattered on the rock floor.

This second betrayal rendered Igwarl moveless.

Quarmal snapped the fingers of his left hand thrice with measured rapidity, slipping his spatulate middle finger off his thumb and bringing it down precisely upon the crevice between his ring finger and his thumb's root with a crack loud as that of a carter's whip. And again. And yet again.

At the first crack the girl halted her forward movement with her knife a handsbreadth short of Igwarl's belly and her eyes widened.

At the second crack realization grew in them of the enormity of the deed she had attempted. She paled.

At the third crack their pupils rolled upward and they fluttered shut as self-horrified unconsciousness enwrapped her. The knife slipped from her fingers and dashed on the rock floor. She swayed forward. Quarmal's rod darted past the bemused boy's shoulder and its brass ferrule took her a handsbreadth below a point midway between the nipplets of her budding breasts. She winced shut-eyed and went a shade paler.

'Catch Issa ere she falls,' Quarmal directed his son. To his credit Igwarl managed to comply swiftly enough, supporting her supine slim form with one arm beneath her shoulders, the other under her thighs.

'Dispose her here,' said Quarmal, indicating the narrow table.

Igwarl did that too. The ability to act in crisis with a certain precision and a minimum of fuss seemed to run in the family, it occurred to the Mouser.

QUARMAL: You were not expecting an instructive demonstration. (Quarmal pointed this out matter-of-factly, almost casually.) Ensconced in our cavern world, you were not on guard against assault. A sister, no matter how well trained, is not to be fully trusted if there are those can undercut your training. To teach you a lesson I entranced Issa to attack you without her conscious knowledge, then countermanded her before the end.

IGWARL: Your sinister fingers' treble snap? (Old Quarmal nodded.) What if the countermand had failed to work?

QUARMAL: You saw the celerity and sureness with which I used this rod, both to stay Issa's fall and prevent you from shortening your lesson and wasting one of Quarmall's more promising female servants.

IGWARL: But what if the rod had failed also?

QUARMAL: Why, there are always more where you came from, youngster. Do you suppose a father who for Quarmall's good would let your gifted elder brothers kill each other, would spare you in like circumstance? Besides, my demonstration was designed to teach you not to trust me overmuch.

IGWARL: You have proven your point, devious parent.

QUARMAL: (lifting Issa's left foot to display angry red circles upon heel and toe) And why this damage and disfigurement to Quarmall's precious property?

IGWARL: (sulkily) It was needful to correct. Those are not regions normally seen, contributing to beauty.

QUARMAL: A limp's a beauty mark? There was the instep to be considered, not to mention the armpits.

IGWARL: I bow to your superior wisdom, sire. Impart to me the skill of enchantment.

QUARMAL: All in good time, my son. I must reassure Issa.

The old man tweaked her left breast sharply, bringing her awake with a gasp. But when he would have spoken to her, his red eyes lifted away and went distant. His right hand fixed on Igwarl's shoulder and bore down. The boy grimaced with the pain.

662

'A hostile force is in the rocks surrounding us,' the old man hissed. 'It came on whilst I was rapt instructing you.'

His two children, looking up, quaked at what they saw in his ruby orbs.

In his grainy retreat the Mouser was aware of the intrusion. The pressure of the earth around him on his body increased, reached a breath-stopping maximum, then slackened off till he felt almost free to shoot off at the speed of light and reach the ends of Nehwon in a trice, then began to tighten up again. It happened over and over in a vast chthonian pulse, as though a giant were pacing overhead.

In his spell-casting map room and library, red-orbed old Quarmal found words. 'It's my old enemy of twelve years back, Gwaay's champion, that cutpurse of empires and spoiler of dominions, the Gray Mouser. He's somehow learned of my plot against his pal and (mayhap with aid from his wizards Sheelba and Ningauble) come to spy upon me. Loose the boreworms and poison moles against him! The rock-tunnelling spiders and the acid slugs that eat through stone!'

These dire threats, clearly heard by the Mouser and half believed, were too much. When the next surge of tremendous pressure came together with the dizzy pulse of freedom, he blacked out.

26

Since Pshawri's self-rule was to do the necessary with least effort, he laid no plans, looking to find inspiration and allies in the developing situation. So when he surmounted Darkfire's crater rim and felt the full force of the north blast, having climbed her by her moonlit east face, he anticipated nothing.

The first thing his eyes lit on was a black rock the size and shape of a narrow man-skull. He reached forward crouching and budged it. Instead of being foamed or clear wave volcanic rock, it was something far heavier, leadstone at least – which explained its being free yet staying where it was in the gale.

Bracing himself, he scanned around the cloud-streaked night, again sensing menace to the southwest – something on tall invisible legs or shouldering down out of the sullied moonshine.

He advanced three paces and peered down into the volcano's narrow-throated fire pit.

The tiny rose-red lake of molten lava flooring it looked very far down and startlingly still, yet on his windchilled cheeks and chin he felt the prick of its radiant heat.

His hands shot toward the pouch between his legs so he might take from it the strange talisman of the foreign god who was his captain-father's foe and hurl it down before hostile night could gather its powers.

But the next instant, as if it had read his mind, the small massy Whirlpool Queller came alive and dashed back and forth, this way and that, seeking escape, outdinting the pouch confining it, drubbing him about the thighs and genitals, inflicting jolts of sickening pain.

His actions shaped themselves without pause to this supernatural flurry. His horny hands closed on the dodging Queller in its bag. He turned around, lunged to the leadstone skull-rock, and pressed tightly against it the encindered and empouched (and certainly ensorceled!) gold talisman. It shook strongly. He was glad it had no teeth. He felt night's awfulest powers looming over him.

He did not look up. Keeping the vibrating Queller confined against the leadstone with left hand and knee, he used his right to draw his dirk and cut the straps by which his pouch hung from his belt. Then, holding his dirk in his teeth by its cork-covered grip, he used the coil of thin climbing line hanging at his side to bind together firmly the skull-rock and the tight-woven wool pouch along with its frantic contents – with many a thoughtful look and hardest knots.

While concentrating on this job with blind automatism, steadily resisting the urge to look over his shoulder, his mind roved. He recalled what his co-mate Mikkidu had told him about how Captain Mouser had had them double the lashing of the deck cargo of *Sea Hawk* so that the galley retained its integrity and buoyancy when foundered by leviathan's dive beside it, and how he'd lectured them on a man's need to bind securely all his possessions to be sure of them, and how he was guessed to have treated the same a beauteous slim she-demon who had sought to enthrall him and secure the ship.

Next came the memory of a tranquil twilight hour when the day's work ashore was done and Captain Mouser, wine cup in hand and in a rare mood of philosophizing familiarity, confided, 'I distrust all serious thought, reasoned analysis, and such. When faced with difficulties, it is my practice to dive but once, deeply, into the pool of the problem, with supreme confidence in my ability to pluck up the answer.'

That had been before Freg's letter had transformed his captain and mentor into his hero and sire – and set him seeking special ways to prove himself. And in so seeking he'd loosed, poor fool, his father's fellest foe.

Where was his father now?

And could he now recoup?

His task was done, the last loop drawn tight, the last knot tied, bag firmly lashed to stone. Again, without one instant's hesitation, he tightly gripped the weighty package in both hands, turned, took two steps into the icy gale and toward the pit, lifted it to its apex, and then very suddenly (and with the feeling that if he took one moment more, something very big above him would snatch it from him) hurled it straight down at the rosy-red target.

He ended in a low crouch on the rim, which he immediately gripped, shooting his legs back so that he lay flat – prone with his face thrust over, peering down. And it was well that he effected this additional descent for he was smitten by a chill gust from above which else had knocked him after his projectile – and crosswise brushed by a huge wing which would have done the same had he been inches higher.

He kept his eye upon the black grain of the plummeting skull-rock package. From it two tiny, whitely incandescent eyes glared up at him. One of them winked. He saw the grain enter the molten pool, from which a single like-sized red drop rebounded, whereupon the whole small lake 'gan to seethe and shake and churn and coruscate, its level crawling upward, as if a dam had burst. The speed of this ascent of the lava pool 'gan to increase as he watched. The crawl became a scramble, then a rush. And what did this portend? Had he saved the Gray Mouser? Or doomed him? – if there were connection between man and talisman.

A blast of hot air travelling ahead of the upgushing lava near seared his slitted eyes. Without pause, groping thought gave way to arrow-swift action. Escape was the one word or he'd not live to think. Pushing himself to his feet and twisting around, he began a skipping moonlit descent of the black cone he'd but now laboriously climbed. Perilous to the point of madness and beyond, yet utterly necessary were he to live to tell.

His eyes were fully occupied spotting the landing points of the successive leaps toward which he steered his feet. The moonlight turned bright pink. There was a giant hissing. He smelled sulphur and brimstone. There was a mighty roar, as if a cosmic lion had coughed, and a hot gust clapped his back heartily, turning three of his leaps into one, speeding his flight. Red missiles flashed past him and burst on impact to either side of his course ahead of him like angry stars. The steep slope gentled. His leaps became a lope. The leonine coughing reechoed like thunder rolling away. The pink moonshine paled and darkened.

At last he risked a backward look, expecting scenes of destruction, but there was only a great wall of sooty darkness that reeked of acid smoke and billowed overhead to besprinkle Skama with black.

He shrugged. For good or ill, his work was done and he was headed south on the front of a second monstrous weather change.

27

Fingers knew she was dreaming because there was a rainbow in the cave. But that was all right because the six colours were more like those of pastel chalk than light and there was a blackboard at which she was being taught to pleasure Ilthmar sailormen by her mother and an old old man, both wearing long black robes and hoods which hid their upper faces.

For teaching, her mother bore her witch's wand and the old

666

man a long silver spoon with which he managed the cleverest demonstrations.

But then, perhaps to illustrate some virtue – persistence? – he began to tap the bowl of his spoon on the hollow top of the desk at which they all three sat. He beat softly with a slow funeral rhythm that fascinated her until that doleful sound was all that was left in the world.

She woke to hear water a-drip, in the same slow beat as the dream-spoon, upon the thin horn pane of a slanting roof window close overhead.

She realized she had grown warm and thrown back her blanket, and as she listened to the drip she thought, *The frosty spell has broken. It's the thaw*.

From the pillow beside her, Gale, who'd also thrown back her bedclothes, murmured ungently in exactly the same rhythm as the water drops: '*Faf-hrd, Faf-hrd, Un-cle Fafhrd.*'

Which told Fingers that the drops were a message from the engaging red-haired captain, boding his return. And she told herself that she had a closer relationship to him than Gale's or even Afreyt's and must bestir herself and venture out and assure his safe return.

This decision once made, she wormed her way off the bed – it seemed important to make no stir – and drew on her short robe and soft fur boots.

After a moment's study and thought, she dropped the thin sheet back across Gale's frowsy supine sprawl and stole from the room.

Passing the bedroom where Cif and Afreyt lodged, she heard sounds of someone rising and turned down the stairs, tiptoeing next the wall to avoid the treads creaking.

Arriving in the banked warmth of the dark kitchen, she smelled gahveh heating and heard footsteps above and behind her. Without haste she made her way to the door of the bath and concealed herself behind Fafhrd's robe of coarse towelling hanging beside it in such a way as to be able to observe without herself being seen, she trusted.

It was Cif descended the stairs, dressed for the day's work. The short woman threw wide the outer door and the sounds of the thaw came in and the low white beams of the setting moon.

Standing in them, she set to her lips a thin whistle and blew – without audible results, but Fingers judged a signal had been sent.

Then Cif went to the banked fire, poured herself a mug of gahveh and took it back to the doorway where she sipped and waited. For a while she gazed straight at Fingers. But if Cif saw the girl, the woman made no sign.

With a jingle of bells but no other sound, a dogcart and pair drew up beyond her – without driver, so far as Fingers could see.

Cif walked out to it, stepped aboard, took the whip from its vertical socket and, sitting very erect, cracked it once high in the air.

Fingers came out from behind Fafhrd's robe and hurried to the door in time to see Cif and her small vehicle moving west beneath the barely diminished descending disc of Satyrs Moon as the two big dogs bore them off toward the spot where they sought Captain Mouser. For a long moment Fingers enjoyed the feeling of being a member of this household of silently occupied witchwomen.

But then the drip of the thaw reminded her of her own quest. She fetched Fafhrd's robe from its peg, and hanging it over her left arm and leaving the house door open behind her, as Cif had, Fingers circled the dwelling and headed out across the open field toward the sea, treading the steaming grass and feeling the caress of the soft south wind that set its seal on the great change of weather.

The moon was directly behind her now. She walked straight up the long shadow of herself it cast, which stretched to the low moondial. Overhead the brighter stars could be discerned, though dimmed by their moon mistress. To the southeast a cloud bank was rising to cover them.

As Fingers watched, a slender single cloud separated itself from the bank and headed toward her. It came coasting down out of the night sky, moving a little faster than the balmy breeze which drove on its fellows and lightly stroked her. The last of the moonlight shone brightly on its swan-rounded prow and sleek straight sides – for it truly did look more like a delicate ship of the air then any proper cloud of aqueous vapour should, so that a spider-webbing shiver of wonder and gossamer fear

668

went along Fingers' rosy flesh beneath her belted robe and she crouched a little and went more softly.

She was nearing the moondial now, passing it just to the south. Where its curving gnomon did not shadow it, its moon-pale round crawled with Rimic runes and half-familiar figures.

Beyond the dial, a bare spearcast distant, the eerie ship-cloud came coasting down, moving in a direction opposite to the girl, and settled to a stop.

At the same instant, almost as if it were part of the same movement, Fingers spread Fafhrd's robe across the wet grass ahead of her and gently stretched herself out upon it so that the moondial's low kerb was sufficient to conceal her. She held still, intently studying the strange cloud's pale hull.

The last bright splinter of Satyrs Moon vanished behind Rime Isle's central peaks. At the opposite end of the sky the dawn glow grew.

From a direction midway between, out of the cloud ship there came the doleful music of a flute and small drum sounding a funeral march.

Simultaneously and silently there thrust down out of the heart of the cloud and touched down a third of the distance between it and Fingers a light gangplank which appeared broad enough for two to go abreast.

Then down this travelway as the dawn lightened and the music swelled there came slowly and solemnly a small procession headed by two slim girls in garments of close-fitting black, like pages, and bearing the flute and small drum from which the sad notes came.

Following these there came two by two and footing with a grave dignity six slender women in the black hoods and form-fitting robes of the nuns of Lankhmar whose plackets showed the pastel tints of underthings of violet, blue, green, yellow, orange, and red.

Upon their shoulders they bore with ease and great solicitude a black-draped, wide-shouldered, slender-hipped tall male form.

Following these there strolled a final slim, tall, black-clad female figure in brimless conical hat and veils of a priestess of the Gods of Lankhmar. She bore a long wand tipped with a tiny, glowing pentagram, with which she sketched an endless row of hieroglyphs upon the twilit air.

Fingers, watching the strange funeral from her hidden point of vantage, could not name their language.

As the procession debouched upon the meadow, it swung west. When the turn had been fully completed, the figure of the priestess lifted her wand in a gesture of command, bringing the dim star to a stop. Instantly the girl-pages stopped their playing, the nuns their dancing forward march, and Fingers felt herself seized by a paralysis that rendered her incapable of speech and froze her every muscle save those controlling the direction in which she looked.

In a concerted movement the nuns lifted the corpse they carried on high, brought it down to the grass with an uncomfortable swiftness, and then twitched aloft the empty shroud.

The point where they had deposited the corpse was just out of Fingers' range of vision, but there was nothing the girl could do about that except grow cold and shiver.

Nor did it help when the priestess lowered her wand.

One by one the nuns knelt with hands out of view and performed a not overlong manipulation, then each dipped her head briefly out of sight and finally all rose together.

One by one the six nuns did this thing.

The priestess touched the last nun's shoulder with her wand to attract her attention and handed her a white silken ribbon. The latter knelt, and when she rose no longer had the ribbon in her hand.

With more speed than solemnity, the priestess once again raised her star-tipped wand, the page-girls struck up a jolly quick-step, the nuns briskly folded the shroud they'd borne so solemnly, the whole procession about-faced and quick-marched back aboard the cloud ship no less swiftly than it takes to write it down, and the crew set sail.

And still Fingers could not move one.

In the interval the sky had brightened markedly, sunrise was close at hand, and as the cloud-ship sailed away west at a surprisingly fast rate, it and its crew, momentarily less substantial, were suddenly on the verge of fading out, while the music gave way to a ripple of affectionate laughter.

Fingers felt all constraints lift from her muscles. She darted forward, and the next moment, it seemed, was looking down into the very shallow depression wherein the dancing nuns had laid their mortal burden.

There on a bed of new-sprung milky mushrooms stretched out serenely the tall, handsome, faintly smiling form of a man she knew as Captain Fafhrd and toward whom she felt such a puzzling mixture of feelings. He was doubly naked because recently close-shaven everywhere, save for eyebrows and lashes, and those trimmed short, and quite unclad except for ribbons of the six spectral colours and white tied in big bows around his limp genital member.

'Keepsakes of his six lady loves who were his pallbearers, or dancers, and from their mistress or chieftainess,' the girl pronounced wisely.

And noting the organ's extreme flaccidity and the depth of satisfaction in his smile, she added with professional approval, 'And loved most thoroughly.'

At first she felt a strong pang of grief, thinking him dead, but a closer look showed his chest to be gently rising and falling, and also brought her within range of his warm exhalations.

She prodded him gently in the chest over his breastbone, saying, 'Wake up, Captain Fafhrd.'

The warmth of his skin surprised her, though not enough to make her think of fever.

The smoothness of his skin truly startled her. It was shaved more closely than she'd thought possible, with sharpest eastern steel. Bending down just as the new-risen sun sent out a wave of brightness, she could see only the faintest copper-pink flecks as of fresh-scoured metal. Yesterday she'd noticed grey and white hairs among the red. He'd merited Gale's 'Uncle' fully. But now – the effect was of rejuvenation, the skin looked babyish, fair as hers was. He continued to smile in his sleep.

Fingers gripped him firmly by the shoulders and shook him.

'Wake up, Captain Fafhrd,' she cried. 'Arise and shine!' Then, in an impish mood, irked by his smile, which now began to seem merely foolish and stupid, 'Cabingirl Fingers reporting for duty.'

She knew that was wrong as soon as she heard herself utter it when in response to her shaking he reared up into a sitting position, though without opening his eyes or changing expression. Suddenly these things became frightening.

To give herself time to think about the situation and consider what to do next, Fingers returned to fetch his robe from where she'd left it spread out on the wet grass back at the moondial. She doubted he'd want to be seen naked, and certainly not wearing his ladies' colours. Yet the sun was up and at any moment Gale, Afreyt, or some visitor might appear.

'For although your ladies playing nuns had every right to mark you as their lover – seeing you'd been most free (I think) with all of them, that does not mean I have to go along with their naughty joke, though I do think it funny,' the girl said as she came hurrying with his robe, speaking aloud because she thought he really did still sleep and wanted in any case to check upon this fact.

In the interval she had jumped to the rather romantic conclusion that Fafhrd was in the situation of the Handsome Tranced One, a male equivalent of Sleeping Beauty in Lankhmar legend – a youth with a sleep spell on him that can be lifted only by his true love's kiss.

Which at once suggested to Fingers that she convey the sleeping (and strangely transformed, even frightening) hero to the Lady Afreyt for the reviving kiss.

After all, they had been introduced to her as lovers (and proper gentlefolk) except for Fafhrd's straying with the naughty nuns, which was the sort of straying to be expected of men, according to her mother's teaching. Moreover he'd been under all the strain of directing the search for his comrade Captain who'd slipped underground.

Surely to bring Fafhrd and Afreyt back together would be a most proper return for all the courtesies they'd shown her, beginning with her rescue from *Weasel*.

Back at the mushroom bed Fafhrd had made no further progress toward awakening. So she draped the sun-warmed robe around him, gently urging him by words and assisting movements to don it.

'Arise, Captain Fafhrd,' she suggested, 'and I will help you into your robe and then to some shadowed and comfortable spot where you may have your full sleep out.'

When with some repetitions of this routine and patter she'd got him up (safely asleep on his feet, as it were) with his robe belted about him so his colourful honours were completely concealed – and a long look around showed they were still unobserved – she breathed a sigh of relief and set about to lead him back to Cif's house using the same methods.

But they'd got no farther than the moondial when it occurred to Fingers to ask herself, Where's everyone?

It was a question easier to ask than answer.

You'd think after the second great weather change, every last soul would be out to see, soaking in the heat and talking about the wonder.

Yet wherever you looked there wasn't a person to be seen or heard. It was eerie.

All yesterday the digging for Captain Mouser had kept up a steady traffic between the diggings, the barracks, and Cif's place. Today no trace of that since Cif's departure by moon-light hours ago.

It was as if Fafhrd's sleep spell were on everyone in Salthaven save herself. Maybe it was.

And the somnambulistic spell on Fafhrd was a lot stronger than she'd judged at first. Here, he and she were halfway back to Cif's and it showed no signs of falling off.

She began to doubt the power of Afreyt's kiss to dispel it. Perhaps it would be better if he had his full sleep out, as she'd been suggesting to him in her patter.

And what if Afreyt didn't go for her idea of the Handsome Tranced One and the revivifying kiss? Or tried it and it didn't? And then they both tried to wake Fafhrd and couldn't? And Lady Afreyt blamed her for that?

Suddenly she lost all faith in the ideas that had seemed so brilliant to her moments before. Getting Fafhrd back to full sleep again (as she had been promising him over and over in her patter) as soon as they'd reached a suitable place for that seemed the thing to do. She recalled an infallible sleep spell her mother had taught her. The sooner she recited it to Fafhrd, the better. Fully asleep again, he'd no longer be her responsibility.

Perhaps it would work on her too – and perhaps that was just what she needed to straighten her out – a good sleep.

The idea of falling asleep with Captain Fafhrd seemed vastly attractive.

They'd just got back to Cif's without encountering anyone. She was relieved to find the door ajar. She thought she'd closed it.

Stopping her soft talk to Fafhrd, but keeping up a pressure on his arm, she worked the thick door open and guided him inside. The house was silent, she was pleased to find, and that Captain Fafhrd, being barefoot, made no more noise than she.

Then, as they were halfway across the kitchen, nearer the cellar stairs than those to the second floor (or the sauna door), she heard footsteps overhead in Cif's bedroom. Afreyt's, she thought.

She decided at once on flight and chose the cellar because it was nearest and also the place where she had first met Fafhrd. She stuck with her choice because the Northerner responded instantly to her silent guidance, as if it would have been his choice too.

And then they were down in the cellar and the die was cast – simply a matter of whether the firm, decisive footsteps of Afreyt followed him down into the cellar or did not. Fingers had led him out of the space at the foot of the stairs visible from the kitchen and sat him down on the bench facing the large square of unpaved loamy earth, illuminated, she now saw, by one of the long-lasting cool leviathan-oil lamps. But she dared not turn that off now, no matter how unsuitable for sleeping, for if Afreyt saw the light dim in the cellar, she'd surely come down to investigate.

The footsteps finished the upper stairs, came five paces across the kitchen, and then stopped dead. Had she noticed the light on in the cellar and would she come down to turn it off?

But moments gave way to seconds and seconds to minutes, or at least lengthened unendurably, and still there'd been no sound. It was as if Afreyt had died up there or just evaporated. Until Fingers, to stop herself growing tired or numb and getting a crick in her neck or shoulder and making a violent involuntary move, edged forward step by silent step and seated herself on the bench beside the northern Captain, facing away from the unpaved square of earth.

She felt herself growing more and more tired, forgot about Afreyt hearing, and hastened to recite the sleep spell softly so that she and Captain Fafhrd would receive the full benefit of it.

Meanwhile something very interesting and quite unsuspected by Fingers had actually been happening to Afreyt.

She had wakened alone just before dawn and heard the thaw, opened the window overlooking the headland and moondial just in time to observe the wondrous sailing of the Arilian moon pinnace with Fafhrd's mistress and her naughty train, and heard the last notes of the quick march give way to the ripple of derisive laughter.

Thereafter, Afreyt had watched from the distance the tricksy and ambitious cabingirl Fingers seemingly rouse, then robe her magically rejuvenated father (for the woman had noted many other resemblances between parent and offspring besides hair colour), and then work their way at leisure back to Cif's place, getting their two stories straight, thought Afreyt, but above all murmuring of great incestuous love (for after all, what else did they really have to talk about?), and while Fafhrd's lady was thus reacting to their manifold treacheries, she furiously laced on her shoes and belted her robe and hurried downstairs to confront the miscreants.

When she found them gone, Afreyt made the deduction Fingers had anticipated about the cellar light. She thought for a moment, then to surprise them, knelt and silently undid the shoes she had so furiously laced, stepped out of them and tiptoed downstairs without a sound.

But when she stepped out suddenly into full view she found them both faced away from her on the bench, gazing at the unpaved square of earth, Fafhrd resting his head against Fingers' chest, 'lying in her lap', as it's expressed, just as the girl started to recite in a small bell-like voice what she thought was her mother's sleep spell but was in truth, as she had inadvertently revealed to Gale and Afreyt the second morning of the cold by reciting its last five individually harmless lines, the direst of Quarmallian death spells taught her under hypnosis by the infinitely vengeful and devious Lord Quarmal of Quarmall.

> *'Call for the robin red breast and the wren*
> *Since o'er shady groves they hover*
> *And with leaves and flowers do cover*
> *The friendless bodies of unburied men.*
>
> *Call unto his funeral dole*
> *The ant, the field mouse, and the mole*
> *To rear him hillocks that shall keep him warm*
> *And safe from any savage hurt or harm . . .'**

As Afreyt heard Fingers recite the first of those eight lines, she saw emerge vertically upward from the soft earth of the left forefront of the unpaved square a small serpent's head or tentacle tip, followed almost at once close to either side by a second and third at the same even rate, then a short fourth in line at the same short distance to the left, and lastly a thick fifth erecting alone two inches in front of the rest, and then she saw that the four serpents' heads or tentacles were joined at their bases to a palm, and taken with the thick separate member, constituted the fingers and thumb of a buried hand digging itself upward and bursting from the ground, while down off it the revealing earth sifted and tumbled.

As Afreyt, all a-shiver at this prodigy, listened to the recitation of the innocuous-seeming second and third lines and realized that the situation must be different, with Fafhrd playing a more passive role than she'd suspected, a second and larger emergence started, that of a head behind and to the right of the hand and with its hairy earth-mired crown beginning at the level of the palm.

The forward-facing brow, as it emerged at the same even rate as had the hand, showed more bright yellow in its illumination than white leviathan light would account for, which reminded

---

*The White Devil by John Webster, Act V, Scene 4. Sometimes called Cornelia's dirge, this ends in the play:

> *'To rear him hillocks, that shall keep him warm*
> *And (when gay tombs are robbed) sustain no harm,*
> *But keep the wolf far thence, that's foe to men,*
> *For with his nails he'll dig him up again.'*

676

Afreyt of Cif's dream of the Mouser wearing a glowing yellow mask and was Afreyt's first clue to the identity of the underground traveller. By now it was apparent that the escaping hand was attached to and directed by the rising head, and Afreyt, shaking with terror at the unnatural sight, at least need not fear the dartings, scuttlings, and gropings of a hostile, detached and independently roving hand.

As she heard the child's clear little voice recite the somewhat sinister fourth line of the Quarmallian death spell, which Afreyt already suspected to be something of the sort (which Fingers did not as yet), the eyes beneath the rising brow came into view and opened wide.

Afreyt at once recognized the gray eyes of the Mouser, saw that they were fixed upon Fafhrd and full of fear for him and that it was the very fear of death. At that moment she would have given a great deal to know whether Fafhrd's own eyes were open or closed, if the Mouser had made his deduction from the expression in them or from his comrade's extreme pallor or other physical symptom. She did not think (at least as yet) of getting up and looking for herself – her awe of what was happening, rather than her fear (though that was great), kept her frozen.

As a matter of fact his eyes were closed with the spell's workings, which operated by degrees, line by line, from sleep to death.

Fingers, reciting the death spell Quarmal had taught her hypnotically after her kidnapping and which she now thought of as a sleep spell of her mother's (as he'd told her 'twas), saw the same figure emerging from the earth that Afreyt did, but it did not catch her interest. She hoped it would not interfere with her recital of the spell and its working on Fafhrd and herself. Perhaps it was the beginning of a dream they'd share.

The Mouser had last lost consciousness underground spying on old Quarmal's buried map room and chamber of necromancy while asking himself questions about Rime Isle.

He came to awareness now with head, shoulders, and one arm emerged into a familiar cellar on the latter island and with the answers to his questions in plain view: Fafhrd dying in the arms and against the breasts of his daughter by (the Quarmallian) slave girl Friska, and the child's unwitting recitation of the death spell.

Who else could be the assassin indicated by the lone red dot on Quarmal's world map? And so what Mouser must do at once to save his dearest friend from life's worst ill – even before Mou inhaled the unrationed breaths he longed to, stretched the cramped muscles, or tasted the wine for which his dry throat cried – was to countermand that death spell by snapping his fingers thrice, as he'd just now seen Quarmal do to stay the instructional assassination of his son Igwarl by the latter's sister Issa.

And, if Mou knew anything about the rules of magic and the ways of Quarmal, those snaps must be perfectly executed, delivered without delay, and loud as thundercracks – or else he could go whistle for Faf's life forevermore.

And so it happened that as Afreyt listened to Fingers recite the idyllic fifth, sixth, seventh, and eighth lines of the spell (but getting closer to the nasty ones she'd 'spelled' to them in her fatigue the second morning of the cold), the Rime Isle woman was puzzled and nonplussed to see the earth-traveller – just as there rose into view Mouser's mouth set in a narrow slit for air scavenging – wave his limply held free hand vigorously, as if it were a dusting rag from which he shook the dirt, and then carefully settle the pad at end of his middle finger against the ball of his thumb above ring and little finger bent back against the palm, and against which the poised and powerfully tensed middle finger now flashed down.

It was, quite simply, the loudest fingersnap she'd ever heard. So might a most impatient god summon a reprehensibly straying angel.

And as if that prodigious snap were not enough to prove whatever point was being contested, it was followed with preternatural swiftness by not one, but two repetitions of the same sound, each one a little louder than the previous one, which as any knowledgeable gambler knows, is not a bet to be backed, an achievement to set a wager on.

The Mouser's fingerbolts had their desired effect on the others in the cellar, including their sender.

They brought Afreyt to her feet. Fingers was silenced, Quarmal's death spell cancelled. The bell tones ceased to sound, the cabingirl fell backward. Fafhrd collapsed, sank sidewise against her.

This should have made it easier for Afreyt to see the Mouser, but it didn't. The effort he'd put into his fingerbolts had taken it out of him. As if time had been turned back to that night of full Satyrs Moon on Gallows Hill, his outline grew fainter, the steady leviathan light flickered, his emergence slowed and stopped, without reaching his waist, and he began to slip backward into the earth.

His eyes fixed on Afreyt's most dolefully. His lips opened and a low moaning came out, such as a ghost utters at cockcrow, infinitely sad.

Afreyt plunged to her knees before the unpaved square. Her grasping digging hands encountered only loose dirt. She clambered to her feet and turned back to the fallen figures.

The man with the child's skin and the child lay as if dead. But a closer inspection showed them to be but sleeping.

28

Cif scraped the wooden scoop four times across the earthen tunnel face before her, detaching small chunks and granules of loosened sand, which pattered down on and around her boots.

The leviathan-oil lamp behind her cast her head's shadow on the fresh area of tunnel face thus uncovered and the newly attached snow-serpent hide (which was the twenty-third in from the shaft) puffed warm air upon it from outside, where Satyrs Moon was two hours set and the bright sun almost as long arisen.

She had been working at the tunnel face all of that time, advancing it at least two feet (and making room for another length of the flexible snowy piping, which had just now been attached).

With her free hand she felt, deep in her pouch, the reassuring touch of the brazen loop, wide enough to be a ring for two fingers, with which Mikkidu had greeted her this morn, telling her that it had been recovered during the digging last night and was (as she well knew) an item the Captain was seldom parted from.

She judged she had another hour of face work in her before she lost her freshness and must give place to Rill, who now assisted her and only had been below for half an hour.

But now 'twas time for one of the quarter-hourly checks she made.

'Cover the lamp,' she called back to Rill.

The lady with the crippled left hand pulled up around the coolly burning lamp a thick black sack and drew it together at the top.

The tunnel grew black as pitch.

Cif stared ahead and this time seemed to see, floating at eye level, a phosphorescent yellow mask such as she'd seen the Mouser wearing in the dream she'd had the first night of the cold. It was dim but truly seemed there.

Letting fall the scoop and withdrawing her left hand from her pouch, she dug her gloved fingers into the sandy face where the mask was drifting. It stayed there, did not fade out or waver, but grew brighter. The featureless black ovals that were its eyes seemed to stare back at her commandingly.

'Uncover the lamp,' she managed to enunciate.

Rill obeyed, not trusting herself to ask questions. Almost with a rush the white light flooded back, revealing Cif staring fiercely at the tunnel face. Rill could no longer contain herself.

'You think . . . ?' she managed to ask in a voice fraught with awe.

'We'll soon know,' the other replied, drawing back her clawed right hand and driving it into the loosened sand of the tunnel face at the level of her chin, twisting it this way and that, back and forth, feeling around before withdrawing it. (Small chunks and grains showered around.) She repeated this action twice, but on the second occasion paused with her hand still dug in.

Her gloved fingers had encountered and were now uncovering two hard, serrated, semicircular ridges with a half-inch gap between them.

Wetting her lips with her tongue and guiding them with her gloved hands held close beside her cheeks, she pressed them against the dry and gritty pair of lips that closely framed the serrated ridges that opposed and almost touched her own teeth.

Puffing a breath of air ahead of it, she ran her tongue's wet tip around the inside of the dry lips hers pressed, repeated that tender action and then inhaled.

Her nostrils and foremouth filled with the exciting acrid reek of the Gray Mouser, familiar to her from a long season's lovemaking.

It made her tremble and shake to realize this was so, that she held between her hands his precious face returned from the grave.

She exhaled to one side that wonder breath, drew in a fresh one from the serpent's mouth, again clamped her lips down upon his still-dry ones and gently blew that breath deep into him, praying it retained its healing serpent's character.

'Dearest, beloved,' she heard him croak.

She realized she was staring deep into his eyes, but was so close the two appeared as one.

'Owl eyes,' she replied foolishly, recalling their lovers' name for that two-equals-one phenomenon.

Then recollecting more of her situation, she said, 'Dear Rill, our captain's back. He's in my arms and I am feeding him air. Do you work in your hands from behind me and dig and brush the earth away from's body and speed his freeing from its dreadful grip.'

'I will be very grateful, Rill, I assure you,' the Mouser broke in *sotto voce*, croaking rather less than he had on 'dearest'.

The witch-whore complied, gingerly at first, then with larger strokes as she realized the amount of earth there was to be moved. She found the scoop Cif had dropped and used it to increase the scoop of first her right hand, then her crippled left, where the advantage it provided was greater.

Meanwhile Cif continued to brush dirt from his cheeks as she alternately kissed him and fed him air, working her hands nearer to the back of his head and a full embrace, with each stroke freeing more of the margins of his eye sockets and ears.

The Mouser said, 'I'll keep my eyes closed, Cif, save when you tell me I may open them,' and was emboldened to ask, 'And would you be a bit more generous with your perfumed saliva, dear? That is, if you've to spare. I've been without refreshment all of two days (or is it three, perchance?) save for such moisture as I've sucked from stones. Or begged from passing worms.'

'I have,' Rill mentioned ingenuously. 'I happen to have been chewing mint the past half hour. The smallest leaves.'

'You *are* a witch, dear Rill,' Cif commented cattily.

Fafhrd's lieutenant Skor chose that moment to appear behind Rill, filling the tunnel with his stooped tall form and reporting past her to Cif as commander of the diggings, 'The Captain's returned from wherever he was yesterday and last night, milady. I gather strange things have been happening, some in the sky. He just arrived by dogcart with the Lady Afreyt and with them the child Gale and the Ilthmar cabingirl.'

At that point he got a good look at what was going on in the tunnel, recognized the Mouser's face and became speechless. (Later he tried to describe what he saw to Skullick and Pshawri. 'She was kissing him out of the sandstone, I tell you, kissing and caressing, working a mighty magic whether she knew it or not. While her sister witch worked a like sorcery upon his bottom half, his nether limbs and members. Our captains are fortunate to enjoy the favour of such women of power.')

Cif turned her head back toward him and straightened up, bringing the Mouser with her out of the tunnel face and shedding sandy debris.

'Things have been happening here too, as you can see,' she said briskly. 'Now harken, Skor. Return aloft and tell the Lady Afreyt and Captain Fafhrd I wish to speak with them down here. But do *not* tell them (or *anyone* up there) of Captain Mouser's passing strange return, else everyone will be crowding down to view and celebrate the wonder.'

'That's true enough,' the tall man with thinning hair agreed, doing his best to sound rational.

'Do as she tells you, Skor,' the Mouser put in. 'There's wisdom in her rede.'

'Don't *you* return down here, of course,' Cif continued. 'Take charge up there, maintain order, and keep the dragon breathing.' She nodded toward the pulsing white snow-serpent piping. 'Here, take the ring of command off my top middle finger and wear it on your thumb.' She held out the hand on which was

Fafhrd's ring. He obeyed. She had an afterthought. 'Send the two girls down also, Fingers and Gale. Else they'll make mischief while your hands are full.'

'Harkening in obedience,' Skor responded, bowing to Cif as he turned around and made off speedily.

'That last thought of yours was inspired, my dear,' the Mouser said breezily, turning from Rill to Cif. 'Mischief? Yes, indeed! – for it turns out that the Ilthmar cabingirl Fingers is the assassin sent to wipe out her father Fafhrd by reciting an outlandish death spell – sent out by our old enemy Quarmal, Lord of Quarmall, as I learned when I breakfasted there al fresco this morn's morn on cave dew, boreworm bread, and toadstool wine – and spied on Quarmal in his most secret lair.'

'Fingers Fafhrd's get?' Rill remarked. 'I suspected it from the red hair. And there's a definite facial resemblance. And something about her cool manner . . .'

The Mouser nodded emphatically. 'Though, to be fair to Fingers, I don't think she knew what she was doing – old Quarmal had her most securely hypnotized. Fortunately I learned at the same time how to scotch his spells ('twas as easy as snap your fingers, and as hard) by observing him foil at the last moment his son Igwarl's murder by *his* sister Issa, which he had masterminded for purposes of instruction. (He makes a positive religion of treachery and mistrust, the old man does.) If I hadn't studied his finger-snapping trick and been able to repeat it perfectly, Fafhrd would be dead as mutton by his daughter's unknowing agency. Whereas, if we can trust Skor, he's as fit as a fiddle.'

'My, my,' observed Cif, 'we *have* managed to keep busy underground, haven't we?'

'You *do* know more about the worser side of human nature than any man I know. Or woman for that matter,' Rill chimed in.

The Mouser shrugged apologetically. The comic gesture caused him to really look at himself and his garments for the first time since coming out of the wall.

His reaction caused Cif and Rill to do the same thing.

His gray jerkin, which had been stout, thick cloth when last observed by any of them, had somehow grown fine as gossamer and quite translucent, while his exposed skin looked as if it had been pumiced.

As if on his journey underground he had endured for hours a blasting sandstorm, suffering such wear and tear as might be accounted for by a trip to Quarmall. The *strangeness* of it all gripped their minds.

At that long moment Fafhrd appeared in the tunnel, followed closely by Fingers and Afreyt, with a wide-eyed Gale bringing up the rear. He was wearing a winter jacket with attached hood fallen away behind, revealing his close-shaven pate.

'I *knew* you had been found,' he said excitedly. 'I read it in Skor's face when he returned with Cif's summons. Though he's fooled the rest, I think. Make no mistake, it was a good idea to keep it a secret for a bit. There are things to be said before we face a celebration. It appears that I owe you my life, old friend – and my child her memory as well. Look here, you rogue, however did you learn old Quarmal's finger-snapping dodge?'

'Why, by travelling underground to his buried city, of course, and spying on him,' the Mouser replied airily. 'And studying his maps,' he added. 'Either I did that in the body or else my ka did in horn-gate dreams. If his boreworms got to me, and I believe they did, it argues for the former.'

'Oh well,' Fafhrd said philosophically, 'boreworms don't kill, only excruciate.'

'And then only if you're awake while they're entering you,' Fingers piped up consolingly. 'But truly, Uncle Mouser, I'm grateful to you beyond words for saving my father's life and me from parricide and madness.'

'Tut, tut, child! No need for melodrama. I believe you,' the Mouser said, 'and entreat your pardon for my earlier doubts. You are the daughter of your mother Friska, truly, who resisted all my efforts to seduce her, which were neither few nor unskillful, to my recollection.'

'I believe you,' Fingers assured him. 'As she's oft told me, your seduction attempts were responsible for her friend (and your lover, Uncle Mouser) Ivivis quitting the escape party at Tovilyis and persuading my mother to quit with her and have me there.'

'I truly planned to get gold and return to Tovilyis and rejoin her,' Fafhrd apologized. 'But something always intervened, generally the absence of gold.'

'Friska never blamed you,' Fingers assured him. 'She always came to your defence when Aunt Ivivis made you the target of one of her tirades. Aunty would say, "He should have stayed with you and let the little jackanapes go on alone," and Mother would answer, "That would have been too much to hope for. Remember, they're lifelong comrades."'

'Friska was always most forgiving,' Fafhrd averred. 'Just as Fingers is to you, Mouser,' he added, shaking his middle digit under the Gray One's nose. 'Do you realize that that terrible treble fingersnap that saved my lift almost slew Fingers at the same time? Stretching her senseless and unconscious across the bench where we'd sat watching you emerge from earth like a pale vengeful mole – I was knocked out myself as well, stretched out across my daughter on the bench. As Afreyt here can attest, who was a full quarter hour eliciting from either of us the least sign of life.'

'That's most true, masters,' the tall blonde averred, her violet eyes flashing. 'I breathed for Fafhrd fully that long before his wits returned. Meanwhile Gale, who'd awakened and come downstairs fortuitously, performed a like service for Fingers.'

'Yes, I did that,' the child confirmed, 'and when you came to, you beast, you bit my nose, like an ungrateful and confused kitten.'

'You should have spanked me,' the girl from Ilthmar told her piously.

'I'll remember that at the first opportunity,' Gale threatened darkly.

'For that matter, *I* lost consciousness myself completely at the climax,' the Mouser asserted, getting back into the game. 'So much depended on getting those fingersnaps of old Quarmal just right, each one a little louder than the last. It literally took everything out of me, so that my task accomplished, I sank back into the earth like a dying ghost, to be transported here by whatever potent agency has guided my long journey, and await dear Cif's revivifying kiss.'

And he slowly shook his head from side to side, raising his

brows and parting his hands a little in a gesture of uncomprehending wonder.

Relaxing then a little from this posture (one got the impression everyone in the tunnel let out a small sigh), he turned with a sweet and gracious smile to Fafhrd and inquired, 'But now tell me, old friend, how came you to be parted from your hair? And so very thoroughly, judging from the portions of you I'm able to see. In my underground travels I've lost some skin (and body hair presumably) from friction with sand, gravel, clay, and rock. My garments certainly have suffered a diminishment, as is plain to see. But you, my friend, have not that excuse.'

'Let me answer that,' Afreyt demanded with such resolution that no one, even Fafhrd, seemed inclined to contest her claim. She took a deep breath and addressed, chiefly to the Gray Mouser (though all heard, for she spoke very clearly) the following remarkable extended statement.

'Dear Captain Mouser, when you first slipped down into the earth early upon the night of Satyrs full and the second of the coming of the cold, it was Captain Fafhrd who set us digging after you here on Goddess Hill. Not all of us agreed with his idea, but when the digging turned up evidence of your passage (your hood, your dagger Cat's Claw, et cetera) we were logically compelled to change our minds. The work begun then has now culminated in the rescue of Captain Mouser by the ladies Cif and Rill after today's miraculous survival underground. All honour to Captain Fafhrd for laying the foundations of this wonderful achievement!'

Gale started to applaud, but none of the others took it up, and when Fingers shook her head at the other girl, she broke off.

Afreyt resumed her extended statement, ignoring the interruption.

'It was at this point, I think, that it began to become apparent, dimly at first, that a supernatural power, or powers, were taking a hand in the developing events.

'In the matter of Captain Mouser, it was the dowsing for him by the Lady Cif and his lieutenant Pshawri which seemed to indicate the Mouser was moving underground at unlikely speeds over incredible distances far beyond the limits of these diggings, even extending out under the Outer Sea.

686

'Besides that, there's an altogether amazing action that occurred this morning in the cellar of the Lady Cif's house and which Fingers and I both witnessed: the Mouser's saving of Fafhrd from a horrid outlandish death spell by employment of information he could hardly have obtained anywhere in Nehwon nearer than buried Quarmall.' And she gazed fiercely, almost accusingly, at the Mouser.

Gale parted her hands to start another round of applause, but then made a face at Fingers and forbore.

The Mouser endured the steely stare a moment more, then said apologetically, 'I'm sorry, Lady Afreyt. I can't fully satisfy your curiosity as to how far I went or all I did below ground. Mostly I recall sucking pebbles to quench my thirst and breathing most shallowly to make best use of the air I scavenged (often having to make do with mephitic gases), and meditating on my sins and those of others (very interesting, some of those). Otherwise I seem to have slept a lot (doubtless a good thing since it reduced my consumption of air) and dreamed some remarkable dreams. So please, Lady Afreyt, continue with your fascinating hypothetical reconstruction of what's happened to us the last two mysterious days – always remembering to end with an explanation of how Fafhrd came to lose his hair. Which was, I believe, the question you set out to answer in the first place.'

'That's true,' she said. 'Well, Captain Mouser, just as a supernatural element entered your movements underground, enabling you to move to far places at fantastic speeds and causing you considerable wear and tear—' She eyed his translucent jerkin. '—a like element began to influence Fafhrd, though functioning in the opposite direction, not below ground, but above.

'Late on the night of Satyrs full he got drunk and set out for Salthaven next morning under the influence. For this part of the story we have the evidence of the children Gale and Fingers, who followed him. They saw him set to swimming through the fog and then mount up into the sky in widening spirals.

'Somewhere aloft above Salthaven he disrobed (to lighten ship, he tells me) and dropped his boots, belt, pouch, bracelet, and other gear, which fell on roofs and treetops, whence they

687

were brought to me yesterday, forming a set of objects not unlike the items Captain Mouser left behind him as he travelled through the earth.

'For the rest of my narrative I must depend chiefly on the testimony of its principal actor, given to me earlier today after he recovered from Captain Mouser's spell-breaking.

'To summarize, a short time after lightening ship, Captain Fafhrd was picked up by a cloud-pinnace captained by Queen Frix of Arilia, his one-time paramour, and crewed by a company of her notorious ladies. Being still somewhat under the influence, he was easily enticed into an orgy, during the course of which he was completely shaven, upon the pretext of increasing his pleasure.'

'Half the civilized races of Nehwon believe that firmly and act accordingly,' Fingers commented. 'They regard all hair as a disfigurement, eyelashes being the one exception.'

'Don't come the old hooker on me! Or presume to instruct us in the sexual fashions of so-called civilized races, you cabingirl princess!' Afreyt told her tartly, violet eyes flashing. 'So far I've been inclined to forgive you all the evil you've innocently been mixed up with, but it wouldn't take much to make me change my mind and give you that shrewd spanking you have been asking for!'

The girl drooped her eyes, gave her lips a reproving tap with her fingertips, covered her mouth with a palm and dropped a submissive curtsey. Gale poked her surreptitiously a little above the hips, where the side is soft.

'But is this true, old friend?' the Mouser asked Fafhrd concernedly. 'Pardon me, Lady Afreyt, but I'm somewhat shocked.'

'I am content with Afreyt's statement of my case,' Fafhrd said stolidly, 'and grateful to her saving me embarrassment.'

'Well, then,' the Mouser said, 'since we're talking so freely, resolve us: does shaving augment carnal delight? In your case, at any rate?'

'That's not a suitable question for public discussion,' Fafhrd responded somewhat primly. 'Ask me in private and I may give you an answer.'

Afreyt looked at the Mouser sweetly and gave a little nod before continuing her statement.

'At some point during the night's licentious doings aboard the aerial warehouse of Queen Frix, Fafhrd succumbed, but whether from an excess of carnal delight, or of brandy and poppy and other narcotic drugs that may have been administered to him, we have no way of knowing.

'Just before dawn the abominable cloud-pinnace landed on Rime Isle on the headland between Salthaven and the Maelstrom and Fafhrd was given a mock funeral which was secretly observed by his long-lost daughter Fingers.'

The girl, her eyes still downcast, nodded twice, rapidly.

'With derisive ceremony and soft music,' Afreyt went on, 'Fafhrd was.laid to rest – abandoned – on a bed of new-sprung mushrooms wet with dew, naked in the dawn's chill save for some ribbons the colour of the underclothes of Frix's whores tied in unsightly mockery around his limp member, his flaccid Wand of Eros.'

'Lovers' Mementos,' Fingers explained, 'a custom observed in—' she began, then broke off. 'Oh pardon me, Lady Afreyt, I didn't mean to speak, I got carried away . . .'

'I am glad to hear you say so,' that one observed neutrally. '*When* the sinister funmakers had departed, Fingers' first action was to enrobe her father decently, then guide him still in a stupor to Cif's abode and make her hypnotically-enforced attempt upon his life, which was providentially foiled by Captain Mouser's most timely emergence, as I'm sure you've all heard by now.'

'Yes indeed, we've had quite enough of that,' the Gray One said modestly. Then, bowing low, 'Thank you, Lady Afreyt, for answering my questions as fully as was possible for you, I'm sure.' Then turning to Fafhrd, 'And now, old friend, could you not be induced to add a few words of your own, sort of wrap the whole matter up, as it were?'

Setting his hands on his hips, Fafhrd replied, 'Listen, little man, we've had enough of this nonsense. I recall something you said last winter at the dinner we had for you at the Sea Wrack to celebrate your successful trading voyage to No-Ombrulsk. Cif was teasing you about your erotic involvement (bondage and discipline, et cetera) with the Simorgyan sea demoness Ississi, who almost scuppered you and *Sea Hawk*.

'You replied to her teasing – manfully, it seemed to me (you blushed) – that you had attempted something somewhat beyond your powers.

'Well, so had I, I confess most emphatically, in this business of Frix and her ladies! I met total defeat in a war of pleasure! So let's have no more of it! For today, at least! I'm sorry, Afreyt, but that had to be said.'

'I think so too,' she told him. 'Let's all cool down.'

'Before some fresh surprises refire our interest,' Rill put in, who was standing close behind the Mouser in the somewhat crowded section of tunnel.

Her words were prophetic, for just then Pshawri, coming from the shaft, edged his way into the press. He was still stripped for running, wearing only loin-cloth, belt, and pouch, carrying over one arm a robe he'd been handed above but not yet donned. When he saw the Mouser, the young lieutenant's weary face lit up wonderfully, but it was Cif to whom he first spoke.

'Lady,' he said, bowing, 'at midnight, following your instructions, I threw into Darkfire's lava pool the talismanic Whirlpool Queller I'd won from the Maelstrom and with which we'd dowsed for Captain Mouser. There was an eruption from which I barely escaped, racing the ensuing weather change south and losing badly. When I crossed the headland I noted Maelstrom had calmed once more.'

'That's wondrous news, brave Lieutenant,' Cif replied in a ringing voice. Then turning to the Mouser, who was frowning, she dipped rapidly into her pouch. 'Before you say anything, Captain, here's something you should read.'

The Mouser spread the worn violet-inked sheet, but had not got very far before he mentioned Fafhrd to come view Freg's letter with him. So they read it side by side and line by line.

When they got to the bit about the Mouser's tricksiness, Fafhrd muttered, 'I always suspected you got at her, you dog,' and he replied, 'Cheer up, at least she recognizes your moral superiority.'

'Is that my uncouthness or my love?' the big man grumbled.

And when they got to the 'triads of moles', Rill, who'd been sneaking glances, could not resist touching with three fingers the three shoulder moles that showed clearly by leviathan light through the worn-to-gossamer fabric of the Mouser's jerkin. When he glared at her, she laughed and said, 'Look at mates to these on Pshawri's side. We're packed too close here to hide anything.'

Afreyt lifted the robe from Pshawri's arm and held it for him, saying, 'You have my thanks too, Lieutenant.' He thanked her back and let her help him don it.

The reading done, the Mouser gazed quizzically at Pshawri a long moment.

'Still want to work for me, son, now I'm your father? I suppose I could pay you off in some way, if that's your choice.'

'Most certainly, sire,' the young man responded. The Mouser spread his arms and they embraced, quite formally to start with.

'Come,' said Cif, moving past them, 'it's time we told the others the good news.'

They followed her, the Mouser admiring her dragon's breath system of ventilation and going on to praise the bucket lift in the shaft.

Halfway along this route, at the floor of the shaft, Mikkidu appeared, bearing one of the Mouser's gray house robes. The Mouser donned it and thanked him, then stepped in the bucket and was drawn up.

Fafhrd emerged from the tunnel followed by Afreyt and the rest. He drew his hood over his shaven pate, then mounted the shaft swiftly by the ladder of pegs.

As the Mouser swung off at the top, his loosely assembled men gave a cheer. Fafhrd's joined in, redoubling their shouts as their captain came into view and stood beside the Mouser. As the cheering ebbed, they were able to exchange a few words in private as the late summer midday sun shone down from low in the south.

MOUSER (indicating the shallow mound of dug earth near where they stood): Mikkidu tells me there's talk of renaming Goddess Hill (formerly Gallows Hill), Mount Mouser.

FAFHRD (a shade resentfully): That's losing no time.

MOUSER: Should I suggest Mount Faf-Mou?

691

FAFHRD: Forget it. I must say, you're looking remarkably fit after your incredibly long sojourn buried.

MOUSER: I don't feel that way. I died down there so many times, I doubt I'll ever trust life again.

FAFHRD: For every time you died, you were reborn. Contrariwise, I think you have become Death's dearest friend.

MOUSER: That's a most dubious distinction. I'm tired of killing.

FAFHRD: Agreed. Fingers is a joy. She came along barely in time to rescue me from boredom.

MOUSER: I'm doubly fortunate – to have been able to instruct my son before I knew he was one.

FAFHRD: I think we can expect more of these strays.

MOUSER: Perish the thought!

29

That day the chief topic of gossip in Godsland was the mysterious vanishment of the troublesome stranger divinity Loki. One of the few deities to know the true explanation was the spider-god Mog.

On a whim Death had sought Mog out to inform him of the continued survival of his chief worshipper, the Gray Mouser, who'd been under Loki's curse, and to boast a bit of trickery by which he'd managed this, for even Death is vain.

'Actually,' Death confided, 'the one to consign Loki firmly to the lava lake was none other than the Gray Mouser's son, who promises also to become a very useful character to me.'

'I've good news too of my man Fafhrd, my lapsed Lankhmar acolyte,' limp-wristed Issek, who'd been listening along with Kos, Fafhrd's barbarian father-god, interrupted impudently. 'He's had himself shaved entire – in my honour, I presume, as once befell him in Lankhmar.'

'Faugh on such effeminate practices,' Kos pronounced.

'Wherever has Death got to?' Issek asked, looking about.

Mog answered, pointing. 'I fancy he caught sign of his sister Pain approaching and slipped back to the Shadowland. He's much ashamed of the way she parades about naked, preening herself upon her conquests and inflictions.'

And this may very well have been the case, for Death is never cruel or uncouth.

30

A fortnight later Captain Mouser's and Fafhrd's officers threw them a barracks party, without asking permission, on the strength of one of them now being a blood relative and close member of the inner family.

Haste was needful because next morning Sergeant Skullick was sailing on a fast Sarheemar smuggler bound for Ilthmar, on a mission for Fafhrd to Fingers' mother Friska after first determining if she were still a free agent and not a brainwashed tool of old Quarmal once more.

'Fingers' memories have grown uncertain again,' the Captain informed his humorous sergeant. 'Besides, from now on we must keep a watchful eye on that cunningest wizard. He's sure to be seeking revenge, ever since Captain Mouser so cleverly foiled his try on my own life.'

Also aboard the early-sailing smuggler *Ghost* would be Snee, the most knowledgeable of the Mouser's thieves turned sailor, to bear a message from Pshawri to his mother Freg in Lankhmar and gather information of interest on the Thieves Guild, the Overlord's court, and the Grain Merchant's Cartel, which meant chiefly Hisvin and his daughter Hisvet.

A third passenger aboard *Ghost* would be Rill, dispatched by Cif and Afreyt to contact witch covens in Ilthmar, Lankhmar, and (if possible) Tovilyis to get news of Friska and Freg.

'It behooves us,' Cif told her friend, 'to keep our own tabs on our husbands' previous bedmates.'

Afreyt emphatically agreed.

Fafhrd commented, 'I confess I find it strange and somewhat distasteful to be forever sending other men on adventures, rather than setting forth on them myself.' He looked quite youthful in his cap of pale red hair and with pinkish down covering his arms.

'I think my journeying tired me more than yours did you,' the Mouser replied. 'Moreover, I look forward to the days, which surely must come, when Arilia falls on hard times and is forced to hire out its airships with their efficient female crews. Their greater speed should make it possible to run things from a home base while still managing an interesting field assignment from time to time.'

'You see how their minds work?' Afreyt commented to Cif *sotto voce*.

THE END

Fritz Leiber (1910–1992) was born in Chicago. Both his parents were Shakespearean actors and his father appeared in a number of films. He majored in psychology and physiology at the University of Chicago and then spent a year at a theological seminary. He joined his father's acting company in 1934 and even had a few roles in films, including a small part in *Camille*, which starred Greta Garbo. In 1936 he married and turned to writing, although his career also included periods as an editor, mainly with *Science Digest*, and as a drama teacher. His long and distinguished writing career covered science fiction and horror as well as his ground-breaking fantasy, and included such acclaimed titles as *The Big Time*, *The Wanderer*, both of which won Hugos, and *Our Lady of Darkness*. In all, Fritz Leiber won six Hugos and four Nebulas, and more than twenty other awards, including the 1975 Grand Master of Fantasy (Gandalf) Award and the 1976 Life Achievement Lovecraft Award. The 1981 Grand Master Nebula Award was presented for his work as a whole.